# FLYAWAY

# WINDFALL

Desmond Bagley was born in 1923 in Kendal, Westmorland, and brought up in Blackpool. He began his working life, aged 14, in the printing industry and then did a variety of jobs until going into an aircraft factory at the start of the Second World War.

When the war ended, he decided to travel to southern Africa, going overland through Europe and the Sahara. He worked en route, reaching South Africa in 1951.

Bagley became a freelance journalist in Johannesburg and wrote his first published novel, *The Golden Keel*, in 1962. In 1964 he returned to England and lived in Totnes, Devon, for twelve years. He and his wife Joan then moved to Guernsey in the Channel Islands. Here he found the ideal place for combining his writing and his other interests, which included computers, mathematics, military history, and entertaining friends from all over the world.

Desmond Bagley died in April 1983, having become one of the world's top-selling authors, with his 16 books – two of them published after his death – translated into more than 30 languages.

'I've read all Bagley's books and he's marvellous, the best.'
                                        ALISTAIR MACLEAN

By the same author

*The Golden Keel* AND *The Vivero Letter*

*High Citadel* AND *Landslide*

*Running Blind* AND *The Freedom Trap*

*The Snow Tiger* AND *Night of Error*

*The Spoilers* AND *Juggernaut*

*The Tightrope Men* AND *The Enemy*

*Wyatt's Hurricane* AND *Bahama Crisis*

# DESMOND BAGLEY

## *Flyaway*

### AND

## *Windfall*

HARPER

HARPER
an imprint of HarperCollins*Publishers*
77-85 Fulham Palace Road
Hammersmith, London W6 8JB
www.harpercollins.co.uk

This omnibus edition 2009
1

*Flyaway* first published in Great Britain by Collins 1978
*Windfall* first published in Great Britain by Collins 1982
*The Circumstances Surrounding the Crime* first published in the USA
in *I, Witness*, edited by Brian Garfield, by Times Books 1978

Desmond Bagley asserts the moral right to
be identified as the author of these works

Copyright © Brockhurst Publications 1978, 1982

ISBN 978 0 00 730476 9

Printed and bound in Great Britain by
Clays Ltd, St Ives plc

**Mixed Sources**

Product group from well-managed
forests and other controlled sources
www.fsc.org   Cert no. SW-COC-1806
© 1996 Forest Stewardship Council

FSC is a non-profit international organisation established
to promote the responsible management of the world's forests.
Products carrying the FSC label are independently certified
to assure consumers that they come from forests that are managed
to meet the social, economic and ecological needs
of present and future generations.

Find out more about HarperCollins and the environment at
**www.harpercollins.co.uk/green**

# CONTENTS

Flyaway
1

Windfall
333

The Circumstances Surrounding
the Crime
681

# FLYAWAY

*To Lecia and Peter Foston*
*of the Wolery*

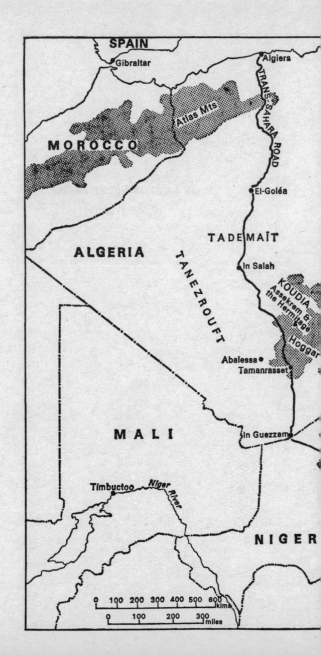

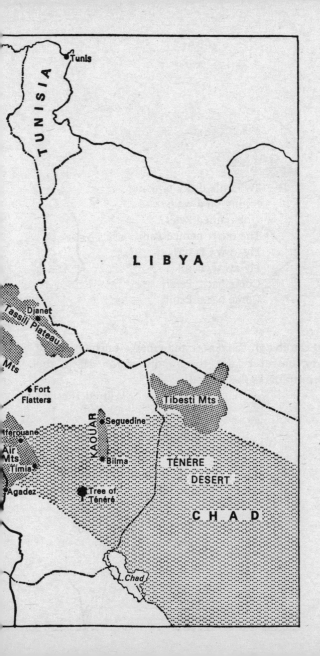

Two little dicky-birds,
Sitting on a wall;
One named Peter,
The other named Paul.
Fly away, Peter!
Fly away, Paul!
Come back, Peter!
Come back, Paul!

No man can live in the desert and emerge unchanged. He will carry, however faint, the imprint of the desert, the brand which marks the nomad.

Wilfred Thesiger

# ONE

We live in the era of instancy. The clever chemists have invented instant coffee; demonstrating students cry in infantile voices, 'We want the world, and we want it *now*!' and the Staffords have contrived the instant flaming row, a violent quarrel without origin or cause.

Our marriage was breaking up and we both knew it. The heat engendered by friction was rapidly becoming unsupportable. On this particular Monday morning a mild enquiry into Gloria's doings over the weekend was wantonly interpreted as meddlesome interference into her private affairs. One thing led to another and I arrived at the office rather frayed at the edges.

Joyce Godwin, my secretary, looked up as I walked in and said brightly, 'Good morning, Mr Stafford.'

'Morning,' I said curtly, and slammed the door of my own office behind me. Once inside I felt a bit ashamed. It's a bad boss who expends his temper on the staff and Joyce didn't deserve it. I snapped down the intercom switch. 'Will you come in, Joyce?'

She entered armed with the secretarial weapons – stenographic pad and sharpened pencil. I said, 'Sorry about that; I'm not feeling too well this morning.'

Her lips twitched in a faint smile. 'Hangover?'

'Something like that,' I agreed. The seven year hangover. 'What's on the boil this morning?'

'Mr Malleson wants to see you about the board meeting this afternoon.'

I nodded. The AGM of Stafford Security Consultants Ltd was a legal formality; three men sitting in a City penthouse cutting up the profits between them. A financial joke. 'Anything else?'

'Mr Hoyland rang up. He wants to talk to you.'

'Hoyland? Who's he?'

'Chief Security Officer at Franklin Engineering in Luton.'

There was once a time when I knew every employee by his given name; now I couldn't even remember the surnames of the line staff. It was a bad situation and would have to be rectified when I had the time. 'Why me?'

'He wanted Mr Ellis, but he's in Manchester until Wednesday; and Mr Daniels is still away with 'flu.'

I grinned. 'So he picked me as third choice. Was it anything important?'

The expression on Joyce's face told me that she thought my hangover was getting the better of me. A Chief Security Officer was expected to handle his job and if he rang the boss it had better be about something bloody important. 'He said he'd ring back,' she said drily.

'Anything else?'

Wordlessly she pointed to my overflowing in-tray. I looked at it distastefully. 'You're a slave-driver. If Hoyland rings I'll be in Mr Malleson's office.'

'But Mr Fergus wants the Electronomics contract signed today,' she wailed.

'Mr Fergus is an old fuddy-duddy,' I said. 'I want to talk to Mr Malleson about it. It won't hurt Electronomics to wait another half-hour.' I picked up the Electronomics file and left, feeling Joyce's disapproving eye boring into my back.

Charlie Malleson was evidently feeling more like work than I – his in-tray was almost half empty. I perched my rump on the edge of his desk and dropped the file in front of him. 'I don't like this one.'

He looked up and sighed. 'What's wrong with it, Max?'

'They want guard dogs without handlers. That's against the rules.'

He raised his eyebrows. 'I didn't catch that.'

'Neither did Fergus and he should have. You know what I think about it. You can build defences around a factory like the Berlin Wall but some bright kid is going to get through at night just for the devil of it. Then he runs up against a dog on the loose and gets mauled – or killed.' Charlie opened the file. 'See Clause 28.'

He checked it. 'That wasn't in the contract I vetted. It must have been slipped in at the last moment.'

'Then it gets slipped out fast or Electronomics can take their business elsewhere. You wanted to see me about the board meeting?'

'His Lordship will be at home at four this afternoon.'

His Lordship was Lord Brinton who owned twenty-five per cent of Stafford Security Consultants Ltd. I got up and went to the window and stared at the tower of the Inter-City Building – Brinton's lair. From the penthouse he over-looked the City, emerging from time to time to gobble up a company here and arrange a profitable merger there. 'Four o'clock is all right; I'll tell Joyce. Is everything in order?'

'As smooth as silk.' Charlie eyed me appraisingly. 'You don't look too good. Got a touch of 'flu coming on?'

'A touch of something. I was told the name of a man this morning and I didn't know he worked for us. That's bad.'

He smiled. 'This business is getting bigger than both of us. The penalty of success.'

I nodded. 'I'm chained to my damned desk seven hours out of eight. Sometimes I wish we were back in the bad old days when we did our own legwork. Now I'm shuffling too many bloody papers around.'

'And a lot of those are crisp, crackling fivers.' Charlie waved at the view – the City of London in all its majesty. 'Don't knock success on this hallowed ground – it's immoral.' The telephone rang and he picked it up, then held it out to me.

It was Joyce. 'Mr Hoyland wants to speak to you.'

'Put him on.' I covered the mouthpiece and said to Charlie, 'You might like to listen to this one. It's about time you administrative types knew what goes on at the sharp end of the business.'

The telephone clicked and clattered. 'Mr Stafford?'

'Max Stafford here.'

'This is Hoyland from . . .'

'I know who you are, Mr Hoyland,' I said, feeling like a con man. 'What's your trouble?'

'I've come up against a funny one, sir,' he said. 'A man called Billson vanished a week ago and I've run into a blank wall.'

'How critical is Billson?'

'He's not on the technical side; he's in the accounts office. But . . .'

'Have you checked the books?'

'They balance to a penny,' said Hoyland. 'It's not that, sir; it's the attitude of the company. I'm getting no cooperation at all.'

'Expand on that.'

'Well, Billson is a bit of a dumb bunny and he's getting paid a lot more than he's worth. He's on £8000 a year and doing the work of an office boy. When I asked Isaacson why, I got a bloody dusty answer. He said the salary structure is no concern of security.'

Hoyland was annoyed, and rightly so. I was annoyed myself because when we took on a contract it was stipulated that *everything* was the concern of security. 'He said that, did he? Who is Isaacson?'

'Chief Accountant,' said Hoyland. 'Can you get on the blower and straighten him out? He's not taking much notice of me.'

'He'll get straightened out,' I said grimly. 'Let's get back to Billson – what do you mean when you say he's vanished?'

'He didn't turn up last week and he sent in no word. When we made enquiries we found he'd left his digs without explanation.' Hoyland paused. 'That's no crime, Mr Stafford.'

'Not unless he took something with him. You say he isn't critical?'

'Definitely not. He's been a fixture in the accounting department for fifteen years. No access to anything that matters.'

'Not that we know of.' I thought about it for a few moments. 'All right, Mr Hoyland; I'll have a word with Isaacson. In the meantime check back on Billson; you never know what you might find.'

'I'll do that, Mr Stafford.' Hoyland seemed relieved. Bucking top management was something he'd rather not do himself.

I put down the telephone and grinned at Charlie. 'See what I mean. How would you handle a thing like that?'

'Franklin Engineering,' he said reflectively. 'Defence contractors, aren't they?'

'They do a bit for the army. Suspension systems for tanks – nothing serious.'

'What are you going to do about it?'

'I'm going to blow hell out of this joker, Isaacson. No money-pusher is going to tell one of my security officers what concerns security and what doesn't.'

Charlie tilted back his chair and regarded me speculatively. 'Why don't you do it personally – face to face? You've been complaining about being tied to your desk, so why don't you pop over to Luton and do some legwork? You can easily get back in time for the board meeting. Get out of the office, Max; it might take that sour look off your face.'

'Is it as bad as that?' But the idea was attractive, all the same. 'All right, Charlie; to hell with the desk!' I rang Joyce. 'Get on to Hoyland at Franklin Engineering – tell him I'm on my way to Luton and to hold himself available.' I cut off her wail of protest. 'Yes, I know the state of the intray – it'll get done tomorrow.'

As I put down the telephone Charlie said, 'I don't suppose it is really important.'

'I shouldn't think so. The man's either gone on a toot or been knocked down by a car or something like that. No, Charlie; this is a day's holiday, expenses paid by the firm.'

# TWO

I should have remembered Hoyland's name because I remembered his competent, square face when I saw it. He was a reliable type and an ex-copper like so many of our security officers. He was surprised to see me; it wasn't often that the top brass of Stafford Security appeared in the front line, more's the pity.

His surprise was mingled with nervousness as he tried to assess why I had come personally. 'Nothing to worry about,' I assured him. 'Only too glad to get away from the desk. Tell me about Billson.'

Hoyland rubbed his chin. 'I don't know much about him. You know I've only been here three months; I was transferred here when Laird retired.'

I didn't know – there was too damned much about my own firm I didn't know. It had grown too big and depersonalized. 'Yes,' I said.

'I took over Laird's files and checked his gradings. Billson came well into the green scale – as safe as houses. He was at the bottom of my priorities.'

'But you've rechecked since he disappeared?'

Hoyland nodded. 'Forty-four years old, worked here fifteen years. As much personality as a castrated rabbit. Lodges with a Mrs Harrison in the town. She's a widow.'

'Anything between him and Mrs Harrison?'

Hoyland grinned. 'She's seventy.'

That didn't mean much; Ninon de L'Enclos was a whore at eighty. 'What about girl-friends?'

'Not Billson – the girls didn't go for him from what I've heard.'

'All right – boy-friends?'

'Not that, either. I don't think he was the type.'

'He doesn't seem much of anything,' I said caustically.

'And that's a fact,' said Hoyland. 'He's so insignificant he hardly exists. You'd walk past him and not know he was there.'

'The original invisible man,' I commented. 'All the qualifications for a sleeper.'

'Isn't fifteen years too long?' queried Hoyland. 'Besides, he left everything in order.'

'As far as we know, that's all. Do the Special Branch boys know about this?'

'They've been poking around and come to the same conclusion as me.'

'Yes,' I said. 'Billson is probably in some hospital, having lost his means of identification. But there is a mystery; why was he overpaid and why is management being coy about it?'

Hoyland nodded. 'I talked to Stewart about it first – he's Billson's immediate boss – and he pushed me on to Isaacson. I got nowhere with him.'

'I'll see what I can do,' I said, and went to find Stewart, who proved to be a sandy Scotsman, one of the new breed of bookkeepers. No dusty ledgers for him; figures were something which danced electronically in the guts of a computer.

No, he had no idea where Billson might have gone. In fact, he knew nothing about Billson, full stop.

'Isn't that a little odd for a department head? Surely you know something about your subordinates?'

'He's a very strange man,' said Stewart. 'Reserved most of the time but capable of the most frantic outbursts occasionally. Sometimes he can be very difficult.'

'In what way?'

Stewart shrugged. 'He goes on about injustice; about people not being given the proper credit for achievement. He's very bitter about it.'

'Meaning himself?'

'No; it was always about others being repressed or cheated.'

'Any political implications?'

'Not at all,' said Stewart positively. 'Politics mean nothing to him.'

'Did he do his work well?'

Stewart offered me a wary look and said over-carefully, 'He did the work we asked of him to our satisfaction.'

'Would you say he was an achiever himself?' I smiled. 'Was he in line for promotion, or anything like that?'

'Nothing like that.' Stewart seemed aware that he had spoken too quickly and emphatically. 'He's not a dynamic man.'

I said, 'When did you join the firm, Mr Stewart?'

'Four years ago. I was brought down from Glasgow when the office was computerized.'

'At that time did you make any attempt to have Billson fired or transferred to another department?'

Stewart jerked. 'I . . . er . . . I did something like that, yes. It was decided to keep him on.'

'By Mr Isaacson, I take it.'

'Yes. You'll have to ask him about that,' he said with an air of relief.

So I did. Isaacson was a more rarefied breed of account-ant than Stewart. Stewart knew how to make figures jump through hoops; Isaacson selected the hoops they jumped through. He was an expert on company law, especially that affecting taxation.

'Billson!' he said, and smiled. 'There's a word in Yiddish which describes a man like Billson. He's a *nebbish*.'

'What's that?'

'A person of less than no account. Let me put it this way; if a man walks out of a room and it feels as though someone has just come in, then he's a *nebbish*.'

I leaned back in my chair and stared at Isaacson. 'So here we have a *nebbish* who draws £8000 for a job worth £2000, if that. How do you account for it?'

'I don't have to,' he said easily. 'You can take that up with our managing director, Mr Grayson.'

'And where will I find Mr Grayson?'

'I regret that will be difficult,' said Isaacson in a most unregretful manner. 'He's in Switzerland for the skiing.'

He looked so damned smug that I wanted to hit him, but I kept my temper and said deliberately, 'Mr Isaacson, my firm is solely responsible for security at Franklin Engineering. A man has disappeared and I find this lack of cooperation very strange. Don't you find it odd yourself?'

He spread his hands. 'I repeat, Mr Stafford, that any questions concerning Mr Billson can be answered only by my managing director.'

'Who is sliding down hills on a couple of planks.' I held Isaacson's eye. 'Stewart wanted to fire Billson but you vetoed it. Why?'

'I didn't. Mr Grayson did. He said Billson must stay.'

'Surely you asked his reasons.'

'Of course.' Isaacson shook his head. 'He gave none.' He paused. 'I know nothing of Billson, Mr Stafford, other than that he was . . . protected, shall we say.'

I thought about that. Why should Grayson be Billson's fairy godfather? 'Did you know that Billson was "protected" when Stewart wanted to fire him?'

'Oh yes.' Isaacson smiled a little sadly. 'I wanted to fire him myself ten years ago. When Stewart brought up the suggestion I thought I'd test it again with Mr Grayson.' He shrugged. 'But the situation was still the same.'

I said, 'Maybe I'd better take this up at a higher level; perhaps with your Chairman.'

'As you wish,' said Isaacson in a cold voice.

I decided to lower the temperature myself. 'Just one more thing, Mr Isaacson. When Mr Hoyland asks you for information you do not – repeat not – tell him that what he wants to know is no concern of security. You give him *all* the information you have, as you have given it to me. I hope I make myself clear?'

'Very clear.' Isaacson's lips had gone very thin.

'Very well; you will allow Mr Hoyland access to everything concerning Billson, especially his salary record. I'll have a word with him before I leave.' I stood up. 'Good morning, Mr Isaacson.'

I checked back with Hoyland and told him what I wanted, then went in search of the Widow Harrison and found her to be a comfortable motherly old soul, supplementing her old age pension by taking in a lodger. According to her, Billson was a very nice gentleman who was no trouble about the house and who caused her no heart-searching about fancy women. She had no idea why he had left and was perturbed about what she was going to do about Billson's room which still contained a lot of his possessions.

'After all, I have me living to make,' she said. 'The pension doesn't go far these days.'

I paid her a month in advance for the room and marked it up to the Franklin Engineering account. If Isaacson queried it he'd get a mouthful from me.

She had not noticed anything unusual about Billson before he walked out 'No, he wasn't any different. Of course, there were times he could get very angry, but that was just his way. I let him go on and didn't take much notice.'

'He was supposed to go to work last Monday, but he didn't. When did you see him last, Mrs Harrison?'

'It was Monday night. I thought he'd been to work as usual. He didn't say he hadn't.'

'Was he in any way angry then?'

'A bit. He was talking about there being no justice, not even in the law. He said rich newspapers could afford expensive lawyers so that poor men like him didn't stand a chance.' She laughed. 'He was that upset he overturned the glue-pot. But it was just his way, Mr Stafford.'

'Oh! What was he doing with the glue-pot?'

'Pasting something into that scrapbook of his. The one that had all the stuff in it about his father. He thought a lot of his father although I don't think he could have remembered him. Stands to reason, doesn't it? He was only a little boy when his father was killed.'

'Did he ever show you the scrapbook?'

'Oh yes; it was one of the first things he did when he came here eight years ago. That was the year after my late husband died. It was full of pictures cut out of newspapers and magazines – all about his father. Lots of aeroplanes – the old-fashioned kind like they had in the First World War.'

'Biplanes?'

'Lots of wings,' she said vaguely. 'I don't know much about aeroplanes. They weren't like the jets we have now. He told me all about his father lots of times; about how he was some kind of hero. After a while I just stopped listening and let it pass over me head. He seemed to think his dad had been cheated or something.'

'Do you mind if I see his room? I'd like to have a look at that scrapbook.'

Her brow wrinkled. 'I don't mind you seeing the room but, come to think of it, I don't think the book's there. It stays on his dressing-table and I didn't see it when I cleaned up.'

'I'd still like to see the room.'

It was not much of a place for a man to live. Not uncomfortable but decidedly bleak. The furniture was Edwardian oversize or 1930s angular and the carpet was clean but threadbare. I sat on the bed and the springs protested. As I looked at the garish reproduction of Holman Hunt's 'The Light of the World' I wondered why an £8000-a-year man should live in a dump like this. 'The scrapbook,' I said.

'It's gone. He must have taken it with him.'

'Is anything else missing?'

'He took his razor and shaving brush,' said Mrs Harrison. 'And his toothbrush. A couple of clean shirts and some socks and other things. Not more than would fill a small suitcase. The police made a list.'

'Do the police know about the scrapbook?'

'It never entered me head.' She was suddenly nervous. 'Do you think I should tell them, sir?'

'Don't worry,' I said. 'I'll tell them.'

'I do hope you can find Mr Billson, sir,' she said, and hesitated. 'I wouldn't want to think he's come to any harm. He really should be married with someone to look after him. His sister came every month but that really wasn't enough.'

'He has a sister?'

'Not a real sister – a half-sister, I think. The name's different and she's not married. A funny foreign name it is – I never can remember it. She comes and keeps him company in the evening about twice a month.'

'Does she know he's gone?'

'I don't know how she can, unless the police told her. I don't know her address but she lives in London.'

'I'll ask them,' I said. 'Did Mr Billson have any girl-friends?'

'Oh no, sir.' She shook her head. 'The problem is, you see, who'd want to marry him? Not that there's anything wrong with him,' she added hastily. 'But he just didn't seem to appeal to the ladies, sir.'

As I walked to the police station I turned that one over. It seemed very much like an epitaph.

Sergeant Kaye was not too perturbed. 'For a man to take it into his head to walk away isn't an offence,' he said. 'If he was a child of six it would be different and we'd be pulling out all the stops, but Billson is a grown man.' He groped for an analogy. 'It's as if you were to say that you feel sorry for him because he's an orphan, if you take my meaning.'

'He may be a grown man,' I said. 'But from what I hear he may not be all there.'

'I don't know,' said Kaye. 'He held down a good job at Franklin Engineering for good pay. It takes more than a half-wit to do that. And he took good care of his money before he walked out and when he walked out.'

'Tell me more.'

'Well, he saved a lot. He kept his current account steady at about the level of a month's salary and he had nearly £12,000 on deposit. He cleared the lot out last Tuesday morning as soon as the bank opened.'

'Well, I'm damned! But wait a minute, Sergeant; it needs seven days' notice to withdraw deposits.'

Kaye smiled. 'Not if you've been a good, undemanding customer for a dozen or more years and then suddenly put the arm on your bank manager.' He unsealed the founts of his wisdom. 'Men walk out on things for a lot of reasons. Some want to get away from a woman and some are running towards one. Some get plain tired of the way they're living and just cut out without any fuss. If we had to put on a full scale investigation every time it happened we'd have our hands full of nothing else, and the yobbos we're supposed to be hammering would be laughing fit to bust. It isn't as though he's committed an offence, is it?'

'I wouldn't know. What does the Special Branch say?'

'The cloak-and-dagger boys?' Kaye's voice was tinged with contempt 'They reckon he's clean – and I reckon they're right.'

'I suppose you've checked the hospitals.'

'Those in the area. That's routine.'

'He has a sister – does she know?'

'A half-sister,' he said. 'She was here last week. She seemed a level-headed woman – she didn't create all that much fuss.'

'I'd be glad of her address.'

He scribbled on a note-pad and tore off the sheet. As I put it into my wallet I said, 'And you won't forget the scrap-book?'

'I'll put it in the file,' said Kaye patiently. I could see he didn't attach much significance to it.


I had a late lunch and then phoned Joyce at the office. 'I won't be coming in,' I said. 'Is there anything I ought to know?'

'Mrs Stafford asked me to tell you she won't be in this evening.' Joyce's voice was suspiciously cool and even.

I hoped I kept my irritation from showing. I was becoming pretty damned tired of going home to an empty house. 'All right; I have a job for you. All the Sunday newspapers for November 2nd. Extract anything that refers to a man called Billson. Try the national press first and, if Luton has a Sunday paper, that as well. If you draw a blank try all the dailies for the previous week. I want it on my desk tomorrow.'

'That's a punishment drill.'

'Get someone to help if you must. And tell Mr Malleson I'll meet him at four o'clock at the Inter-City Building for the board meeting.'

# THREE

I don't know if I liked Brinton or not; he was a hard man to get to know. His social life was minimal and, considered objectively, he was just a money-making machine and a very effective one. He didn't seem to reason like other men; he would listen to arguments for and against a project, offered by the lawyers and accountants he hired by the regiment, and then he would make a decision. Often the decision would have nothing to do with what he had been told, or perhaps he could see patterns no one else saw. At any rate some of his exploits had been startlingly like a magician pulling a rabbit out of a hat. Hindsight would show that what he had done was logically sound, but only he had the foresight and that was what made him rich.

When Charlie Malleson and I put together the outfit that later became Stafford Security Consultants Ltd we ran into the usual trouble which afflicts the small firm trying to become a big firm – a hell of a lot of opportunities going begging for lack of finance. Lord Brinton came to the rescue with a sizeable injection of funds for which he took twenty-five per cent of our shares. In return we took over the security of the Brinton empire.

I was a little worried when the deal was going through because of Brinton's reputation as a hot-shot operator. I put it to him firmly that this was going to be a legitimate operation and that our business was solely security and not the other side of the coin, industrial espionage. He smiled slightly, said he respected my integrity, and that I was to run the firm as I pleased.

He kept to that, too, and never interfered, although his bright young whiz-kids would sometimes suggest that we cut a few corners. They didn't come back after I referred them to Brinton.

Industrial espionage is a social disease something akin to VD. Nobody minds admitting to protecting against it, but no one will admit to doing it. I always suspected that Brinton was in it up to his neck as much as any other ruthless financial son-of-a-bitch, and I used the firm's facilities to do a bit of snooping. I was right; he employed a couple of other firms from time to time to do his ferreting. That was all right with me as long as he didn't ask me to do it, but sooner or later he was going to try it on one of our other clients and then he was going to be hammered, twenty-five per cent shareholder or not. So far it hadn't happened.

I arrived a little early for the meeting and found him in his office high above the City. It wasn't very much bigger than a ballroom and one entire wall was of glass so that he could look over his stamping ground. There wasn't a desk in sight; he employed other men to sit behind desks.

He heaved himself creakily out of an armchair. 'Good to see you, Max. Look what I've gotten here.'

He had a new toy, an open fire burning merrily in a fireplace big enough to roast an ox. 'Central heating is all very well,' he said. 'But there's nothing like a good blaze to warm old bones like mine. It's like something else alive in the room – it keeps me company and doesn't talk back.'

I looked at the fireplace full of soft coal. 'Aren't you violating the smokeless zone laws?'

He shook his head. 'There's an electrostatic precipitator built into the chimney. No smoke gets out.'

I had to smile. When Brinton did anything he did it in style. It was another example of the way he thought. You want a fire with no smoke? All right, install a multi-thousand pound gadget to get rid of it. And it wouldn't cost him too much; he owned the factory which made the things and I suppose it would find its way on to the company books under the heading of 'Research and Development – Testing the Product'.

'Drink?' he asked.

'Yes,' I said. 'The working day seems to be over.'

He pressed a button next to the fireplace and a bar unfolded from nowhere. His seamed old face broke into an urchin grin. 'Don't you consider the board meeting to be work?'

'It's playtime.'

He poured a measured amount of Talisker into a glass, added an equal amount of Malvern water, and brought it over to me. 'Yes, I've never regretted the money I put into your firm.'

'Glad to hear it.' I sipped the whisky.

'Did you make a profit this year?'

I grinned. 'You'll have to ask Charlie. He juggles the figures and cooks the books.' I knew to a penny how much we'd made, but old Brinton seemed to like a bit of jocularity mixed into his business.

He looked over my shoulder. 'Here he is now. I'll know very soon if I have something to supplement my old age pension.'

Charlie accepted a drink and we got down to it with Charlie spouting terms like amortization, discounted cash flow, yield and all the jargon you read in the back pages of a newspaper. He doubled as company secretary and accountant, our policy being to keep down overheads, and he owned a slice of the firm which made him properly miserly and disinclined to build any administrative empires which did not add to profits.

It seemed we'd had a good year and I'd be able to feed the wolf at the door on caviare and champagne. We discussed future plans for expansion and the possibility of going into Europe under EEC rules. Finally we came to 'Any Other Business' and I began to think of going home.

Brinton had his hands on the table and seemed intent on studying the liver spots. He said, 'There is one cloud in the sky for you gentlemen. I'm having trouble with Andrew McGovern.'

Charlie raised his eyebrows. 'The Whensley Group?'

'That's it,' said Brinton. 'Sir Andrew McGovern – Chairman of the Whensley Group.'

The Whensley Group of companies was quite a big chunk of Brinton's holdings. At that moment I couldn't remember off-hand whether he held a controlling interest or not. I said, 'What's the trouble?'

'Andrew McGovern reckons his security system is costing too much. He says he can do it cheaper himself.'

I smiled sourly at Charlie. 'If he does it any cheaper it'll be no bloody good. You can't cut corners on that sort of thing, and it's a job for experts who know what they're doing. If he tries it himself he'll fall flat on his face.'

'I know all that,' said Brinton, still looking down at his hands. 'But I'm under some pressure.'

'It's five per cent of our business,' said Charlie. 'I wouldn't want to lose it.'

Brinton looked up. 'I don't think you will lose it – permanently.'

'You mean you're going to let McGovern have his way?' asked Charlie.

Brinton smiled but there was no humour in his face. 'I'm going to let him have the rope he wants – but sooner than he expects it. He can have the responsibility for his own security from the end of the month.'

'Hey!' I said. 'That's only ten days' time.'

'Precisely.' Brinton tapped his finger on the table. 'We'll see how good a job he does at short notice. And then, in a little while, I'll jerk in the rope and see if he's got his neck in the noose.'

I said, 'If his security is to remain as good as it is now he'll have to pay more. It's a specialized field and good men are thin on the ground. If he can find them he'll have to pay well. But he won't find them – I'm running into that kind of trouble already in the expansion programme, and I know what I'm looking for and he doesn't. So his security is going to suffer; there'll be holes in it big enough to march a battalion of industrial spies through.'

'Just so,' said Brinton. 'I know you test your security from time to time.'

'It's essential,' I said. 'We're always doing dry runs to test the defences.'

'I know.' Brinton grinned maliciously. 'In three months I'm going to have a security firm – not yours – run an operation against McGovern's defences and we'll see if his neck is stuck out far enough to be chopped at.'

Charlie said, 'You mean you're going to behead him as well as hanging him?' He wasn't smiling.

'We might throw in the drawing and quartering bit, too. I'm getting a mite tired of Andrew McGovern. You'll get your business back, and maybe a bit more.'

'I hope you're right,' said Charlie. 'The Whensley Group account is only five per cent of our gross but it's a damned sight more than that of our profits. Our overheads won't go down all that much, you know. It might put a crimp in our expansion plans.'

'You'll be all right,' said Brinton. 'I promise.' And with that we had to be satisfied. If a client doesn't want your business you can't ram it down his throat.

Charlie made his excuses and left, but Brinton detained me for a moment. He took me by the arm and led me to the fireplace where he stood warming his hands. 'How is Gloria?'

'Fine,' I said.

Maybe I had not bothered to put enough conviction into that because he snorted and gave me a sharp look. 'I'm a successful man,' he said. 'And the reason is that when a deal goes sour I pull out and take any losses. You don't mind that bit of advice from an old man?'

I smiled. 'The best thing about advice is that you don't have to follow it.'

So I left him and went down to the thronged street in his private lift and joined the hurrying crowds eager to get home after the day's work. I wasn't particularly eager because I didn't have a home; just a few walls and a roof. So I went to my club instead.

# FOUR

I felt a shade better when I arrived at the office next morning. I had visited my fencing club after a long absence and two hours of heavy sabre work had relieved my frustrations and had also done something for the incipient thickening of the waist which comes from too much sitting behind a desk.

But the desk was still there so I sat behind it and looked for the information on Billson I had asked Joyce to look up. When I didn't find it I called her in. 'Didn't you find anything on Billson?'

She blinked at me defensively. 'It's in your in-tray.'

I found it buried at the bottom – an envelope marked 'Billson' – and grinned at her. 'Nice try, Joyce; but I'll work out my own priorities.'

When Brinton had injected funds into the firm it had grown with an almost explosive force and I had resolved to handle at least one case in the field every six months so as not to lose touch with the boys on the ground. Under the pressure of work that went the way of all good resolutions and I hadn't been in the field for fifteen months. Maybe the Billson case was an opportunity to see if my cutting edge was still sharp.

I said abruptly, 'I'll be handing some of my work load to Mr Ellis.'

'He'll not like that,' said Joyce.

'He'd have to take the lot if I was knocked down by a car and broke a leg,' I said. 'It'll do him good. Remind me to speak to him when he gets back from Manchester.'

Joyce went away and I opened the envelope and took out a four-page article, a potted history of the life and times of Peter Billson, Aviation Pioneer – Sunday Supplement instant knowledge without pain. It was headed: *The Strange Case of Flyaway Peter,* and was illustrated with what were originally black-and-white photographs which had been tinted curious shades of blue and yellow to enliven the pages of what, after all, was supposed to be a colour magazine.

It boiled down to this. Billson, a Canadian, was born appropriately in 1903, the year the first aeroplane took to the sky. Too young to see service in the First World War, he was nourished on tales of the air fighting on the Western Front which excited his imagination and he became air mad. He was an engineering apprentice and, by the time he was 21, he had actually built his own plane. It wasn't a good one – it crashed.

He was unlucky. The Golden Age of Aviation was under way and he was missing out on all the plums. Pioneer flying took money or a sponsor with money and he had neither. In the late 1920s Alan Cobham was flying to the Far East, Australia and South Africa; in 1927 Lindbergh flew the Atlantic solo, and then Byrd brought off the North and South Pole double. Came the early' thirties and Amy Johnson, Jim Mollison, Amelia Earhart and Wiley Post were breaking records wholesale and Billson hadn't had a look-in.

But he made it in the next phase. Breaking records was all very well, but now the route-proving stage had arrived which had to precede phase three – the regular commercial flight. Newspapers were cashing in on the public interest and organizing long-distance races such as the

England-Australia Air Race of 1934, won by Scott and Campbell-Black. Billson came second in a race from Vancouver to Hawaii, and first in a mail-carrying test – Vancouver to Montreal. He was in there at last – a real heroic and intrepid birdman. It is hard to believe the adulation awarded those early fliers. Not even our modern astronauts are accorded the same attention.

It was about this time that some smart journalist gave him the nickname of Flyaway Peter, echoing the nursery rhyme. It was good publicity and Billson went along with the gag even to the extent of naming his newborn son Paul and, in 1936, when he entered the London to Cape Town Air Race he christened the Northrop 'Gamma' he flew *Flyaway*. It was one of the first of the all-metal aircraft.

The race was organized by a newspaper which beat the drum enthusiastically and announced that all entrants would be insured to the tune of £100,000 each in the case of a fatality. The race began. Billson put down in Algiers to refuel and then took off again, heading south. The plane was never seen again.

Billson's wife, Helen, was naturally shocked and it was some weeks before she approached the newspaper about the insurance. The newspaper passed her on to the insurance company which dug in its heels and dithered. £100,000 was a lot of money in 1936. Finally it declared unequivocally that no payment would be forthcoming and Mrs Billson brought the case to court.

The courtroom was enlivened by a defence witness, a South African named Hendrik van Niekirk, who swore on oath that he had seen Billson, alive and well, in Durban four weeks after the race was over. It caused a sensation and no doubt the sales of the newspaper went up. The prosecution battered at van Niekirk but he stood up to it well. He had visited Canada and had met Billson there and he was in no doubt about his identification. Did he speak to Billson in Durban? No, he did not.

All very dicey.

The judge summed up and the case went to the jury which deliberated at length and then found for the insurance company. No £100,000 for Mrs Billson – who immediately appealed. The Appellate Court reversed the decision on a technicality – the trial judge had been a shade too precise in his instructions to the jury. The insurance company took it to the House of Lords who refused to have anything to do with it. Mrs Billson got her £100,000. Whether she lived happily ever after the writer of the article didn't say.

So much for the subject matter – the tone was something else. Written by a skilled journalist, it was a very efficient hatchet job on the reputation of a man who could not answer back – dead or alive. It reeked of the envy of a small-minded man who got his kicks by pulling down men better than himself. If this was what Paul Billson had read then it wasn't too surprising if he went off his trolley.

The article ended in a speculative vein. After pointing out that the insurance company had lost on a legal technicality, it went on:

The probability is very strong that Billson did survive the crash, if crash there was, and that Hendrik van Niekirk did see him in Durban. If this is so, and I think it is, then an enormous fraud was perpetrated. £100,000 is a lot of money anywhere and at any time. £100,000 in 1936 is equivalent to over £350,000 in our present-day debased currency.

If Peter Billson is still alive he will be 75 years old and will have lived a life of luxury. Rich men live long and the chances are that he is indeed still alive.

Perhaps he will read these words. He might even conceive these words to be libellous. I am willing to risk it.

Flyaway Peter Billson, come back! Come back!

I was contemplating this bit of nastiness when Charlie Malleson came into the office. He said, 'I've done a preliminary analysis of the consequences of losing the Whensley Group,' and smiled sourly. 'We'll survive.'

'Brinton,' I said, and tilted my chair back. 'He owns a quarter of our shares and accounts for a third of our business. We've got too many eggs in his basket. I'd like to know how much it would hurt if he cut loose from us completely.' I paused, then added, 'Or if we cut loose from him.'

Charlie looked alarmed. 'Christ! it would be like having a leg cut off – without anaesthetic.'

'It might happen.'

'But why would you want to cut loose? The money he pumped in was the making of us.'

'I know,' I said. 'But Brinton is a financial shark. Snapping up a profit is to him as mindless a reflex as when a real shark snaps up a tasty morsel. I think we're vulnerable, Charlie.'

'I don't know why you're getting so bloody hot under the collar all of a sudden,' he said plaintively.

'Don't you?' I leaned forward and the chair legs came down with a soft thud on to the thick pile carpet. 'Last night, in a conversation lasting less than four minutes, we lost fifteen per cent of Brinton's business. And why did we lose it? So that he can put the arm on Andrew McGovern who is apparently getting out of line. Or so Brinton says.'

'Don't you believe him?'

'Whether he's telling the truth or not isn't the point. The point is that our business is being buggered in one of Brinton's private schemes which has nothing to do with us.'

Charlie said slowly, 'Yes, I see what you mean.'

I stared at him. 'Do you, Charlie? I don't think so. Take a good long look at what happened yesterday. We were manipulated by a minority shareholder who twisted us around his little finger.'

'Oh, for God's sake, Max! If McGovern doesn't want us there's not a damn thing we can do about it.'

'I know that, but we could have done something which we didn't. We could have held the Whensley Group to their contract which has just under a year to run. Instead, we all agreed at the AGM to pull out in ten days. We were manoeuvred into that, Charlie; Brinton had us dancing on strings.'

Charlie was silent.

I said, 'And you know why we let it happen? We were too damned scared of losing Brinton's money. We could have outvoted him singly or jointly, but we didn't.'

'No,' said Charlie sharply. 'Your vote would have downed him – you have 51 per cent. But I have only 24 to his 25.'

I sighed. 'Okay, Charlie; my fault. But as I lay in bed last night I felt scared. I was scared of what I hadn't done. And the thing that scared me most of all was the thought of the kind of man I was becoming. I didn't start this business to jerk to any man's string, and that's why I say we have to cut loose from Brinton if possible. That's why I want you to look for alternative sources of finance. We're big enough to get it now.'

'There may be something in what you say,' said Charlie. 'But I still think you're blowing a gasket without due cause. You're over-reacting, Max.' He shrugged. 'Still, I'll look for outside money if only to keep you from blowing your top.' He glanced at the magazine cutting on my desk. 'What's that?'

'A story about Paul Billson's father. You know – the accountant who vanished from Franklin Engineering.'

'What's the score on that one?'

I shook my head. 'I don't know. At first I had Paul Billson taped as being a little devalued in the intellect – running about eighty pence in the pound – but there are a couple of things which don't add up.'

'Well, you won't have to worry about that now. Franklin is part of the Whensley Group.'

I looked up in surprise. 'So it is.' It had slipped my mind.

'I'd hand over what you've got to Sir Andrew McGovern and wish him the best of British luck.'

I thought about that and shook my head. 'No – Billson disappeared when we were in charge of security and there's still a few days to the end of the month.'

'Your sense of ethics is too strongly developed.'

'I think I'll follow up on this one myself,' I said. 'I started it so I might as well finish it. Jack Ellis can stand in for me. It's time he was given more responsibility.'

Charlie nodded approvingly. 'Do you think there's anything in Billson's disappearance – from the point of view of Franklin's security, I mean?'

I grinned at him. 'I'll probably find that he's eloped with someone's wife – and I hope it's Andrew McGovern's.'

# FIVE

I went down to Fleet Street to look for Michael English, the journalist who had written the article on Peter Billson. His office thought he was at the Press Club, the Press Club invited me to try El Vino's. I finally ran him to ground in a pub off the Strand.

He was a tall, willowy, fair-haired man whom I disliked on sight, although what he had written about Billson might have influenced my feelings. He was playing poker dice with a couple of other journalists and looked at me doubtfully when I gave him one of my business cards to prick his curiosity.

'Security!' he said. There was a shade of nervousness.

I smiled reassuringly. 'I'd like to talk to you about Billson.'

'That little twit! What's he put you on to me for?' Apprehension surrounded English like a fog.

'You've seen him recently?'

'Of course I have. He came to the office making trouble. He threatened a law suit.' English snorted with unhumorous laughter. 'Our lawyer saw him off smartly on that one.'

I was deliberately obtuse. 'I'm surprised he bothered you. If your article was correct he stands a good chance of a jail sentence – although his grey hairs might save him, I suppose.'

35

English looked at me in surprise. 'It wasn't the old man. It was someone who claimed to be his son – said he was Paul Billson. He made quite a scene.'

I looked around and saw an empty corner table. 'I'd like to talk to you about it. Over there where it's quiet. What will you have?'

English hesitated, then shrugged. 'I don't mind. Make it a double scotch.'

As I ordered the drinks he said, 'I suppose you're investigating for the insurance company.' I made an ambiguous murmur, and he said, 'I thought they gave up years ago. Isn't there a time limitation on a crime like that?'

I smiled at him as he splashed water perfunctorily in his glass. 'The file is still open.'

English had been called into his editor's office the day after the article had appeared – the day before Billson went missing. He found the editor trying to cope with an angry and agitated man who was making incoherent threats. The editor, Gaydon, said in a loud voice, 'This is Mr English who wrote the article. Sit down, Mike, and let's see if we can sort this out.' He flicked a switch on the intercom. 'Ask Mr Harcourt if he can come to my office.'

English saw trouble looming ahead. Harcourt was the resident lawyer and his presence presaged no good. He cleared his throat and said, 'What's the trouble?'

Gaydon said, 'This is Mr Paul Billson. He appears to be disturbed about the article on his father which appeared in yesterday's issue.'

English looked at Billson and saw a rather nondescript man who, at that moment, was extremely agitated. His face was white and dull red spots burned in his cheeks as he said in a high voice, 'It was nothing but outright libel. I demand a retraction and a public apology.'

Gaydon said in a calming voice, 'I'm sure that Mr English wrote the truth as he saw it. What do you say, Mike?'

'Of course, you're right,' said English. 'Every matter of fact was checked against the original court records and the contemporary newspaper reports.'

'I'm not complaining about the facts,' said Billson. 'It's the damned inferences about my father. I've never read anything so scurrilous in my life. If I don't get a public apology I shall sue.'

Gaydon glanced at English, then said smoothly, 'It shouldn't come to that, Mr Billson. I'm certain we can come to some arrangement or agreement satisfactory to all parties.' He looked up as Harcourt entered the office and said with a slight air of relief, 'This is Mr Harcourt of our legal department.'

Rapidly he explained the point at issue, and Harcourt said, 'Do you have a copy of the article?'

He settled down to read the supplement which Gaydon produced and the office was uneasily quiet until he had finished. Gaydon tapped restlessly with his forefinger; English sat quite still, hoping that the film of sweat on his forehead didn't show; Billson squirmed in his seat as the pressure within him built higher.

After what seemed an interminable period Harcourt laid down the magazine. 'What exactly are you complaining about, Mr Billson?'

'Isn't it evident?' Billson demanded. 'My father has been blackguarded in print. I demand an immediate apology or I sue.' His finger stabbed at English. 'I sue him and the newspaper.'

'I see,' said Harcourt thoughtfully. He leaned forward. 'What do you believe happened to your father?'

'His plane crashed,' said Billson. 'He was killed – that's what I believe.' He slammed his hand on the magazine. 'This is just plain libel.'

'I believe that you will be unable to sue,' said Harcourt. 'You can sue only if your own reputation is at stake. You see, it's an established principle of law that a dead man cannot be libelled.'

There was a moment of silence before Billson said incredulously, 'But this man says my father is *not* dead.'

'But *you* believe he is dead, and *you* would be bringing the case to court. It wouldn't work, Mr Billson. You needn't take my word for it, of course; you can ask your own solicitor. In fact, I strongly advise it.'

'Are you telling me that any cheap journalist can drag my father's name through the mud and get away with it?' Billson was shaking with rage.

Harcourt said gravely, 'I should watch your words, Mr Billson, or the shoe may be on the other foot. Such intemperate language could lead you into trouble.'

Billson knocked over his chair in getting to his feet. 'I shall certainly take legal advice,' he shouted, and glared at English. 'I'll have your hide, damn you!'

The door slammed behind him.

Harcourt picked up the magazine and flipped it to English's article. He avoided looking directly at English, and said to Gaydon, 'I suggest that if you intend to publish work of this nature in future you check with the legal department before publication and not after.'

'Are we in the clear?' asked Gaydon.

'Legally – quite,' said Harcourt, and added distastefully, 'It's not within my province to judge the moral aspect.' He paused. 'If the widow takes action it will be different, of course. There is a clear implication here that she joined with her husband in cheating the insurance company. How else could Peter Billson profit other than with his wife's connivance?'

Gaydon turned to English. 'What about the widow?'

'It's okay,' said English. 'She died a little over a year ago. Helen Billson married a Norwegian during the war and changed her name to Aarvik. It was when I stumbled over that fact that I decided to write up the story of Billson.'

Harcourt snorted and left, and Gaydon grinned at English. 'That was a bit close, Mike.' He picked up a pen. 'Be a good chap and pick up that chair before you leave.'

I bought English another drink. 'So Paul Billson didn't have a leg to stand on.'

English laughed. 'Not a hope. I didn't attack *his* reputation, you see. Christ, I'd forgotten the man existed.'

I said mendaciously, 'I'm not really interested in Paul Billson. Do you really think that Peter Billson faked his death to defraud the insurance company?'

'He could have,' said English. 'It makes a good story.'

'But do you believe it?'

'Does it matter what I believe?' He drank some scotch. 'No, of course I don't believe it. I think Billson was killed, all right.'

'So you were pretty safe in issuing that challenge to come forth.'

'I like to bet on certainties,' said English. He grinned. 'If he *did* defraud the insurance company he wasn't likely to rise to the bait, was he? I was on sure ground until his son popped up.'

I said, 'About that insurance. £100,000 is a hell of a lot of money. The premium must have been devilish high.'

'Not really. You must remember that by 1936 aeroplanes were no longer the unsafe string-and-sealing wax contraptions of the 'twenties. There wasn't a great deal of doubt that an aircraft would get to where it was going – the question was how fast. And this was at the time of a newspaper war; the dailies were cutting each other's throats to buy readers. Any premium would be a drop in the bucket compared with what they were spending elsewhere, and £100,000 is a nice headline-filling sum.'

'Did Billson stand a chance in the race?'

'Sure – he was a hot favourite. *Flyaway* – that Northrop of his – was one of the best aircraft of its time, and he was a good pilot.'

'Who won the race?'

'A German called Helmut Steiner. I think Billson would have won had he survived. Steiner only won because he took a hell of a lot of chances.'

'Oh! What sort of chances?'

English shrugged. 'I don't remember the times personally – I'm not that old – but I've read up on it. This was in the times of the Nazis. The Berlin Olympics were on and the Master Race was busy proving its case. German racing cars were winning on all the circuits because the Auto-Union was State subsidized; German mountaineers were doing damnfool things on every Alpine cliff – I believe some of them dropped off the Eiger at the time. It didn't prove they were good climbers; only that they were good Nazis. Germany had to beat everybody at everything, regardless of cost.'

'And Steiner?'

'Subsidized by the Hitler regime, of course; given a stripped military plane and a crackerjack support team seconded from the Luftwaffe. He was good, all right, but I think he knew Billson was better, so he took chances and they came off. He pressed his machine to the limit and the engine blew up on him as he landed in Cape Town. He was lucky it didn't happen sooner.'

I thought about that. 'Any possibility of Billson being sabotaged?'

English stared at me. 'No one has come up with that idea before. That really is a lulu.'

'What about it?'

'My God, the lengths to which insurance companies will go! What will you do if Billson was sabotaged? Sue the German government for £100,000? I doubt if Bonn would fall for that one.' He shrugged. 'Billson's plane was never found. You haven't a hope.'

I drained my glass. There wasn't much more I could get out of English and I prepared a sharp knife to stick into him. 'So you don't think you'll have any trouble from Paul Billson.'

'Not a chance,' he scoffed. 'Harcourt may be pious and sanctimonious but he tied Billson into knots. You can't libel a dead man – and Billson swears his father is dead.'

I smiled gently. 'A man called Wright once wrote about William Ewart Gladstone imputing that he was a hypocrite, particularly in sexual matters. This was in 1927 and Gladstone was long dead. But his son, the then Lord Gladstone, took umbrage and also legal advice. Like Paul Billson, he was told that the dead cannot be libelled, but he nailed Wright to the cross all the same.'

English gave me a wet-eyed look. 'What did he do?'

'He libelled Wright at every opportunity. He called Wright a liar, a fool and a poltroon in public. He had Wright thrown out of his club. In the end Wright had to bring Gladstone to court to protect his reputation. Gladstone had Norman Birkett appear for him, and Birkett flayed Wright in open court. When the case was finished so was Wright; his professional reputation was smashed.' I slid the knife home. 'It could happen to you.'

English shook his head. 'Billson won't do that – he's not the man for it.'

'He might,' I said. 'With help.' I twisted the knife. 'And it will give me great pleasure to appear for him and to swear that you told me that you thought his father to be dead, in spite of what you wrote in your dirty little article.'

I rose and left him. At the door of the pub I stopped and looked back. He was sitting in the corner, looking as though someone had kicked him in the belly, knocking the wind out of him.

# SIX

I had an early lunch and then belatedly thought to ring Paul Billson's half-sister. I had expected to find her absent from home in the middle of the working day but the telephone was picked up on the third ring and a pleasant voice said, 'Alix Aarvik here.'

I told her who and what I was, then said, 'I take it you haven't heard from your brother, Miss Aarvik.'

'No, I haven't, Mr Stafford.'

'I'd like to talk to you about him. May I come round?'

'Now?' There was uncertainty in her voice.

'Time is of the essence in these matters, Miss Aarvik.' A platitude, but I find they tend to soothe people.

'Very well,' she said. 'I'll be expecting you.'

'Within the half-hour.' I rang off and took a taxi to Kensington.

With a name like hers I had envisaged a big, tow-headed Scandinavian, but she was short and dark and looked in her early thirties. Her flat was comfortable, if sparsely furnished, and I was interested to see that she was apparently moving out. Two suitcases stood in the hall and another on a table was open and half-packed.

She saw me looking around and said, 'You've caught me in the middle of packing.'

I smiled. 'Found another flat?'

She shook her head. 'I'm leaving for Canada. My firm has asked me to go. I'm flying tomorrow afternoon.' She made a gesture which was pathetically helpless. 'I don't know if I'm doing the right thing with Paul still missing, but I have my job to consider.'

'I see,' I said, not seeing a hell of a lot. Her mother had come into a windfall of £100,000 but there was precious little sign of it around, either sticking to Paul Billson or Alix Aarvik. I made a little small talk while I studied her. She was not too well dressed but managed to make the most of what she had, and she didn't overdo the make-up. You could see thousands like her in the streets; a typical specimen of *Stenographica londiniensis* – the London typist.

When I married Gloria I had not a bean to spare and, during my rise to the giddy heights of success, I had become aware of all the subtle variations in women's knick-knackery from the cheap off-the-peg frock to the one-off Paris creation. Not that Gloria had spent much time in the lower reaches of the clothing spectrum – she developed a talent for spending money faster than I earned it, which was one of the points at issue between us. But I knew enough to know that Alix Aarvik was not dressing like an heiress.

I took the chair she offered, and said, 'Now tell me about Paul.'

'What do you want to know?'

'You can start by telling me of his relationship with his father.'

She gave me a startled look. 'You've got that far already?'

'It wasn't difficult.'

'He hero-worshipped his father,' she said. 'Not that he ever knew him to remember. Peter Billson died when Paul was two years old. You know about the air crash?'

'There seems to be a little doubt about that,' I said.

Pain showed in her eyes. 'You, too?' She shook her head. 'It was that uncertainty which preyed on Paul's mind. He wanted his father to be dead – rather a dead hero than a living fraud. Do you understand what that means, Mr Stafford?'

'You tell me.'

'I arranged for Paul to have psychiatric treatment. The psychiatrist told me that it was this that was breaking Paul in two. It's a dreadful thing to hero-worship a man – your father – and to wish him dead simultaneously.'

'So he had a neurosis. What form did it take?'

'Generally, he raged against injustice; the smart-aleck kind of injustice such as when someone takes credit for another's achievement. He collected injustices. Wasn't there a book called *The Injustice Collector?* That's Paul.'

'You say generally – how about specifically?'

'As it related to his father, he thought Peter Billson had been treated unjustly – maligned in death. You know about the court case?' I nodded, and she said, 'He wanted to clear his father's name.'

I said carefully, 'Why do you talk about Paul in the past tense?'

Again she looked startled and turned pale. 'I . . . I didn't know . . .' She intertwined her fingers and whispered, 'I suppose I think he's dead.'

'Why should you think that?'

'I don't know. But I can't think of any reason why he should disappear, either.'

'This neurosis about injustice – did he apply it to himself? Did he think that *he* was treated unjustly?'

She looked straight at me and said firmly, 'Never! He was always concerned about others. Look, Mr Stafford; I'll come right out and say that Paul wasn't – ' she caught herself – 'isn't too bright. Now you're in security at Franklin Engineering and I'll tell you that Paul isn't a thief or anything like that. He may not be an entirely balanced man, but he's honest.'

'I have no doubt about it, Miss Aarvik,' I said. 'My enquiries are as much on behalf of Paul as they are for Franklin Engineering. The management of Franklin are very much concerned about what happens to their employees.'

That was pious piffle which I hoped she'd swallow. Neither Stewart nor Isaacson had shown a whit of concern.

She said, 'Paul knew . . . knows he'll never make his way in the world, but he never showed resentment. I knew he found it hard to make out on only two hundred a month, but he never complained.'

I opened my mouth to contradict her and then closed it firmly. I waited the space of ten heart beats before I said, 'Is that all he got?'

'£2400 a year – it was all he was worth,' she said a little sadly. 'But you must have checked.'

'Yes,' I said bemusedly. 'The exact figure had slipped my memory.'

So Paul had been cheating on his sister. He had told her he earned £2400 a year when he got over three times as much, although according to Hoyland, and now his sister, that was probably as much as he was worth. You think you have a man taped, his life spread before you like a butterfly pinned in a showcase, and he surprises you with an inconsistency.

I said, 'Did you ever help him financially?'

She hesitated. 'Not directly.'

Slowly I coaxed the story from her. She had been supporting their mother in her last illness. Mrs Aarvik had been dying of cancer painfully and protractedly. Alix paid for a nurse and private hospital treatment and, towards the end, for the services of a specialist – all beyond the stark necessities of the National Health Service. It was very expensive and her savings ran out.

'Then Paul needed treatment,' she said. 'The psychiatrist I told you about.'

The psychiatrist was also in private practice and also expensive. Miss Aarvik had an understanding bank manager who allowed her a sizeable overdraft in spite of the prevailing credit squeeze. 'I'm paying it off as quickly as I can.' She smiled ruefully. 'That's why I'm pleased about the Canadian job; it's at a much higher salary.'

Paul Billson contributed nothing.

'I knew he couldn't save,' she said. 'So what else could I do?'

What else, indeed? I thought of the £12,000 tucked away in Paul's deposit account and marvelled at the curious quirks of mankind. Here was a man whom everybody agreed to be a nonentity – a spineless, faceless creature hardly distinguishable from a jellyfish – and he was proving to be human, after all, just like the rest of us. Human enough to have an eye for the main chance and to batten mercilessly on his sister. Which may only go to show that my view of humanity is jaundiced, to say the least of it.

Anyway, it accounted for Miss Aarvik's sparsely furnished flat and for her neat but somewhat aged dress. If she was paying off a big overdraft she wouldn't be spending on luxurious fripperies. Which was a pity – she deserved better.

I said, 'Did the treatment do Paul any good?'

'I think so. He's been much quieter of late, until . . .'

Until English wrote his poisonous article and Paul blew up, nerved himself to tackle a newspaper editor, and then vanished.

'Think carefully,' I said. 'You probably know your brother better than anyone else. If he went off the rails for any reason, what would he be likely to do?'

'I can't think of anything. Unless . . .' She shook her head. 'No, that's silly.'

'It may not be,' I said encouragingly.

'Well, when he was a boy he used to dream of clearing his father's name by finding the aeroplane; actually going out to Africa and looking for it. It was never found, you know. Not a very practicable dream, I'm afraid; but Paul was never a practicable man.'

I thought about it. Somewhere south of the Mediterranean and north of the Congo. The Sahara. Not at all practicable.

'Of course, he gave up the idea long ago,' she said. 'Even Paul realized it was futile. It would need a lot of money, you see, and he never had the money.'

To tell her that her brother had his pockets stuffed with boodle would have been needlessly cruel. But now I had a lead, for what it was worth. '1936 is a long time ago,' I said. 'I doubt if there'd be anything to find now. What did your parents think of Paul's obsession?'

'My mother always said he'd grow out of it, but he never did. She lived with me and didn't see very much of him. She didn't like him talking so much about his father; she thought it was unhealthy. I suppose it was. He never knew his father, you see.'

'And *your* father – what did he think?'

She gave a wry smile. 'You must think we're an odd family. I never knew *my* father, either. He died before I was born. My mother married him during the war and he was killed in action. He was Norwegian, you know.'

'Your mother had a tough life,' I said. Two husbands killed leaving small children to bring up wasn't my idea of a bed of roses.

'Oh, she was always cheerful – right up to the end.'

'One thing puzzles me,' I said. 'Your mother was awarded £100,000 by the court. What happened to it? There must have been something left to keep her more comfortable in her old age.'

'I don't know,' said Miss Aarvik sombrely. 'I've wondered about that myself, but Mother never talked about it. You must realize that I only knew about it years afterwards when I was about thirteen. It didn't mean much then; children don't think of things that happened before they were born – the present is much more exciting.'

'But later – didn't you ask her?'

'I tried, but she would never talk about it.' She looked at me squarely. 'I think I take after my father, Torstein Aarvik; I never knew him, of course, so I can't be certain. But Paul took after Mother; they're alike in so many ways. She could be very silly and thoughtless at times. Not wilfully, you understand; but she did things without thinking too far ahead. Perhaps something happened that she was ashamed to talk about. She wasn't very bright, but I loved her very much.'

So Paul was the not too bright son of a not too bright mother. That didn't get me far. I stood up. 'Well, thank you, Miss Aarvik, for all the information. You've been very frank.'

She rose with me. 'I must thank you for your interest, Mr Stafford.' She smiled wanly. 'You've certainly been more thorough in your inquiries than the police. Do you think you can find Paul?'

That put me in a moral dilemma. As far as Franklin Engineering was concerned the case was finished; Billson hadn't embezzled the petty cash nor had he breached security as far as I knew and I couldn't load further investigation costs on to the Franklin account. Nor could I load the costs on to Stafford Security Consultants Ltd – that wouldn't be fair to Charlie Malleson or Brinton who weren't in business for charity.

Neither was I. As far as I was concerned, Paul Billson was an unbalanced man whom I had discovered to be of an unscrupulous disposition and, as far as I could see, Alix Aarvik was better off without him. I decided to give what I had to the police and call it a day.

I said diplomatically, 'Your information will make it more likely.'

'If I give you a Canadian address will you write to me?' she asked. 'I've been wondering whether I should go at all while Paul is still missing.'

It struck me that Canada was the best place for her – somewhere away from the leeching of her brother. 'There's nothing you can do if you stay here,' I said. 'I'll certainly write to you.'

She scribbled an address on a stenographic note-pad. 'I don't have a home address yet, but that's the firm I'll be working for.'

I glanced at the sheet. Apparently she'd be with the Kisko Nickel Corporation of Vancouver; I'd never heard of it. I folded the paper and dutifully put it into my wallet as she escorted me to the door. Already the street lights were on as darkness descended. I thought of the quiet fortitude with which Alix Aarvik faced a not too happy life. She had not paraded her troubles before me; indeed, it had taken quite a bit of my not inconsiderable skill to extract many of the details from her. I hoped she'd be happy in Canada; she was good value.

I deliberated about the best way to go to find a taxi and turned in the direction of Kensington High Street. As I walked a man got out of a car parked by the kerb just ahead. He waited until I came abreast of him, then said, 'Your name Stafford?' He had a rough Cockney voice.

A door slammed on the other side of the car as someone else got out. 'Yes, I'm Stafford.'

'Got a message for yer, mate. Keep yer bleedin' nose outter fings wot don't concern yer. This'll 'elp yer remember.'

He suddenly drove his fist into my midriff, just below the sternum, and I gasped and doubled up, fighting for breath. I didn't have much of a chance after that. There were three of them and when I went down they got to work with their boots. It wasn't long before I passed out – but long enough to feel the pain.

# SEVEN

A lot of people came to see me in hospital, some of whom surprised me by their appearance. The police came, of course, but they were followed by a man from the Special Branch checking on Billson because of the defence work done at Franklin Engineering. My wife didn't show up but she took the trouble to spend two minutes on the telephone ordering flowers to be sent to the hospital, which surprised me mildly.

Lord Brinton came, his hands behind his back. 'Don't want to drink this London water,' he said, and put a bottle of Malvern water on the bedside table. 'Spoils the taste of the scotch.' A bottle of Talisker joined the Malvern water.

I smiled – a painful process at the time. 'My doctor might not approve.'

'Better than bringing bloody grapes.' He pulled up a chair and sat warming his ancient and expensive bones at the wall radiator. 'Not as good as a real fire,' he grumbled.

'Hospitals don't like open fires.'

'Well,' he said. 'What the hell happened, Max?'

'I was beaten up,' I said patiently.

'So I see,' he said with a straight face. 'Why?'

'I don't know. It seems I was "poking my nose into fings wot don't concern me", to quote the spokesman of the assault committee. He neglected to be more specific.'

'Mistaken identity?'

I began to shake my head and hastily decided against it for fear it should fall off. 'He made sure he knew who I was first.'

'What were you doing in Kensington?'

'Following up on a case.' I told him about Billson and what I had done. 'Miss Aarvik will be in Canada now,' I said.

'Good country,' observed Brinton. 'I was born there.' He said it as though the act of his being born there had conferred a distinction on Canada. 'I don't see how all this relates to your being beaten up.'

'Neither do I. Neither do the police or the Special Branch.'

His eyes sharpened. 'What's their interest?'

'Franklin Engineering makes bits and pieces of tanks.'

'And they're following up on Billson?'

'So it seems – but they're not pushing too hard. For all anyone can find out he hasn't committed a crime – yet.'

'You think he might?'

'Who knows what a man like Billson might or might not do. He's lived like a vegetable for fifteen years at least, and now he's gone charging off God knows where. He could be up to anything.'

'Well, you're out of it,' said Brinton. 'By the time you get out of here Andrew McGovern will have taken over responsibility for the security of Franklin Engineering.'

'How big a piece of the Whensley Group have you got?' I asked.

'About thirty per cent. Why?'

'Then you'll be a big enough shareholder to ask why Billson was paid three times as much as he's worth and why there's a mystery made of it.'

'I'll look into it,' said Brinton. 'Can't have the shareholders diddled like that. All right, if you weren't beaten up because of Billson, what else have you been doing recently to get you into trouble?'

'My life has been blameless.'

Brinton grunted in his throat. 'Don't try to con an old sinner. Nobody's life is blameless. You're sure you haven't been sleeping in any of the wrong beds?' I just looked at him and he said, 'Not that I'd blame you under the circumstances.'

Soon after that he went away.

Charlie Malleson came to see me. He inspected my assortment of bruises, and said, 'Better not go out into the streets just yet. Someone from the Race Relations Board might get you for trying to cross the colour line.'

I sighed. 'You can do better than that, Charlie. If you have to make jokes they'd better be good. How's business?'

'We're coping. How long do you think you'll be laid up?'

'Nobody tells me anything – you know what hospitals are like. From the way I feel now it'll be about six months, but I'll probably be back in a couple of weeks.'

'Take your time,' Charlie advised. 'Jack Ellis is trying on your shoes to see if they fit.'

'Good – but that will teach me to prophesy.' Charlie raised an eyebrow and I explained. 'I told Joyce that Jack was to take some of my work load. When she queried it I said that if I got knocked down in the street he'd have to take the lot. But this wasn't the sort of knocking down I had in mind.' I thought about Jack Ellis, then said, 'It's about time we made him a director, anyway. He's become very good and we don't want to lose him.'

'I agree,' said Charlie. 'And I think old Brinton will. Max, when did you last take a holiday?'

I grinned. 'That's a funny-sounding word. Maybe two years ago.'

'It's been four years,' he said positively. 'You've been knocking yourself out. My advice is to take some time off right now while you have a good enough excuse to fool your subconscious. Take a trip to the Caribbean and soak up some sun for a couple of months.'

I looked out of the window at the slanting rain. 'Sounds good.'

Charlie smiled. 'The truth is I don't want you around while Jack is finding his feet in a top job. You can be a pretty alarming bastard at times and it might be a bit inhibiting for him.'

That made sense, and the more I thought about it the better it became. Gloria and I could go away and perhaps we could paper over some of the cracks in our marriage. I knew that, when a marriage is at breaking-point, the fault is rarely solely on one side, and my drive to set up the firm had certainly been a contributing factor. Perhaps I could do something to stick things together again.

'I'll think about it,' I said. 'But I'd better see Jack. There are one or two things he ought to know before he gets his feet wet.'

Charlie's face cracked into a pleased smile which faded as he said, 'Who assaulted you, Max?'

We kicked the Billson case around for a while and got nowhere. So Charlie left, promising to send Jack Ellis to see me.

The really surprising visitor was Alix Aarvik.

I gaped as she came in and then said, 'Sit down, Miss Aarvik – you'll excuse me if I don't stand. I thought you were in Canada.'

She sat in the leather club chair which Brinton had had installed for his own benefit. 'I changed my mind,' she said. 'I turned down the job.'

'Oh! Why?'

She inspected me. 'I'm sorry about what happened to you, Mr Stafford.'

I laughed. By this time I was able to laugh without my ribs grinding together. 'An occupational hazard.'

Her face was serious. 'Was it because of your enquiries about Paul?'

'I can't see how it could be.'

'The police came to see me again. And some others who . . . weren't ordinary police.'

'Special Branch. Paul did work in a defence industry.'

'I didn't know what to think. They were so uncommunicative.'

I nodded. 'Their job is to ask questions, not to give answers. Besides, they revel in an aura of mystery. May I ask why you turned down the Canadian job?'

She hesitated. 'About a quarter of an hour after you left my flat I went out to post a letter. There was an ambulance not far from the street door and you were being put into it.' She moistened her lips. 'I thought you were dead.'

I said slowly, 'It must have given you a shock. I'm sorry.'

There was a rigidity about her which betrayed extreme tension. She opened her mouth and swallowed as though the words would not come, then she made another attempt and said, 'Did you see who attacked you?'

The penny dropped. 'It wasn't your brother, if that's what you mean.'

She gave a long sigh and relaxed visibly. 'I had to know,' she said. 'I couldn't leave without knowing, and the police wouldn't tell me anything.'

I looked at her thoughtfully. 'If you thought your brother might attack anyone homicidally you should have warned me.'

'But I didn't think that,' she cried. 'Not when we talked together. It was only afterwards, when I saw you in the ambulance, that it occurred to me.'

I said, 'I want the truth. Have you seen Paul since he disappeared?'

'No, I haven't – I haven't.' Her face was aflame with her vehemence.

I said gently, 'I believe you.'

She was suddenly in tears. 'What's happened to Paul, Mr Stafford? What is he *doing*?'

'I don't know. Honestly, I don't know.' It took me some time to quieten her, and lying flat on my back didn't help. In order to divert her I said, 'You were being transferred to Canada. Will the fact that you turned down the offer affect your present job?'

'I don't think so,' she said. 'Sir Andrew was very good about it.'

A frisson ran down my back. 'Sir Andrew?'

'Sir Andrew McGovern. I'm his secretary.'

'You do mean the Chairman of the Whensley Group?'

'That's right. Do you know him?'

'I haven't had that pleasure. How did you come to work for him, Miss Aarvik?'

'I started work at Franklin Engineering eight years ago.' She smiled. 'In the typing pool. I like to think I'm good at my job – anyway I didn't stay long in the typing pool, and four years ago I was transferred to Group Head Office in London – that's Whensley Holdings Ltd.'

'I know,' I said. 'We handle the security.' But not for long I thought.

'Oh! You mean you employ the men who come around and make sure I've destroyed the executive typewriter ribbons?'

'Sort of. What made you start with Franklin Engineering? How did you get the job?'

'I was with a firm which went bust,' she said. 'I needed another job so Paul suggested Franklin. He'd been working there for quite a while and he said it was a good firm.'

So it was – for Paul Billson. Seeing that I'd started to open the can of worms it seemed a good idea to take the top right off. For instance, was Miss Aarvik's salary as inflated as her brother's? 'Do you mind telling me your present salary, Miss Aarvik?'

She looked at me with some surprise. 'I don't think so. I get £4200 a year – before tax.'

I sighed. That was fairly standard for a top secretary; certainly nothing out of the ordinary. And it was the most natural thing in the world to be introduced into the firm by Paul. 'Why the Canadian transfer?' I asked. 'Isn't it a bit odd for the secretary of the boss to be asked to move to another country? Or were you going with Sir Andrew?'

She shook her head. 'The way Sir Andrew put it, I was doing him a favour. The company I was going to – Kisko Nickel – is undergoing reorganization. I was to organize the office procedures, but only on loan for a year.'

'You must have been pleased about that. Wasn't it a step up? From secretarial to executive?'

'I was bucked about it,' she admitted. 'But then Paul . . .' Her voice tailed away.

'When were you offered the job?'

'It came up rather suddenly – last Monday.'

I wrinkled my brow. That was the day Hoyland rang to tell me of Billson's disappearance. There was something bloody funny going on but, for the life of me, I couldn't see how it hung together.

I smiled at her. 'Well, you see that I am very much alive. In the opinion of the police and of my associates at Stafford Security the attack on me had nothing to do with your brother.'

She looked at me squarely. 'What of your opinion?'

I lied. 'I am of the same opinion. If you want my advice you'll go straight to Sir Andrew McGovern and tell him you've reconsidered and you'll take the Canadian job after all.'

'And Paul?'

'There's nothing you can do about Paul, as I said before. He'll be found, but it's better for you to leave it to the professionals. I'll write to you in Canada.'

She nodded. 'Perhaps that would be the best thing to do.'

'One thing – I wouldn't mention to Sir Andrew that this is my advice, or that you've even seen me. My firm and Sir Andrew aren't on very good terms right now; he's fired Stafford Security and is setting up his own security organization for the Whensley Group, so I think any mention of me would be tactless, to say the least.'

Her eyes widened. 'Was this because of Paul?'

'Not at all. It happened before . . .' I stopped short. It hadn't happened before I knew about Billson. Brinton had sprung it on us at the board meeting on the afternoon when I had just returned from Franklin Engineering. I picked up quickly. 'Nothing to do with your brother at all, Miss Aarvik.'

When she had gone I stared at the ceiling for a long time. Then I opened the bedside cupboard, stripped the lead foil from Brinton's bottle of scotch, and poured myself three fingers. Brinton may have been right about it tasting better with Malvern water, but it tasted even better neat. I suddenly really needed that drink.

# EIGHT

I soon became very damned tired of that hospital and especially of the food. I had just been served a so-called lunch which began with a watery soup which looked like old dishwater and ended with an equally watery custard which resembled nothing on God's earth when my doctor walked in, full of that synthetic bonhomie which is taught in medical schools as the bedside manner.

I thrust the tray under his nose. 'Would you eat that?'

He inspected it, his nose wrinkling fastidiously. 'What's wrong with it?'

'That wasn't the question,' I snarled.

His eyes twinkled. 'Well, possibly not,' he conceded.

'That's good enough for me,' I said. 'I'm discharging myself.'

'But you're not ready.'

'And I never will be if I have to eat this slop. I'm going home to get some decent food in my belly.' For all Gloria's faults she wasn't a half-way bad cook when she wanted to be.

'The food can't be all that bad if you're beginning to feel your oats.' I glared at him and he shrugged. 'All right, but the prescribed regimen is another week's rest and then I want you back here for inspection.'

I said, 'Where are my bloody trousers?'

So I went home by taxi and found Gloria in bed with a man. They were both naked and he was a stranger – I'd never seen him before to my knowledge but Gloria had a lot of odd friends. There weren't any fireworks; I just jerked my thumb at the bedroom door and said, 'Out!' He grabbed his clothes and disappeared, looking like a skinned rabbit.

In silence I looked at the heap of tousled bedclothes into which Gloria had vanished. Presently the front door slammed and Gloria emerged, looking aggrieved and a little scared. 'But the hospital said . . .'

'Shut up!'

She was stupid enough to ignore me. She informed me at length about the kind of man I was or, rather, the kind of man I wasn't. She embroidered her diatribe with all the shortcomings she could find in me, culled from seven years of married life, and then informed me that her bedfriend hadn't been the first by a long shot, and whose fault was that? In short, she tried to work up the familiar instant Stafford row to the $n$th degree.

I didn't argue with her – I just hit her. The first time I had ever hit a woman in my life. An open palm to the side of her jaw with plenty of muscle behind it. It knocked her clean out of bed so that she lay sprawling in a tangle of sheets by the dressing-table. She was still for a few moments and then shook her head muzzily as she pushed against the floor to raise herself up. She opened her mouth and closed it again as she caught my eye. Her fingers stroked the dull red blotch on her face and she looked at me unbelievingly.

I ignored her and walked to the wardrobe from which I took a suitcase from the top shelf and began to pack. Presently I broke the silence. 'You'll be hearing from my solicitor. Until then you can have the house.'

'Where are you going?' Her voice was soft and quiet.

'Do you care?'

She had nothing to say to that so I picked up the suitcase
and left the bedroom. I went downstairs to my study and
unlocked the bureau. As I took out my passport I was aware
of Gloria standing by the door. 'You *can't* leave me,' she said
desolately.

I turned my head and looked at her. 'For God's sake, go
and put on some clothes,' I said. 'You'll die of pneumonia.'

When I put the passport and a few other papers into my
pocket and walked into the hall she was trudging disconso-
lately up the stairs. As I walked towards the front door she
screamed, 'Come back, Max!'

I shut the door gently on her shout, closing an era of my
life. *Sic transit Gloria mundi.* A lousy pun but a true one.

# NINE

I suppose if I hadn't left Gloria I wouldn't have gone on with the Billson case. Billson himself had ceased to be a security matter and was merely a half-way maniac gone on an ancestor-worshipping bender. He was of no concern to anyone but himself and, possibly, Alix Aarvik.

But I had left Gloria, which put me in a somewhat ambiguous position. It had already been agreed that I would take a holiday, partly for my own benefit and partly to give free rein to Jack Ellis. The trouble was that I didn't feel like a holiday; I couldn't see myself toasting on the sands of Montego Bay, as Charlie had suggested. And so the devil found work for idle hands.

Besides, I *had* been assaulted, and if nothing else demanded that something should be done, company policy did.

So I asked Jack Ellis to come and see me at my club. Ellis had joined us four years earlier – young, bright and eager to learn. He was still young, but that didn't worry me; Napoleon was only twenty-six when he was General of the French Army in Italy and licked hell out of the Austrians. Jack Ellis was twenty-seven, something that might hinder him when negotiating with some of the stuffier chairmen of companies, but time would cure that. In the meantime he was very good and getting better.

I took him aside into the cardroom which was empty in the afternoon. For a while we talked about his job and then I brought him up-to-date on the Billson story. He was puzzled as anyone about the whole affair.

'Jack,' I said. 'I want you to find Billson.'

He gave me an old-fashioned look. 'But he's not our pigeon any more. Apart from the fact that Whensley are running their own show now, Billson is out of it.'

I said, 'When this firm was started certain rules were laid down. Do you remember Westlake, the security guard we had at Clennel Enterprises?'

Ellis's face was grave. 'I remember. It happened just after I joined the firm. Shot in the leg during a pay-roll snatch. He had to have it amputated.'

'But do you remember what happened to the man who shot him? We got to him before the coppers did. We handed him to the law intact, although I'd have dearly loved to break his leg. We also made sure that the story got around. And that's the rule, Jack – we look after our own. If any gun-happy bandit hurts one of our men he knows he has to cope with the police *and* our boys. And to coin a phrase – "we try harder". Got the picture?'

He smiled faintly and nodded. 'In this business it makes sense,' he acknowledged.

'The top-ranking coppers aren't too happy about it,' I said, 'because they don't like private armies. But we rub along with the middle level very nicely. Anyway, a member of Stafford Security Consultants Ltd has been assaulted, and the fact it was the boss makes no difference to the principle. I'm not on a personal vendetta but I want those boys nailed.'

'Okay – but Billson!'

'He's *got* to be connected somehow, so dig into him. The police aren't doing much because it's no crime to leave a job. They've got him on a list and if they come across him

they'll ask him a few polite questions. I can't wait that long.
All the villains in London know I've been done over, and
they're laughing their heads off.'

'We should be able to get a line on Billson,' said Jack. 'It's
not easy for a man to disappear into thin air.'

'Another thing; no one is to know any of this except me,
you and the man you put on the job.'

'Not even Charlie Malleson?'

'Not even him. I suspect jiggery-pokery at high levels.' I
saw the expression on Ellis's face, and said irascibly, 'Not
Charlie, for God's sake! But I want to cut out even the possibility of a leak. Some of our top industrialists are doing
some queer things – Sir Andrew McGovern for one. Now, I
want a thorough rundown on him; particularly a survey of
any relationship he might have had with Paul Billson and
with his secretary, Alix Aarvik.'

'Okay,' said Jack. 'I'll get it started right away.'

I pondered for a moment. 'Open a routine file on this.
Your clients are Michelmore, Veasey and Templeton; send
them the bills in the normal way.' As he raised his eyebrows
I said shortly, 'They're my solicitors.'

'Right.'

'And good luck with the new job.' It wouldn't be fair to
Jack if he got the idea that when I came back everything
would be as it was before, so I said, 'If you don't drop too
many clangers it's yours for good. I'm destined for higher
things, such as busting into Europe.'

He went away a very happy man.

*It's not easy for a man to disappear into thin air.*

Those praiseworthy citizens who form and join societies
dedicated to the preservation of civil liberties are quite right
in their concern about the 'data bank' society. At Stafford
Security we weren't a whit concerned about civil liberties;
what we were doing was preserving the industrial secrecy of

our clients, which doesn't amount to the same thing at all.
As a corollary, because we protected against snooping we
understood it, and were well equipped to do some snooping
ourselves should the mood take us.

The bloodhounds were turned on to Paul Billson. No
man living in a so-called civilized society can escape docu-
mentation. His name, and sometimes a number attached to
his name, is listed on forms without end – driving licence,
radio and TV licence, dog licence, income tax return, insurance applications, telephone accounts, gas and electricity
accounts, passport applications, visa applications, hire purchase agreements, birth certificate, marriage certificate,
death certificate. It seems that half the population is pushing around pieces of paper concerning the other half – and
vice versa.

It takes a trained man with a hazy sense of ethics to fer-
ret out another man's life from the confusion but it can be
done, given the time and the money – the less time the
more money it takes, that's all. Jack Ellis hoisted
Michelmore, Veasey and Templeton's bill a few notches and
the information started to come in.

Paul Billson applied for a passport the day after he disappeared, appearing in person at the London Passport Office
to fill in the form. The same day he applied for an international driving licence. The following day he bought a Land-
Rover off the shelf at the main London showroom, paid
cash on the barrel and drove it away.

We lost him for a couple of weeks until he picked up
his passport, then a quick tour of the consulates by a
smooth operator revealed that he had applied for and
been granted visas for Niger, Mali, Chad and Libya. That
led to the question of what he was doing with the Land-
Rover. He had got his green insurance card for foreign
travel but a run around the shipping companies found
nothing at all. Then our man at Heathrow turned up an

invoice which told that a Mr Billson had air-freighted a
Land-Rover to Algiers.

Whatever had happened to Paul had blown him wide
open. After a lifetime of inactive griping about injustice, of
cold internal anger, of ineffectual mumblings, he had suddenly erupted and was spending money as though he had a
private mint. Air freight isn't cheap.

What Jack had dug up about Billson's finances was fantastic. The £12,000 in Paul's deposit account was but the tip
of an iceberg, and he had nearly £65,000 to play around
with. 'I don't know where the hell he got it,' said Jack.

'I do,' I said. 'He saved it. When he vanished he was on
£8000 a year and spending about £2500. You do that for
enough years and are careful with your investments and
you'll soon rack up £65,000.'

Jack said, 'I'll tell you something, Max; someone else is
looking for Billson. We've been crossing their tracks.'

'The police?'

'I don't think so. Not their style.'

'The Special Branch, then?'

'Could be. They move in mysterious ways their wonders
to perform.'

I stretched out an arm for the telephone. 'I'll ask.'

Because some of our clients, such as Franklin
Engineering, were into defence work, contact with the
Special Branch was inevitable for Stafford Security. It was
an uneasy relationship and we were tolerated only because
we could take off them some of their work load. If, for
example, we saw signs of subversion we tipped them off
and were rewarded by being left alone. A strictly confiden-
tial relationship, of course; the trades unions would have
raised hell had they known.

The man I rang was politely amused. 'Billson is no concern of ours. We checked back on what you told us; we
even interviewed that bloody journalist – now there's a

slimy bit of work. As far as we're concerned, Billson is a semi-paranoiac who has gone off the rails a bit. He might interest a psychiatrist, but he doesn't interest us.'

'Thanks.' I put down the telephone and said to Jack, 'He says they aren't interested, but would he tell me the truth?' I frowned as I turned the pages of the report 'Algiers! Why didn't Billson apply for an Algerian visa?'

'He didn't need to. British citizens don't need visas for Algeria.' Jack produced another thin file. 'About Sir Andrew McGovern. Relationship with Billson – apart from the fact that they're remotely linked through Franklin Engineering – nil. Relationship with Alix Aarvik – nil. It's a straight master-and-servant deal – they're not even "just good friends". The Kisko Nickel Corporation *is* undergoing an internal reorganization due to a merger which McGovern engineered. But Alix Aarvik didn't go to Canada; she's still operating as McGovern's secretary.'

I shrugged. 'As I once said to Brinton, the best thing about advice is that you needn't take it.' I smiled sourly. 'It turned out that his advice was good, but that's no reason for Alix Aarvik to take mine.'

'Apart from that there's not much to get hold of in McGovern,' said Jack. 'He does seem to live in Brinton's pocket.'

'Not quite,' I said absently. 'Brinton has been having trouble with him. That's why we lost the Whensley account.' I was thinking of the Sahara; of how big and empty it was.

Jack sniffed. 'If they have quarrelled no one would notice it. McGovern entertained Brinton at his home two days ago.'

I said, 'If Brinton pats Andrew McGovern on the back it's just to find a good spot to stick the knife. Thanks, Jack; you've done a good job. I'll take it from here.'

When he had gone I rang Whensley Holdings and asked for Miss Aarvik. When she came on the line I said, 'Max Stafford here. So you didn't go to Canada, after all.'

'Sir Andrew changed his mind.'

'Did he? Miss Aarvik, I have some information about your brother which I think you ought to know. Will you have dinner with me tonight?'

She hesitated, then said, 'Very well. Thank you for your continued interest in my brother, Mr Stafford.'

'I'll call for you at your flat at seven-thirty,' I said.

After that I went down to the club library, took down *The Times Atlas*, and studied a map of the Sahara for a long time. It didn't take me as long as that to find out that the idea burgeoning in my mind was totally fantastic, utterly irresponsible and probably bloody impossible.

# TEN

I picked up Alix Aarvik that evening and took her to a French restaurant, an unpretentious place with good food. It was only after we had chosen from the menu that I opened the subject over a couple of sherries. I told her where Paul Billson was.

'So he *is* trying to find the plane,' she said. 'But it's totally impossible. He's not the man to . . .' She stopped suddenly. 'How can he afford to do that?'

I sighed. Alix Aarvik was due to receive a shock. 'He's been holding out on you. Probably for a long time, judging by the cash he squirrelled away. He was getting £8000 a year from Franklin Engineering.'

It took a while for it to sink in, but as it did her face went pale and pink spots appeared in her cheeks. 'He could do *that*!' she whispered. 'He could let me pay his bills and not put up a penny for Mother's support.'

She was becoming very angry. I liked that; it was time someone got mad at Paul Billson. I wasn't so cool about him myself. I said, 'I'm sorry to have administered the shock, but I thought you ought to know.'

She was silent for a while, looking down into her glass and aimlessly rotating the stem between her fingers. At last she said, 'I just don't understand him.'

'It seems he didn't abandon his boyhood dream. He saved up his money to fulfil it.'

'At my expense,' she snapped. She gave a shaky laugh. 'But you must be wrong, Mr Stafford. I know what Paul was doing at Franklin Engineering. They wouldn't pay him that much.'

'That's another mystery. It seems they did. Your brother had damn near £60,000 to his name when he pushed off – and he turned it all into hard cash. If he's taken it with him to Algiers he's put a hell of a crimp into the currency regulations. I think Paul is now a law-breaker.'

'But this is ridiculous.'

'I agree – but it's also true; Paul has gone to look for his father's plane. I can't think of any other reason why he should shoot off to Algiers with a Land-Rover. He's looking for a plane which crashed over forty years ago and that's a hell of a long time. I was looking at a map this afternoon. Do you know how big the Sahara is?' She shook her head and I said grimly, 'Three million square miles – just about the same size as the United States but a hell of a lot emptier. It'll be like searching the proverbial haystack for the needle, with the difference that the needle might not be there.'

'What do you mean by that?'

'Suppose Hendrik van Niekirk really did see Peter Billson in Durban after he was supposed to have crashed. You can lay ten to one that Billson wouldn't have left that plane lying around for anyone to find. If he was a faker after that insurance money my guess is that he'd ditch off-shore in the Mediterranean. He'd row himself ashore in a collapsible dinghy – they had those in 1936, I've checked – and get himself lost. So Paul might be looking for something in the desert that's not there.'

'I don't like that,' she said coldly. 'You're implying that my mother was party to a fraud.'

'I'm sorry,' I said. 'I don't like it much myself, but it's a possibility that has to be considered. I do it all the time in my business, Miss Aarvik.'

A waiter interrupted us by bringing the first course. Over the onion soup I said, 'Anyway, that's where your brother is – somewhere in Algeria if he isn't already in Niger or Chad or somewhere else as improbable.'

'He must be brought back,' she said. 'Mr Stafford, I don't have much money, but is it at all possible for your detective agency to look for him?'

'I don't run a detective agency,' I said. 'I run a security organization. Lots of people get the two confused. Frankly, I don't see why you want him back. You've just heard of how he's been deceiving you for years. I think you're better off without him.'

'He's my brother,' she said simply. 'He's the only family I have in the world.'

She looked so woebegone that I took pity on her. I suppose it was then the decision was made. Of course I hedged it about with 'ifs' and 'maybes' as a sop to my conscience should I renege, but the decision was made.

I said carefully, 'There's a possibility – just a possibility, mind you – that I may be going to North Africa in the near future. If I do, I'll ask around to see if I can find him.'

She lit up as though I'd given her the key to the Bank of England. 'That's very good of you,' she said warmly.

'Don't go overboard about it,' I warned. 'Even if I do find him your troubles aren't over. Supposing he doesn't want to come back – what am I supposed to do? Kidnap him? He's a free agent, you know.'

'If you find him send me a cable and I'll fly out. If I can talk to Paul I can get him to come back.'

'No doubt you can, but the first problem is to find him. But we have some things going for us. Firstly, there are large areas of the Sahara where he will *not* look for the air-craft.' I paused and then said acidly, 'Not if he has any sense, that is, which I beg leave to doubt'

'Oh! Which areas?'

'The inhabited bits – the Sahara is not all blasted wilderness. Then there's the course Peter Billson intended to fly – that should give us a rough indication of where the plane is likely to be. Is there anyone who'd know such an odd item of information after forty years?'

She shook her head despondently, then said slowly, 'There's a man in the Aeronautical Section of the Science Museum – Paul used to talk to him a lot. He's some sort of aeronautical historian, he has all sorts of details in his records. I don't remember his name, though.'

'I'll check,' I said. 'The other point in our favour is that in a relatively empty land a stranger tends to stand out. If Paul is buzzing about remote areas in a Land-Rover he'll leave a pretty well-defined trail.'

She smiled at me. 'You're making me feel better already.'

'Don't raise your hopes too high. When . . . if I go to North Africa I'll send you an address where you can contact me.'

She nodded briefly and we got on with the meal.

I took her home quite early and then went back to the club to bump into Charlie Malleson who was just coming out. 'I thought I'd missed you,' he said. 'I was just passing and I thought I'd pop in to see you.'

I glanced at my watch. 'The bar's still open. What about a drink?'

'Fine.'

We took our drinks to an isolated table and Charlie said, 'I rang you at home but no one was in, so I took a chance on finding you here.' I merely nodded, and he cleared his throat uncomfortably. 'Is it true what I hear about you and Gloria?'

'Depends what you've heard, but I can guess what it is. Bad news gets around fast. It's true enough. Where did you hear it?'

'Brinton was saying something yesterday. Gloria's been talking to him.'

'Getting her version in first, no doubt. She won't impress Brinton.'

'Well, I'm truly sorry it happened this way. Are you starting a divorce action?'

'It's in the hands of my solicitor now.'

'I see,' he said slowly. I don't know what he saw and I didn't really care. 'How are you feeling otherwise?' he asked. 'You're not long out of hospital.'

I looked at him over the edge of my glass. 'Have you ever been beaten up, Charlie? Given a thorough going-over by experts?'

'I can't say that I have.'

'It's the most degrading thing that can happen to a man,' I said flatly. 'It isn't so much what they do to the body; that can stand a lot of punishment. It's the feeling of utter helplessness. You're no longer your own man – you're in the hands of others who can do with you what they like. And you ask me how I feel.'

'You're bitter about it, aren't you, Max? You know, I didn't expect that of you.'

'Why not?'

'Well, you have the reputation of being a pretty cold fish, you know. You run your end of the business like a computer.'

'There's nothing wrong with being logical and acting logically,' I said.

'No.' There was a pause before Charlie said, 'I suppose the divorce will keep you in England.'

I drained my glass. 'I don't see why it should. I'm thinking of taking your advice to soak up some sun. I'll be glad to get away from London for a while.'

Charlie looked pleased. 'It'll do you good; you'll come back like a new man.'

'How is Jack Ellis settling in?'

'Very well. I'm glad you said what you did to him about the job; it's cleared the air and makes things easier all round. How long do you expect to be away?'

'I don't really know. Hold the fort, double the profits and bank the proceeds. Expect me when you see me.'

We talked idly for a few more minutes and then Charlie took his leave. I had an obscure feeling that he had not 'dropped by in passing' but had come for a reason, to get some question answered. About the divorce? About my health? I went over the conversation and wondered if he had got his answer.

I had an uneasy night. I thought of myself as seen by others – Max Stafford, the cold fish. I hadn't known Charlie had thought of me in that way. We had always been personal friends as well as getting on well with each other in the business. To get a flash of illumination on oneself through the eyes of another can sometimes come as a shock.

I slept and woke again after having bad dreams of vaguely impending doom. I lay with open eyes for a long time and then, finding sleep impossible, I turned on the bedside light and lit a cigarette.

I prided myself on thinking and acting logically, but where in hell was the logic of goose-chasing to Algiers? The sexual bounce, maybe, from Gloria to Alix Aarvik? The desire to be the parfit, gentil knight on a white charger going on a quest to impress the maiden? I rejected that. Alix Aarvik was a nice enough girl but there was certainly no sexual attraction. Maybe Max Stafford was a cold fish, after all.

What, then?

Maybe it was because I thought I was being manipulated. I thought of Andrew McGovern. He had tried to send Alix to Canada. Why? In the event he didn't send her. Why? Was it because I had been a bit too quick and caught her and talked to her the day before she was supposed to leave? If the damage had been done there would be no reason to send her away. I had been beaten up immediately after I had seen her. If McGovern had been responsible for that I'd have to think up some new and novel punishment for him.

Was McGovern deliberately putting pressure on me through Brinton? Brinton, on the day of the board meeting, had said he was under pressure from McGovern. What sort of a hold could McGovern have over a shark like Brinton? And if McGovern was doing the squeezing, why was he doing it?

Then there was Paul Billson. Before he entered my life I had been moderately happy, but from the moment Hoyland rang me up to have his hand held there had been nothing but trouble. Everything seemed to revolve around Paul, a man obsessed.

Logic! If everything revolved around Paul Billson, maybe he was the person to talk to. Maybe going to Algiers wasn't such a bad idea, after all.

I put out the light and slept.

Three days later I flew to Algiers.

# ELEVEN

Algiers is the only city I know where the main post office looks like a mosque and the chief mosque looks like a post office. Not that I spent much time in the mosque but I thought I had made a major error when I entered the post office for the first time to collect letters from poste restante. I gazed in wonder at that vast hushed hall with its fretted screens and arabesques and came to the conclusion that it was an Eastern attempt to emulate the reverential and cathedral-like atmosphere affected by the major British banks. I got to know the post office quite well.

Getting to know the whereabouts of Paul Billson was not as easy. Although my French was good, my Arabic was non-existent, which made it no easier to fight my way through the Byzantine complexities of Algerian bureaucracy, an amorphous structure obeying Parkinson's Law to the $n$th degree.

The track of my wanderings over Algiers, if recorded on a map, would have resembled the meanderings of a demented spider. At the twentieth office where my passport was given the routine fifteen-minute inspection by a suspicion-haunted official for the twentieth time my patience was nearly at snapping point. The trouble was that I was not on my own ground and the Algerians worked to different rules.

My hotel was in Hamma, in the centre of town near the National Museum, and when I returned, early one evening, I was dispirited. After a week in Algiers I had got nowhere, and if I couldn't track Billson in a city what hope would I have in the desert? It seemed that my cutting edge had blunted from lack of practice.

As I walked across the foyer to collect my room key I was accosted by a tall Arab wearing the ubiquitous *djellaba*. 'M'sieur Stafford?'

'Yes, I'm Stafford.'

Wordlessly he handed me an envelope inscribed with my surname and nothing else. I looked at him curiously as I opened it and he returned my gaze with unblinking brown eyes. Inside the envelope was a single sheet of paper, unheaded and with but two typewritten lines:

I believe you are looking for Paul Billson.
Why don't you come to see me?

There was a signature underneath but it was an indecipherable scrawl.

I glanced at the Arab. 'Who sent this?'

He answered with a gesture towards the hotel entrance. 'This way.'

I pondered for a moment and nodded, then followed him from the hotel where he opened the rear door of a big Mercedes. I sat down and he slammed the door smartly and got behind the wheel. As he started the engine I said, 'Where are we going?'

'Bouzarea.' After that he concentrated on his driving and refused to answer questions. I gave up, leaned back in cushioned luxury, and watched Algiers flow by.

The road to Bouzarea climbed steeply out of the city and I twisted to look through the back window and saw Algiers spread below with the Mediterranean beyond, darkening towards the east as the sun set. Already strings of lights were appearing in the streets.

I turned back as the car swung around a corner and pulled up against a long wall, blank except for a small door. The Arab got out and opened the car door and indicated the door in the wall which was already swinging open. I walked through into a large walled garden which appeared to be slightly smaller than Windsor Great Park, but not much. In the middle distance was a low-slung, flat-roofed house which rambled inconsequently over the better part of an acre. The place stank of money.

The door behind closed with the snap of a lock and I turned to confront another Arab, an old man with a seamed, walnut face. I didn't understand what he said but the beckoning gesture was unmistakable, so I followed him towards the house.

He led me through the house and into an inner court-yard, upon which he vanished like a puff of smoke into some hidden recess. A woman lay upon a chaise-longue. 'Stafford?'

'Yes – Max Stafford.'

She was oldish, about sixty plus, I guessed, and was dressed in a style which might have been thought old-fashioned. Her hair was white and she could have been anyone's old mother but for two things. The first was her face, which was tanned to the colour of brown shoe leather. There was a network of deep wrinkles about her eyes which betokened too much sun, and those eyes were a startling blue. The blue eyes and the white hair set against that face made a spectacular combination. The second thing was that she was smoking the biggest Havana cigar I've ever seen.

'What's your poison? Scotch? Rye? Gin? You name it.' Her voice was definitely North American.

I smiled slowly. 'I never take drinks from strangers.'

She laughed. 'I'm Hesther Raulier. Sit down, Max
Stafford, but before you do, pour yourself a drink. Save me
getting up.'

There was an array of bottles on a portable bar so I went
and poured myself a scotch and added water from a silver
jug. As I sat in the wicker chair she said, 'What are you
doing in Algiers?'

She spoke English but when she said 'Algiers' it came out
as *'el Djeza'ir'*. Then she was speaking Arabic. I said,
'Looking for Paul Billson.'

'Why?'

I sipped the scotch. 'What business is it of yours?'

She offered me a gamine grin. 'I'll tell you if you tell me.'

I looked up at the sky. 'Is it always as pleasant here in
winter?'

She laid down her cigar carefully in a big ashtray. 'So
okay, Stafford; you're a hard trader. But just tell me one
thing. Are you here to hurt Paul?'

'Why should I want to hurt him?'

'For Christ's sake!' she said irritably. 'Must you always
answer a question with a question?'

'Yes, I must,' I said sharply. 'Until you declare your
interest.'

'So, all right; let's quit fencing.' She swung her legs off
the chaise-longue and stood up. Her build was stocky and
she was a muscular old bird. 'I was a friend of Paul's father.'

That sounded promising, so I gave measure for measure.
'His sister is worried about him.'

Her voice was sharp. 'His sister? I didn't know Peter
Billson had a daughter.'

'He didn't. His widow remarried during the war to a
Norwegian who was killed. Alix Aarvik is Paul's half-sister.'

Hesther Raulier seemed lost in thought. After a while she
said, 'Poor Helen; she sure had a tough time.'

'Did you know her?'

'I knew them both.' She went over to the bar and poured a hefty slug of neat rye whisky. She downed the lot in one swallow and shuddered a little. 'Paul told me Helen had died but he said nothing about a sister.'

'He wouldn't.'

She swung around. 'What's that supposed to mean?'

'He treated her pretty badly. People don't talk about those to whom they've been unkind. I'll tell you this much – Paul wasn't much help to his mother in her last years.' I picked up my glass again. 'Why should you think I'd hurt Paul?'

She gave me a level stare. 'I'll have to know a lot more about you before I tell you that, Max Stafford.'

'Fair enough,' I said. 'And I'll need to know a lot more about you.'

She smiled faintly. 'Seems we're going to have us a real gabfest. You'd better stay to dinner.'

'Thanks. But tell me something. Where is Paul now?'

'Come with me,' she said, and led me into the garden where she pointed to the south at a low range of hills just visible in the twilight. 'See those? Those are the foothills of the Atlas. Paul Billson is way to hell and gone the other side.'

By the time we went in to dinner our stiff-legged attitude had relaxed. I was curious about this elderly, profane woman who used an antique American slang; any moment I expected her to come out with 'twenty-three, skidoo'. I gave her a carefully edited account and ended up, 'That's it; that's why I'm here.'

She was drinking whisky as though she ran her own distillery at the bottom of the garden but not one white hair had twitched. 'A likely story,' she said sardonically. 'A big important man like you drops everything and comes to Algiers looking for Paul. Are you sweet on Alix Aarvik?'

'I hardly know her. Besides, she's too young for me.'

'No girl is too young for any man – *I know*. You'll have to do better than that, Max.'

'It was a chain of circumstances,' I said tiredly. 'For one thing I'm divorcing my wife and I wanted to get out of it for a while.'

'Divorcing your wife,' she repeated. 'Because of Alix Aarvik?'

'Because the man in her bed wasn't me,' I snapped.

'I *believe* you,' she said soothingly. 'Okay, what's your percentage? What do you get out of it?'

'I don't know what you mean.'

A cold blue eye bored into me. 'Look, buster; don't give me any of that Limey blandness. You tell me what I want to know or you get nothing.'

I sighed. 'Maybe I don't like being beaten up,' I said, and told her the rest of it.

She was silent for a moment, then said, 'That's a hell of a concoction – but I believe it. It's too crazy to be a spur-of-the-moment story.'

'I'm glad to hear you say that,' I said feelingly. 'Now it's my turn. How do you happen to live in Algiers – for starters.'

She looked surprised. 'Hell, I was born here.' It seemed that her father was of French-Arab mixture and her mother was Canadian; how that unlikely match came about she didn't say. Her mother must have been a strong-minded woman because Hesther was sent to school in Canada instead of going to France like most of the children of the wealthy French colonists.

'But I haven't been back in years,' she said. That would account for her outdated slang.

She had met Peter Billson in Canada. 'He was older than I was, of course,' she said. 'Let's see; it must have been 1933, so I'd be seventeen.'

And Billson was thirty. Hesther was on vacation, visiting the home of a schoolfriend, when Billson came into her life. She was the guest of McKenzie, a wealthy Canadian who was interested in the development of air travel, particularly in the more remote parts of Canada. Billson had begun to make a name for himself, so McKenzie had invited him for a long weekend to pick his brains.

Hesther said, 'It was like meeting God – you know what kids are. These days they go nuts over long-haired singers but in those days the fliers were top of the heap.'

'What sort of a man was he?'

'He was a man,' she said simply. She stared blindly back into the past. 'Of course he had his faults – who hasn't? – but they were the faults of his profession. Peter Billson was a good pilot, a brave man ambitious for fame, an exhibitionist – all the early fliers were like that, all touting for the adulation of the idiotic public.'

'How well did you get to know him?'

She gave me a sideways look. 'About as well as a woman can get to know a man. 1933 was the year I lost my virginity.'

It was hard to imagine this tough, leathery woman as a seventeen-year-old in the toils of love. 'Was that before Billson married?'

Hesther shook her head. 'I felt like hell when I had to talk to Helen over the coffee cups. I was sure I had guilt printed right across my forehead.'

'How long did you know him?'

'Until he died. I was supposed to come back here in 1934 but I managed to stretch out another year – because of Peter. He used to see me every time he was in Toronto. Then in 1935 I had to come back because my mother threatened to cut off the funds. The next time I saw Peter was when he landed here during the London to Cape Town Air Race of '36. I saw him take off from here and I never saw him again.' There was a bleakness in her voice when she added, 'I never married, you know.'

There wasn't much to say to that. After a few moments I broke the uncomfortable silence. 'I hope you won't mind telling me a bit more about that. Did you know his flight plan, for instance?'

'I don't mind,' she said a little wearily. 'But I don't know much. I was a girl of twenty, remember – and no technician. He had that beefed-up Northrop which was a freight carrier. Jock Anderson had installed extra gas tanks in the cargo space and the plan was to fly south from Algiers to Kano in Nigeria. The desert crossing was going to be the most difficult leg, so Jock came here with a team to give the plane a thorough check before Peter took off.'

'Jock Anderson – who was he?'

'The flight mechanic. Peter and Jock had been together a long time. Peter flew the planes and pushed them hard, and Jock kept the pieces together when they threatened to bust apart. They made a good team. Jock was a good engineer.'

'What happened to him afterwards?'

'When Peter disappeared he broke up. I've never seen a man get drunk so fast. He went on a three-day splurge, then he sobered-up and left Algiers. I haven't seen him since.'

I pondered on that but it led nowhere. 'What do you think of Paul Billson?'

'I think he's a nut,' she said. 'Hysterical and crazy. Totally unlike his father in every way.'

'How did you get to know him?'

'Same way as I got to know you. I have ears all over this city and when I heard of a man looking into Peter Billson I was curious so I sent for him.'

'All right,' I said. 'Where is he?'

'Gone looking for his Daddy. By now he'll be in Tammanrasset.'

'Where's that?'

Hesther gave me a crooked smile. 'You go south *into* the desert until you're going *out* of the desert. That's Tammanrasset, in the Ahaggar about two thousand kilometres south of here. Plumb in the middle of the Sahara.'

I whistled. 'Why there?'

'If you're looking for something in the Ahaggar, Tam is a good place to start.'

'What's the Ahaggar like?'

Hesther looked at me for a moment before she said, 'Mountainous and dry.'

'How big?'

'Christ, I don't know – I haven't measured it lately. Wait a minute.' She went away and returned with a book. 'The *Annexe du Hoggar* – that's the administrative area – is 380,000 square kilometres.' She looked up. 'I don't know what that is in square miles; you'll have to figure that yourself.'

I did, and it came to nearly 150,000 square miles – three times the area of the United Kingdom. 'Paul Billson *is* crazy,' I said. 'What's the population?'

Hesther consulted the book again. 'About twelve thousand.'

'There doesn't seem much to administer. People are thin on the ground out there.'

'If you go there you'll find out why,' she said. 'Are you thinking of going after him?'

'The idea has crossed my mind,' I admitted. 'Which makes me as crazy as he is, I suppose.'

'Not really. You should find him easy enough. Getting to Tammanrasset is no problem – there are a couple of flights a week.'

'If I can fly that does make it easier.'

She nodded. 'Then all you have to do is to wait in Tammanrasset until he shows up. If he's in the Ahaggar and wants more gas there's no place he can get it except Tam.' She considered for a moment. 'Of course, if you want to chase after him, that's different. You'd need a guide. Luke Byrne is usually in Tam at this time of year – he might fancy the job.'

'Who's he?'

She laughed. 'Another crazy man. It would tickle his fancy to go looking for a lunatic.' She lit an after-dinner cigar. 'If you're going to Tam you'll need a permit. If you try to get one yourself it'll take two weeks – I can get you one in two days. What will you do when you find Paul Billson?'

I shrugged. 'Persuade him to go back to England if I can.'

'You'll find it hard cutting through that obsession.'

'His sister might stand a better chance, and she said she'd come out. Would you help her, as you're helping me?'

'Sure.'

'What do you believe?' I asked. 'Is Peter Billson's body out there somewhere?'

'Sure it is – what's left of it. I know what you mean; I read about that South African son-of-a-bitch who said he'd seen Peter in Durban. I've often wondered how big a bribe the bastard took. I'll tell you this, Max; Peter Billson wasn't an angel, not by a long way, but he was honest about money. And Helen was the next thing to an angel and no one's going to tell me that she perjured herself for half a million bucks. It just wasn't their style.'

She sighed. 'Let's quit talking about it now, shall we? It's not been my practice to look too deeply into the past, and I'm not ready to start now.'

'I'm sorry,' I said. 'Perhaps I'd better go.'

'Hell, no!' she said. 'Stick around and have some more brandy and I'll match you for dirty stories.'

'All right,' I said obligingly, and told her the limerick about the Bishop of Chichester who made all the saints in their niches stir.

I didn't see Hesther again at that time, but she certainly had some pull because I was ready to leave in a day and a half complete with permit and a seat booked on the plane at her expense delivered to my hotel by her Arab chauffeur. In a covering note she wrote:

I hope you don't mind about the plane ticket; it's just that I'd like to do my bit towards the memory of P.B. If you do find that idiot, Paul, club him on the head, put him in a sack and ship him back to Algiers.

I wired Luke Byrne and he'll be expecting you. You'll find him at the Hotel Tin Hinan. Give him my regards.

I don't know if it means anything but someone else is looking for Paul – a man called Kissack. I don't know anything about him because he blew town before I could check on him.

Best of luck, and come back for another visit.

# TWELVE

I didn't know, what to expect of Tammanrasset but it was certainly different from Algiers. From the air it was a scattering of houses set in a mist of green at the foot of barren hills. Transport from the airstrip was by truck along an asphalted road which led between tall, square pillars which were the entrance to the town. They looked like the decor for a fifth-rate B-movie about the Foreign Legion.

I called it a town, but it would be more appropriate to call it a village. Be that as it may, it was the metropolis of the Ahaggar. The main street was wide, shaded by acacia trees, and bordered by single-storey houses apparently made of dried mud which looked as though they'd wash away in a half-way decent shower of rain. The truck driver blared his horn to clear a path through the pedestrians, tall men dressed in blue and white who thronged the centre of the street as though the internal combustion engine hadn't been invented.

The truck drew up outside the Hotel Tin Hinan where there was a tree-shaded courtyard filled with spindly metal tables and chairs at which people sat drinking. From a loudspeaker above the hotel entrance came the nasal wail of an Eastern singer. I went inside into a dusty hall and waited until someone noticed me. There was no reception desk.

Presently I was noticed. A dapper man in none too clean whites asked in massacred French what he could do for me. I said, 'There should be a reservation. My name is Stafford.'

His eyebrows lifted. 'Ah, M'sieur Stafford! M'sieur Byrne awaits you.' He steered me to the door and pointed. *'Voilà!'*

I stared at the man sitting at the table. He was dressed in a long blue robe and a white turban and he looked like nobody who could be called Byrne. I turned back to the receptionist only to find that he had gone back into the hotel, so I walked over to the table and said hesitantly, 'Mr Byrne?'

The man hesitated with a glass of beer half way to his lips and then set it down. 'Yes,' he said, and turned to face me. Under shaggy white eyebrows blue eyes stared out of a deeply tanned face which was thin to the point of emaciation so that the nose jutted out like a beak. Beneath the nose was a wide mouth with thin lips firmly compressed. I could not see his chin because a fold of his turban had somehow become wrapped about his neck, but his cheeks were bearded with white hair. He looked like Moses and twice as old.

I said, 'My name is Stafford.'

'Sit down, Mr Stafford. Have a beer?' He spoke in English with an American accent which, under the circumstances, was incongruous.

As I sat down he beckoned to a waiter. *'Deux bières.'* He turned back to me. 'Hesther told me about you. She said you might need help.'

'I might. I'm looking for a man.'

'So? Most men look for women.'

'His name is Billson. He's around here somewhere.'

'Billson,' Byrne repeated thoughtfully. 'Why do you want him?'

'I don't know that I do,' I said. 'But his sister does. He's looking for a crashed aeroplane. Are there any of those about here?'

'A couple.'

'This one crashed over forty years ago.'

Byrne's expression didn't change. 'None as old as that.' The waiter came back and put down two bottles of lager and two glasses; Byrne nodded at him briefly and he went away. It seemed that Byrne had a line of credit at the Hotel Tin Hinan.

I poured the beer. 'I'm told the Ahaggar is a big place – very mountainous. A wrecked plane may not have been found.'

'It would be,' said Byrne.

'But, surely, with the thin population . . .'

'It would be found.' Byrne was positive. 'How did Billson get here? By air?'

'He has a Land-Rover.'

'How long has he been here?'

I shrugged. 'I don't know. A week – maybe two.'

Byrne stared into the street without moving his eyes and was silent for some time. I leaned back in the chair and let him think it over. This was a man I found hard to assess because I had no notion of the springs which moved him. He was as alien to me as any of the men dressed like him who strolled in the street, in spite of the fact that he spoke English.

Presently he asked, 'How well do you know Hesther Raulier?'

'Hardly at all. I met her only two days ago.'

'She likes you,' he said. 'Got a bag?'

I jerked my thumb in the direction of the hotel entrance. 'In there.'

'Leave it lay – we'll pick it up later. I'm camped just outside Tam; let's take a walk.' He arose and did something complicated with his head cloth, making quite a production of it. When he had finished his face was hidden, and the cloth left only a slit at eye-level through which he looked.

We left the hotel and walked along the main street of Tammanrasset in a direction away from the airstrip. Byrne was a tall man, yet no taller than any of the other men who, similarly dressed, walked languidly in the street. It was I who was the incongruous figure in that place.

'Do you always dress like an Arab?' I asked.

'Not if I can help it. I don't like Arabs.'

I stared at him because his answer was incomprehensible. 'But . . .'

He bent his head and said, with some amusement, 'You have a lot to learn, Stafford. These guys aren't Arab, they're Imazighen – Tuareg, if you prefer.'

Byrne's camp was about two miles outside the village. It consisted of three large leather tents set in a semi-circle, their backs to the wind. The sand in front of them had been swept smooth and, to one side, a small fire crackled, setting off detonations like miniature fireworks. In the middle distance camels browsed.

As we approached, a man who had been squatting next to the fire stood up. 'That's Mokhtar,' said Byrne. 'He'll look after you while I'm away.'

'Where are you going?'

'To snoop around. But first you tell me more about Billson.'

Byrne strode over to the fire and the two men had a brief conversation. Mokhtar was another tall man who wore the veil. Byrne beckoned me to join him in the middle tent where we sat on soft rugs. The inner walls of the tent were made of reeds.

'Right; why does Billson want to find a forty-year-old crash?'

'It killed his father,' I said, and related the story.

I had just finished when Mokhtar laid a brass tray before Byrne; on it was a spouted pot and two brass cups. 'You like mint tea?' asked Byrne.

'Never had any.'

'It's not bad.' He poured liquid and handed a cup to me. 'Would you say Billson was right in the head?'

'No, I wouldn't. He's obsessed.'

'That's what I figured.' He drank from his cup and I followed suit. It was spearminty and oversweet. 'How does Hesther come into this?'

'She knew Billson's father.'

'How well?'

I looked him in the eye. 'If she wants you to know she'll tell you.'

He smiled. 'Okay, Stafford; no need to get sassy. Did you learn this from Hesther herself?' When I nodded, he said, 'You must have got right next to her. She don't talk much about herself.'

I said, 'What chance has Billson of finding the plane?'

'In the Ahaggar? None at all, because it isn't here. Quite a few wrecks scattered further north, though.' He laughed suddenly. 'Hell, I put one of them there myself.'

I glanced at him curiously. 'How did that happen?'

'It was during the war. I was in the Army Air Force, flying Liberators out of Oran. We got jumped by a gang of Focke-Wolfs and had the hell shot out of us. The cockpit was in a mess – no compass working – we didn't know where the hell we were. Then the engines gave up so I put down. I guess that airplane's still where I put it.'

'What happened then?'

'I walked out,' said Byrne laconically. 'Took a week and a half.' He stood up. 'I'll be back in a couple of hours.'

I watched him walk away with the smooth, almost lazy stride I had already noticed was common to the Tuareg, and wondered what the hell he was doing in the desert.

Presently Mokhtar came over with another tray of mint tea together with small round cakes.

* * *

It was three hours before Byrne came back, and he came riding a camel. The sun was setting and the thorn trees cast long shadows. The beast rocked to its knees and Byrne slid from the saddle, then came into the tent carrying my bag. The camel snorted as Mokhtar urged it to its feet and led it away.

Byrne sat down. 'I've found your boy.'

'Where is he?'

He pointed north. 'Out there somewhere – in the mountains. He left five days ago. He applied at Fort Lapperine for a *permis* but they wouldn't give him one, so he left anyway. He's a goddamn fool.'

'That I know,' I said. 'Why wouldn't they give him a *permis?*'

'They won't – not for one man in one truck.'

'He'll be coming back,' I said. 'Hesther said Tam was the only place he can get fuel.'

'I doubt it,' said Byrne. 'If he was coming back he'd be back by now. Those Land-Rovers are thirsty beasts. If you want him you'll have to go get him.'

I leaned back against the reed wall of the tent. 'I'd like that in more detail.'

'Paul Billson is an idiot. He filled his tank with gas and went. No spare. Five days is overlong to be away, and if he has no spare water he'll be dead by now.'

'How do I get there?' I said evenly.

Byrne looked at me for a long time, and sighed. 'If I didn't know Hesther thought something of you I'd tell you to go to hell. As it is, we start at first light.' He grimaced. 'And I'll have to go against my principles and use a stinkpot.'

What he meant by that I didn't know, but I merely said, 'Thanks.'

'Come on,' he said. 'Let's help Mokhtar get chow.'

'Chow' proved to be stringy goat, hard on the teeth and digestion, followed by a strong cheese which I was told

was made of camel's milk. Byrne was taciturn and we
went to sleep early in readiness for an early start. I lay on
my back at the entrance to the tent, staring up at a sky so
full of stars it seemed I could just reach up an arm to grab
a handful.

I wondered what I was doing there and what I was getting into. And I wondered about Byrne, who spoke almost
as archaic a slang as Hesther Raulier, a man who referred to
his food by the World War Two American army term of
'chow'.

# THIRTEEN

Byrne's 'stinkpot' turned out to be a battered Toyota Land
Cruiser which looked as though it had been in a multiple
smash on a motorway. Since there wasn't a motor-way
within two thousand miles, that was unlikely. Byrne saw
my expression and said, 'Rough country,' as though that
was an adequate explanation. However, the engine ran
sweetly enough and the tyres were good.

We left in the dim light of dawn with Byrne driving, me
next to him, and Mokhtar sitting in the back. Jerricans containing petrol and water were strapped all around the truck
wherever there was an available place, and I noted that
Mokhtar had somewhat unobtrusively put a rifle aboard.
He also had a sword, a thing about three feet long in a red
leather scabbard; what the devil he was going to do with
that I couldn't imagine.

We drove north along a rough track, and I said, 'Where
are we going?'

It was a damnfool question because I didn't understand
the answer when it came. Byrne stabbed his finger forward
and said briefly, 'Atakor,' then left me to make of that what
I would.

I was silent for a while, then said, 'Did you get a *permis*?'

'No,' said Byrne shortly. A few minutes went by
before he relented. 'No fat bureaucrat from the Maghreb

is going to tell me where I can, or cannot, go in the desert.'

After that there was no conversation at all, and I began to think that travelling with Byrne was going to be sticky; extracting words from him was like pulling teeth. But perhaps he was always like that in the early morning. I thought of what he had just said and smiled. It reminded me of my own reaction to Isaacson's treatment of Hoyland. But that had been far away in another world, and seemed a thousand years ago.

The country changed from flat gravel plains to low hills, barren of vegetation, and we began to climb. Ahead were mountains, such mountains as I had never seen before. Most mountains begin rising gently from their base, but these soared vertically to the sky, a landscape of jagged teeth.

After two hours of jolting we entered a valley where there was a small encampment. There was a bit more vegetation here, but not much, and there were many sheep or goats – I never could tell the difference in the Sahara because the sheep were thin-fleeced, long-legged creatures and I began to appreciate the Biblical quotation about separating the sheep from the goats. Camels browsed on the thorny acacia and there was a scattering of the leather tents of the Tuareg.

Mokhtar leaned forward and said something to Byrne, who nodded and drew the truck to a halt. As the dust drifted away on the light breeze Mokhtar got out and walked over to the tents. He was wearing his sword slung across his back, the hilt over his left shoulder.

Byrne said, 'These people are of the Tégéhé Mellet. Mokhtar has gone to question them. If a Land-Rover has been anywhere near here they'll know about it.'

'What's the sword for?'

Byrne laughed. 'He'd feel as undressed without it as you would with no pants.' He seemed to be becoming more human.

'The Teg-whatever-it-is-you-said . . . is that a tribe of some kind?'

'That's right. The Tuareg confederation of the Ahaggar consists of three tribes – the Kel Rela, the Tégéhé Mellet and the Taitoq. Mokhtar is of the Kel Rela and of the noble clan. That's why he's gone to ask the questions and not me.'

'Noble!'

'Yeah, but not in the British sense. Mokhtar is related to the *Amenokal* – he's the boss, the paramount chief of the Ahaggar confederation. All you have to know is that when a noble Kel Rela says, "Jump, frog!" everybody jumps.' He paused, then added, 'Except, maybe, another noble Kel Rela.' He shrugged. 'But you didn't come out here to study anthropology.'

'It might come in useful at that,' I said.

He gave me a sideways glance. 'You won't be here long enough.'

Mokhtar came back, accompanied by three men from the camp. All were veiled and wore the long, flowing blue and white gowns that seemed to be characteristic of the Tuareg. I wondered how they kept them so clean in that dusty wilderness. As they came close Byrne hastily adjusted his own veil so that his face was covered.

There were ceremonial greetings and then a slow and casual conversation of which I didn't understand a single word, and I just sat there feeling like a spare part. After a while Byrne reached into the back of the truck and produced a big round biscuit tin. He took out some small packages and handed them round, and Mokhtar added his own contribution. There was much graceful bowing.

As he started the engine Byrne said, 'Billson came through here four days ago. He must have been travelling damned slow.'

'I don't wonder,' I said. 'He's more used to driving on a road. Which way did he go?'

'Towards Assekrem – or further. And that's not going to be any joke.'

'What do you mean?'

He gave me a considering look. 'Assekrem is a Tamachek word – it means, "The End of the World".'

The truck jolted as he moved off. The Tuareg waved languidly and I waved back at them, glad to offer some contribution to the conversation. Then I sat back and chewed over what Byrne had just said. It wasn't comforting.

Presently I said, 'What did you give those men back there?'

'Aspirin, needles, salt. All useful stuff.'

'Oh!'

Three hours later we stopped again. We had been moving steadily into the mountains which Byrne called Atakor and had not seen a living soul or, indeed, anything alive at all except for thin grasses burnt by the sun and the inevitable scattered thorn trees. The mountains were tremendous, great shafts of rock thrusting through the skin of the earth, dizzyingly vertical.

And then, at a word from Mokhtar, we stopped in the middle of nowhere. He got out and walked back a few paces, then peered at the ground. Byrne looked back, keeping the engine running. Mokhtar straightened and walked back to the truck, exchanged a few words with Byrne, and then took the rifle and began to walk away into the middle distance. This time he left his sword.

Byrne put the truck into gear and we moved off. I said, 'Where's he going?'

'To shoot supper. There are some gazelle close by. We'll stop a little further on and wait for him.'

We drove on for about three miles and then came across a ruined building. Byrne drew to a halt. 'This is it. We wait here.'

I got out and stretched, then looked across at the building. There was something strange about it which I couldn't pin down at first, and then I got the impression that it wasn't as much ruined as intended to be that way. It had started life as a ruin.

Byrne nodded towards the tremendous rock which towered three thousand feet above us. 'Ilamen,' he said. 'The finger of God.' I started to walk to the building, and he said sharply, 'Don't go in there.'

'Why not? What is it?'

'The Tuareg don't go much for building,' he said. 'And they're Moslem – in theory, anyway. That's a mosque, more elaborate than most because this is a holy place. Most desert mosques are usually just an outline of stones on the ground.'

'Is it all right if I look at it from the outside?'

'Sure.' He turned away.

The walls of the mosque were of stones piled crazily and haphazardly one upon the other. I suppose the highest bit of wall wasn't more than three feet high. At one end was a higher structure, the only roofed bit, not much bigger than a telephone box, though not as high. The roof was supported by stone pillars. I suppose that would be a sort of pulpit for the imam.

When I returned to the truck Byrne had lit a small fire and was heating water in a miniature kettle. He looked up. 'Like tea?'

'Mint tea?'

'No other kind here.' I nodded, and he said, 'Those stone pillars back there weren't hand-worked; they're natural basalt, but there's none of that around here for twenty miles. Someone brought them.'

'A bit like Stonehenge,' I commented, and sat down.

Byrne grunted. 'Heard of that – never seen it. Never been in England. Bigger, though, isn't it?'

'Much bigger.'

He brought flat cakes of bread from the truck and we ate. The bread was dry and not very flavoursome but a little camel cheese made it eatable. It had sand mixed in the flour which was gritty to the teeth. Byrne poured a small cup of mint tea and gave it to me. 'What are you?' he asked. 'Some sort of private eye?' It was the first time he had shown any curiosity about me.

I laughed at the outdated expression. 'No.' I told him what I did back in England.

He looked towards the mosque and Ilamen beyond. 'Not much call for that stuff around here,' he remarked. 'How did you get into it?'

'It was the only thing I know how to do,' I said. 'It was what I was trained for. I was in the Army in Intelligence, but when I was promoted from half-colonel to colonel I saw the red light and quit.'

He twitched his shaggy eyebrows at me. 'Promotion in your army is *bad*?' he enquired lazily.

'That kind is. Normally, if you're going to stay in the line of command – field officer – you're promoted from lieutenant-colonel to brigadier; battalion CO to brigade CO. If you only go up one step it's a warning that you're being shunted sideways into a specialist job.' I sighed. 'I suppose it was my own fault. It was my pride to be a damned good intelligence officer, and they wanted to keep me that way. Anyway, I resigned my commission and started the firm I've been running for the last seven years.'

'Chicken colonel,' mused Byrne. 'I never made more than sergeant myself. Long time ago, though.'

'During the war,' I said.

'Yeah. Remember I told you I walked away from a crash?'

'Yes.'

'I liked what I saw during that walk – never felt so much alive. The other guys wouldn't come. Two of them couldn't;

too badly injured – and the others stayed to look after them. So I walked out myself.'

'What happened to them?' I asked.

He shrugged. 'I gave the position of the plane and they sent a captured Fiesler Storch to have a look. Those things could land in fifty yards. It was no good; they were all dead.'

'No water?'

He shook his head. 'Goddamn Arabs. They wanted loot and they didn't care how they got it.'

'And you came back here after the war?' I asked.

He shook his head. 'I let the war go on without me. During the time I was walking through the desert I got to thinking. I'd never seen such space, such openness. And the desert is clean. You know, you can go without washing for quite a time here and you're still clean – you don't stink. I liked the place. Couldn't say as much for the people, though.' He poured some more mint tea. 'The Chaamba Arabs around El Golea aren't too bad, but those bastards in the Maghreb would skin a quarter and stretch the skin into a dollar.'

'What's the Maghreb?'

'The coastal strip in between the Mediterranean and the Atlas.' He paused. 'Anyway, early in '43 I got a letter to say my Pop was dead. He was the only family I had, so I had no urge to go back to the States. And General Eisenhower and General Patton and more of the top brass were proposing to go to Italy. I didn't fancy that, so when the army went north I came south looking for more favourable folks than Arabs. I found 'em, and I'm still here.'

I smiled. 'You deserted?'

'It's been known as that,' he admitted. 'But, hell; ain't that what a desert's for?'

I laughed at the unexpected pun. 'What did you do before you joined the army?'

'Fisherman,' he said. 'Me and my Pop sailed a boat out o' Bar Harbor. That's in Maine. Never did like fishing much.'

*Fisherman!* That was a hell of a change of pace. I suppose it worked on the same principle that the best recruiting ground for the US Navy is Kansas. I said, 'You're a long way from the sea now.'

'Yeah, but I can take you to a place in the Ténéré near Bilma – that's down in Niger and over a thousand miles from the nearest ocean – where you can pick up sea-shells from the ground in hundreds. Some of them are real pretty. The sea's been here and gone away. Maybe it'll come back some day.'

'Ever been back to the States?'

'No; I've been here thirty-five years and like to die here,' he said peacefully.

Mokhtar was away a long time, nearly five hours, and when he came back he had the gutted carcass of a gazelle slung across his shoulders. Byrne helped him butcher it, talking the while.

Presently he came over to me and squinted into the sun. 'Getting late,' he said. 'I reckon we'll stay here the night. Billson is either between here and Assekrem or he ain't. If he is, we'll find him tomorrow. If he ain't, a few hours won't make no difference.'

'All right.'

'And we've got fresh meat. Mokhtar tells me he stalked that gazelle for twenty kilometres and downed it in one shot.'

'You mean he walked twenty kilometres!'

'More. He had to come back. But he circled a bit, so say under thirty. That's nothing for a Targui. Anyway, Mokhtar's one of the old school; he learned to shoot with a muzzle-loader. With one of those you have to kill with one shot because the gazelle spooks and gets clear away before you can reload. But he likes a breech-action repeater better.'

And so we stayed under the shadow of Ilamen that night. I lay in the open, wrapped in a *djellaba* provided by Byrne, and looked up at those fantastic stars. A sickle moon arose but did little to dim the splendour of those faraway lights.

I thought of Byrne. Hesther Raulier had compared him with Billson, calling him, 'another crazy man'. But the madness of Byrne was quite different from the neurotic obsession of Billson; his was the madness that had struck many white men – not many Americans, mostly Europeans – Doughty, Burton, Lawrence, Thesiger – the lure of the desert. There was a peacefulness and a sanity about Byrne's manner which was very comforting.

I thought in wonder of the sea-shells to be picked up from the desert a thousand miles from the sea but had no fore-shadowing that I would be picking them myself. The night was calm and still. I suddenly became aware of the startling incongruity of Max Stafford, hot-shot businessman from the City of London, lying in a place improbably called Atakor beneath the Finger of God which was not far from the End of the World.

Suddenly London ceased to matter. Lord Brinton and Andrew McGovern ceased to matter; Charlie Malleson and Jack Ellis ceased to matter; Gloria and Alix Aarvik ceased to matter. All the pettifogging business of our so-called civilization seemed to slough away like an outworn skin and I felt incredibly happy.

I slept.

I woke in the thin light of dawn conscious of movement and sound. When I lifted my head I saw Byrne filling the petrol tank from a jerrican – it was that metallic noise that had roused me. I leaned up on one elbow and saw Mokhtar in the desert mosque; he was making obeisances to the east in the dawn ritual of Islam. I waited until he had finished because I did not want to disturb his devotions, then I arose.

Thirty minutes later after a breakfast of cold roast venison, bread and hot mint tea we were on our way again, a
long plume of dust stretching away behind us. Slowly the
majestic peak of Ilamen receded and new vistas of tortured
rock came into view. According to Byrne, we were on a
well-travelled road but to a man more accustomed to city
streets and motorway driving that seemed improbable. The
so-called road was vestigial, distinguishable only by boulders a shade smaller than those elsewhere, and the truck
was taking a beating. As for it being well-travelled I did not
see a single person moving on it all the time I was in
Atakor.

Nearly three hours later Byrne pointed ahead.
'Assekrem!'

There was a large hill or a small mountain, depending on
how you looked at it, on the top of which appeared to be a
building. 'Is that a house?' I asked, wondering who would
build on a mountain top in the middle of a wilderness.

'It's the Hermitage. Tell you about it later.'

We drove on and, at last, Byrne stopped at the foot of the
mountain. There seemed to be traces of long-gone cultiva-
tion about; the outlines of fields and now dry irrigation
ditches. Byrne said, 'Now we climb to the top.'

'For God's sake, why?'

'To see what's on the other side,' he said sardonically.
'Come on.'

And so we climbed Assekrem. It was by no means a
mountaineering feat; a track zig-zagged up the mountain,
steep but not unbearably so, and yet I felt out of breath and
panted for air. Half way up Byrne obligingly stopped for a
breather, although he did not seem in discomfort.

I leaned against the rock wall. 'I thought I was fitter than
this.'

'Altitude. When you get to the top you'll be nine
thousand feet high.'

I looked down to the plain below where I saw the truck with Mokhtar sitting in its shade. 'This hill isn't nine thousand feet high.'

'Above sea level,' said Byrne. 'At Tam we were four and a half thousand high, and we've been climbing ever since.' He rearranged his veil as he was always doing.

'What's this about a Hermitage?'

'Ever hear of Charles de Foucauld?'

'No.'

'Frenchman, a Trappist monk. In his youth, so I hear, he was a hellion, but he caught religion bad in Morocco. He took his vows and came out here to help the Tuareg. I suppose he did help them in his way. Anyway, most of what the outside world knows about the Tuareg came from de Foucauld.'

'When was this?'

'About 1905. He lived in Tam then, but it wasn't much of a place in those days. In 1911 he moved here and built the Hermitage with his own hands. He was a mystic, you see, and wanted a place for contemplation.'

I looked at the barren landscape. 'Some place!'

'You'll see why when we get to the top. He didn't stay long – it damn near killed him; so he went back to Tam and that did kill him.'

'How so?'

'In 1916 the Germans bribed the Libyan Sennousi to stir up trouble with the desert tribes against the French. The Tuareg of the Tassili n' Ajjer joined with the Sennousi and sent a raiding party against Tam. De Foucauld was caught and shot with his hands bound – and it was an accident. An excitable kid of fifteen let a gun go off. I don't think they meant to kill him. Everyone knew he was a *marabout* – a holy man.' He shrugged. 'Either way he was just as dead.'

I looked at Byrne closely. 'How do you know all this?'

He leaned forward and said gently, 'I can read, Stafford.' I felt myself redden under the implied rebuke, but he laughed suddenly. 'And I talked to some old guys over in the Tassili who had been on the raid against Tam in 1916. Some of the books I read sure are wrong.' He half-turned as if about to set off again, but stopped. 'And there was some-one else in Tam not long ago like de Foucauld – but a woman. English, she was; name of Daisy Wakefield. Said she was related to some English lord – something to do with oil. Is there a Lord Wakefield?'

'There is.'

'Then that must be the guy.'

'Did you know her?'

'Sure, Daisy and I got on fine. That's how I caught up with the news; she subscribed to the London *Times*. A mite out-of-date by the time it got here but that didn't matter.'

'What happened to her?'

'She got old,' he said simply. 'She went north to El Golea and died there, God rest her soul.' He turned. 'Come on.'

'Byrne,' I said. 'Why are we climbing this mountain?'

'To see a guy at the top,' he said without turning.

I trudged after him and thought: *My God! Wakefield oil!* This damned desert seemed littered with improbable peo-ple. In fact, I was following one of them. Maybe two, count-ing Paul Billson.

The building at the top of Assekrem was simple enough. Three small rooms built of stone. There were two men there who ushered us inside. They were dark-skinned men with Negroid features. Byrne said casually, 'Don't handle any of the stuff here; it's de Foucauld's stuff – holy relics.'

I looked about with interest as he talked with the men. There was a simple wooden table on which were some books, a couple of old-fashioned steel pens and a dried-out ink-well. In one corner was a wooden cot with an inch-thick mattress which looked about as comfortable as concrete. On a wall was a picture of the Virgin.

Byrne came over to me. 'Billson went through three days ago, I think. Or it could have been two days because another truck went through the day after, and I'm not sure which was Billson. But that truck came out again yesterday.'

'We didn't see it.'

'Might have gone out the other way – through Akar-Akar.' He rubbed his jaw reflectively and looked at me. I noticed he hadn't bothered to keep up his veil in the presence of these men. He said abruptly, 'I want to show you something frightening – and why de Foucauld built here.'

He turned and went outside and I followed. He walked across the natural rock floor of a sort of patio to a low stone parapet, and then pointed north. 'That's where your boy is.'

I caught my breath. Assekrem was a pimple on the edge of a plateau. Below the parapet were vertiginous cliffs, and spread wide was the most awe-inspiring landscape I had ever seen. Range after range after range of mountains receded into the blue distance, but these were none of your tame mountains of the Scottish Highlands or even the half-tamed Swiss Alps. Some time in the past there had been a fearsome convulsion of the earth here; raw rock had ripped open the earth's belly with fangs of stone – and the fangs were still there. There was no regularity, just a jumble of lava fields and the protruding cores of volcanoes for as far as the eye could see, festering under a brassy sun. It was killer country.

'That's Koudia,' said Byrne. 'The land beyond the end of the world.'

I didn't say anything then, but I wondered about de Foucauld. If he chose to meditate here – did he worship God or the Devil?

# FOURTEEN

Byrne was still talking to the dark-skinned men who had come out to join us. There was much gesticulating and pointing until, at last, Byrne got something settled to his satisfaction. 'These guys say they saw something burning out there two days ago.'

'Christ!' I said. 'What is there to burn?'

'Don't know.' He fumbled in the leather pouch which depended from a cord around his neck and took out a prismatic compass. He looked at me and said with a grin, 'I'm not against all scientific advance. Mokhtar, down there, thinks I'm a genius the way I find my way around.' He put the compass to his eye to take a sight.

'How far away?'

'Don't know that, either. They say it was a column of smoke – black smoke.'

'In the daytime?'

There was astonishment in Byrne's eyes as he looked at me. 'Sure; how the hell else could they see smoke?'

'I was thinking about the Bible,' I said. 'The Israelites in the wilderness, guided by a pillar of smoke by day and a pillar of fire by night.'

'I don't think you've got that right,' he said mildly. 'I read it as a pillar of cloud.' He turned back to take another sight. 'But I guess we'd better take a look. I make

it just about due north of here, on a compass bearing.
I don't bother none about magnetic variation, not on a
short run.'

'What do you call short?'

'Anything up to fifty kilometres. Magnetic deviation is
another thing. These goddamn hills are full of iron and
you've got to check your compass bearing by the sun all
the time.'

He put the compass away, and from another bag he took
a couple of small packages which he gave to the two men.
There was a ceremonial leave-taking, and he said, 'Salt and
tobacco. In these parts you pay for what you get.'

As we set off down the steep path I said, 'There is something that's been puzzling me.'

Byrne grunted. 'Hell of a lot of things puzzle me, too,
from time to time. What's your problem?'

'That veil of yours. I know it's Tuareg dress, but sometimes you muffle yourself up to the bloody eyebrows and
other times you don't bother. For instance, you didn't bother
up there; you let them see your face. I don't understand the
rationale.'

Byrne stopped. 'Still on your anthropological kick, huh?
Okay, I'll tell you. It's the politeness of the country. If you're
in a place and you don't do as everybody does in that place,
you could get yourself very dead. Take a Targui and set him
in the middle of London. If he didn't know he had to cross
the street in a special place, and only when the light is
green, he could get killed. Right?'

'I suppose so.'

Byrne touched his head cloth. 'This thing is a *chech;* it's a
substitute for the real thing, which is a *tagelmoust,* but you
don't see many of those around except on high days and
holidays. They're very precious. Now, nobody knows why
the Tuareg wear the veil. I don't know; the anthropologists
don't know; the Tuareg don't know. I wear mine because it's

handy for keeping the dust out of my throat and keeps a high humidity in the sinuses on a dry day. It also cuts down water loss from the body.'

He sat down on a convenient rock and pointed downwards. 'You've seen Mokhtar's face?'

'Yes. He doesn't seem to bother about me seeing it.'

'He wouldn't – he's a noble of the Kel Rela,' said Byrne cryptically. 'Society here is highly class-structured and a ceremonial has grown up around the veil. It's polite to hide your face from your superiors and, to a lesser extent, from your equals. If Mokhtar met the *Amenokal* you'd see nothing of him except his eyelashes.'

He jerked his thumb upwards. 'Now, those guys up there are Haratin, and the Haratin were here thousands of years ago, long before the Tuareg moved in. But the Tuareg conquered them and made slaves of them, so they're definitely not my superior, so the veil don't matter.'

'But you're not a Tuareg.'

'The male singular is Targui,' said Byrne. 'And I've been a Targui ten years longer than I was an American.' He jabbed his finger at me. 'Now, you'll see lots of Tuareg faces, because you're a no-account European and don't matter. Got it?'

I nodded. 'I feel properly put in my place.'

'Then let's get the hell out of here.'


If I had thought Atakor was bad it was hard to make a comparison with Koudia; I suppose the only comparison could be between Purgatory and Hell. I soon came to realize that the high road I had anathematized in Atakor was a super highway when compared to anything in Koudia.

I put it to Byrne and he explained. 'It's simple. People make roads when they want to go places, and who in God's name would want to come here?'

'But why would anyone want to be in Atakor except a mystic like de Foucauld?'

'The Hermitage is a place of pilgrimage. People go there, Moslem and Christian alike. So the going is easy back there.'

After leaving Assekrem and plunging into the wilderness of Koudia I don't suppose we made more than seven miles in the first two hours – walking pace in any reasonable country. Koudia was anything but reasonable; I don't think there was a single horizontal bit of land more than five paces across. If we weren't going up we were going down, and if we weren't doing either we were going around.

The place was a litter of boulders – anything from head size to as big as St Paul's Cathedral, and the springing of the Toyota was suffering. So was I. We bounced around from rock to rock and I rattled around the cab until I was bruised and sore. Byrne, at least, had the wheel to hold on to, but I don't think that made it any better for him because it twisted in his hands as though it was alive. As for Mokhtar, he spent more of his time out of the truck than in.

Apart from the boulders there were the mountains themselves, and no one could drive up those vertical cliffs so that was when we went around, Byrne keeping his eyes on his compass so as not to lose direction in all the twisting and turning we had to do. He stopped often to take a reciprocal sighting on Assekrem to make sure we were on the right line.

As I say, Mokhtar spent more time on the ground than in the truck, and it wasn't too hard for him to keep up. He had a sharp eye for signs of passage, and once he stopped us to indicate tyre marks on a patch of sand. He and Byrne squatted down to examine them while I investigated my bruises. When we were about to start again Byrne said, 'Superimposed tracks. One vehicle going in and another, later, coming out.'

I had casually inspected those tracks myself but I couldn't have trusted myself to tell which way the vehicles were going. As a Saharan intelligence officer I was a dead loss.

About seven miles in two hours, then we stopped for a rest and food. There was no vegetation in Koudia at all but Mokhtar had thoughtfully gathered a bundle of acacia twigs while waiting for us at Assekrem and soon had a fire going to boil water for the inevitable mint tea. I said to Byrne, 'Don't you ever drink coffee?'

'Sure, but this is better for you in the desert. You can have coffee when we get back to Tam. Expensive, though.'

The sun was past its height and sinking towards the west as we sat in the shade of the Toyota. This was the hottest part of the day and, in Koudia, that meant really hot. The bare rocks were hot enough to fry eggs and the landscape danced in a constant heat shimmer.

I remarked on this to Byrne, and he grinned. 'This is winter – would you like to be here in summer?'

'Christ, no!'

'This is why they wouldn't give Billson a *permis*. And come nightfall the temperature will drop like a rock. You leave water exposed out here and you'll have half an inch of ice on it by three in the morning. If Billson is lost he'll either have burned to death or frozen to death.'

'I like a cheerful man,' I said acidly.

Mokhtar had disappeared about his private business but suddenly he appeared on top of a boulder about two hundred yards away. He gave a shrill whistle which attracted our attention, and waved both his arms. 'He's found something,' said Byrne, scrambling to his feet.

We went over to Mokhtar and that took us more than ten minutes in that ankle-breaking terrain. When we were fifty yards away Mokhtar shouted something, and Byrne said, 'He's found a truck. Let's see if it's a Land-Rover.'

As we scrambled on top of the boulder, which was as big as a moderate-sized stately home, Mokhtar pointed downwards, behind him. We walked over and stared to where his finger was pointing. There was a vehicle down there behind the boulder, and it was a Land-Rover. Or, at least, it had been – it was totally burnt-out. There was no sign of Billson or anyone else, and I suddenly realized that I wouldn't know Billson if I saw him. I was a damn fool for not having a photograph.

Byrne said, 'The black smoke would come from the burning tyres. Let's get down there.'

Going down meant going back the way we had come and walking around the boulder. As we came in sight of the Land-Rover, Byrne, in the lead, spread his arms to stop us. He spoke rapidly to Mokhtar who went on ahead, peering at the ground. Presently he waved and Byrne walked over to him, and they had a brief discussion before Byrne beckoned to me.

'There's been another truck here; its tracks are on top of those of the Land-Rover, and it went that way.' He pointed back in the general direction of the Toyota.

'Where's Billson?' My mouth was dry.

Byrne jerked his head at the Land-Rover. 'Probably in there – what's left of him. Let's see.'

He stood up and we walked over to the Land-Rover. It was a total wreck – a burnt-out carcass; it sat on the ground, the wheel rims entangled in the steel reinforcing wires of what had been tyres. There was still a lingering stench of burning rubber in the air.

The window glass had cracked and some of it had melted, and the windscreen was totally opaque so that it was difficult to see inside. Byrne reached out and tugged at the handle of the door on the driver's side and cursed as it came away in his hand. He walked around and tried the other door. He jerked it open and looked inside, with me looking over his shoulder.

The inside was a mess. The upholstery had burned, releasing blackened coil springs, and even the plastic coating of the driving wheel had burnt away, leaving bare metal. But there was no body, either in front or on the rear seats.

We went around to the back and got the tailgate open, to find scant remnants of what appeared to be two suitcases. Again, no body. I said, 'The other truck must have taken him away.'

'Maybe,' said Byrne noncommittally. He poked around a bit more in the ruined Land-Rover, then he straightened up. 'Did Paul Billson have any enemies?'

'He may have had.' I went cold as I realized we were speaking of Billson in the past tense just as his half-sister had done. I said, 'I hardly think he'd have the kind of enemy who would follow him to the middle of the Sahara to kill him.'

'Mmm.' Byrne made a nondescript noise and continued his examination. 'I've seen lots of burnt-out trucks,' he said. He picked up a jerrican lying to one side, snapped open the cap, and sniffed. 'He had gas in here. He must have been carrying it in the back there, because he had no cans strapped on the side when he left. This is empty now.'

'Perhaps there was an accident when he was refilling the main tank.'

'Then where's the body?'

'As I say – the other truck rescued him.'

Byrne stood back and looked at the Land-Rover, then talked more to himself than to me. 'Let's see; twenty-eight gallons in the main tank plus about four in the can – that's thirty-two. He'd need at least twenty to get here, so he was in trouble without a fire – he didn't have enough gas to get back to Tam. That leaves twelve gallons – eight in the tank and four in this can, I'd say.'

'How do you know the can wasn't empty? He could have refilled his main tank anywhere – even before Assekrem.'

'There's been gas in the can until quite recently – it smells too strong. And when I picked it up the cap was still closed. Now, if that can had been full of gas during the fire it would have exploded – but it hasn't.'

Byrne seemed to be arguing in circles. 'So he put it in the main tank,' I said exasperatedly.

'No,' said Byrne definitely. 'I've seen a lot of burnt-out trucks in the desert, but never one like this – not with all four tyres gone like that, not with so much fire damage up front.' He bent down to examine the petrol tank, and then crawled under.

When he emerged he stood up and tossed something in his hand. 'That was lying on the ground.' It was a small screw cap with a broken wire hanging from it. 'That's the drain cap for the gas tank. The wire which is supposed to stop it unscrewing has been cut. That makes it certain. Someone doused this truck with gas from the can, then decided it would be a good idea to have more. So he drained another four gallons from the tank – maybe eight – to do a really good job of arson. You don't get auto tyres burning all that easily. Then he tossed in a match and went away, and the guy who would do that wouldn't be rescuing Billson.'

'So where's Billson?'

'Don't know. Maybe we'll find his body around here some place.'

I remembered something. 'The man I put on Billson's track back in England seemed to think that someone else was also looking for him.' I frowned. 'And then Hesther Raulier . . .' I pulled out my wallet and found the note she had enclosed with the air ticket. I scanned it and handed it to Byrne.

He read it through, then said, 'Know this guy, Kissack?'

'Never heard of him.'

'Neither have I.' He gave me back the note.

'Another thing,' I said. 'Billson might have had a lot of money with him. I think he smuggled it out of the UK.'

'What do you call a lot of money?'

'The thick end of £60,000.'

Byrne whistled. 'I'd call that a lot, too.' He swung around and rooted in the back of the Land-Rover where all that was left of two suitcases were the locks, hinges, metal frames and a pile of ashes. He said, 'Whether Billson's money was in here when the fire bust out we'll never know without a forensic laboratory, and those are a mite scarce around here. Was it common knowledge that Billson would be carrying so much loose dough?'

'I shouldn't think so,' I said. 'It's really only a guess on my part.'

'You don't have a monopoly on guesses,' said Byrne. 'And a lot of guys have been killed for less than that.'

As we walked away from the Land-Rover I said, 'Funny that the chap who did this should close the cap on that empty jerrican; especially as he was going to leave it.'

'Probably automatic,' said Byrne. 'I do it myself. Good habit to have.'

'I'd still like to know what Billson was doing here,' I said.

'He was looking for a wrecked airplane, like you said. And he'd have found it, too – it's about five miles further north of here. I was going to head there if we hadn't found this. Billson must have heard about it back in Tam so he came for a look-see, the goddamned fool!'

'It couldn't be . . .' I began.

'Of course it couldn't be his father's plane,' said Byrne tiredly. 'It's a French military airplane that force-landed back when they were getting ready to blow an atom bomb up at Arak. They got the crew out by chopper, then went back to take out the engines and some of the instruments. Then they left the carcass to rot.'

He went to talk to Mokhtar, and I sat on a rock feeling depressed. Billson must have been the biggest damned fool in the history of the Sahara. He had probably read the

Land-Rover's Owner's Manual and taken the manufacturer's fuel consumption claim as gospel, but it's one thing tool-
ing along a motorway and another fighting your way
through Koudia. I doubt if we'd been getting more than five
miles to the imperial gallon since we left Assekrem and perhaps ten or twelve in Atakor. I don't think it's disrespectful
to British Leyland to suggest that the Land-Rover was averaging about the same.

But Billson had probably measured straight lines on a
map and set out on that basis. But that was water under the
bridge or, more accurately, vapour through the carburettor.
What we had now was an entirely different set of circumstances in which Billson's idiocy didn't figure because, if we
found his body it would be because he had been murdered
by a man, and the man was possibly called Kissack.

It was then that I made the discovery. Mokhtar or Byrne
would probably have done it, but they didn't – I did, and it
brought back some of my self-respect as a working member
of this crazy expedition and made me feel something less of
a hanger-on while others did the work.

I was looking down idly at the rock on which I sat when
I noticed a small brown stain over which an ant was scurrying. For a moment I wondered how even an ant could live
in Koudia, and then I noticed another and then another.
There was quite a trail of them going backwards and forwards between a crack in the rock and the stain.

I stood up, looked at the Land-Rover, took a line on it,
and then explored further away. Sure enough ten yards further on there was another stained rock, and a little way
along there was another. I turned. 'Hey!'

'What is it?'

'I think I've found something.' Byrne and Mokhtar came
up and I said, 'Is that dried blood?'

Mokhtar moistened the tip of his little finger and rubbed
it on the stain, then he sniffed his fingertip delicately,

looked at Byrne, and said one word. 'Yeah,' said Byrne. 'It's blood.'

'There's a line of it coming from the Land-Rover.' I turned and pointed towards a narrow ravine. 'I think he went up there.'

'Okay – Mokhtar goes first; he's better at this than we are. He can see a sign you wouldn't know was there.'

Billson, if it was Billson's blood, had gone up the ravine but fairly soon it became obvious that he hadn't travelled in a straight line. Not because of the difficulty of the terrain because he had dodged about quite a bit when he had no obvious need to, and on occasion he had reversed his course. And the blood splashes got bigger.

'Hell!' I said. 'What was he doing? Playing hide-and-seek?'

'Maybe he was at that,' said Byrne grimly. 'Maybe he was being chased.'

We found him at last, tumbled into a narrow crack between two rocks where there was shade. Mokhtar gave a cry of triumph and pointed downwards and I saw him sprawled on sand which was bloodstained. His face wasn't visible so Byrne gently turned him over. 'This Billson?'

'I wouldn't know,' I said. 'I've never seen him.'

Byrne grunted and felt about the body. The face of the man was puffy and swollen and his skin was blackened. Incongruously, he was wearing a normal business suit – normal for England, that is. At least I had had the sense to visit a tailor to buy what was recommended as suitable attire for the desert, even if the tailor had been wrong to the point of being out of his mind. The probability rose that this was indeed Billson.

Byrne said, 'Whoever the guy is, he has a hole in him. He's been shot.' He held out his fingers, red with liquid blood.

'He's alive!' I said.

'Not for long if we don't do something.' Byrne spoke to Mokhtar, who went away fast. He then turned the man over so that he lay more easily and put his hand inside his jacket to withdraw a passport and a wallet from the inside breast pocket. He flipped open the passport one-handedly. 'This is your boy; this is Paul Billson.' He gave me the passport and wallet.

I opened the wallet. It contained a sheaf of Algerian currency, a smaller wad of British fivers, and a few miscellaneous papers. I didn't bother to examine them then, but put the passport and the wallet into my pocket.

'We're in trouble,' said Byrne. He indicated Billson. 'Or he is. If he stays another night he'll die for sure. If we try to take him out he'll probably die. You know how rough it'll be getting back to Assekrem; I don't know if he can take it in his condition.'

'It's a question of the lesser of two evils.'

'Yeah. So we try to take him out and hope he survives.' He looked down at Billson. 'Poor, obstinate bastard,' he said softly. 'I wonder how well Hesther knew his old man? She said in her note to you that she'd wired me. I didn't tell you it was a ten-page cable, and she was pretty firm and detailed in her instructions.'

'Has the flow of blood stopped?' I asked.

'Yeah; I have the tail of his shirt wadded into the hole. We can't do much until Mokhtar gets back. He won't be long.'

'You must have known about Paul Billson before I arrived.'

'Sure I did, but he'd taken off by then.'

I said, 'If you hadn't waited for me you could have got here earlier.'

'Not much. I got Hesther's cable the morning you came. I don't know when she sent it, but the communications in this country aren't noted for reliability.'

'But you did lead me a little way up the garden path.' It seemed odd to be making conversation over the body of a man who was probably dying.

Byrne said, 'I wanted time to size you up. I don't like to travel with people I can't trust. Hereabouts it can be fatal.'

'So I passed the examination,' I said flatly.

He grinned. 'Just by a hair.'

A shadow fell athwart us. Mokhtar had come back. He had brought cloth for bandages, water, and a couple of sand ladders. The sand ladders, as Byrne had earlier explained, were to put under the wheels of the Toyota if we got stuck in sand. They were about six feet long and of stout tubular steel. 'Only stinkpots need them,' Byrne had said. 'Camels don't.'

Byrne tore off a strip of cloth, soaked it in water and put it in Billson's mouth; being careful not to choke him. Then he proceeded to dress the wound while Mokhtar and I lashed the sand ladders together to make an improvised stretcher.

It took us over an hour to get Billson the comparatively short distance back to the Toyota.

# FIFTEEN

We had travelled two hours' worth into Koudia but it took us four hours to get out from the time Byrne started the engine until we drove beneath the peak of Assekrem. He picked his way as delicately as he could through that rocky desolation but, even so, Billson took a beating. Fortunately, he knew nothing of it; he was unconscious. I tended him as best I could, cushioning his body with my own, bathing his face, and trying to get some water into him. He did not move voluntarily nor did he make a sound.

I had expected Byrne to stop at Assekrem where perhaps we could have got help from the Haratin at the Hermitage, but he drove past the beginning of the path up the cliff and we camped about three miles further on. Mokhtar took a roll of cloth from the back of the Toyota and very soon had a windbreak erected behind which we laid Billson. It was now dark so Byrne redressed the wound in the acid light of a glaring pressure lantern.

He sat back on his heels and watched Mokhtar administer a salve to Billson's blackened face. 'If we can get some water into him he might survive,' he said. 'That's only a shoulder wound and the bullet went right through without hitting bone. Weakening but not killing. He's suffered more from exposure than the wound.'

I said, 'Why didn't you stop at Assekrem? They might have had something to help him.'

'Not a chance.' He nodded towards the Toyota. 'I have more stuff in my first aid kit than there is in the whole of the Ahaggar, if you except the hospital at Tam. Besides . . .' His voice tailed away, which was odd in Byrne because he was usually pretty damned decisive.

'What's the matter?'

'Do you know anything about Algerian law?'

'Not a thing.'

'Well, Billson broke one of them. He came out here without a *permis*.'

'So did you.'

'But I didn't apply for one – he did. You can be sure that when he disappeared from Tam they knew where he'd gone. There are police posts on all the main tracks out of Tam and when he didn't show up at any of those they'd be sure. So when he shows up in Tam he'll be arrested.'

'At least he'll get hospital treatment,' I said. 'And when he's out of hospital I'll stand bail.'

'You'll be lucky,' said Byrne drily. 'Because this guy is going to show up with a bullet hole in him and Algerian cops are no different than any other cops – they don't like mysterious bullet wounds. It's going to be a mess.'

He held up a finger. 'One – Billson has broken the law, and it's a serious offence. The Algerians are nuts on security and they don't like foreign nationals floating around the desert tribes unobserved. That could mean prison and I wouldn't wish my worst enemy in an Algerian prison.' A second finger joined the first. 'Two – he comes back with a bullet wound and that the cops won't like either. It's not an offence to be shot but it means someone else ought to be in jail, and that means trouble where there ought to be no trouble.' A third finger went up. 'Three –

the guy who was shot is a foreigner and that brings Algiers
into the act complete with a gaggle of diplomats. As far as
I know Britain broke off diplomatic relations with Algeria
years ago. I don't know who represents British nationals
here – could be the Swiss – but that means a three-
cornered international hassle, and no one is going to like
that.'

'I begin to see the problems,' I said thoughtfully.

'Four,' said Byrne remorselessly. 'And this is the big one.
Supposing we take Billson into Tam and he goes into hospital. It's only a small place and within twelve hours everybody is going to know about the man in hospital who was
shot – including the guy who shot him . . .'

'. . . and who thinks he's dead,' I chipped in.

'. . . and whom Billson can identify. What's to stop him
having another crack and finishing the job?'

'If he's still around.'

'What makes you think he won't be?' Byrne stood up
and looked down at Billson. 'This guy is giving everybody a
pain in the ass – including me.' He shook his head irritably.
'If it wasn't for Hesther . . .' His voice tailed away again.

'Is there an alternative to Tam?'

'Yeah.' He kicked at the sand. 'But I'll have to think
about it.'

He went over to the truck and came back with the rifle,
then spoke to Mokhtar who took a full magazine from the
pouch hung on his neck. Byrne slipped it into the rifle with
a metallic click, worked the action to put a bullet up the
spout, and carefully set the safety-catch. 'I suppose you
know how to use one of these, Colonel, sir?'

'I have been known to.'

'You might have to use it. It shoots a shade to the left and
upwards; say, two inches at ten o'clock at a hundred yards.
We'll stand watches tonight.'

I frowned. 'Expecting trouble? I'd have thought . . .'

He broke in. 'Not really, but Billson will have to be watched throughout the night.' He held up the rifle. 'This is for unexpected trouble.'

I stood the middle watch in order to give both Byrne and Mokhtar an uninterrupted run of sleep; I didn't know where we were going if it wasn't Tammanrasset, but wherever it was they would have to take me there, so they were more important than me.

Billson was unmoving but still breathing, and I thought he looked a shade better than he had. For one exasperated moment that evening I had thought of quitting and going back to London. As Byrne had said – though less politely – Billson was nothing but trouble for everyone who came near him, and I did think of leaving him to stew in his own juice.

But the thought of going back and telling Alix Aarvik about all this made my blood run cold. Besides, it wouldn't be fair on Byrne and Mokhtar who had gone to a great deal of trouble to help a man they didn't know. Also, I would have to be on hand when Billson recovered because someone had to get him out of the country as he had very little money left. And London was far away and receding fast, and I found I quite enjoyed the desert in a masochistic way.

I took the rifle and looked at it in the dim light of the fire. it was an old British Lee-Enfield .303 and, judging by its low number, it had seen service in the First World War, as well as the Second. I took out the magazine and worked the action to eject the round in the breech, then looked down the barrel into the fire. It was as clean as a whistle and any hardened sergeant would have had to give Mokhtar full marks. He had looked after it well. I reloaded and laid the rifle aside, then checked Billson again.

Towards the end of my watch he began to stir and, just before I woke Byrne, he had begun to mutter, but his

ramblings were incoherent. I put my hand to his brow but
he did not seem to be running a temperature.

I woke Byrne. 'Billson's coming to life.'

'Okay; I'll tend to him.' Byrne looked at the sky to get the
time. He wore no watch. 'You get some sleep. We start early;
our next camp is at Abalessa.'

I wrapped myself in my *djellaba* because it was very cold,
and lay down. I wasted no time wondering about Abalessa
but fell asleep immediately.

Billson was obviously better in the morning, but he was
dazed and I doubt if he knew where he was or what was
happening to him. We bedded him down in the back of
the Toyota on the camel hair cloth that had served as a
wind-break and on a couple of *djellabas*. 'We can get some
camel milk once we're out of Atakor,' said Byrne. 'And
maybe scare up some hot soup. That'll bring him around
better than anything else.'

We travelled fast because Byrne said we had a long way
to go. Coming out of Atakor we encountered the Tuareg
camp we had passed on the way in. They were packing up
to go somewhere but found some warm camel milk for
Mokhtar. Byrne had thrown a *djellaba* casually into the back
of the truck, covering Billson, and stood guard. 'There's no
need for anyone to see him.'

We left the camp and stopped for a while a little later
while we spooned milk into Billson. He seemed even better
after that, even though the skin was peeling from his face
and the backs of his hands in long strips. Mokhtar applied
more salve and then we set off again, with Byrne really piling on the speed now that the country was much better.

These things are relative. Coming from the green land of
England, I would have judged this place to be a howling
wilderness. All sand, no soil, and the only vegetation an
occasional clump of rank grass and a scattering of thorn

trees which, however desirable they may have been to a camel, did nothing for me. But I had not just come from England; I had come from Koudia and Atakor and what a hell of a difference that made. This country was beautiful.

We travelled hard and fast, making few stops, usually to top up the tank with petrol from the jerricans. Billson finished the milk and was able to drink water which put a bit more life into him, although he still wandered in his wits – assuming he had any to begin with. Once Byrne stopped and sent Mokhtar on ahead. He disappeared over a rise, then reappeared and waved. Byrne let out the clutch and we went ahead at a rush, topping the rise and down the other side to cross what, for the Sahara, was an arterial highway.

'The main road north from Tam,' said Byrne. 'I'd just as soon not be seen crossing it.'

'Where are we going?'

'We're going round Tam to the other side – to Abalessa.' He fell silent and concentrated on his driving.

Abalessa, when we got there, was a low hill on the horizon. We didn't drive up to it but made camp about a mile away. There was still some gazelle meat left so Mokhtar seethed it in a pot to make soup for Billson before putting on the kettle for the mint tea. Byrne grunted. 'You can have your coffee when we go into Tam tomorrow. Me, I'm looking forward to a cold beer.'

'But I thought . . .'

'Not Billson,' said Byrne. 'He stays here with Mokhtar. Just you and me. We've got to make you legal.'

I scratched my chin. I hadn't shaved during the past few days and it felt bristly. Maybe I'd grow a beard. I said, 'You'll have to explain that.'

'Strictly speaking, you should have reported at the *poste de police* at Fort Lapperine as soon as you got into Tam. Your name will have been on the airplane manifest, so by now the cops will be wondering where you are.'

'Nobody told me that. Specifically, you didn't tell me.'

'You'd have been told if you'd registered at the hotel. Anyway, I just told you.' He pointed to the hill in the distance. 'That's your alibi – the Tomb of Tin Hinan.' He paused. 'Mine, too.'

'The previous owner of the hotel, I suppose.'

He grinned. 'The legendary ancestress of the Tuareg. I did see a camera in your bag, didn't I?'

'Yes; I have a camera.'

'Then tomorrow we climb up there and you take a whole raft of photographs and we take them into Tam to be developed. That proves we have been here if anyone gets nosey. I don't want anyone getting the idea we went the other way – up into Atakor. Not immediately, anyway.'

'How long do we stay in Tam?'

'As long as it takes to satisfy that fat little guy behind the desk that we're on the level – no longer. The story is this; you came into Tam, got talking to me, and asked about the Tomb of Tin Hinan – you'd heard about it – it's famous. I said I'd take you there and we left immediately, and we've been here ever since while you've been rootling around like an archaeologist. *But* you don't bear down on that too heavily because to do real archaeology you need a licence. Only, tonight I discovered you hadn't registered with the cops so I've brought you back to get things right. Got the story?'

I repeated the gist of it, and Byrne said, 'There's more. The fat little guy will ask about your future plans, and you tell him you're going south to Agadez – that's in Niger.'

I looked at him blankly. 'Am I?'

'Yeah.' He pointed at Billson. 'We've got to get this guy out of Algeria fast. Clear out of the country.'

I scratched my bristles again. 'I have no Niger visa. First, I didn't have time to get one, and secondly I had no intention of going. Looking at this place from England, I decided that there's a limit to what I could do.'

'You'll get by without a visa if you stick with me.'

'Have you got a visa for Niger?'

'Don't need one – I live there. Got a pretty nice place in the Aïr ou Azbine, to the north of Agadez. I come up to Tam once a year to look after a couple of things for Hesther. She's got interests here.'

Mokhtar served up mint tea. I sat down, feeling comfortably tired after a long day's drive. 'How did you come to know Hesther?' I sipped the tea and found I was coming to like the stuff.

'When she was younger she used to come down to the Ahaggar quite a lot; that was when the French were here. One time she got into trouble in the Tademaït – that's about 700 kilometres north of here. Damn place fries your brains out on a hot day. Wasn't bad trouble but could have gotten worse. Anyway, I helped her out of it and she was grateful. Offered me a job in Algiers but I said I wasn't going to the damned Maghreb, so she asked me to help her out in Tam. That went on for a couple of years, then once, when she came down to Tam, we got to talking, and the upshot was that she staked me to my place in the Aïr, down in Niger.'

'What do you do down there?' I asked curiously. Byrne had to earn a living somehow; he just couldn't go around helping strangers in distress.

'I'm a camel breeder,' he said. 'And I run a few salt caravans across to Bilma.'

I didn't know where Bilma was and a salt caravan sounded improbable, but the camel breeding I could understand. 'How many camels have you got?'

He paused, obviously calculating. 'Pack animals and breeding stock together, I'd say about three hundred. I had more but the goddamn drought hit me hard. Seven lean years, just like in the Bible. But I'm building up the herd again.'

'Who is looking after them now?'

He smiled. 'If this was Arizona you'd call Mokhtar's brother the ranch foreman. His name is Hamiada.' He stretched. 'Got film for your camera?'

'Yes.'

'That's okay then. I reckon I'll go to sleep.'

'Aren't you going to eat?'

'We'll eat well in Tam tomorrow. There's just enough chow left to feed Mokhtar and Billson until we come back. Wake me at midnight.' With that he rolled over and was instantly asleep.

So I went hungry that night but I didn't mind. I looked around and saw that Mokhtar was asleep, as was Billson. It seemed as though I had been elected to stand first watch.

At about eleven Billson awoke and was coherent for the first time. He muttered a little, then said clearly, 'It's dark. Why is it dark?'

'It's night time,' I said softly.

'Who are you?' His voice was weak but quite clear.

'My name is Stafford. Don't worry about it now, Paul; you're quite safe.'

He didn't say anything for some time, then he said, 'He shot me.'

'I know,' I said. 'But you're all right now. Go to sleep and we'll talk tomorrow.'

He fell silent and when I looked at him closely five minutes later I saw that his eyes were closed and that he was breathing deeply and evenly.

At midnight I woke Byrne and told him about it, then went to sleep myself.

# SIXTEEN

We didn't have much time for Billson in the morning because Byrne wanted to get back to Tam and we still had to go to the mound of Abalessa to take photographs, and so we had time to exchange only a few words. Mine were consoling – Byrne's were more in the nature of threats.

Billson was very weak, but rational. He had some more of the soup that Mokhtar prepared and managed to eat a few bits of the meat. As I knelt next to him he said, 'Who are you?'

'I'm Max Stafford. Your sister sent me to find you.'

'Alix? How did she know where I'd gone?'

'It wasn't too hard to figure,' I said drily. 'I suppose you know you did a damn silly thing – bolting like that.'

He swallowed. 'I suppose so,' he said reluctantly. He looked past me. 'Who are those Arabs?'

'They're not Arabs. Now listen, Paul. You made a bigger mistake when you went into Atakor without a permit. Did you know that you didn't have enough petrol to get back to Tam?' His eyes widened a little and he shook his head. 'And then you were shot. Who shot you – and why?'

His face went blank and then he frowned and shook his head. 'I don't remember much about that.'

'Never mind,' I said gently. 'All you have to do is to get well. Paul, if the police find you they'll arrest you and you'll go to prison. We are trying to stop that happening.'

I turned as Byrne called, 'Are you ready?' There was impatience in his voice.

'Coming.' I stood up and said to Billson, 'Rest easy.'

Byrne was more forthright. A Tuareg in full fig can be pretty awe-inspiring but, to the recumbent Billson, Byrne towering over him must have seemed a mile high. There is also something particularly menacing about a man who utters threats when you can't see his face.

Byrne said, 'Now, listen, stupid. You stay here with this man and you don't do a goddamn thing. If you step out of line just once Mokhtar will cut your crazy head off. Hear me?'

Paul nodded weakly. I noted that Mokhtar was wearing his sword and that the rifle was prominently displayed. Byrne said, 'If you do one more screwball thing we'll leave you for the vultures and the fennecs.' He strode away and I followed him to the Toyota.


On top of the mound of Abalessa were the ruins of a stone building, very unTuareglike. 'French?' I asked. 'Foreign Legion?'

'Hell, no!' said Byrne. 'Older than that. There's one theory that this was the southernmost post of the Romans; it has a likeness to some of the Roman forts up north. Another theory is that it was built by the remnants of a defeated legion that was driven down here. The Romans did lose a couple of legions in North Africa.' He shrugged. 'But they're just theories.'

'What's this about Tin Hinan?'

'Over here.' I followed him. 'She was found down there.' I peered into the small stone chamber which had obviously been covered by a hand-worked stone slab that lay nearby.

'It's still a mystery. The Tuareg have a story that a couple called Yunis and Izubahil were sent from Byzantium to rule over them; that would be about the year 1400. Some of the jewellery found on her was East Roman of that period, but some of the coins dated back to the fifth and sixth century. And there were some iron arm rings which the Byzantines didn't wear.'

He changed his tone and said abruptly, 'We're not here for a history lesson – get busy with your snapshots. Put me in one of them, and I'll do the same for you. Fool tourists are always doing that.'

So I ran off a spool of pictures and Byrne took a couple of me and we went away although I should have liked to have stayed longer. I have always liked a good mystery which, I suppose, was the reason I was in the Sahara anyway.

Abalessa was about sixty miles from Tammanrasset and we made it in just about two and a half hours, being helped during the last stretch by the asphalted road from the air-strip to Tam. That ten-mile bit was the only paved road I saw in the whole Sahara and I never found out why it had been put there.

Byrne pulled up outside the Hotel Tin Hinan. 'Go in and make your peace,' he said. 'I'm going to nose around. I'll meet you back here in, maybe, an hour. You can have a beer while you're waiting.'

'Am I staying here tonight?'

'No, you'll be with me. But you'll probably have to pay for your room reservation. Give me your film.'

So I took the film from the camera, gave it to him and got out, and he drove away blasting the horn. There was the predictable confusion in the hotel with reproaches which I soothed by paying the full room charge even though I had not used it. The manager's French was bad but good enough for me to hear that the police had been looking for me. I promised faithfully to report to the *poste de police*.

Then I went into the courtyard, sat at a table, and ordered a beer, and nothing had ever tasted so good. Nothing had changed in Tammanrasset since the day I had flown in and seen it with new eyes. The Tuareg walked down the sandy street in their languid, majestic manner, or stood about in small groups discussing whatever it was that Tuareg discuss. Probably the price of camels and the difficulty of shooting gazelle. A lot of them wore swords.

Of course, there was no reason why Tam should have changed. It was I who had changed. Those few days in Atakor and Koudia had made the devil of a difference. And now it seemed I was to go down to Niger – to a place called Agadez and where was it? Ah yes; the Aïr ou something or other. I didn't know how far it was and I wondered if I could buy a map.

There were other things I needed. I looked down at myself. The natty tropical suiting the London tailor had foisted on me was showing the strain of desert travel. I gave the jacket an open-handed blow and a cloud of dust arose. With those travel stains and my unshaven appearance I probably looked like a tramp; any London bobby would have run me in on sight. But I saw no chance of buying European-style clothing in Tam. I'd ask Byrne about that.

I finished the beer and ordered a coffee which came thick and sugary and in very small quantity, which was just as well, and I decided I'd rather stay with the mint tea. I was half way through the second beer when Byrne pitched up. His first act was to order a beer and his second to drain the glass in one swallow. Then he ordered another, and said, 'No one called Kissack has been around.'

'So?'

He sighed. 'Don't mean much, of course. A guy can change his name. There's a party of German tourists going through.' He laughed. 'Some of them are wearing *Lederhosen.*'

I wasn't very much amused. In the desert *Lederhosen* weren't any more ridiculous than the suit I was wearing. I said, 'Have you any maps? I'd like to know where I'm going.'

'Don't use them myself, but I can get you one.'

'And I can do with some clothes.'

He inspected me. 'Wait until we get further south,' he advised. 'Nothing much here; better in Agadez. Your prints will be ready in an hour; I put the arm on the photographer.' He drained his glass. 'Now let's go tell the tale to the cops.'

Outside the entrance to the *poste de police* he said, 'Got your passport?'

I pulled it out of my pocket and hesitated. 'Look, if I say I'm going to Niger it's going to look funny when he finds no Niger visa in here.'

'No problem,' said Byrne. 'He won't give a damn about that. Niger is another country and it's not his worry what trouble you find yourself in there. He'll be only too happy to get you out of Algeria. Now go in and act the idiot tourist. I'll be right behind you.'

So I reported to the plump uniformed policeman behind the desk, and laid down my passport. 'I've been waiting for you, M'sieur Stafford,' he said coldly. 'What kept you?' He spoke heavily accented French.

'*Merde!*' said Byrne. 'It was only a couple of days.' I supposed I shouldn't have been surprised that Byrne spoke French, but I was. It was ungrammatical but serviceable.

'Three and a half, M'sieur Byrne,' said the policeman flatly.

'I thought he'd reported – I only found out last night, and we came straight in.'

'Where were you?'

'Abalessa.' He added something in a guttural language totally unlike that in which he spoke to Mokhtar. I took it to be Arabic.

'Nowhere else?'

'Where else is there to go out there?' asked Byrne.

I said, 'I suppose it's my fault. I jumped at the chance to go out there as soon as I met Mr Byrne. I didn't know I had to report here until he told me last night.' I paused, and added, 'It's quite a place out there; I'm not sure it's Roman, though.'

The policeman didn't comment on that. 'Are you staying in Tammanrasset long, M'sieur Stafford?'

I glanced at Byrne. 'No; I'm going down to Agadez and the Aïr.'

'With M'sieur Byrne?'

'Yes.'

He suddenly seemed more cheerful as he picked up my passport. 'We have much trouble with you tourists. You don't understand that there are strict rules that you must follow. There is another Englishman we are looking for. It all wastes our time.' He opened the passport, checked me against the photograph, and flicked the pages. 'There is no visa for Algeria here,' he said sharply.

'You know it's not necessary,' said Byrne.

'Of course.' The policeman's eyes narrowed as he looked at Byrne. 'Very good of you to instruct me in my work.' He put his hands flat on the table. 'I think a lot about you, M'sieur Byrne. I do not think you are a good influence in the Ahaggar. It may be that I shall write a report on you.'

'It won't get past the Commissioner of Police in Algiers,' said Byrne. 'You can depend on that.'

The policeman said nothing to that. His face was expressionless as he stamped my passport and pushed it across the desk. 'You will fill out *fiches* in triplicate. If you do not know how I am sure M'sieur Byrne will instruct you.' He indicated a side table.

The *fiche* was a small card, somewhat smaller than a standard postcard and printed in Arabic and French. I scanned it, then said to Byrne, 'Standard bureaucratic stuff – but what the hell do I put down under "Tribe"?'

Byrne grinned. 'A couple of years ago there was a guy here from the Isle of Man. He put down Manx.' He wilted a little under my glare and said, 'Just put a stroke through it.'

I filled in all three *fiches* and put them on the policeman's desk. He said, 'When are you leaving for Niger?'

I looked at Byrne, who said, 'Now. We just have to go to Abalessa to pick up some gear.'

The policeman nodded. 'Don't forget to report at the checkpoint outside town. You have an unfortunate habit of going around it, M'sieur Byrne.'

'Me? I never!' said Byrne righteously.

We left and, just outside the office, passed a man carrying a sub-machine-gun. Once in the street I said, 'He doesn't like you. What was all that about?'

'Just a general principle. The boys in the Maghreb don't like foreigners getting too close to the Tuareg. That guy is an Arab from Sidi-bel-Abbès. It's about time they recruited their police from the Tuareg.'

'Can he get you into trouble?'

'Fat chance. The Commissioner of Police lives in Hesther Raulier's pocket.'

I digested that thoughtfully, then said, 'What did you say to him in Arabic?'

Byrne smiled. 'Just something I wouldn't want to say to your face. I told him you were a goddamn stupid tourist who didn't know which end was up. I also managed to slip in that we were waiting for a roll of film to be developed. With a bit of luck he'll check on that.'

We went shopping. Byrne seemed well known and there was a lot of good-natured chaffing and laughter – also a lot of mint tea. He bought salt, sugar and flour, small quantities of each in many places, spreading his custom wide. He also bought a map for me and then we went back to the hotel for a final beer.

As we sat down he said, 'No trace of Kissack, but the word is out to look for him.'

The map was the Michelin North and West Africa, and the scale was 40 kilometres to the centimetre, about 63 miles to the inch. Even so, it was a big map and more than covered the small table at which we were sitting. I folded it to more comfortable proportions and looked at the area around Tammanrasset. The ground we had covered in the last few days occupied an astonishingly small portion of that map. I could cover it with the first joint of my thumb.

I observed the vast areas of blankness, and said, 'Where are we going?'

Byrne took the map and put his finger on Tammanrasset. 'South from here, but not by the main road. We take this track here, and as soon as we get to Fort Flatters we're in Niger.' He turned the map over. 'So we enter the Aïr from the north – through Iferouane and down to Timia. My place is near there. The Aïr is good country.'

I used my thumb to estimate the distance. It was a crow's flight of about four hundred miles, probably six hundred on the ground and, as far as I could see, through a lot of damn all. The Aïr seemed to be mountainous country.

I said, 'What's an *erg*?'

Byrne clicked his tongue. 'I guess it's best described as a sea of sand.'

I noted with relief that there was no *erg* on the route to the Aïr.

We drank our beer leisurely and then wandered down the street to pick up the photographs. Suddenly Byrne nudged me. 'Look!' A policeman came out of a doorway just ahead and crossed the road to go into the *poste de police*. 'What did I tell you,' said Byrne. 'He's been checking those goddamn pictures.'

'Hell!' I said. 'I didn't think he'd do it. A suspicious crowd, aren't they.'

'Keeping the Revolution pure breeds suspicion.'

We collected the photographs, picked up the Toyota at a garage where it had been refuelled and the water cans filled, and drove back to Abalessa.

Mokhtar reported no problems, but Billson suddenly became voluble and wanted to talk. He seemed a lot stronger and, since he hadn't been able to talk to Mokhtar, it all came bursting out of him.

But Byrne would have none of it. 'No time for that now. I want to get out of here. Let's go.'

Again we picked up speed as we hit the asphalted section of road and, because we had to go through Tam, Billson was put in the back of the truck and covered with a couple of *djellabas*. The road to the south left Tam from Fort Lapperine and, as we turned the corner, I was conscious of the man standing outside the *poste de police*, cradling a sub-machinegun in his arms, and sighed with relief as we bumped out of sight.

About four miles out of town Byrne stopped and went to the back of the truck where I joined him. He uncovered Billson, and said, 'How are you?'

'I'm all right.'

Byrne looked at him thoughtfully. 'Can you walk?'

'Walk?'

Byrne said to me, 'There's a police checkpoint just around the corner there. I bet that son of a bitch back there has told them to lay for me.' He turned to Billson. 'Yes, walk. Not far – two or three kilometres. Mokhtar will be with you.'

'I think I could do that,' said Billson.

Byrne nodded and went to talk to Mokhtar. I said to Billson, 'You're sure you can do it?'

He looked at me wanly. 'I can try.' He turned to look at Byrne. 'Who is that man?'

'Someone who saved your life,' I said. 'Now he's saving your neck.' I went back and got into the cab. Presently Byrne got in and we drove on. I looked back to see Billson and Mokhtar disappear behind some rocks by the roadside.

Byrne was right. They gave us a real going-over at the checkpoint, more than was usual, he told me afterwards – much more. But you don't argue with the man with the gun. They searched the truck and opened every bag and container, not bothering to repack which Byrne and I had to do. They pondered over my passport for a long time before handing it back and then we had to fill in more *fiches*, again in triplicate.

'This is damn silly,' I said. 'I did this only this morning.'

'Do it,' said Byrne shortly. So I did it.

At last we were allowed to go on and soon after leaving the checkpoint Byrne swerved off the main track on to a minor track which was unsignposted.

'The main road goes to In Guezzam,' he said. 'But it would be tricky getting you over the border there. Fort Flatters will be better.' He drove on a little way and then stopped. 'We'll wait for Mokhtar here.'

We got out of the truck and I looked at the map. After a few minutes I said, 'I'm surprised they're not here by now. We were a fair time at the checkpoint and it doesn't take long to walk three kilometres.'

'More like eight,' said Byrne calmly. 'If I'd told him the truth he might have jibbed.'

'Oh!'

Presently Mokhtar emerged on to the side of the road. He was carrying Billson slung over his shoulder like a sack. We put him in the back of the truck and made him as comfortable as possible, revived him with water, and then drove on.

# SEVENTEEN

We drove to the Aïr in easy stages, doing little more than a hundred miles a day. It was during this period that I got to know Paul Billson, assuming that I got to know him at all because he was a hard man to fathom. I think Byrne got to know him a lot better than I did.

In spite of his garrulity at Abalessa, he felt a lot less like talking after passing out while going around the check-point, but he was a lot better that evening when we made camp. We now had tents which were carried on a rack on top of the truck, and while Byrne and Mokhtar were erecting them I dressed Billson's wound. It was clean and already beginning to heal, but I puffed some penicillin powder into it before putting on fresh bandages.

He was bewildered. 'I don't know what's going on,' he said pathetically. 'Who are you?'

'I told you – Max Stafford.'

'That means nothing.'

'If I said that I was responsible for security at Franklin Engineering would that mean anything?'

He looked up. 'For God's sake! You mean you've chased all the way out here because I left Franklin's in a hurry?'

'Not entirely – but you get the drift. There's a lot you can tell me.'

He looked around. We were camped on the lee side of a ridge almost at the top. I had queried that when Byrne picked the spot; camping on the flats at the bottom of the ridge would have been better, in my opinion. Byrne had shaken his head. 'Never camp on low ground. More men die of drowning in the Sahara than die of thirst.' When I expressed incredulity he pointed to mountains in the northeast. 'You could have a thunderstorm there and not know it. But a flash flood sweeping through the wadis could come right through here.' I conceded his point.

Billson said, 'Where are we?'

'About fifty miles south-east of Tammanrasset.'

'Where are we going?'

'Niger. We're getting you out of Algeria; the police are looking for you. You bent the rules.'

'Why are you doing this for me?'

I put the last knot in the bandage and snipped off the loose ends. 'Damned if I know,' I said. 'You've certainly proved to be a bloody nuisance. Niger is probably the last place in the world I want to go to.'

He shook his head. 'I still don't understand.'

'Have you remembered anything about the man who shot you?'

'A bit,' said Billson. 'I stopped because one of the tyres was going soft and I thought I might have to change a wheel. I was looking at it when this other car came along.'

'Car or truck?' A car seemed improbable in Koudia.

'A Range-Rover. I thought he might help me so I waved. He came up and stopped about ten yards away – then he shot me.'

'Just like that?'

'Just like that. I felt this blow in my shoulder – it knocked me down. It didn't hurt; not then.'

I looked at Billson speculatively. This sounded an improbable story, but then, Billson collected improbabilities about him as another man might collect postage stamps. And I never forgot for one moment that I had been badly beaten up in a quiet street in Kensington.

'Did you see the man?'

'Yes. He – they chased me.'

'How many?'

'Two of them.'

'Were they locals? I mean, were they Arabs or Tuareg?'

'No, they were white men, like you and me.'

'Didn't he say anything before he shot you?'

'No. As I said, the car just stopped and he shot me.'

I sighed. 'So what happened then?'

'Well, when I fell down they couldn't see me because I was behind the Land-Rover. Close by there was a gap between two rocks and I nipped in there. I heard them getting out of their car so I went between the rocks and up a sort of cleft and ran for it.'

He fell silent so I prompted him. 'And they chased you. Did they shoot at you again?'

He nodded. 'Just the one man. He didn't hit me.' He touched his shoulder. 'Then this started to hurt and I became dizzy. I don't remember any more.'

He had collapsed and fortunately fallen out of sight down a cleft in the rocks. The men had probably searched for him and missed him, not too difficult in Koudia. But burning his Land-Rover was another way of killing him; I couldn't imagine a man with a gunshot wound and no water walking out of Koudia.

'How did you find me?' he asked.

'We were looking for you.'

He stared at me. 'Impossible. Nobody knew where I'd gone.'

'Paul, you left a trail as wide as an eight-lane motorway,' I said. 'It wasn't difficult for me, nor for someone else, evidently. Do you have any enemies? Anyone who hates you badly enough to kill you? So badly that they'd follow you to the middle of the Sahara to do it?'

'You're mad,' he said.

'Someone is,' I observed. 'But it's not me. Does the name of Kissack mean anything to you?'

'Not a thing.' He brooded a moment. 'What happened to my Land-Rover? Where is it?'

'They burned it.'

He looked stricken. *'They burned it!'* he whispered. 'But what about . . .' He stopped suddenly.

'How much money did you have in those suitcases?' I asked softly. He didn't answer, so I said, 'My assessment is about £56,000.'

He nodded dully.

'Whether they searched those cases before dousing them with petrol or not doesn't matter. You've lost it.' I stood up and looked down at him. 'You're a great big law-breaker, Paul. The British can nail you for breaking currency regulations, and now the Algerians are looking for you. If they find you with a bullet hole in you that'll bring more grief to someone. Jesus, you're a walking disaster.'

'Sorry to have been the cause of trouble,' he mumbled. His hand twitched, the fingers plucking at his jacket.

I contemplated that piece of understatement with quiet fury. I bent down and stuck my finger under his nose. 'Paul, from now on you don't do a single thing – not a single bloody thing, understand, even if it's only unzipping your fly – without consulting either me or Byrne.'

His head jerked towards Byrne. 'Is that him?'

'That's Byrne. And walk carefully around him. He's as mad at you as I am.'

They had finished putting up the tents and Mokhtar had a fire going. I told Byrne what I had got from Billson, and he said contemplatively, 'Two Europeans in a Range-Rover.

They shouldn't be hard to trace. And they shot him just like that? Without even passing the time of day?'

'According to Paul – just like that.'

'Seems hard to believe. Who'd want to shoot a guy like that?'

I said tiredly, 'He was driving around with 56,000 quid in British bank notes packed in his suitcase. I shouldn't think it went up in flames in the Land-Rover. He probably opened his mouth too wide somewhere along the line, and someone got greedy.'

'Yeah, you could be right. But that doesn't explain Kissack.'

'I don't believe he exists.'

'If Hesther says he was looking for Paul Billson, then he exists,' said Byrne firmly. 'Hesther don't make mistakes.'

We had mutton that night because Mokhtar had bought a sheep that morning from a passing Targui at Abalessa. He grilled some of it kebab-style over the fire and we ate it with our fingers. It was quite tasty. Byrne pressed Billson to eat. 'I'm trying to fatten you up,' he said. 'When we get to Fort Flatters you've got to walk some more.'

'How much more?' asked Billson.

'Quite a piece – maybe thirty kilometres. We've got to get you round the Algerian border post.' He turned to me. 'You'll have a walk, too; around the Niger border post.'

I didn't look forward to it.

The next night I tackled Paul again, this time not about what he'd been up to in North Africa, but about the puzzling circumstances of his life in England. I could have questioned him as we drove but I didn't want to do it in front of Byrne. Paul might unburden himself to a single interrogator but he might not before an audience.

I dressed his wound again. It was much better. As I re-wrapped the bandage I said, 'How much did you earn at Franklin Engineering, Paul?'

'£200 a month.'

'You're a damned liar,' I said without heat. 'But you always have been, haven't you? You were on £8000 a year – that's nearly four times as much. Now, tell me again – how much did you earn?' He stayed sullenly silent, and I said, 'Tell me, Paul; I want to hear it from you.'

'All right. It was £8000 a year.'

'Now, here comes the £8000 question,' I said. 'Do you consider that you were worth it to Franklin Engineering?'

'Yes – or they wouldn't have paid it to me.'

'You don't really believe that, do you?' Again he maintained silence. 'Do you know that Mr Isaacson wanted to fire you ten years ago, but the managing director wouldn't agree?'

'No.'

'Do you know that Mr Stewart wanted to fire you when he arrived from Glasgow to reorganize the accounts office, and again the managing director wouldn't have it?'

'No.'

'Who is your guardian angel, Paul?'

'I don't know what you mean.'

'For God's sake!' I said. 'You were doing work that any sixteen-year-old office boy could do. Do you think that was worth eight thousand quid a year?'

He avoided my eye. 'Maybe not,' he muttered.

'Then how come you were paid it? There must have been some reason. Who were you blackmailing?'

That got him angry. 'That's a damnable thing to say,' he spluttered. 'You've no right . . .'

I cut in. 'How did you get the job?'

'It was offered to me. I got a letter.'

'When was this? How long ago?'

Billson frowned in thought, then said, 'Must have been 1963.'

'Who sent the letter?'

'A man called McGovern. He was managing director of Franklin.'

McGovern! Then managing director of Franklin Engineering, later Chairman of the Board, now Chairman of the entire Whensley Group and knighted for his services to industry. Sir Andrew McGovern, who ran like a thread through Billson's life and who wanted to run his own security operation as soon as Billson disappeared.

I said, 'What was in the letter?'

'McGovern offered me a post at £2000 a year.' Billson looked up. 'I grabbed it.'

He would! £2000 wasn't a bad salary back in 1963 when the average pay was considerably less than £1000. 'Didn't you wonder why McGovern was offering that?'

'Of course I did.' Billson stared at me. 'But what did you expect me to say? I wasn't going to turn it down because it was too much.'

I had to smile at that. Billson might be stupid, but not stupid enough to say, 'But, Mr McGovern; I'm not worth half that.' I said, 'So you just took the money and kept your mouth shut.'

'That's right. I thought it was all right at first – that I'd have to earn it. It worried me because I didn't know if I could hold down that sort of job. But then I found the job was simple.'

'And not worth £2000 then or £8000 now,' I commented. 'Now tell me; why was McGovern grossly overpaying you?'

'I don't know.' Billson shrugged and said again, almost angrily, 'I tell you – I don't know. I've thought about it for years and come to no answer.' He glowered at me. 'But I wasn't going to ask McGovern.'

No, he wouldn't; he'd be frightened of killing the goose that laid the golden eggs. I laid that aspect aside and turned to something else. 'How did Alix come to work for Franklin Engineering?'

'There was a vacancy in the typing pool,' said Billson. 'I told her about it and she applied. She got the job but she wasn't in the typing pool long. She became McGovern's secretary and he took her with him when he moved to London. Alix is a clever girl – she has brains.'

'Did McGovern know she's your half-sister?'

'I don't know. I didn't tell him.' He gave a deep sigh. 'Look, it was like this. I hardly *saw* McGovern. I wasn't in the kind of job where you hob-nob with the managing director. During the first six years I don't think I saw McGovern as many times, and I haven't seen him at all since. That's when he moved to London.'

Very curious indeed! I said, 'Now, it's a fact that you kept your enhanced pay a secret from your sister. Why did you do that?'

'Oh, hell!' Billson suddenly grabbed a handful of sand. 'I've just told you – Alix is smart. If she knew she'd ask me why – and I couldn't tell her. Then she'd dig into it and perhaps find out.' He wagged his head. 'I didn't want to know.'

He was afraid that Alix would shake all the leaves off the money tree. Billson might be a stupid man in many ways but he had cunning. Before he started work for Franklin Engineering he had already lived for many years at low pay and was quite content to continue to do while he amassed a small fortune. But to what end?

'You've acted the bastard towards Alix, haven't you, Paul?' I said. 'You must have known she was in financial difficulties and had to borrow money from the bank. And it was to help you, damn it!'

He said nothing. All he did was to pour fine sand from one hand to the other. I suppose a psychologist would call that a displacement activity.

'But the psychiatrist didn't help much, did he? You had a sudden brainstorm.'

'What the hell do you know about it?' he said petulantly. 'You don't know why I'm here. No one does.'

'Do you think I'm a damned fool?' I demanded. 'You've come out here to find your father's aeroplane.'

His jaw dropped. 'How do you know that? You couldn't . . . no one could.'

'Jesus, Paul; you're as transparent as a window-pane. You read that article by Michael English in the Sunday supplement and it sent you off your rocker. I talked to English and he told me what happened in the editor's office.'

'You've seen English?' He dropped the sand and dusted off his hands. 'Why have you been following me? Why come out here?'

It was a good question. My original idea had just been to ask a few questions in Algiers and let it go at that. I certainly hadn't expected to be on my way to Niger in the company of one Targui, one pseudo-Targui and one man who was half way round the bend. It had been a chain of circumstances, each link not very important in itself, excepting perhaps when we found Billson half dead.

I said wearily, 'Let's say it's for Alix and leave it at that, shall we?' It was the truth, perhaps, but only a fraction of it. 'She worries about you, and I'm damned if you deserve it.'

'If I hadn't been shot I'd have found it,' he said. 'The plane, I mean. I was within a few miles of it.' He drove his fist into the sand. 'And now I'm going in the opposite direction,' he said exasperatedly.

'You're wrong,' I said flatly. 'That crashed aircraft in Koudia is French. Byrne knows all about it. Ask him. You went at that in the way you go about everything – at half-cock. Will you, for once in your life, for God's sake, stop and think before you take action? You've been nothing but a packet of trouble ever since you left Franklin.'

I didn't wait for an answer but got up and left him and, for once, I didn't confide my findings to Byrne. This bit really had nothing to do with him; he knew nothing of England or of London and could contribute nothing.

I walked out of camp a couple of hundred yards and sat down to think about it. I believed Billson – that was the devil of it. I had told him that he was as transparent as glass, and it was true. Which brought me to McGovern.

I thought about that pillar of British industry for a long time and got precisely nowhere.

# EIGHTEEN

And so we travelled south.

At the Algerian border post Mokhtar guided Billson on foot around it while Byrne and I went through. There were more *fiches* to fill in – in triplicate, but we didn't get the full treatment we had had at the police post outside Tammanrasset. We went on and waited for Billson in the no-man's-land between the Algerian post and Fort Flatters in Niger, then it was my turn to walk, and Mokhtar took me on a long and circuitous route around the fort. If the two border posts compared notes, which Byrne doubted they would, then two men would have gone through both.

When Mokhtar and I rejoined the truck beyond Fort Flatters Byrne seemed considerably more cheerful. I was footsore and leg-stretched and was glad to ease myself down creakily into the seat next to him. As he let out the clutch he said gaily, 'Nice to be home.'

We were eighty miles into Niger when we camped that night and the country hadn't changed enough to justify Byrne's cheeriness, but thereafter it became better. There was more vegetation – thorn trees, it's true – but there was also more grass as we penetrated the mountains, and I saw my first running water, a brook about a foot across. According to Byrne, we had left the desert but, as I have said, these things are relative and this was still a wilderness to the untutored eye.

'The Aïr is an intrusion of the Sahel into the desert,' said Byrne.

'You've lost me,' I said. 'What's the Sahel?'

'The savannah land between the desert and the forest in the south. It's a geographer's word. Once they called it the Sudan but when the British pulled out they left a state called the Sudan so the geographers had to find another word because they didn't want to mix geography and politics. They came up with Sahel.'

'Doesn't look much different from desert.'

'It's different,' said Byrne positively. 'These uplands get as much as six inches of rain a year.'

'That's a lot?'

'A hell of a lot more than Tam,' he said. 'There've been periods of up to ten years when it hasn't rained there at all.'

We stopped at a small village called Iferouane which must have been important in the Aïr because it had an airstrip. Although the people here were Tuareg there was a more settled look about them. 'Still nomadic,' said Byrne. 'But there's more feed around here, so they don't have to move as far or as often.'

There were more animals to be seen, herds of camels, sheep and goats, with a few hump-backed cattle. The Tuareg seemed to be less formal here than in the north and some of the faces I saw were decidedly Negroid. I mentioned that to Byrne, and he shook his head. 'Those people are either Haratin or slaves.'

'Slaves!'

'Sure. The Tuareg used to go raiding across the Niger Bend to bring back slaves.'

'Is there still slavery?'

'Theoretically – no. But I wouldn't bet on it. A few years ago a British novelist bought a slave in Timbouctou just to prove that it could be done. Then he set the man free which was a damnfool thing to do.' He saw my frown. 'He had no land, so he couldn't grow anything; he had no money so he couldn't buy anything – so what was the poor bastard to do? He went back to his old master.'

'But slavery!'

'Don't get the wrong idea,' said Byrne. 'It's not what you think and they don't do too badly.' He smiled. 'No whips, or anything like that. Here, in the Aïr, they grow millet and cultivate the date palms on a share-cropping basis. Theoretically they get a fifth of the crop but a smart guy can get as much as half.'

Byrne seemed well-known and popular in Iferouane. He talked gravely with the village elders, chaffed the young women, and distributed sweets and other largesse among the children. We stayed there a day, then pushed on south over rougher country until we arrived at Timia and Byrne's home.

Ever since we had left Fort Flatters, Billson had avoided me. He couldn't help being close in the truck but he didn't talk and, out of the truck, he kept away from me. I suppose I had not hidden my contempt of him and, naturally enough, he didn't like it. I had penetrated his thick skin and wounded whatever *amour propre* he had, so he resented me. I noticed that he talked a lot with Byrne during this time and that Byrne appeared to show interest in what he was saying. But Byrne said nothing to me at the time.

Byrne was un Tuareg enough to have built himself a small house on the slopes of what passed for a pleasantly-wooded valley in the Aïr. The Tuareg in the area lived, not in leather tents as they did in the desert to the north, but in reed huts, cleverly made with dismountable panels so that they could be collapsed for loading on the back of a pack camel. But Byrne had built a house – a minimal house, it is true, with not much in the way of walls – but a house with rooms. A permanent dwelling and, as such, foreign to the Tuareg.

We arrived there late and in darkness and I didn't see much that night because we ate and slept almost immediately. But next morning, Byrne showed me around his kingdom. Close by there was something which, had it been permanent, would have been called a village and Byrne talked to a man whom he told me was Hamiada, Mokhtar's brother. Hamiada was tall, even for a Targui, and his skin, what little I could see of it above his veil, was almost as white as my own.

Byrne said to me, 'Most of the herd's grazing out towards Telouess – about twenty kilometres away. I'm going out there tomorrow. Like to come?'

'I'd like that,' I said. 'But what about Billson?' Billson was not with us; when we had left that morning he was still asleep.

Byrne looked troubled. 'I want to talk to you about him – but later. Now I want to show you something.'

Hamiada had gone away but he returned a few minutes later leading a camel. It was one of the biggest beasts I had seen and looked to be about ten feet high at the hump, although it could hardly have been that. It was of a colour I had never seen before, a peculiar smokey-grey. Byrne said, 'This is my beauty – the cream of my herd. Her name is Yendjelan.'

He spoke with such obvious pride that I felt I had to echo it even though I was no expert on the finer points of camel-breeding. 'She's a very fine animal,' I said. 'A racing camel?'

He chuckled. 'There's no such thing. She's a Mehari – a riding camel.'

'I thought they raced.'

'Camels don't run – not unless they're urged. And if they run too far they drop dead. Fragile animals. When you come with me tomorrow you'll be riding one. Not Yendjelan, though; she's mine.'

Yendjelan looked at me in the supercilious way of a camel, and her lip curled. She thought as much of the idea of me riding a camel as I did.

We looked at some more of Byrne's herd, the few that were browsing close by. As I watched them chewing up branches of acacia, three-inch thorns included, I wondered how in hell you controlled a camel. Their mouths would be as hard as iron.

We accepted Hamiada's hospitality – cold roast kid, bread and camel milk. Byrne said abruptly, 'About Billson.'

'Yes.'

'What was your intention?'

I sighed. 'I don't quite know. I thought if we could get him further south into Nigeria, then I could get him on to a plane back to England.'

Byrne nodded. 'Yes, south to Kano, a plane from there to Lagos, and so home.' He paused, chewing thoughtfully like one of his own camels. 'I don't know if that would be such a good thing.'

'Why not?'

'The guy's unstable enough as it is. He's come out here and made a bust of it so far. If he goes home now he knows he'll never be able to come back, and that might knock him off his perch entirely. He could end up in a looney-bin. I don't know that I'd like that. Would you?'

I thought of the biblical bit about being one's brother's keeper. Also the Chinese bit to the effect that if you save a man's life you are responsible for him until he dies. Also the Sinbad bit about the Old Man of the Sea. 'What's he to you?' I asked.

Byrne shrugged. 'Not much. Something to Hesther, though.'

I wondered, not for the first time, about the exact relationship between Byrne and Hesther Raulier. She'd said she'd never married but that did not necessarily mean much between a man and a woman. I said, 'What are you suggesting? That we indulge him in his fantasies?'

'Fantasies? Oh, sure, they're fantasies as far as Billson is concerned. I mean, it's fantastic for Billson to suppose that he could come out here and find that airplane unaided. But, as far as the plane itself is concerned, I've been talking to him and what he says makes a weird kind of sense.'

'You mean he's talked you into believing that the plane's still here?'

'Must be,' said Byrne simply. 'It was never found.'

'Not necessarily so,' I said. 'Not if Billson did defraud the insurance company.'

'I thought Hesther had talked you out of that way of thinking.'

'Maybe – but for Christ's sake, the Sahara is a bloody big place. Where the hell would we start?'

Byrne drained a bowl of camel milk. 'Billson really studied that last flight of his father. He's got all the details at his fingertips. For instance, he knew that when his old man took off from Algiers he intended to fly a great circle course for Kano.' He chuckled. 'I borrowed your map and traced that course. It's been a few years since I had to do spherical trigonometry but I managed.'

'And what conclusion did you come to?'

'Okay; the distance is 2800 kilometres – about 1500 nautical miles, which is the unit he'd work in for navigational purposes. It would take him over the Ahaggar about 150 kilometres east of Tam. It would take him right over here, and smack bang over Agadez. Paul wasn't all that crazy when he went to look at an airplane in the Ahaggar. 'Course he should have checked with someone first – me, for instance – but the idea was good.'

'Where is all this leading?'

Byrne said, 'All the planes in that race took the great circle course because a great circle is the shortest distance between

two points on the earth's surface. Now, Agadez lies *exactly* on
that course and so it made a good aiming point. Furthermore,
it was a condition of that leg of the race that the planes had
to fly low over Agadez – it was a sort of checkpoint. Every
plane except two buzzed Agadez and was identified. One of
the planes that wasn't seen at Agadez was Billson's.'

'And the other?'

'Some Italian who got a mite lost. But he arrived in
Kano, anyway.'

'Maybe Peter Billson had weather trouble,' I said. 'Forced
down.'

'He was forced down all right,' agreed Byrne. 'But not
by weather. Paul has checked that out; got meteorological
data for the time of flight. He's been real thorough
about this investigation. The weather was good – no sand-
storms.'

'Obsessionally thorough.'

'Yeah,' said Byrne. 'But thorough all the same. Now,
when Peter Billson went down it would be likely to be to
the north of Agadez, and one thing's for sure – it wasn't in
the Aïr. There are too many people around here and the
plane would have been found. The same applies anywhere
north of the Ahaggar. If it went down there it would have
been found by some Chaamba bedouin.'

'So that leaves the Ahaggar and you're certain it's not
there. You're talking yourself into a corner.'

He said, 'When the French were getting ready to blow
that atom bomb at Arak they lost three planes in the
Ahaggar. I've told you about one of them. They gave
the Ahaggar a real going-over, both from the air and on the
ground. They found three planes which was all they expected
to find. I'm pretty sure that if Billson's plane had been there
the French would have found it.'

'Perhaps they did,' I said. 'And didn't bother to mention it.'

Byrne disagreed. 'It would have made big news. You don't suppose Billson was the only record-breaking airman lost in the Sahara, do you? There was a guy called Lancaster went down in 1933 south of Reggan in the Tanezrouft. He wasn't found until 1962 and it made the headlines.'

I worked it out. 'Twenty-nine years.'

'He was still with the plane, and he left a diary,' said Byrne. 'It made bad reading. Paul knows all about Lancaster; he *knows* how long a crashed plane can remain undetected here. That's why he thinks he can still find his father.'

'This place where Lancaster crashed – where is it?'

'In the Tanezrouft, about 200 kilometres south of Reggan. It's hell country – *reg,* that's gravel plain for as far and farther than you can see. I know a bit of what happened to Lancaster because I read about it back in '62 and Paul has refreshed my memory. Lancaster was flying a light plane and put down at Reggan to refuel. He took off, got into a sandstorm and lost direction; he flew *east* damn near as far as In Salah before he put down at Aoulef to find out where he was. He'd intended to fly to Gao on the Niger Bend and that was due south, but he'd used up too much fuel so he went back to Reggan. He left next day and after a while his engine quit. So he crashed.'

'Didn't they search for him?'

'Sure they did – by air and ground. I don't know how good their air search was back in 1933, but they did their best. Trouble was they were looking mostly in the wrong place, towards Gao. Anyway, he had two gallons of water and no more, because he had an air-cooled engine. He died eight days later, and was found twenty-nine years later. That's the story of Lancaster.'

'Who found him?'

'A routine French patrol working out of Bidon Cinq. What the hell they were doing in the Tanezrouft I don't know. Probably on a vehicle-testing kick – I can think of no other reason for going into that hell hole.'

'All right,' I said. 'You've made a point. So Peter Billson and his plane can still be in the desert. Are you proposing that we go look for it in this place – the Tanezrouft?'

'Not goddamn likely,' said Byrne. 'I think it possible that Billson went off course. When he disappeared there was a search but, just like Lancaster, he wasn't found because they weren't looking in the right place.'

'And you know the right place, I suppose.'

'No, but think of this. Lancaster's plane was found by the French. For all we know it might have been seen much earlier by, say, some Hartani or even a Targui. But why would they want to report it? It would mean nothing to them. Don't forget, this plane crashed only three years after the final battle between the French and the Tuareg when the French got the upper hand at last. The Tuareg felt they didn't owe the French a goddamn thing. Sure, if they'd found Lancaster alive they'd have brought him out, but they wouldn't care much about a dead guy in a dead plane.'

'All right,' I said. 'Spit it out. What are you getting at?'

Byrne said, 'Would you put up, say, five camels to help find Paul's old man?'

The question was so unexpected that I blinked with astonishment and I suppose I was testy. 'What the devil do you mean?'

'I mean put up the price of five camels.'

'How much is a camel worth?' I asked suspiciously.

Byrne scratched his jaw through his veil. 'An ordinary pack camel will go for about a hundred pounds sterling. A reasonable Mehari will fetch between a hundred fifty and two hundred.' He laughed. 'You couldn't buy Yendjelan for a thousand. Okay, let's say five hundred.'

'You want me to put up £500,' I said carefully. 'To find Paul's father.'

'I'd put up the same,' he said. 'In camels.'

'So now we have ten camels,' I said. 'How do they help? Do we ride them spaced a hundred yards apart in a sweep of the bloody Sahara?'

'No,' said Byrne calmly. 'They're a reward for a sighting of a plane that crashed in 1936 – payable when we're taken to see it.'

It was a good idea provided I was willing to fork out £500 to help Paul Billson, which wasn't a cast-iron certainty. A good idea but for one thing – the time element. I said, 'For God's sake! How long will it take for news of this reward to get around? Two months? Three months? I don't have that much time to spend here, and if I go, then Billson goes, even if I have to do what Hesther suggested – club him and put him in a sack.'

Byrne laughed quietly. 'You don't know much about the desert. There are trucks going up from Agadez to Tam every day – two days' journey at the most. Those truck drivers waste no time in sight-seeing; they've seen it already. From Tam to In Salah – another day. From Agadez east to Bilma – two days. From Bilma to Djanet in the Tassili n' Ajjer – two more days driving fast. In six days minimum I can get news to all the important oases in the desert. The whole Sahara is a big sounding-board if the news is important enough.'

I was sceptical. 'Word of mouth?'

'Word of mouth – hell!' Byrne snorted. 'Ten thousand leaflets handed out. Printed in Arabic, of course. Those who can't read will go to the public letter-writers for a reading as soon as they hear of a ten-camel reward.'

'You're crazy,' I said. I looked around at the thorn trees and the browsing camels. 'Where the blazes are you going to get ten thousand leaflets printed here?'

'I'll draw it up tonight,' he said. 'Then have them Xeroxed in Agadez. They have a machine in the bank.' He leaned forward and peered at me. 'Something the matter?' he enquired gently.

'No,' I said weakly. 'Nothing the matter. It's just the idea of blanketing the Sahara with leaflets seems a bit weird. You've never worked for J. Walter Thompson, have you?'

'Who's he?'

'A small advertising agency back in the States – and elsewhere.'

'Never heard of him.'

'If you ever leave the desert I'd apply for a job with him. You'd do well.'

'You're nuts!' he said. 'Well, what about it?'

I started to laugh. Between chuckles I said, 'All right . . . I'll do it . . . but it won't be for Paul Billson. It'll be worth it just to say I've done a saturation advertising campaign in the Sahara.'

Byrne wagged his head. 'Okay – I don't care why you do it so long as you do it.'

'What do I do?' I said. 'Give you a cheque?'

'Now what in hell would I do with a cheque?' he asked. 'I'll put up your half and you get the cash to Hesther in Algiers as and when you can.' He paused. 'Pity we don't have pictures of the plane. Paul had some but they went up with the Land-Rover.'

'I can help there. I got some photocopies from the Aeronautical Department of the Science Museum in London. Not Billson's plane but one exactly like it.'

'Good,' said Byrne. 'We'll put those on the hand-out. Or maybe drawings might be better.' He adjusted his veil and stood up. 'There's one thing you maybe haven't thought of.'

'What's that?'

'If the guy who shot Paul is still around he might get to know of these leaflets if he has local connections. If he does he'll be drawn down here like a hornet to a honey-pot. It might turn out real interesting.'

It might indeed!

# NINETEEN

When Paul Billson heard what we were going to do he took it as his due. He didn't even thank us, and I could have picked him up and shaken him as you would try to shake sense into a puppy. But that was the man, and he wasn't going to change. Byrne settled down to draw up his leaflet and I wandered away to think about things – mostly about Byrne, because I was fed up with thinking about Paul.

From what I had seen of Byrne's camels he seemed to take pride in breeding a superior animal. If his information on the price of camels was correct and a pack camel would cost £100, then it would be reasonable to assume that his might average, say, £150. That would make him worth £45,000 in stock alone, regardless of his other interests. He had said he ran salt caravans; I didn't know if that was profitable but I assumed it was. Then there was whatever he got from Hesther Raulier for looking after her affairs in the desert, and there were probably other sources of income.

It seemed likely that Byrne was a wealthy man in his society. I don't know how far the Tuareg had been forced into a cash economy – I had seen very little money changing hands – but even on a barter basis Byrne would be rich by desert standards.

\* \* \*

Next day Byrne and I went into Agadez, Paul staying behind on Byrne's insistence. 'I don't want you seen in Agadez,' he said. 'You'd stand out like the Tree of Ténéré. You spend the day here – and stay put. Understand?'

Paul understood. It wasn't what Byrne said, it was the way he said it that drove it home into Paul's skull.

As we drove away Byrne said, 'And Hamiada will see that he stays put.' There was a touch of amusement in his voice.

I said, 'What was that you said about a tree?'

'The Tree of Ténéré?' He pointed east. 'It's out there. Only tree I've ever heard of being put on the maps. It's on your map – take a look.'

So I did, and there it was – *L'Arbre du Ténéré,* about a hundred and sixty miles north-east of Agadez in the *Erg du Ténéré,* an area marked yellow on the map – the colour of sand. 'Why should a tree be marked?'

'There's not another tree in any direction for about fifty kilometres,' said Byrne. 'It's the most isolated tree in the world. Even so, a fool French truck driver ran into it back in 1960. It's old – been there for hundreds of years. There's a well there, but the water's not too good.'

So the map indicated – *eau trés mauvaise à 40 m.*

It was a little over a hundred miles to Agadez over roughish country. Even though we were able to pick up speed over the last forty miles of reasonable track it took us five hours, averaging twenty miles an hour for the whole trip.

Agadez seemed a prosperous little town by Saharan standards. It even had a mosque, something I had not seen in Tam. We parked the truck outside the Hotel de l'Aïr and went inside to have a beer, then Byrne went to the bank to have his leaflets printed. Before he left he said, 'You might like to do some shopping; it's better here than in Tam. Got any money?'

It occurred to me that Byrne was laying out considerable sums during our travels and he would need recompense. I dug out my wallet and checked it. I had the equivalent of about a hundred pounds in Algerian currency, another four hundred in travellers' cheques and a small case stuffed with credit cards.

Byrne looked at my offerings and said, 'None of that is much use here. You give anyone a strange piece of paper or a bit of plastic and he'll laugh at you.' He produced a small wad of local currency. 'Here. Don't worry, I'll bill you when you leave, and you can settle it with Hesther in Algiers.'

And I had to make do with that.

I walked along the dusty street and found that American influence had even penetrated as far as Agadez – there was a supermarket! Not that an American would have recognized it as such but it was passable, although the stock of European-style clothing was limited. I bought a pair of Levi's and a couple of shirts and stocked up with two cartons of English cigarettes. Then I blinked at an array of Scotch whisky, not so much in astonishment that it was there at all but at the price, which was two-thirds the London price. I bought two bottles.

I took my booty and stowed it in the Toyota, then had another beer in the hotel while waiting for Byrne. When he came back we took the Toyota to a filling station to refuel and there, standing next to the pumps, was a giraffe.

I stared at it incredulously. 'For God's sake! What the hell . . .'

The giraffe bent its neck and looked down at us with mild eyes. 'What's the matter?' asked Byrne. 'Haven't you seen a giraffe before?'

'Not at a filling station.'

Byrne didn't seem in the least surprised. 'I'll be a little while here. This is where we start the distribution of our message.'

I nodded wordlessly and watched the giraffe amble away up the main street of Agadez. As Byrne opened the door I said, 'Hang on. Satisfy my curiosity.'

'What about?'

I pointed. 'That bloody giraffe.'

'Oh, that. It's from the zoo. They let it out every morning, and it goes back every night to feed.'

'Oh!' Well, it *was* an explanation.

We arrived back at Byrne's place in the Air the next day, having camped on the way. I was getting to like those nightly camps. The peace was incredible and there was nothing more arduous to think about than the best place to make the fire and the best place to sleep after testing the wind direction. It was a long way from the busy – and now meaningless – activities of Stafford Security Consultants Ltd.

At that particular camp I offered Byrne a scotch, but he shook his head. 'I don't touch the hard stuff, just have the occasional beer.'

I said, 'I can't get over the fact that it's cheaper than in England.'

'No tax on it,' he said. 'In England you need a lot of money to build essentials like Concorde airplanes so your taxes are high.' His tone was sardonic. 'Out here who needs it?' He picked up the bottle. 'This stuff is brought up from Nigeria, mostly for the tourist trade. Same with the cigarettes. Might even have come up on the back of a camel.'

The whisky tasted good, but after the first I found I didn't want another. I said, 'The most incredible thing today was that bloody giraffe.'

'Civilized people hereabouts,' said Byrne. 'Don't like to keep things in cages. Same with camels.'

'What do you mean?'

'Well, a Tuareg-trained camel is worth more than one trained by an Arab, all other things being equal. A Targui is kinder about it and the camel responds. Real nice people.'

Looking up at the stars that night I thought a lot about that.

After that nothing very much happened except that I got a new suit of clothes and learned how to ride a camel, and the two were connected. Byrne was going out to inspect his herd, and when I arrived for my camel-riding lesson in jeans he shook his head solemnly. 'I don't think so,' he said. 'I really don't think so.'

And so I dressed like a Targui – loose, baggy trousers in black cotton cloth fitting tight around the ankles, a white *gandoura*, the Tuareg gown, and another blue *gandoura* on top of that. There was a *djellaba* too, to be worn in cold weather or at night. Literally topping it off was the *chech*, twenty feet of black cotton, about eighteen inches wide, which Byrne painstakingly showed me how to arrange.

When I was dressed in all my finery I felt a bit of a fool and very self-conscious, but that wore off quickly because no one else took any notice except Billson and I didn't give a damn for his opinion. He wouldn't change his clothing nor ride a camel; I think he had slightly Empire notions about 'going native'.

A camel, I found, is not steered from the mouth like a horse. Once in the saddle, the Tuareg saddle with its arm-chair back and high cross-shaped pommel, you put your bare feet on the animal's neck and guide it by rubbing one side or the other. Being on a camel when it rises to its feet is the nearest thing to being in an earthquake and quite alarming until one gets used to it.

Byrne, Hamiada and I set out with two pack camels for the grazing grounds near Telouess and were going to be away for over a week, Byrne commenting that he could not reasonably expect any reaction from his leaflet campaign for at least a fortnight. He had arranged with the owner of the filling station for the distribution of the leaflets in packets of 500 to the twenty most important oases south of the Atlas mountains.

'And it'll take that time to bring Paul up to the mark,' he said. 'Because one thing is certain – if we find that airplane it's going to be in some of the lousiest country you've ever seen, else the French would have found it years ago.'

What Billson did while we were away I don't know. I never found out and I didn't ask.

Looking back, I think those days spent wandering in the Aïr was the most idyllic time of my life. The pace was slow, geared to the stride of a camel, and the land was wide and empty. One fell into an easy rhythm, governed not by the needs of other men but by the passage of the sun across the sky, the empty belly, the natural requirements of the beast one was riding.

We found Byrne's herd and he looked at the animals and found their condition good. They were looked after by a family of Tuareg headed by a man called Radbane. 'These people are of the Kel Ilbakan,' said Byrne. 'A vassal tribe from south of Agadez. They graze their stock here in the winter and help me with mine.'

We accepted Radbane's hospitality and stayed at his camp for two days, and then struck west, skirting the base of a mountain called Bagzans. We were striking camp on the ninth day out of Timia when Hamiada gave a shout and pointed. We had visitors; three camels were approaching, two with riders. As they came closer Byrne said, 'That's Billson.'

He frowned, and I knew why. It would need something urgent to get Billson up on to a camel.

They came up to the camp and I noted that Billson's camel was on a leading rein held by the Targui who accompanied him. The camels sank to their knees and Billson rocked violently in the saddle. He slid to the ground painfully, still incongruously dressed in his city suit, now worn and weary. His face was grey with fatigue and he was obviously saddle-sore. I had been, too, but it had worn off.

I said, 'Come over here, Paul, and sit down.' Byrne and Hamiada were talking to the Targui. I dug into my saddle-bag and brought out the bottle of whisky which was still half full. I poured some into one of the small brass cups we used for mint tea and gave it to Paul. It was something he appreciated and, for once, he said, 'Thanks.'

'What are you doing out here?' I asked.

'I saw him,' he said.

'Who did you see?'

'The man who shot me. He was in Timia asking questions, and then came on to Byrne's place.' He paused. 'In the Range-Rover.'

'And you saw him? To recognize him?'

Paul nodded. 'I was bored – I had no one to talk to – so I went down among the Tuareg. There's a man who can speak a little French, about as much as me, but we can get on. I was outside his hut when I saw the Range-Rover coming so I ducked inside. The walls are only of reeds, there are plenty of cracks to look through. Yes, I saw him – and I knew him.'

'Was he alone?'

'No; he had the other man with him.'

'Then what happened?' I looked up. Byrne had come over and was listening.

'He started to talk to the people, asking questions.'

'In Tamachek?' asked Byrne abruptly.

'No, in French. He didn't get very far until he spoke to the man I'd been with.'

'That would be old Bukrum,' said Byrne. 'He was in the Camel Corps when the French were here. Go on.'

'They just talked to the old man for a bit, then they went away. Bukrum said they asked him if there were any Europeans about. They described me – my clothes.' His fingers plucked at his jacket. 'Bukrum told them nothing.'

Byrne smiled grimly. 'He was told to say nothing – they all were. Can you describe these men?'

'The man who asked the questions – the one who shot me – he was nearly six feet but not big, if you see what I mean. He was thin. Fair hair, very sunburned. The other was shorter but broader. Dark hair, sallow complexion.'

'Both in European clothes?'

'Yes.' Paul eased his legs painfully. 'Bukrum and I had a talk. He said he'd better send me to you because the men might come back. He said you'd be where wheels wouldn't go.'

I looked at the jumble of rocks about the slopes of Bagzans. Bukrum had been right. I said, 'I've asked this question before but I'll ask it again. Can you think of any reason – any conceivable reason – why two men should be looking for you in the Sahara in order to kill you?'

'I don't know!' said Paul in a shout. 'For Christ's sake, I don't know!'

I looked at Byrne and shrugged. Byrne said, 'Hamiada and I will go to Timia and nose around. We'll make better time on our own.' He pointed to the Targui who was talking to Hamiada. 'His name is Azelouane; he's Bukrum's son. He'll take you to a place in the hills behind Timia and you stay there until I send for you. There's water there, so you'll be all right.' He looked at the three camels which Azelouane had brought. 'You stay here today; those beasts need resting. Move off at first light tomorrow.'

Within ten minutes he and Hamiada were mounted and on their way.

*   *   *

It took us two days to get to the place in the hills behind Timia so, with the day's enforced rest, that was three days. There was a pool of water which Azelouane called a *guelta*. He, too, had a small smattering of French so we could talk in a minimal way with the help of a lot of hand language. We were there for three more days before Byrne came.

During this time Billson was morose. He was a very frightened man and showed it. Having a hole put in you with intent to kill tends to take the pith out of a man, but Paul had not really been scared until now. Probably he had reasoned that it was a case of mistaken identity and it was over, his attacker having given him up for dead after burning the Land-Rover. The knowledge that he was still being pursued really shook him and ate at his guts. He kept muttering, 'Why me? Why *me*?' He found no answer and neither did I. He also got rid of the rest of my whisky in short order.

Byrne arrived late at night, riding tall on Yendjelan and coming out of the darkness like a ghost. Yendjelan sank to her knees, protesting noisily as all camels do, and he slid from the saddle. Azelouane unsaddled her while I brewed up some hot tea for Byrne. It was a cold night.

He sat by the fire, still huddled in his *djellaba* with the hood over his head, and said, 'You making out all right?'

'Not bad.' I pointed to where Billson was asleep. 'He's not doing too well, though.'

'He's scared,' said Byrne matter-of-factly.

'Find anything?'

'Yeah. Two guys – one called Kissack, a Britisher; the other called Bailly. He's French, I think. They're scouring the Aïr looking for Billson.' He paused. 'Looking for me, too. They don't know about you.'

'How do they know about you?'

'My name had to go on that leaflet,' he said. 'That's how I figured it. No point in issuing a reward unless you give the name and place of the guy offering it.'

'Where are they now?'

'Gone to Agadez to fill up with gas. I think they'll be back.'

I thought about it, then said slowly, 'That tells us something. They're not just looking for Billson; they're after anybody who is looking for that bloody plane. Billson's name wasn't on the leaflet, was it?'

'No,' said Byrne shortly.

'That does it,' I said. 'It must be the plane.' I put my hand on his arm. 'Luke, you'd better watch it. They put a bullet into Billson on sight. They could do the same to you.' I realized that I had addressed him by his given name for the first time.

He nodded. 'That's what I thought.'

'Christ, I'm sorry to have got you into this.'

'Make never no mind,' he said. 'I'm not going to stick my head up as a target. And you didn't get me into this. I did.'

I said, 'So it's Peter Billson's plane. But why? Why should somebody want to stop us finding it?'

'Don't know.' Byrne fumbled under his *djellaba* and his hand came out holding a piece of paper. 'First results have started to come in. Maybe we should have just offered one camel; they're reporting every goddamned crashed airplane in the desert. Fifteen claimants so far. Five are duplications – reporting the same plane – so that cuts it down to ten. Six of those I know about myself, including that French plane in Koudia I told you of. That leaves four. Three of those are improbable because they're in areas where any crash should have been seen. That leaves one possible.'

'Where is it?'

'Up on the Tassili n' Ajjer. Trouble is it's way off Peter Billson's great circle course.'

'How far off?'

'About fifteen degrees on the compass. I know I argued that Billson must have been off course – that's why the search didn't find him. But fifteen degrees is too much.' He accepted a cup of tea.

'So what do we do now?'

'Sit tight and wait for more returns to come in.' He sipped the tea and added as an afterthought, 'And keep out of Kissack's way.'

'Couldn't we do something about him?'

'Like what?'

'Well, couldn't Paul go to the police in Agadez and lay a charge of attempted murder?'

Byrne snorted. 'The first thing they'd ask is why he didn't tell the Algerian authorities. Anyway, the cops here wouldn't be too interested in a crime that happened in Algeria.' He was probably right; I doubted if there'd be any Interpol co-operation in the Sahara. He said, 'I'm tired,' and rolled over and went to sleep in his sudden way.

I beat my brains out wondering why Kissack and Bailly should want to kill anyone searching for an aircraft that had crashed over forty years before. Presently I stopped thinking. I wasn't aware of it. I was asleep, too.


Byrne had brought us some provisions. Millet to be pounded in a mortar and boiled to a thin gruel before having crushed dates added, and flour and salt to make flapjacks. Azelouane went off somewhere and returned with a goat kid which he killed by slitting its throat, so we had fresh meat.

And so we sat tight in the hills, half a day's journey from Timia.

Three days later Byrne went back, leaving early in the morning and returning the same night. He reported that Kissack was still active. 'He's really scraping the bottom of the barrel,' he said. 'Tassil Oued, Grup-Grup, El Maki – all the little places. But Timia seems to attract him. He knows I live near there. He was in Timia again at midday today.'

'Hell!' I said. 'Be careful.'

He laughed. 'I was standing six feet from him and I was just another Targui. How was he to know different unless someone told him, and my people wouldn't give him a drink of water in the Tanezrouft.' There was a tinge of pride in the way he said 'my people'.

I thought that the Tuareg veil certainly did have its advantages, as did the fact that all the Tuareg dress alike in blue and white.

He said, 'There's another batch of sightings from hopefuls who'd like to win ten camels each. Twenty-two. Most of them duplicating the first lot.'

'Any possibles?'

He shrugged. 'Just that one on the Tassili n' Ajjer. Let's go talk to Paul. Where is he?'

'Down by the *guelta*. He spends a lot of time just looking at the water.'

So we went looking for Paul and found him, as I thought we would, sitting on the little sandy beach by the pool. Byrne sat on a rock and said, 'Paul, I want to talk to you.'

'What about?'

'I reckon you know more about your father's last flight than anyone in the world. I'd like your opinion on something.' He clicked his fingers at me. 'The map.'

The sun was dipping behind the hills but there was still enough light to see by. Byrne spread the map on the sand and traced a line with his finger. 'Algiers to Kano – that's the great circle course your father intended to fly. Right?'

Paul examined the line Byrne had drawn. 'Yes, that's about it.'

'It's not *about* anything,' said Byrne. 'That's the line.' He took the stub of pencil from the wallet which hung from his neck. 'Now we have one possibility – and it's here.' He marked the map with a cross.

Paul turned the map around. 'No,' he said firmly.

'Why not?'

'My father was a good pilot. He'd never have gone so far off course.'

Byrne said, 'Remember I was a flier, too, so I know what I'm talking about. What time of day did he take off from Algiers?'

Paul said, 'He landed in Algiers just after midday. He didn't refuel immediately because his mechanic wanted to check the plane. That woman in Algiers said . . .'

'You mean Hesther Raulier?'

'Yes.'

'Then call her by her name,' said Byrne harshly. 'She is *not* "that woman in Algiers". Go on.'

Paul flinched. 'Hesther Raulier said there was an argument about that. My father wanted to refuel immediately and take off, but the mechanic wouldn't have it. He said he wanted to have the plane just right.'

I said, 'Paul, in this race was time on the ground deducted from the elapsed time, or was it a case of whoever got to Cape Town first had won?'

'Whoever got to Cape Town first won outright.'

I said to Byrne, 'Then every minute Peter Billson spent on the ground was a minute lost. It's not surprising he argued for a quick take-off.'

Byrne nodded. 'Who won the argument?'

'Must have been the mechanic,' said Paid. 'The wo – Hesther Raulier said she took my father to an hotel where he got some sleep.'

'Then when did he take off?'

'At five that afternoon.'

'That time of year it would be dark at six,' said Byrne. 'He was making a night flight. He wouldn't be able to tell from the ground whether he was on course or not. He couldn't see the ground.'

'Hesther Raulier said it worried my father,' said Paul. 'Not the night flying, but he'd be landing at Kano in the dark. He didn't know if the airstrip would be illuminated.'

'Yeah,' said Byrne. 'That Northrop cruised at 215 mph, but he'd be pushing it a bit. Say eight hours to Kano landing at one in the morning. But he didn't get that far.'

It was now too dark to see the map clearly. I said, 'So what's the next move?'

'That's up to Paul,' said Byrne. 'I still think the plane was off course, and now I know it was a night flight that makes it certain to my mind.' He tapped the map. 'This could be Peter Billson's plane.'

I said, 'You'd be willing to take us there?'

'If that's what Paul wants.'

I looked towards Paul. I couldn't see his face but his movements showed indecision. At last he said hesitantly, 'Yes. All right.' Again no mention of thanks.

Byrne clapped his hands together lightly. 'We leave at dawn.'

# TWENTY

We arrived at Byrne's house at eleven next morning, Byrne having scouted ahead to see if it was safe to go in. Once there he wasted no time. 'I thought Paul would make that decision,' he said to me. 'We have to go through Agadez to tank up on gas, but Paul mustn't – not with Kissack about. I've sent Hamiada on ahead. He'll be waiting with camels this side of Agadez to take Paul around.'

That reminded me of something. 'I haven't seen Mokhtar around. He just seemed to evaporate as soon as we got here from Algeria.'

Byrne laughed. 'He'll be half way to Bilma by now. He's my *madugu*.'

'What's that?'

'Caravan master. He's taking millet to Bilma and bringing back salt. We should catch up with him the other side of Fachi.'

'We're going to Bilma?'

'Through Bilma,' corrected Byrne. 'And away to hell and gone the other side.'

I went to study my invaluable map, and I didn't much like what I saw. We'd be crossing the *Erg du Ténéré* and there was no track marked. And beyond that was the *Grand Erg du Bilma*. It seemed that I was going to see the Tree of Ténéré, very bad water at forty metres included.

When I next saw Byrne he was cleaning and oiling an automatic pistol and another lay by his side. 'You're an old army man; take your pick,' he invited.

They were both German; one was a Walther and the other a Luger. I said, 'Where did you get those?'

'There was a bit of trouble up north, if you remember,' he said. 'The trouble I walked away from. A lot of guns, too; and quite a few came south.'

I nodded. Both the pistols were standard German side-arms, officers for the use of. I picked the Walther and Byrne nodded approvingly. I said, 'I wouldn't give one of these to Paul.'

Byrne looked at me disgustedly. 'Think I'm crazy? If I'm going to be shot it had better be by the right guy.' He handed me a packet of ammunition and a spare magazine. 'Load up.'

I loaded the magazines and slipped one into the butt of the pistol. Then I had a problem; I didn't know where to put the damned thing. There was an inside pocket in the breast of the *gandoura* but it wasn't good enough to take anything as heavy as an automatic pistol. Byrne watched me with a sardonic eye, then said, 'There's a belt and holster in the closet behind you.'

There was a pocket built into the holster to take the spare magazine. I strapped the belt around my waist under the *gandoura*. There was no problem of access because the arm-holes of a *gandoura* are cut very low and one can withdraw one's arms right inside. A *djellaba* is made the same way, and on a cold night among the Tuareg one could be excused for thinking one was among a people without arms.

We left within the hour, just Byrne, Billson and myself in the Toyota, heading for Agadez. Four hours later Byrne swung off the track and we found Hamiada camped in a grove of doum palms. 'This is where you leave us,' Byrne said to Paul. 'Hamiada will take you to the other side of Agadez. We'll join you later tonight.' He had a few words with Hamiada, then we left them and rejoined the track.

We filled up with petrol and water at the filling station in Agadez and I noticed Byrne paying special attention to the tyres. He talked briefly with the owner and then we set off again. Byrne said, 'There's another batch of sightings but they're all duplicate.'

Going by the mosque we were held up for a moment by the giraffe which was strolling up the street. Byrne nudged me. 'Look there.' He nodded towards the Hotel de l'Air. A Range-Rover was parked outside.

'Kissack?'

'Could be. Let's find out.' He swung across the dusty street and parked next to the Range-Rover. We got out and he studied it, then produced a knife and bent down to the rear wheel.

'What are you doing?'

He straightened and put the knife away. 'Just put my mark on a tyre,' he said. 'It'll be comforting to know if Kissack's around or not.' He looked at the hotel entrance. 'Let's go talk to him.'

'Is that wise?'

'He's looking for me, ain't he? And I know it. It would be the neighbourly thing to do. If this is Kissack he has a bad habit of shooting folks without as much as a word of greeting. If a guy's going to shoot at me I'd like to get to know him before he does. That's what I didn't like about the Army Air Force – you got shot at by strangers.'

I said, 'You're the boss.'

'Damn right,' he said. 'Now, pull up your veil, and when we go in there don't sit down – just stand behind me. And don't say a goddamn word under any circumstances.' He reached into the back of the Toyota and pulled out a sword. 'Put that on.'

I slung on the sword in the way I had seen Mokhtar wear his, and followed Byrne into the hotel. So I was a Targui, a good enough disguise. I wasn't worried about my colour; all anyone could see of me were my eyes and my hands, and the backs of my hands were deeply tanned. Anyway, many of the Tuareg were lighter coloured than I was.

Byrne went up to the bar and questioned the barman who jerked a thumb towards an inner room. We went in to find it deserted except for two men sitting at a table. Paul had described them well. Kissack was a tall, thin man with fair hair who was not so much tanned as burned, the way the sun often affects fair-skinned people. Strips of skin were peeling from his forehead. Bailly was swarthy and the sun wouldn't affect him much.

Byrne said, 'I'm Byrne. I hear you've been looking for me.'

Kissack looked up and his eyes widened. '*You* are Byrne?'

'Yeah.' Byrne lowered his veil. I wondered if Kissack knew that was a mark of contempt.

Kissack smiled. 'Sit down, Mr Byrne. Have a drink?' He was English, probably a Londoner to judge by his accent.

'Thanks.' Byrne sat down. 'I'll have a beer.' Kissack's eyes wandered past him to rest on me thoughtfully. Byrne jerked his thumb at me. 'He don't drink; it's against his religion. He'll have a lemonade.'

Kissack held up his arm and a waiter came and took the order. 'My name is Kissack. This is M'sieur Bailly.'

Bailly merely grunted, and Byrne nodded shortly. Kissack said, 'I understand you are interested in aeroplanes, Mr Byrne.'

'Yeah.'

'Crashed aeroplanes.'

'Yeah.'

Kissack narrowed his eyes as he studied Byrne. He was getting the answers he wanted, but they were too mono-syllabic for his taste. 'May I ask why?' he said smoothly.

'Guess it's because I used to be a flier myself.'

'I see. Just a general interest.'

'Yeah.'

Kissack's eyes flickered to Bailly, who grunted again. It was a sound of disbelief. 'Any particular aircraft you're interested in.'

'Not really. They're all interesting.'

'I see. What's the most interesting aeroplane you've come across so far?'

The waiter came back. He put a beer on the table and handed me a glass of lemonade. Byrne didn't answer immediately but picked up his glass and studied the bubbles. 'I guess it's the wreck of an Avro Avian up in the Tanezrouft. Got quite a history. Name of *Southern Cross Minor*. Owned by Kingsford-Smith who flew it from Australia to England in 1931. Then a guy called Lancaster bought it to try to beat Amy Mollison's record to Cape Town.' He drank some beer, then added drily, 'He didn't.'

Kissack seemed interested. 'When was this?'

'1933. The wreck wasn't found until 1962. The desert hides things, Mr Kissack.'

'Any other old aeroplanes?'

'None as old as that – far as I know.'

Byrne was playing with Kissack, teasing him to say out-right what he wanted. I pushed the glass of lemonade under my veil and sipped. It was quite refreshing.

'Any about as old?'

'Well, let's see,' said Byrne reflectively. 'There are a couple of dozen wrecks from the war littered about in places too difficult to get them out. I wrecked one of those myself.'

'No – from before the war?'

'Not many of those. What's *your* interest, Mr Kissack?'

'I'm a reporter,' said Kissack. 'Investigative stuff.'

'In the Sahara?' queried Byrne sardonically.

Kissack spread his hands. 'Busman's holiday. I'm just touring around and I guess my journalistic instincts got the better of me.'

Byrne nodded his head towards Bailly. 'He a reporter, too?'

'Oh no. M'sieur Bailly is my guide.'

Bailly looked more suited to be a guide to the murkier regions of the Kasbah in Algiers. Byrne said, 'Is that all you wanted me for?' He drained his glass.

Kissack stretched out his hand. 'How long have you lived here, Mr Byrne?'

'Thirty-five years.'

'Then please stay. I'd like to talk to you. It's nice to be able to talk to someone again in my own language. I have very little French and M'sieur Bailly has no English at all.' He was a damned liar; Bailly was taking in every word. Kissack said, 'Have another beer, Mr Byrne – that is, if you're not in a hurry.'

Byrne appeared to hesitate, then said, 'I'm going no place. All right, I'll have another beer. You want to pick my brains, that's the payment.'

'Good,' said Kissack enthusiastically, and signalled for a waiter. 'You'll be able to fill me in on local colour – it's hard for Bailly to get it across.'

'I'll do my best,' said Byrne modestly.

The waiter took the order and I gave him my empty glass. Kissack said casually, 'Ever come across a man called Billson?'

'Know of him. Never did get to meet him.'

'Ah!' Kissack was pleased. 'Do you know where he is?'

'He's dead, Mr Kissack,' said Byrne.

'Are you sure of that?'

'Well, I can't say I am,' admitted Byrne. 'There was no death certificate. But I reckon he's dead, all right.'

Kissack frowned. 'How do you know?'

'Hell!' said Byrne. 'He must be. His airplane crashed over forty years ago. You don't suppose he's still walking across the desert like the children of Israel?'

Kissack said in a choked voice, 'That's not the Billson I meant.'

'No?' said Byrne. 'I thought you were still on the airplane kick.' The waiter put a beer in front of him and he picked it up.

'Your Billson,' said Kissack softly. 'When did that happen?'

'Was in 1936 during the London to Cape Town Air Race.' He shrugged. 'And he's not my Billson.'

'Do you know where *that* aeroplane is?'

'Nobody knows where it is,' said Byrne. 'I told you – the desert hides things. Hell, you could hide an air fleet in three million square miles.' He drank some beer. 'Not that I wouldn't be interested in it if someone found it.'

'You wouldn't be looking for it?' asked Kissack.

'Why in hell would I be doing that? I've better things to do with my time. When that airplane is found it'll be in a goddamn nasty part of the desert, else it would have shown up by now. I've better things to do than risk my neck like that.'

Kissack put his hand to his breast pocket. From it he extracted a piece of paper which he unfolded and laid on the table. It was one of Byrne's leaflets. 'I'm unable to read this myself but Bailly translated it for me,' he said. 'I found it remarkably interesting.'

'Yeah, I suppose a reporter might.'

'And you still say you're not looking for that aeroplane?'

'Not specifically – no.' Byrne pointed to the leaflet. 'That's something I distribute every three-four years – more in hope than anything else. I told you, I was a flier during the war. Flying in North Africa, too. I'm interested in desert air-planes, especially since I put one there myself. Might write a book about them.'

'A scholarly monograph, no doubt,' said Kissack sarcastically. *'Some Aspects of Air Disasters in the Sahara.'*

'I know it sounds nutty,' said Byrne. 'But it's my hobby.
Most folks' hobbies seem nutty to someone or other. Ever
thought how crazy stamp collecting is?'

'Expensive, too,' said Kissack. 'Ten camels must be worth
a lot of money.'

'Might seem so to you.' Byrne shrugged. 'I breed them.'
He grinned at Kissack. 'Get them at cost price, as you might
say. And it ain't much, spread over three or four years.'

Kissack wore a baffled look. The yarn Byrne was spinning was just mad enough to be true. He took a deep breath,
and said, 'The man I'm looking for is Paul Billson.'

*'Paul* Billson.' Byrne tasted the word along with some
beer. *'Paul* Billson.' He shook his head. 'Can't say I've heard
of him. Any relation?'

'I don't know,' said Kissack flatly. He prodded the leaflet
with his forefinger. 'Get any results from that?'

'Not so far. Just the same goddamn list I got last time I
put it out.'

Kissack looked at him for a long time wordlessly. Byrne
stirred, and said, 'Anything more you'd like to know?'

'Not for the moment,' said Kissack.

Byrne stood up. 'Well, you know where to find me again
if you want me. Up near Timia. Nice to have visited with
you, Mr Kissack. Hope I've been of help.' He nodded pleasantly to Bailly. *'Bonjour, M'sieur Bailly.'*

Bailly grunted.

As we drove away from the hotel I said, 'Well, now we
know.'

'Yeah,' said Byrne laconically. After a while he said, 'That
guy gives me a real creepy feeling.'

'Why should he be looking for Paul? He must have written him off as dead.'

'It must have come as a hell of a shock to him,' said Byrne. 'He knocks off Paul, then the whole goddamn Sahara is flooded with questionnaires about crashed airplanes – and coming from Niger, for God's sake! He must have been a confused boy.'

'But he was quick off the mark.' I thought about it. 'Good thing we didn't bring Paul into town.' I laughed. 'That was a crazy yarn you spun him.'

'It won't hold him long,' said Byrne. 'He'll ask around and find I've never done a damnfool thing like that before. I'm hoping he'll go up to Timia – that'll give us some space between us. If he wastes his time on Timia we'll be the other side of Bilma before he finds out he's lost us.'

# TWENTY-ONE

We drove east out of Agadez for about five miles, then left the track to rendezvous with Hamiada at the place appointed. Hamiada had already made camp and had a tent erected. We stayed there the night and slept early in preparation for an early start to cross the Ténéré.

Next morning I gave Billson the jeans and shirts I had bought. 'You can't wander around the Sahara in a business suit,' I said. 'You'd better wear these. I think they'll fit.'

He rejected them and I said, 'Paul, you're a damned fool! Kissack, back there, has your description and he knows what you're wearing.' I shrugged. 'But please yourself.'

Paul changed his clothing fast.

I noticed that Hamiada had cut a lot of acacia branches which he tied in bundles and put in the back of the truck. When I asked Byrne about this he said, 'If we want hot food we have to have fuel.' He nodded towards the east. 'There's nothing out there.'

Hamiada left, taking the camels and going back to Timia. We went in the opposite direction, at first due east, and then curving to the north-east. For the first fifty miles it wasn't too bad; the track was reasonably good and we were able to hold an average speed of about thirty miles an hour. But then the track petered out and we were on rough ground which gradually gave way to drifts of sand, and finally, the sand dunes themselves.

'So this is what you call an *erg*,' I said.

Byrne laughed shortly. 'Not yet.' He indicated a crescent-shaped dune we were passing. 'These are barchan dunes. They're on the move all the time, driven by the wind. Not very fast – but they move. All the sand is on the move, that's why there's no track here.'

Presently the isolated barchan dunes gave way to bigger sand structures, rolling hills of sand. The mountains of the Air had long disappeared below the horizon behind us. Byrne drove skilfully, keeping to the bottom of the valleys and threading his way among the dunes. I wondered how he knew which way to go, but he didn't seem worried. As we went he discoursed on the different types of sand.

'This ain't too bad,' he said. 'At least you can stop without getting into trouble. *Fech-fech* is the worst.'

'What's that?'

'Sometimes you get times of high humidity – high for the desert, anyway. At night in winter the moisture freezes out of the air and forms dew on the surface of the sand. That makes a hard crust on the top with soft sand underneath. Driving on that is okay if you keep moving, but if you stop you're likely to break through and go down to your axles.' He paused and said reflectively, 'Don't bother a camel none, though.'

Another time he said, 'A few years ago I was up north, round about Hassi-Messaoud where the oil-wells are. I came across a big truck – could carry a hundred tons. Russian, it was; used for carrying oil rigs about. The guys who were driving it were Russians, too, and they showed me how it worked. It had eight axles, sixteen big balloon tyres and you could let air out and pump air in by pressing buttons in the cab. They reckoned that with a full load they could jiggle things so that the weight on the ground per square inch was no more than that of a camel. A real nice toy it was.'

'Ingenious.'

'Yeah.' He laughed. 'But they were sloppy about it. They had five of the tyres on wrong way around. Anyway, a few weeks later I heard what happened to it. They were driving along and decided to stop for the night. So they stopped, had something to eat, and went to sleep. But they stopped on *fech-fech* and during the night the truck broke through. The Russians were sleeping underneath it and it killed them both. They never did get it out.'

A nice illustrative and macabre story of the dangers of the desert. Byrne said, 'Lousy stinkpots! Never have liked them except when I'm in a hurry, like now.'

After a while the sand dunes levelled off into a plain of sand, and presently Byrne said, 'The Tree!' On the far horizon ahead was a black dot which might well have been an optical illusion – a speck of dust on the eyeball – but which proved to be a solitary wide-spreading thorn tree. There was a well near the tree and the ground all about was littered with the olive-shaped pellets of camel dung. There were also several skeletons of camels, some still covered with hide, mummified in the dry, hot desert air.

Byrne said, 'We'll stop here for something to eat – but not near the well. Too many biting bugs.'

As we drove past, Paul, behind me, said, 'There's someone standing by the tree.'

'So there is,' said Byrne. 'Just one man. That's unusual here. Let's go see who he is.'

He pulled over the wheel and we stopped just by the tree. The man standing there was not a Targui because he wore no veil and his skin was darker, a deep rich brown. He was shorter than the average Targui and not as well dressed. His *gandoura* was black and his head cloth in ill array.

Byrne got out and talked to the man for a few minutes, then came back to the truck. 'He's a Teda from the Tibesti. He's been hanging around here for three days waiting for someone to come along. He's heading east and he can't do the next stretch alone.'

'How did he get here?'

'Walked. Only just made it, too. Did the last two days without water. Do you mind if we give him a lift as far east as we're going?'

'It's your truck,' I said. 'And you're the boss.'

Byrne nodded and waved to the man, who came over to the Toyota. He was carrying a shaggy goatskin bag which Byrne said was a *djerba*, used for holding water. Byrne tapped the bag and asked a question, pointing to the well. The man answered and then, at a command from Byrne, emptied the contents of the bag on the ground.

'It's okay to drink that stuff if you have to,' said Byrne. 'But not unless. An addax antelope fell into the well a few years ago and it's been no goddamn good since.'

As we drove away I said, 'What's his name?'

'He didn't say. He said his name used to be Konti.'

I frowned. 'That's a funny thing to say.'

'Not really,' said Byrne. 'It means he's a murderer.' He seemed unperturbed.

I twisted around to look at the man in the back of the truck, whose name used to be Konti. 'What the hell . . .'

'It's okay,' said Byrne. 'He won't kill us. He's not a professional murderer. He probably killed somebody in a blood feud back home and had to take it on the lam. Maybe he reckons it's now safe to go back or he's got word his family has paid the blood money.'

He stopped the truck about a mile the other side of the Tree. 'This will do.' We got out. From the back of the truck Byrne took what appeared to be a length of metal pipe. 'Help me fill this.'

There was a brass cap on the top which he unscrewed. I held a funnel while Byrne filled the contraption with water from a jerrican. As he did so he said, 'This is a volcano – the most economic way of boiling water there is.'

It was simple, really, consisting of a water jacket, holding about two pints, around a central chimney. Byrne poked a lighted spill of paper into a hole in the bottom, added a few twigs of acacia and, when the fire had taken hold of those, popped in a handful of pellets of dried camel dung which he had picked up near the tree. They burned fiercely, but with no smell. Within five minutes we had boiling water.

We lunched on bread and cheese and mint tea, our murderer joining in. 'Ask him his name,' I said. 'I can't keep on referring to him as the man who used to be Konti.'

As Byrne talked to the man Paul said, 'I'm not going to ride with any murderer. Nobody asked me if he could come along.'

Byrne stopped abruptly and turned to Paul. 'Then you'll walk the rest of the way, either forward or back.' He jerked his head. 'He's probably a better man than you. And the reason you weren't asked is that I don't give a good goddamn what you like or what you don't like. Got it?' He didn't wait for a reply but went back to talking in guttural tones.

I looked at Paul, whose face was as red as a boiled beet. I said softly, 'I told you to walk carefully around Byrne. You never learn, do you?'

'He can't talk to me like that,' he muttered.

'He just did,' I pointed out. 'And what the hell are you going to do about it? I'll tell you – you're going to do nothing, because Byrne is the only thing standing between you and being dead.'

He lapsed into a sulky silence.

Byrne finished his interrogation and turned back to me. 'He says it's okay for you to call him Konti now. I don't speak his lingo well, but he has some Arabic – and I was just about right. He killed a man three years ago in the Tibesti and ran away. He's just learned that the blood money has been paid so he's going back.' He paused. 'Blood camels, really; there's not much hard cash in the Tibesti.'

'How many camels are worth a man's life?'

'Five.'

'Half a 1930s aeroplane,' I commented.

'You could put it that way,' he said. 'The change of name is a pure ritual, of course. You know what he'd do when he ran away? He'd kill an antelope, take a length of its large intestine, and pull it on to his feet like socks. Then he'd jump up and down till it broke. Symbolic breaking of the trail, you see.'

'Weird,' I said.

'Yeah; funny people, the Teda. Related to the Tuareg but a long ways back.' He looked up at the sun. 'Let's go. I want to be the other side of Fachi before nightfall.'

We pressed on and entered an area where again there were large dunes, some of them several hundred feet high. I realized that Byrne was doing all the driving and offered to spell him but he rejected the idea. 'Later, maybe; but not now. You'd get us stuck. There's an art in driving in soft sand, and you have to hit these rises at just the right angle.'

Once I glimpsed an animal with large ears scurrying over the edge of a dune. Byrne said it was a fennec. 'Desert fox. Gets its moisture from eating insects and jerboas. Jerboas make water right in their own bodies. Least, that's what a guy told me who was out here studying them. That fennec wouldn't show himself in daytime in summer; too goddamn hot.'

Fachi was a small, miserable oasis a little over a hundred miles from the Tree of Ténéré. The people were Negroid and the women wore rings in their noses. 'These people are

Fulani,' said Byrne with an edge of contempt in his voice. 'The Tuareg don't like 'em, and they don't like the Tuareg. We're not staying here – they'd steal us blind.'

We stopped only long enough to fill the water cans and to buy a goat kid which Byrne efficiently killed and butchered, then we went on for ten miles and camped just as the sun was setting. We cooked a meal, then ate and slept, and were on our way again at dawn next day.

We drove mile after rolling mile among the dunes and sometimes over them when there was no other recourse. Once I said to Byrne, 'How the devil do you know which way to go?'

'There's an art in that, too,' he said. 'You've got to know what the prevailing wind was during the last few months. That sets the angle of the dunes and you can tell your direction by that. It don't change much from year to year but enough to throw you off and get you lost. And you keep an eye on the sun.'

It was nearly midday when we rose over the crest of a dune and Byrne said, 'There's the *azelai*.'

'What?'

'The salt caravan Mokhtar is taking to Bilma. He's two days out of Fachi.'

That gave me a clue as to the difference between the speed of a camel and that of a Toyota. 'How long from Agadez to Bilma?'

'Four weeks. Two or three weeks in Bilma to rest up, then back again with the salt. Best part of three months for the round trip.'

The caravan consisted of about three hundred camels and perhaps twenty camel drivers. 'Fifty of these are mine,' said Byrne, and hailed Mokhtar. He came towards the truck with the slow, lazy saunter of the Tuareg, looked at me in surprise, and then laughed and said something to Byrne who chuckled and said, 'Mokhtar thinks I've got a convert.

He wants to know if I'm setting up in competition with the Prophet.'

He examined his animals and expressed satisfaction at their condition, and then we went on, and the caravan, plodding its slow three-miles-an-hour pace, was soon left behind.

It was at about three that afternoon when the offside front tyre burst and the steering-wheel slewed violently in Byrne's hands. 'Goddamn!' he said, and brought us to a halt.

There was a whipcrack at my ear and the windscreen shattered. I had been shot at in Korea and I knew a bullet when I heard one, even without the evidence of the broken windscreen. 'Everyone out,' I yelled. 'We're under fire.'

I jerked at the door handle and jumped out. The bullet had come from my side, so I ran around the truck to get into cover. As I did so a fountain of sand spurted a yard ahead of me. Paul was still in the truck, not being quick enough off the mark, and I found Byrne hauling him out. I discovered that I was holding the Walther pistol in my hand although I couldn't remember drawing it.

The shooting was still going on, sharp cracks in the dead, dry air. I judged it to be a rifle. But no bullets were coming anywhere near us. Byrne nudged me. 'Look!' He pointed upwards to the dune behind us.

Konti, the Teda, was running up the dune and was already three-quarters of the way to the top, which was about sixty feet. His *gandoura* fluttered in the breeze of his passage, and bullets sent the sand flying about his feet. At the top, silhouetted against the sky, he seemed to stumble, then he fell rather than jumped over the other side of the dune and was gone from sight. The shooting stopped.

'Think he was hit?'

'Don't know,' said Byrne, and opened the rear door of the Toyota. He put his arm inside and withdrew the

Lee-Enfield rifle. 'I think Kissack got ahead of us.' He took a full magazine from the pouch at his neck and loaded the rifle.

There was another shot and a thump, then the metallic howl of a ricochet off metal. The truck quivered on its springs. 'The bastards have us pinned down,' said Byrne. 'If we try to make a run for it now we'll be dead meat.' He looked up at the dune behind us. 'That guy only got away because he did the unexpected. I guess he's been shot at before.'

'If he did get away.'

Another bullet slammed into the side of the truck.

'Yeah.'

I looked around for Billson and found him scrunched up behind the rear wheel, making himself as small as possible. Byrne followed my glance. 'He won't be much help,' he said flatly. 'We can count him out.'

'So what do we do?'

'Shoot back.'

There was a *thunk* and a soft explosive blast of air as another tyre went. Byrne said, 'He does that once more and we're stuck. I only have two spares. See if you can locate the son of a bitch.'

Carefully I raised my head, looking through the windows of the Toyota. I stared at the dune I saw which was about a hundred feet high, and ran my eye along the line of the crest. There was another shot which hit the truck and then I saw a slight movement.

I ducked down. 'He's on top of the dune and about twenty degrees to the left.'

'How far?'

'Hard to say. Two fifty to three hundred yards. It'll be an uphill shot.'

'Uh-huh!' Byrne adjusted the sight on the rifle. 'Now let the dog see the rabbit. And, for Christ's sake, keep that handgun ready and watch our flanks.'

I stood back at a crouch as Byrne pushed the barrel of the rifle through the open window in the door of the truck. I glanced from side to side but nothing moved. 'I see him,' said Byrne softly. They fired together and Byrne ducked. The truck shivered on its springs. 'I think I put some sand in his eyes,' he said.

There was silence broken only by metallic creakings from the cooling engine and a soft liquid gurgling noise. I was beginning to think Byrne was right when there came another shot and a bullet went right through both open windows of the truck, breaking the sound barrier about six inches above my head with a vicious crack.

Byrne said, 'I'll bet he moved. If I can do that again be ready to make a break for it. Then try to out-flank them. If we don't do something we'll be shot to bits just standing here.'

'All right.'

He raised his head and looked up at the dune. 'Yeah, he moved. Now where in hell is he?' Another bullet came our way with disastrous effect. It slammed into the tyre on the wheel behind which Billson crouched and there was a *whoosh* as the air escaped.

'That's buggered it!' said Byrne. Paul was whimpering and trying to burrow his way into the soft sand. 'We won't get far on three wheels, but I've got the bastard spotted.'

He brought up the rifle again and prepared to fire. I said, 'Hold it, Luke!' and put all the urgency I could into my voice.

He lowered his head. 'What is it?'

I knew what that gurgling noise had meant. 'He's either got the petrol tank or one of the fuel cans. Can't you smell it?' Byrne sniffed the stink of petrol. I said, 'You shoot that thing and we could go up in flames in a big way. It only needs a spark.'

'Jesus!' He withdrew the rifle and stared at me, and the same thing was in both our minds. It would need only a spark from a ricochet off metal to fire the vapourizing petrol.

I said, 'I made that mistake in Korea, and I've got burned skin to prove it.'

'I wondered about that puckering on your chest. We'd better run for it then. Different directions. I think there's only one guy shooting; he won't get us both.'

'What about Paul?'

'He can do what the hell he likes.'

A bullet smashed into a headlight and glass flew.

'All right,' I said. 'Immediately after the next shot.'

Byrne nodded.

There was no next shot – not from the rifle, but faintly in the distance someone screamed, an ululating noise of pure agony which went on and on. I jerked, torn from the tension of waiting to run into a greater tension. I stared at Byrne. 'What's that?'

The scream still went on, now broken into sobbing screeches as someone fought for breath. 'Someone's hurting, that's for sure,' he said. There were distant shots, not from the rifle but from pistols in my judgement. Then the screaming stopped and again there was silence.

We listened for a long time and heard nothing at all. After a while I said, 'I think . . .'

'Quiet!' snapped Byrne.

In the distance was the unmistakable noise of a balky starter turning an engine over. It whined a few more times and then the quieter engine must have fired because the noise stopped. Byrne said, 'Maybe they're leaving.'

'Maybe it's a trick to get us in the open.' He nodded at that so we stayed there.

After perhaps ten minutes there was a shout and I looked up at the dune, careful to keep cover. Standing up there was Konti and he was shouting and waving. Byrne took a deep breath. 'I'll be goddamned! Let's go see.'

We climbed the dune and Konti started to jabber at Byrne with much gesticulation. He was very excited and understandably so; it had been an exciting fifteen minutes. He pointed down to the valley on the other side of the dune and he and Byrne walked down with me following because I wanted to know what was going on.

There were tyre tracks down there and someone had shed a lot of blood, perhaps a pint or more. Byrne squatted down and pointed to where a tyre had gone over blood-dampened sand. 'Kissack,' he said. 'That's the mark I put in his rear tyre.'

'What happened?'

'What happened is that you can thank God we picked up Konti yesterday. He probably saved our lives.'

'How?'

Byrne talked to Konti for a few minutes then said to me, 'He says there were three men here. From the description he gives they were Kissack, Bailly and another guy, probably an Arab. Kissack and the Arab were up top on the dune with Kissack doing the shooting. Bailly was standing here by the car. So Konti came around here and threw a knife at him.'

'A knife!' I said blankly. 'And that was what all the screaming was about?' I couldn't think why. A man with a knife in him didn't usually make that kind of row, but of course it would depend where the knife hit him. I looked around, then said, 'How did Konti get close enough to throw a knife? There's no cover.'

'You ain't seen the knife,' said Byrne. 'After it hit Bailly it buried itself in the sand. Konti picked it up before he called us.'

He said something to Konti and held out his hand. Konti fumbled about his person and produced the knife, which was like no knife I'd ever seen before. It was about eighteen inches long and made out of a single piece of flat steel an eighth of an inch thick. The handle was a foot long but the rest of it is hard to describe. It curved in a half-circle and two other blades projected at right-angles with hooks on the end. There seemed to be a multiplicity of cutting edges, each as sharp as a razor. It was very rusty.

'That's a *mouzeri*,' said Byrne. 'The Teda throwing knife. It's thrown horizontally from below waist level and it'll stop a horse going at full gallop. It's used for hunting addax and oryx but it'll also chop a man off at the ankles at sixty yards. Bailly didn't know what hit him, but Konti says it damn near took his left foot right off and badly injured his right ankle.'

I looked at the rusty blades. 'If he doesn't die of loss of blood it'll be by blood-poisoning,' I observed. What this thing had done to Bailly was enough to make anyone scream.

'I hope so,' said Byrne harshly. He took the queer-shaped knife and gave it back to Konti, who grinned cheerfully. 'Konti says it's the same knife he used to kill his enemy with in the Tibesti.' He looked down at the blood on the sand and shrugged. 'Let's go see what the damage is.'

The damage was bad. Three tyres shot to pieces and only two spares. But that wasn't the worst, because the petrol tank had a hole in it. We had refilled from the jerricans not long before the shooting and there wasn't nearly enough petrol to take us to Bilma even if we had good tyres.

I said, 'Well, we've got plenty water and food. All we have to do is to sit tight until Mokhtar comes along, then we can hitch a ride on a camel.'

'Yeah,' said Byrne. 'Good thinking – but for one thing. He ain't coming this way.'

# TWENTY-TWO

Billson had still not got over his fit of the quivers. I couldn't say that I blamed him; being shot at takes different men in different ways, and Paul had not been the most stable man to begin with. And there was something else that Paul had to contend with which did not obtain under war conditions. He lived with the knowledge that he was being hunted personally, that someone malevolent was pursuing him with intent to kill. Every bullet that came our way had Paul's name engraved upon it.

And so he was in no shape to take an immediate part in the discussion. Konti, while being wise in desert ways, knew little about the Ténéré; it was not his stamping ground. The same applied to me except the bit about desert ways, and so most of the decisions were made by Byrne.

After the flat statement that Mokhtar was not coming our way I merely said, 'Oh!' and waited for what he'd say next.

What he did say was: 'That *djerba* is going to come in useful. We're going to walk a piece.'

'How far?'

He said, 'I came this way because it's a short cut and okay for a truck. The camel trail is fifteen miles to the south.'

After leaving Fachi I would have sworn that Byrne had navigated from camel skeleton to camel skeleton but I had seen none in the last few miles. And he had just given the reason why. 'Fifteen miles,' I said, feeling relieved. 'That's not far.'

Byrne said, 'We'll need to take water – as much as we can carry.'

'To walk fifteen miles?'

Byrne took me by the elbow and walked me out of Paul's hearing. He said, 'It'll take us the rest of today and all day tomorrow. You ever walked in soft sand?'

'Not far.' I looked up the valley. 'But it doesn't seem too difficult.'

He followed my glance. 'The camel trail to Bilma is successful because it follows the grain of the country. You can go up the long valleys between the dunes. We'll be walking against the grain; you'll be going up and down dunes until you're dizzy. It's fifteen miles across country plus five miles of climbing up and another five miles going down. And there are other things to keep in mind.'

'Such as?'

He shook his head. 'I'll tell you if it's necessary. No point in you worrying about what may not happen. Let me do the worrying.'

He only succeeded in making me uneasy.

The first thing we did was to fill the *djerba* with water from a jerrican, then Byrne looked me up and down. 'How much weight do you reckon you can carry?'

I remembered army route marches which were not so much for use in these mechanized days as to toughen the men. Officers were supposed to do better than the men. I picked a figure, then hastily revised it downwards as I thought of climbing interminably in soft sand. 'Forty pounds.'

Byrne shook his head. 'Too much. A jerrican half-full for you and Paul; that's about thirty pounds each. Konti can take his *djerba*; he's used to it.'

We took a full jerrican and split it between two, then made slings so the jerricans could be back-packed, taking care to put in plenty of padding to avoid chafe. Byrne made us take the *djellabas*. 'It gets cold at night.' I noted that the jerrican he picked to carry himself was full. That would be a killing load for a man on the wrong side of sixty if what he had said about our journey was true, but I said nothing about it. He knew what he was doing.

We then ate and stuffed what was left of the bread and cheese and a few scraps of meat into the breast pockets of our *gandouras*. 'Drink hearty,' advised Byrne. 'Water is better in you than out. Any camel knows that.'

When Byrne had spoken of water in the past he had referred to litres or gallons interchangeably, but his gallons were American. I estimated that we moved away carrying eight and a half imperial gallons in jerricans plus what was in the *djerba* which was difficult to estimate – say, nearly twelve gallons in all. It seemed a lot of water to take for a fifteen-mile hike and I wondered what possibilities were lurking in Byrne's mind.

My memories of the journey I seldom care to reflect upon. The most insistent thing that comes to mind is the soft, yet gritty, sand. A building contractor would have delighted in it because it would be ideal for making high-quality cement and concrete and, no doubt, some sharp entrepreneur will find some way of shipping it out and making a profit. God knows, there's enough of it. But I can never now look upon an expanse of sand without feeling, in imagination, the cruel tug of that damned jerrican on my back.

We passed the place where Konti had hamstrung Bailly, crossed the valley and climbed another of the dunes which, in that place, were running from sixty to a hundred feet high. I suppose we were lucky in a way because the forward slopes which we had to climb were not as steep as the reverse slopes. Had we been going north instead of south it would have been much worse.

I watched Byrne going ahead of me across a valley floor and it came to me that there was some significance to that languid, gliding walk of the Tuareg – it came from much walking in sand, using the most economical means possible. I tried to imitate it without much success; you had to have been born with it or trained by the years like Byrne. My feet were more accustomed to city pavements.

We climbed another dune, feet digging into the sand against insistent pull of the back packs, and sometimes slipping backwards. On the crest I paused for breath and looked around. Byrne had well described an *erg* as a sea of sand. The Ténéré was like a still picture of a storm at sea, the waves frozen in mid-heave. But these waves were bigger than any wave of water and stretched interminably as far as I could see.

The sun was setting, casting long shadows into the troughs, and the crest of the dune on which I was standing wound sinuously for many miles until it dipped out of sight. The dunes themselves were soft and smooth, sculptured by the wind, unmarked by footprint, whether of man or animal.

Byrne gestured impatiently and we went slipping and sliding down the other and steeper side. Many times during that awful journey I lost control during these descents. The jerrican on my back would seem to push and I would lose my balance and fall headlong. Luckily the sand was soft and cushiony, but not so soft in individual grains that it wasn't also abrasive, and the skin of my hands became tender.

If I was suffering like that, what of Billson? I had lived a sedentary city life but had tried to temper myself and keep in condition by gymnastics and fencing. Paul had worked for fifteen years in the same dreary office in Luton and, from what I had gathered during the course of investigating his life he hadn't done much to keep fit. But the odd thing was that during this time he didn't complain once. He stolidly climbed and just as stolidly picked himself up when he slipped and fell, and kept up the same speed as the rest of us, which wasn't all that slow with Byrne setting the pace.

I was slowly coming to a conclusion about Paul. Some men may be sprinters, good in the short haul and competent in a crisis. Paul might prove to be the reverse. While not handling crises particularly well he was tenacious and stubborn, as proved by his lifelong obsession about his father, and this stroll across the Ténéré was bringing out his best qualities. Be that as it may, he did as well as anyone on that journey, ill-conditioned though his body was for it.

We stopped on top of a dune just as the sun was dipping below the horizon, and Byrne said, 'Okay; you can take off your packs.'

It was a great relief to get rid of that jerrican which had seemed to increase in weight with every step I took. Billson slumped down and in the red light of the setting sun his face was grey. I remembered that he had been shot in the shoulder not many weeks before, and said gently, 'Here, Paul; let me help you.' I helped him divest himself of his back pack, and said, 'How's your shoulder?'

'All right,' he said dully.

'Let me look at it.' His chest was heaving as he drew panting breaths after that last climb and he made no move, so I unbuttoned the front of his shirt and looked at his shoulder before it became too dark to see. The wound, which had been healing well, was now inflamed and red. It would seem that the pull of the jerrican on the improvised harness was chafing him. I said, 'Luke, look at this.'

Byrne came over and inspected Paul. He said, 'We drink the water out of his can first.'

'And perhaps we can transfer some into my can.'

'Maybe,' he said noncommittally. 'Let's eat.'

Our dinner that night was cold and unappetizing. The stars came out as the light ebbed away in the west and the temperature dropped. Byrne said, 'Better wear *djellabas.*'

As I put mine on I asked, 'How far have we come?'

'Mile and a half – maybe two miles.'

'Is that all?' I was shattered. It seemed more like five or six.

'More'n I expected.' Byrne nodded towards Billson. 'I thought he'd hold us up. He still might. I suggest you take some of his water. Do it now before we leave.'

'Leave! You're not going on in the dark?'

'Damn right I am. We're in a hurry. Don't worry; I have a compass and the moon will rise later.'

I put half of Billson's water into my jerrican, reflecting that Byrne was still carrying a full one. He gathered us together. 'We're moving off now. So far you've not done much talking. That's good because you needed your breath. But now you talk because it's dark – you don't lose contact with anyone and you don't let them lose contact with you. It'll be slow going but we need every yard we can make.'

He said something to Konti, probably repeating what he'd told us, then we descended from the top of the dune. It was damned difficult in the dark, and Byrne kept up a constant grunting, 'Ho! Ho! Ho!', sounding like a demented Santa Claus. But it was enough to let us know where he was, and I was encouraged to raise my own voice in song.

At the bottom he rounded us up and we set off across the valley floor under those glittering stars. I sang again; a ditty from my army days:

> 'Uncle George and Auntie Mabel
> Fainted at the breakfast table.
> Let this be an awful warning
> Not to do it in the morning.'

I paused. 'Billson, are you all right?'

'Yes,' he said wearily. 'I'm all right.'

From the left Konti made a whickering noise. He sounded like a horse. Byrne grunted, 'Ho! Ho! Ho!'

> 'Ovaltine has put them right,
> Now they do it morn and night;
> Uncle George is hoping soon
> To do it in the afternoon.
> Hark the Herald Angels sing,
> "Ovaltine is damned good thing."'

Billson made the first attempt at a witticism that I had heard pass his lips. 'Were you a Little Ovaltiney?'

I bumped into Byrne. 'Now we've had the commercial,' he said acidly. 'Let's get climbing.'

So up we went – slowly.

I didn't know then how long we stumbled along in the dark but it seemed like hours. Later Byrne said he'd called a halt just before midnight, so that meant a six-hour night march at probably not more than half a mile an hour. He stopped unexpectedly when we were half way up a slope, and said, 'This is it. Dig in.'

Thankfully I eased the jerrican from me and massaged my aching shoulders. In the light of the moon I saw Billson just lying there. I crawled over to him and helped him out of his harness, then made sure his *djellaba* was wrapped around him, and built up a small rampart of sand on the downhill side of him to prevent him rolling to the bottom in his sleep. Before I left him he had passed out.

I crawled over to Byrne and demanded in an angry whisper, 'What the hell's the flaming hurry? Paul's half dead.'

'He will be dead if we don't get to where we're going by nightfall tomorrow,' said Byrne unemotionally.

'What do you mean?'

'Well, an *azelai* don't stop at sunset like we've usually been doing. Mokhtar will push on until about eleven every night. 'Course, it's easy for them, they're going along the valley bottoms.'

'How does he navigate?'

'Stars,' said Byrne. 'And experience. Now, I figure to get to where he'll be passing through before sundown, and I also figure that he'll be passing through some time during the night. Camels don't have headlights and tail lights, you know; and an *azelai* moves along goddamn quiet, like. At night a caravan could pass within two hundred yards of you and you wouldn't know it, even though in daylight it would be in plain sight. That's why I want to get there when I can see.'

'See what?'

'I'll figure that out when I get there. Now go to sleep.'

I was about to turn away when I thought of something. 'What happens if we miss the caravan?'

'Then we walk to Bilma – that's why we brought all the water. Konti and I would make it. You might. Billson wouldn't.'

That was plain enough. I dug out a trench in the side of the dune to lie in, and hoped it didn't look too much like a grave. Then I pulled the *djellaba* closer around me, and lay down. I looked up at the pock-marked moon for a long time before I went to sleep. It must have been all of three minutes.

We drank all of Billson's remaining water the following morning and abandoned his jerrican. 'Soak yourselves in it,' advised Byrne. 'Get as much water into you as you can hold.'

Breakfast in the light of dawn was frugal and soon done with. I cleaned out the last few crumbs from my pocket, hoisted the jerrican on to my back with distaste, and was ready to go.

Billson said, 'Stafford, why don't we put half your water in here?' He kicked the discarded jerrican with a clang. 'I could carry it.'

I looked at him in surprise. That was the first time he had offered to do anything for anyone so far. Maybe there was hope of reclaiming him for the human race, after all. I said, 'Better put that to Byrne; his can is full.'

Byrne stepped over to Billson. 'Let's see your shoulder.' He examined it and shook his head. 'You couldn't do it, Paul. More abrasion and more sand in there and you'll get gangrene. Keep it wrapped up. Let's move.'

And so we set off again – 'Up the airy mountain, down the rushy glen' – the mountain bit was real enough and it was certainly airy on that cold morning, but there were no rushes and the valleys were anything but glen-like, although welcome enough because they gave a brief respite for level walking.

I pictured us as four ants toiling across a sand-box in a children's playground. At mid-morning, when we stopped to take on water, I said, 'To think I liked building sand castles when I was a kid.'

Byrne chuckled. 'I remember a drawing I once saw, a cartoon, you know. It was in a magazine Daisy Wakefield had up in Tam. There was a detachment of the Foreign Legion doing a march across country like this, and one guy is saying to the other, "I joined the Legion to forget her, but her name is Sandra." I thought that was real funny.'

'I'm glad you're keeping your sense of humour.'

Billson was doing all right. He didn't say much, but kept up with us just in front of Konti. I had the idea that Byrne had detailed Konti as rearguard to keep an eye on Paul. Although he kept up with us I doubt if he'd have been able to if he still had water to carry. His wound was troubling him; not that he complained about it, but I noticed he favoured his right arm when he took a tumble and fell.

There wasn't much point in stopping long at midday because we had nothing to eat and only needed to drink water. Byrne said, 'Okay, Max; take off your pack.'

We had drunk from my jerrican at the mid-morning stop, so I said, 'No; you take off yours.'

The wrinkles about his eyes deepened as he stared at me, but then he said obligingly, 'Okay.' So we lightened his load by a few pounds between us.

That day I found I was glad to be wearing the Tuareg veil and the rest of the fancy dress. I could see that Paul, apart from anything else, was beginning to suffer from exposure whereas I was protected.

The rest of the day until sunset passed in a blur of exhaustion. Up one side, down the other, and still another one to come. Against the grain of the land, Byrne had said. It was a good descriptive phrase and I was now really beginning to find how good it was.

I fell into a blind, mindless rhythm and a chant was created in my mind – what the Germans call an 'earworm' – something that goes round and round in your head and you can't get rid of it. *One bloody foot before the next bloody foot. One bloody dune after the next bloody dune. One bloody foot before the next bloody foot. One bloody dune after the next bloody dune. One bloody . . .* It went on and on and on . . .

Maybe it helped me.

And so it went on for hour after hour until I staggered into Byrne who had stopped. So did my bloody foot. 'We made it just in time.' He looked at the sun. 'Three-quarters of an hour to nightfall.'

'We're there?' I said thickly, and looked down the side of the dune. The valley bottom didn't look much different than any of the others we'd crossed.

'Yeah. Mokhtar will be coming along there.'

I looked around. 'Where's Billson?'

'Maybe a quarter-mile back. Konti's looking after him. Let's go down.'

When we got to the bottom I looked up and saw Paul and Konti silhouetted against the sky at the top of the dune. 'You mean we can rest now?'

'No,' said Byrne relentlessly. He started to walk up the valley so I followed. I was tired but at least this was reasonably level ground and I didn't have to go up and down. The dunes began to close in on either side and then the valley widened. Byrne stopped. 'This is the place. How wide would you say this valley is?'

'Quarter of a mile.'

'More. Six hundred yards. I want three trenches dug going up and down the valley. Each maybe ten yards long but I'd like more.'

That sounded like work and I wasn't in the mood for it. 'How deep?'

'Not much; just so that your feet can recognize it in the dark. We're all going to stand sentry tonight.'

The idea was simple and good. The trenches divided the width of the valley into four equal parts and the four of us would patrol back and forth, each on our 150-yard stretch. When our feet encountered a trench we'd know it was time to turn around smartly and go back, just like a sentry in front of Buck House. If the caravan was coming through, then statistically it was highly likely that one of us was going to run into a camel. And the walking would keep us awake.

I began to dig where Byrne indicated, heaping the soft sand aside with my hands because I had nothing else to dig with. But first I unloaded the jerrican and had some water. Billson and Konti came down and were put to work, and by nightfall we had done all we could do, not to Byrne's satisfaction but that couldn't be helped.

Then came the patrolling back and forth across the width of the valley, each in our own sector. I was weary and the slow trudge in the thick sand didn't help. Every so often my feet encountered the edge of the trench and I turned to go back. Say three hundred yards for the round trip, about six to the mile. I wondered how many miles I was going to walk that night. Still, it was better than the bloody dunes.

On a couple of occasions at a trench I met Byrne and we exchanged a word before we turned and went our opposite ways. If we could have synchronized our speeds we could have met every time, but there was no way of doing that in the darkness.

The night wore on and my pace became slower. I was desperately tired and it was only because I had to walk that I kept awake, although sometimes I wonder if at times I wasn't walking in my sleep. But the walking and a few hunger pangs kept me going.

I encountered Byrne again, and he said, 'Have you seen Konti?'

'We met a couple of patrols ago. He's awake, if that's what's worrying you.'

'It's not. I should be finding Billson, and I'm not.'

I sighed. 'He's had a harder day than most of us. He's clapped out.'

'It leaves a hole in the line. I'll feel better when the moon comes up.'

We didn't have to wait that long. There was a yell from Konti and a startled cry of *'Hai! Hai! Hai!'* as someone strove to quieten a plunging camel. Then a couple of Tuareg came up from *behind* us, from up the valley. Half of that caravan had got past us without anyone knowing until Konti had bumped into someone.

I sat down, exactly where I was. 'Luke,' I said. 'I'm going to sleep.'

# TWENTY-THREE

And so I went into Bilma by camel. Paul did, too, but Byrne walked after the first day. Konti walked all the time. These men were seemingly indestructible. Mokhtar had camped where he found us, but we continued the next day and, as Byrne had said, well into the darkness before we camped again.

Then Byrne began to walk, as did all the Tuareg, and I noted his feet were bare. He walked lithely by the side of the camel I rode. I said, 'Is it normal to walk?'

'Yeah.'

'All the way from Agadez to Bilma?'

'And back.' He looked up. 'We're all humble camel drivers – like the Prophet.'

I thought about it, thinking how quickly we had traversed that vastness in the Toyota. 'I would have thought it would be more efficient to use trucks.'

'Oh, sure.' He pointed ahead. 'Bilma produces 4000 tons of salt a year. The whole export job could be done with twenty 20-tonners. If this was Algeria they'd use trucks. The bastards in the Maghreb are nuts on efficiency when it's profitable.'

'Then why not here?'

'Because the Niger government is sensible. A camel can carry a seventh of a ton so, to shift a year's salt you need

28,000 camels. Like I said, a camel is a fragile animal – for every day's work it must have a day's rest. So – three months on the salt trail means another three months' resting-up time and feeding. That's six months, which takes care of the winter season. No one comes across here in summer. So you do have to have 28,000 camels because each makes but one journey. At $180 each that's a capital investment of better than five million dollars. Add harness, wrappings, drivers' pay and all that and you can make it six million.'

'God!' I said. 'It would certainly pay to use trucks.'

'I haven't finished,' said Byrne. 'A camel can last four years in the business, so that means 7000 new animals needed every year. Somebody has to breed them; guys like me, but more usually like Hamiada. What with one thing and another there's two million dollars going to the breeders from the Bilma salt trade. And Bilma's not the only source of salt. In the Western Sahara there's Taoudenni which supplies Timbouctou and the whole Niger Bend area – that's much bigger than the Bilma trade.' He looked up at me. 'So it's illegal to carry salt on trucks. It would ruin the traditional economy and destroy the structure of the desert tribes if trucks were allowed.'

'I see,' I said thoughtfully. 'Humanitarianism versus efficiency.' It made sense, but I doubt if a hard-headed City businessman would have agreed.

'Look,' said Byrne. 'The Kaouar.'

Stretching across the horizon was a wall of mountains, blue-hazed with distance. 'Bilma?'

'Bilma,' he said with satisfaction.

Half a day later I could see welcome tints of green, the first sight of vegetation since leaving Fachi, and soon I could distinguish individual date palms. Byrne hastened ahead to talk to Mokhtar, then came back. 'We won't go into Bilma – not yet,' he said. 'Kissack might be there and so we have to go in carefully. We'll stop at the salt workings at Kalala.'

Kalala proved to be a plain with heaps of soil thrown up from the salt workings. There were many men and more camels as several other caravans were in residence. Our camels were unloaded of their cargo and Byrne pointed out the sights. He indicated the group of men around Mokhtar. 'More Tuareg from the Aïr. I guess they'll be going back tomorrow. They look ready.' He swung around. 'Those guys, there, are Kanuri up from Chad. Salt is the most important substance in Africa. If the animals don't get it they go sick. The Kanuri from Chad are cattlemen, so they need salt. So are the Hausa from around Kano in Nigeria.'

'How long has this been going on?'

'I wouldn't know. A thousand years – maybe more. You stay here, Max; see that Paul doesn't wander. I'm going into Bilma to borrow a truck – I want to retrieve the Toyota. Also to see if Kissack is here.'

'Be careful.'

'I'm just another Targui,' he said. 'The veil is useful.'

He went away and I collected Billson and we went to look at the salt workings. Billson had improved a lot. Although a long camel ride is not popularly regarded as being a rest cure, there is no doubt that it is when compared to running up and down sand dunes. Mokhtar had provided an ointment of which Byrne approved, and the angry inflamation around Paul's wound had receded.

Paul had improved in spirit, too, and for a man who normally kept a sulky silence he became quite chatty. Maybe the desert had something to do with it.

Looking down at the salt pans was like viewing a less salubrious section of Dante's Inferno. Salt-bearing earth was dug from pits and thrown into evaporating pans where an impure salt was deposited on the surface as the water evaporated under the hot sun. This, laboriously scraped away, was packed into moulds and shaped into pillars about three feet high.

Paul said suddenly, 'You know, it's the first time that bit of the Bible has made sense – about Lot's wife being turned into a pillar of salt. I've never understood about a pillar of salt until now.'

I thought of the caravan trails across the Sahara and wondered if salt from Bilma had found its way to ancient Israel. It was improbable – the Dead Sea was saltier than other seas – but the method of manufacture was probably old.

We went back to the caravan and rested. The camels were resting, too, and some of them were lying flat on their sides after they had been unloaded. I had never seen camels do that. I was studying one of them when Mokhtar passed. He saw my interest and struggled for words. After a lot of thought he came out with *'Fatigué – très fatigué.'*

I nodded. If I'd walked for a month, sixteen hours a day, I'd be bloody tired, too. But Mokhtar had walked and he looked as fresh as a daisy. The camel's ribs were showing through its hide. I said, 'It's thin – *maigre.'* I patted my own flank, and repeated, *'Maigre.'*

Mokhtar said something in Tamachek which I couldn't understand. Seeing my incomprehension, he took the camel's halter and brought it to its feet. He beckoned, so I followed him as he led the camel about a quarter of a mile to a stone trough which was being laboriously filled with water from a well.

The camel dipped its head and drank. It drank for ten minutes without stopping and filled out before my eyes. It must have drunk more than twenty gallons of water and when it had finished it was as plump and well-conditioned a beast as I'd seen.

Byrne did not come back until mid-morning of the next day, but he came in the Toyota. Apart from the smashed wind-screen it looked no different than before it had been shot up, but then, it had looked battered to begin with. A few holes were neither here nor there, and a difference that makes no difference is no difference.

Billson and I were well rested – a good night's sleep does make a difference – but for the first time Byrne looked weary. I said, 'You need sleep.'

He nodded. 'I'll rest this afternoon and sleep tonight, but we have something to do first. Get in.'

I climbed into the Toyota and Byrne let out the clutch. As we drove away a breeze swept through the cab. 'It's going to be draughty from now on,' I said. 'Where are we going?'

'To waylay a gang of tourists,' he said to my surprise. 'How's your German?'

'Adequate – no more.'

'Maybe it'll do. Kissack's in Bilma. He took Bailly to what passes for a hospital and spun a yarn about an auto accident to explain Bailly's foot. It passed because there's no doctor. Bailly is being flown out tomorrow.'

'He could hardly report being assaulted – not after what he did to us. But why don't we report to the police?'

'And how would we explain you? You're in Niger illegally.' Byrne shook his head decisively. 'Hell, we'd be tied up for months, with or without you. Besides, I'd like to settle with Kissack myself and in my own way.'

'So where do German tourists come in?'

'It struck me that Kissack doesn't know about you.'

I thought about that and found it was probably true. I hadn't told anyone in England where I was going. As far as anyone knew I was sunning myself in Jamaica, as Charlie Malleson had suggested, instead of doing the same in an improbable place like Bilma. And even though I had been close enough to Kissack to touch him he only knew me as an anonymous Targui. The only times he had seen me were

in the Hotel de l'Aïr and over the sights of a rifle in the
Ténéré.

Byrne said, 'I want to put you next to Kissack. Find out
what he's doing.'

'But the German tourists?'

'I was talking to a Ténéré guide, a Targui I know called
Rhossi. He says there's a German crowd coming in from the
north and they should be hitting Bilma this afternoon – he's
going to take them across the Ténéré. It's a government
regulation that all tour groups must have a guide in the
Ténéré.'

I wasn't surprised. 'So?'

'There aren't many Europeans in Bilma so you can't just
walk in to chat with Kissack. The local law would spot
you and want to see your papers. But if you arrive with a
gang of Germans you can merge into the background. I'm
going to drop you about five miles out of Bilma and you can
bum a lift.'

It would work. Any party of Europeans would give a
lone European hitch-hiker a lift for a few miles. 'What do I
tell them?'

'Hell, tell them anything you like. No. There's some rock
carvings about seven miles out just off the road. Tell them
that you walked out of Bilma to look at them, but now
you're tired and you'd appreciate a lift back.' He thought for
a moment. 'You'd better see the carvings.'

So we went to look at rock carvings up the rough track
north of Bilma. I suppose they were more engravings than
carvings, cut into the vertical sides of rocks but not too
deeply. The subjects were interesting; there were many
cattle with spreading horns, a rider on a horse which
was unmistakably a stallion though the rider was depicted
as a mere stick figure, and, surprisingly, an elephant
drawn with a fluent line which Picasso would have been
proud of.

'An elephant?'

'Why not?' asked Byrne. 'Where do you suppose Hannibal got the elephants to cross the Alps?'

That question had never troubled me.

Byrne said, 'The North African elephant went extinct about two thousand years ago. I've seen skeletons, though. They were midgets – about half the size of an Indian elephant.'

I looked at the barren waste around us; there wasn't enough vegetation to support a half-sized rabbit. I looked back at the engraving. 'How old?'

'Maybe three thousand years. Not as old as the paintings in the Tassili.' He pointed to a series of marks – crosses, circles, squares and dots. 'That's more recent; it's Tifinagh, the written form of Tamachek.'

'What does it say?'

'I wouldn't know; I can't read it.' He smiled. 'Probably something like "I love Lucy", or "Kilroy was here". You'd better change your clothes.'

So I reverted to being a European and the clothing seemed oddly restricting after the freedom of a *gandoura*. As Byrne drove back to the track he said, 'The tour leader will probably collect all the passports and take them into the fort for inspection. He won't ask for yours, of course. Just mingle with the group enough so it looks as though you're one of them. They'll split up to have a look at Bilma pretty soon and that gives you your chance to hunt up Kissack.'

'That's all right as long as the cops don't do a head count.' Byrne shook his head at that. 'Where am I likely to find Kissack?'

'Anywhere – look for the Range-Rover – but there's a broken-down shack that calls itself a restaurant. You might find him there. Anyway, it's a chance to have a beer.'

He dropped me by the side of the track and drove away after thoughtfully leaving a small canteen of water which looked as though it had started life in the British army.

The German group pitched up three hours later, eighteen people in four long-wheelbase Land-Rovers. I stood up and held out my hand as the first Land-Rover came up, and it drew to a halt. My German, learned when I was with the Army of the Rhine, was about as grammatical as Byrne's French, but just as serviceable. No foreigner minds you speaking his language badly providing you make the attempt. Excepting the French, of course.

The driver of the first Land-Rover was the group leader, and he willingly agreed to take me into Bilma if I didn't mind a squash in the front seat. He looked at me curiously. 'What are you doing out here?'

'I walked out from Bilma to look at some rock engravings.' I smiled. 'I'd rather not walk back.'

'Didn't know there were any around here. Plenty up north at the Col des Chandeliers. Where are they?'

'About three kilometres back, just off the track.'

'Can you show me? My people would be interested.'

'Of course; only too glad.'

So we went back to look at the engravings, and I reflected that it was just as well that Byrne had taken me there. We spent twenty minutes there, the Germans clicking away busily with their Japanese cameras. They were a mixed lot ranging from teenagers to old folk and I wondered what had brought them into the desert. It certainly wasn't the normal package deal.

Less than half an hour after that we were driving up the long slope which leads to the fort in Bilma. The Land-Rovers parked with Teutonic precision in a neat rank just by the gate and I opened the door. 'Thanks for the lift.'

He nodded. 'Helmut Shaeffer. Perhaps we will have a beer in the restaurant, eh?'

'I'm Max Stafford. That's a good idea. Where is the restaurant?'

'Don't you know?' There was surprise in his voice.

'I haven't seen much of Bilma itself. We got in late last night.'

'Oh.' He pointed down the slope and to the right. 'Over there; you can't miss it.'

As Byrne had predicted, he began collecting passports. I lingered, talking with a middle-aged man who discoursed on the wonders he had seen in the north. Shaeffer took the pile of passports into the fort and the group began to break up. I wandered off casually following a trio heading in the general direction of the restaurant.

It was as Byrne had described it; a broken-down shack. The Germans looked at the sun-blasted sign and the peeling walls and muttered dubiously, then made up their minds and went inside. I followed closely on their heels.

It was a bare room with a counter on one side. There were a few rough deal tables, a scattering of chairs, and a wooden bench which ran along two sides of the room. My hackles rose as I saw Kissack sitting on the bench at a corner table next to a man in local dress – not a Targui because he did not wear the veil. That would be the Arab Konti had seen. Kissack was eating an omelette.

He looked up and inspected us curiously, so I turned and started to talk in German to the man next to me, asking if he thought the food here would be hygienically prepared. He advised me to stick to eggs. When I looked back at Kissack he had lost interest in us and seemed more intent on what was on his plate.

That gave me an idea. I crossed the room and stood before him, and asked in German if he recommended the omelette.

He looked up and frowned. 'Huh! Don't you speak English?'

I put a smile on my face and it felt odd because I didn't feel like smiling at this assassin. 'I was asking if you could recommend the omelette. Sorry about that, but I've been travelling with this crowd so long that the German came automatically.'

He grunted. 'It's all right.'

'Thanks. That and a beer should go down well.' I sat at the next table quite close to him.

He turned away and started to talk in a low voice to the Arab. The sun was not dealing kindly with Kissack. His face was burned an angry red and the skin was still peeling from him. I was glad about that; he wasn't earning his murderer's pay easily.

As a waiter came to take my order an aircraft flew over quite low. Kissack made a sharp gesture and the Arab got up and walked out. I ordered beer and an omelette, then I twisted and looked through the window behind me. The Arab was walking towards the fort.

Presently a bottle of beer and a not too clean glass was put in front of me. As I poured the beer I wondered how to tackle Kissack. It was all right for Byrne to talk airily about putting me next to Kissack – that had been done – but what next? I could hardly ask, *'Killed any good men recently?'*

But I had to make a start and old ploys are best, so I said, 'Haven't we met before?'

He grunted and looked at me sideways. 'Where have you come from?'

'Up north. Over the Col des Chandeliers.'

'Never been there.' His eyes returned to his plate.

I persisted. 'Then it must have been in England.'

'No,' he said flatly without looking up.

I drank some beer and cursed Byrne. It had seemed a good idea at the time; fellow countrymen meeting on their travels are usually glad to chat, but Kissack was bad-tempered, grouchy and uncommunicative. I said, 'I could have sworn . . .'

Kissack turned to me. 'Look, chum; I haven't been in England for ten years.' He put a lot of finality in his voice, indicating quite clearly that the subject was closed.

I drank some more beer and waited for my omelette. I was becoming annoyed at Kissack and was just about to put in the needle when someone called, 'Herr Stafford!' I froze, then looked up to see Shaeffer who had just come in. I glanced sideways at Kissack to see if the name had meant anything to him, but apparently it didn't and I breathed easier.

'Hi, Helmut,' I said, hoping he wouldn't show surprise at easy familiarity with his given name from a casual acquaintance. 'Have a beer.' As he sat down I immediately regretted my invitation. Shaeffer could unknowingly drop a clanger and reveal that I was not a part of his group. The only thing going for me was that his English was not too good.

'Everything all right at the fort?' I asked in German.

He shrugged. 'They're too busy to bother with us now. A plane came in from Agadez to take an injured man to hospital. I left the passports; I'll pick them up later.'

The waiter put an omelette in front of me and I ordered a beer for Shaeffer. Kissack ordered another beer for himself so he'd be staying a while. I tinned to him. 'You know, I *have* seen you before.'

'For Christ's sake!' he said tiredly.

'Wasn't it in Tammanrasset? You were driving a Range-Rover.'

That got through to him. He went very still, a glass half way to his lips. Then he turned and looked at me with stony eyes. 'What are you getting at, chummy?'

'Nothing,' I said coolly. 'It's just that a thing like that niggles me. Nice to know I wasn't mistaken. You were in Tam, then.'

'And what if I was? What's it to you?'

I tackled my omelette. 'Nothing.' I turned to Shaeffer and switched to German. 'I forgot to tell you. Rhossi, your guide, is here in Bilma. Someone told me he was waiting for a German party so I assume it's you. Have you seen him?' Out of the corner of my eye I saw Kissack staring at me. I hoped his lack of German was complete.

Shaeffer shook his head. 'He'll be camped at Kalala near the salt workings.'

I turned back to Kissack. 'I was just asking Helmut, here, if he's seen the guide yet. You need a guide to cross the Ténéré.'

'When were you in Tammanrasset?' Kissack asked suddenly.

'Evidently when you were,' I said. 'Oh, by the way; did you hear anything about that chap who disappeared? Another Englishman. There was a devil of a brouhaha going on about it when I left.'

Kissack moistened his lips. 'What was his name?'

'Wilson,' I said. 'No, that's not right. Williamson? No, not that, either. My memory really is playing me up – first you, now this chap.' I frowned. 'Billson!' I said in triumph. 'That was his name. Billson. The police were really in a stew about him, but you know what Algerians are like. Bloody bureaucrats with sub-machine-guns!'

The waiter put a bottle of beer and a glass in front of Shaeffer and another bottle before Kissack. He ignored it. 'What happened to this Billson?' His voice was over-controlled.

I didn't answer immediately but popped a slice of omelette into my mouth. I'd got Kissack interested enough to ask questions and that was progress, and the omelette was quite good. I swallowed and said, 'He went up into Atakor without asking permission and didn't come back. There were a hell of a lot of rumours floating around when I left.'

'What sort of rumours?'

'Oh, the usual stuff that goes around when anything like that happens. Unbelievable, most of it.'

I had Kissack hooked because he asked, 'Such as?'

I shrugged. 'Well, for instance, someone said his Land-Rover had been found burnt out the other side of Assekrem. You know those parts?'

'Not well,' said Kissack tightly.

'This is a damned good omelette,' I observed. 'Anyway, someone else said his body had been brought out and he'd died of exposure. But then there was a buzz that he'd been brought out alive but he'd been shot. I told you – unbelievable stuff. Those things don't happen these days, do they? The desert is pretty civilized now.'

'What are you talking about?' asked Shaeffer. He grinned. 'My Tamachek is better than my English – I heard Tammanrasset and Atakor and Assekrem.'

'Oh, just about an Englishman who vanished near Tam.'

Kissack was looking bleak. He said, 'Any rumours about what finally happened to Billson?'

'The last I heard was that he was in hospital in Tam with a police guard – sort of house arrest. Just another bloody rumour, though.'

Kissack fell silent and poured his beer. He was thinking hard; I could almost see the damned wheels going round. I turned to Shaeffer and started to chat about the problems of crossing the Ténéré, all in German. After a while Kissack said, 'Stafford . . . it is Stafford, isn't it?'

I turned. 'Yes?'

'How did you get from Tam to here?'

That was a stumer; a damned good question. I visualized the Michelin map I had pored over, and said lightly, 'Flew across to Djanet from Tam, then came south. I was already booked into the party. Why?'

'What were you doing in Tam?'

I frowned. 'Not that it's any of your business but I'm interested in Charles de Foucauld. I wanted to see where and how he lived.'

Kissack said, 'I think you're a damned liar.' He nodded towards Shaeffer. 'Any tour group coming down from Djanet is going to go through Tammanrasset anyway. Why should you want to go there twice?'

I stood up. 'Because I'm leaving the group at Agadez and going south to Kano. That's why. Now get up off that damned bench. No man calls me a liar.'

Kissack looked up at me but didn't move. Shaeffer said, 'What's the matter?' He hadn't understood what was said but the changed atmosphere needed no language to understand.

'This man called me a liar.' I was suddenly infuriated with Kissack and I wanted to belt hell out of him. I stooped, grabbed his shirt, and hauled him to his feet. The table went flying and a glass smashed on the floor. Kissack made a grab for the inside of his jacket so I rammed my elbow into his side and felt the hardness of a gun.

Then Shaeffer grabbed me from behind and hauled me away. 'Herr Stafford; this is no place to make trouble,' he said, his mouth close to my ear. 'The prison here is not good.'

Kissack had his hand inside his jacket. I shook off Shaeffer's hands and stuck a finger at Kissack. 'You don't want the coppers here, either – not with what you have there. You'd have too much explaining to do.'

The barman came from behind the bar carrying a foot-long bar of iron, but stopped as Shaeffer said something in Arabic. Kissack withdrew his hand and it came out empty. 'I don't know what you mean.' His eyes flickered towards the barman. 'Hell; this is a lousy place, anyway.' He dipped his hand into his pocket and tossed a couple of bank notes on to the floor, then walked towards the door.

From a distance someone said in German, 'Brawling Englishmen – I bet they're drunk.'

I said to Shaeffer, 'Tell the owner I'll pay for any damage. Your Arabic sounds better than his French.'

He nodded and rattled off some throat-scratching Arabic. The barman nodded curtly without smiling, picked up the money, and returned to the bar. Shaeffer said, 'You should not cause fighting here, Herr Stafford.' He shook his head. 'It is not wise.'

'I was provoked.' I looked through the window and saw Kissack walking towards the mud-coloured huddle of houses that was Bilma. I had blown it. I hadn't got a damned thing out of him that was of any use. What's more, I had probably given him grounds for suspicion.

But perhaps something could be retrieved if I was quick about it. I went to the bar and laid a bank note down. The barman looked at me unblinkingly so I put down another. I had to add two more before he nodded curtly. Then I went out fast, looking for Kissack. If I could get him alone he was going to tell me quite a few things, gun or no gun.

# TWENTY-FOUR

Bilma is constructed on something like the lines of Daedalus's Labyrinth; no streets, just a warren of alleys and passages, and if I had met the Minotaur I wouldn't have been particularly surprised. It was difficult keeping up with Kissack and twice I lost him and had to cast about. Not that he was being evasive – he didn't look behind him to see if he was being followed or anything like that. In fact, I think he was lost himself at times, not very difficult in Bilma, and I swear we passed the same corner three times.

I followed him deeper and deeper into the maze. There were very few people about and those I encountered regarded me incuriously. They looked to be the same kind that I had seen at Fachi and whom Byrne had called Kanuri. Every so often I would pass a more or less open space where sheep or goats were penned or where chickens scratched, but in general there were just mud walls set with secretive doors every so often. A good shower of rain would have dissolved Bilma in one night, sending it back to the earth from which it had arisen.

At last I peered around a corner to see Kissack open a door and vanish inside. I walked up and looked at the door and then at the expanse of windowless wall. It wouldn't be too difficult to climb but doing the burglar bit in broad daylight would be unwise – even a blank-minded Kanuri would regard that as anti-social, and I was uncomfortably aware of an old toothless crone who had stopped at the end of the alley and was looking at me.

While I was debating the next step my mind was made up for me by a voice saying in French, 'Why didn't he wait at the restaurant?' It floated from the corner I had just turned.

That did it. There was just one thing to do so I opened the door and slipped inside. I found myself in a courtyard just big enough to hold Kissack's Range-Rover and very little else. Around the sides of the courtyard were hovels made of the ubiquitous mud.

Behind me, on the other side of the door, the voice said, 'Is this it?' There wasn't much else to do but what I did. I hurled myself forward and dived under the Range-Rover, being thankful for the generous ground clearance. I was only just in time because the door opened wide just as I got hidden and several men came into the courtyard. I twisted my head, counted feet, and divided by two – four men.

'Where is Kissack?' said the man who had queried about the restaurant. He still spoke French. '*Kissack!*' he bellowed.

'In here.' Kissack's voice came from one of the mud buildings.

The French-speaker switched to English. 'You come out here.' A door slammed and Kissack's feet came into view. 'If you think I'm going into that flea-ridden kennel you're mistaken.' The tone was distasteful and the accent standard BBC grade announcer's English.

'Hello, Lash,' said Kissack.

'Don't hello me,' said Lash acidly. 'And it's Mr Lash to you.' He went back into French. 'You lot get lost for the next half-hour but then be findable.'

'How about the restaurant?' someone asked.

'That's all right – but stay there so I can find you.' Three men went away and the door slammed. Lash said, 'Now just what in hell have you been doing, Kissack?'

'Just doing what I was told,' said Kissack sullenly.

'Like hell you have!' said Lash explosively. 'There's a contract out on Billson and he's still alive. Why?'

'Christ, I don't know,' said Kissack. 'He should be dead. I shot him in some of the most God-awful country you've ever seen. He *couldn't* have walked out.'

'So he was helped, and the next thing is someone is advertising for that bloody aeroplane. Advertising, by God! Leaflets all over the bloody desert! The idea, Kissack, was not to draw attention to that aeroplane but, because you're ham-fisted, everybody and his bloody Arab uncle is looking for it.'

'That's not my fault,' yelled Kissack. 'I didn't know about Byrne.'

'He's the man who put out the leaflets?'

'Yes. He's a sodding Yank who's gone native.'

'I'm not going to stand here and fry my brains out,' said Lash. 'Get in the car.'

The Range-Rover rocked on its springs as they got in, and I took the opportunity of easing my position because a stone was digging into my hip. The arrival of Lash changed everything. Kissack having failed twice had sent for reinforcements – and the boss had arrived. From what I heard, Lash was certainly more incisive than Kissack.

And I could still hear them because they had the windows down. Lash said, 'When we heard about the leaflets I told you to stay put in Agadez. So what happens? I arrive to find you've gone into the damned desert. Then we get a message that Bailly's been in a motor smash. What happened to him?'

'It wasn't a smash,' said Kissack. He told Lash of how he had ambushed us. 'I had them nailed down, all but one who got away – and I reckoned he couldn't get far on foot. They didn't have a chance. Then Bailly started to scream his bloody head off.'

'What happened?'

'Christ knows! This Arab did something to him. What or how I don't know, but he's going to lose his foot. There was Bailly wriggling around on the sand and yelling fit to bust, and the Arab was dodging away among the dunes. We chased him a bit but he got away.'

'You were scared,' said Lash flatly.

'You'd be bloody scared if you'd seen what he did to Bailly,' Kissack retorted. 'He wouldn't stop screaming. I had to slug him to shut him up.'

'So then you put him in this car and brought him to Bilma. Kissack, you're stupid.'

'What else was there to do?'

'You could have killed Bailly to shut him up and then attended to the others. You said you had them nailed down.'

'Jesus, you . . .' Kissack's voice caught. 'You're a cold-hearted bastard.'

'I'm a realist,' said Lash. 'Now, who were these men you were shooting at?'

'One of them was Byrne, the Yank who got out the leaflets. He spun me a yarn back in Agadez but I saw through it. Another I'm pretty sure was Billson. The other two were Arabs.'

'Arabs or Tuareg?'

'Who cares? They're all the same to me.'

'I repeat, and I don't like repeating myself – you're stupid, Kissack. Did they wear veils?'

'Byrne did – and one of the others. The one who did for Bailly had no veil.' There was a pause while Lash digested that, and Kissack said defensively, 'What's the difference? Christ, I hate this bloody desert.'

'Shut up!' Lash was silent for a while, then said, 'What happened to them?'

'I don't know. They aren't here. I shot up that Toyota pretty good; got three of the tyres. And no one is going to walk out of all that sodding sand out there, Mr Lash.'

'You said that before about Billson, and you were wrong.' Lash was contemptuous. 'And I'm betting you're wrong again because you're stupid. Before I flew down from Algiers I took the trouble to find out about this American, Byrne. He's been in the desert thirty-five years, Kissack. The Algerians don't like him much but he has friends with political clout so he still hangs around. Anyway, he spends most of his time here in Niger. If you didn't kill him, then I'm saying he's going to get out because he knows how. Did you kill him?'

'No,' said Kissack sullenly.

'Tomorrow you take me and show me that shot-up Toyota. If it's not there you're going to wish you were Bailly.'

'It'll be there, Mr Lash. I know where I put the bullets.'

'Don't bet on it,' said Lash coldly. 'Because I'm assuming it's not there. Now I told you to stay in Agadez and wait for me. Why the hell didn't you?'

Kissack had an access of courage. 'Remember what you said when you came in here. You said there was a contract out on Billson and you asked why he was still alive. I was just doing the job.'

'Good God Almighty!' said Lash violently. 'Those bloody leaflets changed all that. Even a cretin like you should have realized that. Whether Billson is alive or dead, that plane is going to be found now. If it is, then my principal is going to be up a gum tree and he's not going to like that.'

'If I'd got Byrne there'd be nobody to give the reward. That's why I had a crack at him.'

'I don't deal in damned ifs,' snapped Lash. 'I want certainties. And you're wrong. If that crashed plane is worth maybe a thousand pounds to Byrne, then anyone who finds it will figure it's worth something to someone else, whether Byrne is around or not. I tell you, that plane is going to be found and talked about.'

'What's so bloody special about it?' asked Kissack.

'None of your business.' Lash fell silent. Presently he said, 'Any idea why Byrne and Billson suddenly took off in this direction? Do you know where they were going?'

'I didn't ask.'

'Working in the dark as usual,' said Lash acidly. 'Now this is how we work it from now on. I'm betting that Byrne and Billson are still around – so we find them. And when we do you don't lay a bloody finger on them. What's more, if they're in trouble you get them out of it. Understand?'

'Hell! One minute you want to know why they're not dead, and the next you want me to pick 'em up and dust 'em off.' Kissack was disgusted.

Lash was heavily patient. 'We don't know where that plane is, do we? But Byrne might have a good idea by now – he's the one who's been advertising for it. So we let him find it and, if necessary, we help him. Then, when we've got Byrne, Billson and the plane all in one place . . .'

'Bingo!' said Kissack.

'And I'll be along to see you don't make a balls-up of it,' said Lash. 'Now, is there anything else you think I ought to know? It doesn't matter how insignificant it is.'

'Can't think of anything, except there's been some funny rumours going round Tammanrasset.'

'What rumours?'

'Well, I heard that Billson was in some sort of hospital jail in Tam. But he couldn't be, could he? Not if he was in the Ténéré.'

'When did you hear this?'

'Today – in the restaurant. A British tourist travelling with a German crowd was shooting his mouth off. Billson dead of exposure, Billson alive with a bullet in him, Billson alive and in jail. But all just rumours, this chap Stafford said.'

'*What!*'

'He said they were just rumours; nothing certain.'

'What did you say the name was?'

'Whose name?'

'The British tourist, for Christ's sake! Who else are we talking about?'

'Oh! He called himself Stafford. No, he didn't; but his German mate called him Stafford.'

'Good God Almighty!' said Lash softly.

'And he answered to Stafford when I talked to him. Is he important?'

'Did he say where he'd come from? He's been in Tammanrasset, you say.'

'He came down from Djanet with a German tour group. Said he'd flown to Djanet from Tam. I thought that was a bit funny but he explained it. Said he was leaving the tour at Agadez and going down to Kano.'

'And he had a German friend?' Lash sounded puzzled.

'That's right. They jabbered a lot in German. I think he was the tour leader. They were talking about a guide to take them across the Ténéré.'

'Coming down from the *north* with Germans? But how . . .' Lash cut himself short. 'When was this?'

'Not long ago. I came straight here from the restaurant and then you pitched up a couple of minutes later.'

'Then he might still be there?'

'He was there when I left.' There was a hint of a shrug in Kissack's voice. 'We had a bit of a barney; he was getting on my wick.'

'How?'

'All his talk about Billson in Tam was making me edgy.'

'So you do have some imagination, after all. Come on; let's see if he's there.'

'So who is he?'

They got out of the Range-Rover and walked across the courtyard. Lash said, 'Trouble!'

The door slammed.

# TWENTY-FIVE

I got out from under the Range-Rover and looked about. A minor puzzlement which had been a fugitive at the back of my mind during that interesting conversation had been how they had got the Range-Rover into that courtyard. It couldn't be driven through Bilma, not through alleys four feet wide at the most. The puzzle was solved by the sight of a big pair of double doors, so I opened one and found myself on the edge of the town, clear the other side from the restaurant.

I did the three miles to Kalala at a jog-trot, my mind busy with the implications of what I had heard, the most interesting one being that Lash knew me – or of me – and he had been very surprised to hear that I was in Bilma. That, and a phrase that had been dropped a couple of times, made it almost certain that it had been Lash who had me beaten up in Kensington. I owed him something for that.

When I got back to the resting caravan Byrne was asleep but Billson was around. He said, 'Where have you been? Where did he take you?' He looked me up and down, examining my English tailoring. 'And why did you change? Byrne wouldn't tell me anything when he came back.'

If Byrne had decided to keep mum then so would I. Paul had been improving during the last few days, but if he knew what I had just found out he might blow his top. It

229

was the final proof positive that someone wanted him dead
and would go to any length to kill him. And expense was no
object, so it seemed. Touring half a dozen men around the
Sahara by road and air isn't the cheapest pastime in the
world, especially if they're killers – guns for hire.

I said casually, 'I've just been wandering around Bilma to
see what I could see.'

'Did you find the Range-Rover?'

'If it's there it must be hidden.' That was true enough.

'What about Kissack?' he said fretfully.

I remembered that Byrne and I had not said anything to
Paul about meeting Kissack and Bailly in Agadez. I lied. 'I
wouldn't know Kissack if I stood next to him. And he
wouldn't know me. Relax, Paul; you're safe enough here.'

I went to the Toyota, got out my Tuareg gear, and
changed, feeling the better for it. The clothing worn in any
area has been refined over the years and is suited to the
conditions. It made sense to wear Tuareg clothes and I no
longer felt on my way to a fancy dress ball but, instead, cool
and free.

That night, when Paul was asleep, I woke Byrne and told
him my story. When I got to Lash's suggestion to Kissack
about what he ought to have done about Bailly he said
ironically 'This Lash is a really nice guy.'

'He calls himself a realist,' I said, and carried on.

When I had finished he said, 'You did right well, Max;
but you were goddamn lucky.'

'That's true enough,' I admitted. 'I made a mess of tackling Kissack from the start.'

'Luck runs both ways. Take Billson, now; he's lucky you
followed him from England. He'd be dead otherwise, up in
Koudia.'

I smiled. 'We're both of us lucky to have you along,
Luke.'

He grunted. 'There's one thing I don't understand. You said something about a contract. What sort of contract?'

'You've been away from civilization too long. It's under-world jargon imported from the States. If you want a man killed you put out a contract on him on a fee contingency basis.'

'You call that civilization? Out here if a guy wants another man dead he does his own killing, like Konti.'

I smiled but this time it was a bit sour. 'It's called the division of labour.'

'Which brings us back to the big question,' said Byrne. 'Who would want Paul dead? And a bigger question, at least to my mind – who would want me dead?'

'I rather think I'm on the list now,' I said. 'I don't know, Luke; but a name that springs to mind is Sir Andrew McGovern.'

'A British sir!' Byrne said in astonishment.

'I haven't told you much about the English end of this,' I said. 'But now you've got yourself on Lash's list I think you ought to know.' So I told him what I knew, then said, 'I think Lash must have had me beaten up. All contracts aren't for killing. They wanted to discourage me.'

'And this guy McGovern?'

'Everything seems to lead back to him.' I ticked off points on my fingers. 'He employed Paul in the first place and saw that he's been grossly overpaid ever since. As soon as Paul had his brainstorm and disappeared McGovern pulled my firm out of security of the Whensley Group. He couldn't just do it for Franklin Engineering, you see – that would have looked fishy. He didn't want me looking too deeply into Paul and his affairs and that was the only way he could stop me. Then he tried to get Paul's sister out of the way before I could see her by send-ing her to Canada. That didn't work so he called off that plan and kept her in England. It was about that time when

I was beaten up and warned off. Everything goes back to McGovern.'

'Okay,' said Byrne. 'Now tell me why. Why should a titled Britisher get into an uproar about an airplane that crashed in 1936?'

'I'm damned if I know. But Andrew McGovern is going to answer a lot of questions to my satisfaction when I get back to London.'

'You'd better change that to *if* you get back to London,' said Byrne wryly. 'How old is McGovern?'

I hadn't thought of that. 'I don't know. Maybe fifty-five – pushing sixty.'

'Let's take the top figure. If he's sixty now he'd be eighteen in 1936.'

Or thirteen on the lower figure. I said, 'This makes less and less sense. How could a teenager be involved?'

Byrne moved his hand in a dismissive gesture. 'Let's stick to the present. Did you get a look at Lash?'

I shook my head. 'Only his feet. I was flat on my belly under that Range-Rover. I didn't see any of the others, either; except Kissack, of course, and his Arab friend.'

'But there are now five of them?' I nodded, and he said, 'Must have come in on the airplane that's taking Bailly back to Agadez. And Lash's plan now is to do nothing until we find that airplane?'

'As of now it is. He could change his mind.'

'That we'll have to risk. Now, we know what he's going to do, but he doesn't know we know, so that gives us an edge. He wants to help us along until we locate that airplane. Okay, that's fine with me and I propose to let him help, and to do that he'll have to show himself.'

'Maybe. Perhaps he'll be master-minding in the background.'

'I don't think so,' said Byrne. 'He won't use Kissack because he knows I've seen Kissack, and Kissack knows

I tried to screw him so Lash knows it too. And from what you tell me, the other guys along with him are hired muscle from Algiers.'

'Or hired guns,' I said glumly.

'Could you recognize him by voice?'

'I think so, unless he's smart enough to change it.'

'Good enough.' I couldn't see Byrne in the darkness but there was a smile in his voice. 'You know, Max; if these guys follow us and help us on our way I wouldn't be surprised if they got in real trouble. The desert can be a dangerous place, especially when it has help.'

I said, 'How much of this do we tell Paul?'

'Are you out of your mind?' he said. 'We don't tell him a goddamn thing. He's just along for the ride.'

We left early next morning with Konti still with us. 'We'll take him as far as Djado,' said Byrne. 'Then he'll head east, back home to the Tibesti.'

We drove openly around Bilma and past the fort. I didn't see Kissack or anyone who might be Lash. Then we took the track due north, skirting the ramparts of the Kaouar mountains, sheer cliffs for mile after mile. Just after leaving Bilma Byrne said, 'About forty kilometres ahead there's the military post at Dirkou; I'll have to stop there for gas. But not you – they'd want to see your papers and you got none. So I'll park you just outside with Konti. He don't like soldiers, either.'

When we came into sight of distant palm groves he stopped and pointed. 'Head that way as straight as you can. That'll bring you to the road the other side of the post but out of sight. Wait for me there.'

Konti and I got out. Byrne was about to start off again but he paused. 'You got a spare bottle of whisky?'

'In my bag in the back. Why?'

'There's a guy in Dirkou who likes his booze. A sweetener makes life run easier around Dirkou.' He drove off.

Konti and I set off across the desert which, thank God, was flat thereabouts. Presently I stooped and picked up something. Byrne had been right – there were sea-shells in the desert near Bilma.

After about half an hour's trudge we reached the track and waited, being careful to stand behind a convenient rock and not in plain sight. Soon we heard the grind of gear-changing and I looked out to see the Toyota approaching, so we stepped out and Byrne stopped just long enough for us to climb in.

He jerked his thumb back to Dirkou. 'Would you say Lash is a big man?'

'His feet were middling size.'

'There's a Britisher back there. Came in twenty minutes behind me.'

'Don't tell me,' I said. 'In a Range-Rover.'

'No; in an old truck nearly as beat-up as mine. He's pretty tall, pretty broad, dark hair.'

'Anyone with him?'

'Two guys. From the way they spoke Arabic together I'd say they're from the Maghreb – Algiers, most likely. The Britisher don't speak Arabic, he talks to them in French which they don't understand too good.'

'It fits,' I said.

'They'll be more than twenty minutes behind us when they leave Dirkou,' said Byrne with a grin. 'I had a talk with the guy who likes his booze. Right now he's turning them inside out and the English feller is swearing fit to bust a gut. Won't do him no good, though. Seems that whisky has its uses.'

'That might be useful,' I said thoughtfully. 'If your whisky drinker is turning them over that thoroughly he might find guns. He wouldn't like that, would he?'

'That passed through my mind,' agreed Byrne cheerfully. 'Let us not smooth the way of the transgressor.' He laughed at my expression. 'Lots of good things in the Bible.'

From the seat behind me Billson said, 'What are you talking about? Who was that man back there?'

'Just a guy,' said Byrne. 'Maybe nothing to do with Kissack but I like to play safe.'

I said, 'Don't worry about it, Paul.'

The track was bad and got steadily worse. Every so often we would pass a village with the inevitable grove of date palms. There was evidently water under the tall cliffs of the Kaouar mountains. But the villagers hadn't tried to make life easier for themselves by maintaining the track.

We travelled steadily all day and not only the track deteriorated but so did the weather. A wind arose, lifting the sand in a haze which dimmed the sun, and dust filtered everywhere in the truck. It was then that I found the true efficacy of the Tuareg veil and pulled it closer about my face.

Disaster struck in the late afternoon. There was a grinding noise from somewhere at the back of the Toyota and we came to a shuddering halt in soft sand. Byrne said, 'Goddamn it! That's something wrong with the transmission.'

So we got out to look at the damage. The rear wheels were sunk nearly to the axle in the fine sand and I could see it was going to be a devil of a job to get out even if there was nothing wrong with the transmission. And if the transmission had gone we could be stuck there forever. Byrne didn't seem too worried; he merely dug out two jacks from the back of the truck and laid them on the sand. 'Here's where the hard work starts,' he remarked. 'We'll need the sand ladders from up top.'

Paul and I got down the sand ladders. Byrne regarded Paul thoughtfully. 'Would you do me a favour?'

'Of course. What is it?'

'Go to the top of that rise back there and keep your eyes open. If you see anyone coming let us know fast.'

Paul looked at Konti. 'What about him?'

'I need him,' said Byrne briefly.

'Oh! All right.' Paul started off back down the track.

Byrne laughed shortly. 'Paul will keep a better look-out than any of us. He seems to value his skin more.'

'I don't know,' I said. 'I'm pretty attached to mine.'

An hour later we knew the worst, and it was bad. 'The differential gears are pretty near all stripped,' said Byrne. 'No wonder it sounded like my old man's coffee-grinder back home in Bar Harbor. It never could grind coffee worth a damn.'

I regarded the jacked-up Toyota gloomily. 'What do we do? Walk?'

'There's a place called Seguedine a piece up the road – maybe ten kilometres. Not that there's much there, but maybe we could use a team of camels to haul us out.'

'And then what? The differential's busted. There wouldn't be a service station in Seguedine?'

Byrne laughed. 'Not likely. But I've got a spare differential in the back of the truck. The bastards are always stripping so I've made it a habit to keep a spare. But I'd like to get in cover before replacing it. It's going to blow a son of a bitch tonight and this damned sand gets in everywhere. Not good for differentials.'

'Well, who goes? I can't speak the language.'

Byrne grinned. 'I sent Konti on ahead half an hour ago. I was pretty sure of what I'd find.'

I looked around and, sure enough, Konti was missing. But Billson was running towards us at full tilt. 'Someone coming!' he yelled. 'They'll be here in five minutes or less.'

He skidded to a halt in front of us. 'Any idea who it is?' asked Byrne calmly.

'It looked like the truck we saw in Dirkou.'

Byrne's right arm disappeared inside his *gandoura* and when it reappeared he was holding a fistful of gun. He worked the action and set the safety-catch, then put it away again. Paul watched him wide-eyed. 'Go and sit in the front seat, Paul,' said Byrne.

Billson scurried around the truck and I saw to my own pistol. Byrne said, 'If this is Lash we'll pretty soon find out how genuinely he wants to help. Keep your veil up and your mouth shut.' He stooped and put an oil-can upright on the ground. 'If you recognize his voice kick that over, accidental like.'

We waited, the hot desert wind driving at us and flicking grains of sand into our faces. It was as much to protect my face as to hide it when I drew up and tightened the veil in the way Byrne had shown me. Then I stood with my arm inside my *gandoura* hanging straight down with the pistol in my hand; it couldn't be seen and I would waste no time in drawing from the holster.

The truck came over the rise two hundred yards away, travelling fast and trailing a long plume of dust which was blown to one side by the wind. As it approached it slowed, and then drew to a halt abreast of us. The driver was obviously not a European but the man who got out of the front passenger seat was. He was as Byrne had described him, fairly big and with dark hair. His eyes flickered towards Byrne and me, then he looked at Paul in the front seat and said, 'Are you in trouble? Perhaps I can help.'

I didn't hear what Paul answered because I took half a pace to one side and knocked over the oil-can with a metallic clatter. Byrne raised his voice. 'Yeah, you can say we're in trouble. Lousy differential's bust.'

Lash turned his head and stared at Byrne, then came to the back of the truck. 'You an American?' He filled his voice with well-simulated incredulity.

'We get around.'

'You don't look like one,' said Lash in an amused tone. He nodded at me. 'I suppose he's American, too.'

'Nope,' said Byrne. 'He's British like you.'

Lash raised his eyebrows but said nothing. I suppose Byrne had done the right thing. Lash knew I was around and there was no point in me hiding; and it would be difficult to maintain the deception unless I pretended I was deaf and dumb.

He stooped and looked under the Toyota, then said, 'Yes, I'd say you're in trouble.' He straightened. 'By the way, my name is Lash – John Lash.'

'I'm Luke Byrne. This here is Max Stafford and the feller up front is Paul Billson.' I was afraid that Lash would offer to shake hands which would have been difficult with me holding the pistol, but he merely nodded. Byrne said, 'The differential don't matter – I have a spare; but I'd sure appreciate a tow out of this sand and a few kilometres up the road.'

'That shouldn't be too difficult,' said Lash, and turned away and began to talk to the men in his truck. From the intonation he was speaking French although I didn't get the words. I noted he did not introduce them.

Byrne took his right arm from his *gandoura* and his hand was empty. If he was willing to take a chance then so was I, so I unobtrusively holstered the pistol and did the same. He said, 'We'll put in the sand ladders before we let the jacks down; it'll be easier with them.'

Lash's two companions got out of their truck. I walked to the cab of the Toyota. Paul said in a low voice, 'That's the man who was at Dirkou.'

'So?'

'So wasn't Byrne suspicious of him?'

'Hell!' I said. 'He's just a Good Samaritan come to get us out of trouble. Don't be paranoiac, Paul. Get out and help.'

We put the sand ladders under the rear wheels, then let the Toyota down on to them and took away the jacks. Lash didn't have a towing chain but Byrne did, and we were ready to go within ten minutes. It was then I noticed that one of Lash's men had disappeared.

Lash and the other man got into their truck and the engine fired. In a low voice I said to Byrne, 'Where's the other thug?'

'Gone back over the rise – and I know why.'

'Why, for God's sake?'

'It ain't because he's shy of exposing himself,' Byrne said sardonically. 'My guess he's gone back to flag down Kissack and stop him. The Range-Rover won't be far behind.'

It made sense. Lash wouldn't want us to see Kissack. I said, 'One thing – don't talk about Lash while we're being towed or you'll spook Paul.'

'I'll watch it.' He raised his voice. 'Paul, you stand on this side and Max on the other. If you think we're getting deeper into trouble, then yell.' He got behind the wheel and waved at Lash, who revved his engine.

There was no trouble. Lash's truck was more powerful than it looked and pulled us out of the sand easily, though what it did to one of the sand ladders was indescribable. Byrne threw away that twisted bit of junk as being unusable and we collected the few tools that were lying around. As we did so, the missing man came walking at a smart pace up the road. He saw us looking at him and zipped up the fly of his trousers. Byrne looked at me and grinned faintly.

So the man who was going to kill us towed us into Seguedine, which wasn't much of a place, but there was a ruin with three standing walls and a decrepit roof which was enough to shelter the Toyota from the wind. Lash helped us push it in. 'Mind if I stay the night here with you?' he asked. 'Perhaps I could help you strip the transmission.'

'No call for that,' said Byrne. 'I can manage.'

Lash smiled. 'And I don't feel like driving on in a sand-storm. A man could lose his way. I have a feeling that could be bad.'

'Sure could,' Byrne agreed. 'You could get dead. You want to stay, you stay. It's a free country. Thanks for your help, Mr Lash; you got us out of a nasty hole, but there's no call for you to get your hands dirty.'

But Lash helped us anyway. I suppose he thought it in his own interest to put us on our way as fast as possible. His henchmen disappeared, probably to tell Kissack what was happening. Lash wasn't all that much of a help, though, and his aid was confined to handing over tools when asked, as indeed was mine. Byrne could have done the job quite handily himself and, for a man who professed hatred of 'stinkpots' he was American enough to understand them well.

Paul came and went restlessly. Once, in Lash's absence, Byrne said to him enthusiastically, 'Lash is a real nice guy, don't you think? Him getting us out of the sand and helping us like this and all.'

I said, 'Yes; a Good Samaritan, Paul.' I looked over Byrne's shoulder and saw Lash come slowly out of the shadows, and wondered if Byrne had known that Lash was behind him, listening. Probably he had known; there were no flies on Luke Byrne.

We finished the job in the glare of a pressure lantern after nightfall, then cleaned up and prepared a meal just as Konti showed up. Byrne talked to him for a moment then said to me, 'He walked as far as here, found no one, so he went up the track a long ways with no success. Walking fools, these Teda.'

Lash contributed a bottle of whisky for after-dinner drinks. I accepted a tot, and so did Paul, but Byrne refused politely. 'Where are your friends, Mr Lash?'

Lash raised his eyebrows. 'Friends? Oh, you mean . . . They're just showing me around. Professional guides.' I glanced at Byrne who didn't bat an eyelid at that preposterous statement. 'They prefer to eat their own food.' Lash looked around in the darkness. 'What is this place?'

'Seguedine? Used to be people here – three or four families of Kanuri. Must have moved out since I was here last. The Tassili Tuareg come from the north when the feed gives out there. Where are you heading?'

Lash shrugged. 'Nowhere in particular. Just looking around.' That was supposed to give him an excuse for popping up out of nowhere at any time and occasioning no surprise, but it was a stupid thing to say. Even a tyro like myself had observed that desert crossings were most carefully prepared with times and distances collated and fuel and water carefully metered. No one in his right mind would flutter hither and yon like a carefree butterfly. To risk running out of fuel or water was dangerous.

Lash sipped his whisky. 'And you?'

'Pretty much the same,' said Byrne uninformatively.

I would have thought Lash might have pursued the subject of our further travels, but he didn't. He made desultory conversation, telling us he was the managing director of a firm in Birmingham which specialized in packaging and that this was the first real holiday he'd had in seven years. 'I decided to do something different,' he said.

He tried to draw me out on what I did in England so I told him the truth because he knew all about me anyway and to lie would arouse his suspicions. 'Recuperating from an illness,' I said, then added, 'and getting over a divorce.' Both statements were true; he'd probably been the cause of the 'illness' and the bit about Gloria could confuse him by its truth. The truth can be a better weapon than lies.

After a while he excused himself, after getting nowhere with Billson, and went to his truck where he bedded down. Soon thereafter Konti came out of the darkness and spoke to Byrne, who questioned him closely. Paul said to me, 'Inquisitive, isn't he?'

'Not abnormally so. Chit-chat between ships that pass in the night.'

'I don't like him.' Paul pulled his *djellaba* closer about him. 'I don't think he's what he says he is.' I *knew* it, but Paul was showing an acuity which surprised me. Perhaps it was the sixth sense of the hunted animal.

A few minutes later, out of Paul's hearing, Byrne said, 'Kissack is camped about a mile from here. I sent Konti to scout him out.' He chuckled. 'I don't think Kissack will be comfortable out there. The wind's still rising.'

'Do we stand watches?'

Byrne shook his head. 'Konti will watch all night.'

'Bit hard on him, isn't it?'

'Hell, no! He'll sleep in the Toyota tomorrow. For a Teda to sleep while on the move is sheer unaccustomed luxury.'

Next morning the storm had blown itself out and Lash had gone together with his truck. 'Went just before dawn,' said Byrne. 'Sudden guys, these friends of yours. Kissack shoots folks without saying a word and Lash goes, just like that. Unneighbourly, I call it.'

'So what now?'

'On to Chirfa and Djanet.'


Chirfa was nearly a hundred and fifty kilometres north of Seguedine and consisted of a Tuareg camp and one deserted Foreign Legion fortress which might have stood in for Fort Zinderneuf in *Beau Geste* but for one thing – there was an anchor carved above the main gate. Because we were about as far away from the sea as a human being can get on this planet I stared at this improbable emblem and asked Byrne about it.

'I wouldn't know. Maybe it was built by French marines.'

The Tuareg seemed different from those I had met before, being more shabbily dressed. Byrne said they were of the Tassili Tuareg. From them he bought a donkey, which he gave to Konti. 'This is where he leaves us,' he said. 'He'll go east, past Djado and on to the Tibesti.'

'How far to the Tibesti?'

'Maybe five hundred kilometres; it's over in Chad.'

'Walking all the way?'

'Yeah. But the donkey'll help.'

'My God!' I watched Konti walk out of sight, towing the donkey.

As he walked back to where the Toyota was parked Byrne said, 'We've been followed most of the way here, but I lost sight of them about an hour ago. Two trucks.'

'Lash and Kissack.'

'I guess so. Wish I hadn't lost them; they're a couple of guys I like to keep my eye on.'

# TWENTY-SIX

About ten kilometres out of Chirfa we climbed the pass that is called the Col des Chandeliers for no apparent reason because I didn't see anything that looked like a candlestick. At the top Byrne stopped under a cliff on which was a huge engraving about twenty feet high of a barbaric figure holding a spear. He ignored it, having seen many rock engravings before, and climbed up a little way to where he could get a good view of the way we had just come.

Presently he came down again. 'No one in sight.' He seemed disappointed. 'I'd just as lief know where that bastard is.'

'I knew it,' said Paul. 'You mean Lash.'

Byrne shrugged. 'You're a big boy now, Paul. Yeah, I mean Lash.'

'Who is he? I felt there was something wrong with him.'

I sighed. 'He might as well know, Luke.' I looked at Paul and said deliberately, 'Lash is Kissack's boss.'

He was hurt. 'Why didn't you tell me before?'

'Because we didn't know how you'd take it,' I said. 'You're apt to go off half cock. We found out about him back in Bilma.'

'But who is he?'

'I don't know, but he's in the packaging industry like I'm a candidate for the *Playboy* centrefold. My guess is that he's a big noise in the London underworld.'

'Why would anyone like th—'

'For God's sake, Paul! I don't know. Stop asking unanswerable questions.' I turned to Byrne. 'Let's go.'

He shook his head. 'Either they're behind us or they're ahead of us. If they're ahead, then we'll run into them sooner or later. If they're behind, I'd just as soon know it. We'll wait here awhile. Paul, climb up there and keep watch.'

Paul hesitated, then nodded briefly and climbed up to where Byrne indicated. Byrne said, 'We'll give them an hour.' He turned and walked away and I fell into step beside him. 'You wouldn't be holding out on me, would you, Max? I mean, there isn't anything you haven't told me.'

'You know as much as I do.'

'Then maybe it's Paul. We may have to talk to him seriously.'

I shook my head. 'I've done that – filleted him. He knows nothing.'

Byrne gave a soft exclamation, then stooped and picked up something. He examined it then handed it to me. 'A souvenir of the Sahara.'

It was a small blade carved from stone and about an inch long and half an inch wide. It was beautifully polished and the cutting edge was still keen. 'A small chopper,' he said.

'Tuareg?'

'Hell, no!' He pointed upwards at the engraving of the giant with the spear. 'His people. If you keep your eyes open you can find dozens of things like that around here. Three thousand years old – maybe more.'

I passed my finger over the polished stone. *Three millennia!* It seemed to put me and my doings into an oddly dwindled perspective. Three-quarters of an hour later when Paul shouted I had found another, larger, axe-head and a couple of arrow-heads. I hastily pocketed them and ran for the Toyota.

Byrne was up on the cliff. 'Maybe six kilometres back,' he reported when he got down. 'Both trucks – that suits me fine. Let's go.' So off we went, bouncing down the other side of the Col des Chandeliers and heading north-west.

I kept an eye to the rear and presently saw the faint dots trailing dust plumes like comet tails. They kept an even distance behind, not dropping back and not catching up, and we went on like that for perhaps a couple of hours. Then we came to a beacon by the side of the track. Byrne said, 'Balise 593. Check the odometer – I want exactly fifty kilometres on top of what we've got now.'

I kept an eye on the odometer, watching the kilometres roll by. None of us talked much. Byrne because he was concentrating on his driving, me because I had nothing much to say, and Paul, I suspect, because his thoughts were occupied by the trucks behind. When fifty kilometres had been added on to the score I said, 'This is it.'

'Not quite,' said Byrne, and drove on for another half kilometre before he stopped. He got out and swung himself up on top of the Toyota where he stood gazing back. Then he got back into the cab and remarked, 'I wouldn't want them to lose us now.'

'Why not?'

He pointed off to the left. 'That, believe it or not, is supposed to be a track, and that's the way we're going. We'll soon find out how professional Lash's guides are.' He waited five minutes and then moved off, swinging on to the track which was hardly distinguishable.

The country changed and we lost sight of the mountains, being on an immense gravel plain as flat as a billiard table from horizon to horizon. 'This is called *reg*,' he said. 'Not bad for travelling on if you don't mind the monotony. I guess it was sea bottom at one time.'

Monotonous it certainly was and I began to become sleepy. I looked back at Paul and saw that weariness had conquered whatever terrors he had of Lash and Kissack. He was heavily asleep. The kilometres and miles flowed away beneath our wheels and still the view was unchanged. At one time I said, 'This must be the biggest plain in the desert.'

'Hell, no!' Byrne said. 'That's the Tanezrouft – about as big as France. Makes this look like a postage stamp. It'll be changing in a while – for the worse.'

And it did. First there were isolated barchan dunes, yellow crescents against the black gravel, then bigger patches of sand which Byrne avoided. Finally there was more sand than gravel and he couldn't avoid it. He said conversationally, 'In desert driving this is what separates the men from the boys. This is *fech-fech* – remember what I told you about it?'

I remembered the macabre tale of the big truck breaking through. 'Now you tell me!'

He turned his head and grinned. 'It's okay if you keep up your speed – sort of skim along the surface. Trouble might come if you slow down. I'm betting that those goons of Lash's don't know that.'

'You knew it was here?'

'Yeah. I was stuck here myself once about twenty years back. There's usually *fech-fech* here at this time of year.'

I said, 'It looks like ordinary sand to me.'

'Different colour. And if you look back you'll see we're not kicking up as much dust. One thing's for certain – we don't stop to find out for sure.'

Presently, after about an hour, he changed direction and soon after came to a stop. He climbed again on to the top of the cab and looked around, and when he got back he was grinning. 'Not a sign of them. Mr Lash might have helped us back at Seguedine but I don't think we should help him now. We join the main track to Djanet over there. That's Balise Berliet 21. Know what Djanet means?'

'I don't even know what Balise Berliet 21 means.'

'The Berliet Motor Company tested their heavy trucks out here and signposted the desert. And Djanet is Arabic for Paradise.'

# TWENTY-SEVEN

Paradise was built partly on the desert floor and partly on a rocky hillside and provided more amenities than most oasis towns. The hotel was spartan but clean and better than most; bedroom accommodation was in *zeribas*, grass huts with the walls hung with gaily-coloured blankets, and there were showers which actually worked. As I sponged myself down I reflected that Byrne had been right – the desert is a clean place and a man doesn't stink. This was the first shower I'd had in nearly a month.

Byrne had left the Toyota in the hotel compound and had gone looking for his informant, the putative lucky winner of ten camels. He came back some time later with two Tuareg whom he introduced as Atitel and his son, Hami. 'Have you got those photocopies of the Northrop?'

'Sure.' I dug into my bag and gave them to him.

He unfolded them. 'Where did you get these?'

'The Science Museum in London – they're from Jane's *All the World's Aircraft*, 1935 edition.'

He spread the photocopies on the table and began to interrogate Atitel, pointing frequently to the photograph of the Northrop 'Gamma'. This particular specimen must have been one of the first aircraft to be used by Trans-World Airlines because the TWA emblem was on the fuselage near the tail. It was a stylishly designed plane, long and sleek, with the cockpit set far back near the tail. It had, of course, been designed in the days when aircraft had cockpits and not flight decks, and it had a non-retracting undercarriage with the struts and wheels enclosed in streamlined casings. The caption described it as a freight and mail-carrying monoplane.

At last Byrne straightened. 'This could be it. He says there's a metal bird of the *Kel Ehendeset* up on the Tassili about three days' march in from Tamrit.'

'How far is that, and what the devil is a *Kel* whosit?'

'Maybe seventy kilometres. The *Kel Ehendeset* are you and me – anyone who knows about machines.' He turned to Atitel and they talked briefly, then he said, 'He says the *Kel Ehendeset* have power over the *angeloussen* – the angels – and it's the *angeloussen* who make the trucks move and lift the airplanes.'

'Sounds logical. If it's three days' march then it's about six hours by *angeloussen* power.'

Byrne looked at me disgustedly as though I ought to know better. 'We won't get the Toyota on to the plateau. When we go we walk.' He tapped the photograph. 'Atitel seems pretty certain that the wreck on the Tassili is just like this. He insists there are no engine nacelles on the wings and that the fuselage is cylindrical up front just like in the picture. That's the big radial engine there.'

'Then it may be Billson's?'

'Could be.' Byrne shook his head. 'But the Tuareg don't go much for pictures – like all Moslems. Against their religion, so they have no experience of pictures. I've known a guy hang a picture on the wall of his tent in imitation of what he's seen Europeans do in their houses. It was something he'd cut out of a magazine because he liked it. He'd put it upside-down.' He smiled. 'It was a picture of a square-rigger in full sail, but he'd never seen a ship or even the goddamn sea, so all it made was a pretty pattern which maybe looked just as well upside-down.'

'But if Atitel *has* seen a plane, then he should be able to compare it with a picture.'

'I wouldn't bet my life on it, but I suppose we'll have to take the chance. We didn't come all this way for nothing.'

'When do we start?'

He began to dicker with Atitel and a lot of palavering went on with Hami putting in his tuppence-worth from time to time. It was fifteen minutes before Byrne said, 'He says he can't start until late tomorrow or, maybe, early the day after. He's got to round up some donkeys that have strayed. The plane is about fifty kilometres from Tamrit – that's on the edge of the plateau at the top. We won't be doing much more than fifteen kilometres a day up there so it means taking water for at least a week, preferably ten days. That means baggage animals and more donkeys than he can lay his hands on right now.'

He turned back to Atitel and money changed hands. When the Tuareg had gone I said, 'That money was Algerian.'

Byrne looked at me in surprise. 'Yeah; because we're in Algeria.'

'When did that happen?'

He grinned. 'Remember the detour we took to lose Lash? Well, it took around the border posts, too. You're okay, Max; you're legal in Algeria.'

'But Billson may not be.'

He grunted. 'Relax. There's a hell of a lot of desert between here and Tam; the word may not have filtered through.' He held up the photocopies. 'Mind if I hang on to these? I have some figuring to do.' I nodded. 'Where's Paul?'

'Still in the shower.'

He laughed. 'I told you a guy could drown in the desert.' Then he sat at the table, took out his stub of pencil and began making calculations on the back of one of the photo-copies, referring constantly to the specifications of the Northrop 'Gamma'.

We didn't start next day or even the day after, but the day after that. Byrne grumbled ferociously. 'Sometimes these people give me a pain in the ass.'

I grinned. 'I thought you were one of them – a proper Targui.'

'Yeah; but I revert to type at times. I'm thinking of Lash and Kissack. I don't know how badly they were sanded in, but it won't take them forever to get out. I want to get clear before they get here.'

'What makes you think they'll come to Djanet?'

'Only place they can get gas.'

But it gave me the chance of unwinding and relaxing after the heavy pounding in the Toyota. And I slept in a bed for the first time since leaving Algiers – the hotel mattress wasn't much harder than the sand I'd become accustomed to. And we all had a few welcome beers.

On the third day after arrival we drove out of Djanet in the Toyota and we still hadn't seen Lash. I said, 'Perhaps he's still out there where you stranded him.'

'My heart bleeds for him,' said Byrne. He cocked his head and looked back at Paul. 'What do you think?'

'I hope he rots,' said Paul vindictively. 'Kissack, too. All of them.'

Paul was becoming bloodthirsty, but it wasn't too surprising. It's hard to be charitable towards people who shoot at you without telling you why.

We drove towards the mountains, towards steep cliffs which reared up like a great stone barrier. At last we bumped to a halt in a grove of tamarisk trees among which donkeys were grazing. Atitel and Hami waved in greeting as we got out. Byrne grunted in disgust.

'Those goddamn animals should have been loaded by now.'

'Where are we going?'

His arm rose forty-five degrees above the horizontal as he pointed and I got a crick in my neck as I looked up. 'Up there.'

'My God!' The cliffs rose vertically for about two thousand feet and Byrne was pointing to a cleft, a ravine which cut into them, leaving a v-shaped notch at the top which looked like a gunsight. 'I'm no bloody mountaineer.'

'Neither is a donkey and any man can go where a donkey can. It's not as steep as it looks.' He cocked an eye at the sun. 'Let's get started. I want to be at the top before nightfall.'

He chivvied Atitel and Hami into loading the donkeys. The goatskin *djerbas* of the Tuareg were kinder to the animals than the jerricans which held the rest of our water supply because they caused less chafe, but there weren't enough *djerbas* and so the jerricans had to be used. Most of the load was water for man and animal.

'I'm figuring on ten days,' said Byrne. ''Course we may be lucky and find a *guelta* – that's a rock pool – but we can't depend on it. Now you see 'em, now you don't.'

So we loaded water and food for five men and seven donkeys for ten days, and Byrne added a cloth-wrapped parcel which clinked metallically. He also added the Lee-Enfield rifle to the top of one load, being careful to strap it tight. 'I'll be back in ten minutes,' he said, and got into the Toyota and drove away.

I watched him out of sight, then turned to Paul. 'What about this? Think you can make it?'

He looked up at the cliffs. 'I think I can; I won't be carrying anything. Not like when we were crossing the dunes in the Ténéré.'

His face was drawn and pale in spite of the tan he had acquired. I don't think he had been a fit man even when he left England because his life had been sedentary. Since then he had been shot and nearly died of exposure, and what we had been doing since had been no rest cure. I said, 'Maybe it would be better if you stayed. I'll talk to Byrne about it.'

'No,' he said sharply. 'He'd agree with you. I want to come. There may be – ' he swallowed – 'may be a body.'

The obsession which had driven him all his life was nearing its culmination. Within only a few days he had the chance of finding out the truth about his father, and he wasn't going to give up now. I nodded in agreement and looked up at the cliffs again. It still looked a killer of a climb.

Byrne came back on foot. 'I've put the truck where it won't be found easily. Let's move.'

I drew him on one side. 'Have you been up there before?'

'Sure. I've been most places.'

'What's the travelling like once we get on top?'

'Not bad – if we stick to the water-courses.'

'Water-courses!' I said incredulously.

'You'll see,' he said with a grim smile. 'It's the damnedest country you're ever likely to see. Like a maze – easy to get lost. What's your point?'

'I'm thinking of Paul.'

Byrne nodded. 'Yeah, he's been on my mind, too. But if he can get to the top here he'll be okay.'

'*Tassili n' Ajjer*,' I said thoughtfully. 'What does that translate as?'

'The Plateau of Goats – not that I've ever seen any. A few wild camels, though.' He shook his head irritably. 'Let's move, for God's sake!'

And so we started. It wasn't bad at first because we were on gently rising ground approaching the base of the cliffs. When we got to the ravine it was bigger than it looked at first, maybe half a mile wide at the bottom and narrowing as it rose. There was a path of sorts which zig-zagged from side to side so that for every hundred yards of forward travel we walked perhaps six hundred. And climbed, of course, but not as much.

It was a steady toil which put a strain on the calf muscles and on to the heart and lungs, a battle for altitude. It wasn't any kind of a mountaineering feat, just damned hard work which went on and on. There was no sound but the steady rasping of breath in my throat, the occasional clatter as a stone was dislodged to go bounding down the ravine, and the clink of a jerrican as it hit a rock. Sometimes a donkey would snort but no one had breath for talking.

I think we would have made the top quicker had it not been for Paul who held us back. We stopped frequently for him to catch up, and waited while he rested. It gave me time to rest my own lungs, for which I was thankful. Atitel and Hami didn't seem worried by the effort; they would smoke a half-cigarette and carefully put away the stubs before resuming the climb. As for Byrne, he was all whip-cord and leather, as usual, but his nose was beakier and his cheeks more sunken than I had noticed before.

So it was that it took us over four hours to climb two thousand feet and I doubt if the ground distance we had covered would be more than a mile and a half when measured on a map. As soon as the ground began to level we stopped and within minutes Atitel and Hami had the inevitable miniature Tuareg camp fires going and water on the boil to make tea. I said breathlessly, 'Are we there?'

'Nearly. The worst is over.' Byrne pointed towards the setting sun. 'I reckon you can see over eighty kilometres from here.'

The view was fantastic – dun-coloured hills close by changing to blue and purple in the distance. Byrne pointed towards a jumble of dunes. 'The *Erg d'Admer*; all that sand was washed down from the plateau. Must have been one of the biggest waterfalls in the world right here – a fall of two thousand feet.'

'Waterfall!' I said weakly.

'Sure; the Tassili was well watered at one time. Real big rivers. And it was good cattle country with plenty of feed. Long time ago, of course.'

Of course!

I sipped sweet tea from a small brass cup and regarded Paul, who was lying flat on his back and seemed completely exhausted. He'd made it but only just. I went over to him. 'Have some tea, Paul.'

His chest heaved. 'Later,' he gasped.

'Max!' said Byrne. His voice was soft but there was a snap of command in it. I looked up and he jerked his head so I went and joined him where he stood looking down the ravine. He pointed to the desert floor and there, two miles away and nearly half a mile below was a movement of sand.

'Dust devils?' They were familiar in the desert; miniature whirlwinds caused by the convection currents stirred up by the heat.

Byrne looked up at the sun. 'Not at this hour. I think we've got company. There are two.'

'How the hell would Lash know we came here?'

Byrne shrugged. 'Anyone going up to the Tassili from Djanet would come this way. No other way as easy.' Easy! 'He'll have been asking around in Djanet; it would have been no trick to trace us – just a few enquiries at the hotel.'

'We ought to have been more discreet.'

'It wouldn't have worked. No one can hire men and animals in Djanet without the word getting round. Lash's men might speak Tamachek, but even if they have only Arabic they'd have no trouble in finding out what they wanted to know.'

I looked down the cliffside and there was no movement to be seen. 'So we're in trouble.'

'Not too much,' said Byrne unperturbedly. 'They won't climb up here in the dark, and the sun will set in an hour.

I guess they'll wait until tomorrow. That gives us a chance to get lost.' He looked back at Paul. 'We'll give him time to rest up then push on.'

'Where to?'

'Over the rise there – to Tamrit and Assakaô.'

Never could I have imagined a landscape such as that of the Tassili n' Ajjer. We walked in the beds of long-gone rivers which, when in flood, had carved deeply into the soft sandstone, making what were now canyons, the walls of which were scalloped into whole series of shallow caves on all sides. When desiccation set in and the water had gone the wind had continued to work on the Tassili, abrading the sandstone for thousands of years and sculpturing the rock into pillars and pinnacles of fantastic shape, some towering two hundred or more feet, others undercut at the base and felled as a woodsman would fell a tree.

The land had a baked appearance like an ill-made pie left too long in the oven and, indeed, the Tassili had been under the furnace of the sun for too long without the amelioration of vegetative cover. The sandstone was blackened and covered with a patina of what Byrne called desert varnish. 'You get dew on the stone some nights,' he said. 'And it draws iron and manganese to the surface. Next day the dew evaporates and the iron and manganese oxidize. Have that happening for a few hundred or thousand years and you get a good coating of varnish.'

As he had said, it was a maze, the canyons that had been water-courses joining, linking and separating. I had the feeling that this had been some sort of delta, the end of a journey for a mighty river, once fast but now slow and heavy with silt like the delta of the Nile. But then it had come to Tamrit and the edge of the Tassili to plunge two thousand feet to the land below, taking the silt to what were now the huge dunes of the *Erg d'Admer*. And now there was no water. The land was dry as a camel bone found in the Ténéré, but not bleached – rather sun-scorched and hardened like a mummified corpse.

That I saw during the first hour before the sun set and then, at Byrne's insistence, we continued, aided by the lamp of a full moon, until nine that night when he relented and we made camp. By this time Paul was near collapse and I was wearier than I'd been since our stroll through the Ténéré. Too tired to eat, I crawled into one of the shallow caves in the rock and fell asleep huddled in my *djellaba*.

I awoke in daylight to find a man looking down at me. He was dark-skinned and wore nothing but a loincloth and, in his right hand, he carried a spear. Behind him was a herd of cattle, healthy-looking beasts with piebald hides and wide' spreading horns. And beyond them was a group of hunters carrying bows, some with arrows nocked to the string.

I blinked in surprise and sat up and stared. The man was nothing but paint on the wall of the cave, and so were the cattle and the hunters. I jerked my head around and saw Byrne squatting outside the cave, feeding the water-boiling contraption he called a volcano. Behind him Hami was loading *djerbas* on to a donkey.

'Luke,' I said, 'have you seen this?'

He looked up. 'Time you were awake. Sure, I've seen it – one of the Tassili frescoes.'

I turned back to stare at it. The colours seemed as fresh as though it had been painted the week before and there was a fluency and elegance of line in the drawing of the cattle which any modern painter would envy. 'How old is this?'

Byrne came into the cave. 'The cattle? Three thousand years, could be four.' He moved along the wall of the cave until he came to the end. 'This is older – this mouflon.' I scrambled to my feet and joined him. The wild sheep was more crudely executed. 'Eight thousand years,' said Byrne. 'Maybe more, I wouldn't know.'

I began to examine the wall more carefully, looking for more treasures, but he said brusquely, 'No time for that. We've a long way to go. Wake Billson.'

Reluctantly I turned away, woke Paul, and then helped to make our breakfast. Not more than half an hour after I had woken we were on our way again, threading the canyons of the Tassili. An hour later I saw the green of trees, big ones lofting more than fifty feet. The branches were wide spread but twisted and gnarled.

I said, 'There must be water here,' and pointed.

'Cypress,' said Byrne. 'Those can have a tap root a hundred feet long and going straight down. And they're older than Methuselah; maybe they were here at the time the guy was painting those cattle back there in the cave.'

We left the trees behind and marched in silence and again all was silence except for the clatter of stones and the snorting of the donkeys and an occasional word passing between Atitel and Hami. There wasn't much to say about what we were looking for – everything had been said to exhaustion. And there wasn't much to say about Lash, either. If he was coming up behind he'd either catch us or he wouldn't.

We stopped briefly at midday to eat, and again at sunset, and then pressed on into the moonlit night. I thought it unsafe and said so, but Byrne was confident that Atitel knew what he was doing, more confident than I. Again we stopped at about nine and I found another cave. To my surprise I was not as tired as I had expected to be, and Paul was better, too. I looked at him as he unslung a jerrican from a donkey and thought of what Isaacson, back in Luton, had called him. A *nebbish*! The total nonentity.

It was true! Hours had gone by at a time when, even in Paul's presence, I had not given him a thought. When we drove in the Toyota he always sat in the back and wasn't under my eye. On this, and other, desert marches he always brought up the rear. He said little, never commenting on what he saw, however wondrous, but just stubbornly put one foot in front of the other. And he never complained, no matter how he felt. It was something to say for Paul but, all the same, he might just as well not have been there. The *nebbish!*

As for Luton – that was a million miles away, on another planet.

We fed on dates and dried mutton and I asked Byrne what progress we were making. He chewed vigorously, then swallowed. 'Not too bad. Atitel reckons on less than a day and a half. He says he'll see a landmark he knows before dark tomorrow.'

'What about Lash?' I said. 'And Kissack?'

'What about them? At Tamrit we left them at least eight hours behind, and you can add another three hours tonight because they won't be moving at night. I guess we're a full day ahead. And they don't know where we're going.'

'We've been leaving tracks. I've noticed. Prints in the sand and donkey droppings.'

He nodded. 'Sure. But we've also been moving a lot on rock and leaving no trail. They can follow us if they know how but it'll take up a lot of time, casting around and all. That puts us another day ahead, maybe two.' He took another bite of mutton and said casually, 'We might run into them on the way back.'

'That's nice.'

He grinned. 'I'll ask Atitel to take us back another way.'

When I awoke the next morning I eagerly scanned the wall of the cave but, to my disappointment, it was bare rock. Hami had baked bread in the hot sand under a fire, and it was crunchy in the crust and very tasty if you ignored the gritty sand. After breakfast we set off again, Atitel leading the way through the shattered wastes of the Tassili n' Ajjer.

The worst thing that could possibly have happened occurred at mid-afternoon. We were picking our way through a particularly bad patch where, for some reason or other, the wind action on the sandstone columns had been accentuated. The grinding action of sand-laden wind against the bases of the columns had felled a lot of them and, in their fall they had smashed and broken, leaving a chaos of debris through which it was difficult to negotiate our way.

Suddenly the donkey which Atitel was leading brayed vigorously and plunged, butting him in the back so that he fell. He gave a cry and Byrne ran up and stamped at something on the ground. When I got to him I saw it was a snake. 'Horned viper,' said Byrne, and ground its head to pulp under his heel. 'It scared the donkey.'

It had done more than that because Atitel was sitting up holding his leg and groaning. Byrne examined it and looked up at me. 'It's broken,' he said flatly.

'Christ!' I said. 'What do we do now?'

'Make a splint for a start.'

That wasn't as easy as it sounded because we had nothing suitable for a splint other than the barrel of the rifle. Unexpectedly, it was Paul who came up with a good idea. He tapped a jerrican which was hanging on the flank of a donkey and it rang hollowly. 'This empty?'

'Yeah.'

'We can bash it with rocks,' said Paul. 'Flatten it. We ought to be able to make some sort of rigid splint.'

'We can do better than rocks,' said Byrne, and went to a donkey and unpacked the cloth-covered bundle he had brought. From it he produced a hammer and a cold chisel. 'Get that can on the ground.'

It took time and the desert rang with the sound as it echoed from column to column but eventually we splinted

Atitel's leg, padding it first and then binding the metal with strips ripped from a *gandoura*. He had stopped groaning and looked on interestedly as we did it.

When we had finished Byrne squatted next to him and uttered the first words of what proved to be a long conversation. I said to Paul, 'God knows what we'll do now. From what Byrne told me last night we're ten or twelve kilometres from where the old man said he saw the plane.'

'We'll go on.' Paul's face was set in stubbornness.

'Be reasonable.' I waved my hand at the chaos all about us. 'How the hell can we find it without a guide? This, Paul – this bloody Godforsaken land – is the reason it wasn't found in the first place. You could walk within ten yards and never see it.'

'We'll go on,' he said. 'And we'll find it.'

I shook my head and looked to where Atitel was drawing with his finger in the sand. Byrne was asking questions. I shrugged and went to help Hami adjust the harness on one of the donkeys where the edge of a jerrican had chafed and worn a sore spot in its hide.

Half an hour later Byrne stood up. 'Okay; Atitel and Hami are going back. The old man can ride a donkey and Hami will lead another with enough food and water for the two of them. He'll take Atitel to Tamrit and then go down into Djanet for help.'

I said, 'They might run into Lash.'

'I've told them about Lash. They know enough to keep clear of him. Hami will go back a different way.' He laughed shortly. 'I said it's a blood feud; they understand that.'

'And us?'

'We go on.' I looked at Paul, who was grinning. 'Atitel's landmark is unmistakable, according to him. It's a big rock column about two hundred feet high and split from the top to half way down as though someone has driven a wedge into it – you know, like splitting timber. He says all we have to do is to keep going the way we are now and we should see it in a couple of hours.'

'And the plane?' Paul's voice was shrill.

'Is about three kilometres north-west of the split column.'

It was chancy. Atitel's idea of north-west might not coincide with Byrne's compass, and I didn't like the sound of that '*about* three kilometres' – it could be anything from two to four, more or less. I figured we might have to search five or six square kilometres. Still, it was better than the situation I had envisaged when talking to Paul.

I said, 'Can you guide us back to Tamrit? I don't know that I could.'

'Yeah. I've been taking compass bearings.' Byrne looked from me to Paul. 'Well, what about it?'

Paul nodded vigorously, so I shrugged. If it was a question of taking a vote I was out-voted. I said, 'It's all right with me as long as Atitel will be okay. It's a long way back to Tamrit and then he'll have to wait alone while Hami goes down that bloody ravine and on into Djanet. Do you think it's fair on him?'

'It's his idea,' said Byrne. 'He don't mind the broken leg just as long as he can get it set properly. He says he's broken that leg before. What he's really worried about is his ten goddamned camels. He wants them.'

'Then tell him to pray to Allah that this is the aeroplane we're looking for.'

We redistributed loads on the donkeys and then the two Tuareg went back, with Atitel riding a donkey led by Hami, his splinted leg sticking out grotesquely at right-angles. Then there were just the three of us left with five donkeys. I led two and so did Paul, while Byrne coped with one so that he could have a hand free for his compass.

I was mildly surprised when we saw Atitel's landmark after a two-hour march. It didn't seem possible that things

could go right for us – I had half expected that we'd have to
search for the damn thing – but there it stood unmistakably
as Byrne had described it, a tall tower which looked as
though a giant had taken a swipe at it with an axe and had
cleft it from the top.

We camped at its base. Paul was all for going on the further three kilometres to the north-west but Byrne wouldn't
have it. 'It's late,' he said. 'I didn't mind night marches with
Atitel; I trusted him. But any one of us could bust a leg in
the dark. We'll leave it until morning.'

So we left it until morning and breakfasted before dawn,
then set out as soon as it was light enough to see clearly. In
all my years, even in the army, there was never a period
during which I made as many dawn starts as in the desert.
We marched three kilometres, Byrne setting the direction
and pacing us. That took an hour. Then we stopped in the
middle of nowhere and unloaded the donkeys and hobbled
them so they wouldn't stray.

The landscape was anarchic; a disorder of rock columns,
a hugger-mugger of hiding places. Peter Billson's plane
could be within a hundred yards but there was no way
of knowing. I said into the silence, 'It could have burnt
out.'

'No,' said Byrne. 'Atitel said it was intact. He's seen
planes before at the airstrip at In Debiren and he said that
this plane still had its wings on. He said it was *exactly* like the
plane in the picture.'

'That's incredible! You mean Billson landed in the middle
of all this in the dark without bending anything. I don't
believe it.'

'He was a good pilot,' protested Paul.

'I don't care if he could fly as well as the Archangel
Gabriel – it still seems bloody impossible.'

'Maybe the *angeloussen* helped him,' said Byrne. 'Now,
we've got to do this real careful. No one goes off alone.

We keep in sight or sound of each other. If you're out of sight keep hollering.' He stared at Paul. 'In this mess a guy can get lost awful easy so mind what I say.'

Paul mumbled assent. He was quivering like an eager dog who wanted to go and chase rabbits. I said, 'I didn't look at those photocopies too closely. How big is this Northrop?'

'Forty-eight feet wingspan,' said Paul. 'Length, thirty-two feet. Maximum height, nine feet.'

It was bigger than I had assumed. We were looking for something in an area of, say, fifteen hundred square feet. I felt a bit better, but not much.

'We spread out in a line, Paul in the middle,' said Byrne. 'And you take your direction from me.'

And so began the search. We quartered the area in over-lapping sweeps so as not to miss anything, and it was damned hard work. This was not a mere matter of making a march; we had to cover and inspect an area, which meant scrambling over rocks and looking behind every column in that broken wilderness.

We searched all day without finding anything but rocks.

That night Paul was dispirited. He huddled in his *djellaba* and aimlessly tossed a stone from one hand to the other while staring blankly with unmoving eyes. I didn't feel too good myself and said to Byrne, 'What do you think?'

He shrugged. 'Maybe Atitel was out in his distance and direction. We'll look again tomorrow. Get some sleep.'

'God!' I said. 'Talk about needles in haystacks. And there's that proverb about leaving no bloody stone unturned.'

Byrne grunted. 'If it was easy to see it would have been found years ago. Atitel says he came on it only by chance four years ago. He'd come up here trying to trap wild camel foals and got himself lost.'

'Why didn't he report it when he got back to Djanet?'

'It didn't mean that much to him. If there had been a body he might have, but he said there was no body near.'

'Do you think Billson tried to walk out?'

'He was a damned fool if he did.'

Paul came alive. 'He wouldn't try that,' he said positively. 'He knew the rules about that. All the pilots in the race were told to stay by the plane if they came down.'

'Yeah,' said Byrne. 'It's the sensible thing to do and, from what I've heard of him, Peter Billson was a sensible guy.' He paused. 'Sorry to bring this up, Paul; but when Atitel told me there was no body I had my doubts about this being the right airplane. What in hell would a good flier like your old man be doing way over here anyway? He'd be off course by nearly two hundred miles.'

'Atitel identified the plane,' said Paul obstinately.

'Yeah, but when I first suggested the Tassili you said yourself your father was too good a pilot to be fifteen degrees out.'

It was all very depressing.

We found it next morning only ten minutes after restarting the search. I found it, and it was infuriating to think that if Byrne hadn't called off the search the previous night another ten minutes would have done it.

I scaled the side of a pillar of rock that had fallen intact and walked across it to see what was on the other side. There, in a sixty-foot-wide gully was an aeroplane looking as pristine as though it had just been delivered from the manufacturer. It stood in that incongruous place as it might have stood on the tarmac outside a hangar.

'Luke!' I yelled. 'Paul! It's here!'

I scrambled down to it, and they both arrived breathless. 'That's it!' shouted Paul. 'That's my father's plane.'

I looked at Byrne. 'Is it?'

'It's a Northrop "Gamma",' he said, and passed his hand almost reverentially over the fuselage. 'Yeah, this is Peter Billson's plane. Look!'

Over forty years of wind-driven sand had worn away the painted registration marks but on the fuselage one could still detect the outline of the letters which made up a word – *Flyaway*.

'Oh, God!' said Paul, and leaned on the trailing edge of the wing. Suddenly he burst into tears. All the pent-up emotion of a lifetime came out of him in one rush and he just stood there and wept, racked with sobs. To those brought up in our stiff-upper-lip society the sight of a man in tears is apt to be unnerving, so Byrne and I tactfully walked away until Paul could get a grip on himself.

We walked a little way down the gully away from the plane, then Byrne turned and said, 'Now how in hell did he put it down there?' There was wonder in his voice.

I saw what he meant. There was not much clearance at the end of each wingtip and beyond the plane the gully narrowed sharply and if the aircraft had rolled a few feet further the wings would have been ripped off. I said as much.

'That's not what I mean,' said Byrne. He turned and studied the terrain with narrowed eyes. 'This airplane is in a goddamn box.' He pointed to the wall of rock at the wider end of the gully. 'So how did it get in the box?' He shook his head and looked up at the sky. 'He must have brought it down like a helicopter.'

'Is that possible?'

'Unlikely. Look, the guy is in trouble; it's night time and something has gone wrong, so he has to put down. He can't see worth a damn, his landing speed is sixty miles an hour, and yet he sets that thing down right way up on its wheels in a space that should be impossible.'

I looked around. 'No wonder it wasn't found. Who'd look on the Tassili anyway? And if they did it's in an impossible place.'

'Let's go get the gear,' he said. 'We'll set up camp here.'

He called out, telling Paul to stay there, and we went to round up the donkeys, load them, and take them back to the plane. It was difficult to find a way in but we found a cleft big enough to take one donkey at a time, and unloaded and set up camp in the clear space just behind *Flyaway*. After that the donkeys were taken out again, hobbled, and turned loose to feed on what sparse vegetation they could find.

When we got back Paul had recovered, although his eyes were still red. 'Sorry about that.'

'That's all right, Paul,' I said. 'I didn't expect an icy calmness.'

Byrne was pacing the distance from the rock wall at the end of the gully to the tail of the plane. I walked towards him. 'Sixty yards,' he said, and blew out his cheeks expressively. 'I still don't believe it. Paul okay?'

I nodded and put my hand up to touch the rudder. 'She looks ready to fly.'

'You'd have to lift her out of here with a crane,' said Byrne. 'And then build a runway. But there's more. Look!' He pointed down to the tail wheel which was flat. When he kicked it, it fell apart in a powdery heap. 'That's the weak link. The airplane is fine – all metal. 24ST Alclad according to the specification, and the desert wouldn't hurt that. The engine will be fine, too; it'll just need the dried oil cleaning out and it'll run as sweetly as new. But all the sealings will have gone, and all the gaskets, and anything made of rubber. And I guess any plastic parts, too. I hear those early plastics weren't too stable chemically.' He sighed. 'No, she'll not fly again – ever.'

As Paul joined us Byrne said, 'Mind if I take a look in the cockpit?' Paul looked puzzled, as well he might, because this was the first time Byrne had asked his permission to do anything. Byrne explained, 'I guess this is your airplane – by inheritance, Paul.'

Paul swallowed, and I saw the glisten of tears in his eyes. 'No,' he said huskily. 'I don't mind.'

Byrne walked around the tailplane and put his foot on the step on the wing fillet, then swung himself up to look into the cockpit. The cockpit cover was slid back and he looked down and said, 'Fair amount of sand in here.'

I left him to it and walked back to get my camera. I spent some time cleaning the lens, which wasn't easy because the air was dry and the static electricity such that you could see the fine dust jumping on to the surface of the lens under its attraction. I did my best and then loaded the camera with a film and went back to take pictures.

Byrne had got into the cockpit and was fiddling around with the controls. The rudder moved, but with a squeaking and grating noise, and then the ailerons went up and down with less disturbance. Paul was standing on one side, doing nothing but just looking at *Flyaway*. I have never seen a man look so peaceful, and I hoped he would now be cured of what ailed him, because there was no doubt that he had been a man badly disturbed to the point of insanity.

I used up the whole roll of film, taking pictures from various angles, including two of the faded name on the side of the fuselage. Then I rewound the film into its cassette and packed it away with my unused shaving gear.

Presently Byrne called me and I went back to the plane. He was still in the cockpit. 'Come up here.'

I put my foot on the step and hoisted myself up. He had his pocket prismatic compass in his hand. 'Look at this!' He tapped an instrument set at the top of the windscreen.

'What is it?'

'The compass. It reads one hundred eighty-two degrees.'
He held up the prismatic compass so I could see it 'Mine
reads one hundred seventy-five.'

'Seven degrees difference. Which is right?'

'Mine's not wrong,' he said evenly.

'An error of seven degrees wouldn't account for Billson
being fifteen degrees off course.'

'Maybe not.' He handed me the prismatic compass.
'I want you to go back there – well away from the airplane.
Take a sighting on the rudder; I want you lined up exactly
the way the airplane is. Then take a reading and come back
and tell me what it is.'

I nodded and climbed down, then went back as far as
I had left the baggage. I sighted on the rudder and got a
reading of 168°. I thought I'd made an error so I checked my
position and tried again and got the same result. I went back
to Byrne. 'A hundred and sixty-eight.'

He nodded. 'Fourteen degrees difference – that would be
about right to put him here.' He tapped the aircraft compass again. 'Look, Billson is flying at night, right? So he's
flying by compass. Let's say he sets a course of one eighty
degrees. He's actually going one sixty-six and way off
course.'

'His compass was that much out?'

'Looks like it. And it must have gone wrong in Algiers
because he got that far without trouble.'

I said, 'Why did your compass give different readings in
here and out there?'

'Magnetic deviation,' he said. 'Remember what I told
you at Assekrem about iron in the mountains causing
trouble? Well, there's a lot of iron here. Up front there's a
goddamn hunk of iron called an engine. That affects the
compass reading. Now, that's a Wright Cyclone with nine
cylinders and, in flight, all the spark plugs are busy
sparking and sending out radiation. They tell you they can

be screened but I've never seen anyone do a good
job of screening yet And there'll be other bits of iron
about the airplane – the oleo struts, for instance.' He
tapped the metal of the fuselage. 'This don't matter – it's
aluminum.'

I said, 'What are you trying to tell me?'

'I'm getting to it.' Byrne stared thoughtfully at the compass. 'Now, you build an airplane, and you take a perfectly
good compass and put it in that airplane and it gives you a
wrong reading because of all the iron around. So you have
to adjust it to bring it back to what it was before you put it
in the airplane.' He pointed to the compass. 'Built in back of
there are some small magnets put in just the right places to
compensate for all the other iron.'

'And you think one of them fell off? Because of
vibration, perhaps?'

'Nope,' he said shortly. 'They're not built to fall off;
they're screwed in real tight. And there's something else –
any compass, no matter how good, will give a reading that's
a bit off when you're flying on different courses. You see,
the needle is always pointing in the same direction, to magnetic north; so when you change course you're swinging all
your iron around the needle.'

'It's getting more complicated.'

'This is the real point. Every compass in every airplane is
tested individually because all airplanes have different
magnetic characteristics – even the same models. The airplane is flown along different known courses and the compass readings are checked. Then a compass adjuster does
his bit with his magnets. It's a real skilled job, more of an
art than a science. He works out his calculations and maybe
adds in the date last Tuesday, then he makes out a deviation card for the residual errors he can't get rid of on various courses. I've been looking for Billson's deviation card
and I can't find it.'

'Not surprising, after forty-two years. What are you really getting at, Luke?'

'You can bet your last cent that Billson would have had his compass checked out real good before the race. His life depended on it.'

'And it let him down.'

'Yeah; but only after Algiers. And compasses don't go fourteen degrees wrong that easy.'

I stared at him. '*Sabotage!*'

'Could be. Can't think of anything else.'

My thoughts went back to English, the journalist who had set fire to Paul. 'That idea has come up before,' I said slowly. 'A German won the race – a Nazi. I don't suppose he could have done it personally, but a friend of his might.'

'I'd like to take this compass out,' said Byrne. 'There's a screwdriver in that kit of tools I brought.'

'I wondered about that,' I said. 'Were you expecting this?'

'I was expecting something. Don't forget there's a son of a bitch who is willing to kill to prevent this plane being found.'

'I'll get the screwdriver.'

As I dropped to the ground Byrne said, 'Don't tell Paul.'

Paul was sitting on the ground in front of *Flyaway* just looking at her. I walked away, got the screwdriver and came back, concealing it in the folds of my *gandoura*. Byrne attacked the first of the four screws which held the compass in place. It seemed locked solid but an extra effort moved it and then it rotated freely.

He took out all four screws and gently eased the compass out of place and turned it over in his hands. 'Yeah,' he said. 'You see these two brass tubes here? Inside those are small pole magnets. This screw here makes the tubes move like scissor blades – that's how the compass adjuster gets his results. And this is a locking nut to make sure the tubes can't move once they're set.'

He tested it with his fingers. 'It's locked tight – which means . . .'

'. . . that if the compass is fourteen degrees out of true it was done deliberately?'

'That's right,' said Byrne.

# TWENTY-EIGHT

Sabotage! An ugly word. An uglier deed.

I said, 'How long would it take to do it?'

'You saw how easy it was to take out this compass. To make the change and put back the compass wouldn't take long. A maximum of fifteen minutes for the whole job.'

'I'm taking that compass back to England with me,' I said. 'Just as it is. I'm beginning to develop peculiar ideas.'

'It only tells half the story,' said Byrne. 'We have to solve the other half – why did he come down? I have ideas on that. I want to look at the plumbing of this airplane.'

'I'll leave you to it.' I climbed down from the wing and joined Paul. 'Well, Paul, this is it – journey's end.'

'Yes,' he said softly. He looked up. 'He wasn't a cheat. That South African was lying.'

'No, he wasn't a cheat.' I certainly wasn't going to tell Paul that the compass had been gimmicked – that would really send him round the twist. I said carefully, 'Byrne is trying to find out what was wrong with *Flyaway* to make her come down. Do you mind?'

'Of course not. I'd like to know.' He rubbed his shoulder absently. 'That newspaper back in England. Do you think the editor will publish an apology?'

'An apology? By God, Paul, it'll be more than that. It will be headline news. There'll be a complete vindication.' But it would be better if we could find the body, I thought.

I looked around and tried to put myself in Billson's place. He had either tried to walk out or he hadn't, and both Paul and Byrne were fairly certain that he'd do the right thing and stick close to *Flyaway*; it was standard operating procedure. He must have known that an air search would be laid on and that an aeroplane is easier to spot than a man on foot. What he didn't know was that no one dreamed of searching the Tassili area.

So if he hadn't walked out where was he? Atitel had said he hadn't seen a body, but had he searched?

I said nothing to Paul but walked away and climbed the side of the fallen rock pillar from which I first saw *Flyaway*, and began to walk along it. It was my idea that Billson would want to get out of the sun, so I was looking for a cave.

I found the remains of the body half an hour later. It was in one of the shallow scooped-out caves peculiar to the Tassili and the walls were covered with paintings of men and cattle and hunting scenes. I use the word 'remains' advisedly because scavengers had been at the body after Billson had died and there were pieces missing. What was left was half covered in blown sand, and near by was the dull gleam of a metal box which could have been a biscuit tin.

I touched nothing but went back immediately. Paul hadn't moved but Byrne was on top of *Flyaway* and had opened some kind of a hatch on the side of the fuselage. As I climbed up he said, 'I think I've got it figured.'

'Never mind that,' I said. 'I've found the body.'

'Oh!' He turned his head and looked at Paul, then turned back to me. 'Bad?'

'Not good. I haven't told Paul yet. You know what he's like.'

'You'll have to tell him,' said Byrne definitely. 'He'll have to know and he'll have to see it. If he doesn't he'll be wondering for the rest of his life.' I knew he was right. 'But don't tell him yet. Let's get this figured out first'

'What have you found?'

'If you look in the cockpit you'll see a brass handle on the left. It's a sort of two-way switch governing the flow of gas to the engine. In the position it's set at now it's drawing fuel from the main tank. It was in that position when I found it. Turn it the other way and gasoline is drawn from an auxiliary tank which has been built into the cargo space here. Got the picture?'

'He was drawing from his main tank when he crashed.'

'That's it.' He fumbled in his *gandoura* and came out with the photocopies I had given him. 'According to this, the main tank holds 334 gallons which gives a range of seventeen hundred miles at three-quarters power – that's cruising. But Billson was in a race – he wouldn't be cruising. I reckon he'd be flying on ninety per cent power, so his range would be less. I figure about fifteen hundred miles. It's eighteen hundred from Algiers to Kano, so that's a shortfall of three hundred miles.'

'Hence the auxiliary tank.'

'Yeah. So he needs another three hundred miles of fuel – and more. He'd need more because he might run into head winds, and he'd need a further reserve because he wouldn't want to do anything hairy like finding Kano in the dark and coming in on his last pint of gas. At the same time he wouldn't want this auxiliary tank to be full because that means weight and that would slow him down. I've been trying to figure like Billson and I've come up with the notion that he'd put a hundred fifty gallons in this tank. And you know what?'

'Tell me.'

'That's just about enough to bring him from Algiers to here on the course he was heading.'

'You mean when he switched over from the auxiliary to the main tank his engine failed. Empty main tank?'

'Hell, no! Billson wasn't an idiot – he'd supervise the filling himself. Besides, there are gauges in the cockpit. The engine quit all right, but it wasn't because the tank was empty. I'd like to find out why.'

'How?'

'I'd like to open up the main tank. Think Paul would mind?'

'I'll ask him.'

Paul said he didn't mind; in fact, he developed an interest as Byrne stood with hammer in one hand and cold chisel in the other surveying *Flyaway*, 'I've been tracing the gas lines and I'd say the main tank is in this mid-section here – might even extend into the wing fillets. I'll start there.'

He knelt down, laid the cutting edge of the chisel against the fuselage, and poised the hammer. 'Wait!' said Paul quickly. 'You might strike a spark.'

Byrne turned his head. 'So?'

'The petrol . . .'

'There ain't no petrol – no gasoline – in here, Paul. Not after forty-two years. It'll have evaporated.'

'From a sealed tank?' said Paul sceptically.

'No fuel tank is sealed,' said Byrne. 'There's a venting system. You try to pull gas from a tank without letting air in and you'll get nowhere. It's okay, Paul; there's no fuel in here now.'

There was a clang as he struck the head of the chisel. He struck again and again and presently I went to help him by holding the chisel so he could strike a harder blow. But first I cautioned him to make sure he hit the chisel and not my hand. Slowly we cut a hole into the side of *Flyaway* and, oddly, I thought it an act of desecration.

The hole was about a foot by six inches and at last Byrne was able to bend back the flap of aluminium so that he could look inside. As he did so some brown powder dropped out to lie on the sand. 'Yeah,' he said. 'An integral fuel tank.'

'What's the powder?'

'You always get gunk in the bottom of a tank no matter what you do. The gasoline is filtered going in and filtered coming out but no gas is pure anyway, and you have chemical instabilities and changes.' He put his hand inside and withdrew it holding a handful of the powder. 'More in here than I would have thought, though. If I was Billson and entering a race I'd have the tanks scoured and steam-cleaned before starting.'

I looked at the handful of dried sludge as he put it to his nose. 'More than you would have thought,' I repeated.

'Don't put too much into that,' he advised. 'This is the first time I've looked inside a fuel tank. It ain't a job that's come my way before. There were over three hundred gallons in this tank and God knows what was happening to it while it was evaporating. Constant changes of temperature like you get here could have started all kinds of reaction.'

'All the same,' I said, 'I'd like to have a sample of that stuff.'

'Then find something to put it in.'

I'm old-fashioned enough to use a soap shaving-stick and mine came in a plastic case. It hadn't seen much use in the desert and I'd grown a respectable beard which, Byrne told me, was necked with grey. 'Pretty soon you'll look as distinguished as me,' he had said. I broke off the column of soap and we filled the case with the brown powder and I screwed the cap back on and, for safety, secured it with an adhesive dressing from Byrne's first aid kit.

By that time it was past midday so we prepared a meal. As we ate Paul said, 'When are we leaving?'

Byrne glanced at me and I knew the same thought was in both our minds – we had a burial detail to attend to. He said, 'Early tomorrow.'

I said nothing to Paul until we had finished eating and had drunk our tea. Then I put a new film in my camera because I wanted a full record. I said, 'Paul, brace yourself; there's something I must tell you.'

His head jerked and he stared at me wide-eyed, and I knew he'd guessed. 'You've found him. You've found my father.'

'Yes.'

He got to his feet. 'Where?'

'Not far from here. Are you sure you want to see him? Luke and I can do what's necessary.'

He shook his head slowly. 'No – I must see him.'

'All right. I'll take you.'

The three of us went to the cave and the tears streamed down Paul's face as he looked down at what was left of his father. There were still scraps of flesh and skin left attached to the bones but it was brown and mummified, and a few tendrils of hair clung to the skull which otherwise was picked clean.

I took some photographs and then we began to brush the sand from the skeleton. Underneath the thin layer of sand was rock so we could not bury Peter Billson. Instead we piled a cairn of stones over the remains, Paul sobbing all the time. Then we went back to *Flyaway*, Byrne carrying under his arm the tin box which had been next to the body. There were a couple of other things we had buried with Billson; two packets bearing the name of Brock, the pyrotechnic company. One contained flares, the other smoke signals. Neither had been used because a rescue plane had neither been seen nor heard.

Standing next to *Flyaway* Byrne held out the box to Paul. 'Yours,' he said simply.

He took it and then sat down on the sand and laid the box in front of him. He looked at it for a long time in silence before he stretched out with trembling fingers to open it. This was nothing like opening a Christmas present. There were a lot of papers inside.

In his last days Peter Billson had kept a diary, written in his log-book. I don't propose to go into this in detail because it is most harrowing. A proposal has been made that it be published in a future edition of the *Journal of the Royal Aeronautical Society*. I'm against the idea. A man's mental agonies when facing death ought to be private.

There was Billson's flying licence, a sealed envelope addressed 'To my darling, Helen', a worn leather wallet, a pipe and an empty tobacco pouch, a Shell petrol carnet, a sheaf of bank notes – British, French and Nigerian, and it was strange to see the old big British five-pound note – and a few other small odds and ends.

Paul picked up the letter addressed to his mother. His lower lip trembled. 'I ought to have treated her better,' he whispered, then handed it to me. 'Will you burn that, please? Don't open it.'

I nodded. Byrne stooped and picked up a card. 'The compass deviation card,' he said. 'Not more than a degree and a half out on any course.' He handed it to me. 'It don't matter if a compass has deviation as long as you know what it is.'

Printed on the card was a compass rose around which were written figures in ink. It was signed by the compass adjuster and dated the 4th of January, 1936. I turned it over and saw something scrawled on the back. *I wonder how bloody true this damn thing is?* I nudged Byrne and showed it to him, and said in a low voice, 'He was beginning to guess in the end.'

The diary told Byrne what he wanted to know about the landing. 'He *was* a good flier, Paul,' he said. 'This is how he got down. His engine had quit and he was coming down in a glide with an airspeed of fifty-five knots. There was a low moon and suddenly he saw rocks between him and the moon, so he stalled her. He pulled her nose right up and that lost his speed and his lift at the same time, so he fell out of the sky damn near vertically. What he called a pancake landing. Never heard it called that before. He says, "The old girl pancaked beautifully but I'm afraid both oleo legs are broken – one badly. Never mind, she wouldn't take off from here anyway."'

I read the diary. He had lasted twelve days on two and a half gallons of water. At first the handwriting was firm and decisive but towards the end it degenerated into a scrawl. During the last few days he was apparently feverish and had hallucinations, communing with the painted men on the wall of the cave. The last entry was in a surprisingly firm hand and was a plea that his wife and young son be well looked after. The thought of the £100,000 insurance on his life seemed to comfort him a lot.

Byrne grunted and stood up. 'A guy like that deserves better than a heap of stones. He needs a marker.' He strode to *Flyaway* and jumped up on to the wing, then made his way up the fuselage until he was astride the cowling of the big radial engine. There was a banging and I saw he was un-shipping the propeller.

That gave me an idea. I found the piece of aluminium we had cut from the side of the fuselage and, using the chisel and a small hammer began to incise letters. Paul came over to see what I was doing and stayed to help. When I thought we had finished I said, 'That's it, Paul.'

'No – there's something I want to add.'

So he guided the blade of the chisel while I thumped with the hammer and we added the fourth line so that our rough plaque read:

PETER BILLSON
AIRMAN
1903–1936
Fly away, Peter

# TWENTY-NINE

That seemingly small task took longer than I thought and by the time we had finished the sun was setting. We had our evening meal and went to sleep early. At dawn the following morning Paul and I helped Byrne take out the last two bolts that held the propeller to the shaft and we lowered it to the ground using a rope made up of bits and pieces of the donkey harness. Byrne and I carried it to the grave in the cave while Paul brought the plaque. We set the propeller upright near the grave and Byrne fastened the plaque to the boss using some wire he had found in *Flyaway*.

Then we stood there for a while, doing nothing, but just standing there. Byrne said, 'I guess Billson was the first guy to see those pictures in here in a few thousand years. Maybe this propeller and the inscription will still be there in a thousand years from now. Aluminum don't rust and things change slow in the desert. It's a good marker.'

After a while we went away, leaving Paul to his own thoughts.

In spite of the hobbles the donkeys had moved a fair way in search of grazing and it took us a while to find them and it was an hour before we got them back to the camp. Paul had come back looking sombre and helped us load them. It was time to go.

We took one last long look at *Flyaway* and then began the awkward business of coaxing the donkeys through the narrow cleft in the rock. When we got them out Byrne said, 'Okay – back to Tamrit. Maybe three days.'

Paul said, 'Do you mind waiting a minute? I won't be long. I just want . . .' He swallowed convulsively and looked at me. 'You didn't take a picture of the plaque. I'd like that.'

I glanced at Byrne who said, 'All right, Paul, but not more than fifteen minutes. Tether those donkeys firmly. We'll stroll ahead.' He pointed. 'That's the line we take.'

I unfastened my bag and took out my camera. 'Shall I come with you, or can you take the pictures?'

'I can do it,' he said, so I gave him the camera and he went back through the cleft.

Byrne said, 'Funny thing, this flesh and blood. You wouldn't think he'd feel like that about a man he hardly knew.' He tugged at the donkey rein. 'Let's go; he can catch up.'

We went at an easy pace, threading our way among the rocks for about half a mile. I looked back and said, 'Perhaps we'd better wait for Paul.'

'Huh?' said Byrne abstractedly. He was staring at the ground. 'Been camels here.'

I looked down at the enormous pad marks in the sand. 'You said there were wild camels.'

Byrne dropped on one knee. 'Yeah, I know I did – but wild camels don't repair their own pads.' He traced a line on one of the footprints. 'This one cut its foot and someone put a leather patch on.'

I frowned. 'Can that be done?'

'Sure. I just said so, didn't I?' He stood up and looked around. 'And there it is.'

I turned and, coming up from behind us was a man riding a camel – the Arab who had been with Kissack. He whistled shrilly and from our front came an answering whistle. There were five of them altogether; Kissack and the Arab, and Lash and his two musclemen, all mounted on camels and with no less than six baggage animals. There were no weapons in sight but that didn't mean a thing.

Lash looked down at us from the enormous height a camel confers. 'Mr Byrne,' he said pleasantly. 'And Mr Stafford. Well met. I didn't expect to find you here. Looking for frescoes, I take it?'

Kissack said, 'You're a long way from Kano, Stafford. You've come the wrong way.'

'And there's someone missing.' Lash snapped his fingers. 'What was his name? Ah, yes – Billson. Where is Mr Billson?' One of the men behind him muttered something, and he added, 'And the Tuareg who were with you?'

Byrne dropped the leading rein of his donkey and put his foot on it. 'Paul went sick so they took him back to Djanet.' It was a good improvised lie.

'Strange that we didn't meet him,' observed Lash. He beckoned to the Arab, who came close to him. Lash tossed him the camel reins and the Arab coaxed the camel to its knees and Lash dismounted awkwardly. He had not been riding in the Tuareg manner with his feet on the neck of the camel, but had stirrups. He grimaced. 'Damned uncomfortable beasts.'

'No call to ride them if you don't want,' said Byrne. 'You'd do better with a Tuareg saddle instead of that Chaamba rig.' He jerked his head at the Arab. 'His, I suppose.'

'You suppose correctly.' Lash waved his hand and all the men dismounted, the camels grunting discontentedly. 'Cat got your tongue, Mr Stafford?'

'I've found nothing interesting to say, so far.'

'Oh, you will,' he assured me. 'I'm certain you will. You've both already met Kissack so there's no need to introduce him. As for my other friends, they have no English.'

'Friends!' I said. 'Not guides?'

Lash smiled thinly. 'Propinquity breeds friendship. From the direction you're taking it seems you are returning to Tamrit. Do I gather that you've found what you were looking for?'

'Yeah, we found some paintings,' said Byrne. 'And I guess these are new ones – not seen before.'

'You weren't looking for frescoes,' said Lash flatly. 'Let's cut the cat and mouse act, shall we? You were looking for an aeroplane. Did you find it?'

'I don't know what business it is of yours,' I said.

Lash looked at me unsmilingly. 'Or yours, either. You wouldn't take a warning back in London. You had to play the thick-headed hero and meddle in things that don't concern you.'

So there it was said outright – Lash had been responsible for having me beaten up. 'Who's paying you?' I asked.

'Still meddling? That's dangerous. Now, where's Billson?'

'You've just been told,' I said. 'He went back to Djanet three days ago. He had an injury which was inflamed.' I touched my own shoulder. 'Here.' I was careful not to look at Kissack.

The play of expression on Lash's face was interesting because what I had just said could be circumstantially true. He dismissed Billson for the moment. 'And the aeroplane – where is it?'

'What airplane?' asked Byrne.

Lash sighed. 'Look, Byrne; don't play with me. That's just being stupid.' He turned away and began to talk to the Arab in low tones. The Arab remounted his camel, urged it to its feet, and began to backtrack along the way we had come. If he went far enough he'd find the donkeys Paul had left tethered outside the cleft in the rock. He might even find Paul.

Lash turned back to face us. 'Where's that aeroplane? And don't ask which aeroplane. It's a Northrop "Gamma"

2 – D, built in 1934 and called *Flyaway*. It was crashed around here in 1936 by Peter Billson.' As Byrne opened his mouth Lash held up his hand. 'Don't tell me you don't know what I'm talking about. That would be a big mistake.'

Before Byrne could reply Kissack said, 'You're wasting time, Mr Lash. Let me try.'

'Shut up!' said Lash coldly.

Byrne said, 'I don't know what you're talking about.'

'All right,' said Lash wearily. 'We'll try it your way, Kissack.'

There was suddenly a gun in Kissack's hand. He stepped forward and looked at us speculatively. 'The old geezer knows more about the desert than Stafford, I reckon; so he'd be a better guide.' I looked at the pistol he lifted; the muzzle was pointing directly between my eyes and I knew I was close to death. 'If you don't tell us, Stafford will be dead meat.'

It seemed an eternity before Byrne said, 'Okay – it's about ten kilometres back.'

A grunt of satisfaction came from Lash, and Kissack said, 'Do I kill him anyway, Mr Lash?'

'No,' said Lash. 'We might need him again – and for the same reason. Search them.'

They found our pistols, of course. Kissack checked the loads on the three donkeys. 'You had a rifle – where is it?'

I realized it had been packed on one of Paul's donkeys. Byrne said, 'Left it behind in the Ténéré. Too much sand and the action jammed. That's the only reason you're still alive, Kissack.'

Kissack's face whitened and he lifted the pistol again and pointed at Byrne. 'What, for Christ's sake, did you do to Bailly?'

'That's enough,' commanded Lash. 'We're wasting time. Help me get up on this bloody camel.' They all remounted and now they all had guns showing except Lash, who seemed to be unarmed. 'About face,' he ordered. 'Now, take us to that aeroplane. No tricks, Byrne, or you'll be shot in the back where you stand.'

And so we retraced our steps. I glanced sideways at Byrne whose nose was beakier than ever. He didn't look at me but gazed ahead with a bleak expression. All he had bought was time – ten kilometres' worth of it – say, four or five hours. Then it would all start again.

I wondered about Paul – Byrne had given him fifteen minutes and he ought to have shown up by now. I prayed to God that he would live up to his reputation. Be a *nebbish*, Paul, I thought. Be the invisible man,

I tramped along, conscious of the guns at my back, and a rhyme chittered insanely through my mind over and over again:

> As I was going up the stair,
> I met a man who wasn't there;
> He wasn't there again today,
> I wish to hell he'd go away!

We hadn't been moving long when the Arab appeared and reined his camel alongside Lash. There was a muttered conversation, and Lash called 'Stop!' I stopped and looked back. Lash said silkily, 'More tricks, Byrne? I warned you about that. Follow Zayid.'

The Arab moved in front of us and veered to the left on a course which would take us directly to where we had left Paul. Byrne grunted and shrugged imperceptibly. It seemed that Zayid was a good tracker – good enough to call Byrne's bluff.

We came to the cleft in the rock and there were no donkeys and no sign of Paul. If he was a *nebbish* he had also the characteristics of a boojum because, wraithlike, he had 'softly and suddenly vanished away'. Byrne looked at me and raised his eyebrows, and I shook my head to indicate that I didn't know, either. The little man who wasn't there had indeed gone away.

There was a bit of discussion in French with Zayid pointing out the imprint of donkey hooves in the sand and a clear indication they had gone through the cleft. Lash said, 'Kissack, get down and go through there, and tell me what you see.'

Kissack dismounted and, with drawn gun, went through the cleft. He disappeared from sight because there was a bend half way through and then all was silence except for the snuffling of a camel behind me. Suddenly there was a shout, incoherent and without words, which echoed among the rock pillars, and Kissack came back, yelling excitedly, 'It's there, Mr Lash; the bloody plane is there!'

'Is it?' Lash seemed unmoved. 'Zayid!' The Arab helped him dismount 'Now let's all go and look at this aeroplane which is unaccountably ten kilometres out of position according to Mr Byrne's reckoning.'

There was no choice for it so we went. The camels were too big to go through the cleft so Zayid hobbled them and left them outside, but they took the donkeys through. And there stood *Flyaway* just as we had left her. Zayid and Lash's hired thugs from Algiers weren't very much interested, but Lash and Kissack were. They went towards her, Lash at a steady pace and Kissack practically dancing a jig. 'Is it the one, Mr Lash?' he asked excitedly. 'Is it the one?'

Lash took a paper from his pocket and unfolded it, then studied it and compared it with what was before him. He peered at the side of the fuselage and said, 'Yes, Kissack, my boy; this is indeed the one.'

'Christ!' said Kissack, and jumped up and down. 'Five thousand quid! Five grand!'

'Keep your damned mouth shut,' said Lash. 'You talk too much.' He swung on his heel and stared back at us. 'You – come here!' Byrne and I were hustled forward, and Lash pointed to the hole we had cut. 'Did you do that?'

'Yeah,' said Byrne.

'Why?'

'We found Billson's body. We wanted to mark the grave.' He nodded up towards the engine. 'That's also why we took the propeller.'

'You buried the body?'

'What there was of it. The ground is pretty hard. We built a cairn over it.'

Lash showed his teeth in a grim smile. 'So that's what you did. Then all is not lost.' I didn't know what he meant by that. 'Where is the body?'

Byrne told him. 'Get that propeller, Kissack,' said Lash. 'Take Zayid with you. But first tie these two – arms behind them and ankles secured.'

So we were tied up and left to lie under the rock wall of the gully. Kissack and Zayid went off to find the grave and Lash and the other two ducked into the cleft. Where they were going I didn't know. I said, 'Sorry to have got you into this, Luke.'

He merely grunted and wriggled, and in his struggles with his bonds he fell against me and knocked me over. I fell heavily and a stone dug into my breastbone. When I got back into a sitting position I was panting. 'It's no good,' he said. 'They know how to tie a guy. Struggle and the knots tighten.'

'Yes. What do you think he's going to do?'

'About the airplane – I don't know. But if you're right about what you heard in Bilma he's sure as hell going to kill us. Why he hasn't done it yet I don't know.'

I looked down at the sand on which I had fallen. The imprint of my body was there, but there was no stone. And yet I had felt it. 'Luke! Remember that stone axe-head you found at the Col des Chandeliers? It's in the pocket of my *gandoura*. Think you can get it out?'

I fell on my side and he wriggled around with his back to me, his bound arms groping for my chest. It was a grotesque business, but he got his hands into the pocket and explored around. 'It's right at the bottom.'

'Got it!' Slowly his hands came out under my nose and I saw he grasped the small object between his fingers. It wasn't very big – not more than an inch long – and was probably more of a stone scraper than an axe-head. But the edge was keen enough.

'Trying to bite free?' said an amused voice behind us. Byrne dropped the scraper and it fell to the sand and I rolled on to it. 'You'll need strong teeth to bite through leather thongs,' said Lash.

I turned my head and looked at him. 'Do you blame me for trying?'

'Of course not, Colonel Stafford. It's the duty of every officer to try to escape, isn't it?' He squatted on his heels. 'But you won't, you know.'

'Get lost,' I said sourly.

'No – it will be you who are lost. If your bodies are ever found they'll look something like Billson's, I imagine. But they won't be found near here – oh, dear me, no! We couldn't have a coincidence like that.'

He turned his head at the clanging of metal on rock, and I followed his gaze to see his men coming through the cleft, each carrying two jerricans. They carried them over to *Flyaway* and set them down, then went away again. Lash's attention returned to us. He said to Byrne, 'I've been going over what you've told me since we met this morning and I've come to a conclusion, Byrne. You're a damned liar!'

Byrne grinned tightly. 'You wouldn't say that if I had my hands free.'

'Yes, you lied about practically everything – about the position of this aeroplane, about looking for frescoes – so why shouldn't you have lied about Billson? It would fit your pattern. Where is he?'

'He left us three days ago!' said Byrne. 'His shoulder was bad and getting worse. That was where Kissack shot him. He'd had a hard time in the Ténéré and it had opened up again and, like the goddamned fool he is, he said nothing about it because he wanted to find his Pappy's airplane.'

'So you know about that.' Lash glanced at me. 'Both of you.'

'When I found out how bad his shoulder was I was feared of gangrene,' said Byrne. 'So I sent him back with Atitel and Hami. I guess he's travelling slow, so he should be going down from Tamrit about now.'

'I wish I could believe you.'

'I don't give a hoot in hell whether you believe me or not.'

The men came back carrying four more jerricans which they put with the others. I watched them go back through the cleft. Lash clapped his hands together lightly. 'So, according to you, Billson never came here.'

'Not if he went back three days ago.'

'It doesn't matter,' said Lash, and stood up. 'I won't take the chance. Billson won't leave North Africa. He's a dead man, as dead as you are.'

He went away and Byrne said, 'A real cheerful feller.'

'I wonder where Paul is?' I said in an undertone.

'Don't know, but I ain't putting my trust in a guy like him. Any help from him is as likely as a snowstorm on the Tassili. Where's that goddamn cutter?'

I groped around for a full five minutes, sifting the sand. 'Got it!'

'Then hold on to it, and don't let go. We may have a chance yet.'

Kissack and Zayid came back carrying the propeller. Kissack showed the plaque to Lash who laughed. He didn't toss it aside but walked over to where the donkeys were patiently waiting and carefully stowed it. Then he climbed up on to the wing of *Flyaway* and looked into the cockpit. 'He'll see that the compass is missing,' I muttered.

'Maybe not,' said Byrne.

Lash made only a superficial investigation of the cockpit but then climbed up on to the fuselage and opened the cargo hatch. He peered inside, then said something to Kissack who was standing below. He seemed highly satisfied. He next made his way up the fuselage towards the engine where he sat astride the cowling just as Byrne had done. He picked up something and examined it, laughed again and tossed it down to Kissack, and pointed to us.

Kissack walked in our direction. He stood over us and held something in his fingers. 'Where's the spanner that fits this?' It was one of the nuts that secured the propeller to the engine shaft.

'Find it yourself,' said Byrne.

Kissack kicked him in the ribs. I said quickly, 'It's packed in a tool kit aboard that donkey – the one in the middle.'

Kissack grinned at me and went away. Byrne said, 'No need to help them, Max.'

'I'm not. I don't want them searching all the loads. The compass is packed among my kit.' I looked across at Lash. 'Did you leave all the nuts there?'

'Yeah – in a neat row on top of the engine cowling. I'm a real tidy guy.' His voice was bitter.

Lash's men came through the cleft carrying four more jerricans; that made twelve and they apparently went back for more. A jerrican holds a nominal four gallons – actually a little more – so there was fifty gallons standing there on the sand. I said, 'What the hell do they want with all that water?'

'What makes you think it's water?'

I blinked in astonishment. 'You think it's petrol!'

'They're putting the propeller back, ain't they?'

'They're crazy,' I said. 'They can't fly it out of here.'

'They don't intend to,' said Byrne. 'Remember Paul's Land-Rover? I figure they're going to burn it.'

Destroying evidence of what? I watched them replace the propeller. It was a much more laborious task for them to put it back than it was for us to take it off. At one time all five of them were engaged on the job and it was then that I took a chance and had a go at cutting the thongs around Byrne's wrists. Holding the polished and sharpened stone blade I sawed at the leather without being able to see what I was doing because Byrne and I were back to back.

Suddenly he said, 'Enough! They've finished.' I palmed the blade and twisted around again to look at *Flyaway*. Kissack and Zayid were handing up jerricans to Lash, who stood on the wing and was pouring petrol into the auxiliary tank. The other two were still engaged in ferrying more jerricans. Lash put fifty gallons into the tank and there was still another fifty available because I counted twenty-four jerricans in all.

'Three camel loads,' said Byrne. 'I did wonder about all those pack animals.'

Lash and Kissack came over to us. Byrne looked up at them. 'I said it to Wilbur and I said it to Orville – "It'll never get off the ground."'

'Very funny,' said Lash. 'Kissack's come up with a suggestion. He thinks we ought to put one of you into the cockpit.' He studied us, then turned to Kissack and said objectively, 'It can't be Byrne – he's too old and it might show. If it's anybody at all it'll be Stafford.'

Kissack shrugged. 'Suits me.'

Lash looked at me. 'I don't know,' he said reflectively. 'The clothes are wrong.'

'They'd be burnt.'

'Mmm. Then there are the teeth. This plane's going to be found sometime, Kissack, and someone might decide to do a thorough investigative job. If they discover the wrong man in the cockpit, then a hell of a lot of questions are going to be asked.'

'After more than forty years!'

'Stranger things have happened. No, on balance I think we'll leave things as they are. We have Billson's body so let's leave it at that. It'll look as though he got out before the plane went up.' Lash looked down at me and smiled. 'Don't let your hopes soar, Stafford. It's merely a reprieve.'

I said, 'You're a cold-blooded bastard!'

Kissack kicked me in the ribs and Lash caught his arm. 'Don't do that. I detest gratuitous violence.'

Kissack said, 'Gratty-what violence?'

'I mean I don't get my kicks out of it as you do.' Lash turned and looked at *Flyaway*. 'It doesn't *look* crashed,' he complained. 'Not so it would burn out. We'll have to raise the tail and tip the whole plane forward on to the engine.'

'Hell, that thing's heavy!'

'Not as heavy as all that, and there are five of us. All we have to do is to lift up the tail and put stones under it. When we get the pile of stones high enough it'll tip forward like a see-saw. But first, some petrol, I think.'

They walked away towards *Flyaway* and Lash climbed up on to the wing again. Kissack handed him a full jerrican and Lash poured it into the cockpit, and then poured another into the cargo compartment. Then he did the same thing again with two more jerricans and I saw the shimmering haze of evaporating petrol above the aircraft. It was like a bomb and only needed a spark to explode.

All five of them assembled at the tail. While four of them lifted the other piled stones underneath and gradually the tail rose higher and higher. While all eyes were off me I got busy with the stone blade at Byrne's wrists. I didn't see *Flyaway* tip over but when I looked her fuselage was at forty-five degrees and her tail was pointing to the sky. The rending noise had been the propeller bending under the sudden weight of the engine as it hit the ground.

They poured more petrol into her and Kissack used the last can to lay a trail across the sand. He didn't want to be too close when he tossed in a naked flame. He was quite a competent arsonist. Lash, standing close by us, took a paper from his pocket; I think it was the same one he had used to identify *Flyaway*. 'I won't need this any more,' he said conversationally, and lit one corner with a cigarette lighter. He held it up to make sure it was aflame, then tossed it into the petrol-soaked sand.

At first nothing happened. In the bright glare of the sun it was impossible to see the flames as they ran towards *Flyaway*. But then she exploded in fire; flames gouted out of the cockpit with a roar as though under forced draught, and ran up the fuselage right up to the tail and rudder until she was totally enveloped.

The donkeys brayed and plunged in fright. Lash shouted, 'Get those bloody donkeys out of here!' I don't think he had realized until then how much heat so much petrol would generate. They rounded up the donkeys and pushed them through the cleft, then went through themselves, leaving us lying there.

I took the opportunity of trying to cut the thongs at Byrne's wrists again, but he snatched himself away. 'For Christ's sake!' he said. 'Roll over against the rock and keep your head down. That goddamn auxiliary tank will be going up any second.'

We rolled over and huddled against the rock, keeping our faces away from the burning aeroplane. Behind us, seventy yards away, the auxiliary fuel tank exploded like a bomb and I felt a wave of searing heat. There was a pattering noise

all about and something hit me in the small of the back.
When I looked at *Flyaway* again she had blown in two, and
her tailplane and rudder were lying some distance from the
forward section. One wing was also detached.

And I had lost my stone blade.

After that the flames died down very quickly and Lash
came back. He looked down at us quizzically. 'Feeling a trifle singed? Never mind, it will make your hair grow.'

'Go to hell!' said Byrne.

Lash ignored him and looked at the wreck of *Flyaway*. 'A
really nice job,' he said with satisfaction. 'I had considered
using gelignite but it might not have looked right. This
looks perfectly natural. Anyone who goes to the movies
knows that crashed aircraft burn well.' He beckoned to
Kissack. 'Get these two on their feet and walking. We'll
visit the grave.'

Kissack bent down and cut the thongs at my ankles and
he wasn't particularly considerate about it because he cut
me, too. I got to my feet laboriously because my hands
were still tied behind my back and I lost my balance. Lash
and Zayid led the way, with Byrne and me following,
Kissack behind us with a pistol in his hand. The other two
tagged on behind.

The cairn of stones had been disarranged and Billson's
skull was showing. Lash looked down at it unemotionally.
'Well, we've got the body but we can't leave it like this, can
we? I mean, the man wouldn't have died and conveniently
buried himself.'

He gave orders in French and his men began to disman-
tle the cairn. I said, 'How did you know the plane would
need burning?'

Lash shrugged. 'I didn't. If it had burned forty years ago
it would have saved me a considerable amount of trouble.
But I didn't take the chance. I never take chances. I came
prepared for anything.'

He looked down as the desiccated corpse was revealed. 'Kissack wanted to put this in the cockpit before we burned the plane – but Kissack is a fool, as I'm sure you've learned. As soon as he told me there was an arm missing I vetoed that suggestion. Everything must not only look right – it must *be* right. I never take chances.'

The body was soon wholly uncovered. Lash looked down at it. 'Is this as you found it?'

'Yes.'

'I don't believe you. He would have left a message of some kind – left his papers.' His head came up and he stared at us. 'Where are they?'

'Maybe you just burned them,' said Byrne. 'You didn't search that airplane too well.'

'But you did,' said Lash. He turned to Kissack and said abruptly, 'When we get back down there I want those donkeys unloaded and everything searched.'

'All right,' said Kissack. He held the pistol negligently in his hand, muzzle down.

I wasn't worried about Billson's papers because Paul had them, wherever Paul was, which was probably a long way over the horizon by now. But if our stuff was searched they'd find the compass. Why in hell I was worried about that I don't know; it should have been the least of my worries.

I said, 'Kissack!'

'What?'

'When you burned Paul Billson's Land-Rover did you search it first?'

'What the hell? No, I didn't. What's it to you?'

'Nothing. You're getting paid five thousand pounds for this job, aren't you? I bet Lash is getting ten times as much.'

Lash's eyes flickered. 'Mr Stafford exaggerates.'

I stared at Kissack. 'Didn't Lash tell you?'

'Tell me what, for God's sake? What's Billson's Land-Rover got to do with my five thousand quid?'

I shrugged. 'Just that Billson was carrying quite a lot of cash. More than five thousand – much more. I can't believe Lash didn't tell you.'

'How much more?' Kissack said hoarsely.

'Fifty-six thousand in British currency. It was in his suit-cases in the back of the Land-Rover.'

Kissack's eyes widened, and he whirled on Lash. 'Is that true?'

'How would I know?' said Lash in a bored voice. 'Keep your cool, man. Stafford's just trying to needle you.'

'Is he, now? I wonder?'

Lash lost his boredom. 'Damn it, if I'd known do you think I wouldn't have told you? Do you think I'd have stood by and let you burn money? I'm not such a – '

He had no time to say more because there was a shock-ingly loud bang from quite close and the top of Kissack's head blew off, spattering grey fragments of brain all about. His knees buckled and he collapsed to the ground, letting the pistol fall as he did so.

Paul Billson always did over-react.

# THIRTY

An army rifle, even one of First World War vintage, is intended to kill men at ranges of up to a thousand yards or more, and an averagely good marksman finds it a comfortably good tool at four hundred yards. Paul Billson was not an averagely good marksman; in fact, he was not a marksman at all and later confessed that it was the first shot he had ever fired, whether in anger or otherwise. But even Paul Billson could not miss killing Kissack at a range of fifteen feet.

By his account he had gone to the grave and taken his photographs, then spent some minutes in contemplation. He had then gone back, picked up his two donkeys and followed the line Byrne had given him. He had spotted us surrounded by Lash's men on camels and tactfully drew aside. Luckily for him – and us – he had gone over rock, otherwise Zayid might have seen his tracks. He watched us led into captivity and wondered what to do about it.

He didn't say so but I think his first instinct was to make a run for it, yet I might be maligning him. Anyway, where was he to run? It was three days on foot back to Tamrit and he must have known that he could never find his way there by himself. But whatever his thoughts were he decided to stick around. And he discovered that Byrne's Lee-Enfield was packed on one of his donkeys.

He went away and found a hole among the rocks and tethered the donkeys. One of them was inclined to bray, which frightened him because he thought it might be heard and they'd come looking for him. But he did the right thing. He unloaded the donkeys, hobbled them as he had seen Byrne do, and turned them loose. Then he looked at the rifle.

He had seen guns at a distance but had never handled one, nothing unusual in an Englishman of his age who had missed war service because of physical unfitness. There are not that many guns floating loose about Luton. He fiddled about with it, being careful not to touch the trigger, and worked the bolt action, trying to find the principle by which it worked. Eventually, more or less by accident, he pressed a catch and the magazine fell into the palm of his hand. It was empty, which was why no bullets were being inserted into the breech.

He thought about that for a moment and soon came to the conclusion that the ammunition would not be kept far from the weapon. He knew that Byrne was in the habit of keeping a full magazine in the pouch slung around his neck but surely there must be more bullets somewhere. He began to search through the loads he had taken from the donkeys and eventually found an opened packet containing eleven rounds.

When he tried to put bullets into the magazine they wouldn't fit so he tried them the other way around and they went in sweetly, compressing the leaf spring in the magazine. He found that it held five bullets. He pushed the magazine into the rifle and worked the action slowly and was rewarded by the sight of a cartridge being pushed firmly and smoothly into the breech. He now had the rifle loaded.

He knew there was such a thing as a safety-catch and soon found the small switch-like lever on the side of the rifle which would cover or uncover a red spot. His problem

was that he didn't know when it was on and when it was
off. It never occurred to him to take out the magazine,
eject the round from the breech and then test the trigger
with an empty gun. At last he reasoned that red would
mean danger, so that when the red spot showed the safety-
catch was off. He covered the red spot and stood up,
holding the rifle.

Paul was not a man of action, rather a man of reaction.
He could be pushed – by men, by circumstances, or as
English, the journalist, had pushed – but it was not his habit
to initiate action. So he stood there, irresolute, wondering
what was the best thing to do. He then decided that it would
not be a good idea to walk in on Lash and company by way
of the cleft in the rocks which was now the common highway to *Flyaway*; instead, he would try to approach from the
other direction. That was a good idea.

He found a canteen and filled it with water, put the
remaining six bullets into his pocket, and then set off to
explore, carrying the rifle somewhat gingerly as though it
might explode of its own volition. He knew his direction to
the cleft so he set off at right-angles to that, skirting the base
of a rock pillar. To anyone knowing Paul Billson it must
have been an unlikely sight.

He kept track of his progress by counting his paces, and
when he had counted two hundred double strides
he veered to the left and carried on. After five minutes he
stopped in his tracks because he heard voices. Cautiously he
peered round a rock and saw Kissack and Zayid passing by
within spitting distance. They were carrying a propeller.

That gave him his location; he was somewhere near his
father's grave. He waited a while and then stepped out to
where they had walked and immediately knew where he
was, so he walked a little way until he came to the cave
where his father was buried. The rocks of the cairn had been
rudely tumbled aside and he saw the white bone of his

father's skull. That angered him very much and he trembled with rage.

His impulse was to walk down to *Flyaway* and shoot Kissack, but he reined himself in. He had no illusions about his prowess with a rifle and seriously doubted if, when it came to the push, he *could* kill Kissack – not in a straight shooting match. And then there were the others. I rather doubt if the plight of Byrne and myself crossed his mind at that time.

He stopped over the grave and picked up a rock, intending to rebuild the cairn. Then he paused with the rock still held in his hand and thought about it. Logical thought did not come naturally to Paul Billson; as I have said, he was a man who reacted to stimuli. But he thought now and carefully replaced the rock where he had found it, then went away and sat behind a rock out of sight of the cave to work things out.

Presently he saw smoke drifting overhead, and then came the dull, echoing thud as the auxiliary fuel tank of *Flyaway* exploded. He assumed, correctly, that *Flyaway* was being destroyed. He didn't know why, but then, very few people did. He stood up and looked towards the source of the smoke, again irresolute.

Then he turned and looked through a gap in the rocks towards the grave. Paul didn't know it but he was standing by what a rifleman would consider a perfect loophole. Two rocks standing on a third, the gap between them about six inches. The depth of the gap was nearly three feet, and from where he was standing he could see the grave, about twenty feet away. There were even two flat ledges on which he could plant his elbows to give aiming support.

Chance, circumstance, and the odd workings of Paul's mind had put him in exactly the right place at the right time. Soon he heard voices.

A little later he fired the rifle.

* * *

The muzzle blast of an army rifle fired at close range can be quite frightening. I suspect that, given the standard army firing squad of eight men, even if they all missed the victim would probably die of shock. That single shot, coming unexpectedly, froze everybody into a tableau as Kissack fell bonelessly to the ground.

The bullet that smashed into the back of Kissack's head passed through him as though he wasn't there. It entered the cave, ricocheted around the walls and came out *spaaang*, giving Zayid a fright. But it wasn't that which broke the tableau; it was the dry metallic clatter, coming from nowhere in particular, as Paul worked the action to put another round up the spout.

Lash pulled a pistol from nowhere at exactly the same time as Byrne dived for the gun Kissack had dropped. It's difficult to do a rugby tackle when your hands are tied behind your back but I did my best and went for Lash's legs. His pistol exploded and I felt a smashing blow in my left arm and tumbled to one side. But I had brought him down.

Then bullets were buzzing over me like bees as Byrne shot over and past me, and out of the corner of my eye I saw Zayid go down in a tumbled heap. Paul added to the row with another blast just as Lash recovered enough to raise his gun intending to shoot at Byrne. I swung my legs around and booted at his wrist just before Byrne got him. Byrne was shooting police-fashion; square on to the target and in a crouch, with arms extended and both hands on the butt of the pistol. He pumped three shots into Lash who jerked convulsively, then flopped about on the ground and began to scream.

Paul fired again and the bullet ricocheted from rock to rock. Byrne yelled above Lash's screams, 'Paul, stop shooting, for Christ's sake! You'll kill us all.'

I tried to lever myself up, but I used the wrong arm and got a jolt of pain. When I finally sat up and looked around

I saw the bodies of Zayid and Kissack and Lash, who was screaming just as Bailly had screamed in the Ténéré. The other two had vanished. It had all happened within, perhaps, twenty seconds.

Byrne yelled again. 'Come out, Paul. Show yourself.'

Paul came from behind a rock. His face was white as paper and his hands shook uncontrollably. Byrne stepped forward and caught the rifle as it fell. 'Did you fill the magazine?'

Paul nodded wordlessly.

'Any more ammunition?'

Paul dug his hand into his pockets and passed the cartridges over. He stared at Lash and then clapped his hands over his ears to shut out the endless screaming. I wanted to do the same but I couldn't lift my left arm. When a man is killed in the films he folds up decorously and has the decency to die quietly; in real life it's different.

Byrne pulled back the bolt of the rifle and an empty brass case flew out He slammed the bolt forward and locked it and then, without warning, stepped over to Lash, put the muzzle of the rifle to his temple, and pulled the trigger.

The shot crashed out and after the echoes had died away the silence was shocking. Byrne looked at me and his face was drawn and haggard. 'My responsibility,' he said harshly. 'Three bullets – one in the belly. He wouldn't have lived. Best this way.'

'Okay, Luke,' I said quietly. So died a man who said he detested gratuitous violence but who would kill coldly to a plan. In my book Lash had been worse than Kissack.

Byrne was reloading the rifle. 'You hurt?'

'I caught one in the arm – I'm flying on one wing.'

He grunted. 'You two wait here,' he said, and went off without another word.

Paul walked over and looked down at Lash. 'So quick,' he whispered. Whether he was referring to what Byrne had done or to the entire action I didn't know. He turned his head. 'You all right?'

'Help me up.' My left arm was beginning to really hurt; it felt as though an electric shock was being applied at irregular intervals. As he hoisted me to my feet I said, 'You did well, Paul; very well.'

'Did I?' he said colourlessly.

'These bastards were seriously considering burning me in the plane,' I said. 'And if I know Kissack he'd have liked to burn me alive – and so would Lash if he thought it would contribute to realism.' I paused; I was waiting for the sound of shots but all was silent.

Paul turned a puzzled face towards me. 'What was it all about, Max?'

'I don't know,' I said. 'But I'm going to find out. And now, for God's sake, will you cut me loose? But be careful with my arm.'

Byrne came back half an hour later. The rifle was slung over his shoulder and he was leading two pack camels. He leaned the rifle against a rock and said, 'No problem,' then held out his wrists. 'I don't remember breaking free,' he said. 'I just did it. You did well with that stone chopper.'

'The other two men?'

He indicated Lash. 'The paymaster is dead, so no pay – no fight. Trash from the Maghreb. I gave them three camels and water and told them to get to hell out of it. They won't bother us none.' He tossed the leading rein to Paul and unslung a box from the pack saddle. 'Let's see your arm.'

He pronounced it to be broken, which I already knew, set it in a rough and ready way and put it in an improvised sling. 'We'd better get you back to civilization,' he said.

But there was much to do before that. Paul helped him load the three bodies on to the camels and they went away. Where they went I don't know but they came back two hours later without the bodies. In that time I had finished rebuilding the cairn over Billson's body. Byrne laid the aluminium plaque on top. 'No propeller,' he said wryly. 'Can't shift it again.'

We cleaned up around the cave, picking up spent cartridge cases and other evidence, then went back to *Flyaway*, and Paul looked at the blackened wreckage and shook his head. 'Why?' he asked again.

No one answered him.

'We leave tomorrow at dawn,' said Byrne. 'But this time we ride.'

And so we did, with Byrne grumbling incessantly about the damnfool way the Chaambas rigged their camels for riding.

# THIRTY-ONE

As Edward FitzGerald might have put it, 'Djanet was Paradise enow'. Four days later Byrne saw me settled comfortably in a hotel room, then went away, probably to see Atitel and to tell him that his broken leg was worth ten camels, after all – delivered to Bilma at the beginning of next season. I wondered how much a broken arm was worth.

When he came back he had done that, and more. He had also gone to the telegraph office and cabled Hesther Raulier. I don't know exactly what he'd put in the cable but it was enough for Hesther to promise to send a chartered aircraft to Djanet to return Paul and me to Algiers. 'I'd like for you to get that arm fixed,' he said. 'But not here. Hesther knows the right people in Algiers – it can be arranged quietly.'

I nodded. 'Then we've got things to do,' I said. 'Is there such a thing as a Commissioner for Oaths in Djanet?'

'Huh?'

'An American would call him a Notary Public.'

His brow cleared. 'Sure there is. Why?'

'I want to put down in writing everything we found wrong with *Flyaway* – all about the compass and the stuff in the bottom of the main fuel tank. And I want you to sign it before an official witness. I'll sign it too, but we'll keep

Paul out of it. Do you think you can find a typewriter anywhere?'

'There's one in the hotel office,' he said. 'I'll borrow that.'

So I spent half a day typing the statement, with many references to Byrne to elucidate the more technical bits. I did it one-handedly but that was no hardship because my typing is of the hunt-and-peck order, anyway. Next morning we went to the notary public and both of us signed every page which also had the embossed seal of the notary public. It didn't matter that he couldn't understand the content; it was our signatures he was witnessing.

Then I brought out my plastic shaving-soap container and that was put into an envelope and sealed and Byrne and I signed our names across the flap. I watched Byrne laboriously writing his name in an unformed handwriting, his tongue sticking out of the side of his mouth like that of a small schoolboy. But it came out clear enough – Lucas Byrne.

As we left the official's office Byrne said, 'You got ideas?'

'Some – but they're pretty weird.'

'Could be nothing but. It figures. If you find any answers let me know.'

'I'll do that,' I said.

The three of us lunched at a restaurant and inhaled a few beers and then Byrne drove us back to the hotel to pick up our bags and then the few miles to In Debiren where the airstrip was and where a Piper Comanche awaited us. Paul, who once didn't have the grace to thank anyone for anything, positively embarrassed Byrne, who adopted a 'Shucks, 't'warn't nuthin'' attitude.

I said, 'Paul, get in the plane – I want a couple of last words with Luke.' Once he was out of earshot I said, 'He's right, you know; thanks aren't enough.'

Byrne smiled. 'I hope to God you're right.' He produced an envelope, sealed and with my name on it. 'This is for you. I told you I'd bill you. You can settle it with Hesther.'

I grinned and tucked it in the pocket of my *gandoura* unopened. 'What will you do now?'

'Get back to the Aïr and my own business – go back to leading the quiet life. Give my regards to Hesther.'

'I'll give her your love,' I said.

He looked at me quizzically. 'You do that and she'll laugh like a hyaena.' He took my hand. 'Look after yourself, now. From what I hear, the big cities can be more dangerous than the desert.'

'I'll bear that in mind,' I promised and got into the Comanche.

So we took off and, as the plane circled the airstrip I saw that Byrne hadn't waited. The Toyota was trailing a cloud of dust and heading south to Bilma and, from there, to the Aïr.

At first, during the flight north, I was preoccupied with my own thoughts and gazed sightlessly at the vast dun expanse which flowed below. There were too many damn loose ends to tie up and I couldn't begin to see where to start.

Presently I took out Byrne's envelope and handed it to Paul. 'Can you open that for me?'

'Of course.' He ripped off the end, shook out the contents and gave it back to me.

As Byrne had promised he'd billed me, and it was all set out clearly, payable in pounds sterling. His own services he had put down as a guide at £30 a day; at thirty-three days that came to £990. Then there was the purchase of gasoline – so many litres at such-and-such; oil and new tyres; camel hire – and the purchase of five camels at £100 each. He also added in half the cost of a new Toyota Land Cruiser which seemed quite steep until I remembered how Kissack had shot Byrne's truck full of holes in the Ténéré. Altogether the bill came to a little over £5000.

There was no charge for saving life. Byrne was one hell of a fellow.

As I put it away Paul said happily, 'I'm looking forward to seeing that editor's face again.'

'Um – Paul; do me a favour. Don't go off pop as soon as we get to London. I don't want you to tell anyone a damn thing until I give you the word. Please!'

'Why not?'

I sighed. 'I can't tell you now, but will you believe me when I say it's for your own good? In any case, you can't tell anyone about Lash and Kissack.'

Again he said, 'Why not?'

'Jesus!' I said. 'Paul, you *killed* a man! Shot the top of his head right off. You don't want to open that can of worms. Look, you can tell the newspapers about finding *Flyaway* and your father's body, but just give me time to find out something, will you? I want to discover what the hell it was all about.'

'All right,' he said. 'I won't say anything until you say I can.'

'And you won't *do* anything, either. Promise?'

'I promise.' He was silent for a while, then he said, 'I don't remember much about my father. I was only two when he died, you know.'

'I know.'

'About the only thing I can remember was him bouncing me on his knee and singing that nursery rhyme; you know, the one that goes, "Fly away, Peter! Fly away, Paul!" I thought that was a great joke.' So would Billson. Paul rubbed his chin. 'But I didn't like my stepfather much.'

I cocked my eye at him. 'Aarvik? What was wrong with him?'

'Oh, not Aarvik; he came later. I mean the other one.'

I said, 'Are you telling me your mother married *three* times?'

'That's right. Didn't you know?'

'No, I didn't,' I said thoughtfully. 'What was his name?'

'Can't remember. He wasn't around much, and I was only a kid. After I was about four years old he wasn't around at all. It's all a long time ago.'

Indeed it is, Paul; indeed it is!

He didn't say much after that revelation and neither did I. We lapsed into silence and I was still mulling it over when we landed at Algiers.

The big Mercedes with the Arab chauffeur was waiting by the hangar as the Comanche taxied up and we were soon wafted luxuriously to the heights of Bouzarea overlooking Algiers. If the chauffeur was surprised at carrying a Targui he didn't show it.

We stopped at the small door in the wall which opened as silently and mysteriously as before, and Paul and I walked towards the house. Hesther Raulier was still lying on the chaise-longue and might never have moved but that she was wearing a different dress. As we approached she put down her cigar and stood up.

Suddenly her monkey face cracked into a big grin and she laughed raucously. 'Jesus, Stafford! What in hell do you think you're doing? Auditioning for *The Desert Song*?'

She put me to bed fast and summoned the doctor who, apparently, was on tap immediately. She said, 'Luke put a couple of words into his cable that meant something bad – stuff I hadn't heard since the Revolution – so I got in Fahkri. He's used to gunshot wounds and knows how to keep his mouth shut.'

Dr Fahkri examined my arm, asked how long ago it had happened, and then told me the bullet was still in there. He deadened the arm, sliced it open and took out the bullet, stitched it up again and put on a proper splint. I said to

Hesther, 'Better have him look at Paul. He took a bullet in the shoulder about a month ago.'

She spoke to Fahkri in Arabic and he nodded and went away, then she turned to me. 'What happened out there?'

'Kissack happened,' I said. 'He and a man called Lash – and four others.' I gave her an edited version of what had happened, and ended up by saying, 'I don't know what we'd have done without Luke Byrne.'

'Luke's a good man,' she said simply. 'But what was it all about?'

'Whatever set it off was in England. I suppose Paul really started the ball rolling but he triggered something, a sort of time bomb that was lying around for forty-two years. I've got a few questions to ask. If I find any answers I'll let you know.'

'You do that.' She stood up. 'You can't go back to England dressed as a Targui.'

I shrugged. 'Why not? London is full of Arabs these days, and nobody there could tell the difference.'

'Nonsense. I'll get a tailor in tomorrow and you'll have a suit the day after. You and Paul both.'

We stayed in Algiers for four days, more so I could recuperate from Fahkri's surgery than anything else. I lazed about and read the English newspapers that Hesther bought me so that I could catch up on the news. Everything was going to hell in a handcart, as usual.

Once, referring to Paul, she said, 'That guy's changed – changed a lot. He's quieter and not as nervy.'

I grinned. 'God knows why. What happened to him is enough to make anyone go screaming up the wall.'

On the fourth day we left on an Air Algérie flight to Orly. The interior of the plane was decorated in a tasteful shade of emerald green. Green may be the Arab colour but this plane had pictures of jaunting cars and scenes from Killarney because it had been bought second-hand from Aer Lingus. However, it got us to Orly all right and we transferred to the London flight.

An hour later we were at Heathrow. It was raining and it looked as though it had never stopped since I had left.

# THIRTY-TWO

I had telephoned Heathrow from Orly and so there was a car waiting with a driver, since I could not drive a car with a broken arm. He drove us the short distance to the Post House Hotel and I told him to stick around while I booked in. There were reservations for Paul and me in adjoining rooms, so we went up and I got him settled.

Paul, of course, was dead broke – he hadn't a penny – and that suited me fine because I wanted him immobilized. I didn't give him any money, but said, 'Paul, stay here until I get back. If you want anything, order it – it's on the house. But don't leave the hotel.'

'Where are you going?'

'I have things to do,' I said uninformatively.

I went down to the lobby, cashed a sheaf of travellers' cheques, picked up the driver, and gave him an address in Marlow. As we left the hotel-studded environs of Heathrow I reflected that the Post House was the ideal sort of anonymous caravanserai to hide Paul; I didn't want his presence in England known yet, nor mine, either.

The car pulled up outside Jack Ellis's house and I walked up and rang the doorbell. Judy Ellis opened it, looked at me uncertainly, and said, 'Yes?' interrogatively.

I had met Jack's wife only three or four times. Stafford Security Consultants Ltd was not the kind of firm that drew

wives into the business orbit; we had other ways of ensur-
ing company loyalty, such as good pay. I said, 'Is Jack in?
I'm Max Stafford.'

'Oh, I didn't recognize you. Yes, he's just got back. Come
in.' She held the door wide and let me into the hall while
making all the usual excuses wives make when the boss
drops in on an unexpected visit. The place didn't look all
that untidy to me. 'Jack,' she called. 'Mr Stafford's here.'

As I stood in the doorway of the living-room Ellis rose
from an armchair, laying aside a newspaper. He looked at
me questioningly. 'Max?'

I was suddenly aware of the beard – now neatly trimmed
by a barber Hesther had brought in, the light-coloured suit
of a decidedly foreign cut, and the black silk sling which cradled my left arm. I suppose that to Jack it was a disguise.
'Hello, Jack.'

'Well, for God's sake! Come in.' He seemed glad to
see me.

I was aware of Judy hovering in the background. 'Er . . .
this isn't a social call, Jack. I want to talk to you.'

'I hope to God it isn't,' he said. 'And I want to talk to you.
Where have you been? Come into my study.'

He hustled me away and I smiled pleasantly at Judy in
passing. In the study he offered me a chair. 'What's wrong
with the arm?'

'Just broken.' I smiled. 'It only hurts when I laugh.'

'God, I'm glad to see you. You just disappeared, and I
didn't know where to look. All hell's been breaking loose.'

'I've not been away long – just over a month,' I said
mildly. 'You haven't lost your grip in so short a time?'

'If you want to put it that way, I suppose I have.' His
voice was grim. 'But I never had much grip to begin with,
did I?'

It was evident that something was griping him so I said,
'Give me a drink, sit down and tell me all about it.'

He took a deep breath, then said, 'Sorry.' He left the room and returned with a tray on which were bottles and glasses. 'Scotch okay?' I nodded, and as he poured the drinks he said, 'As soon as you left the whole character of the company changed.'

'In what way?'

'Well, as a minor example, we're now letting dogs out without handlers.' He handed me a glass.

'Starting with Electronomics,' I suggested.

He looked at me in surprise. 'How did you know that?'

'Never mind. Go on.'

He sat down and looked broodingly into the glass which he held cradled in his hands. 'The big thing is that we're now up to our necks in industrial espionage. You've been away six weeks and I'm already running three penetration exercises.'

'Are you, by God? On whose authority?'

'Charlie Malleson twisted my arm.'

I stared at him. 'Jack, you're not there to take instructions from Charlie. He's just the bloody accountant – a number juggler. You're supposed to be standing in for me – running the operational side – and that doesn't mean penetration operations. We're in security; that's what the name of the firm means. Now, how did Charlie twist your arm?'

Ellis shrugged. 'He just told me to do it.'

'Didn't you squawk?'

'Of course I bloody well squawked.' His ire was rising. 'But what the hell could I do? I'm not a shareholder, and he brought Brinton in to back him up, and when the bosses say "Do!", you do. Max, this last week I've been on the verge of quitting, but I held on in the hope that you'd come back.' He stuck his finger out at me. 'Any moment from now I'm going to get instructions to penetrate one of our own clients. That would be a laugh, wouldn't it? Playing both ends against the middle. But it's not what I joined the firm for.'

'Not very ethical,' I agreed. 'Take it easy, Jack; we'll sort this out. You say Charlie brought in Lord Brinton?'

'The old bastard is in and out all the time now.' Jack caught himself. 'Sorry. I forgot he's a friend of yours.'

'Not particularly. You say he comes to the office frequently?'

'Two or three times a week. He has himself driven two whole blocks in his Rolls-Royce.'

'Does he have access to files?'

Jack shrugged. 'Not through me. I don't know about Charlie.'

'Oh, we can't have that.' I thought about it for a moment, then said, 'I talked about you to Charlie before I left. It was agreed that if you could handle my job then you'd be made managing director. That would entitle you to a parcel of shares because that's the way we work. I was going to start operations in Europe – go for the multinationals. Didn't Charlie say anything about this?'

'Not a word.'

'I see.' I sipped my scotch. 'This is a surprising development but it's not what I came to see you about. Remember what we were doing just before I left?'

He nodded. 'Looking for a half-wit called Billson.'

'Well, I found him, and that led to other things. I want you to re-open the account of Michelmore, Veasey and Templeton, but do it quietly. Don't open a formal file, and keep all details locked away from prying eyes.'

'Same as before?'

'Exactly the same as before. No one sees it – especially not Charlie or Brinton. Now, this is what I want you to do.' As I reeled off my requirements Jack's eyes got bigger. I ended up by saying, 'Oh yes; and that analytical chemist must be a forensic type, able to go on to the stand in court as an expert witness.'

He looked up from the notebook in which he was scribbling. 'Quite a packet.'

'Yes. Now, don't worry about what's happening to the firm. Leave that in my hands and I'll sort it out. Carry on as usual. One more thing, Jack; I'm not in England. You haven't seen me tonight. I'll arrive at the office unexpectedly one day. Okay?'

He grinned. 'Catching them in the act?'

'Something like that.'

I went away leaving Jack a great deal less troubled in the mind than when I'd arrived. I gave the driver Alix Aarvik's address in Kensington and sat back wondering how that pair of cheapjack bastards thought they could get away with it. It was very puzzling because I was the majority shareholder.

Alix Aarvik was in and pleased to see me. As she ushered me in to the living-room she said, 'Oh, you've hurt yourself.'

'Not irrevocably. Have you been keeping well?'

'I'm all right. Would you like coffee?'

'Thank you.'

She was busily domestic for a few minutes, then she said, 'I like your beard – it suits you.' She suddenly blushed because she'd said something personal to a comparative stranger.

'Thank you. I might keep it on that recommendation.' I paused. 'Miss Aarvik, I've found your brother.' I raised my hand. 'He's quite well and undamaged and he's back in England.'

She sat down with a bump. 'Oh, thank God!'

'Rather thank a man called Byrne; he got Paul out of most of the holes he got himself into. Paul will tell you about it.'

'Where was he?'

I thought of Koudia and Atakor and the Tassili. 'In North Africa. He found his father, Miss Aarvik.' Her hand flew to her mouth. 'I suppose the story will be breaking in the newspapers quite soon. A complete vindication, making nonsense of all the malicious speculation.'

'Oh, I'm so glad!' she said. 'But where is Paul now?'

I wondered whether or not to take her into my confidence. She was much more level-headed than Paul, but in the end I decided against it. The truth, if and when it came out, would be so explosive that the fewer in the know the better, and there must be no possible way of Paul getting to know it.

I said carefully, 'Newspapermen in a hurry can be highly inaccurate. We'll be holding a press conference in a few days' time and Paul and I are honing our statements – making sure they're just right I'd rather he wasn't disturbed until then.'

She nodded understandingly. 'Yes,' she said. 'I know Paul. That would be better.'

'You may find that Paul has changed,' I said. 'He's different'

'How?'

I shrugged. 'I think you'll find that he's a better man than he was.'

She thought about that for a moment but couldn't make anything of it. 'Were you with Paul when you found . . . the body?'

'Yes, and so was Byrne. We helped Paul bury it.' I neglected to say that we'd helped him twice.

'Who is Byrne?'

I smiled. 'A difficult man to describe. You could call him a white Targui, except that a lot of Tuareg are as white as we are. He says he used to be an American. A very fine man. Your brother owes him a lot.'

'And you, too.'

I changed the subject. 'Are you still with Andrew McGovern as his secretary?'

'Yes.'

'I'd like you to do me a favour. I'd like to meet him.'

'That can be arranged,' she said.

'But not very easily the way I want to do it. I want to meet him *not* at his office, and without him knowing who I am. This is a matter of some discretion, an assignment on behalf of a client.'

'That *will* be difficult,' she said, and fell into thought. 'His lunches are usually business affairs. Can't you see him at his home?'

'I'd rather not. I prefer not to take business into people's homes.' Considering that I'd just busted in on Jack Ellis and here I was in Alix Aarvik's flat that was a non-starter, but she didn't notice.

'He has no lunch appointment for the day after tomorrow,' she said. 'On those occasions he hardly eats at all and, if it's fine, he nearly always takes a walk in the gardens of Lincoln's Inn. If it's not raining he'll probably be there. Would you know him if you saw him?'

'Oh yes.'

She spread her hands. 'Then, there you are.'

I made leave-taking motions, and she said, 'When will I be seeing Paul?'

'Oh, not long. A week, perhaps; not more than ten days.' I thought that if I didn't get what I wanted within ten days I probably wouldn't get it at all.

I didn't leave all the work to Ellis. For instance, I spent an interesting morning in the Public Records Office, and on my way to see McGovern I called in at Hatchard's and browsed through the current edition of *Whitaker's Almanac*. Although it told me what I wanted to know I bought it anyway as part of the dossier.

Eight days later I had all I needed. I primed Ellis to let me know the next time Lord Brinton visited the office, then sat waiting by the telephone.

# THIRTY-THREE

I pressed the button in the lift and ascended to the floor which held the offices of Stafford Security Consultants Ltd. The girl travelling up with me was one of our junior typists; probably somebody had sent her out to buy a packet of cigarettes or a bar of chocolate or something illicit like that. She looked at me and turned away, then looked at me again as though I were someone she ought to recognize. It was the beard that did it.

I stepped into the familiar hallway, walked into Reception and straight on through towards my own office. Barbara the receptionist said, hastily, 'Here, you can't . . .'

I turned and grinned at her. 'Don't you recognize your own boss?'

I carried on, hearing, 'Oh, Mr Stafford!' I went into my office and found Joyce hammering a typewriter. 'Hi, Joyce; is Mr Ellis in?'

'You've hurt your arm.'

'And gone all hairy. I know. Is he in?'

'Yes.'

I walked in on Ellis. 'Morning, Jack. Got the rest of the bits and pieces?'

'Yes.' He unlocked the drawer of his desk. 'The chemist's report and the marriage certificate. It was 1937, not '36.'

I nodded. 'There'd be a mourning period, of course.'

'What's this all about, Max?'

I unlocked my briefcase, using one hand, and he dropped the papers into it. 'Better you don't know. Is Brinton here?'

'His Nibs is with Charlie.'

'Right – stand by for fireworks.'

I walked in on Charlie cold, without announcement, ignoring the flapping of his secretary. He was sitting behind his desk and Brinton was in an armchair by his side. The armchair was new, but Brinton was noted for attending to his own creature comforts. If Charlie had seen fit to get an armchair then it meant Brinton was a frequent visitor.

Charlie looked up at me blankly, and then the penny dropped. 'Max!'

'Hello, Charlie.' I nodded at Brinton. 'Morning, my lord.'

'Well, I'm damned!' said Brinton. 'Where did you spring from? I see you've hurt your arm. How did you do that?'

'Skiing can be dangerous.' A perfectly truthful statement, if not responsive to the question. I drew up a chair, sat down, and put the briefcase on the floor.

'Where were you? Gstaad?' Brinton was his old genial self but Charlie Malleson seemed tongue-tied and wore a hunted look.

I said, 'I've been hearing some bloody funny stories about the company so I came back.'

Charlie's eyes slid to Brinton who didn't seem to notice. He still retained his smile as he said, 'From Ellis, I suppose. Well, it's true enough. We've made some changes to improve the profitability.'

'Without my knowledge,' I said coldly. 'Or my consent.'

'What's the matter, Max?' said Brinton. 'Don't you like money?'

'As much as the next man – but I'm particular how I earn it.' I turned to Charlie. 'You didn't take that clause from the Electronomics contract. So this was being cooked up as long ago as that. What the hell's got into you?' He didn't answer, so I said, 'All right; from now on we go back to square one.'

Brinton's voice was almost regretful as he said, ''Fraid not, Max. You don't have all that much of a say any more.'

I looked at him. He still wore the big smile but it didn't reach his eyes which were cold as ice. 'What the devil are you talking about? I own fifty-one per cent of the shares – a controlling interest.'

He shook his head. 'You did. You don't now. You made a mistake, the elementary mistake of a man in love. You trusted someone.'

I knew it then. 'Gloria!'

'Yes, Gloria. You went off in a hurry and forgot about the seven per cent interest in the firm you'd given her. I bought her shares.' He wagged his head. 'You should pay more attention to proverbial sayings; there's a lot of truth in them. Hell hath no fury like a woman scorned. See what I mean?'

I said, 'Seven plus twenty-five makes thirty-two. That's still not control.'

His grin had turned reptilian. 'It is if Charlie votes with me – and he will. It seems he's been a trifle worried lately – his financial affairs have become somewhat disordered and it's definitely in his interest to increase the profitability of the company. It fell to me to point out that simple fact.'

'I don't suppose you had anything to do with his financial disorder,' I said acidly. Brinton's grin widened as I turned to Charlie and asked quietly, 'Will you vote with him?'

He swallowed. 'I must!'

'Well, by God! What a bloody pair you are. I was prepared for his lordship to pull a fast one, but I didn't think it of you, Charlie.' He reddened. 'You came to see me at my

club just before I left. I thought then that you wanted
something but I couldn't figure what it was. Now I know.
You wanted to find out if I was still going on holiday even
though I'd left Gloria.' I jerked my thumb at Brinton. 'He
sent you to find out. No wonder both of you were urging
me to go. You were giving me the fast shuffle so that
Brinton could grab Gloria's shares.'

Brinton chuckled. 'It was her idea, really. She came and
offered them to me. Max, you're a simpleton. You don't
think I'd let all the valuable information in your files go to
waste. A man could make millions with what you've got
here.'

'You let me build up the reputation of the company, and
now you're going to rape it. Is that it?'

'Something along those lines,' he said carelessly. 'But
legally – always legally.'

I said, 'Brinton, I have something for your ears only –
something I don't think you'd like Charlie to know about.'

'There's nothing you can say to me that anyone can't
hear. If you have something in your gullet, spit it out.'

'All right,' I said. 'Kissack won't be coming back.'

'What the devil are you talking about?' he demanded.
'Kissack? Who the hell is he?'

I hadn't scored with that one. Of course, he might not
know of Kissack who was pretty low on the totem pole – a
hired hand. I tried again. 'Lash won't be coming back,
either.'

That got to him! I knew by the fractional change in the
planes of his face. But he kept his end up well. 'And who is
Lash?'

'Lash is the man who hired the men who beat me up,'
I said deliberately. 'Lash is the man who hired Kissack
to k—'

Brinton held up his hand abruptly. 'I can't stay here all
day. I have things to do at my place. You can come with

me and get rid of this nonsense there.' He got to his feet creakily.

I cheered internally. I had the old bastard by the short hairs, and he knew it. He went ahead of me and I paused at the door and looked back at Charlie. 'You louse!' I said. 'I'll deal with you later.'

I went with Brinton to the basement and we solemnly drove two blocks to the basement of another building and ascended to his penthouse where the coal fire still blazed cheerfully. All the time he didn't say a thing, but once on his own ground, he said, 'Stafford, you'd better be careful with your statements or I'll have your balls!'

I grinned, walked past him and sat in an armchair by the fire, and put down my briefcase. He didn't like that; he didn't like not being in central, and that meant he'd have to follow me. He sank into an opposing chair. 'Well, what is it?'

'I'd like to tell you a story about a bright, ambitious young engineer who married a woman who had just come into money. She hadn't won the pools or anything like that, but the life of her previous husband had been insured for a hundred thousand pounds. This was in 1937, so that's a lot more money than it sounds like now – maybe half a million in our terms.'

I stopped but Brinton made no comment. He merely stared at me with cold eyes. 'But what this woman didn't know was that this bright young engineer who, incidentally, was Canadian like yourself, had murdered her husband. His name was John Grenville Anderson, but he was commonly known as Jock. He was born in 1898 which, by another coincidence, would make him exactly as old as you.'

Brinton whispered, 'If you repeat those words in public I'll take you to court and strip you naked.'

'It was the name that foxed me,' I said. 'We've had quite a few Canadian peers but none of them have tried to hide behind a name. Beaverbrook was obviously Canadian;

Thomson of Fleet not only retained his own name but advertised his newspaper connection. But Brinton doesn't mean a damned thing, either here or in Canada. There's a little place called Brinton in Norfolk but you've never been near it to my knowledge.'

I leaned down and opened the briefcase. 'Exhibit One – a photocopy of a page from *Whitaker's Almanac*.' I read the relevant line. '"Created 1947, Brinton (1st.) John Grenville Anderson, born 1898." A most anonymous title, don't you think?'

'Get on with this preposterous nonsense.'

'Exhibit Two – a copy of your marriage lines to Helen Billson early in 1937. You didn't stick with her long, did you, Jock? Just long enough to part her from her money. A hundred thousand quid was just what a man like you needed to start a good little engineering company. Then the war came, and Lord, how the money rolled in! You were in air-craft manufacture, of course, on cost plus a percentage until your compatriot, Beaverbrook, put a stop to that. But by the end of the war you'd built up your nest-egg to a couple of millions, plus the grateful thanks of your sovereign who ennobled you for contributing funds to the right political party. And not just a tatty old life peerage like we have now. Not that that made any difference – you had no legitimate children.'

His lips compressed. 'I'm being very patient.'

'So you are. You ought to have me thrown out neck and crop. Why don't you?'

His eyes flickered. 'You amuse me. I'd like to hear the end of this fairy story.'

'No one can say I'm not obliging,' I said. 'All right; by 1946 you'd just got started. You discovered you had a flair for finance; in the property boom of the 'fifties you made millions – you're still making millions because money makes money. And it all came out of the murder of Peter Billson whose widow you married.'

'And how am I supposed to have murdered Billson?'

'You were his mechanic in the London to Cape Town Air Race of 1936. In Algiers you delayed him so he'd have to fly to Kano at night. Then you gimmicked his compass so that he flew off course.'

'You can never prove that. You're getting into dangerous waters, Stafford.'

'Exhibit Three – an eight-by-ten colour photograph of *Flyaway*, Billson's aircraft, taken by myself less than two weeks ago. Note how intact it is. Exhibit Four – an affidavit witnessed by a notary public and signed by myself and the man who took out the compass and tested it.'

Brinton studied the photograph, then read the document. I said, 'By the way, that's also a photocopy – all these papers are. Those that are a matter of public record are in the appropriate place, and the others are in the vaults of my bank. My solicitor knows what to do with them should anything happen to me.'

He grunted. 'Who is Lucas Byrne?'

'An aeronautical engineer,' I said, stretching a point. 'You'll note he mentions a substance found in the main fuel tank. Here's a report by a chemist who analysed the stuff. He says he found mostly hydrocarbons of petroleum derivation.'

'Naturally,' sneered Brinton.

'He said mostly,' I pointed out. 'He also found other hydrocarbons – disaccharides, D-glucopyranose, D-fructopyranose and others. Translated into English it means that you'd put sugar into the fuel tank, and when Billson switched over from the auxiliary his engine froze solid.' I sat back. 'But let's come to modern times.'

Brinton stretched out his hand and dropped Byrne's statement on to the fire. I laughed. 'Plenty more where that came from.'

'What about modern times?'

'You became really worried about Paul Billson, didn't you, when you found he was practically insane about his

father? He was the one man who had the incentive and the
obsessiveness to go out to find *Flyaway* in order to clear his
father's name. You weren't as worried about Alix Aarvik but
you really anchored Paul. I had a long chat with Andrew
McGovern about that the other day.'

Brinton's head came up with a jerk. 'You've seen
McGovern?'

'Yes – didn't he tell you? I suppose I must have thrown
a bit of a scare into him. He had no objection to employ-
ing Paul because you were paying all of Paul's inflated
salary. He jumped to the natural conclusion: that Paul was
one of your byblows, a souvenir of your misspent youth
whom you were tactfully looking after. And so you tethered Paul for fifteen years by giving him a salary that he
knew he wasn't worth. It's ironic that it was you who
financed his trip to the Sahara when he blew up. I dare say
the payments you made through the Whensley Group can
be traced.'

His lips twisted. 'I doubt it.'

'McGovern told me something else. He didn't want
Stafford Security pulled out of the Whensley Group – it
was your idea. You twisted his arm. I don't know what
hold you have on McGovern, but whatever it is you used
it. That was to stop me carrying on the investigation into
Paul Billson. You also got McGovern to send Alix
Aarvik to Canada but that didn't work out, did it? Because
I got to her first. So you had Lash have me beaten up.
I don't think McGovern likes you any more. I suppose
that's why he didn't report back to you that he'd seen
me – that and the fact that I told him he'd better keep his
nose clean.'

Brinton dismissed McGovern with a twitch of a finger.
'You said Lash isn't coming back. What happened to him?'

'Two bullets through his lungs, one through the belly,
and another through the head at close range – that's what

happened to Lash. There are three dead men out there, and another with an amputated foot, and all because of you, Jock. All because you were so scared of what Paul Billson might find that you put out a contract on him.' I tapped my arm in its sling. 'Not Gstaad, Jock; the Tassili. You owe me something for this.'

'I owe you nothing,' he said contemptuously.

'Then we come to a man called Torstein Aarvik who married Helen Billson.' I drew a photocopy of the marriage certificate from my briefcase. 'This really shook me when I saw it because legally she was Anderson, wasn't she? Helen had lost sight of you so she took a chance. She married Aarvik as the widow Billson without divorcing you. It was wartime and things were pretty free and easy and, besides, she wasn't too bright – I have Alix Aarvik's word for that. But you knew where she was because you'd been keeping tabs on her. I don't know how you separated her from her money in the first place but you used her bigamous marriage to keep her quiet for the rest of her life. She couldn't fight you, could she? And maybe she wasn't bright but perhaps she was decent enough to prevent Alix knowing that she's a bastard. Now who's the bastard here, you son of a bitch?'

'You'll never make this stick,' he said. 'Not after forty-two years.'

'I believe I will, and so do you, or you wouldn't have been so bloody worried about Paul Billson. There's no statute of limitations on murder, Jock.'

'Stop calling me Jock,' he said irritably.

'You're an old man,' I said. 'Eighty years old. You're going to die soon. Tomorrow, next year, five years, ten – you'll be as dead as Lash. But they don't have capital punishment now, so you'll probably die in a prison hospital. Unless . . .'

He was suddenly alert, scenting a bargain, a deal. 'Unless what?'

'What's the use of putting you in jail? You wouldn't live as luxuriously as you do now but you'd get by. They're tender-minded about murderous old men these days, and that wouldn't satisfy me, nor would it help the people you've cheated all these years.'

I put my hand into my pocket, drew out a calculator, punched a few keys, then wrote the figure on a piece of paper. It made a nice sum if not a round one – £1,714,425.68. I tossed it across to him. 'That's a hundred thousand compounded at a nominal seven per cent for forty-two years.'

I said, 'Even if Scotland Yard or the Director of Public Prosecutions take no action the newspapers would love it. The Insight team of the *Sunday Times* would make a meal of it. Think of all the juicy bits – Lady Brinton dying of cancer in virtual poverty while her husband lived high on the hog. Your name would stink, even in the City where they have strong stomachs. Do you think any decent or even any moderately indecent man would have anything to do with you after that?'

I stuck my finger under his nose. 'And another thing – Paul Billson knows nothing about this. But I can prime him with it and point him at you like a gun. He'd kill you – you wouldn't stand a flaming chance. You'd better get out your cheque book.'

He flinched but made a last try. 'This figure is impossible. You don't suppose I'm as fluid as all that?'

'Don't try to con me, you old bastard,' I said. 'Any bank in the City will lend you that amount if you just pick up the telephone and ask. Do it!'

He stood up. 'You're a hard man.'

'I've had a good teacher. You make out two cheques; one to the Peter Billson Memorial Trust for a million and a half. The rest to me – that's my twelve-and-a-half per cent commission. Expenses have been high. And I get Gloria's

shares, and you sell out of Stafford Security. I don't care
who you sell your shares to but it mustn't be Charlie
Malleson.'

'How do I know you won't renege? I want all the papers
you have.'

'Not a chance in hell! Those are my insurance policies.
I wouldn't want another Lash turning up in my life.'

He sat down and wrote the cheques.

I walked the streets of London for a long time that afternoon with cheques in my pocket for more money than
I had ever carried. Alix Aarvik and Paul Billson would
now be all right for the rest of their lives. I had put
the money into a trust because I didn't want Paul getting
his hands on it – he didn't deserve that. But the not-too-
bright son of a not-too-bright mother would be looked
after.

As for me, I thought $12\frac{1}{2}$% was a reasonable fee. It
would enable me to buy out Charlie Malleson, a regret-
table necessity because I could no longer work with him.
Jack Ellis would continue to be a high flier and he'd get his
stake in the firm, and we'd hire an accountant and pay
him well. And Byrne would get something unexpectedly
higher than the ridiculous fee he'd asked for saving lives
and being shot at.

At the thought of Byrne I stopped suddenly and looked
about me. I was in Piccadilly, at the Circus, and the lights
and crowds were all about me in the evening dusk. And it
all seemed unreal. This, the heart of the city at the heart of
the world, wasn't reality. Reality lay in Ataker, in Koudia, in
the Aïr, in the Ténéré, on the Tassili.

I felt an awful sense of loss. I wanted to be with Byrne
and Mokhtar and Hamiada, with the cheerful man who,
because his name used to be Konti, was a murderer. I
wanted to say hello again to the giraffe in Agadez, to sit

beside a small fire at an evening camp and look at the stars, to feel again the freedom of a Targui.

I stopped and pondered, there among the hurrying crowds of Londoners, and decided to give Byrne his fee in person. Besides, it would also give me the opportunity of swapping dirty limericks with Hesther Raulier.

# WINDFALL

*To*

*Jan Hemsing*

*and an unknown number of Kenyan cats*

# ONE

It is difficult to know when this business began. Certainly it was not with Ben Hardin. But possibly it began when Jomo Kenyatta instructed the Kenyan delegation to the United Nations to lead a move to expel South Africa from the UN. That was on the 25th of October, 1974, and it was probably soon thereafter that the South Africans decided they had to do something about it.

Max Stafford himself dated his involvement to the first day back at the London office after an exhaustive, and exhausting, trip around Europe – Paris, Frankfurt, Hamburg, Amsterdam, Milan. Three years earlier he had decided that since his clients were multinational he, perforce, would also have to go multinational. It had been a hard slog setting up the European offices but now Stafford Security Consultants, as well as sporting the tag 'Ltd' after the company name, had added 'SA', 'GmbH', 'SpA' and a couple of other assortments of initials. Stafford was now looking with a speculative eye across the Atlantic in the hope of adding 'Inc'.

He paused in the ante-room of his office. 'Is Mr Ellis around?'

Joyce, his secretary, said, 'I saw him five minutes ago. Did you have a good trip?'

'Wearing, but good.' He put a small package on her desk. 'Your favourite man-bait from Paris; Canal something-or-other. I'll be in Mr Ellis's office until further notice.'

Joyce squeaked. 'Thanks, Mr Stafford.'

Jack Ellis ran the United Kingdom operation. He was young, but coming along nicely, and ran a taut ship. Stafford had promoted him to the position when he had made the decision to move into Europe. It had been risky using so young a man in a top post where he would have to negotiate with some of the stuffier and elderly Chairmen of companies, but it had worked out and Stafford had never regretted it.

They talked for a while about the European trip and then Ellis looked at his watch. 'Bernstein will be here any minute.' He gestured to a side table on which lay several fat files. 'Have you read the reports?'

Stafford grimaced. 'Not in detail.' Having determined to expand he had gone the whole hog and commissioned an independent company to do a world-wide investigation into possibilities. It was costing a lot but he thought it would be worthwhile in the long run. However, he liked to deal with people rather than paper and he wanted to match the man against the words he had written. He said, 'We'll go over it once lightly with Bernstein.'

Two hours later he was satisfied. Bernstein, an American, was acute and sensible; he had both feet firmly planted on the ground and was not a man to indulge in impossible blue sky speculation. Stafford thought he could trust his written reports.

Bernstein tossed a file aside. 'So much for Australasia. Now we come to Africa.' He picked up another file. 'The problem in general with Africa is political instability.'

Stafford said, 'Stick to the English-speaking countries. We're not ready to go into francophone Africa.' He paused. 'Not yet.'

Bernstein nodded. 'That means the ex-British colonies. South Africa, of course, is the big one.' They discussed

South Africa for some time and Bernstein made some interesting suggestions. Then he said, 'Next is Zimbabwe. It's just attained independence with a black government. Nobody knows which way it's going to go right now and I wouldn't recommend it for you. Tanzania is out; the country is virtually bankrupt and there's no free enterprise. The same goes for Uganda. Now, Kenya is different.'

'How?' asked Ellis.

Bernstein turned several pages. 'It has a mixed economy, very much like Britain. The government is moderate and there is less corruption than is usual in Africa. The Western banks think highly of Kenya and there's a lot of money going into the country to build up the infrastructure – modernization of the road system, for instance.' He looked up. 'Of course, you'd have competition – Securicor is already established there.'

Securicor was Stafford's biggest competitor in Britain. He smiled and said, 'I can get along with that.' Then he frowned. 'But is Kenya really stable? What about that Mau-Mau business some years ago?'

'That was quite a while ago,' said Bernstein. 'When the British were still there. Anyway, there are a lot of misconceptions about the Mau-Mau insurrection. It was blown up in the Western press as a rebellion against the British and even the black Kenyans have done some rewriting of history because they like to think of that period as when they got rid of the British oppressor. The fact remains that in the seven years of the Mau-Mau rebellion only thirty-eight whites were killed. If it was a rebellion against the British it was goddamn inefficient.'

'You surprise me,' said Ellis. 'Then what was it all about?'

Bernstein tented his fingers. 'Everyone knew the British would be giving up jurisdiction over Kenya – the tide of history was running against the British Empire.

The Mau-Mau insurrection was a private fight among
black Kenyans, mainly along tribal lines, to figure out
who'd be on top when the British abdicated. A lot of people died and the few whites were killed mainly because
they happened to be caught in the middle – in the wrong
place at the wrong time. When it was all over, the British
knew who was going to hold the reins of government.
Jomo Kenyatta was intelligent, educated and had all the
qualifications to be the leader of a country, including the
prime qualification.'

'What was that?' asked Ellis.

Bernstein smiled. 'He'd served time in a British jail,' he
said dryly. 'Kenyatta proved to be surprisingly moderate. He
didn't go hog-wild like some of the other African leaders.
He encouraged the whites to stay because he knew he
needed their skills, and he built up the trade of the country.
A while ago there was considerable speculation as to what
would happen when he died. People expected another civil
war on the lines of the Mau-Mau but, surprisingly, the tran-
sition was orderly in the democratic manner and Moi
became President. Tribalism is officially discouraged and,
yes, I'd say Kenya is a stable country.' He flicked the pages
he held. 'It's all here in detail.'

'All right,' said Stafford. 'What's next?'

'Now we turn to Nigeria.'

The discussion continued for another hour and then
Stafford checked the time. 'We'll have to call a halt now. I
have a luncheon appointment.' He looked with some distaste at the foot-thick stack of papers on the desk. 'It'll take
some time to get through that lot. Thanks for your help, Mr
Bernstein; you've been very efficient.'

'Anything you can't figure out, come right back at me,'
said Bernstein.

'I think we'll give Africa a miss,' said Stafford thoughtfully. 'My inclination is to set up in the States and then,

perhaps, in Australia. But I'm lunching with a South African. Perhaps he'll change my mind.'

Stafford's appointment was with Alix and Dirk Hendriks. He had met Alix a few years earlier when she had been Alix Aarvik, the daughter of an English mother and a Norwegian father who had been killed during the war. It was in the course of a professional investigation and, one thing leading to another, he had gone to North Africa to return to Britain with a bullet wound in the shoulder and a sizeable fortune for Alix Aarvik. His divorce was ratified about that time and he had contemplated marrying Alix, but there was not that spark between them and he had not pursued the idea although they remained good friends.

Since then she had married Dirk Hendriks. Stafford did not think a great deal of Hendriks. He distrusted the super-ficial veneer of charm and suspected that Hendriks had married Alix for her money. Certainly Hendriks did not appear to be gainfully employed. Still, Stafford was honest enough to admit to himself that his dislike of Hendriks might be motivated by an all-too-human dog in the manger attitude. Alix was expecting a baby.

Over lunch Alix complained that she did not see enough of him. 'You suddenly dropped out of my life.'

'For men must work,' said Stafford lightly, not worrying too much that his remark was a direct dig at Dirk Hendriks. 'I've been scurrying around Europe, making the fortunes of a couple of airlines.'

'Still intent on expansion, I see.'

'As long as people have secrets to protect there'll be work for people like me. I'm thinking of moving into the States.' He leaned back to let a waiter remove a plate. 'A chap this morning recommended that we expand our activities into South Africa. What do you think about that, Dirk?'

Hendriks laughed. 'Plenty of secrets in South Africa. It's not a bad idea.'

Stafford shook his head. 'I've decided to keep out of Africa altogether. There's plenty of scope in other directions and the Dark Continent doesn't appeal to me.'

He was to remember that remark with bitterness in the not too distant future.

# TWO

Three thousand miles away Ben Hardin knew nothing about Max Stafford and Kenya was the last thing on his mind. And he was in total ignorance of the fact that, in more senses than one, he was the man in the middle. True, he had been in Kenya back in 1974, but it was in another job and in quite a different connection. Yet he was the unwitting key which unlocked the door to reveal the whole damn mess.

It was one of those hot, sticky days in late July when New York fries. Hardin had taken time off to visit his favourite bar to sink a couple of welcome cold beers and, when he got back to the office, Jack Richardson at the next desk said, 'Gunnarsson has been asking for you.'

'Oh; what does he want?'

Richardson shrugged. 'He didn't say.'

Hardin paused in the act of taking off his jacket and put it back on. 'When does he want to see me?'

'Yesterday,' said Richardson dryly. 'He sounded mad.'

'Then I guess I'd better see the old bastard,' said Hardin sourly.

Gunnarsson greeted him with, 'Where the hell have you been?'

'Checking a contact on the Myerson case,' said Hardin inventively, making a mental note to record the visit in the Myerson file. Gunnarsson sometimes checked back.

Gunnarsson put his hands flat on the desk and glowered at him. He was a burly, square man who looked as though he had been hacked out of a block of granite and in spite of the heat he wore his coat. Rumour had it that Gunnarsson lacked sweat glands. He said, 'You can forget that, Ben; I'm taking you off the case. I have something else for you.'

'Okay,' said Hardin.

Gunnarsson tossed a thin file across the desk. 'Let's get this straight. You clear this one and you get a bonus. You crap on it and you get canned. We've been carrying you long enough.'

Hardin looked at him levelly. 'You make yourself clear. How important is this one?'

Gunnarsson flapped his hand. 'I wouldn't know. A Limey lawyer wants an answer. You're to find out what happened to a South African called Adriaan Hendriks who came to the States some time in the 1930s. Find out all about him, especially whether he married and had kids. Find them too.'

'That's going to take some legwork,' said Hardin thoughtfully. 'Who can I use?'

'No one; you use your own damn legs.' Gunnarsson was blunt, if you can't clear us a pisswilly job like this then I'll know you're no use to Gunnarsson Associates. Now you'll do it this way. You take your car and you go on the road and you find what happened to this guy. And you do it yourself. If you have to leave New York I don't want you going near any of the regional offices.'

'Why not?'

'Because that's the way I want it. And I'm the boss. Now get going.'

So Hardin went away and, as he laid the file on his desk, he thought glumly that he had just received an ultimatum. He sat down, opened the file, and found the reason for its lack of bulk. It contained a single sheet of computer print-out which told him nothing that Gunnarsson had not already told him; that a man called Adriaan Hendriks was believed to have entered the United States in the late thirties. The port of entry was not even recorded.

'Jesus wept!' said Hardin.

Ben Hardin wished, for perhaps the thousandth time, or it could have been the ten thousandth, that he was in another line of work. Every morning when he woke up in whatever crummy motel room it happened to be it was the thought that came into his mind: 'I wish I was doing something else.' And that was followed by the automatic: 'Goddamn that bastard, Gunnarsson,' and by the equally automatic first cigarette of the day which made him cough.

And every morning when he was confronted by breakfast, invariably the junk food of the interstate highways, the same thought came into his mind. And when he knocked on a door, any door, to ask the questions, the thought was fleetingly at the back of his mind. As with the Frenchman who said that everything reminded him of sex so everything reminded Hardin of the cruel condition of his life, and it had made him an irritable and cynical man.

On the occasion of the latest reiteration of his wish he was beset by water. The rain poured from the sky, not in drops but in a steady sheet. It swirled along the gutters a foot or more deep because the drains were unable to cope, and Hardin had the impression that his car was in imminent danger of being swept away. Trapped in the metal box of the car he could only wait until the downpour ceased. He was certainly not going to get out because he would be soaked to the skin and damn near drowned in ten seconds flat.

And this was happening in California – in Los Angeles, the City of the Angels. No more angels, he thought; the birds will all have drowned. He visualized a crowd of angels sitting on a dark cloud, their wings bedraggled, and managed a tired grin. They said that what California did today New York would do tomorrow. If that was true someone in

New York should be building a goddamn Ark. He wondered if there was a Mr Noah in the New York telephone book.

While he waited he looked back on the last few weeks. The first and obvious step had been to check with the Immigration and Naturalization Service. He found that the 1930s had been a lean decade for immigrants – there were a mere 528,431 fortunate people admitted into the country. McDowell, the immigration officer he checked with, observed dryly that Hardin was lucky – in the 1920s the crop had been over four million. Hardin doubted his luck.

'South Africa,' said McDowell. 'That won't be too bad. Not many South Africans emigrate.'

A check through the files proved him right – but there was no one called Adriaan Hendriks.

'They change their names,' said McDowell some time later. 'Sometimes to Americanize the spelling. There's a guy here called Adrian Hendrix . . .' He spelled it out. 'Would that be the guy you want? He entered the country in New Orleans.'

'That's my man,' said Hardin with satisfaction.

The search so far had taken two weeks.

Further searches revealed that Hendrix had taken out naturalization papers eight years later in Clarksville, Tennessee. More to the point he had married there. Establishing these simple facts took another three weeks and a fair amount of mileage.

Adrian Hendrix had married the daughter of a grain and feed merchant and seemed in a fair way to prosper had it not been for his one fault. On the death of his father-in-law in 1950 he proceeded to drink away the profits of the business he had inherited and died therefrom but not before he sired a son, Henry Hendrix.

Hardin looked at his notebook bleakly. The substitution of the son for the father had not made his task any easier.

He had reported to Gunnarsson only to be told abruptly to
find young Hendrix and to stop belly-aching, and there followed further weeks of searching because Henry Hendrix
had become a drop-out – an undocumented man – after
leaving high school, but a combination of legwork, persis-
tence and luck had brought Hardin to the San Fernando
Valley in California where he was marooned in his car.

It was nearly three-quarters of an hour before the rain
eased off and he decided to take a chance and get out. He
swore as he put his foot into six inches of water and then
squelched across the street towards the neat white house.
He sheltered on the porch, shaking the wetness from his
coat, then pressed the bell and heard chimes.

Presently the door opened cautiously, held by a chain,
and an eye and a nose appeared at the narrow opening. 'I'm
looking for Henry Hendrix,' Hardin said, and flipped open a
notebook. 'I'm told he lives here.'

'No one by that name here.' The door began to close.

Hardin said quickly, 'This *is* 82, Thorndale?'

'Yeah, but my name's Parker. No one called Hendrix
here.'

'How long have you lived here, Mr Parker?'

'Who wants to know?'

'I'm sorry.' Hardin extracted a card from his wallet and
poked it at the three-inch crack in the doorway. 'My name
is Hardin.'

The card was taken in two fingers and vanished. Parker
said, 'Gunnarsson Associates. You a private dick?'

'I guess you could call me that,' said Hardin tiredly.

'This Hendrix in trouble?'

'Not that I know of, Mr Parker. Could be the other way
round, from what I hear. Could be good news for Hendrix.'

'Well, I'll tell you,' said Parker. 'We've lived here eight
months.'

'Who did you buy the house from?'

'Didn't buy,' said Parker. 'We rent. The owner's an old biddy who lives in Pasadena.'

'And you don't know the name of the previous tenant? He left no forwarding address?' There was not much hope in Hardin's voice.

'Nope.' Parker paused. 'Course, my wife might know. She did all the renting business.'

'Would it be possible to ask her?'

'I guess so. Wait a minute.' The door closed leaving Hardin looking at a peeling wooden panel. He heard a murmur of voices from inside the house and presently the door opened again and a woman peered at him then disappeared. He heard her say, 'Take the chain off the door, Pete.'

'Hell, Milly; you know what they told us about LA.'

'Take the chain off,' said Milly firmly. 'What kind of a life is it living behind bolts and bars?'

The door closed, there was a rattle, and then it opened wide. 'Come on in,' said Mrs Parker. 'It ain't fit for a dog being out today.'

Thankfully Hardin stepped over the threshold. Parker was a burly man of about forty-five with a closed, tight face, but Milly Parker smiled at Hardin. 'You want to know about the Hendersons, Mr Hardin?'

Hardin repressed the sinking feeling. 'Hendrix, Mrs Parker.'

'Could have sworn it was Henderson. But come into the living room and sit down.'

Hardin shook his head. 'I'm wet; don't want to mess up your furniture. Besides, I won't take up too much of your time. You think the previous tenant was called Henderson?'

'That's what I thought. I could have been wrong.' She laughed merrily, 'I often am.'

'Was there a forwarding address?'

'I guess so; there was a piece of paper,' she said vaguely. 'I'll look in the bureau.' She went away.

Hardin looked at Parker and tried to make light conversation. 'Get this kind of weather often?'

'I wouldn't know,' said Parker briefly. 'Haven't been here long.'

Hardin heard drawers open in the next room and there was the rustle of papers. 'The way I hear it this is supposed to be the Sunshine State. Or is that Florida?'

Parker grunted. 'Rains both places; but you wouldn't know to hear the Chambers of Commerce tell it.'

Mrs Parker came back. 'Can't find it,' she announced, 'It was just a little bitty piece of paper.' She frowned. 'Seems I recollect an address. I know it was off Ventura Boulevard; perhaps in Sherman Oaks or, maybe, Encino.'

Hardin winced; Ventura Boulevard was a hundred miles long. Parker said abruptly, 'Didn't you give the paper to that other guy?'

'What other guy?' asked Hardin.

'Why, yes; I think I did,' said Mrs Parker. 'Now I think of it. A nice young man. He was looking for Henderson, too.'

Hardin sighed. 'Hendrix,' he said. 'Who was this young man?'

'Didn't bother to ask,' said Parker. 'But he was a foreigner – not American. He had a funny accent like I've never heard before.'

Hardin questioned them further but got nothing more, then said, 'Well, could I have the address of the owner of the house. She might know.' He got the address and also the address of the local realtor who had negotiated the rental. He looked at his watch and found it was late. 'Looks like the day's shot. Know of a good motel around here?'

'Why, yes,' she said. 'Go south until you hit Riverside, then turn west. There are a couple along there before you hit the turning to Laurel Canyon.'

He thanked them and left, hearing the door slam behind him and the rattle of the chain. It was still raining; not so hard as before but still enough to drench him before he reached the shelter of his car. He was wet and gloomy as he drove away.

His motel room was standard issue and dry. He took off his wet suit and hung it over the bath, regarded it critically, and decided it needed pressing. He wondered if Gunnarsson would stand for that on the expense account. Then he took off his shirt, hung it next to the suit, and padded into the bedroom in his underwear. He sat at the table, opened his briefcase, and took out a sheaf of papers which he spread out and regarded dispiritedly. His shoulders sagged and he looked exactly what he was – a failure. A man pushing fifty-five-with a pot belly, his once muscular body now running to fat, his brains turning to mush, and the damned dandruff was making his hair fall out. Every time he looked at his comb he was disgusted.

Ben Hardin once had such high hopes. He had majored in languages at the University of Illinois and when he had been approached by the recruiter he had been flattered. Although the approach had been subtle he was not fooled; the campus was rife with rumours about the recruiters and everyone knew what they were recruiting for. And so he had fallen for the flattery and responded to the appeals to his patriotism because this was the height of the Cold War and everyone knew the Reds were the enemy.

So they had taken him and taught him to shoot – handgun, rifle, machine-gun – taught him unarmed combat, how to hold his liquor and how to make others drunk. They told him of drops and cut-outs, of codes and cyphers, how to operate a radio and many other more esoteric things. Then he had reported to Langley as a fully fledged member of the CIA only to be told bluntly that he knew nothing and was the lowest of the low on the totem pole.

In the years that followed he gained in experience. He
worked in Australia, England, Germany and East Africa.
Sometimes he found himself working inside his own country which he found strange because the continental United
States was supposed to be the stamping ground of the FBI
and off-limits to the CIA. But he obeyed orders and did
what he was told and eventually found that more than half
his work was in the United States.

Then came Watergate and everything broke loose. The
Company sprang more holes than a sieve and everyone
rushed to plug up the leaks, but there seemed to be more
informers than loyal Company men. Newspaper pages
looked like extracts from the CIA files, and the shit began to
fly. There were violent upheavals as the top brass defended
themselves against the politicians, director followed director, each one publicly dedicated to cleaning house, and
heads duly rolled, Hardin's among them.

He had been genuinely shocked at what had happened to
the Company and to himself. In his view he had been a
loyal servant of his country and now his country had turned
against him. He was in despair, and it was then that
Gunnarsson approached him. They met by appointment in
a Washington bar which claimed to sell every brand of beer
made in the world. He arrived early and, while waiting for
Gunnarsson, ordered a bottle of Swan for which he had
developed a taste in Australia.

When Gunnarsson arrived they talked for a while of how
the country was going to hell in a handcart and of the current situation at Langley. Then Gunnarsson said, 'What are
you going to do now, Ben?'

Hardin shrugged. 'What's to do? I'm a trained agent,
that's all. Not many skills for civilian life.'

'Don't you believe it,' said Gunnarsson earnestly. 'Look,
Fletcher and I are setting up shop in New York.'

'Doing what?'

'Same racket, but in civilian form. The big corporations are no different than countries. Why, some of the internationals are bigger than goddamn countries, and they've all got secrets to protect – and secrets to find. My God, Ben; the field's wide open but we've got to get in fast before some of the other guys who were canned from Langley have the same idea. We wait too long the competition could be fierce. If this Watergate bullshit goes on much longer retired spooks will be a drug on the market.'

Hardin took a swig of beer. 'You want me in?'

'Yeah. I'm getting together a few guys, all hand picked, and you are one of them – if you want in. With our experience we ought to clean up.' He grinned. 'Our experience and the pipelines we've still got into Langley.'

'Sounds good,' said Hardin.

'Only thing is it'll take dough,' said Gunnarsson. 'How much can you chip in?'

Money and Hardin bore a curious relationship. A dollar bill and Hardin were separated by some form of anti-glue – they never could get together. He had tried; God, how he had tried. But his bets never came off, his investments failed, and Hardin was the centre of a circle surrounded by dollar bills moving away by some sort of centrifugal force. He had once been married and the marriage had failed as much by his inability to keep money as by the strain imposed by his work. The alimony payments now due each quarter merely added to the centrifugal force.

Now he shook his head. 'Not a thin dime,' he said. 'I'm broke and getting broker. Annette's cheque is due Tuesday and I don't know how I'm going to meet that.'

Gunnarsson looked disappointed. 'As bad as that?'

'Worse,' said Hardin glumly. 'I've got to get a job fast and I have to sweet talk Annette. Those two things are holding my whole attention.'

'Gee, Ben; I was hoping you'd be with us. There's nobody I'd rather have along, and Fletcher agrees with me. Only the other day he was talking about how ingeniously you shafted that guy in Dar-es-Salaam.' He drummed his fingers on the table. 'Okay, you don't have money, but maybe something can be worked out. It won't be as sweet a deal as if you came in as a partner but it'll be better than anything else you can get. And we still want you along because we think you're a good guy and you know the business.'

So a deal had been worked out and Hardin went to work for Gunnarsson and Fletcher Inc not as a partner but as an employee with a reasonable salary. At first he was happy, but over the years things began to go wrong. Gunnarsson became increasingly hard-nosed and the so-called partnership fell apart. Fletcher was squeezed out and Gunnarsson and Fletcher Inc became Gunnarsson Associates. Gunnarsson was the ramrod and let no one forget it.

And Hardin himself lost his drive and initiative. No longer buoyed by patriotism he became increasingly dissatisfied with the work he was doing which in his view fulfilled no more elevating a function than to increase the dividends of shareholders and buttress the positions of corporate fatcats. And he was uneasy because a lot of it was down-right illegal.

He fell down on a couple of jobs and Gunnarsson turned frosty and from then on he noted that he had been downgraded as a field agent and was relegated to the minor investigations about which no one gave a damn. Like the Hendrix case.

Hardin lay on the bed in the motel and blew a smoke ring at the ceiling. Come on, Hardin, he thought. You've nearly got a Hendrix – you're nearly there, man. Think of the bonus Gunnarsson will pay you. Think of Annette's alimony.

He smiled wryly as he remembered that Parker had referred to him as a 'private dick'. Parker had been reading too many mysteries. Natural enough, though; wasn't this Chandler country; Philip Marlowe country; 'down these mean streets a man must go' country? Come on, you imitation Marlowe, he said to himself. Get off your ass and do something.

He swung his legs sideways, sat on the edge of the bed, and reached for the telephone. From what he had gathered the owner of the Parker house operated from her home in Pasadena, and it was still not too late in the evening to talk to her. He checked the number in his notebook and dialled. After a few buzzes a voice said in his ear, 'The White residence.'

The White House! He suppressed an inane chuckle, and said, 'Mrs White?'

'It is she speaking.'

'My name is Hardin, and I represent Gunnarsson Associates of New York. I understand you own a house in North Hollywood.'

'I own several houses in North Hollywood,' she said. 'To which do you refer?'

'It would be 82, Thorndale; at present rented by Mr Parker.'

'Yes, I own that property, but it is rented to Mrs Parker.'

'I see; but I have no interest in the Parkers, Mrs White. I am interested in a previous tenant, a man called Hendrix, Henry Hendrix.'

'Oh, him!' There was a sudden sharpness to Mrs White's voice. 'What is your business, Mr Hardin?'

'I'm a private investigator.'

'A private eye,' said Mrs White, confirming his theory that he was in mystery readers' country. 'Very interesting, I must say. What do you want *him* for? Nothing trivial, I hope.'

He explored the nuances of her voice, and said, 'I can't tell you, Mrs White. I just find them; what happens to them is out of my hands.'

'Well, I hope that young man gets his comeuppance,' she said bitterly. 'He *wrecked* that house. It took me thirty-five hundred dollars to repair the damage done by him and his friends.'

'I'm sorry to hear that,' said Hardin, injecting sincerity into his voice. 'How did it happen?'

'He – Hendrix, I mean – rented the house and agreed to abide by all the conditions. What I didn't know was that he was leader of what they call a commune. You *know;* those young people who go around with dirty feet and the men wearing head bands.' Hardin smiled. 'Mrs Parker tells me the place still stinks of marijuana. And the filth they left there you wouldn't believe.'

'And when did they leave?'

'They didn't *leave,* they were thrown out,' said Mrs White triumphantly, 'I had to call the Sheriff's Department.'

'But when was this?'

'Must be nine . . . no, ten months ago.'

'Any idea where they went?'

'I don't know, and I don't care. For all I care they could go drown, only it would dirty up the ocean.'

'You say Hendrix was the leader of the commune?'

'He paid the rent.' Mrs White paused. 'But no; I don't reckon he was the leader. I think they used him as a front man because he was cleanest. The leader was a man they called Biggie. Big man – tall as a skyscraper and wide as a barn door.'

Hardin made a note. 'Do you know his name – his last name?'

'No; they just called him Biggie. He had long blond hair,' she said. 'Hadn't been washed for months. Kept it out of his eyes with one of those head bands. Shaggy beard. He walked around with his shirt open to the waist. Disgusting! Oh, and he wore something funny round his neck.'

'What sort of funny?'

'A cross. Not a decent Christian cross but a funny cross with a loop at the top. It looked like gold and he wore it on a chain. You couldn't help but notice it the way he wore his shirt open.'

'Were there any women in the commune, Mrs White?'

'There were. A lot of brazen hussies. But I didn't have any truck with them. But I'll tell you something, Mr Hardin. There were so many of those folks in that little house they must have slept head-to-foot. I don't think there could have been a virgin among them, and I don't think they were married, either.'

'You're probably right,' said Hardin.

'Orgies!' said Mrs White, relishing the word. 'We found a lot of incense sticks in the house and some funny statues, and they weren't made in the way God made man. I knew then I was right to get rid of that man. Could have been another Charles Manson. You heard of him back East?'

'Yes, I've heard of Charles Manson.' Hardin closed his notebook. 'Thank you for your information, Mrs White; you've been very co-operative.'

'Are you going to put those folks in jail where they belong?'

'I'm a private investigator, Mrs White; but if I find evidence of wrongdoing I'll pass the information on to the authorities. Thanks for your help.'

He put down the telephone, lit another cigarette, and lay back on the bed. Incense sticks and strange statues! And the funny cross with the loop at the top was probably an Egyptian ankh. He shook his head. God, the things the kids were up to these days.

He wondered briefly who else was looking for Hendrix and then closed his eyes.

# THREE

Hardin walked out of his room next morning into a day that was rainwashed and crisp. He put his bags into his car and drove to the front of the motel. As he got out he looked in astonishment towards the north. There, stretched across the horizon, was a range of mountains with snow-capped peaks rising to a height of maybe 10,000 feet. They had not been there the previous day and they looked like a theatrical backdrop.

'Hollywood!' he muttered, as he went into the inside for breakfast.

Later, as he was tucking his credit card back into his wallet, he said, 'What are those mountains over there?'

The woman behind the desk did not raise her head. 'What mountains?' she asked in an uninterested way.

'That range of mountains with snow on the top.'

She looked up. 'Are you kidding, mister? There are no mountains out there.'

He said irritably, 'Goddamn it! They're practically on your doorstep. I'm not kidding.'

'This I've got to see.' She came from behind the desk and accompanied him to the door where she stopped and gasped. 'Jesus, those are the San Gabriels! I haven't seen them in ten years.'

'Now who's kidding who?' asked Hardin. 'How could you miss a thing like that?'

Her eyes were shining. 'Musta been the rain,' she said. 'Washed all the smog outa the air. Mister, take a good look; you ain't likely to see a sight like that for a long time.'

'Nuts!' said Hardin shaking his head, and walked towards his car.

As he drove downtown he pondered on the peculiarities of Los Angeles. Any community that could lose a range of mountains 10,000 feet high and 40 miles long was definitely out of whack. Hardin disliked Los Angeles and would not visit it for pleasure. He did not like the urban sprawl, so featureless and monotonous that any section of the city was like any other section. He did not like the nutty architecture; for his money it was a waste of time to drive down to Anaheim to visit Disneyland – you could see Disneyland anywhere in LA. And he did not like the Los Angeles version of the much lauded Californian climate. The smog veiled the sun and set up irritation is his mucous membranes. If it did not rain, bush fires raged over the hills burning out whole tracts of houses. When it rained you got a year's supply inside twelve hours and mud slides pushed houses into the sea at Malibu. And any day now the San Andreas Fault was expected to crack and rip the whole tacky place apart. Who would voluntarily live in such a hell of a city?

Answer: five million nuts. Which brought his mind back smartly to Hendrix, Biggie and the commune. To hell with Gunnarsson; he would go see Charlie Wainwright.

The Los Angeles office of Gunnarsson Associates was on Hollywood Boulevard at the corner of Highland, near Grauman's Chinese Theatre. His card got him in to see Charlie Wainwright, boss of the West Coast region, who said, 'Hi, Ben; what are you doing over here?'

'Slumming,' said Hardin as he sat down. 'You don't think I'd come here if I had a choice?'

'Still the same old grouch.' Wainwright waved his hand to the window. 'What's wrong with this? It's a beautiful day.'

'Yeah; and the last for ten years,' said Hardin. 'I had that on authority. I'll give you a tip, Charlie. You can get a hell of a view of the San Gabriels today from the top of Mullholland Drive. But don't wait too long; they'll be gone by tomorrow.'

'Maybe I'll take a drive up there.' Wainwright leaned back in his chair. 'What can we do for you, Ben?'

'Have you got a pipeline into the Sheriff's office?'

'That depends on what you want to come down it,' said Wainwright cautiously.

Hardin decided not to mention Hendrix. 'I'm looking for a guy called Biggie. Seems he's mixed up in a commune. They were busted by sheriff's deputies about ten months ago over in North Hollywood.'

'Not the LAPD?' queried Wainwright. 'Don't they have jurisdiction in North Hollywood?'

Hardin was sure Mrs White had not mentioned the Los Angeles Police Department, but he checked his notebook. 'No; my informant referred to the Sheriff's Department.'

'So what do you want?'

Hardin looked at Wainwright in silence for a moment before saying patiently, 'I want Biggie.'

'That shouldn't be too difficult to arrange.' Wainwright thought a while. 'Might take a little time.'

'Not too long, I hope.' Hardin stood up. 'And do me a favour, Charlie; you haven't seen me. I haven't been here. Especially if Gunnarsson wants to know. He's playing this one close to his chest.'

'How are you getting on with the old bastard?'

'Not bad,' said Hardin noncommittally.


Two hours later he was in a coffee shop across from City Hall waiting for a deputy from the Sheriff's Department.

Wainwright had said, 'Better not see him in his office – might compromise him. You don't have an investigator's licence for this state. What's Gunnarsson up to, Ben? He's not done this before. These things are usually handled by the local office.'

'Maybe he doesn't like me,' said Hardin feelingly, thinking of the miles of interstate highways he had driven.

He was about to order another coffee when a shadow fell across the table. 'You the guy looking for Olaf Hamsun?'

Hardin looked up and saw a tall, lean man in uniform. 'Who?'

'Also known as Biggie,' said the deputy. 'Big blond Scandahoovian – monster size.'

'That's the guy.' He held out his hand. 'I'm Ben Hardin. Coffee?' At the deputy's nod he held up two fingers to a passing waitress.

The deputy sat opposite. 'Jack Sawyer. What do you want with Biggie?'

'Nothing at all. But he's running with Henry Hendrix, and I want to visit with Hank.'

'Hendrix,' said Sawyer ruminatively. 'Youngish – say, twenty-six or twenty-seven; height about five ten; small scar above left eyebrow.'

'That's probably my boy.'

'What do you want with him?'

'Just to establish that he's his father's son, and then report back to New York.'

'Who wants to know?'

'Some British lawyer according to my boss. That's all I know; Gunnarsson doesn't confide in me. Operates on need to know.'

'Just like all the other ex-CIA cloak and dagger boys,' said Sawyer scornfully. He looked at Hardin carefully. 'You were a Company man, too, weren't you?'

'Don't hold it against me,' said Hardin, forcing a grin.

'Even if I don't that doesn't mean I have to like it. And you don't have an investigator's licence good in California. If I didn't owe Charlie Wainwright a couple I wouldn't be here now. I don't like you guys and I never have.'

'Now wait a minute,' said Hardin. 'What's eating you?'

'I'll tell you.' Sawyer leaned forward. 'Last year we busted a gang smuggling cocaine from Mexico. Turned out that half of them were bastards from the CIA. *They* claimed we'd wrecked one of their best Mexican operations. *We* said they were breaking the law of the United States and we were going to jail them. But do you think we could? Those sons of bitches are walking around free as air right now.'

Hardin said, 'You can't blame that on me.'

'I guess not,' said Sawyer tiredly. 'Okay, I'll tell you where to find Biggie.' He stuck out his forefinger. 'But step out of line one inch and I'll nail your hide to the barn door, even if it's for spitting on the sidewalk.'

'Thanks,' said Hardin ironically.

'You'll find the gang down at Playa del Rey. If they're not there try Santa Monica, down near the Bristol Pier. There's a greasy spoon called Bernie's where they hang out.'

Hardin wrote in his notebook. 'Does Hendrix have a record? Or Hamsun?'

'Hamsun's been busted for peddling pot. He had a fraction under an ounce on him, so it didn't come to much. Nothing on Hendrix; at least, not here.'

'I've been wondering about something,' said Hardin, putting away his notebook. 'When you cracked down on the commune in North Hollywood you found some funny things in the house, I hear. Statues of some kind, and not the kind a good, Christian woman would like.'

'The good, Christian woman being Mrs White,' said Sawyer ironically. 'The old witch. There's nothing to it, Hardin. It's just that the kids tried their hand at pottery; reckoned they could sell the stuff at the Farmer's Market and make a few dollars. That pottery kiln did most of the damage to the house when it blew up.'

'Is that all?'

'That's all,' said Sawyer, and laughed. 'Turned out they weren't very good at sculpting. They didn't know enough anatomy; least, not the kind you need for sculpting.' He became philosophical. 'They're not a bad crowd of kids, not as things are these days. Sure, they smoke pot, but who doesn't? I bet my own kids do when I'm not around. They're just mostly beach bums, and that's not illegal yet.'

'Sure,' said Hardin. He had a sudden thought. 'Does Biggie still wear the ankh?'

'The *what*?'

'The ankh.' He sketched it on the back of the menu.

'Yeah, he still wears that thing. Didn't know it had a name. It should be valuable. It's big and looks as though it's solid gold. But it would take some real crazy guy to rip it off Biggie.'

Hardin spent two days at Playa del Rey and drew a blank, so he went up the coast to Santa Monica. He found Bernie's and had a cup of coffee, steering clear of the hamburgers. The place stank of rancid oil and he judged the level of hygiene was good for a jail sentence. The coffee was lousy, too, and there was lipstick on his cup.

He questioned the harassed waitress intermittently as she passed and repassed his table and again drew a blank. Yes, she knew Biggie but had not seen him for some time. No, she didn't know anyone called Hendrix. Hardin pushed aside the unfinished coffee and left.

For another two days he roamed the Santa Monica water front, questioning the kids – the beach bums and surfing freaks – and made little progress. Biggie was well known but no one had seen him around. Hendrix was less known and no one had seen him, either. Hardin looked gloomily at the offshore oil rigs which periodically sprang leaks to poison the fish and kill the seabirds, and he cursed Gunnarsson.

On the evening of the second day he checked again at Bernie's. As he stared distastefully at the grease floating on the surface of his coffee a girl sidled up next to him. 'You the guy looking for Biggie?'

He turned his head. Her long uncombed hair was a dirty blonde and her make-up had been applied sloppily so that she looked like a kid who had just used the contents of her mother's dressing table for the first time. 'I'm the guy,' he said briefly.

'He don't like it.'

'I'm broken hearted.'

She made a face. 'But he'll talk to you.'

'When and where?'

'Tonight – eight o'clock. There's an old warehouse on Twenty-seventh Street at Carlyle. He'll be there.'

'Look,' said Hardin, 'I'm not interested in Biggie, but he has a sidekick called Hendrix – Hank Hendrix. Know him?'

'Sure.'

'He's the guy I want to talk with. Let him be at the warehouse. I don't give a damn about Biggie.'

The girl shrugged. 'I'll pass the word.'


Hardin was at the rendezvous an hour early. The abandoned warehouse was in a depressed area long overdue for urban renewal; the few windows still intact were grimy, and the place looked as though it would collapse if an over-zealous puff of air blew in from the Pacific. He tested a door, found it unlocked, and went inside.

It took only a few minutes to find that the building was empty. He explored thoroughly, his footsteps echoing in the cavernous interior, and found a locked door at the back. He unlocked it and returned to his car where he sat with a good view of the front entrance and lit a cigarette.

Biggie and Hendrix showed up halfway through the third cigarette. Biggie was unmistakable; tall and broad he looked like a circus strong man, and there was a glint of gold on his bare chest. Hendrix, who walked next to him, was no light-weight but next to Biggie he looked like a midget. They went into the warehouse and Hardin finished his cigarette before getting out of the car and crossing the road.

He entered the warehouse and found Biggie sitting on a crate. Hendrix was nowhere to be seen. Biggie stood up as he approached, 'I'm Ben Hardin. You'll be Olaf Hamsun, right?'

'Could be,' conceded Biggie.

'Where's Hendrix?'

Biggie ignored the question. 'You a pig?' he asked.

Hardin suppressed an insane desire to giggle; the thought of describing himself as a private pig was crazy. Instead, he said mildly, 'Watch your mouth.'

Biggie shrugged. 'Just a manner of speaking. No offence meant. What do you want with Hank?'

'If he wants you to know he'll tell you. Where is he?'

Biggie jerked his thumb over his shoulder. 'Back there. But you talk to me.'

'No way,' said Hardin decidedly.

'Suit yourself. Now shut up and listen to me, buster. I don't like creeps like you asking questions around town. Christ, every Joe I've talked to in the last couple days tells me I'm a wanted man. Hurts my reputation, see?'

'You shouldn't be hard to find.'

'I'm not hiding,' said Biggie. 'But you and your foreign friend bug me.'

'I don't have a foreign friend,' said Hardin.

'No? Then how come he's been asking around, too?'

Hardin frowned. 'Tell me more,' he said. 'How do you know he's foreign?'

'His accent, dummy.'

'I told you to watch your mouth,' said Hardin sharply. He thought for a moment and remembered that Gunnarsson had mentioned a British lawyer. 'Could it be a British accent?'

'You mean like we hear on those longhair programs on TV?' Biggie shook his head. 'No; not like that. This guy has a real foreign accent.' He paused. 'Could be a Kraut,' he offered.

'So you've talked with him.'

'Naw. I had a friend talk with him at Bernie's. I was in the next booth.'

'What did he want?'

'Same as you. He wants to visit with Hank.'

'Can you describe him?'

'Sure. Big guy, well set up; looks like he can handle himself. Short hair, crewcut like a soldier boy.' Biggie scratched his chest absently, his hand moving the golden ankh aside. 'Scar on his cheek.'

'Which side?'

'Left.'

Hardin pondered. All this was adding up to the classic picture of a German soldier except that ritual duelling was no longer acceptable. 'How old is he?'

'Thirty-five – maybe forty. Not more. So you really don't know the guy.'

'I don't give a damn about him and I don't give a damn about you. All I want is to talk to Hendrix. Go get him.'

'You don't give a damn about me, and you don't listen good.' Biggie stuck out his forefinger then tapped himself on the chest. 'The only way to get to Hendrix is through me.'

'Does he know that?' asked Hardin. 'What is he, anyway? Your fancy boy?'

'Christ, that does it,' said Biggie, enraged.

'Oh, shit!' said Hardin resignedly as Biggie flexed his muscles, 'I'm not mad at you, Biggie; I don't want to fight.'

'Well, I want to fight you.' Biggie plunged forward.

It was no contest. Hardin was full of frustrations; his anger at Gunnarsson, the weary miles of travel, his sense of personal failure – all these he worked out on Biggie. He had several advantages; one was that Biggie had never learned to fight – he never had to because what idiot would want to tangle with a man who was obviously a meat grinder? The idiot was Hardin who had been trained in unarmed combat by experts. In spite of his age and flabbiness he still knew the chopping places and pressure points, the vulnerable parts of a man's body, and he used his knowledge mercilessly. It was only by a deliberate act of will that he restrained himself from the final deadly blow that would have killed.

Breathing heavily he bent down and reached for the pulse at the side of Biggie's neck and sighed with relief as he felt it beating strongly. Then he straightened and turned to see Hendrix watching him.

'Jesus!' said Hendrix. He was wide-eyed as he stared at the prostrate Biggie, 'I didn't think you could beat him.'

'I've taken a lot of shit on this job,' said Hardin, and found his voice was shaking. 'But I wasn't going to take any from him.' He bent down and ripped the golden ankh from Biggie's neck, breaking the chain. 'And I've been insulted by a cop, a cop who told me this couldn't be done.' He tossed the golden cross down by Biggie's side. 'Now let's you and me talk.'

Hendrix eyed him warily. 'What about?'

'You can start off by telling me your father's name.'

'What's my old man got to do with anything?' said Hendrix in surprise.

'His name, sonny,' said Hardin impatiently.

'Hendrix, of course. Adrian Hendrix.'

'Where was he born?'

'Africa. Some place in South Africa. But he's dead.'

Hardin took a deep breath. This was the one; this was the right Hendrix. 'You got brothers? Sisters? Your Mom still alive?'

'No. What's this all about?'

Hardin said, 'I wouldn't know, but a man in New York called Gunnarsson wants to know.'

'Why?'

'Because a British lawyer wants to know. Maybe you're inheriting something. What about going to New York with me to find out?'

Hendrix scratched his jaw. 'Gee, I don't know. I don't like the East much.'

'Expenses paid,' said Hardin.

Biggie stirred and groaned, and Hendrix looked down at him. 'I guess Biggie will be hard to live with now,' he said reflectively. 'He won't want anyone around who's seen him slaughtered like that. Might not be a bad idea to split for a while.'

'Okay,' said Hardin, 'Is there anything you want to take?'

'Not much,' said Hendrix, and grinned, 'I have a good surfboard but that won't be much use in New York. I'd better take some clothes, though.'

'I'll come help you pack,' said Hardin, and added pointedly, 'I've had a hard time finding you, and I don't want to lose you now.'

# FOUR

Hendrix told Hardin where he lived and, as he drove, Hardin thought about the other man looking for Hendrix. Or other men. The man described by Biggie was hardly likely to be the 'nice young man' as described by Mrs Parker. All right then; two or more men. He said, 'Did Biggie ever say anything about another guy looking for you? Could be a German.'

'Yeah.' Hendrix lit a cigarette. 'He told me. He thought you were together but he wanted to make sure first before . . .' He broke off suddenly.

'Before what?'

Hendrix laughed shortly. 'Biggie thought there might be some dough in it somewhere. If you and the foreign guy were together, then okay; but if you weren't he figured he could make a trade.'

'Sell you off to the highest bidder?' Hardin grimaced. 'What did you think of that?'

Hendrix shrugged. 'Biggie's all right. It's just that he was short of dough, that's all. We're all short of dough.'

'All?'

'The gang.' He sighed. 'Things haven't been the same since we were busted over in the San Fernando Valley.'

'When you blew up Mrs White's house?'

Hendrix turned his head sharply. 'You've been getting around.' He sounded as though he did not like it. 'But it wasn't all that much. Just some smoky walls and busted glass.'

Hardin came back to his main problem. 'The foreigner. Did you ever meet him?'

'No. Biggie set up a meeting for tonight in case he had something to trade. That's why he wanted to blow you off fast.'

'Where's the meeting?'

'I don't know – we didn't get that far. Man, you sure cooled him.' He pointed. 'That's our place.'

Hardin drew up in front of the dilapidated house. 'I'll come in with you.' He escorted Hendrix to the door and they went in. In the narrow hall they met the girl who had set up the meeting with Biggie. She looked at Hardin with surprise and he thought he detected something of alarm in her eyes.

She turned to Hendrix. 'Where's Biggie?'

'He'll be along. He . . . uh . . . had something to attend to,' said Hendrix. 'Come on, Mr Hardin; we'd better make this fast.'

As they climbed the stairs Hardin thought with amusement that Hendrix had every reason for speed. If Biggie came back and found him in the act of packing he would want to know why and Hendrix would not want to tell him. 'How many in the gang?' he asked.

'It varies; there's six of us now. Have been as many as twelve.' Hendrix opened the door of a room. 'This won't take long.'

It took less time than Hardin would have thought. Hendrix was a nomad and had few possessions, all of which went into a metal-framed backpack. He lifted it effortlessly and then looked regretfully at the surfboard lying against the wall behind the unmade bed. 'Can't take that along, I guess. You sure there are dollars in this, Mr Hardin?'

'No,' said Hardin honestly. 'But I can't think of anything else.'

'You said a British lawyer. I don't know any Britishers and I've never been out of the States.' Hendrix shook his head. 'Still, you said you'll pay my way so it's worth a chance.'

They went downstairs and met the blonde girl again. 'When'll Biggie be back?' she asked.

'He didn't say,' said Hendrix briefly.

She looked at the backpack. 'You going some place?'

'Not far.' Hendrix coughed. 'Just down to . . . uh . . . Mexico, Mr Hardin and me. Got to pick up a package in Tijuana.'

She nodded understandingly. 'Be careful. Those Customs bastards are real nosy. What is it? Pot or snow?'

'Snow,' he said. 'Come on, Mr Hardin.' As they got into the car Hendrix forced a smile. 'No use in letting the world know where we're going.'

'Sure,' said Hardin. 'No point at all.' He switched on the ignition and, as he took off the handbrake, something whined like a bee in front of his nose. Hendrix gave a sharp cry, and Hardin shot a glance at him. He had his hand to his shoulder and blood was oozing through his fingers.

Hardin had been shot at before. He took off, burning rubber, and turned the first corner at top speed. Only then did he look in the mirror to check for pursuers. The corner receded behind him and nothing came into sight so he slowed until he was just below the speed limit. Then he said, 'You all right, Hank?'

'What the hell!' said Hendrix, looking unbelievingly at the blood on his hand. 'What happened?'

'You were stung by a bee,' said Hardin. 'From a silenced gun. Hurt much?'

'You mean I've been shot?' said Hendrix incredulously. 'Who'd want to shoot me?'

'Maybe a guy with a German accent and a scar on his left cheek. Perhaps it's just as well you and Biggie couldn't keep that appointment tonight. How do you feel?'

'Numb,' said Hendrix. 'My shoulder feels numb.'

'The pain comes later.' Hardin still watched the mirror. Everything behind still seemed normal. But he made a couple of random turns before he said, 'We've got to get you off the streets. Can you hold on for a few more minutes?'

'I guess so.'

'There's Kleenex in the glove compartment. Put a pad of it over the wound.'

Hardin drove on to the Santa Monica Freeway and made the interchange on to the San Diego Freeway heading north. As he drove his mind was busy with speculations. Who had fired the shot? And who was the intended victim? He said, 'I don't know of anyone who wants to kill me. How about you, Hank?'

Hendrix was holding the pad of tissues to his shoulder beneath his shirt. His face was pale. 'Hell, no!'

'You told the girl back there we were going to Tijuana to pick up a package of cocaine.'

'Ella? I had to tell her something to put Biggie off.'

'She didn't seem surprised. You've done that often? The cocaine bit, I mean.'

'A couple of times,' Hendrix admitted. 'But it's small time stuff.'

'A man can make enemies that way,' said Hardin. 'You might have stepped on someone's turf. The big boys don't like that and they don't forget.'

'No way,' said Hendrix. 'The last time I did it was over a year ago.' He nursed his shoulder. 'What the hell are you getting me into, Hardin?'

'I'm not getting you into anything; I'm doing my best to get you out.'

They were silent for a long time after that, each busy with his thoughts. Hardin changed on to the Ventura Freeway and headed east. 'Where are we going?' asked Hendrix.

'To a motel. But we'll stop by a drugstore first and pick up some bandages and medication.'

'Jesus! I need a doctor.'

'We'll see about that when you're under cover and rested.' Hardin did not add that gunshot wounds had to be reported to the police. He had to think about that.

He pulled into the motel on Riverside Drive where he had stayed before and booked two rooms. The woman behind the desk was the one he had seen before. He said casually, 'The San Gabriels have vanished again.'

'Yeah; it's a damn shame,' she said, a little forlornly. 'I bet we don't see them again for another ten years.'

He smiled. 'Still, it's nice to see the air we're breathing.'

He got Hendrix into his room, examined his shoulder, and was relieved by what he saw. It was a flesh wound and the bullet had missed the bone; however, it had not come out the other side and was still in Hendrix. He said, 'You'll live. It's only a .22 – a pee-wee.'

Hendrix grunted. 'It feels like I've been kicked by a horse.'

As he dressed the wound Hardin puzzled over the calibre of the bullet. It could mean one of two things; the gun had been fired either by an amateur or a very good professional. Only a good professional killer would use a .22, a man who could put his bullets where he wanted them. He tied the last knot and adjusted the sling. 'I have a bottle in my bag,' he said. 'I guess we both need a drink.'

He brought the whiskey and some ice and made two drinks, then he departed for his own room, the glass still in his hand. 'Stick around,' he said on leaving. 'Lie low like

Brer Rabbit. I won't be long.' He wanted to talk to Gunnarsson.

'Where would I go?' asked Hendrix plaintively.

On the telephone Gunnarsson was brusque. 'Make it quick, Ben; I'm busy.'

'I've got young Hendrix,' said Hardin without preamble. 'Only trouble is someone just put a bullet in him.'

'God damn it!' said Gunnarsson explosively. 'When?'

'Less than an hour ago. I'd just picked him up.'

'How bad is he?'

'He's okay, but the slug's still in him. It's only a .22 but the wound might go bad. He needs a doctor.'

'Is he mobile?'

'Sure,' said Hardin. 'He can't run a four-minute mile but he can move. It's a flesh wound in the shoulder.'

There was a pause before Gunnarsson said, 'Who knows about this?'

'You, me, Hendrix and the guy who shot him,' said Hardin factually.

'And who the hell was that?'

'I don't know. Someone else is looking for Hendrix; I've crossed his tracks a couple of times. A foreign guy – could be German. That's all I know.' Hardin sipped his whiskey. 'What is all this with Hendrix? Is there something I should know that you haven't told me? I wouldn't like that.'

'Ben; it beats me, it really does,' said Gunnarsson sincerely. 'Now, look, Ben; no doctor. Get that kid to New York as fast as you can. Come by air. I'll have a doctor standing by here.'

'But what about my car?'

'You'll get it back,' said Gunnarsson soothingly. 'The company will pay for delivery.'

Hardin did not like that idea. The car would be entrusted to some punk kid who would drive too fast, mistreat the engine, forget to check the oil, and most likely end up in a total wreck. 'All right,' he said reluctantly. 'But I won't fly from Los Angeles. I think there's more than one guy looking for Hendrix and the airport might be covered. I'll drive up to San Francisco and fly from there. You'll have your boy the day after tomorrow.'

'Good thinking, Ben,' said Gunnarsson, and rang off.

They left for San Francisco early next morning. It was over 300 miles but Hardin made good time on Interstate 5 ignoring the 55 mph speed limit like everyone else. He went with the traffic flow, only slowing a little when he had the road to himself. If you stayed inside the speed limit you could get run down, and modern cars were not designed to travel so slowly on good roads.

Hendrix seemed all right although he favoured his wounded shoulder. He had complained about not being seen by a doctor, but shut up when Hardin said, 'That means getting into a hassle with the law. You want that?' Apparently not, and neither did Hardin. He had not forgotten what Deputy Sawyer had said about spitting on the sidewalk.

Hendrix had also been naturally curious about why he was being taken to New York. 'Don't ask me questions, son,' Hardin said, 'because I don't know the answers. I just do what the man says.'

He was irked himself at not knowing the answers so, when they stopped for gas, he took Hendrix into a Howard Johnson for coffee and doughnuts and did a little pumping of his own. Although he knew the answer he said, 'Maybe your old man left you a pile.'

'Fat chance,' said Hendrix. 'He died years ago when I was a kid.' He shook his head. 'Mom said he was a dead beat, anyway.'

'You said she was dead too, right?'

'Yeah.' Hendrix smiled wryly, 'I guess you could call me an orphan.'

'Got any other folks? Uncles, maybe?'

'No.' Hendrix paused as he stirred his coffee. 'Yeah, I have a cousin in England. He wrote to me when I was in high school, said he was coming to the States and would like to meet me. He never did, but he wrote a couple more times. Not lately, though. I guess he's lost track of me. I've been moving around.'

'What's his name?'

'Funny thing about that. Same as mine but spelled differently. Dirk Hendriks. H-E-N-D-R-I-K-S.'

'Your father spelled his name the same way when he was in South Africa,' said Hardin. 'Have you got your cousin's address?'

'Somewhere in London, that's all I know. I had it written down but I lost it. You know how it is when you're moving around.'

'Yeah,' said Hardin. 'Maybe he's died and left you something. Or maybe he's just looking for you.'

Hendrix felt his shoulder. 'Someone sure is,' he said.

So it was that Hardin saw Gunnarsson sooner than he expected. Hardin and Hendrix took a cab from Kennedy Airport direct to Gunnarsson Associates and he was shown into Gunnarsson's office fast. Gunnarsson was sitting behind his desk and said abruptly, 'You've got the Hendrix kid?'

'He's right there in your outer office. You got a doctor? He's in pain.'

Gunnarsson laughed. 'I've got something to cure his pain. Are you sure he's the guy?'

'He checks out right down the line.'

Gunnarsson frowned. 'You're sure.'

'I'm sure. But you'll check yourself, of course.'

'Yeah,' said Gunnarsson. 'I'll check.' He doodled on a piece of paper. 'Does the guy have kids?'

'None that he'll plead guilty to – he's not married.' Hardin was wondering why Gunnarsson did not invite him to sit.

Gunnarsson said, 'Now tell me how Hendrix got shot.'

So Hardin told it all in detail and they kicked it around for a while. At last he said, 'I guess I earned that bonus. This case got a mite tough at the end.'

'What bonus?'

Hardin stared. 'You said I'd get a bonus if I tracked down any Hendrixes.'

Gunnarsson was blank-faced. 'That's not my recollection.'

'Well, I'll be goddamned,' said Hardin softly. 'My memory isn't that bad.'

'Why would I offer you a bonus?' asked Gunnarsson. 'You know damned well we've been carrying you the last couple of years. Some of the guys have been bending my ear about it; they said they were tired of carrying a passenger.'

'Which guys?' demanded Hardin. 'Name the names.'

'You're on the wrong side of the desk to be asking the questions.'

Hardin was trembling. He could not remember when he had been so angry. He said tightly, 'As you get older you become more of a cheapskate, Gunnarsson.'

'That I don't have to take.' Gunnarsson put his hands flat on the desk. 'You're fired. By the time you've cleaned out your desk the cashier will have your severance pay ready. Now get the hell out of my office.' As he picked up the telephone Hardin turned away blindly. The door slammed and Gunnarsson snorted in derision.

Hardin took the elevator to the lobby and crossed the street to the Irish bar where, in the past, he had spent more time than was good for either his liver or his wallet. He sat on a stool and said brusquely, 'Double bourbon.'

Over the drink he brooded on his fate. Damn Gunnarsson! It had never been Hardin's style to complain that life was unfair; in his view life was what you made it. Yet now he thought that Gunnarsson had not only been unfair but vindictive. Canned and out on his ear after five minutes' conversation – the bum's rush.

He viewed the future glumly. What was a man aged fifty-five with no particular marketable skills to do? He could set up on his own, he supposed; find an office, put some ads in the paper, and sit back and wait for clients – a seedy Sam Spade. Likely he'd have to wait a long time and starve while waiting. More likely he'd end up carrying a gun for Brinks or become a bank guard and get corns on his feet from too much standing.

And his car, goddamn it! He and his car were separated by three thousand miles. He knew that if he went back to Gunnarsson and reminded him of the promise to bring the car back to New York Gunnarsson would laugh in his face.

He ordered another drink and went over the events of the last few weeks. Gunnarsson *had* promised him a bonus if he cracked the Hendrix case, so why had he reneged on the offer? It wasn't as though Gunnarsson Associates were broke – the money was rolling in as though there was a pipeline from Fort Knox. There had to be a definite reason.

Come to think of it the Hendrix case had been a funny one right from the beginning. It was not Gunnarsson Associates' style to send a man freelancing all over the country – not when they had all those regional offices. So why had Gunnarsson handled it that way? And the way he had been fired was too damned fast. Gunnarsson had delib-erately needled him, forcing an argument and wanting Hardin to blow his top. Any boss was entitled to fire a man who called him a cheapskate.

Dim suspicions burgeoned in Hardin's mind.

His musings were interrupted by a hand on his shoulder and a voice said, 'Hi, Ben; I thought you were on the West Coast.'

Hardin turned his head and saw Jack Richardson. 'I was,' he said sourly. 'But how did you know?'

'I had to call the Los Angeles office this morning. Wainwright said you'd been around. What's your poison?'

'Make it bourbon.' So Wainwright couldn't keep his big mouth shut after all. Richardson ran the files at Gunnarsson Associates; the records were totally computerized and Richardson knew which buttons to push. Now Hardin regarded him with interest. 'Jack, did you hear any of the guys in the office beefing about me? Complaining of how I do my work, for instance?'

Richardson looked surprised. 'Not around me. No more than the usual anyway. Everyone beefs some, you know that.'

'Yeah.' Hardin sipped his whiskey. 'Gunnarsson canned me this morning.'

Richardson whistled. 'Just like that?'

Hardin snapped his fingers. 'Just like that. Took him about thirty seconds.'

'Why?'

'I called him a cheapskate for one thing.'

'I'd have liked to have seen his face,' said Richardson. 'No wonder he fired you.'

'I don't think it was the reason,' said Hardin, 'I think it was something else. Could you do me a favour?'

'I might, depending on what it is. Don't ask for dough, Ben. I'm broke.'

'Who isn't?' said Hardin feelingly, 'I'd like you to ask your metal friend across the street for the name and address of the British lawyer who started the Hendrix case.'

'The Hendrix case,' repeated Richardson, and frowned. 'Gunnarsson seems to be keeping that one under wraps.

He says he's handling it personally. I don't have any information on it so far.'

Hardin found that interesting but he made no comment. 'But the details of the original letter from England should be in the files.'

'I guess so,' said Richardson without enthusiasm. 'But you know how Gunnarsson is about security. The computer logs every inquiry into any case and Gunnarsson checks the log.'

'He can't check every log; he'd be doing nothing else.'

'Spot checks mostly,' admitted Richardson. 'But if he's handling the Hendrix case personally that's one log he might very well check. I can't risk it, Ben. I don't want to get fired, too.'

'For Christ's sake!' said Hardin in disgust. 'You know enough about the computer to gimmick a log. You wrote the goddamn programs for the data base.'

'What's your interest in this?'

'I'm damned if I know; I've got to do some hard thinking. There's something wrong somewhere. I feel it in my bones. But, for your information, Gunnarsson isn't handling the Hendrix case. I've been handling it, and I cracked it. Then I get fired. I'd like to figure out why I was fired.'

'Okay, Ben; I'll see what I can do,' said Richardson. 'But you don't talk about this. You keep your mouth zipped.'

'Who would I talk to? When can I have it?'

'I'll see what I can do tomorrow. I'll meet you in here at midday.'

'That's fine,' said Hardin and drained his glass. 'This one's on me. Then I'll go clean out my desk like a good boy.' He signalled the bartender, 'I wonder what Gunnarsson's idea of severance pay is.'

# FIVE

Gunnarsson's idea of severance pay made Hardin madder than ever. He tried to complain but could not get past the acidulated spinster who guarded Gunnarsson's office, and neither could he get through on the phone. Gunnarsson's castle was impregnable.

But Richardson came up with the information he needed next day. He gave Hardin an envelope and said, 'You don't know where you got it.'

'Okay.' Hardin opened the envelope and took out a single piece of paper. 'This isn't a computer print-out.'

'You're damned right it isn't,' said Richardson, if Gunnarsson found a printout with that information floating loose he'd head straight for me. Is it what you want?'

Hardin scanned it. A London inquiry agency, Peacemore, Willis and Franks, requested Gunnarsson Associates to search for any living relatives of Jan-Willem Hendrykxx – Hardin blinked at the spelling – and to pass the word back. Hendrykxx was reputed to have married in South Africa and to have had two sons, one of whom was believed to have emigrated to the United States in the 1930s. There was also the address and telephone number of a lawyer in Jersey.

It told Hardin nothing he did not know already except for the unusual spelling of Hendrix, and the Jersey address

confused him until he realized that it referred to the original Jersey in the Channel Islands and not the state of New
Jersey. He nodded. 'This is it.' There was something more.
Peacemore, Willis and Franks was the British end of
Gunnarsson Associates, a fact not generally known. It
meant that Gunnarsson had been in it right from the start,
whatever 'it' was. 'Thanks. It's worth a drink, Jack.'

If Hardin was mad at Gunnarsson he was also broke. He
moved out of his apartment on the East Side and into a
rooming house in the Bronx. It cost more in subway and
bus fares to get into Manhattan but it was still cheaper. He
wired instructions to San Francisco to sell his car and wire
the money. He did not expect much but he needed the cash,
and a car was a needless luxury in the city.

He carefully maintained his pipelines into the offices of
Gunnarsson Associates, mainly through Jack Richardson,
although there were a couple of secretaries whom he took
to frugal lunches and pumped carefully, trying to get a line
on what Gunnarsson was doing in the matter of Hank
Hendrix. The answer, apparently, was nothing at all. Worse
still, Hendrix had vanished.

'Maybe Gunnarsson sent him to England,' Richardson
said one day.

'You can check that,' said Hardin thoughtfully. 'There'll
be an expense account for the air fare. Do me a favour.'

'Goddamn it!' said Richardson heatedly. 'You'll get me
fired.' But he checked and found no record of transatlantic
flights since Hendrix had arrived in New York. On his own
initiative he checked for any record of medical expenses
paid out for the treatment of Hendrix's wound and, again,
found nothing. He was a good friend to Hardin.

'Gunnarsson is playing this one close,' commented
Hardin. 'He's usually damned hot on record keeping. I'm
more and more convinced that the bastard's up to no good.
But what the hell is it?'

Richardson had no suggestions.

Probably Hardin would not have pressed on but for a genuine stroke of luck. Nearly a month had passed and he knew he had to get a job. His resentment at Gunnarsson had fuelled him thus far but an eroding bank account was a stronger argument. He had set aside enough for Annette's next payment and that he would not touch, but his own reserves were melting.

Then he got a wire from Annette. 'GOT MARRIED THIS MORNING STOP NOW MRS KREISS STOP WISH ME LUCK ANNETTE.'

'Thank God!' he said to Richardson. 'Now some other guy can maintain her.' Briefly he wondered what sort of a man this stranger, Kreiss, was then put the matter out of his mind. For he was now the master of unexpected wealth and his heart was filled with jubilation. 'Now I can do it,' he said.

'Do what?' asked Richardson.

'I'm flying to England.'

'You're nuts!' Richardson protested. 'Ben, this obsession is doing you no good. What can you do in England?'

'I don't know,' said Hardin cheerfully. 'But I'll find out when I get there. I haven't had a vacation in years.'

Before leaving for England he flew to Washington on the shuttle where he renewed acquaintance with some of his old buddies in the Company and armed himself with some British addresses, and he visited the British Embassy where he ran into problems. No one knew much about Jersey.

'They're autonomous,' he was told. 'They have their own way of doing things. You say you want to know about a will?'

'That's right.'

'In London a copy would be kept in Somerset House,' said the attaché. 'But I don't think that applies to Jersey wills.' He thought for a moment then his face lightened.

'I do believe we have someone who would know.' He picked up a telephone and dialled, then said, 'Pearson here. Mark, you're a Jerseyman, aren't you? Yes I thought so. Would you mind popping in here for a moment?' Pearson put down the telephone. 'Mark le Tissier should know about it.'

And Mark le Tissier did. 'Wills are kept in the Greffe,' he said.

'The *what*?'

'The Greffe.' Le Tissier smiled. 'The Public Records Office. I had the same problem a couple of years ago. They'll give you a copy.'

'All I have to do is to go to this place, the Greffe, and ask?'

'Oh you don't have *to go*. Just drop a line to the Greffier. We'll go into the library and dig out his address.'

So Hardin went back to New York and wrote to Jersey, giving as return address *poste restante* at the London office of American Express. A few days later he flew and the day he left from Kennedy Airport the rooming house in the Bronx in which he lived burned to the ground though he did not know about it until long after. Still, it could have been chance; there are, after all, whole blocks burned out in the Bronx.

In the employment of Gunnarsson Associates Hardin had learned how to travel light. He freshened up before landing at Heathrow in the early morning and cleared Customs quickly while the rest of the passengers were waiting for their baggage, then took the Underground into London where he registered at an inexpensive hotel near Victora Station. He then walked through St James's Park towards the Haymarket where he picked up his mail.

He enjoyed the walk. The sun was shining and he felt oddly contented and in a holiday mood as he strolled by the lake. It was true that it had been some years since he had taken a real vacation. Perhaps he had been getting in a rut and the split with Gunnarsson was to be good for him in the long run. He had little money and no prospects but he was happy.

After leaving the American Express office Hardin bought a street plan of London from a news vendor because, although he was no stranger to London, it was many years since he had been there. Then he went into a pub to inspect the single letter he had received. The envelope was bulky and bore Jersey stamps. He ordered a half pint of beer at the bar and took it to a corner table, then opened the envelope.

The will was seven pages long. Jan-Willem Hendrykxx had left £10,000 to Dr Morton, his physician, as a token of esteem for keeping him alive so long, £20,000 to Mr and Mrs Adams, his butler and housekeeper, and various sums of between £1,000 and £4,000 to various members of his staff, which appeared to be large.

Detailed instructions were given for the sale of his real property of which he had a plenitude; a house in Jersey, another in the South of France, yet another in Belgium, and a whole island in the Caribbean. The sums arising from these sales and from the sale of his other possessions were to be added to the main part of his estate. Hendrykxx had evidently been a careful man because the will was up-to-date and he had estimated the current market values of his properties. Thenceforth the terms were expressed in percentages; 85 per cent of his estate was to go to the Ol Njorowa Foundation of Kenya, and 15 per cent to be divided equally among his living descendants.

The name of the executor was given as Harold Farrar of the firm of Farrar, Windsor and Markham, a Jersey law firm. Hardin made a note of the address and the telephone

number. His hand trembled a little as he noted the size of
the estate.

It was estimated at forty million pounds sterling.

Hardin drank his beer, ordered another, and contemplated
what he had discovered. Hank Hendrix and Dirk Hendriks,
if he was still around, stood to split £6 million between
them. He translated it into more familiar terms. The rate of
the dollar to the pound sterling had been volatile of late but
had settled at about two to one. That made twelve million
bucks to split between two if there were no other heirs and
he knew of none, unless Dirk Hendriks had children. That
dope-smuggling drop-out, Hank Hendrix, was a multi-
millionaire. The main bulk of the fortune might be going to
the foundation with the funny name but the residue was
not peanuts.

Hardin smiled to himself. No wonder Gunnarsson had
been so interested. He always knew the value of a dollar and
would not resist the temptation to put himself alongside six
million of them in the hope of cutting himself a slice. He
had isolated Hendrix and that young man would be no
match for Gunnarsson who could charm birds from a tree
when he wanted to. Gunnarsson would cook up some kind
of deal to guarantee that some of those dollars would stick
to his fingers.

So what was the next step? Hardin walked to the corner
of the bar where there was a telephone and checked the
directory which lay on a shelf next to it. He turned to 'H'
and found the Hendriks's; there were more than he expected
of that spelling, perhaps fifteen. He ran his fingers down the
column and found 'Hendriks, D.' On impulse he checked
the variant spelling of 'Hendrykxx' but found no entry.

He returned to his table and consulted the street map.
The address was near Sloane Square and the map of the
London Underground gave his route. He patted his jacket

over his breast pocket where he had put the will. Then he finished his drink and went on his way.

Coming up from the subway at Sloane Square he discovered himself in what was obviously an upper class section of London comparable to the 70s and 80s of Manhattan's East Side. He found the street he was looking for, and then the house, and gave a low whistle. If Dirk Hendriks lived in this style he was in no particular need of a few extra millions.

Hardin hesitated, feeling a bit of a fool. He had found what he wanted to know – why Gunnarsson had been so secretive – and there was nothing in it for him. He shrugged and thought that perhaps Hank was in there with his cousin; the place looked big enough to hold an army of Hendrixes. He would like to see the kid again. After saving his life and ministering to his wounds he felt a proprietary interest. He walked up the short flight of steps to the front door and put his finger on the bellpush.

The door was opened by a young woman in a nurse's uniform. Someone sick? 'I'd like to see Mr Hendriks – Dirk Hendriks,' he said.

The young woman looked doubtful. 'Er . . . I don't think he's here,' she said. 'You see, I'm new. I haven't been here long.'

Hardin said, 'What about Henry Hendrix?'

She shook her head. 'There's no one of the name here,' she said. 'I'd know that. Would you like to see Mrs Hendriks? She's been resting but she's up now.'

'Is she sick? I wouldn't want to disturb her.'

The nurse laughed. 'She's just had a baby, Mr . . . er . . .'

'Sorry. Hardin, Ben Hardin.'

She opened the door wider. if you come in I'll tell her you're here, Mr Hardin.'

Hardin waited in a spacious hall which showed all the evidences of casual wealth. Presently the nurse came back. 'Come this way, Mr Hardin.' She led him up the wide stairs and into a room which had large windows overlooking a small park. 'Mrs Hendriks; this is Mr Hardin.' The nurse withdrew.

Mrs Hendriks was a woman in her mid-thirties. She was short and dark, not particularly beautiful but not unattractive, either. She used make-up well. As they shook hands she said, 'I'm sorry my husband isn't here, Mr Hardin. You've missed him by twenty-four hours. He went to South Africa yesterday. Do you know my husband?'

'Not personally,' said Hardin.

'Then you may not know that he's a South African.' She gestured. 'Please sit down.'

Hardin sat in the easy chair. 'It's not your husband I really want to see,' said Hardin, 'It's Han . . . Henry Hendrix I'd like to visit with.'

'Henry?' she said doubtfully.

'Your husband's cousin.'

She shook her head, 'I think you're mistaken. My husband has no cousin.'

Hardin smiled. 'You may not know of him. He's an American and they've never met. Least, that's what Hank told me. That's how he's known back home. Hank Hendrix; only the name is spelled different with an "X" at the end.'

'I see. But I still think you're mistaken, Mr Hardin. I'm sure my husband would have told me.'

'They've never met. A few letters is all, and those some years ago.' Hardin was vaguely troubled. 'Then Hank hasn't been here?'

'Of course not.' She paused. 'He might have come when I was in confinement. I've just had a baby, Mr Hardin, and modern doctors prefer maternity wards.'

'The nurse told me,' said Hardin. 'Congratulations! Boy or girl?'

'I have a son,' she said proudly. 'Thank you, Mr Hardin.' She reverted to the problem. 'But Dirk would have told me, I'm sure, if a long-lost cousin had arrived out of the blue.'

'I'm sure he would have,' said Hardin sincerely, and his sense of trouble deepened. If Hank had come to England he would have certainly looked Dirk up; all it took was a phone book. Damn it, the Jersey lawyer would have certainly introduced them. Jack Richardson had checked that flight tickets had not been bought, so where in hell was Hank and what game was Gunnarsson playing?

His worry must have shown on his face because Mrs Hendriks said gently, 'You look troubled, Mr Hardin. Is there anything I can do to help?'

Hardin felt the copy of the will in his pocket. At least that was real. He said, 'Has Mr Hendriks heard from a lawyer about his grandfather's will?'

Mrs Hendriks was astonished. 'His grandfather! My husband's grandfather died years ago in South Africa. Or, at least, I've always assumed so. Dirk has never mentioned him.'

Hardin took a deep breath. 'Mrs Hendriks; I have something to tell you and it may take a while. It's like this . . .'

# SIX

Max Stafford was contemplating the tag end of the day and thinking about going home when his telephone rang. It was Joyce, his secretary. 'Mrs Hendriks is on the line and wants to talk to you.'

'Put her through.'

There was a click. 'Max?'

'Hello, Alix. How is motherhood suiting you?'

'Great. I'm blooming. Thank you for the christening mug you sent young Max. A *very* elegant piece of Georgian silver. He'll drink your health from it on his coming-of-age.'

Stafford smiled. 'Is it eighteen or twenty-one these days? I'll be a bit long in the tooth then.'

She laughed. 'But that's not why I rang; there's a proper "Thank you" letter in the post. Max, I need your advice. A man, an American called Hardin, came to me yesterday with a strange story concerning Dirk. Now, Dirk isn't here – he's in South Africa. I tried to ring him last night but he seems to be on the move and no one knows exactly where he is. I'd like you to see this man before he goes back to America.'

'What sort of strange yarn is he spinning?'

'It's a bit difficult to explain and I probably wouldn't get it right. It's complicated. Please see him, Max.'

Stafford pondered for a moment, 'Is Dirk in trouble?'

'Nothing like that. In fact it might be the other way round. Dirk might inherit something according to Hardin, but there's something odd going on.'

'How odd?'

'I don't know,' she said, 'I can't get the hang of it.'

'When is Hardin going back to the States?'

'Tomorrow or the day after. I don't think he can afford to stay.' She hesitated, 'I would like your advice, Max; you've always been wise. Things have been difficult lately. Dirk has been broody for quite a while – ever since I told him I was pregnant. It's been worrying me. And now this.'

'This Hardin character isn't blackmailing you, is he?'

'It's nothing like that,' she protested. 'Can you come to lunch? I'll see that Hardin is here.'

Stafford thought about it. His in-tray was overflowing and Joyce was a strict secretary. Still, this might be something he could sort out in an hour. 'All right,' he said. 'I'll be with you at twelve-thirty.'

'Thank you, Max,' said Alix warmly, 'I knew I could depend on you.'

Stafford put down the telephone and sat thinking. Presently he became aware that Ellis was standing before him snapping his fingers. 'Come out of your trance. Got a problem?'

Stafford started. 'Not me – Alix Hendriks. It seems that Dirk doesn't relish being a father. He's whistled off to South Africa and left Alix holding the three-week-old baby which I consider bloody inconsiderate. And now she's come up against someone who sounds like a con man, and Dirk isn't around. She wants my advice.'

'The last time you helped Alix you came to the office with your arm in a sling,' said Ellis. 'Watch it, Max.'

'That kind of lightning doesn't strike twice,' said Stafford.

*  *  *

Stafford soon found that the problem presented by Alix was not to be sorted out in an hour. He arrived on time at the house in Belgravia and found Hardin already there, a balding man in his mid-fifties with a pot belly like a football. To Stafford's eye he looked seedy and rundown. After gravely inspecting and admiring Stafford's three-week-old namesake the three of them adjourned to the dining room for lunch and Hardin retold his story.

It was three in the afternoon when Stafford held up the sheaf of papers. 'And this is purported to be the will?'

Hardin's face reddened, 'It *is* the goddamn will. If you don't believe me you can get your own copy. Hell, I'll even stand the cost myself.'

'All right, Mr Hardin; cool down.'

During Hardin's narrative Stafford had been revising his opinion of the man. If this was a con trick he found it difficult to see the point because there was nothing in it for Hardin. The will was obviously genuine because its source could be so easily checked and the passing of a fake will through the Probate Court was inconceivable. Besides, there was Gunnarsson.

He said, 'What do you think Gunnarsson has done with Hendrix?'

Hardin shrugged, 'I wouldn't know.'

'Would you call Gunnarsson an ethical man?'

'Christ, no!'

'Neither would I,' said Stafford dryly.

'You know him?' said Hardin in surprise.

'Not personally, but he has caused me a considerable amount of trouble in the past. We happen to be in the same line of business but reverse sides of the coin, as you might say. I run Stafford Security Consultants.'

Hardin was even more surprised. 'You're *that* Stafford? Well I'll be damned!'

Stafford inspected the will. 'Old Hendrykxx was either wise or had good advice.'

Alix poured more coffee. 'Why?'

'Setting up in the Channel Islands. No death duties, capital gains tax or capital transfer tax. It looks as though Dirk will get about three million quid free and clear. I know quite a bit about that aspect. When we went multinational we began to put our business through the Channel Islands.' He laid the will on the table. 'Who do you think shot Hendrix in Los Angeles?'

'That I don't know, either,' said Hardin, 'I can only guess. There were other guys looking for Hendrix besides me. I told you that.'

'Who could be German,' said Stafford. 'All right, Mr Hardin; why did you come to England?'

'I was so mad about the way Gunnarsson shafted me that I wanted to do something about it. Call it revenge, if you like. I drew a blank in New York and when I got a few unexpected dollars I came over here.' Hardin shrugged and pointed at the will. 'When I saw that, I knew damn well what Gunnarsson was doing, but there's not a thing I can do about it. But I came here to see Hank and to tell him to watch his step with Gunnarsson and to put a zipper on his wallet.'

Stafford was pensive for a while. At last he said, 'How long are you staying in England?'

'I'm leaving tomorrow or maybe the day after. Depends on when I can get a reservation.' Hardin smiled wryly. 'I have to get home and go back to earning a living.'

'I'd like you to stay a little longer. Your expenses will be paid, of course.' Stafford glanced at Alix, who nodded. He did not know exactly why he wanted Hardin to stay. He just had an obscure feeling that the man would be handy to have around.

'I don't mind staying on that basis,' said Hardin.

Stafford stood up. 'If you let me have the name of your hotel I'll be in touch.'

'I have it,' said Alix.

'Then that's it for the moment. Thank you, Mr Hardin.' When Hardin had gone Stafford said, 'May I use your phone?'

Alix looked up from clearing away the coffee cups. 'Of course. You know where it is.'

Stafford was absent for five minutes. When he came back he said, 'Jan-Willem Hendrykxx really did exist. I've been talking to my man in Jersey who looked him up in the telephone book. His name is still listed. I think Hendrykxx is a Flemish name.' He picked up the will. 'That would account for the house in Belgium. I've asked my chap to give me a discreet report on the executor of the estate and to find out when and how Hendrykxx died.'

Alix frowned. 'You don't suspect anything . . .? I mean he must have been an old man.'

Stafford smiled. 'I was trained in military intelligence. You never know when a bit of apparently irrelevant information will fit into the jigsaw.' He scanned the will. 'The Ol Njorowa Foundation stands to inherit about thirty-four million pounds. I wonder what it does?' He sat down. 'Alix, what's this with you and Dirk? You sounded a shade drear on the phone this morning.'

She looked unhappy. 'I can't make him out, Max. I don't think fatherhood suits him. We were happy enough until I got in the family way and then he changed.'

'In what way?'

'He became moody and abstracted. And now he's pushed off back to South Africa just when I need him. The baby's just three weeks old – you'd think he'd stay around, wouldn't you?'

'Um,' said Stafford obscurely. 'He never mentioned his grandfather at any time?'

'Not that I can remember.' She made a sudden gesture as if brushing away an inopportune fly. 'Oh, Max; this is ridiculous. This man – this Fleming with the funny way of spelling his name – is probably no relation at all. It must be a case of mistaken identity.'

'I don't think so. Hardin came straight to this house like a homing pigeon.' Stafford ticked off points on his fingers. 'The American, Hank Hendrix, told him that Dirk was his cousin; Hardin saw the instructions to Gunnarsson from Peacemore, Willis and Franks to turn up descendants of Jan-Willem Hendrykxx with the funny name; in doing so Hardin turns up Hank Hendrix. It's a perfectly logical chain.'

'I suppose so,' said Alix. 'But can you tell me why I'm worried about Dirk inheriting millions?'

'I think I can,' he said. 'You're worried about a bit that doesn't seem to fit. The shooting of Hank Hendrix in Los Angeles. And I've got one other thing on my mind. Why haven't the Peacemore mob turned up Dirk? Hardin did it in thirty seconds.'

Curtis, Stafford's manservant, was mildly surprised at seeing him. 'The Colonel is back early,' he observed.

'Yes, I got sidetracked. It wasn't worth going back to the office.'

'Would the Colonel like afternoon tea?'

'No; but you can bring me a scotch in the study.'

'As the Colonel wishes,' said Curtis with a disapproving air which stopped just short of insolence.

Curtis was a combination of butler, valet, chauffeur, handyman and nanny. He was ex-Royal Marines, having joined in 1943 and electing to stay in the service after the war. A 37-year man. At the statutory retiring age of 55 he had been tossed into the strange civilian world of the 1980s, no longer a Colour-Sergeant with authority but just another man-in-the-street. A fish out of water and somewhat baffled by the indiscipline of civilian life. He was a widower, his wife Amy having died five years before of cancer; and his only daughter was married, living in Australia, and about to present him with a third grandchild.

When Stafford had divorced his wife he had stayed at his club before moving into a smaller flat more suitable for a bachelor. It was then that he remembered Curtis whom he had known from the days when he had been a young officer serving with the British Army of the Rhine. One night, in one of the less salubrious quarters of Hamburg, he had found himself in a tight spot from which he had been rescued by a tough, hammer-fisted Marine sergeant. He had never forgotten Curtis and they had kept in touch, and so he acquired Curtis – or did Curtis acquire Stafford? Whichever way it was they suited each other; Curtis finding a congenial niche in a strange world, and Stafford lucky enough to have an efficient, if somewhat military, Jeeves. Curtis's only fault was that he would persist in addressing Stafford in the third person by his army title.

Stafford looked at the chunky, hard man with something approaching affection. 'How's your daughter, Sergeant?'

'I had a letter this morning. She says she's well, sir.'

'What will it be? Boy or girl?'

'Just so that it has one head and the usual number of arms, legs and fingers. Boy or girl – either will suit me.'

'Tell me when it comes. We must send a suitable christening present.'

'Thank you, sir. When would the Colonel like his bath drawn?'

'At the usual time. Let me have that scotch now.' Stafford went into his study.

He sat at his desk and thought about Gunnarsson. He had never met Gunnarsson but had sampled his methods through the machinations of Peacemore, Willis and Franks which was the wholly-owned London subsidiary of Gunnarsson Associates, and what he had found he did not like.

It was the work of Stafford Security Consultants to protect the secrets of the organizations which were their clients. A lot of people imagine security to be a matter of patrolling guards and heavy mesh fencing but that is only a part of it. The weakest part of any organization is the people in it, from the boss at the top down to the charwomen who scrub the floors. A Managing Director making an indiscreet remark at his golf club could blow a secret worth millions. A charwoman suborned can find lots of interesting items in waste paper baskets.

It followed that if the firm of Stafford Security Consultants was making a profit out of guarding secrets – and it was making a handsome profit – then others were equally interested in ferreting them out, and the people who employed Gunnarsson Associates were the sort who were not too fussy about the methods used. And that went for the Peacemore mob in the United Kingdom.

Stafford remembered a conversation he had had with Jack Ellis just before he left for the Continent. 'We've had trouble with the Peacemore crowd,' said Ellis. 'They penetrated Electronomics just before the merger when Electronomics was taken over. Got right through our defences.'

'How?'

Jack shrugged. 'We can guard against everything but stupidity. They got the goods on Pascoe, the General Manager. In bed with a gilded youth. Filthy pictures, the lot. Of course, it was a Peacemore set-up, but I'd have a hell of a job proving it.'

'In this permissive age homosexuality isn't the handle it once was,' observed Stafford.

'It was a good handle this time. Pascoe's wife didn't know he was double-gaited. He has teenage daughters and it

would have ruined his marriage so he caved in. After the
merger we lost the Electronomics contract, of course.
Peacemore got it.'

'And Pascoe's peccadilloes came to light anyway.'

'Sure. After the merger he was fired and they gave full
reasons. He'd proved he couldn't be trusted.'

'The bastards have no mercy,' said Stafford.

Industrial espionage is not much different from the work
of the department called MI6 which the British government
refuses to admit exists, or the KGB which everyone knows
to exist, or the CIA which is practically an open book. A car
company would find it useful to know the opposition's
designs years in advance. One airline, after planning an
advertising campaign costing half a million, was taken very
much by surprise when its principal rival came out with the
identical campaign a week before its own was due to start.

A company wanting to take over another, as in the
Electronomics case, would like to know the victim's defensive strategy. Someone wanted to know what bid price
Electronomics would jib at, and employed Peacemore to
find out.

Of course, no one on the Board comes right out and says,
'Let's run an espionage exercise against so-and-so.' The
Chairman or Managing Director might be thinking aloud
and says dreamily, 'Wouldn't it be nice if we knew what so-
and-so are doing.' Sharp ears pick up the wishful think and
the second echelon boys get to work, the hatchet men hungry for promotion. Intermediaries are used, analogous to
the cut-outs used in military and political intelligence, the
job gets done with no one on the Board getting his hands
dirty, and an under-manager becomes a manager.

Defence is difficult because the espionage boys go for the
jugular. All the security guards in creation are of no avail
against human weakness. So Stafford Security Consultants
investigated the personnel of their clients, weeding out

doubtful characters, and if that was an offence against human rights it was too bad.

And sometimes we fail, thought Stafford.

He sighed and picked up the neglected whisky which Curtis had brought in. And now Gunnarsson was mixed up in the affairs of a friend. Not that Stafford felt particularly friendly towards Dirk Hendriks, but Alix was his friend and he did not want her hurt in any way. And Gunnarsson was not acting in a straightforward manner. Why had he not produced the missing heirs?

Stafford checked the time. It was probably after office hours in Jersey but he would try to talk with the Jersey law firm. There was no reply.

# SEVEN

The next morning, just after he arrived at the office, Stafford took a call from Peter Hartwell, the director of the Jersey holding company whom he had queried the day before. Hartwell said, 'Your man, Hendrykxx, died a little over four months ago. The body was cremated. I checked the newspapers and it went unreported except for the usual formal announcement.'

'What was the cause of death?'

'Heart attack. It was expected; he had a history of heart trouble. I discovered we shared the same doctor so I was able to ask a few questions. I went to the Greffe and saw the will. Makes bloody interesting reading, doesn't it?'

Stafford said, 'I'm surprised the newpapers didn't get hold of it. It's not often multi-millionaires hop their twig.'

Hartwell laughed. 'Millionaires are not uncommon here – they're just plain, ordinary folk. Besides, Hendrykxx lived very quietly and didn't make waves. The news boys don't read every will deposited in the Greffe, anyway.'

'How long had he lived on Jersey?' asked Stafford.

'He came in 1974 – not all that long ago.'

'What about the executor? What's he like?'

'Old Farrar? Good man, but damned stuffy. What's your interest in this, Max? Isn't it a bit out of your line?'

'Just doing a favour for a friend. Thanks, Peter; I'll get back to you if I need anything more.'

'There is one odd point,' said Hartwell. 'The clerk in the Greffe said there's been quite a run on copies of that particular will. One from England, two from America and another from South Africa.' Hartwell laughed. 'He said he was considering printing a limited edition.'

After he put down the phone Stafford leaned back and thought for a moment. So far, so uninteresting, except possibly for the requests for copies of the will. He snapped a switch, and said, 'Joyce, get me Mr Farrar of Farrar, Windsor and Markham, St Helier, Jersey. It's a law firm.'

Five minutes later he was speaking to Farrar. He introduced himself, then said, 'I'm interested in the late Mr Jan-Willem Hendrykxx. He died about four months ago.'

'That is correct.'

'I believe you are having difficulty in tracing the heirs.'

'In that you are mistaken,' said Farrar. He had a dry, pedantic voice.

Stafford waited for him to continue but Farrar remained silent. Well, Hartwell had said he was stuffy. Stafford said, 'I take it you refer to Henry Hendrix of Los Angeles and Dirk Hendriks of London.'

'You appear to be well informed. May I ask how you obtained your information?'

'I've been reading the will.'

'That would not give you the names,' said Farrar dryly. 'But essentially you are correct. Mr Henry Hendrix is flying from the United States tomorrow, and Mr Dirk Hendriks has been informed.' Farrar paused. 'It is true that I was surprised at the length of time taken by . . .' He stopped as though aware of being on the edge of an unlawyerly indiscretion. 'May I ask your interest in this matter, Mr Stafford?'

Stafford sighed. 'My interest has just evaporated. Thanks for letting me take up your time, Mr Farrar.' He hung up.

The telephone rang almost immediately and Alix came on the line. 'It's true, Max,' she said excitedly. 'It's all true.'

'If you mean about Dirk's inheritance, I know. I've just been talking to Farrar.'

'Who?'

'The executor of the estate. The Jersey solicitor.'

'That's funny. The letter came from a solicitor called Mandeville in the City.' Alix hurried on. 'Dirk knew all the time. He said he didn't want to excite me when I was having the baby. He had to go to South Africa to collect evidence of identity. He got back this morning and he's seeing the solicitor tomorrow. And there *is* a long-lost cousin, Max. He'll be there too.'

'All very exciting,' said Stafford unemotionally. 'Congratulations.' He paused. 'What do you want me to do about Hardin?'

'What would you suggest?'

'He strikes me as being an honest man,' said Stafford. 'From the way it looked there *could* have been jiggery-pokery, and Hardin did his best to put it right at considerable personal effort. I suggest you pay his London expenses and his total air fare. And you might add a small honorarium. Shall I take care of it?'

'If you would,' she said. 'Send me the bill.'

'I'll break the news to him at lunch. 'Bye.' He rang off, asked Joyce to make a lunch appointment with Hardin, and then sat back, his fingers drumming on the desk, to consider the matter.

There did not seem much to consider. Mandeville was probably Farrar's London correspondent; law firms did arrange their affairs that way. Stafford wondered why Dirk Hendriks had not told Alix before he went to South Africa – she had had the baby by then – but he always had been an inconsiderate bastard. There were a couple of minor points that did not add up. Who shot Hendrix and why? And why hadn't Gunnarsson produced Hendrix in England as soon as he had been found? But he had only Hardin's word for those events. Perhaps Hardin really was a con man and playing his own devious game. Stafford, who prided himself on being a good judge of men, shook his head in perplexity.

He got on with his work.


Stafford stood Hardin to lunch in a good restaurant. The news may have been good for Hendrykxx's heirs but it was bad news for Hardin, and he judged a good meal would make the medicine go down better. Hardin said ruefully, 'I guess I made a fool of myself.'

'The man who never made a mistake never made anything,' said Stafford unoriginally. 'Mrs Hendriks doesn't want you to be out of pocket because of this affair. How long is it since you left Gunnarsson Associates?'

'Just about a month.'

'What did he pay you?'

'Thirty thousand bucks a year, plus bonuses.' Hardin shrugged. 'The bonuses got a little thin towards the end, but in good years I averaged forty thousand.'

'All right.' Stafford took out his chequebook. 'Mrs Hendriks will stand your air fare both ways, your London expenses, and a month's standard pay. Does that suit you?'

'That's generous and unexpected,' said Hardin sincerely.

Again Stafford wondered about Hardin, then reflected that sincerity was the con man's stock in trade. They settled the amount in dollars, Stafford rounded it up to the nearest thousand, converted it into sterling, and wrote the cheque. As Hardin put it into his wallet he said, 'This will keep me going until I get settled again back home.'

'When will you be leaving?'

'Nothing to keep me here now. Maybe tomorrow if I can get a seat.'

'Well, good luck,' said Stafford, and changed the subject.

Over the rest of lunch they talked of other things. Hardin learned that Stafford had been in Military Intelligence and opened up a bit on his own experiences in the CIA. He said he had worked in England, Germany and Africa, but he talked in generalities, was discreet, and told no tales out of school, 'I can't talk much about that,' he said frankly. 'I'm not one of the kiss-and-tell guys who sprang out of the woodwork with Watergate.'

Stafford silently approved, his judgment of Hardin oscillating rapidly.

Lunch over, Stafford paid the bill and they left the restaurant, pausing for a final handshake on the pavement. Stafford watched Hardin walk away, a somehow pathetic figure, and wondered what was to become of him.

Dirk Hendriks rang up next day, and Stafford sighed in exasperation; he was becoming fed up with *l'affaire* Hendriks. Dirk's voice came over strongly and Stafford noted yet again that the telephone tends to accentuate accent. 'I've seen the solicitor, Max. We're going to Jersey tomorrow to see Farrar, the executor.'

'We?'

'Me and my unexpected cousin. I met him in Mandeville's office.'

'Happy family reunion,' said Stafford. 'What's your cousin like?'

'Seems a nice enough chap. Very American, of course. He was wearing the damnedest gaudy broadcheck jacket you've ever seen.'

'Three million will cure any eyestrain, Dirk,' said Stafford dryly. 'Did you find out about the Ol Njorowa Foundation?'

'Yes. It's some sort of agricultural college and experimental farm in Kenya.' Hendriks hesitated. 'There's a funny condition to the will. I have to spend one month each year working for the Foundation. What do you make of that?'

Stafford had noted the clause. His tone became drier. 'A month a year isn't much to pay for three million quid.'

'I suppose not. Look, Max; this character, Hardin. What did you make of him?'

Stafford decided to give Hardin the benefit of the doubt. 'Seems a good chap.'

'So Alix says. She liked him. When is he going back to the States?'

'He's probably gone by now. He said there wasn't anything to keep him here, and he has to find a job.'

'I see. Could you give me his address in New York? He must have run up some expenses and I'd like to reimburse him.'

'It's all taken care of, Dirk,' said Stafford. 'I'll send you the bill; you can afford it now. In any case, he didn't leave an address.'

'Oh!' In that brief monosyllable Stafford thought he detected disappointment. There was an appreciable pause before Hendriks said, 'Thanks, Max.' He went on more briskly, 'I must get on now. We've just left Mandeville who seems satisfied, and Cousin Henry, Alix and I are having a celebratory drink. Why don't you join us?'

'Sorry, Dirk; I'm not a bloated millionaire and I have work to do.'

'All right, then. I'll see you around.' Hendriks rang off.

Stafford had told a white lie. Already he was packing papers into a briefcase in preparation to go home. There was a Test match that afternoon and he rather thought England would beat Australia this time. He wanted to watch it on television.

He walked into his flat and found Curtis waiting for him. 'The Colonel has a visitor. An American gentleman, name of Mr Hardin. I rang the office but the Colonel had already left.'

'Oh! Where is he?'

'I settled him in the living room with a highball.'

Stafford looked at Curtis sharply. 'What the devil do you know about highballs?'

'I have been drunk with the United States Navy on many occasions, sir,' said Curtis with a straight face. 'That was in my younger days.'

'Well, I'll join Mr Hardin with my usual scotch.'

Stafford found Hardin nursing a depleted drink and examining the book shelves, 'I thought you'd have gone by now.'

'I almost made it, but I decided to stay.' Hardin straightened. 'Did Hank Hendrix arrive?'

'Yes; I had a call from Dirk. They met the lawyer this afternoon. He seemed satisfied with their credentials, so Dirk says.'

'The lawyer's name being Mandeville?'

'Yes. How do you know that?'

Stafford had thought Hardin had appeared strained but now he looked cheerful, 'I bumped into Gunnarsson this morning at Heathrow Airport. Well, not bumped exactly – I don't think he saw me. I decided not to leave right then because I wanted to follow him.'

Curtis came in with a tray and Stafford reached for his whisky. 'Why?'

'Because the young guy with him wasn't the Hank Hendrix I picked up in Los Angeles.'

Stafford was so startled that he almost dropped the glass. 'Wasn't he, by God?'

Hardin shook his head decidedly. 'No way. Same height, same colouring – a good lookalike but not Hank Hendrix.'

Stafford thought of his conversation with Dirk. 'What was the colour of his jacket?'

Hardin grinned crookedly. 'You couldn't mistake him for anyone but an American – Joseph's coat of many colours.'

That did it. Curtis was about to leave the room and Stafford said abruptly, 'Stick around, Sergeant, and listen to this. It might save a lot of explanations later. But first get Mr Hardin another highball, and you might as well have one yourself. Mr Hardin; this is Colour-Sergeant Curtis, late of the Royal Marines.'

Hardin gave Stafford a curious look then stood up and held out his hand. 'Glad to know you, Sergeant Curtis.'

'Likewise, Mr Hardin.' They shook hands then Curtis turned to Stafford, 'If the Colonel doesn't mind I'd rather have a beer.'

Stafford nodded and Curtis left to return two minutes later with the drinks. Stafford said, 'So you followed Gunnarsson?'

'Yeah. Your London taxi drivers don't surprise worth a damn. I told mine that if he kept track of Gunnarsson's cab it was worth an extra tip. He said he could do better than that – they were on the same radio net. Five minutes later he said Gunnarsson was going to the Dorchester. I got there before him and had the cab wait. It ran up quite a tab on the meter.'

'You'll get your expenses.'

Hardin grinned, 'It's on the house, Mr Stafford. Because I'm feeling so good.'

He sipped his replenished highball. 'Gunnarsson and the other guy registered at the desk and then went upstairs. They were up there nearly two hours while I was sitting in the lobby getting callouses on my butt and hoping that the house dick wouldn't latch on to me and throw me out. When they came down I followed them again and they took me to Lincoln's Inn Fields.'

'Where Mandeville has his chambers. Right? That's where you got the name.'

'Right. I still kept the cab and hung on for a while. Gunnarsson came out just as Mrs Hendriks went in with a guy. Would he be Dirk Hendriks?'

'Big broad-shouldered man built like a tank?' Like a lot of South Africans Hendriks was designed to play rugby scrum half.

'That's the guy.' Stafford nodded sharply, and Hardin said, 'They went into the same place. I followed Gunnarsson to the office of Peacemore, Willis and Franks. I didn't think I could do much more so I came here and paid off the taxi.' He looked up. 'I thought it was better I came here instead of your office.'

Stafford nodded absently, mulling it over, then he said, 'All right; let's do a reconstruction. You found Henry Hendrix and took him to Gunnarsson in New York. Gunnarsson, who had been hoping for a gold mine, realized he'd found it. Hendrix had no family, he'd never been out of the States, and it wouldn't be too hard to drain him of information and put someone else in as a substitute here in London.'

Curtis coughed. 'I don't really know what this is about yet, but where is the real Henry Hendrix?'

Hardin gave him a sideways glance, 'I wouldn't care to guess.' There was a silence while they digested that, then he asked, 'So what do we do now?'

'I suppose I should tell Farrar he's being taken,' Stafford said slowly. 'But I'm not going to.' Hardin brightened. 'If I do then Gunnarsson can slide right out from under.'

'Yeah,' said Hardin. 'The young guy takes his lumps for being an impostor, and Gunnarsson spreads his hands and says he's been as deceived as anyone else. All injured innocence.'

'And no one would believe you,' commented Stafford. 'He'd call you a liar; a disgruntled ex-employee who was fired for incompetence.'

'That he would.' Hardin scratched his jaw. 'There's still Biggie and the commune. They'd know this guy isn't Hank.'

'Christ, they're seven thousand miles away,' said Stafford irritably. 'This man, whoever he is, has committed no crime in the States. He'd be tried here under British law or perhaps Jersey law, for all I know.'

'What's the sentence for impersonation over here?'

'It wouldn't be much. Maybe two years.'

Hardin snorted, but Stafford ignored him. He was deep in thought and looked upon Hardin with new eyes. The man had proved to be right, after all, and here he had at hand an unemployed Intelligence agent and a man who hated Gunnarsson's guts. If Stafford was going against Gunnarsson it occurred to him that Hardin would be handy to have around. He knew Gunnarsson and how he operated, and the first rule of any kind of warfare is: 'Know your enemy.'

He said, 'You told me you worked in Africa. Do you know Kenya?'

'Sure.' Hardin shrugged. 'It will have changed since I was there, but I know Kenya.'

'Are you *persona grata*?'

'I'm okay in Kenya.' He smiled. 'I wouldn't like to say what would happen if I stuck my nose into Tanzania.'

Stafford said, 'You told me your salary at Gunnarsson Associates. I think we can match that, and maybe a bit more. How would you like to work for Stafford Security Consultants?'

Hardin did not jump at it. 'Are you in the same business as Gunnarsson?'

'Not exactly. We try to stop the bastards.'

Hardin held out his hand, 'I'm your man. Thanks, Mr Stafford.'

Stafford smiled, 'I'm Max, you are Ben, and the Sergeant is the Sergeant.'

Hardin had given up his hotel room so Stafford told him he could use the spare bedroom until he got fixed up. 'You can pay your rent by briefing Sergeant Curtis on this thing.'

'What's this with Kenya?'

Stafford said, 'That's where I think the action will be.' He was thinking that an awful lot of money was going to the Ol Njorowa Foundation, a hell of a lot more than the six million dollars going to the fake Hendrix. The Foundation would be awash with cash – something like seventy million American dollars – and he was sure that Gunnarsson had got the heady scent of it in his nostrils.

# EIGHT

Stafford discussed the Gunnarsson affair with Jack Ellis who was the next biggest shareholder in Stafford Security after himself. He felt he could not run up costs on the firm without informing Ellis. He outlined the situation and Ellis said thoughtfully, 'Gunnarsson. He's the Peacemore mob, isn't he?'

'That's right.'

'We've been having trouble with that crowd. Remember Electronomics?'

'All too clearly,' said Stafford. 'Jack, our next logical expansion is into the States. We're going to come up slap hard against Gunnarsson sooner or later. I'd rather it was sooner, before we set up operations over there. I want to go after him now when he's not on his home ground.'

Ellis nodded. 'That should make it easier. Who knows about all this? I mean that Gunnarsson has run in a substitute for Hendrix.'

'Just four; you, me, Hardin and the Sergeant.'

'Not Alix Hendriks?'

Stafford shook his head. 'Nor Dirk. I want to keep this tight.'

'And why Kenya?'

Stafford said, 'There was once an American bank robber called Willie Sutton. Someone asked him why he robbed banks. He looked a bit disgusted, and said, "That's where the money is." There's a hell of a lot of money going into Kenya. Gunnarsson will go where the money is.'

'What do we know about this Foundation in Kenya?'

'Not a damned thing; but that can be cured.'

'And you want to handle this personally?'

'With help.' Stafford shrugged. 'I've been working damned hard in Europe, and I haven't had a holiday for three years. Let's call this paid leave of absence.'

Ellis smiled wryly, 'I have an odd feeling of *déjà vu* as though we've had this conversation before.'

Stafford said, 'Make no mistake, Jack; this isn't a favour for Alix Hendriks. This is for the future benefit of Stafford Security.'

Ellis agreed.

Stafford sent Hardin to Kenya as a one man advance party. He did not want Hardin to meet either Gunnarsson or Hendrix by accident and, although there are eight million people in London, he was taking no chances. The West End covers a comparatively small area and it would be plain bad luck if they met face to face in, say, Jermyn Street. In Kenya Hardin was to arrange hotel accommodation and hire cars. He was also to do a preliminary check into the Ol Njorowa Foundation.

Gunnarsson and the fake Hendrix were kept under discreet observation. Stafford arranged to get a look at them so that he would know them again when he saw them. Gunnarsson did nothing much; he frequented the offices of Peacemore, Willis and Franks, which was natural since he owned the place, and he gambled in casinos, winning often. His luck was uncanny. Hendrix, after looking around London, hired a car and went on a tour of the West Country.

It was then that Stafford invited Alix and Dirk Hendriks to dinner; they were his spies behind the enemy lines. Over the aperitifs he said, 'How did you get on in Jersey?'

Dirk laughed, 'I signed a lot of papers and got writer's cramp. The old man had a fantastic head for business. His investments are widespread.'

'Did you know your grandfather?'

Dirk shook his head, and Alix said, 'You've never mentioned him, Dirk.'

'I thought he was killed in the Red Revolt of 1922,' said Dirk. 'There was a revolution on the Rand, a real civil war which Smuts put down with artillery and bombers. That's when he disappeared, or so I was told. It's a bit spooky to know that he really died only a few months ago.'

'And your grandmother – did you know her?' asked Stafford.

'I have vague recollections,' said Dirk, frowning. 'She used to tell me stories. It must have been she who told me about my grandfather. She died when I was a kid. They all did.'

'All?' said Alix questioningly.

'Both my parents, my sister and my grandmother were killed in a car crash. The only reason I wasn't in the car was because I was in hospital. Scarlet fever, I believe. I was six years old.' He put on a mock lugubrious expression. 'I'm a lone orphan.'

Alix put her hand over his. 'My poor darling. I didn't know.'

Stafford thought it odd that Dirk had not told Alix this before but made no comment. Instead he said, 'What's this Foundation in Kenya?'

'Ol Njorowa?' Dirk shook his head, 'I don't know much about it other than what I've already told you. We're going out next Wednesday to inspect it. Since I have to spend a month a year there I'd better learn about it. The Director is a man called Brice. Mandeville thinks a lot of him.'

'How does Mandeville come into it? He's a QC, isn't he? I thought Farrar was the executor.' Stafford held up a finger to a passing waiter.

'He did a lot of legal work for my grandfather. Apparently they were on terms of friendship because he said he used to stay at my grandfather's house whenever he went to Jersey.'

'Is he going to Kenya with you?'

Dirk laughed. 'Lord, no! He's a bigwig; he doesn't go to people – they go to him. But Farrar is coming along; he has business to discuss with Brice.'

Stafford turned to Alix. 'Are you going, too?'

She smiled ruefully. 'I'd like to, but I couldn't take young Max. Perhaps we'll go next time.'

'And Henry Hendrix is going, of course. Where is he, by the way? I thought you'd be together.'

'He's sightseeing in the country,' said Dirk, and added tartly, 'We're not going to live in each other's pockets. It's only now that I appreciate the saying, "You can choose your friends but not your relatives."'

'Don't you like him?'

'He's not my type,' said Dirk briefly. 'I think we'll choose different months to stay at Ol Njorowa. But, yes; he will be going with Farrar and me.'

'I might bump into you in Nairobi,' said Stafford casually. 'I'm taking a holiday out there. My flight is on Tuesday.'

'Oh?' Dirk looked at him intently. 'When did you decide that?'

'I booked the trip a couple of weeks ago – at least, my secretary did.'

The waiter came up, and Alix said, 'I won't have another drink, Max.'

'Then we'll go in to dine,' he said, and rose, satisfied with his probing.

\* \* \*

Next day he learned that Gunnarsson had visited a travel
agent and a discreet enquiry elicited his destination –
Nairobi. Stafford had Curtis book two seats on the Tuesday
flight and cabled Hardin, advising him to lie low. Curtis
said, 'Am I going, sir?'

'Yes; I might want someone to hang my trousers. What
kind of natty gent's clothing would be suitable for Kenya?'

'The Colonel doesn't want to trouble his head about that.
Any of the Indian stores will make him up a suit within
twenty-four hours. Cheap too, and good for the climate.'

'You're a mine of information, Sergeant. Where did you
pick up that bit?'

'I've been there,' Curtis said unexpectedly. 'I was in
Mombasa a few years ago during the Mau-Mau business.
I got a bit of travel up-country to Nairobi and beyond.' He
paused. 'What kind of trouble is the Colonel expecting –
fisticuffs or guns?' Stafford regarded him thoughtfully, and
Curtis said, 'It's just that I'd like to know what preparations
to make.'

Stafford said, 'You know as much as I do. Make what
preparations you think advisable.' The first thing any green
lieutenant learns is when to say 'Carry on, Sergeant.' The
non-commissioned officers of any service run the nuts and
bolts of the outfit and the wise officer knows it.

Curtis said, 'Then have I the Colonel's permission to take
the afternoon off? I have things to do.'

'Yes; but don't tell me what they are. I don't want to
know.'

The only matter of consequence that happened before they
went to Kenya was that Hendrix crashed his car when career-
ing down a steep hill in Cornwall near Tintagel. He came out
with a few scratches but the car was a total write-off.

They flew to Nairobi first class on the night flight. Curtis was
a big man and Stafford no midget and he saw no reason to be

cramped in economy class where the seats are tailored for the inhabitants of Munchkinland. If all went well Gunnarsson would be paying ultimately. Stafford resisted the attempts of the cabin staff to anaesthetize him with alcohol so he would be less trouble but, since he found it difficult to sleep on air-craft, at 3 a.m. he went to the upstairs lounge where he read a thriller over a long, cold beer while intermittently watching the chief steward jiggle the accounts. The thriller had a hero who always knew when he was being followed by a prickling at the nape of his neck; this handy accomplishment helped the plot along on no fewer than four occasions.

Curtis slept like a baby.

They landed just after eight in the morning and, even at that early hour, the sun was like a hammer. Stafford sniffed and caught the faintly spicy, dusty smell he had first encountered in Algeria – the smell of Africa. They went through Immigration and Customs and found Hardin waiting. ''Lo, Max; 'lo, Sergeant. Have a good flight?'

'Not bad.' Stafford felt the bristles on his jaw. 'A day flight would have been better.'

'The pilots don't like that,' said Hardin. 'This airport is nearly six thousand feet high and the midday air is hot and thin. They reckon it's a bit risky landing at noon.'

Stafford's eyes felt gritty. 'You're as bad as the Sergeant, here, for unexpected nuggets of information.'

'I have wheels outside. Let me help you with your bags. Don't let these porters get their hands on them; they want an arm and a leg for a tip.'

They followed Hardin and Stafford stared unbelievingly at the vehicle to which he was led. It was a Nissan van, an eight-seater with an opening roof, and it was dazzlingly painted in zebra stripes barely veiled in a thin film of dust. He said, 'For Christ's sake, Ben! We're trying to be incon-spicuous and you get us a circus van. That thing shouts at you from a bloody mile away.'

'Don't worry,' Hardin said reassuringly. 'These safari trucks are as common as fleas on a dog out here, and they'll go anywhere. We're disguised as tourists. You'll see.'

Hardin drove, Stafford sat next to him, and Curtis got in the back. There was an unexpectedly good divided highway. Stafford said, 'How far is the city?'

'About seven miles.' Hardin jerked his thumb. 'See that fence? On the other side is the Nairobi National Game Park. Lots of animals back there.' He laughed, 'it's goddamn funny to see giraffes roaming free with skyscrapers in the background.'

'I didn't send you here to look at animals.'

'Hell, it was Sunday morning. My way of going to church. Don't be a grouch, Max.'

Hardin had a point. 'Sorry, Ben. I suppose it's the lack of sleep.'

'That's okay.' Hardin was silent for a while, then he said, 'I was talking to one of the local inhabitants in the bar of the Hilton. He lives at Langata, that's a suburb of Nairobi. He said all hell had broken loose early that morning because a lion had taken a horse from the riding stables next door. Even in Manhattan we don't live that dangerously.'

Stafford thought Hardin had turned into the perfect goggling tourist. He was not there to hear small talk about lions. He said, 'What about the Foundation?'

Hardin caught the acerbity in Stafford's voice and gave him a sideways glance. He said quietly, 'Yeah, I got some information on that from the same guy who told me about the lion. He's one of the Trustees; Indian guy called Patterjee.'

Stafford sighed. 'Sorry again, Ben. This doesn't seem to be my day.'

'That's okay. We all have off days.'

'Did you get anything interesting out of Patterjee?'

'A few names – members of the Board and so on. He gave me a printed handout which describes the work of the Foundation. It runs agricultural schools, experimental laboratories – things like that. And a Co-operative. The Director responsible to the Board is called Brice; he's not in Nairobi – he's at Ol Njorowa. That's near Naivasha in the Rift Valley, about fifty miles from here.'

'Who started the Foundation – and when?'

'It was started just after the war, in the fifties. The handout doesn't say who by. I did some poking around Naivasha but I didn't see Brice; I thought I'd leave him for you. He's English and I thought you'd handle him better, maybe.'

'Did Patterjee say anything about the Hendrykxx inheritance?'

'Not a murmur. But he wasn't likely to talk about that to a stranger he met in a bar. The news isn't out yet. I checked the back issues in a newspaper office.'

They were coming into the city. Stafford had not known what to expect but was mildly surprised. He knew enough not to expect mud huts but the buildings were high rise and modern and the streets were well kept. Hardin braked hard. 'When you're driving around here watch out for guys on bicycles. They think traffic lights don't apply to them.'

The lights changed and Hardin let out the clutch. 'We're on Uhuru Highway. Over to the left is Uhuru Park.' Stafford saw black schoolgirls dressed in gym slips playing handball. There were flowers everywhere in a riot of colour. They turned a corner and then another, and Hardin said, 'Harry Thuku Road, named after a revolutionary hero who got on the wrong side of the British in colonial days. And there's the Norfolk where we're staying.'

He put the vehicle into a slot between two identically zebra-striped Nissans. 'One of those is ours. I thought we'd better have two sets of wheels.'

'Good thinking.' Stafford twisted and looked back at Curtis. 'You're very loquacious, Sergeant; you've been positively babbling. Anything on your mind?'

'Got things to do if the Colonel will excuse me,' he said stolidly, 'I could do with a street map.'

'I have one here,' said Hardin. 'But you'd better register first.'

They went into the hotel as a horde of porters descended on the Nissan. After registering Curtis gave Stafford a brief nod and went away, walking out of the hotel and into the street. Hardin stared after him. 'The strong, silent type,' he commented. 'Where's he going?'

'Better you not ask,' said Stafford. 'He's going his mysterious ways his wonders to perform.'

Their rooms were across an inner courtyard alive with the noise of birds from two large aviaries. 'The Sergeant is bunking in with me,' said Hardin. 'You're on your own. I've ordered breakfast in your room; I reckoned you might be tired and not want to use the dining room.' They ascended stairs and he opened a door. 'Here you are.'

A waiter was stooping over a loaded tray which he had just set down. He straightened and said, with a wide grin, 'Breakfast, sah; guaranteed finest English breakfast.'

Hardin tipped him and he left. 'The refrigerator is full of booze.'

Stafford shuddered. 'Too early in the morning.'

'Tell me something,' said Hardin. 'What's with you and the Sergeant? I thought you had the class system in England. It doesn't show with you two.'

'I don't happen to believe in the class system,' said Stafford, uncovering a dish to reveal bacon and eggs. He picked up a glass of orange juice and sipped it, noting appreciatively that it was freshly squeezed. 'Have you anything more to tell me before I demolish this lot and fall on that bed?'

'Yeah. The name of the Foundation. Ol Njorowa is the name of a place near Naivasha. It's Masai. I don't know what the translation into English would be but the British settlers call it Hell's Gate. When do you want to be wakened?'

'Twelve-thirty.'

Stafford had breakfast and went to bed thinking of Hell's Gate. It was a hell of a name to give to a charitable foundation.

# NINE

Hardin woke Stafford on time. He felt hot and sticky but a shower washed away the sweat. As he came out of the bathroom Hardin said, 'The Sergeant is back – with friends.'

'What friends?'

'You'll see them in the Delamere Bar.'

Stafford dressed and they went downstairs. As they crossed the courtyard in the midday sun Stafford felt the sweat break out again, and made a note to ask Curtis about his tailor.

The Delamere Bar was a large patio at the front of the hotel scattered with tables, each individually shaded, from which one could survey the passing throng. It was crowded, but the Sergeant had secured a table. He stood up as they approached, 'I would like the Colonel to meet Pete Chipende and Nair Singh.'

They shook hands. Chipende was a black African who offered a grin full of white teeth. 'Call me Chip; everyone does.' His English was almost accentless; just a hint of East African sing-song. Nair Singh was a turbanned Sikh with a ferocious black beard and a gentle smile.

As Stafford sat down Hardin said, 'The beer's not bad; cold and not too alcoholic.'

'Okay, a beer.' Stafford noted that it was probably too alcoholic for the Sikh who sat in front of a soft drink. He looked at Curtis and raised his eyebrows.

Curtis said, 'Back in London I thought we might need friends who know the territory and the language, so I made a few enquiries and got an address.'

'Our address,' said Chip. 'We work well; turn our hands to anything.'

Stafford kept his eye on Curtis. 'Where did you get the address?'

He shrugged. 'Friends, and friends of friends,' he said carelessly.

'You have useful friends.' Curtis was playing the old soldier, and Stafford knew he would get nothing more out of him – not then. He turned to the others. 'Do you know the score?'

Nair said, 'You want people watched.'

'Unobtrusively,' added Chip. He paused. 'And maybe you'll want more.'

'Maybe.' A waiter put down glasses and beer bottles. 'All right. A man arrives tomorrow from London. Gunnarsson, an American. I want to know where he goes and what he does.'

Chip poured himself some beer. 'Can be done.'

'There'll be two others; Hendrix, another American; and Farrar, an Englishman. Hendrix is important – Farrar less so. And there'll be another man – also Hendriks, but spelled differently.' He explained the difference.

Hardin said, 'You want Dirk tailed?' His voice held mild surprise.

'Why not?' Stafford poured beer, tasted it and found it refreshingly cold. 'Does anyone know anything about the Ol Njorowa Foundation?'

'Ol Njorowa?' said Chip. The name slipped more smoothly off his tongue than it had off Stafford's. 'That's near Naivasha.'

'An agricultural college,' said Nair. 'Doing good work, so I hear. I know someone there; a scientist called Hunt.'

That interested Stafford. 'How well do you know him?'

'We were at university together.' Nair pointed. 'Across the road there. We drank too much beer in this place.' He smiled. 'That was before I returned to my religion. I see him from time to time.'

'Could you introduce me? In an unobtrusive way?'

Nair thought for a moment, 'It's possible. When?'

'Today, if you can. I'd like to find out more about the Foundation before Gunnarsson arrives.'

'It will have to be at Naivasha. Who will be going apart from you?'

'Ben will be along. The Sergeant and Chip will stay to look after Gunnarsson tomorrow morning.'

Nair nodded and stood up. 'I'll make the arrangements. Be back soon.'

Stafford took a bigger sample of beer. 'Sergeant; I need suitable clothing or I'll melt away.'

He said, 'I'll see that the Colonel is fitted out.'

'You want a safari suit like this,' said Chip, fingering his own jacket. He smiled. 'You'd better go with Nair after lunch. You look too much the tourist. He'll get you a better price.'

Hardin handed Stafford a menu. 'Talking about lunch . . .'

They ordered lunch and another beer all round – a soft drink for Nair. When he came back he said, 'Everything fixed. We'll have dinner with Alan Hunt and his sister at the Lake Naivasha Hotel. It's part of the same chain as the Norfolk so I booked rooms for tonight. Is that all right?'

'That's fine.'

Lunch arrived and they got down to it.

That afternoon Stafford was fitted out with a safari suit in less than an hour in one of the Indian shops near the market. Nair did the chaffering and brought the price down to a remarkably low level. Stafford ordered two more suits,

then they set out for Naivasha, Nair driving and Hardin
sitting in the back of the Nissan.

Outside town the road deteriorated, becoming pot-holed
with badly repaired patches. When Stafford commented
on this Nair said ruefully, 'It is not good. You would not
think that this is an arterial highway – the main road to
Uganda. The government should repair it properly and stop
the big trucks.'

'Yeah,' said Hardin. 'The main liquids in this country
seem to be beer and gasoline.'

Stafford found what he meant when they passed Limuru
and started the descent of the escarpment into the Rift
Valley. The drop was precipitous and the road wound tortu-
ously round hairpin bends. They were stuck behind a petrol
tanker and in front of that was a big truck and trailer loaded
with Tusker beer. The Nissan ground down in low gear,
unable to overtake in safety, until Nair made a sound of
exasperation and pulled off the road.

'We'll let them get ahead,' he said. 'This low gear work
makes the engine overheat.' He opened the door of the car.
'I will show you something spectacular.'

Stafford and Hardin followed him through trees to the
edge of a cliff. He waved. 'The Rift!'

It was a tremendous gash in the earth's surface as though
a giant had struck with a cleaver. Stafford estimated a width
of twenty miles or more. In the distance the waters of a lake
glinted. Nair pointed to the hills on the other side. 'The Mau
Escarpment – and that is Lake Naivasha. The mountain
there is Longonot, a volcano, and the Ol Njorowa College is
just the other side. You can't see the buildings from this
angle.'

'How far does the Rift stretch?' asked Hardin.

Nair laughed. 'A long way. Four thousand miles, from
the Lebanon to Mozambique. It's the biggest geological scar
on the face of the earth. Gregory, the first white man to

identify it, said it would be visible from the moon. Neil
Armstrong proved it. Here, at this place, Africa is being torn
in two.' He caught Stafford eyeing him speculatively. 'I
studied geology at university,' he said dryly.

'And what do you do now, Nair?'

'I'm a courier, showing tourists around Kenya.' He
turned. 'The road should be clear now.'

As Stafford walked back to the car he wondered about
that courier bit. Perhaps it was true, perhaps not. And perhaps it was true but not the entire truth. This friend of a
friend of Sergeant Curtis was a shade too enigmatic for his
liking. 'And Chip? Is he a courier, too?'

'Why, yes,' said Nair.

They got to the floor of the Rift Valley unhampered
by beer trucks, although a steady procession was grinding
up the hill, going the other way. Once on the level Nair
increased speed. They passed a road going off to the
left across the valley. Nair said, 'That's the road to Narok
and the Masai Mara. You ought to go there – many
animals.'

Stafford grunted. 'I'm not here for sightseeing.' Thereafter Nair was silent until they arrived at the hotel.

It was a low-slung building, painted white with a red,
tiled roof and, but for the row of rooms set to one side, it
could have been a gentleman's country house. They registered and found their rooms. Stafford shared with Hardin
and, as soon as they were alone, he said, 'What do you
know about this pair – Chip and Nair?'

Hardin shrugged. 'No more than you. The Sergeant was
tight-mouthed.'

'He said he had connections here, but that was a long
time ago, during the Mau-Mau business. At that time Chip
and Nair wouldn't have been long out of kindergarten.
I think I'll have to have a serious talk with him when we get
back to Nairobi.'

Stafford had a quick shower before they assembled on the lawn in front of the hotel. It was six o'clock, the cocktail hour, and groups of guests were sitting at tables knocking back the pre-prandial booze while watching the sun dip below the Mau Escarpment beyond the lake. He ordered gin and tonic, Hardin had a Seagram's, while Nair stuck to his lemon squash.

A dachshund was chasing large black and white birds quite unsuccessfully; they avoided his mad rushes contemptuously. Nair said, 'Those are ibis; quite a lot of them around here. There are also pelicans, marabou storks and cormorants all around the lake.' He pointed at an incredibly multi-coloured bird, gleaming iridescently in blues, greens and reds, which was hopping among the tables. 'And that's a superb starling.'

'You seem to know a lot about birds,' Stafford said. 'For a geologist.'

'A courier must know a lot if he's to please his clients,' Nair said blandly. 'Will you need a cover story for Alan Hunt?'

The switch in subject matter was startling. Stafford looked at him thoughtfully, and said, 'I thought Hunt was your friend. Would you con him?'

Nair shrugged. 'As I said, I try to please my clients. I told him you were about to visit the geo-thermal project at Ol Karia; that's about two kilometres the other side of Hell's Gate.'

'But I know damn-all about it.'

'You don't have to know anything. You're going there as a vaguely interested visitor. They're drilling for steam to power an electricity generating plant. It's very interesting.'

'No doubt. Tell me, Nair; why are you doing this for me? Why are you playing along?'

He toyed with the iron bangle he wore on his wrist. 'Because I was asked,' he said. 'By a good friend in England.'

Stafford looked at Hardin. 'What do you think of that?'
He grinned. 'Not much.'

Nair said earnestly, 'Just be thankful that we're here to help you, Mr Stafford.'

Stafford sighed. 'Since we're on first name terms you'd better call me Max.' He added something pungent in Punjabi. Nair lit up and responded with Punjabi in full flow. Stafford said, 'Whoa, there! I wasn't in the Punjab long enough to learn more than the swear words. I was there for a short time as a boy just after the war; my father was in the Army. It was at the time of Partition.'

'That must have been a bad time,' Nair said seriously. 'But I've never been to India; I was born in Kenya.' He looked over Stafford's shoulder. 'Here is Alan Hunt now.'

Hunt was a tall, tanned man, blond with hair bleached almost white by the sun. He was accompanied by his sister, a shade darker but not much. Nair made the introductions and Stafford found her name was Judy. A hovering waiter took the order for another round of drinks.

'Is this your first visit to Kenya?' asked Judy, launching into the inevitable introductory smalltalk.

'Yes.' Stafford looked at his watch. 'I've been here about ten hours.'

'You get around quickly.'

'The car is a great invention.' Alan Hunt was talking to Nair. 'Are you with your brother at the Ol Njorowa College?'

'Yes; I'm an agronomist and Alan is a soil scientist. I suppose we complement each other. What do you do, Mr Stafford?'

'Max, please. I'm your original City of London business-man.' He tugged at the sleeve of his jacket. 'When I'm not wearing this I'm kitted out in a black suit, bowler hat and umbrella.'

She laughed, 'I don't believe it.'

'Take my word for it. It's still *de rigueur*.'

'I've never been to England,' she said a little wistfully.

'It's cold and wet,' Stafford said. 'You're better off here. Tell me something. I've been hearing about Hell's Gate – that's Ol Njorowa, isn't it?'

'In a way. It's what the English call it.'

'It sounds like the entrance to Dante's Inferno. What is it really?'

'It's a pass which runs along the western flank of Longonot; that's the big volcano near here. There are a lot of hot springs and steam vents which gave it its name, I suppose. But really it used to be an outlet for Lake Naivasha when the lake was a lot bigger than it is now.'

'How long ago was that?'

She smiled. She had a good smile. 'I wouldn't know. Maybe a million years.'

Nair stood up. 'We'd better go inside. The lake flies will be coming out now the sun has set.'

'Bad?' asked Hardin.

'Definitely not good,' said Hunt.

Over dinner Stafford got to know something about Hunt – and the Foundation. Hunt told about his work as a soil scientist. 'Jack of all trades,' he said. 'Something of geology, something of botany, something of microbiology, a smidgin of chemistry. It's a wide field.' He had been with the Foundation for two years and was enthusiastic about it. 'We're doing good work, but it's slow. You can't transform a people in a generation.'

When Stafford asked what he meant he said, 'Well, the tribes here were subsistence farmers; the growing of cash crops is a different matter. It demands better land management and a touch of science. But they're learning.'

Stafford looked across at Judy. 'Don't they object to being taught by a woman?'

Hunt laughed. 'Just the opposite. You see, the Kikuyu women are traditionally the cultivators of land and Judy gets on well with them. Her problem is that she loses her young, unmarried women too fast.'

'How come?'

'They marry Masai men. The Masai are to the south of here – nomadic cattle breeders. Their women won't cultivate so the men like to marry Kikuyu women who will take care of their patches of maize and millet.'

Stafford smiled. 'An unexpected problem.'

'There are many problems,' Hunt said seriously. 'But we're licking them. The Commonwealth Development Corporation and the World Bank are funding projects. Up near Baringo there's a CDC outfit doing the same thing among the Njemps. It's a matter of finding the right crops to suit the soil. Our Foundation is more of a home grown project and we're a bit squeezed for cash, although there's a rumour going around that the Foundation has been left a bit of money.'

Not for long, Stafford thought. He said, 'When was the Foundation started?'

'Just after the war. It took a knock during the Mau-Mau troubles, went moribund and nearly died on its feet, but it perked up five or six years ago when Brice came. He's our Director.'

'A good man?'

'The best; a real live wire – a good administrator even though he doesn't know much about agriculture. But he has the sense to leave that to those who do. You must come to see us while you're here. Combine it with your visit to Ol Karia.'

'I'd like that,' said Stafford. He did not want to be at Ol Njorowa when Dirk Hendriks was around because his curiosity might arouse comment. 'Could we make it next week?'

'Of course. Give me a ring.'

They went into the lounge for coffee and brandy. Hunt was about to sit down when he paused. 'There's Brice now, having a drink with Patterson. He's one of the animal study boys. I can clear your visit to the College right away.' He went over and talked with Brice then he turned and beckoned.

He introduced Stafford and Hardin to Brice who was a square man of medium height and with a skin tanned to the colour of cordovan leather. His speech was *almost* standard Oxford English but there was a barely perceptible broadening of the vowels which betrayed his Southern Africa origins. It was so faint that Hardin could be excused for identifying him as English.

He shook hands with a muscular grip. 'Glad to have you with us, Mr Stafford; we don't get too many visitors from England. Have you been in Kenya long?' The standard ice-breaking question.

'I arrived this morning. It's a beautiful country.'

'Indeed it is,' Brice said, 'It's not my own country – not yet-but I like it.'

Judy said questioningly, 'Not yet?'

Brice laughed jovially, 'I'm taking out Kenyan citizenship. My papers should be through in a couple of months.'

'Then you're English,' Stafford said.

He laughed again. 'Not me; I'm Rhodesian. Can't you tell by my accent?' He raised his eyebrows at Stafford's silence. 'No? Well, I lived in England a while, so I suppose I've lost it. I got out of Rhodesia when that idiot Smith took over with UDI.'

'What's that?' asked Hardin.

'The Unilateral Declaration of Independence.' Brice smiled, 'I believe you Americans made a similar Declaration a couple of hundred years ago.'

'Of course,' said Hardin, 'I was here in Africa when it happened, but I never got that far south. How did it come out in the end? African affairs aren't very well reported back home.'

'It couldn't last,' said Brice. 'You couldn't have a hundred thousand whites ruling millions of blacks and make it stick. There was a period of guerilla warfare and then the whites caved in. The British government supervised elections and the Prime Minister is now Mugabe, a black; and the name of the country is now Zimbabwe.'

'Do you have any intention of going back now that Mugabe is in command?' asked Stafford.

Brice shook his head. 'No,' he said. 'Never go back – that's my motto. Besides, I have precious little to go back to. I had a farm up near Umtali, and that's where the war was.' His face hardened. 'My parents were killed and I heard that the farmhouse my father built was burned out – a total loss. No, this will be my country from now on.' He sipped from his glass. 'Mind you, I couldn't leave Africa. I didn't like England; it was too bloody cold for my liking.'

He turned to Hunt, 'I don't see any reason why Mr Stafford shouldn't take a look at the College. When would that be?'

'Some time next week?' suggested Stafford.

They arranged a day and Brice noted it in his diary. He smiled, and said, 'That will probably be the day I kill the rumours.'

Stafford lifted his eyebrows. 'What rumours?'

'About the unexpected inflow of cash,' said Hunt. He looked at Brice. 'Is it true?'

'Quite true,' said Brice. 'An unexpected windfall. Could be as much as six or seven million.'

'Kenya shillings?' queried Hunt.

Brice laughed. 'Pounds sterling,' he said, and Hunt gave a long whistle.

Stafford kept a poker face and wondered what had happened to the rest of the cash. There was a shortfall of about twenty-seven million.

Brice said, 'Keep it under your hat, Alan, until I make the official announcement. I'm seeing the Trustees and a lawyer in the next few days.'

They had a few more moments of conversation and then Stafford and Hunt returned to their own table. Stafford was abstracted, mulling over what Brice had said, but presently he got talking to Judy, 'If you're coming to the College you must go ballooning with us,' she said.

He stared at her. 'Ballooning! You must be kidding.'

'No, I'm not. Alan has a hot air balloon. He *says* he finds it useful in his work.' She laughed, 'I think that is just an excuse, though; it's for the sport mostly. It's great fun. A good way of spotting animals.'

'Can you steer it?'

'Not very well. You go where the wind listeth, like a thistledown. Alan talks learnedly about wind shear and other technicalities, and says he can go pretty much where he wants. But I don't think he has all that much control.'

'What happens if you blow over the lake?'

'You don't go up if the wind is in that direction; but if it changes you swim until the chase boat catches up, and you hope there aren't any crocodiles about.'

Stafford said, 'I call that living dangerously.'

'It's not really dangerous; we haven't had as much as a sprained wrist yet. Alan caught the ballooning bug from another Alan – Alan Root. Have you heard of him?'

'The wildlife man? Yes; I've seen him on television back home.'

'He lives near here,' said Judy. 'He does a lot of filming from his balloon. And he went over Kilimanjaro. Ballooning is becoming popular here. Down at Keekorok in the Masai Mara they take tourists up and call it a balloon safari.'

It was pleasant sitting there chatting. Stafford learned a bit more about the Foundation, but not much, and was sorry when the Hunts departed at about eleven, their parting words urging him to come back soon. When they had gone he, Hardin and Nair pooled their knowledge and found it wouldn't fill an egg-cup.

Stafford said, 'Ben, I'm sending you back to England to do something we should have done before. In any case you're too conspicuous here; Nairobi is a small town and you could come face to face with Gunnarsson all too easily.'

'Yeah,' he said, 'I suppose I am your hole card. What do I do in England?'

'You study the life and times of Jan-Willem Hendrykxx. I could bear to know how he made his boodle and why he left it to the Ol Njorowa Foundation. Find the Kenya connection, Ben. And nose around Jersey while Farrar is away. The old man must have talked to *someone* in the seven years he was there.'

'When do I leave?'

'Tomorrow.' Stafford turned to Nair. 'And I'd like to know more about the Foundation. Can you dig out anything on it?'

He nodded. 'That should be easy.'

'Then we leave for Nairobi immediately after breakfast tomorrow.'

# TEN

They got back to Nairobi just after eleven next morning and, as Nair parked the car outside the Norfolk, Stafford saw Curtis in the Delamere Bar sinking a beer. He said to Hardin, 'Tell the Sergeant I'll see him in my room now.'

'Okay,' said Hardin.

'I'll find Chip,' said Nair.

Stafford nodded and got out of the car. He went into the bar to buy cigarettes and then went up to his room where Curtis and Hardin awaited him. He looked at Curtis and said, 'Where's Gunnarsson?'

'At the Hilton,' said Curtis. 'Chip is covering him.'

'Chip is covering him,' Stafford repeated. 'All right, Sergeant; exactly who are Chip and Nair?'

He wore an injured look, 'I told you.'

'Don't come the old soldier with me,' said Stafford. 'I've had better men than you booked for dumb insolence. You've told me nothing. Now, out with it. I want to know if I can trust them. I want to know if they'll sell me should Gunnarsson offer a higher price. How much are we paying them, anyway?'

'Nothing,' Curtis said. 'It's a favour.'

Stafford looked at him in silence for a while, then said, 'That does it. Now you've *got* to tell me.'

'I'm a mite interested, too,' said Hardin.

Curtis sighed. 'All right; but I don't want anyone getting into trouble. No names, no pack drill; see? I told the Colonel I'd been in Kenya before, but that wasn't the only time. I spent a leave here in 1973. The Colonel knows how it's done.'

'You talked to a Chief Petty Officer and came over as a supernumerary in one of Her Majesty's ships. A free ride.'

He nodded. 'She was one of the ships on the Beira patrol.'

'What's that?' asked Hardin.

'A blockade of Beira to try to stop oil getting into Rhodesia,' said Stafford. 'And bloody ineffectual it was. Carry on, Sergeant.'

Curtis said, 'I went ashore at Mombasa, had a look around there, then came up here on the train. I'd been here three or four days when I went to have a look at that big building – the tall round one.'

'The Kenyatta Conference Centre,' said Hardin.

'That's it,' said Curtis. 'It wasn't finished then. There was a lot of builder's junk around; it was a mess. I'd left it a bit late in the day and before I knew it the twilight had come, and that doesn't last long here. Anyway I heard a scuffle and when I turned a corner I saw four black Africans attacking an old Indian and a girl. They'd beat up the old man and he was lying on the ground, and now they were taking care of the girl. It was going to be a gang rape, I reckon. It didn't happen.' He held up his fists, 'I'm pretty good with these.'

Stafford knew that; Curtis had been runner-up in the Marine Boxing Championships in his time. And a tough Marine Colour-Sergeant would be more than a match for four unskilled yobbos. 'Go on.'

'The girl was fifteen years old, and the man was her grandfather. The girl was unhurt if scared, but the old man had been badly beaten-up. Anyway the upshot of it was that I took them home. They made quite a fuss of me then – gave me a meal. It was good curry,' he said reminiscently.

'We'll leave your gourmet experiences until later,' Stafford said. 'What next?'

'The Indians were in a bad way then. Kenyatta had declared that holders of British passports must turn them in for Kenyan passports.'

'It was the Kenya for the Kenyans bit,' remarked Hardin. 'I was here then. The word for it was "localization".'

'The Indians didn't want to give up their British passports but they knew that if they didn't the government would deport them,' Curtis said. 'India wouldn't have them and the only place they could go to was the UK. They didn't mind that but they weren't allowed to take any currency with them, and their baggage was searched for valuables before leaving.'

'Yeah,' said Hardin. 'They were between the rock and a hard place.' He shrugged. 'But I don't know that you could blame Kenyatta. He didn't want a big foreign enclave in the country. It applied to the British, too, you know. Become Kenyans or leave.'

Curtis said, 'They asked me to help them. I'd told them how I had come to Kenya and they wanted me to take something back to England.'

'What was it?' Stafford asked.

He sketched a small package in the air. 'A small box sewn up in leather.'

'What was in it?'

'I don't know. I didn't open it.'

'What do you think was in it?'

Curtis hesitated, then said, 'I reckon diamonds.'

Stafford said, 'Sergeant, you were a damned fool. If you'd have been caught you'd have been jailed and lost your service pension. So you took it to England.'

'Yes. Landed at Portsmouth and then went up to London to an address in the East End.'

'What did you charge for your services?'

He looked surprised. 'Nothing, sir.' Stafford regarded him thoughtfully, and Curtis said, 'They were good people. You see, they got to England and settled. And after that my Amy was a fearsome time in dying and I had a hard officer. I applied for compassionate leave and he wouldn't let me have it. I got it at the end, though; I was there when she died. And I found those Indians had been looking after her – taking flowers and fruit and things to the hospital. Seeing she was eased.' He was silent for a while, then repeated, 'Good people.'

Stafford sighed and went to the refrigerator. He broke the paper seal and took out a bottle. 'Have a beer, Sergeant.'

'Thank you, sir.'

He gave another to Hardin and opened one for himself. 'So when you knew we were coming to Kenya you went and asked for assistance. Is that it?'

'Yes, sir.'

'What's the name of this Indian family?' Curtis held his silence, and Stafford said gently, 'It's safe with me, Sergeant.'

Reluctantly he said, 'Pillay.'

A snort came from Hardin. 'Every second Gujarati is called Pillay; those that aren't are called Patel. It's like meeting a Britisher called Smith or Jones.'

Stafford paused in the pouring of the beer. 'Gujarati? This is where it stops making sense. Nair Singh is a Sikh, and since when have Sikhs and Gujaratis been chums? Not to mention Pete Chipende – he's a black African and that's a combination even less likely. And you say these two are helping us free of charge? Come *on*, Sergeant!'

'Hold it a minute,' said Hardin. 'Max, you need a short course in Kenyan political history. I was working here, remember? The Company was very interested in political activities in Kenya, and I was in it up to my neck so I know the score.'

'Well?'

He held up a finger. 'A one party state – the Kenya African National Union; that's KANU. Kenyatta was President, and the vice-President was Oginga Odinga. But even in a one party state there are factions, and Odinga broke away and formed the Kenya People's Union – the KPU. Kenyatta wasn't having that. There was a power struggle and, in the end, the KPU was banned. Odinga spent quite a time in jail. That was back in 1969. Of course, being Africa the brawl was about tribal loyalties as much as anything else. Kenyatta was a Kikuyu and Odinga a Luo. I've been keeping my ear to the ground while I've been here, and even now KANU is losing ground among the Luos. Of course, there's ideology involved, too.'

'So what's this got to do with anything?'

'Odinga had to get his money from somewhere; he had to have a war chest. I know he got some from the Chinese and some from the Russians. Kenyatta wasn't having anything to do with the Commies – he closed down their embassies – so they'd do anything to embarrass him. But there was a strong feeling that Odinga was getting funds from the expatriate Indian community in Britain. They'd been thrown out and they didn't bear Kenyatta any love, either.'

'So what's your conclusion?'

'My guess is that Chip and Nair are Odinga's supporters, KPU men. The KPU is banned but it's still going strong underground. If a source of UK funds should request a favour it wouldn't be refused.'

'Damn!' said Stafford. 'Bloody politics is the last thing I want to get mixed up in.'

'You're not mixing in politics,' said Hardin. 'You're not attacking the government. Just accept the favour and keep your mouth shut. Those guys could be useful. They *are* being useful.'

Curtis looked woebegone. Stafford smiled, and said, 'Cheer up, Sergeant; the Good Samaritan nearly always gets the chop in this weary world. It's really my fault. I told you back in England that I didn't want to know what you were up to.'

Curtis drank some beer and Stafford could see him take heart. Hardin said, 'You can bet there'll be more than Chip and Nair. They may not show but they'll be there.'

'What tells you that?'

'Past experience,' he said, and drained his glass.

So that was that. Stafford had allies thrust upon him that he could very well do without. But Hardin was right – they could be useful. He determined to accept their help up to a point and to keep his mouth shut as Hardin advised. Hear no evil, see no evil, speak no evil. But trust them he would not.

Chip showed up early in the afternoon. It seemed that Gunnarsson was doing what Stafford had done – sleeping away his travel weariness. But he had not appeared for lunch and had a meal sent up to his room. 'Who is keeping an eye on him now?'

Chip showed a mouthful of teeth. 'Don't worry. He's being watched.'

So Hardin was right; Chip and Nair were not alone. Chip said, 'Mr Farrar's party is coming in from London on the morning flight.'

'How do you know?'

Again the teeth. 'My brother-in-law is an official at the airport.'

Nair turned up a few minutes later. He brought with him a thick envelope which he handed to Stafford. It proved to be a rundown on the Ol Njorowa Foundation. It was quite detailed and he wondered how Nair had got hold of all this information at such short notice. Very efficient.

There were five Trustees; K. J. Patterjee, B. J. Peters, D. W. Ngotho, Col S. T. Lovejoy and the Rev A. T. Peacock. He said, 'Who are these people?'

Chip lounged over and looked over his shoulder. 'One Indian, a Parsee; three Brits and a black Kenyan.'

'People of influence? Of standing in the community?'

Stafford heard a chuckle and looked up to see that Nair's face was wreathed in a smile as well as a beard. Chip said, 'We wouldn't go as far as to say that; would we, Nair?'

Nair laughed outright, 'I don't think so.'

Chip's hand came over Stafford's shoulder and tapped on the paper. 'Patterjee was jailed for trying to smuggle 12,000 kilogrammes of cloves from Mombasa. That's highly illegal in this country. Peters was convicted of evading currency regulations and jailed. Ngotho was convicted of being a business prostitute; also jailed.'

'What the hell is a business prostitute?'

Nair said, 'Non-citizens cannot hold controlling interests in businesses in Kenya. There was a brisk trade in front men – Kenyans who would apparently own shares but who did not actually do so. Pure legal fakery. It was Mzee Kenyatta who coined the phrase, "business prostitute", wasn't it?'

'That's right,' said Chip. 'He made it illegal. Colonel Lovejoy is okay, though; he's been in Kenya forever. An old man now. Peacock is a missionary.'

Stafford was baffled. It was a curious mixture. 'How in hell did three crooks get made Trustees of the Ol Njorowa Foundation?'

'It *is* odd,' agreed Chip. 'What is your interest in the Foundation, Max?'

'I don't know that I have any interest in the Foundation itself. The Foundation is peripheral to my investigation.'

'I wonder . . .' mused Nair.

Chip said, 'You wonder what?'

'If the Foundation is really peripheral to Max's investigation.'

'Since we don't know what Max is investigating that's hard to say,' observed Chip judiciously.

Stafford sighed and leaned back in his chair. 'All right, boys; suppose we stop talking with forked tongues.'

Chip said, 'Well, if we knew what we were doing it would help. Wouldn't it, Nair?'

'I should think so.'

Stafford said, 'I'll think about it. Meanwhile, if you crosstalk comedians will allow me, I'll get on with this.' He turned pages. There were plans of the College which appeared to be quite extensive, involving lecture rooms, laboratories, studies, a library and a residential area. There were sports facilities including a swimming pool, tennis courts and a football field. There was also a large area devoted to experimental plots, something like British garden allotments but more scientific.

Stafford flipped a few pages and found a list of the faculty and caught the name of Alan Hunt. He tapped the name at the top of the page. 'This man, Brice, the Director. Your friend, Hunt, seems to think he's a good man, good for the Foundation. Would you agree?'

'Yes, I would. He's built up the place since he's been there. He works in well with the agronomists at the University, too.' Nair shrugged, 'I think the University – and the Government – are pleased that the Foundation can take up some of the financial load. Research is expensive.'

But Hunt had said that cash was tight. Stafford ignored that for the moment and flipped back the pages to the beginning – to the Trustees. 'How long have these three jokers been on the Board of Trustees?'

'I don't know,' said Chip. 'But we can find out. Can't we, Nair?'

'I should think so,' said Nair. 'Not much difficulty there.'

The telephone rang and Stafford picked it up, then held it out to Chip. 'For you.'

He listened, answering in monosyllables and not speaking English. Then he put down the phone, and said, 'Gunnarsson is up and about. He's at the New Stanley, having a coffee at the Thorn Tree.' He stood up. 'I'll be about his business. Coming, Nair?'

'Might as well. Nothing to do here except drink Max's beer, and I can't.' He joined Chip at the door.

Chip turned, and said softly, 'I hope you'll make up your mind about telling us what this is about, Max. It would be better for all of us.' The door closed behind them.

Stafford seriously doubted that. If Hardin was right and a proscribed political party was looking for loot to replenish its war chest there was too much of it about floating relatively loose for him to take chances. He spent the rest of the afternoon concocting a suitable story which would satisfy Chip and Nair, and then went to see Hardin who was in his room packing.

Hardin went back to London. Farrar duly arrived and wasted no time. He whisked the two heirs down to Naivasha. Unknown to him Gunnarsson went, too, and they all stayed at the Lake Naivasha Hotel. And, unknown to any of them, Chip and Nair were there. A real cosy gathering. Stafford stayed in Nairobi digging a little deeper into the curious matter of the Trustees, although he would dearly have liked to be a fly on the wall when Farrar, Hendrix, Hendriks and Brice got together in Brice's office.

They stayed in Naivasha for a total of three days and then returned to Nairobi. Farrar and Dirk took the night flight to London, and Stafford wired Hardin to expect them.

Gunnarsson moved into the New Stanley with Hendrix, and Stafford sat back wondering what was to happen next. Sooner or later he would have to make a move, but he didn't know the move to make. It was like playing chess blindfold, but he knew he would have to do something before distribution of the estate was made and Gunnarsson and Hendrix departed over the horizon, disappearing with three million pounds. Stafford badly needed ammunition – bullets to shoot – and he hoped Hardin would find something.

Chip came to see him. 'You wanted to know when the various Trustees of the Foundation were appointed.'

'I could bear to know.'

Chip grinned. 'Lovejoy and Peacock are founder Trustees; they've been on the Board since 1950. The others all came on at the same time in 1975.'

Stafford sat back to think. 'When did Brice take over as Director? When exactly?'

Chip said, 'Early 1976.'

'Interesting. Try this on for size, Chip. The Foundation was started in the 1950s but, according to Alan Hunt, it went moribund just after Kenya went independent. But that doesn't mean to say it had no money. I'll bet it had more than ever. The Charities Commission in the UK has done a survey and found scores of charities not doing what their charters have called for, but piling up investment money. No jiggery-pokery intended, just apathy and laxity on the part of the Trustees.'

'So?'

'So the Foundation *must* have had money. Where else could Brice have got it for his revitalizing programme? Now, take three vultures called Patterjee, Peters and Ngotho who realize there's a fat pigeon to be picked over. Somehow, I don't know how, they get themselves elected on to the Board of Trustees. They appoint as Director a non-Kenyan, a stranger called Brice, a man who doesn't know the country or its customs and they think they can pull the wool over his eyes.'

'While they milk the Foundation?' said Chip. He nodded. 'It would fit. But what about Lovejoy and Peacock?'

'I've done a little check on that pair,' said Stafford. 'Colonel Lovejoy is, as you say, an old man. He's eighty-two and senile, and no longer takes any active role in any business. Peacock, the missionary, used to be active in the Naivasha area but he moved to Uganda when Amin was kicked out. Now he's doing famine relief work there up in Karamoja. I don't think they'd be any problem to our thieves. But Brice is too sharp. He's no figurehead; he's proved that while he's been Director. Our trio have hardly got their hands into the cash register before he's really taken charge. He's got his hands on the accounts and they can't do a damned thing about it.'

'And they couldn't fire him,' said Chip. He laughed. 'If he caught them at it he'd have them by the short and curlies. And if he was sharp enough he'd keep them on as Trustees. That would put him in as top dog in the Foundation. He wouldn't want a stronger Board – it might get in his way.'

'Maybe he'd sweeten them by letting them take a healthy honorarium this side of larceny. That's what I'd do,' said Stafford. 'Just to keep them really quiet.'

Chip said, 'Max, you have a devious mind. You could just be right about this.'

'And what it means is that Brice is an honest man. The take could have been split four ways instead of three, but he really built up the Foundation into a going concern. I'd like to see this man; I have a standing invitation from Alan Hunt.' Stafford looked at his watch. 'I'll ring him now.'

'I'll drive you to Naivasha,' Chip offered.

'No, I'll go alone. But stay in touch. And keep a careful eye on Gunnarsson and Hendrix. If they move I want to know.'

# ELEVEN

Ol Njorowa College was about twelve kilometres from the Lake Naivasha Hotel. Stafford showered to wash away the travel stains and then drove there, first along the all-weather road that skirted the lake, and then along the rough track which would, no doubt, be dicey in wet weather. He found the College under the slopes of brooding Longonot.

There was a heavy meshed high fence and a gatehouse with closed gates, which surprised him. A toot on the horn brought a man running, and he wound the window right down as the man approached. He stopped and brought a gnarled, lined face to Stafford's level. 'Yes, sah?'

'Max Stafford to see Mr Hunt.'

'Dr Hunt? Yes, sah.' The lines of suspicion smoothed from the face. 'You're expected.' He straightened, issued a piercing whistle, then bent again. 'Straight through, sah, and follow the arrows. You can't miss it.'

The gates were opening so Stafford let out the clutch and drove through the gateway. The road inside the College grounds was asphalted and in good condition. There were 'sleeping policemen' every fifty yards, humps right across the road to cut down the speed of cars. They did, and as Stafford bumped over the first he checked the rear view mirror; the gates were closing behind and there was no evidence of anyone pushing them. Most of the buildings were long, low structures but there was a two-storey building ahead. The grounds were kept in good condition with mown lawns, and flowering trees were everywhere, bougainvillea and jacaranda.

Outside the big building he put the car into a slot between neatly painted white lines. When he got out he felt the hammer blow of the sun striking vertically on to his head. Because the elevation cut the heat one tended to forget that this was equatorial Africa, with the Equator not very far away. Hunt was waiting in the shade under the portico at the entrance and came forward.

They shook hands. 'Glad you could come.'

'Glad to be here.' Stafford looked around. 'Nice place you have.'

Hunt nodded. 'We like to think so. I'll give you the Grand Tour. Would you like it before or after a beer?'

'Lead me to your beer,' Stafford said fervently, and Hunt chuckled.

As they went inside he said, 'This block is mostly for administration, offices and so on. Plus those laboratories that need special facilities such as refrigeration. We have our own diesel-electric generators at the back.'

'Then you're not on mains power? That surprises me. I saw a lot of high tension pylons as I drove around the lake. Big ones.'

'Those are the new ones from the geothermal electric plant at Ol Karia. It's not on line yet. The power lines are being erected by the Japanese, and the geothermal project has advisors from Iceland and New Zealand. Those boys know about geothermal stuff. Have you been out there yet?'

'It's next on my list.'

'When we get mains power we'll still keep our own generators for standby in case of a power cut.' He opened a door. 'This way.'

He led Stafford into a recreation room. There was a half-size billiards table, a ping-pong table, several card tables scattered about, and comfortable armchairs. At the far end there was a bar behind which stood a black Kenyan in a white coat polishing a glass. Hunt walked forward and flopped into a chair. 'Billy,' he called. 'Two beers.'

'Yes, sah; two beers coming. Premium?'

'*Hapana*; White Cap.' Hunt gave Stafford half smile.

'Premium is a bit too strong if we're going to walk in the midday sun.'

'Mad dogs and Englishmen,' Stafford suggested.

'Something like that.' Hunt laughed. 'You know, the Victorians had entirely the wrong idea, what with their pith helmets and flannel spinal pads. They were more likely to get heatstroke indoors than outdoors in their day; their roofs were of corrugated iron and they cooked on wood-burning stoves. The rooms must have been like ovens.'

Stafford looked at Hunt's sun-bleached hair. 'So you're not worried about sunstroke?'

'You're all right once you're acclimatized and as long as you don't overdo it.' The bartender put a tray on the table. 'Put it on my chit,' said Hunt. He poured his beer. 'Cheers!'

Stafford waited until he had swallowed the first stinging, cold freshness before he said, 'Tell me something. Isn't a place like this eligible for a government grant?'

Hunt stretched his legs and absently rubbed a red scratch on his thigh. 'Oh, we get a grant but it doesn't go far enough. They never do. But things are changing. You heard what Brice said the other day. He still hasn't made the official announcement, though.' Hunt paused, then added, 'Anyway, it was enough to bring the Trustees out of the woodwork. They came this week and it's the first time I've seen them here, and that's been two years.'

Stafford said, 'I'd have thought, if money was tight, they'd have been in your hair seeing there wasn't any wastage.'

'Oh, Brice keeps them informed.' There was a slight hesitation as though he had meant to say something else, and Stafford guessed it was that Brice kept the Trustees in line, 'I wouldn't say he's machiavellian about it, but it suits me if I never see the Trustees. I have enough to bother about.' He looked up and waved. 'Here's Judy and Jim Odhiambo.'

Stafford stood up but Judy waved him back into the chair. 'Sit down, Max. I'd give my soul for an ice-cold tonic.'

He was introduced. Odhiambo was a short and stocky black with muscular arms. Hunt said, 'Dr Odhiambo is our resident expert on cereals – maize, millet, wheat – you name it.'

'Dr Hunt exaggerates,' said Odhiambo deprecatingly.

He ordered a beer for himself and a tonic for Judy. Hunt said, 'I've got something for you, Jim. I came across a paper in the Abstracts about primitive, ancestral forms of maize in Peru and I remembered what you said about preserving the gene pool. If you're interested I'll dig it out.'

Within two minutes they were engaged in a technical conversation. Judy said ruefully, 'This must be very dull for you.'

'Not at all,' Stafford said lightly, 'I like to hear experts talk, even though I don't understand one word in ten.' He looked at the bubbles rising in his glass. 'Alan has been telling me about the Foundation's good fortune.'

She lit up. 'Yes, isn't it wonderful.' And more soberly she said, 'Not that I'm cheering about the death of an old man in England, but I never knew him, and we can do so much good with the money here.'

'Who was he?'

'I haven't the slightest idea.'

A cul-de-sac. A bit of offensive was needed or he would never get anywhere. 'Why the fortifications?'

Judy wrinkled her brow. 'What fortifications?'

Stafford said, 'The fence around the grounds, and the gatehouse with closed gates.'

'Oh, that.' Her voice was rueful again. 'We like to give visitors to Kenya a good impression, but there are some awfully light-fingered people around here. We were losing things; not much – just minor agricultural implements, seeds, petrol – stuff like that. Most of it didn't matter very much, but when Jim Odhiambo breeds a special kind of maize for a certain soil and the seed is stolen and probably ends up in the stewpot of some ignorant wananchi then it hurts. It really does.'

'*Wananchi*?'

'Indigenous Kenyan. You can't really blame them, I suppose. The seed would look like any other seed, and they don't really understand what we're doing here.' She shook her head. 'Anyway, with the fence and the gates we tightened security.'

Hunt drained his glass. 'Come and see my little empire, Max. The bit of it that's upstairs.'

Stafford followed him and, on the way, said, 'Is Brice here today?'

'You'll probably meet him at lunch.' Hunt led the way along a corridor. 'Here we are.' He opened a door.

It was a laboratory filled with incomprehensible equipment and instruments the uses of which Hunt explained with gusto and, although much of it was over Stafford's head, he could not but admire Hunt's enthusiasm. 'Perhaps, with this new money, I can get the gas chromatograph I've been pushing for,' Hunt said, 'I need it to identify trace elements.'

Stafford wandered over to the window. Being on the top storey he had quite an extensive view. Away in the distance he could see the fence around the College grounds, and there was a man walking along it as though on patrol. He wore a rifle slung over his shoulder. He said, 'Why do you need armed guards?'

Hunt stopped in full spate. 'Huh?'

'Armed guards; why do you need them?'

'We don't.'

Stafford pointed. 'Then what's he doing out there?'

Hunt crossed to the window. 'Oh, we've been having a problem with a leopard lately, but how the devil it gets over the fence we don't know. It's taken a couple of dogs and the resident staff are disturbed – some of them have children here just about the size to attract a leopard.'

'And you don't know how it gets in?'

'Brice thinks there must be a tree, probably an acacia, which is growing too near the fence. He was organizing an exploration of the perimeter this morning. That's why he wasn't around.'

'How long is your perimeter?'

'I wouldn't know,' said Hunt lightly, 'I haven't measured it.'

Lunch was in the staff canteen which would not have disgraced a moderately good hotel as a dining room. It was spacious with good napery and silverware, and the food was very good. It seemed to Stafford that for a Foundation supposed to be hard up for money the senior staff did themselves well.

He was introduced to most of the staff over a pre-lunch drink at the bar. Their names and faces were forgotten as soon as the introductions were made, as usually happens on these occasions, but he estimated that they were black Kenyans, Indians and whites in roughly equal proportions, and honorifics like 'Doctor' and 'Professor' were bandied about with enthusiasm.

Hunt grinned at him, and said *sotto voce*, 'We have an almost Germanic regard for academic titles out here. You don't happened to be a PhD, do you?'

'Not a hope.'

'Pity.'

Stafford was re-introduced to Brice who said, 'Is Alan looking after you, Mr Stafford?'

Stafford smiled. 'Like royalty.'

They had a few moments more of conversation and then Brice drifted away, going easily from group to group with a word and a laugh for everyone. A jovial man with an instinct for leadership. Stafford had it himself to some degree and recognized it in another.

A few minutes later they adjourned for lunch and he found himself sitting with the Hunts and Odhiambo. He nodded towards Brice who was at what could be called the top table. 'Nice chap.'

Odhiambo nodded. 'For a non-scientist.' He leaned forward. 'Do you know he hardly understands a thing about what we're doing here. Odd in such an intelligent man. But he's a good administrator.'

Judy said, 'But, Jim, you don't really understand literature, do you?'

'I appreciate it,' he said stiffly. 'Even if I don't wholly understand it. But Brice doesn't *want* to know about our work.' He shook his head and looked at Stafford. 'We have a review meeting each week for the senior staff which Brice used to chair. It was impossible because he simply didn't understand. In the end he gave up and left it to us.'

Alan Hunt said, 'You must agree he knows his limitations and leaves us alone.'

'There is that,' agreed Odhiambo.

'Then who does the forward planning?' Stafford asked. 'The scientific work, I mean.'

'The weekly meeting reviews progress and decides on what must be done,' said Odhiambo.

'That's right,' said Hunt. 'Brice only digs his heels in when it comes to a matter of costs. He runs the financial end. I must say he does it very well.'

The meal was very good. They were ending with fresh fruit when Brice tapped on a glass with the edge of a knife and the hum of conversation quietened. He stood up. 'Ladies and gentlemen, friends and colleagues. I understand that certain rumours are circulating about a change in the fortunes of our College – a favourable change, I might add. I don't like rumours – they add to the uncertainty of life – and so this is to be regarded as an official statement.'

He paused and there was dead silence. 'The Foundation is the fortunate recipient of a certain sum of money from a gentleman in Europe now dead. The sum involved is five, perhaps six, maybe even seven . . .' He paused again with a fine sense of timing '. . . million pounds sterling.'

Pandemonium erupted. There was a storm of applause and everyone stood, clapping and cheering. Stafford joined in, smiling as much as anyone, but wondering what had happened to the rest of the loot. Judy, her eyes shining, said, 'Isn't it just great?'

'Great,' he agreed.

Brice held up his hands and the applause died away. 'Now that doesn't mean you can go hog-wild on your financial requisitions,' he said genially, and there was a murmur of amusement. 'There are legal procedures before we get the money and it may be some months yet. So, for the time being, we carry on as usual.' He sat down and a hubbub of noisy conversation arose again.

Stafford was still puzzled. He had assessed Brice, on his record, as being an honest man. Under the will 85 per cent of more than forty million pounds was to go to the

Foundation so why was Brice lying? Or was he? Could it be that the Hendrykxx estate was being looted by someone else? Farrar, perhaps. A crooked lawyer was not entirely unknown – someone had once made the crack that the term 'criminal lawyer' is a tautology.

Hunt said something, rousing Stafford from his abstraction. 'What's that?'

'I'll show you around the College,' he repeated.

'All right.'

They did the rounds in a Land-Rover and Stafford found the place to be more extensive than he had thought. The research was not only into agricultural science concerning the growing of crops, but animal husbandry was involved and also a small amount of arboriculture. Hunt said, 'We're trying to develop better shrubs to give ground cover in the dry lands. Once the cover is destroyed the land just blows away.' He laughed. 'There's a chap here trying to develop a shrub that the bloody goats won't eat. Good luck to him.'

An extensive area was given over to experimental plots which looked like a patchwork quilt. Hunt said, 'It's based on a Graeco-Latin square,' and when Stafford asked what that was Hunt launched into an explanation replete with mathematics which was entirely beyond him, but he gathered it had something to do with the design of experiments. He commented that mathematics seemed to enter everything these days.

They were on their way back to the Admin Block when his attention was caught by something not usually associated with an agricultural college – a dish antenna about twelve feet across and looking up almost vertically. 'Stop a minute,' he said. 'What's that for?'

Hunt braked. 'Oh, that's the animal boys. It's a bit peripheral to us.'

'That,' Stafford said positively, 'is a radar dish and nothing to do with bloody animals.'

'Wrong,' said Hunt. 'It's a transmitter-receiver on communication with a satellite up there.' He jerked his thumb upwards. 'And it has everything to do with animals.'

'All right; I'll buy it.'

'Well, it's no use us developing super crops if animals wreck the fields. You've no idea how much damage an elephant can do, and hippos are even worse. A hippo going through a maize field is like a combine harvester, and what it doesn't eat it tramples. So there's basic research going on into the movement of animals; we want to know how far they move, and where they're likely to move, and when. Selected animals are tagged with a small radio, and a geostationary satellite traces their movements.'

'What will you scientists get up to next?'

Hunt shrugged, 'It's of more use in tracing truly migratory animals like the Alaskan caribou. They used this method when they were planning the oil pipeline across Alaska. An elephant doesn't migrate in the true sense of the word although the herds do get around, and a hippo might go on a twenty-mile stomp.' He nodded towards the dish on the top of the building. 'But they're also using this to trace the annual migration of wildebeest from the Serengeti.' He released the brake.

'That's in Tanzania, isn't it?'

'Yes; but wildebeest don't respect national boundaries.'

Stafford laughed. 'Neither do radio waves.'

As they drove off Hunt said, 'I'd take you in there but there's no one about right now. As I said, it's peripheral to our work here. The radio crowd isn't financed by the Foundation; we just give them space here. They're a bit clannish; too; they don't mix well. We very rarely see them.'

He pulled up in front of the Admin Block, and Stafford said, 'Thanks for the guided tour. What about coming to the hotel for dinner?'

Hunt shook his head regretfully. 'Sorry, I've got something else on – a committee meeting. But what about coming up with me in the balloon tomorrow? Jim Odhiambo wants me to do some photography.'

Always something new. 'I'd like that,' said Stafford.

'I'll pick you up at the hotel – seven o'clock.'

Stafford drove back to the hotel and found a message waiting. Ring Curtis. He used the telephone in his room and got Curtis on the line who said, 'Chip wants to speak with the Colonel if the Colonel will hold on a minute.'

Stafford held on. Presently Chip said, 'Max?'

'Speaking.'

'Gunnarsson and Hendrix are going on safari.'

'And just what does that mean?'

'Going to a game lodge to see animals. Our main tourist attraction. They've booked with a tour group going to the Masai Mara down on the Tanzanian border. They'll be staying at the lodge at Keekorok. Don't worry; we'll be keeping an eye on them. No need for you to change any plans.'

Stafford said, 'Are you sure this is just an ordinary tour group?'

'Sure,' said Chip soothingly, 'I used to do the courier bit with them. It's standard operational procedure for tourists, showing them the big five – lion, leopard, elephant, rhino and buffalo.' He laughed, 'If they're lucky they see the lot; sometimes they aren't lucky.'

'What have our pair been doing?'

'Sightseeing around town. They had lunch once in the revolving restaurant on top of the Kenyatta Conference Centre. Gunnarsson's been playing the tables in the International Casino. Just the usual tourist stuff.'

'When are they going on safari?'

'Day after tomorrow.'

Stafford made up his mind. 'Can you lay me alongside Gunnarsson? I'd like to get a closer look at him.'

'You want to go to the Mara?' Chip paused. 'Sure, that can be arranged. When?'

'I'd like to be there when Gunnarsson arrives.'

'Stay where you are. We'll pick you up tomorrow morning.'

'Bring the Sergeant,' said Stafford, and hung up.

He had no idea why he wanted to see Gunnarsson but inactivity irked him, and he wanted to know why Gunnarsson was sticking around. It could not be to see animals – he doubted if Gunnarsson was a wild life enthusiast – so he was possibly waiting for something. If so, what? Anyway, this was more important than ballooning so Stafford picked up the telephone to cancel the appointment with Hunt.

# TWELVE

Chip came early next morning accompanied by Nair and Curtis. 'We won't need two trucks,' he said to Stafford. 'We'll leave yours here and pick it up on the way back.'

Stafford took Curtis on one side. 'Any problems, Sergeant?'

'No, sir.'

'I hope you've been keeping your ears open. Did Chip or Nair let anything drop to give a reason why they're being so bloody helpful?'

'Nothing I heard, sir.' Curtis paused, waiting for Stafford to continue, then he said, 'I'll pack the Colonel's case.'

Stafford had already packed so they wasted no time and were soon on the road. It was a good road, if narrow, and went straight as an arrow across the Rift Valley, and they made good time. They skirted the Mau Escarpment and eventually arrived at Narok which was nothing more than a village.

On the way Chip probed a little. 'Did you find what you wanted to know about Brice?'

'Not exactly,' said Stafford. 'He tells me he's applying for Kenyan citizenship. I would have thought a white colonial Rhodesian would be *persona non grata* here.'

'Normally you'd be right,' said Chip. 'But Brice's credentials are impeccable. He was anti-UDI, anti-Smith, anti-white rule. He left Zimbabwe – Rhodesia as it was then – at the right time. Brice is a liberal of the liberals, isn't that so, Nair?'

'Oh, yes; he's very liberal,' said Nair.

'You seem to know a lot about him,' observed Stafford.

'Just interested,' said Chip. 'He's not a secretive man. He talks a lot and we listen. We listen to lots of people, including you. But you don't say anything.'

'I don't go much for light conversation.'

'No, you don't,' he agreed. 'But some things don't need words. That scar on your shoulder, for instance. I saw it this morning before you put your shirt on. A bullet wound, of course.'

Stafford's hand automatically went up to touch his shoulder. 'Not unusual in a soldier,' he said. Actually the bullet had been taken out three years before by Dr Fahkri in Algiers; he had not done a good job and the wound had gone bad in England and so the scarring was particularly noticeable.

'You left the army ten years ago,' said Chip. 'That scar is more recent.'

Stafford looked sideways at him. 'Then you *have* been investigating me.'

Chip shrugged. 'To protect our own interests. That's all.'

'I hope I came out clean.'

'As much as anyone can. What's your interest in Brice?'

'He's come into a lot of money,' said Stafford. 'Or the Foundation has.'

'We know,' said Nair. 'It's in today's *Standard*.' He passed the newspaper forward from the back seat.

It was on the front page. The Ol Njorowa Foundation had inherited a sum of money from the estate of Jan-Willem Hendrykxx, a mysterious millionaire. The exact amount was not yet known but was believed to be in the region of £7 million. It was a thin story which told Stafford nothing he did not know already except that someone was pulling a fast one.

Chip said, 'Yet another spelling of the name. Are they all connected?'

Stafford nodded. 'Dirk Hendriks and Henry Hendrix are both heirs under the Hendrykxx estate.'

'A South African and an American,' said Chip thoughtfully. 'Sounds improbable, doesn't it, Nair?'

'Highly improbable,' said Nair, the eternal echo.

'They're both grandsons of old Hendrykxx,' said Stafford. 'The family got scattered and the names got changed. Nothing impossible about that.'

'I didn't say impossible,' said Chip, and added, 'Seven million sterling is a lot of money. I wonder what the Trustees think of it, Nair.'

Nair smiled through his beard. 'I should think they are delighted.'

Stafford said, 'I wish I could check out Brice; he seems too good to be true.'

'What would you want to know?' asked Chip.

'I'd like to know if Mr and Mrs Brice had a farm near Umtali in Zimbabwe. I'd like to know if the farm was burned and the Brices killed by guerillas. I'd like to know if their son . . . what's his name, anyway?'

'Charles,' said Nair. 'Charles Brice.'

'I'd like to know if their son, Charlie, left when he says he did.'

'I think we could find that out,' said Chip seriously.

'How?'

'I think our brothers in Zimbabwe would co-operate. Wouldn't you say so, Nair?'

'I think they would,' said Nair. 'I'll see to it.'

Stafford took a deep breath. 'You boys seem to have an extensive organization.'

'People are supposed to help and support each other,' said Chip, smiling. 'Isn't that what Christianity teaches? So we're helping *you*.'

'At the request of some Indian in London?' said Stafford incredulously. 'At the request of Curtis? Pull the other leg, it's got bells on it. What do you think, Sergeant?'

'It does seem rum, sir,' said Curtis.

Chip looked hurt, 'I don't think Max appreciates us, Nair.'

Nair said, 'Suspicion corrodes the soul, Max.'

'Oh, balls!' he said. 'Look, I appreciate your help but I doubt your motives. I'll be quite plain about that. I don't know who you are and I don't know what you want. The helping hand you are so kindly offering is bloody unnatural, and Christianity hasn't got a damned thing to do with it. Nair isn't even a Christian, and I doubt if you are, Chip.'

Chip smiled. '"Him that is weak in the faith receive ye, but not to doubtful disputations." Romans 14:1. I was educated in a mission school, Max; I'll bet I know more of the Bible than you. Don't be weak in the faith, Max; and let's not have any doubtful disputations. Just accept.'

'Chip is right,' said Nair. 'Is there anything else you'd like us to do?'

It was obvious to Stafford that he was not going to get anything out of this pair that they did not want him to know. If they were members of a banned political organization then it was obvious they would be careful. But he wished he knew why they were being so damned helpful. He was sure it was not because they liked the colour of his eyes.

Chip had been driving but at Narok Nair took over. Chip said, 'He's the better driver.'

'Will a better driver be needed?'

'You'll see.'

After Narok they left the asphalt and encountered the most God-awful road it had been Stafford's fate to be driven over. He had been more comfortable in a tank going across

country in NATO exercises in Germany. Where heavy rains
had washed gullies across the road they had not been filled
in and repaired, and the traffic of heavy trucks had worn
deep longitudinal grooves. Several times Nair got stuck in
those and Stafford heard the underside of the chassis scraping the ground.

'Manufacturers of exhausts must do a roaring trade
out here.' He looked back and saw they were creating
a long rooster's tail of dust. 'Why the hell don't they
repair this road? Don't they encourage visitors to Masai
Mara?'

Chip said, 'Narok District and the Government are having an argument about who pays. So far no one pays –
except to the repair shops.'

Stafford took out the map he had bought in Nairobi and
discovered they were driving across the Loita Plains. Every
so often they passed villages of huts and sometimes a herds-
man with his cattle. They were tall men with even taller
spears and dressed in long gowns. Chip said they were
Masai.

'What tribe are you?' Stafford asked.

'Kikuyu.'

Stafford remembered Hardin's lecture on African tribal
politics. 'Not Luo?'

Chip slanted his eyes at Stafford. 'What makes you think
I'd be Luo?'

'I haven't the slightest idea.' Chip frowned but said
nothing.

They passed a petrol tanker that had not made it. It was
overturned by the side of the road and burnt out. They
crossed a narrow bridge and Stafford checked the map.
There were only two bridges marked and, after the second,
the road changed status from being a main road to a
secondary road. He commented on this with feeling and
Nair burst out laughing.

Oddly enough, after the second bridge the road improved somewhat. Game began to appear, small herds of antelope and zebra and some ostriches. Chip played courier to the ignorant tourist and identified them. 'Impala,' he would say, or 'Thomson's gazelle.' There were also eland and kongoni.

'Are we in the Reserve yet?' Stafford asked.

'Not until we pass the Police Post.'

'Then there are more animals in the Reserve than here?'

'More?' Chip laughed. 'Two million wildebeest make the migration from the Serengeti to the Mara every year.' Stafford thought that was a lot of venison on the hoof. Chip rummaged around and found a map. 'Here's a map of the Mara. I thought you'd like to see what you're getting into.'

At first glance Stafford thought he was not getting into much. He checked the scale and found there were large chunks of damn-all cut through by what were described as 'motorable tracks.' Since the horrible road from Narok had been described as a main road he regarded that with reservation. There were two lodges, Keekorok and Mara Serena, and Governor's Camp; also about a dozen camp sites scattered mainly in the north. Streams and rivers abounded, there were a couple of swamps thrown in and, as Chip had said, a couple of million wildebeest and an unknown number of other animals, some of which were illustrated on the map.

He said, 'Is there really a bird called a drongo? I thought that was an Australian epithet.'

They arrived at the Police Post at the Olemelepo Gate and Nair drew to a halt. Chip said, 'I'll see to it. Be my guest.' He got out and strolled across to the police officer who sat at a table outside the Post.

Stafford got out to stretch his legs and when he slapped his jacket a cloud of dust arose. Curtis joined him. 'Enjoying yourself, Sergeant?'

Curtis brushed himself down and said ironically, 'Not so dusty.'

'People pay thousands for what you're going through.'

'If I have a beer it'll hiss going down.'

Stafford unfolded the map and checked the distance to Keekorok Lodge. 'Not long to go – only eight miles to your beer.'

Chip came back and they started off again and well within the hour the beer was hissing in the Sergeant's throat.

# THIRTEEN

Keekorok was 105 miles south of the Equator and at an altitude of 5,258 feet; there was a sign at the front of the Lodge which said so. It was a pleasant sprawling place with an unbuttoned air about it, a place to relax and be comfortable. There was a patio with a bar overlooking a wide lawn and that evening Stafford and Chip sat over drinks chatting desultorily while watching vervet monkeys scamper about in the fading light of sunset.

'We might as well do the tourist bit tomorrow,' said Chip. 'We'll go and look at the animals. I'll be courier – I know the Mara well.'

Stafford said, 'I want to be here when Gunnarsson and Hendrix arrive.'

'They won't be here until six in the evening.'

'How do you know?'

'Because that's what the courier has been told,' said Chip patiently.

Stafford sat up straight. 'What do you mean by that?'

'I mean that Adam Muliro, the driver, has been told when to deliver the party. I told him.' Chip paused and added with a grin. 'He's my brother-in-law.'

'Another?' said Stafford sceptically.

'You know us Third World people – we believe in the extended family. Now take it easy, Max.' He spread out a

461

map on the table. 'I'll show you hippo here, at Mara New Bridge.' He tapped his finger on the map.

The River Mara ran a twisting course north to south and the place where it was bridged was close to the Tanzanian border. If the scale of the map was anything to go by the road ran within three hundred yards of the border. Stafford thought of the different political philosophies of the two countries; the Marxist state of Tanzania and Kenya with its mixed economy. He had heard there was no love lost between them. 'Does Kenya have problems with Tanzania?'

Chip shrugged. 'The border is closed from time to time. There's a bit of friction; nothing much. Some poaching. There's an anti-poaching post here at Ngiro Are.' He spoke of the collapse of the East African Federation; the attempt of the three ex-British African nations to work in unison. 'It couldn't work – the ideas were too different. Tanzania went socialist – a totally different political philosophy from ours. As for Uganda . . .' He made a dismissive gesture. 'With Amin in power it was impossible.' He tapped the map again. 'You see the problem?'

Stafford frowned. 'Not really.'

'I have my finger on it,' Chip said. 'South of the border is Tanzania. Until 1918 it was German East Africa, then it was British Tanganyika, and now Tanzania. But look at the border – a line drawn straight with a ruler by nineteenth-century European bureaucrats. The country is the same on both sides and so are the people. Here they are Masai.' His finger moved south to Tanzania. 'And there they are Masai. A people separated by nineteenth-century politics.' He sounded bitter. 'That's why we have the Shifta trouble in the north.'

'What's the Shifta trouble?'

'The same thing. A line drawn with a ruler. On one side the Somali Republic, on the other side, Kenya; on both sides, Somalis. There's been a civil war running up there ever since I can remember. Nobody talks about it much. It's referred to in the press as Shifta trouble – banditry. Cattle raids and so forth. What it is really is an attempt to get a United Somalia.' Chip smiled grimly. 'Tourists aren't welcome on the North East Frontier.'

There was a diversion. In the fading light a bull elephant had come up from the river and was now strolling on the lawn, making its way purposefully towards the swimming pool. There were cries of alarm and then white-coated staff erupted from the kitchen, clattering spoons on saucepans. The elephant stopped uncertainly and then backed away, its ears flapping. Ponderously it turned and lumbered away back to the river.

Stafford said, 'That's one problem we don't have in English gardens.' He realized that the elephant had crossed the path he would have to walk to go to his room that night. 'Are those things dangerous?'

'Not if you don't get too close. But you're quite safe.' Chip jerked his head. 'Look.'

Stafford turned and saw a man in uniform standing on the edge of the patio who was holding a rifle unobtrusively, and thought that if Stafford Security Consultants were to move into Africa they would have to learn new tricks and techniques.

So next day they went to look at animals and saw them in profusion; wildebeest, impala, gazelle, topi, zebra. Also lion, elephant and giraffe. Stafford was astonished to realize that what he saw was but a fraction of the vast herds which roamed the plains in the nineteenth century. Although he was not in Kenya as a sightseer he found that he really enjoyed the day, and Chip, whatever he might be otherwise, knew his stuff as a guide.

They returned to Keekorok at five in the afternoon and, after cleaning away the travel stains, Stafford settled down to wait for Gunnarsson and Hendrix while settling the dust in his throat with the inevitable and welcome cold beer. They arrived on time in a party of six travelling in the usual zebra-striped Nissan, booked in at the desk and then went to the room they shared. Stafford marked it.

Later they appeared on the patio for drinks and he was able to assess them at close hand for the first time. Gunnarsson looked to be in his mid-fifties and his hair was turning iron-grey. He was a hard-looking man with a flat belly and appeared to be in good physical condition. His height was an even six feet and what there was on his bones was muscle and not fat. His eyes were pale blue and watchful, constantly on the move. He looked formidable.

The fake Hendrix was in his late twenties, a gangling and loose-jointed young man with a fresh face and innocent expression, and stood about five feet, nine inches. He was blond with a fair complexion and if he missed shaving one day no one would notice, unlike Gunnarsson who had a blue chin.

Chip joined Stafford at his table. 'So they're here. Now what?'

Stafford sighed. 'I don't know.'

'Max, for God's sake!' he said exasperatedly. 'I'm doing my best to help but what can I do if you don't trust me? Nair is becoming really annoyed. He thinks you're wasting our time and we should quit. I'm beginning to agree with him.'

During the past couple of days Stafford had come to like Chip; his style was easy and his conversation intelligent. He didn't want Chip to leave because he suspected he would need someone who really knew his way about Kenya. That was the role he had planned for Hardin but Hardin wasn't around.

He said, 'All right; I'll tell you. That young man has just come into a fortune – three million pounds sterling from the Hendrykxx estate.'

Chip whistled. 'And you want to take it from him?'

'Don't be a damned fool,' Stafford said without heat.

Chip grinned. 'Sorry. I really didn't put you down as a crook.'

'The whole point is that he isn't Hendrix. He's a fake rung in by Gunnarsson.' He told Chip the story.

'But why didn't you just tell the police in London?' asked Chip.

'Because Gunnarsson would have slid out from under, all injured innocence, and I want Gunnarsson. He's a cheap, unethical bastard who has got in my way before, and I want his hide. The trouble is I can't find a way of doing it. I've been beating my brains silly.'

'I'll have to think about this,' said Chip. 'This is a big one.'

Stafford watched Hendrix. He was chatting up a girl who was in his party. 'Who is she? Do you know?'

'Her name is Michele Roche. She's doing the tour with her parents. They're French. Her father's a retired business-man from Bordeaux; he was in the wine trade until six months ago.'

'You don't miss much,' Stafford said.

Chip grinned widely, 'I told Adam Muliro to find out as much as he could. The other member of the tour group is a young Dutchman called Kosters, Frederik Kosters. He and Hendrix don't like each other. They're both trying to get to know Michele better and they get in each other's way. Kosters is something in the diamond business in Amsterdam. Here he comes now.'

Stafford turned and looked at the young man making his way to the bar. He greeted the girl and she smiled at him warmly. Chip said, 'Kosters speaks French which gives him an advantage.'

'Your Adam Muliro is a fund of information. What did he find out about Gunnarsson?'

'He's an insurance broker from New York.'

'In a pig's eye. He runs an industrial espionage outfit. He's ex-CIA.'

'Is he, now?' said Chip thoughtfully. 'That's interesting.'

'And Hendrix; what about him?'

'According to Adam he smokes bhang. You'll know it better as marijuana. That's an offence in Kenya, of course, but it could be useful. If you want him held at any time the police could be tipped off. I could make sure that bhang would be found in his possession.'

'And you accused me of having a devious mind,' Stafford remarked. 'Anything else? Is he bragging about new found wealth, for instance?'

'Not according to Adam. He doesn't talk much about himself.'

'I don't suppose he can, seeing that he's someone else.'

Chip nodded. 'Adam says that Gunnarsson jumped on Hendrix a couple of times and made a change of subject but he didn't know why. We know why now.'

'Yes,' said Stafford. 'Hendrix must have been opening his mouth a bit too wide. Making trifling errors and in danger of blowing his cover. It must be wearing for Gunnarsson to be riding shotgun on three million pounds.'

'When is Hendrix getting the money?'

'I don't know, but it will be very soon. Farrar is fixing that now.' Stafford shook his head. 'I'd like to know why Gunnarsson and Hendrix are hanging about here in Kenya when the cash is in England. If I were Hendrix I'd be twisting Farrar's arm; urging him to get a move on.'

'You would if you were innocent,' said Chip. 'But Hendrix isn't. Perhaps Gunnarsson thinks he can keep closer to Hendrix here than in England. I wouldn't suppose there's all that much trust between them.'

'No honour among thieves? That might be it. Gunnarsson won't want Hendrix vanishing with the loot as soon as he lays hands on it. He's certainly sticking close to him now.'

Chip stretched his arms. 'Now I understand your problem better, but I don't know how to solve it. What do we do?'

'What we've been doing; we watch and wait. I can't think of anything else.'

Next day they went game spotting again, but this time with a difference; they stayed within easy reach of Gunnarsson's tour group. That was not difficult because Adam Muliro co-operated, never getting too far away. If Gunnarsson spotted them they would just be another group in the distance, and they were careful never to get too close. Stafford did not know why he was taking the trouble because it was a pretty pointless exercise. Action for the sake of action and born out of frustration.

And, of course, they saw animals – sometimes. Stafford found how difficult it is to see an unmoving animal, even one so grotesque as a giraffe. Once Nair pointed out a giraffe and he could not see it until it moved and he found he had been staring between its legs. And the grass was long and the exact colour of a lion. Of them all it was, oddly enough, Curtis who was the best at game spotting.

They were on the way back to Keekorok when Nair braked to a halt. 'We're getting too close,' he said. The Nissan ahead of them topped a rise and disappeared over the other side. 'We'll be able to see it when it rounds the bend over there.' He pointed to where the road curved about a mile away.

Stafford produced a packet of cigarettes and offered them around. Chip said, 'This isn't getting us far, Max.'

Nair smiled. 'Call it a holiday, Chip. Look at the pretty impala over there.'

Curtis said, 'With due respect I think the Colonel is wasting his time.'

Those were strong words coming from the Sergeant who had few words to spare at any time. Stafford said, 'And what would you suggest?'

'Get hold of Hendrix on his own and beat the bejesus out him until he admits he's an impostor,' he said bluntly.

'Sergeant Curtis has a point,' said Chip.

'It's an idea,' said Stafford. 'The problem will be to separate him from Gunnarsson. I don't want to tip him off.' Or anyone else, he thought. There was the peculiar conduct of Brice back at Ol Njorowa College; Stafford had not told Chip about the twenty-seven or so million pounds unaccounted for. That did not tie in at all.

They kicked it around a while, then Nair said, 'Funny. They're not in sight yet.' There was no sign of the Nissan that had gone ahead.

'They've probably found a lion over the hill,' said Chip. 'Tourists stop a long time with lions. They're probably making a fortune for Kodak.'

'Not Gunnarsson and Hendrix,' said Nair.

They talked some more and then Nair moved restlessly. 'Still no sign of them. A long time even for a lion.'

'Perhaps there's a track leading off the road just over the hill,' said Stafford.

'No track,' said Nair positively.

He said, 'Then he's gone off the road, track or no track.'

'Adam wouldn't do that; not without giving us a signal.' Chip stubbed out his cigarette. 'Let's move it, Nair. Just to the top there.'

Nair turned the key in the ignition and they moved off. At the top of the rise they stopped and looked down into the little valley. The Nissan was standing in the centre of the road below them about 400 yards away. There was nothing unusual about that; tour buses stood stationary like that all over the Reserve and it was normally the sign that something unusual had been spotted – a kill, perhaps.

Chip took binoculars and scanned the vehicle. 'Get down there, Nair,' he said quietly.

They coasted down the hill and came to a halt next to the Nissan. There was not a living soul in it.

The first bizarre thought that came into Stafford's head was the story of the *Mary Celeste*. Chip shot a spate of words to Nair in a language he did not understand, probably Swahili, and they both got out, ignoring the deserted vehicle and looking about at the landscape. There must have been a watercourse in the valley, now dried up, because there was a small culvert to take water under the road, and the bush was particularly thick and green.

Stafford and Curtis got out to join them, and Chip said sharply, 'Don't come closer.'

Stafford said, 'Where the hell have they all gone?' It was an offence to get out of a car in the Reserve; you could lose tourists that way, and that would be bad for business.

Chip stooped and picked up something which glittered in the sun – a pair of dark glasses with one lens broken. 'They didn't go voluntarily.'

'Kidnapped!' Stafford said incredulously. 'Who'd want to do that?'

'The *Jeshi la Mgambo?* said Nair. 'Right, Chip?'

'I'd say so.' Chip opened the door of the Nissan and looked inside. 'It's stripped,' he said. 'No cameras, binoculars or anything else. Everything gone.'

Nair looked back along the road. 'They'll have had a man up there watching us.' He turned and pointed. 'Up there, too. They could still be around.'

'Too damned right,' said Chip. He moved quickly to their own Nissan and opened the door at the back. Stafford had inspected the vehicle so he did not know where he got them but when he turned around Chip was holding two rifles. He tossed one to Nair and said to Stafford, 'Can you use one of these?'

'I have been known to,' Stafford said dryly. 'Now will you kindly tell me what's happening?'

'Later,' Chip said, and gave him the rifle.

'I can use one of those, too,' said Curtis.

'You're going to Keekorok as fast as you can drive,' said Chip. He took a notebook and pen from his pocket and scribbled rapidly. 'Give this to the manager of the Lodge; he'll radio the Police Post at Mara New Bridge.' Going to the driver's seat he fished out the map of Masai Mara and marked it. 'That's where we are now. Okay, Sergeant; move!'

Curtis looked at Stafford, who nodded. 'Which truck?' he asked.

'Ours,' said Chip. 'But wait.' He went to the back again and when he straightened he was holding a sub-machine-gun, one of the little Israeli Uzis which are supposed to be one of the best designs in the world. He also had two packs of rifle ammunition and a spare magazine for the Uzi. 'On your way,' he said. 'Don't stop for anyone. If anyone tries, keep your head down and run them over.'

The crackle of authority in Chip's voice brought an automatic, 'Yes, sir,' from Curtis. He climbed into the driver's seat, the wheels spun, and he was away in a cloud of dust.

Stafford checked the rifle. A sporting and not a military weapon, it was bolt action with a five-round magazine. The magazine was full so he put a round up the spout, set the safety catch, took out the magazine to put another round in, then put the rest of the ammunition into his pockets. Chip watched and nodded approvingly. 'You've been there before,' he said.

Nair was kneeling by the Nissan looking at the dusty road. 'Six of them,' he said. 'Six, I think.'

'Six of who?' Stafford demanded irascibly.

'*Jeshi la Mgambo,*' said Chip. 'Tanzanians. The so-called Tanzanian Police Reserve. A paramilitary force with bad discipline. This has happened three or four times before. They come across the border, pick up a busload of tourists, and hustle them across the border. Then they're picked clean of everything they've got and left to walk back to Keekorok. The government has sent several protest notes to the Tanzanians.' He shrugged, 'it stops for a while but then they start again.'

'And they're armed?'

His reply was brief and chilling. 'Kalashnikovs.'

Stafford winced and looked down at the rifle he held. The Russian Kalashnikov is a fully automatic weapon which can spew out bullets as water from a hosepipe. The sporting rifle, while not exactly a toy, was not in the same league. 'And we're going after them?'

Chip gave him a quick glance. 'What else would you suggest? Curtis is the oldest; nearly sixty. That's why I sent him back. It could be a rough trip.'

Stafford said mildly, 'On those grounds Curtis could have given you an argument.'

'Besides, we have only three guns.'

Nair said, 'The border is over there – two miles. They can't have got much of a start and the prisoners will slow them down. Also they'll have to cross the Losemai.'

'Easy at this time of year,' said Chip. 'Let's go.'

They went on foot because to track from a Nissan is impossible, and it was Chip who did the tracking. He went confidently, going by signs which eluded Stafford and as he marched behind he wondered about these men who could produce an armoury at the drop of a hat. An Uzi isn't something you pick up casually at the corner shop.

# FOURTEEN

In the African bush there is a species of acacia known as the wait-a-bit thorn. It is well named. Chip and Nair knew enough to avoid them while Stafford, trailing in the rear, did not. He found it was like being trapped in barbed wire and his temper suffered, as did his suit and his skin.

After a while he got the hang of it and learned to travel in the master's footsteps and then it became better. Chip kept up a cracking pace, stopping occasionally to cast around. Twice he pointed out the signs of passage of those they were pursuing – footprints on the dusty earth. Nair nodded, and said in a low voice, 'Military boots.'

Once Chip threw his arms wide and the party came to a sudden halt. He waved and they made a wide circuit of a patch of ground on which Stafford saw a snake, not very long but with a body as thick as a man's brawny arm. Afterwards Chip told him it was a puff adder, and added, 'Most snakes get out of the way when they sense you're coming, but not the puff adder – he's lazy. So, if you're not careful you tread on him and he strikes. Very poisonous. Don't walk about at night.'

It was hot and Stafford sweated copiously. Heavy physical exercise on the Equator at an altitude of 5,000 feet is not to be recommended if you are not acclimatized. The

Kenyan Olympics Team has a training camp at 9,000 feet where the oxygen is thin and the body becomes accustomed to its lack. When they go to sea level that gives a competitive edge, an advantage over the others. But Stafford was a reverse case and he suffered, while Chip and Nair were in better shape.

The terrain consisted of rolling plains with an occasional outcrop of rock. The trees, mostly flat-topped acacias, were scattered except where they tended to grow more thickly in the now dry watercourses, and the grass was waist high. The ground was so open that anyone looking back would surely see a long way.

Consequently they made good time in the valleys between the ridges but slowed as they came to a crest, creeping on their bellies to peer into the next shallow valley. As they came up to the top of one such ridge Chip said quietly, 'We're in Tanzania. There's the Losemai.'

Ahead, stretching widely, was a green belt of thicker vegetation which marked the Losemai River. It looked no different from any similar place in the Kenyan Masai Mara. Chip took his binoculars, and said, 'Hold up your hand to shade these from the sun.'

Stafford put up his hand to cast a shadow on the lenses, and reflected that Chip was up to all the tricks of the trade. He didn't want a warning flash of light to be reflected; it would have been like a semaphore signal. He wondered where Chip had learned his trade. More and more there were certain things about Chip and Nair which didn't add up into anything that made sense.

Chip surveyed the land ahead, the binoculars moving in a slow arc. Suddenly he stopped, pointing like a hunting dog. 'There – entering the trees at two o'clock.' Another military expression.

Away in the distance Stafford saw the minute dots and strained his eyes to count. Chip said, 'I make it thirteen. You

were right, Nair; *Jeshi la Mgambo,* six of them. And six in the
tour group plus Adam. They're all there.'

Nair said, 'Do you think they'll stop at the Losemai?
What happened before?'

'They might,' said Chip. 'They've got good cover down
there and it's a convenient place to strip the tourists.'

Stafford said, 'It seems a lot of trouble for little profit.'

Chip snorted. 'Oh, there's profit. Take your tourist; he
comes here to photograph animals so he usually has a good
camera, still or cine. Plus telephoto lenses and other goodies
such as a wristwatch. He also has money, traveller's cheques
and credit cards, and there's a good trade in cheques and
cards. A tourist, particularly a German or American, can be
worth up to £1,000 on the hoof, and that's a damn sight
more than the average Tanzanian makes in a year.'

'Don't bother about convincing Max of what he can see
with his eyes,' said Nair acidly. 'How do we get there?'

'The last of them has gone into the trees,' said Chip.
He took the glasses from his eyes, withdrew from the top of
the ridge and rolled over on to his back, then looked about
him. He jerked his thumb. 'We can't follow them that way;
they might have someone keeping watch. I know they're
undisciplined, but we can't take that chance.'

Nair looked along the ridge. 'That thin line of trees there
might be a stream going down to join the Losemai. It could
give cover.'

'We'll take a look,' said Chip.

They went along the ridge, keeping below the crest, and
found that it was a stream or, rather, it would be when the
rains came. Now it was dusty and dry although if one dug
deep enough one would find dampness, enough to keep the
acacias green in the dry season. The force of rushing water
during the rains had carved into the soft soil making a channel which averaged a couple of feet deep. It would provide
cover of a minimal kind.

So they went down on their bellies, following the winding of the watercourse. It was something Stafford had not done since his early days in the Army and he was out of practice. Once he jerked his hand up as he was about to put it on something which moved. It scuttled away and he saw it was a scorpion. He sweated and it was not all because of the African heat.

It took a long time but finally they got down to the shelter of the trees which fringed the Losemai and were able to stand up. Chip put his fingers to his lips and cautiously they made their way to the river and lay close to the bank, hidden by tall grass. Stafford parted the stems and looked to the other side.

It was not a big river by any standards; the depth at that time of year was minimal and Stafford supposed one could cross dry shod by jumping from sandbank to sandbank. The flow of water was turgidly slow and muddy brown. In a clearing on the other side a giraffe was at the water's edge, legs astraddle and drinking. Something on a sandbank moved and he saw a crocodile slip into the water with barely a ripple, and changed his mind about jumping from sandbank to sandbank.

Chip said softly, 'I don't think they've crossed; that giraffe wouldn't be there. We'll go up river on this side very slowly.'

They went up river in military formation. Chip, with the sub-machine-gun, was point; behind him Stafford was back-up, and Nair was flanker, moving parallel but about fifty yards away and only visible momentarily as he flitted among the trees, his rifle at high port.

It was very slow and very sweaty work. The river bank was full of noises; the croaking of frogs and the chirping of grasshoppers and cicadas. Occasionally Stafford jerked as he caught a movement out of the corner of his eye but always it was the quick flash of a brightly coloured bird crossing the river. Once there was a splash from the water and he saw a small brown animal swimming away because Chip had disturbed it in its waterside home.

Suddenly Chip went down on one knee and held the Uzi over his head with both hands. Stafford stopped and snapped off the safety catch on the rifle. Chip motioned him forward so he went up to him and knelt beside him. There was a distant murmur of voices and a louder burst of laughter. 'Cover me,' said Chip, and went forward on his belly.

For a moment Stafford lost sight of him in the long grass, then he came into view again. Chip beckoned and Stafford dropped flat and went to join him. Chip had parted the grass and was staring at something. 'Take a look,' he said quietly. The voices were louder.

Stafford parted the stems of grass and found that he was looking into a clearing by the river. They were all there, the Tanzanians and the tour group. The Tanzanians wore camouflaged battle fatigues and were all armed with automatic rifles. Two of them wore grenades attached to their belts and one, with sergeant's stripes, had a pistol in a holster.

The tour group was in a bad way. They had been stripped of most of their clothing and Mam'selle and Madame Roche were down to their bras and panties. Madame Roche's face was blotchy as though she had been crying and her husband, a ridiculous figure with his big belly swelling over his underpants, was trying to comfort her. Michele Roche had paled under her tan so that her face was a jaundiced yellow. She looked scared, and young Kosters was talking quietly to her, his hand on her arm.

If Gunnarsson was frightened he did not show it. His face was dark with anger as he stooped to pick up a shoe and as a rifle was nudged into his back he straightened with a quick truculence and shouted, 'Goddamn it, you've gotta leave us shoes.' The answer was a shake of the head and another dig with the rifle. He dropped the shoe and glowered.

Hendrix, also stripped, was standing separately from the group flanked by two Tanzanians. The young black sitting on the ground with a set, expressionless face would be Adam Muliro, the courier. Before him, striking dazzling reflections from the sun, was the loot – cameras, lenses, binoculars and other equipment, together with a pile of clothing.

Slowly Stafford let the grass escape from his fingers to form a screen. Chip put his mouth to Stafford's ear. 'We can do nothing. We could cause a massacre.'

That was certainly true. Those Kalashnikov rifles scared Stafford and the sight of the grenades frightened him even more. He had been a soldier and he knew what those weapons could do. If, as had happened before, the prisoners were turned loose to walk back to Keekorok, the only discomfort they would suffer would be sunburn and cut and sore feet. Under the circumstances a shooting match was out of the question. They were outnumbered and outgunned and the safety of the prisoners could not be risked.

Chip indicated that Stafford should withdraw so he wriggled backwards and then turned, still lying flat. Then he looked back to see Chip running towards him at a crouch. Chip waved his arm wildly as he passed and then flung himself headlong into a thick patch of long grass and vanished from sight. Stafford got the message and picked himself up and ran for the nearest tree.

Just as he got there he heard voices. The tree trunk was not as thick as his body and he set himself edge on to it, moving slowly around so as to keep it between him and the approaching men. They came closer and he could distinguish a baritone and a lighter voice; and could even catch words but did not understand the language. As they went by he risked a glance. Hendrix was hobbling by the river bank, walking painfully because of his bare feet. He was clad only in his underpants and behind him came two

Tanzanians, one of them prodding him in the back with a rifle. They disappeared from view.

Chip's head came out of the grass. He waved his arm in a wide circle and then ran to the river bank and began to follow. Stafford turned to find Nair and saw him emerge from hiding. He waved him to follow Chip and then took off, making a wide circle. Chip was still at the point, Stafford was now flanker and Nair was rearguard. Stafford stayed about fifty or sixty yards from the river and kept parallel with it, occasionally going in as closely as he dared to keep track of Hendrix and his captors.

Once he got close enough to hear Hendrix wail, 'Where are you taking me? What have I done?' There was a thump and a muffled grunt and a short silence before he said desolately, 'Christ! Oh, my Christ!' Stafford guessed he had been hit in the kidneys by a rifle butt but did not risk going close enough to see.

They went on in this manner for quite a distance, perhaps half a mile, and then Stafford lost them. He backtracked a hundred yards and found that they had stopped. Hendrix was standing quite close to the edge of the river facing the Tanzanians, one quite young, the other an older man. The young one had Hendrix at rifle point keeping him covered; the other had his rifle slung and was smoking. He took the cigarette stub from his mouth, examined it critically, then casually dropped it and put his foot on it before he unslung his rifle. He lifted it to his shoulder and aimed at Hendrix, his finger on the trigger.

Hastily Stafford brought up his own rifle but it was then that Chip cut loose with the Uzi. The burst of fire caught the man in the back and he was flung forward. The young Tanzanian whirled around and Stafford shot him in the head. He grew a third eye in the middle of his forehead and staggered back and fell into the river with a splash. After that sudden outburst of noise there was a silence broken only by insect noises and the whimpering of Hendrix who was on his knees staring unbelievingly at the sprawling body before him.

Chip came into sight, gun first and cautiously, and then Nair. Stafford went to join them. He said, 'The bastard was going to shoot Hendrix,' and heard the incredulity in his own voice. He snapped his fingers. 'Just like that.'

Chip stirred the body with his foot, then bent down to check the pulse at the side of the neck. He straightened up. 'They've gone crazy,' he said blankly. 'They've never tried anything like this before.' He turned to Nair. 'Get back there – about a hundred yards – and keep watch.'

Stafford went over to Hendrix. Tears streaked his face and he was making gagging noises at the back of his throat. Stafford tried to help him to his feet but he went limp and lay down in a foetal position. 'For God's sake, man,' said Stafford. 'Get up. Do you *want* to be killed?'

'He's been nearly frightened to death,' said Chip.

'He'll be the death of us if he doesn't move,' Stafford said grimly. 'They'll have heard those shots.'

'They were expecting to hear shots,' said Chip. 'Let's hope they can't tell the difference between an Uzi and a Kalashnikov. But they're pretty far away.' He bent down and began going through the pockets of the dead man.

Stafford walked to the river bank which here was about six feet high. The river moved sluggishly and the body of the man he had shot had not drifted far. He was the first man Stafford had ever killed as far as he knew and he felt a little sick. His soldiering had been mostly in peacetime and even in those faraway days in Korea it was surprising how rarely you saw the enemy you were shooting at. And later they did not go too much for bodies in Military Intelligence.

Chip said, 'No identification; just this.' He held up a wad of currency. 'Kenya twenty-shilling notes.' He put them into his pocket. 'Help me get his clothes off.'

'Why strip him?'

Chip nodded towards Hendrix. 'He's not going to move far or fast without clothes and boots. And we don't have much time; not more than a few minutes. These men will be expected back and when they don't show someone will come looking.'

While Stafford was unlacing the Tanzanian's boots Chip stripped him of his bloody and bullet-ripped jacket and, together, they took off his trousers. Undressing a dead man is peculiarly difficult. He does not co-operate. Then they rolled the body to the edge of the bank and dropped it over the side. It fell with a splash into the muddy water. The other body had gone.

'No one will find them now,' said Chip. 'This looks like a likely pool for crocodiles. The crocs will take them and wedge them under water until they ripen enough to eat.' It was a gruesome thought.

They dressed Hendrix and he did not co-operate, either. He was almost in a state of catatonia. Stafford noted that Hendrix had no scar on either shoulder, a scar which ought to have been there. He said nothing, and looked up when Chip said, 'One of your problems is solved; you've separated Hendrix from Gunnarsson. How long do you want to keep it that way?'

That hadn't occurred to Stafford. He said, 'We'll discuss it later. Let's get the hell out of here.'

They hoisted Hendrix to his feet and Stafford slapped his face hard twice with an open palm. Hendrix shook his head and put up his hand to rub his cheek. 'What did you do that for?' he asked, but the imbecile vacuous look in his eyes was fading.

'To pound some sense into you,' Stafford said, if you don't want to die you've got to move.'

A slow comprehension came to him. 'Christ, yes!' he said.

Chip was brushing the ground with a leafy branch, scattering dust over the few bloodstains and eliminating all signs of their presence. He walked over to where he had fired the sub-machine-gun and picked up all the cartridge cases he could find, then he tossed them and the two Kalashnikovs into the river. 'Let's get Nair,' he said, so Stafford picked up his rifle and they went from that place.

They struck away from the river and headed north-east for the border, going up the narrow gully they had come down until they got to the comparative safety of the other side of the ridge where they rested a while and had a brief council of war. At a gesture from Chip Nair stood guard on Hendrix and he and Stafford withdrew from earshot. 'What now?' said Chip.

Up to that moment Stafford had had no opportunity for constructive thinking; all his efforts had been bent on staying alive and out of trouble and he had not considered the implications of what he had seen. Those people stripped to trek back to Keekorok troubled him. If they travelled when the sun was up they would get terribly sunburned, and Chip had indicated that travel at night could be dangerous. He said, 'How far is it to Keekorok from here?'

'About eleven or twelve miles – in a straight line. But no one travels in a straight line in the bush. Say fifteen miles.'

That was a long way; a day's march. Stafford was not worried about Gunnarsson or Kosters. Gunnarsson was tough enough and the young Dutchman looked fit. Michele Roche could probably take it, too, but her parents were something else. A sedentary wine merchant who looked as though he liked to sample his own product freely and his elderly wife were going to have a hell of a tough time. He said, 'This is a funny one, Chip. These border raids: has anyone been killed previously?'

Chip shook his head. 'Just robbery. No deaths and not even a rape. They took three Nissans full of Germans about a year ago but they all came back safely.'

'Then why this time?' asked Stafford. 'That was nearly a deliberate murder. It looked almost like a bloody execution.'

'I don't know,' Chip said. 'It beats me.'

'That charming scene in the clearing when Gunnarsson wanted his shoes. Did you notice anything about Hendrix?'

'Yes, he was separated from the others.'

'And under guard. Now, why should Tanzanians want to cut Hendrix from the herd to kill him? If you could give me the answer to that I'd be very happy because I think it would give us an answer to this whole mess.'

'I don't *have* an answer,' Chip said frankly.

'Neither do I,' said Stafford, and brooded for a while.

'Well; you've got Hendrix now,' said Chip. 'If you want to question him now's the time to do it before he joins the others.'

'Whoever wanted Hendrix out of the way wanted it to be bloody permanent,' Stafford said ruminatively. 'And it wasn't a matter of secrecy, either. Chip, supposing you were in that tour group and you saw Hendrix marched away. A little later you hear shots, and then the Tanzanians who took Hendrix away return wearing broad grins. What would you think?'

'I'd think Hendrix had been shot, probably trying to escape.'

'So would I,' said Stafford. 'And that's probably what the rest of the group think right now, except that Hendrix's guards didn't return. But they'll have heard the shots. Does that sound reasonable?'

'It could be.'

Nair gave a peculiar warbling whistle and beckoned. They went back to the crest of the ridge and Nair pointed to the belt of trees by the Losemai. 'They're coming out.'

Minute figures were emerging on to the open plain. Chip, his binoculars to his eyes, counted them. '. . . four . . . five . . . six.'

'No more.'

'No more. Just the group minus Hendrix. The Tanzanians have sent them home.' He looked at the setting sun. 'They won't make good time, not without shoes. They'll be spending a night in the bush.'

'Dangerous?'

He shook his head. 'Not if they're careful; just scary. But Adam will look after them if they have the sense to let him. We'll wait for them up here.'

Stafford said, 'Let's have a chat.'

Hendrix stirred at Nair's side. 'Say, who *are* you guys?'

'Lifesavers,' said Stafford. 'Your life. Now shut up.' He looked at Nair. 'Keep him quiet. If he doesn't want to be quiet then quieten him.' He did not want Hendrix to get any wrong ideas about his rescuers. He wanted him softened up and it was best that Hendrix should think he'd jumped out of a moderately warm frying pan into a bloody hot fire.

Stafford jerked his head at Chip and they walked away again. He said, 'I don't know the motives for the attempted murder of Hendrix but, so far, only four people know he's not dead. You, me, Nair and Hendrix himself. And he would have been very dead if you hadn't let go with the Uzi when you did. It was a matter of a split second.'

'What are you getting at?'

'Supposing he doesn't join the others? Supposing he stays dead? That's going to confuse the hell out of somebody.'

'Which somebody?'

'How the devil would I know? But six Tanzanians don't deliberately try to murder the inheritor of three million pounds just for kicks. The average Tanzanian wouldn't even know Hendrix existed. Somebody, somewhere, must have given the orders. Now, that somebody will think

Hendrix is dead as per orders. He might be mystified about the disappearance of two Tanzanians, but Hendrix will have disappeared, too. The survivors of the group will tell their tale and it will add up to Hendrix's death because, if he isn't dead, why doesn't he show up? But I'll have him. He's not a trump card but a joker to be played at the correct time.'

Chip stared at Stafford for a long time in silence. Eventually he said, 'You don't want much, do you?' He ticked off points on his fingers. 'One, we kidnap Hendrix; two, we have to smuggle him out of the Mara because he can't go through any of the gates; three, we have to keep him alive with food and water while all this is going on; four, we have to find a place to put him when we get him out of the Mara; five, that means guards to be supplied; six . . .' He stopped. 'You know; a man could run out of fingers this way.'

'In the past you've always proved to be a resourceful chap,' Stafford said engagingly.

Chip gave him a thin smile. 'All hell is going to break loose,' he said. 'This is going to make headlines in the world press. An American multi-millionaire kidnapped and killed – a first-rate front page story full of diplomatic dynamite. The Kenyan government will be forced to protest to Tanzania and the American government will probably join in. So what happens when we finally turn him loose? Then our heads are on the chopping block.'

'Not at all,' Stafford said. 'He won't say a damned thing. He *can't* say a thing. You're forgetting that he isn't really Hendrix.'

'I'm forgetting nothing,' said Chip coldly. 'All I know is what you've told me. You haven't proved anything yet.'

Stafford turned his head and looked at Hendrix. 'Let's ask him his name,' he proposed.

'Yes, but not here. Let's get out of Tanzania.'

Stafford hesitated because he was worried about the tour group, particularly the Roches. 'The others,' he said. 'Will they be all right?'

'I told you; Adam will take care of them,' said Chip impatiently. 'They'll be all right. Look, Max; we'll be able to make better time on our own. We can get back to Keekorok and have cars sent to pick them up on the border. And on the way you can have your talk with Hendrix.'

Put that way it was a good solution. 'All right,' Stafford said at length. 'Let's get going.'

'But I promise nothing until you prove your point about Hendrix,' said Chip. 'You have to do that.'

# FIFTEEN

So they went back into Kenya but not the same way they had come out. They changed direction and headed north-west, in the direction of Mara New Bridge. Chip said, 'Whatever happens we'll have to come up with a story for the police, and it will have to be a story with no guns in it. Dr Robert Ouko isn't going to take kindly to civilians who make armed incursions into Tanzania.'

'Who's he?'

'Minister for Foreign Affairs. He'll be sending a strong diplomatic note to Dar-es-Salaam and he won't want it weakened by talk of guns.'

'How are you going to keep Hendrix's mouth shut?'

'Don't think it isn't on my mind.'

On the way they concocted a story. After sending Curtis back to Keekorok to raise the alarm they had courageously and somewhat foolishly chased after the Tanzanians. On realizing they were about to infringe Tanzanian territory they stopped and turned back, only to lose their way. After several hours of wandering in the dark they finally found the road near Mara New Bridge and were now reporting like good citizens to the Police Post.

A thin story and not to be carefully examined. It also presupposed the total absence of Hendrix which cheered Stafford because it seemed that Chip was tacitly accepting his proposal to keep Hendrix under wraps. But he suspected that Chip was busy in the construction of another yarn should he have to write Hendrix back into the script.

Meanwhile they marched steadily through the bush until nightfall, with Hendrix protesting at intervals about the speed, and wanting to know who the hell they were, and various other items that came to his mind. He was silenced by Nair who produced a knife; it was the *kirpan*, the ceremonial knife carried by all Sikhs, but by no means purely ornamental, and the sight of it silenced Hendrix as effectively as if Nair had cut out his tongue with it.

They stopped as the last of the light was ebbing from the sky. There was still enough to march by but Chip's decision to halt was coloured by the fact that they discovered a small hollow or dell which was screened from all sides. 'We can build a small fire down there,' he said. 'It won't be seen.'

'Where are we?' Stafford asked. 'Kenya or Tanzania?'

Chip grinned. 'A toss of the coin will tell you.'

So they collected wood to make a fire which wasn't difficult because the bush is scattered with dead wood. The fire wasn't so much for warmth as to keep away animals. Chip said he was worried less about lions and other large predators than about hyenas. 'They'll go for a sleeping man,' he said. They built the fire in such a way so as always to have a burning brand ready to grab for self-defence.

When they got the fire going Chip looked at Stafford then jerked his head at Hendrix. 'Your turn.'

'Okay.' He turned to Hendrix. 'What's your name?'

'Hendrix, Henry Hendrix. Folks call me Hank. Who are you?'

'That doesn't matter,' said Stafford. 'And you're a liar.' He was silent for a moment. 'I notice you haven't thanked anyone for saving your life.'

Hendrix's eyes glimmered in the light of the flames. 'Hell; every time I opened my mouth I was told to shut it.'

'We want you to talk now. In fact, we'll positively encourage it. Who is Gunnarsson?'

'A friend. And, okay; thanks for doing what you did. I really thought I was dead back there. I really did.'

'Think nothing of it,' said Chip dryly.

'Who is Hamsun – Olaf Hamsun?' asked Stafford.

'Never heard of him,' said Hendrix.

'You might know him better as Biggie.'

'Oh, Biggie! He's a guy I knew back in LA. What's with the questions?'

'Who is Hardin?'

'Never heard of the guy.'

'You ought to know him. He took you from Los Angeles to New York.'

'Oh, him. I never knew the guy's name.'

'You went from Los Angeles to New York with a man and never knew his name? You'll have to do better than that. You'll be telling us you don't know your own name next. What is it?'

His eyes flickered. 'Hendrix,' he said sullenly. 'Look, I don't know what you guys want but I don't like all these questions.'

'I don't care what you like or don't like,' Stafford said. 'And I don't care whether you live or die. What does Biggie wear around his neck?'

The switch in pace caught Hendrix flat-footed. 'What kind of a goddamn question is that? How in hell would I know?'

'You were his friend. Where did you meet Gunnarsson?'

'New York.'

'Where's the hole in your shoulder?'

Hendrix looked startled. 'What the hell are you talking about?'

Stafford sighed. 'You took a bullet in your shoulder back in Los Angeles. Hardin bound it up. You should have a hole in you so where is it?'

'I heal real good,' said Hendrix sullenly.

'You're the biggest liar since Ananias,' said Stafford. 'You ought to have your mouth washed out with soap. You're not Hendrix, so who are you?'

He hesitated, and Nair said, 'Why did someone want you dead? Is it because your name is Hendrix?'

'That's it,' said Chip. He laughed. 'There's an open season on Hendrixes. Of course, it's illegal; game shooting is prohibited in Kenya.'

'But not in Tanzania,' said Nair. 'It's legal there. They could get away with it.'

'Maybe someone wants a stuffed Hendrix head on his wall,' said Chip. 'A trophy.'

'The eyes would have to be glass,' said Nair. 'Could they match the colour?'

'I believe they're using plastic these days,' said Chip. 'They can do anything with plastic.'

The crazy crosstalk got to Hendrix. 'Shut up, you nigger bastard!' he shouted.

There was a dead silence before Chip said coldly, 'You don't talk that way to the man with the gun.' In the distance there was a coughing roar and Hendrix jerked. 'A lion,' said Chip. 'Maybe we should leave him to the lions. Maybe *they* want a trophy.'

A choked sob came from Hendrix. Stafford said, 'You've been under observation ever since you left the States. We *know* you're not Hendrix. Tell us who you are and we'll leave you alone.'

'Dear Jesus!' he said. 'Gunnarsson'll kill me.'

'Gunnarsson won't get near you,' said Stafford. 'Leave him to us. And what the devil do you think nearly happened by the river? You stay being Hendrix and you're a dead man.'

The night noises in the bush were growing in intensity. The lion roared again in the distance and, from quite close, something snarled and something else squealed appallingly. The squalling noise was cut off sharply and Chip put another tree branch on the fire. 'A leopard caught a baboon,' he said. Nair picked up his rifle and stood up, staring into the darkness.

It got to Hendrix; his eyes rolled and he shivered violently. He'd had a hard time that day. He'd been kidnapped, nearly murdered, and now he was being interrogated by armed strangers who apparently knew everything about him except his name and in a place where animals were murdering each other. No wonder he cracked.

'You'll keep me safe from Gunnarsson. You guarantee it?'

Stafford glanced at Chip, who nodded. He said, 'We'll put you in a safe place where no one will know where you are. But you'll have to co-operate. Tell us.'

Hendrix still hesitated. 'Anyone got a cigarette?' Chip took a packet from his pocket and shook one out, and Hendrix lit it with a burning twig from the fire. He took a long draught of smoke into his lungs and it seemed to calm him. 'All right. My name's Jack Corliss and Gunnarsson propositioned me a few weeks ago. Christ; I wish he'd never come near me.'

The story was moderately simple. Corliss worked in a bank in New York. He was a computer buff and had found a way to fiddle the electronic books and Gunnarsson had caught him at it. From then on it was straight blackmail. Stafford did not think Gunnarsson had to try too hard because Corliss was bent already.

'I had to read a lot of stuff about Hendrix,' said Corliss. 'About his family. Then there were tape recordings – a lot of them. Hendrix talking with Gunnarsson. I don't think Hendrix knew he was being taped. Gunnarsson got him to talk a lot about himself; it was real friendly. Gunnarsson got him drunk a couple of times and some good stuff came out.'

'Good for anyone wanting to impersonate Hendrix,' said Chip.

Corliss nodded. 'It looked great. Hendrix was a loner; he had no family. Gunnarsson said it would be dead easy.'

'Dead being the operative word,' said Stafford. 'What else was he offering you, apart from the chance of staying out of jail?' Corliss avoided his eyes. 'Let's have it all.'

'A quarter of a million bucks,' he mumbled. 'Gunnarsson said I'd have to have a hunk of dough to make it look good afterwards.'

'One twelfth of the take,' Stafford said. 'You taking the risk and Gunnarsson taking the cream. What a patsy you were, Corliss. Do you think you'd have lived to enjoy it?'

'For Christ's sake! I had no goddamn choice. Gunnarsson had me by the balls.'

'Where is Hendrix now?'

'How would I know?' demanded Corliss. 'I never even met the guy.'

'Terminated with extreme prejudice,' said Chip. 'That's the CIA expression isn't it?'

Stafford nodded. 'No one knew he was in New York except Hardin. I think that's why Hardin was fired, and I think Hardin was bloody lucky – it could have happened to him. But Gunnarsson underestimated Hardin; he never thought resentment would push Hardin into going to England.'

'What happens to me now?' asked Corliss apathetically.

'Chip and Nair will take you away and put you in a safe place. You'll have clothing and food but no freedom until this is all over. After that we'll get you back to the States where you'd better get lost. Agreed, Chip?'

'If he co-operates and makes no trouble,' said Chip. 'If he does anything foolish there are no guarantees any more.'

'I'll make no trouble,' said Corliss eagerly. 'All I want to do is to get out of this damn country.' He listened to the night noises and shivered, drawing the fatigue jacket closer to him although it was not cold. 'It scares me.'

'There's one more thing,' Stafford said. 'People don't usually get shot for no reason at all. Who'd want to kill you, Corliss? Not Gunnarsson; he wouldn't want to kill the goose that lays the golden eggs. Who, then?'

'I don't know,' said Corliss violently. 'No one would want to kill *me*. I don't know about Hendrix. You guys said it was open season on Hendrix.'

'That was a manner of speaking,' said Stafford.

Corliss shook his head as though in wonderment at what was happening to him. He said, 'I had an auto accident in Cornwall, but I'm not that bad a driver. The brakes failed on a hill.'

Stafford shrugged. 'It doesn't have to be guns.'

'*Cui bono*?' said Chip, unexpectedly breaking into Latin. He grinned at Stafford's expression, his teeth gleaming in the firelight. 'This nigger bastard went to university. Who inherits from Hendrix?'

Stafford thought about it, then said slowly, 'The next of kin, I suppose. Corliss, here, says Hendrix had no family but, of course, he had, although he didn't know it. His next of kin would be his cousin, Dirk Hendriks, assuming that Henry Hendrix made no will.'

'I think we can accept that assumption,' said Chip dryly.

Stafford shook his head. 'It's impossible. Dirk went back to England with Farrar. How could he organize a kidnapping into Tanzania? That would take organization on the spot. Anyway, he's inherited three million himself. What's the motive?'

From the darkness on the other side of the fire Nair said, 'Six is better than three. Some people are greedy.'

'I don't see it,' said Stafford. 'Hendriks has no Kenyan connections; he's a South African, damn it. He'd never been in the country until he came with Farrar. How could a man,

not knowing either country, organize a kidnapping in
Kenya by Tanzanians? I'd say South Africans are a damn
sight more unwelcome in Tanzania than they are in Kenya.'

'Yes,' said Chip. 'We're a tolerant people. We don't mind
South Africans as long as they behave themselves. The
Tanzanians aren't so tolerant.'

They batted it around a bit more and got nowhere. At last
Stafford said, 'Perhaps we're barking up the wrong tree. I
know that no tourists have been killed in these Tanzanian
raids but it was bound to happen sooner or later when people carry guns. Perhaps this attempt on Corliss was a statis-
tical inevitability – a Tanzanian aberration.'

'No,' said Chip, 'I can understand a gun going off and
killing someone. I can understand one man going round the
bend and killing someone. But two men deliberately took
Corliss and, as you said, it was the nearest thing to an execution I've witnessed. It was deliberate.'

'Jesus!' said Corliss.

'But why?' Stafford asked.

No one could tell him.


The fire had to be kept going all night so one man stood
watch while the others slept and Stafford stood first watch.
By unspoken agreement Corliss did not stand a watch; no
one was going to sleep having him loose with two rifles and
a sub-machine-gun. When his time was up Stafford
stretched out on the ground not expecting to sleep, but the
next thing he knew Nair was shaking him awake. 'Dawn,'
he said.

When Stafford stood up he was stiff and his bones
creaked. In his time in the army and in the Sahara he had
slept on the ground in the open air many times, but it is a
game for a young man and as he grew older he found that
it ceased to be fun. He looked around, and asked, 'Where's
Chip?'

'He left at first light – ten minutes ago. He said he'll be back in an hour, maybe two.' Nair nodded towards Corliss. 'We have to make arrangements about him. He can't be seen by anyone, including the police.'

Stafford stretched. 'I know that you pair display an amazing efficiency but I'd like to know how Chip is going to fix that. The KPU must still have a lot of pull.'

Nair raised his eyebrows. 'The Kenya People's Union no longer exists. How can it have influence?'

'All right, Nair; have it your own way.'

'Max,' he said, 'a word of warning. It would be most unwise of you to talk openly about the KPU. Loose talk of that nature could put you in prison. It is still a touchy subject in Kenya.'

Stafford held up his hands placatingly. 'Not another word shall pass my lips.' Nair nodded gravely.

It was two and a half hours before Chip came back and he brought with him two men whom he introduced as Daniel Wekesa and Osano Gichure. 'Good friends,' he said.

'Just good friends?' Stafford said sardonically. 'Not brothers-in-law?'

Chip ignored that. 'They'll look after Corliss and get him out of the Mara.'

'Where will they take him?'

'We'll come to that later. The tourists haven't come back yet, and the border is alive with police on the Kenyan side.' He stroked his chin. 'The tour group is probably still in Tanzania. Bare European feet make for slow going. Still, they should come in some time this morning if I know Adam.'

'Which you do.'

'Yes. I want to talk to him. I want to know exactly how the Tanzanians picked him up. I also want breakfast, so let's go.'

Chip talked to Corliss, told him he'd be looked after if he behaved himself, and then they went, again heading north.

They left the rifles and the Uzi with Chip's good friends and he made Stafford empty his pockets of ammunition. 'If the police find so much as a single round you're in trouble,' he said.

On the way he said he had seen the police. 'Just stick to the story we arranged and we'll be fine.'

Chip proved to be right. They walked for an hour and then saw a vehicle coming towards them, bumping through the bush. It contained a police lieutenant and a constable, both armed. They spun their yarn and the lieutenant shook his head. 'It was very unwise to follow those men; it could have been dangerous. I am glad that Mr Chipende had the sense to stop you crossing the border.'

Stafford scowled at Chip who was now a virtuous citizen. The lieutenant smiled. 'I hope this has not spoiled your holiday, Mr Stafford. I assure you that these incidents are rare. Certain wild elements in our neighbouring country get out of control.'

'Is there news of the tour group?' asked Nair.

The lieutenant looked bleak. 'Not yet. They will be given a warm welcome when they arrive. Jump in; I'll take you back to Keekorok in time for a late breakfast.'

So they rode back to the Lodge at Keekorok and got there inside half an hour; not long but long enough for Stafford to wonder if it was habitual for Kenyan police officers to administer a mild slap on the wrist for transgressions such as theirs. He had expected a real rocket and here was the lieutenant actually apologizing for a spoiled holiday. Perhaps it was his view that it was normal for a European tourist to be an idiot.

Their arrival was the occasion for a minor brouhaha. Although the manager met them and tried to ease them into their rooms quietly they were spotted and mobbed by a crowd eagerly asking questions in assorted accents. It was known they had been out all night and that there was another party still missing and, from the look on the manager's face as they briefly answered queries, it was definitely a case of bad public relations.

And Curtis was there, his face set in a wide, relieved smile. He put his broad shoulders between Stafford and a particularly importunate American, and said, 'I hope the Colonel is all right.'

'Tired and a bit travel-worn, that's all, Sergeant. Just point me towards breakfast and a bed.'

'The manager's arranged for you to have breakfast in your room, sir. He thought it would be better.'

'Better for whom?' Stafford said acidly. His guess was that the manager was wishing they would vanish instantly so as not to infect the other guests with the virus of bad news. And it would get worse when the others came back; having tourists kidnapped was not good for the image of Keekorok Lodge. It would get still worse when one tourist didn't come back at all, and even worse than that when the tourist was identified as an American millionaire. The manager wouldn't know what had hit him.

Over breakfast Stafford said, 'I took your advice, Sergeant,' and brought him up to date. 'We separated Hendrix from Gunnarsson.'

Curtis was normally an imperturbable and phlegmatic man but the story made his thick, black eyebrows crawl up his scalp like a couple of hairy caterpillars until they threatened to eliminate his bald patch. When Stafford finished he thought in silence then remembered to close his mouth. 'So we've got Hendrix – I mean Corliss. Where?'

Stafford buttered some toast. 'I don't know. Chip whistled a couple of characters out of nowhere and they went off with him.' He took a bite and said indistinctly, 'Sergeant, I think I'll have to rechristen you Aladdin; you've rubbed a lamp and conjured up a genie. My slightest wish is Chip's command and I don't know how the hell he does it. Sheer magic.'

Curtis said, 'Something's just come to me.'

'What?'

'You remember when we came to the Masai Mara and stopped at the gate. Chip got us in. You have to pay to get into a Reserve – any Reserve.'

Stafford nodded. 'He said we were his guests.'

'But he didn't pay,' said Curtis. 'No money passed. He showed a card and signed a book.'

Stafford was tired and looking longingly at the bed. 'Maybe a season ticket,' he mumbled, but a season ticket for four wasn't likely.

# SIXTEEN

Curtis woke Stafford. 'I'm sure the Colonel would like to know that the other group has come in.'

He came wide awake. 'You're damned right. What time is it?'

'Just after two.' Stafford blinked disorientedly at the closed curtains and Curtis added gently, in the afternoon, sir.'

Stafford dressed in shirt and shorts with swimming trunks beneath and thrust his feet into sandals. Curtis said, 'I'm going with Nair to see Corliss if the Colonel doesn't mind.'

'Why?'

'Chip said they're short of food so we're taking it.' He paused. 'It would be good for us to know where he is, sir.'

Stafford nodded. 'Carry on, Sergeant.'

The lobby was a hubbub of noise and crammed with a welcoming committee of the curious – those guests who had not gone game spotting. There were a lot of them. Stafford suspected that game spotting in the Masai Mara would be a depreciating part of the tourist industry until this storm had blown itself out. Game spotting was one thing and the risk of being kidnapped was another.

He joined Chip who was leaning against a wall. 'How are they?'

'I haven't seen them yet, and we won't be able to talk to them for a while. There's a heavy police escort.'

The rescued tourists came in, spearheaded by a phalanx of police. Six of them – the Roches, Gunnarsson, Kosters and Adam Muliro. They did not walk well, but their feet had been bandaged and clothing had been issued, ill-fitting and incongruous but necessary. The crowd pressed around, shouting questions, and the police kept them back, linking arms.

A senior police officer held up his hands in one of which he held a swagger stick. 'Quiet please! These people are not well. They need urgent medical attention. Now, make way, please.'

There was a brief hush, then someone called, 'There are only six. Who's missing?'

'Mr Hendrix has not yet appeared. We are still looking for him.'

As photo-flashes began to pop Stafford watched Gunnarsson. He had a baffled, almost defeated, expression on his face. So that's how a man looks when he's been cheated of six million dollars. It must have been how many a man looked in New York in the crash of 1929 just before jumping out of the skyscraper window – an expression of unfocused anger at the unfairness of things. Not that Gunnarsson would commit suicide. He was not the type and, anyway, he had not lost the money because he had never had it. Still, it was a hard blow.

Stafford lost sight of him as the party was led away. Chip made a motion of his hand as Adam Muliro went past and Adam nodded almost imperceptibly. Chip said, 'We won't see them for a while. Let's have a swim.'

It was a good idea, so after waiting for the crowd to thin they walked towards the pool. Halfway there someone ran after them. 'Mr Stafford?' He turned and saw the man who had asked who was missing. 'Eddy Ukiru – the *Standard*. Can I have a word with you?'

Behind Ukiru a man was unlimbering what was obviously a press camera. Stafford glanced at Chip who said, 'Why not?'

And so Stafford gave a press interview. Midway through Ukiru was joined, to his displeasure, by another reporter from a rival newspaper, *Nation,* and Stafford had to repeat some of the details but essentially he stuck to the prepared story which Chip corroborated. Ukiru showed minor signs of disbelief. 'So you turned back at the border,' he said. 'How did you *know* it was the border? There is no fence, no mark.'

Stafford shrugged. 'You will have to ask Mr Chipende about that.'

So he did, and Chip switched into fast Swahili. Eventually Ukiru shrugged his acceptance, the photographers took their pictures, and they all went away. Stafford said, 'They got here damned quickly. How?'

'The manager will have telephoned his head office who will have notified the police in Nairobi. Plenty of room for leaks to the press there. They'll have chartered aircraft. There's an airstrip here.'

'Yes, I've seen the airstrip,' said Stafford. 'But I didn't know about the telephone. I've seen no wires.'

Chip smiled. 'It's a radio-phone in the manager's office. And we can't have wires because the elephants knock down the telegraph poles. Let's have that swim.'

Stafford wanted to put himself next to Gunnarsson and found the opportunity during the pre-dinner cocktail hours. All the rescued tour group was there in the bar with the exception of Adam Muliro and they were being quizzed about their experience by the other guests. There was an air of euphoria about them; much laughter from the Roches and Kosters. Now saved, their adventure verged somewhat on unreality and would be something to dine out on for years to come. Adventure is discomfort recollected in tranquillity.

Stafford talked with Kosters and Michele Roche and got their account with no great difficulty, then said with an air of puzzlement, 'But what about Hendrix? What happened to him?'

The euphoric gaiety disappeared fast. 'I don't know,' said Kosters soberly. 'They took him away and there was shooting.'

'You think he's dead?'

Michele's voice was sombre. 'He hasn't come back. We didn't see him again.'

Stafford looked across at Gunnarsson. There was no euphoria about him. He sat with his legs stretched out, gloomily regarding his bandaged feet. Someone had found him a pair of carpet slippers which had been slashed to accommodate the bandages. Stafford took his drink and walked over to Gunnarsson. 'You've had a nasty experience. Oh; my name is Stafford.'

Gunnarsson squinted up at him. 'Stafford? You the guy who tried to come after us?'

'We didn't get very far,' Stafford said ruefully. 'We just got lost and made bloody fools of ourselves.'

'Let me top up your drink.' Stafford sat down. 'I'm John Gunnarsson.' He turned and looked at Stafford, then shook his head. 'You wouldn't have done any good, Mr Stafford – those guys were a walking arsenal – but thanks for trying. What will you have?'

'Gin and tonic.'

Gunnarsson beckoned to a waiter and gave the order, then sighed. 'Christ, what an experience. I've been in some tough spots in my time but that was one of the toughest.'

'They tell me it's happened before,' Stafford said casually.

'Yeah. These damned half-ass Kenyans ought to beef up their border force. You know what was the worst? There's nothing takes the steam out of a guy faster than to strip him bollock naked.' He gave a small snort. 'Well, not quite; they let us keep our underpants.' He brooded. 'It was bad coming back what with the sun and the thorns. My feet feel the size of footballs. And there was the goddamn hyena . . .'

'A hyena?'

'A big son of a bitch. It trotted parallel with us about a hundred yards off, I guess. Waiting for someone to lag or drop out. If it wasn't for the nig . . . the black guy, Adam Somebody, I don't think we'd have made it. He was good.'

'I hear somebody didn't make it,' Stafford said.

'Oh, Jesus!' Gunnarsson's neck swelled.

'What happened to him? Enderby, wasn't it?'

'Hendrix.' Gunnarsson glowered. 'There were six of us, six of them, and Adam, the driver. Trouble was, they were armed. Kalashnikovs. Know what they are?'

Stafford shook his head. 'Things like that don't come my way.'

'You're lucky. They're Russian-made automatic rifles. We couldn't do a goddamn thing. Helpless.' He made a fist in his frustration. 'Then a couple of them took Hendrix away and later there was firing and the four black guys with us burst out laughing. Imagine that.'

'I can't,' Stafford said soberly. 'Were these men in uniform?'

'Yeah. Camouflage gear. A real military set-up. Jesus, but there's going to be trouble when I get back to Nairobi. Nobody's going to get away with doing this to an American citizen.'

'What are you going to do?' Stafford asked interestedly.

'Do! I'm going to raise hell with the American Ambassador, that's what I'm going to do. Hendrix was a real nice young guy and I want him found, dead or alive. And if he's dead I want blood if I have to take it all the way to the United Nations.'

Stafford contemplated that statement. If Gunnarsson was prepared to raise a stink at that level it meant that the real Hendrix was not around to object. Terminated with extreme

prejudice, as Chip had said. The killing of a newly made
American millionaire was certain to find its way into New
York newspapers if Gunnarsson was prepared to push it so
far, which meant that Gunnarsson thought he was safe.

'Had you known him long? Hendrix, I mean.'

'A while – not long,' said Gunnarsson. 'But that's not the
point, Mr Stafford. The point is they can't get away with
doing this to an American citizen and I'm going to scream
that loud and clear.'

Yes, it was his only chance if Hendrix/Corliss was still
alive and in the hands of the Tanzanians. Only strong diplomatic pressure put on Tanzania by Kenya and the United
States could get back Gunnarsson's walking treasure chest.
It would take nerve but Gunnarsson had that in plenty.

'I wish you well,' Stafford said. 'Let me buy you a drink.'

So he bought Gunnarsson a drink and presently took his
leave. As he walked by the back of Gunnarsson's chair he
said, 'Good luck,' and clapped him on the shoulder.
Gunnarsson jumped a foot in the air, let out a scream and
banged both feet on the floor, whereupon he emitted
another piercing yell. Stafford apologized, professing to
have forgotten his sunburn, and made a quick getaway.

# SEVENTEEN

They left for Nairobi next morning and so did a lot of others but for different reasons. After seeing the condition in which the tour group had come back from their unwanted, brief sojourn in Tanzania the front desk was busy as the fearful paid their bills. The manager was gloomy but resigned.

Again they drove that spine-jolting, back-breaking road to Narok and then sat back with relief as they hit the asphalt which led all the way to Nairobi, and pulled into a parking slot in front of the Norfolk Hotel in comfortable time for lunch. There Stafford received a surprise. On opening the door of his room he found an envelope on the floor just inside. It contained the briefest of messages: 'I'm back. Come see me. Room 14. Ben.'

He dumped his bags, went to room 14, and knocked. A guarded voice said, 'Yeah; who is it?'

'Stafford.'

There was the snap of a lock and the door opened and swung wide. He went in and Hardin said, 'Where the hell have you been? I've been telephoning every two hours for the last two days and getting no answer. So I jump a plane and what do I find? No one.' He was aggrieved.

'Calm down, Ben,' Stafford said. 'We had to go away but it had good results.' He paused and examined that statement, then added, 'If I knew what they were.'

Hardin examined Stafford closely. 'Your face is scratched. Been with a dame?'

Stafford sat down. 'When you've stopped being funny we can carry on. You were sent back for a reason. Did you find anything?'

Hardin said, 'I've just ordered from room service. I didn't want to eat in public before I knew where Gunnarsson was. I'll cancel.'

'No, I'll join you,' said Stafford. 'Duplicate the order.'

'Okay.' Hardin telephoned the order before opening the refrigerator and taking out a couple of bottles of beer. 'Jan-Willem Hendrykxx – an old guy and a travelling man. I've been spending a lot of your money, Max; ran up a hell of a phone bill. And I had to go to Belgium.' He held up his hand. 'Don't worry; I flew economy.'

'I think the firm can stand it.'

Hardin gave Stafford an opened bottle and a glass. 'I've written a detailed report but I can give you the guts of it now. Okay?'

'Shoot.'

He sat down. 'Jan-Willem Hendrykxx born in 1899 in – believe it or not – Hoboken.'

Stafford looked up, startled. 'In the States!'

'It got me, too,' Hardin admitted. 'No, the original Hoboken is a little place just outside Antwerp in Belgium. Parents poor but honest, which is more than we can say of Jan-Willem. Reasonable education for those days but he ran away to sea when he was seventeen. Knocked about a bit, I expect, but ended up in South Africa in 1921 where he married Anna Vermuelen.'

He rubbed his jaw. 'There was a strike in Johannesburg in 1922, if that's what you can call it. Both sides had artillery and it sounds more like a civil war to me. Anyway, Jan-Willem disappeared leaving Anna to carry the can – the can being twin babies, Jan and Adriaan. Jan is the father of

Dirk Hendriks, and Adriaan is the father of Hank Hendrix, the guy I picked up in Los Angeles. Follow me so far?'

'It's quite clear,' Stafford said.

'Jan-Willem jumped a freighter going to San Francisco, got to like the Californian climate, and decided to stay. Now, you must remember these were Prohibition days. Most people, when they think of Prohibition, think of Rum Row off Atlantic City, but there was just as much rum running on the West Coast, either from Canada or Mexico, and Hendrykxx got in on the act. By the time Repeal came he was well entrenched in the rackets.'

'You mean he was a genuine dyed-in-the-wool gangster?'

Hardin shrugged. 'You could put it that way. But he made a mistake – he never took out US citizenship. So when he put a foot wrong he wasn't jailed; he was deported back to his country of origin as an undesirable alien. He arrived back in Antwerp in April, 1940.'

Stafford said, 'You've been busy, Ben. How did you discover all this?'

'A hunch. What I found out in Belgium made Hendrykxx a crook. He was supposed to have been killed in Jo'burg in 1922 but we know he wasn't, so I wondered where he'd go, and being a crook he'd likely have a record. I have some good buddies in the FBI dating back to my CIA days. They looked up the files. There's a hell of a dossier on Hendrykxx. When he came to the attention of the FBI they checked him very thoroughly. That's where the phone bill came in; I spent about six hours talking long distance to the States.'

The room waiter came in with lunch and set it on the table. Hardin waited until he had gone before continuing. 'I don't know whether it was good or bad for Hendrykxx that he arrived in Antwerp when he did. Probably good. The German offensive began on May 10th, Holland and Belgium fell like ninepins and France soon after. Antwerp was in

German hands about two weeks after Hendrykxx got there. His wartime history is misty but from what I've picked up he was well into the Belgian rackets, the black market and all that. Of course, in those days it was patriotic but I believe Hendrykxx wasn't above doing deals with the Germans.'

'A collaborator?'

Hardin bit into a club sandwich and said, with his mouth full, 'Never proved. But he came out of the war in better financial shape than he went into it. Then he started import-export corporations and when the EEC was organized he went to town in his own way which, naturally, was the illegal way. There was a whole slew of EEC regulations which could be bent. Bargeloads of butter going up the Rhine from Holland to Germany found themselves relabelled and back in Holland with Hendrykxx creaming off the subsidy. He could do that several times with the same bargeload until the damn stuff went rancid on him. He was into a lot of rackets like that.'

'The bloody crook,' said Stafford.

'On the way through the years there was also a couple of marriages, both bigamous because Anna was still alive back in South Africa. In 1974 he retired and went to live in Jersey, probably for tax reasons. By then he was pretty old. Last year he died, leaving close on a hundred million bucks, most of which went to the Ol Njorowa Foundation in Kenya. End of story.'

Stafford stared at Hardin. 'You must be kidding, Ben. Where's the Kenya connection?'

'There isn't one,' said Hardin airily.

'But there must be.'

'None that I could find.' He leaned forward. 'And I'll tell you something else. Hendrykxx never was all that big time and crooks like him are usually big spenders. I doubt if he made more than five million dollars in his whole life. Maybe ten. Of course, that's not bad but it doesn't make him into any kind of financial giant. So where did the rest of the dough come from?'

'Every time we find anything new this whole business gets crazier,' Stafford said disgustedly.

'I checked a couple of other things,' said Hardin. 'I went to Jersey and saw Hendrykxx's death certificate in the Greffe – that's their Public Record Office. The old guy died of a heart attack. I talked to the doctor, a guy called Morton, and he confirmed it. He said Hendrykxx could have gone any time, but . . .' Hardin shook his head.

'But what?' asked Stafford.

'Nothing to put a finger on definitely, but I had the impression that Morton was uneasy about something.' Hardin refilled his glass. 'Back in London I checked on Mandeville, the lawyer who handled the London end of the legacy business. Very right wing. He's making a name for himself defending neo-Nazi groups, the guys who find themselves in court for race rioting. But I don't see that has anything to do with us.'

'No,' agreed Stafford. 'Did you talk to him?'

'I couldn't. He's vacationing in South Africa.' Hardin drank some beer. 'What's new with you?'

Stafford told him and by the time he had finished it was late afternoon and the undrunk coffee had gone cold. Hardin listened to it all thoughtfully. 'You've had quite a time,' he commented. 'Where's Corliss now?'

'Curtis saw him yesterday,' Stafford said. 'He was in a remote tented camp in the Masai Mara, but I wouldn't want to guarantee he's there now. What do you think of the line Gunnarsson pitched me?'

'Righteous anger isn't Gunnarsson's style,' said Hardin. 'He sure as hell wants Corliss back and if that's the way he's going about it you know what it means – Hendrix is dead.'

'I'd already got that far,' said Stafford.

'But there's more.' Hardin took out his wallet. 'I got this at *poste restante* in London. Jack Richardson sent it, and he got it from Charlie Wainwright in Los Angeles. Charlie remembered I'd been interested in Biggie.'

He took a newspaper clipping from the wallet and passed it to Stafford. It was a brief report from the Los Angeles *Examiner* to the effect that a disastrous fire had broken out in a house in Santa Monica and that all the occupants had died, six of them. The fire was believed to have been caused by an over-heated pottery kiln which had exploded. The names of the dead were given. Five of them were unknown to Stafford, but the sixth was Olaf Hamsun. Biggie.

He looked at Hardin and said slowly, 'Are you thinking what I'm thinking?'

'If you're thinking that Gunnarsson plays for keeps.'

'Ben; you're a bloody lucky man. How did Gunnarsson miss you?'

'You've just said it – sheer goddamn luck. Jack Richardson sent a letter with that clipping; he told me that the rooming house I'd been living in had burned up. Maybe I'd slipped to London just in time.' Hardin rubbed his jaw. 'On the other hand it might not have been Gunnarsson at all. In the Bronx they have a habit of burning buildings for the insurance money. The whole damn place is falling apart.'

Stafford held up the clipping. 'Was this the whole of the commune?'

'Just about, I reckon.'

'Then that means that you are possibly the only person who definitely knows that the Hendrix who claimed the estate is a fake. What's more, it means that Gunnarsson, if he's going to make a big song and dance at the Embassy, is sure that you won't pop up to prove him wrong. If Gunnarsson thinks you're out of the game – and that's the way he's acting – then that gives us an edge.'

'What do I do? Dress in a white sheet and scare him to death?'

'We'll think of something. Let's get back to the main issue. Who would want Hendrix dead? Chip asked the question – who benefits? The answer to that is his cousin and sole relative, Dirk Hendriks. I argued that he couldn't have organized it because he was in England, but these days one can get around really fast.'

'He was in England,' said Hardin. 'I forgot to tell you. He was on the same plane that I came in on this morning.'

'Was he?' said Stafford.

'It's okay, Max; he's never met me. Besides, he travelled first class, and the guys up front don't mix with the *hoi polloi* in economy.'

Stafford said sarcastically, 'I'm mixing with a real egghead crowd. First Chip with Latin, now you with Greek.'

Hardin scratched the angle of his jaw. 'You've had a funny feeling about Hendriks all along, haven't you? Mind telling me why?'

'I'm suspicious about everyone in this case,' Stafford said. 'The more I know about it the stranger it becomes.' He shrugged. 'As for Dirk I suppose it's a gut feeling. I've never really liked him even before you came along and blew the whistle on Gunnarsson.'

Hardin looked at him shrewdly. 'Something to do with his wife?'

'Good God, no! At least, not in the way you're thinking. Alix means nothing to me apart from the fact that we're friends. But you don't like to see friends get hurt. She's a wealthy woman and Dirk is battening on her, or was until this Hendrykxx thing blew up. He's too much the playboy type for my liking.' Stafford changed the subject. 'When you were with the CIA how long did you spend in Kenya?'

'A couple of years.'

'Would you know your way around now?'

'Sure. It hasn't changed much.'

'Do you still have contacts?'

'A few, I guess. It depends on what you want.'

'What I want is to find out more about Pete Chipende and Nair Singh, particularly Chip. I've noticed that he tends to give the orders and Nair jumps.'

Hardin frowned. 'What's the point? They're helping plenty judging by your account.'

'That's just it,' said Stafford. 'They're helping too damn much, and they're too efficient. When we wanted Corliss taken off our hands Chip just pushed off into the bush in the middle of nowhere and turned up two of his friends very conveniently. And there are a few other things. One is that they know soldiering – they're no amateurs at that. In fact, they're thorough all-round professionals. There's also something you said just before you went to England.'

'What was that?'

'You said there'd be others behind Chip and Nair. You said they might not show but they'd be there. I think you're right, and I also think there's an organization, a complex organization, and I want to know what it is before we get into this thing over our heads. Chip is helpful all right, but I'd like to be sure he doesn't help us right into a jail – or a coffin. I don't want to get into any political trouble here.'

Hardin pondered for a moment. 'I don't know who is on the CIA station here right now. I think I'll go along to the Embassy and see if there's anyone there I know.'

'Will they talk to you?'

He shrugged. 'It depends. The CIA is no different than any other outfit; some are bastards, others are right guys.' He grimaced. 'But sometimes it's difficult to tell them apart. Gunnarsson turned out to be a bastard.'

'All right,' Stafford said. 'But don't go to the Embassy until we're sure that Gunnarsson isn't there. I'll see Chip about that.' He smiled. 'He can be helpful in that way as

much as he likes. I'll have him check Gunnarsson and let
you know.'

Stafford went back to his room to find the telephone ringing. It was Chip. 'Where have you been?' he asked. 'You
walked into the hotel and then disappeared off the face of
the earth.'

Stafford looked at his watch. Exchanging information
with Hardin had taken most of the afternoon, 'I had things
to do,' he said uninformatively.

If silence could be said to have surprise in it then that
silence had. At last Chip said, 'Some items have come up. I'd
like to see you.'

'Come up.'

When Chip came in he said, 'What have you got?'

'Brice,' said Chip. 'You wanted to know about Brice in
Zimbabwe. But it was Rhodesia then. Harry and Mary Brice
farmed near Umtali on the Sabi River. They had a son,
Charles Brice. When UDI came and Rhodesia became independent Charles Brice had a quarrel with his parents and
left the country. Later, when the guerillas became active,
the farm was destroyed and Harry and Mary Brice were
killed.'

Stafford said, 'That checks out with Brice's story.'

'Exactly,' said Chip.

'Where did you get it?'

'I told you. The brothers in Zimbabwe are co-operative.
You asked to have Brice checked there. He was checked.'

'And he comes out whiter than white.' Stafford did not
spend much time thinking about that expression because he
was thinking of this, yet another spectacular example of
Chip's efficiency. He said, 'Chip, you must have quite an
organization behind you. A while ago you needled me
because you said I was withholding information. Now, just
who the hell are you?'

'Some questions are better not asked,' Chip said.

'All the same, I'm asking.'

'And some questions are better not answered.'

'That's not good enough.'

'It's all you're going to get,' Chip said bluntly. 'Max, don't stir things up – don't muddy the water. It could cause trouble. Trouble for you, for everybody. Just let it slide and accept the help. We have helped, you know.'

'I know you've helped,' said Stafford. 'But I don't know why. I want to know why.'

'And I'm not going to tell you. Just study Kenyan history since the British left and draw your own conclusions.' He paused. 'I believe you brought up a certain subject with Nair and he told you to keep your mouth shut. It's advice I strongly advise you to follow. Now let's get on with it. Dirk Hendriks flew in from London this morning. He's staying at the New Stanley. Do you still want him watched?'

'Yes. How did you know he came in this morning?'

'As I once said, I have friends at the airport. We check the passenger list of every London flight – every European flight, come to that. That's how we know that your Mr Hardin came in this morning.'

Stafford sat up straight. 'Are you having us watched, too?'

Chip laughed. 'Simmer down. My friend at the airport relayed the information as a matter of course. Is that where you've been all afternoon; talking with Hardin? I ought to have guessed. Did he find out what you wanted to know?'

Two could play at withholding information. Stafford said, 'It was a cold trail, Chip. Hendrykxx was an old man. You can't unravel an eighty-year life all that quickly. Ben is an experienced investigator, I know, but he's not that bloody good.'

'A pity,' said Chip.

'Where is Corliss now?'

'Not far. If you want him we can produce him inside an hour.'

'But you're not going to tell me where he is.'

'Correct. You're learning, Max.' He looked at his watch. 'Gunnarsson will be here before sunset – back in the New Stanley. You know, it's going to be hard to pin him down.'

'What do you mean?'

'Neither he nor Corliss has committed a crime against Kenyan law. Hendrykxx's will was drawn up by a Jersey lawyer and presumably will come under Jersey law. If Gunnarsson puts Corliss in as a substitute for Hendrix that is no crime here; no Kenyan has been defrauded. We can't hold either of them on those grounds. So how are you going to go about it?'

'I don't know,' Stafford said glumly. 'All I know is that you're talking like a lawyer.'

'How do you know I'm not a lawyer?' said Chip.

'I don't. You're a bloody chameleon. If the Kenyan authorities can't hold Gunnarsson then there's nothing to stop him leaving. I don't think he will leave, not until he knows what's happened to Corliss, but he might. It would be nice if something were to stop him.'

'He could always lose his passport,' offered Chip. 'It wouldn't stop him, but it would delay him until he got papers from the American Embassy.'

'And how would he lose his passport?' Stafford asked.

Chip spread his hands. 'People do all the time. Strange, isn't it? It causes considerable work for the consular staffs.' He stood up. 'I must go; I have work to do, arrangements to make. Take it easy, Max; don't work up a sweat.' He turned to go, then dropped some newspapers on the table. 'I thought you might like to read the news.'

He went and Stafford lay on the bed and lit a cigarette. If Chip was a member of the Kenya People's Union he

certainly would not come right out and say so, and he
had not. On the other hand, if he was not a member
why would he imply that he was? Or had that been the
implication? Had Stafford read too much into Chip's
equivocations?

But there was more. Whether he was or was not a
member of a banned political party why was he being so
bloody helpful to Max Stafford to the point of kidnapping
Corliss and stealing Gunnarsson's passport, both of which
were criminal acts? Stafford was damned sure it was not at
the behest of some Indian back in London who liked
Curtis.

He picked up the newspapers and scanned the front
pages. The kidnapping of the tour group and the disappearance of Hendrix had made headlines in both the *Standard*
and the *Nation*. Perhaps, if it had not been for Hendrix, the
story would have been played down; Stafford suspected that
government pressure would suppress anything that made
for a bad public image. But Hendrix made it different – no
one had vanished before.

An editorial in the *Standard* called for an immediate and
extremely strong note of protest to the Tanzanian government and demanded that Hendrix be returned, dead or
alive. Someone from the *Nation* had tried to interview the
American Ambassador but he had not been available for
comment. The inevitable unnamed spokesman said the
American authorities regarded the matter in the most serious light and that steps were being taken. He did not say in
which direction.

In neither newspaper was there a report of the interview
Chip and Stafford had given to Eddy Ukiru, the reporter
from the *Standard*, and his companion from the *Nation*. No
mention of Stafford, of Chip, of Nair, of Curtis. No photographs. It was as though their part in this nine day wonder
had never happened. Of course, they were pretty small

beer compared to Hendrix but it seemed sloppy journalism to Stafford. He tossed the newspapers aside with the thought that perhaps Ukiru and his mate had not met their deadline.

It was only when he was on the verge of sleep that night that he realized he had never told Chip at any time that Hendrykxx's will had been drawn up in Jersey. So how did Chip know?

# EIGHTEEN

Dirk Hendriks drove down the winding road of the escarpment towards the Rift Valley and Naivasha and towards what he always held in his mind but never mentioned aloud – *die Kenya Stasie*. Not that it was fully operational yet but it would be once this business was over. Still, Frans Potgeiter had done a good job considering the slim funding that had been available. He was a good man.

He passed the church at the bottom of the hill which had been built by Italian prisoners during the war and turned towards Naivasha. His eyes flitted over the signpost that indicated the road to Narok and he smiled. Potgeiter had succeeded in the Masai Mara, too, after others had failed miserably. There had been too much bungling, too much interference. As the English proverb said: 'too many cooks spoil the broth'. But everything was coming right at last.

He turned off the main road short of Naivasha and took the road which ran back along the lake edge past the Lake Naivasha Hotel and on to Ol Njorowa. It was precisely midday when he pulled up outside the gatehouse and blew a blast on his horn. The gate keeper came running. 'Yes, sah?'

'Mr Hendriks to see Mr Brice. I'm expected.'

'Sah.' The gate keeper went back and the gates opened. As Hendriks drove through, the gate keeper shouted warningly *'Pole pole!'* Hendriks did not know what that meant until he hit the first sleeping policeman at a speed which jarred his teeth. He slowed the car and reflected that he had better learn Swahili. It would be useful in the future.

He parked outside the Administration Block and went inside. In the cool hall he approached the reception desk behind which sat a muscular young black who was dressed neatly in white shirt and shorts. Another young Kenyan was sitting at a side desk hammering a typewriter. 'Mr Hendriks to see Mr Brice,' Hendriks repeated.

'Yes, sir; he's expecting you. Come this way.' Hendriks followed, passing through a wicker gate and along a corridor towards Brice's office. He nodded approvingly. Potgeiter had it organized well; no one was going to wander about the place unobserved.

Brice was sitting behind his desk and looked up with a smile as Hendriks came in. The Kenyan left, closing the door behind him, and Hendriks said, *'Goeie middag, meneer Potgeiter; hoe gaan dit?'*

The smile abruptly left Brice's face. 'No Afrikaans,' he said sharply. 'And my name is Brice – always Brice. Remember that!'

Hendriks smiled and dropped into a chair. 'Think the place is bugged?'

'I know it isn't.' Brice tapped on the desk for emphasis. 'But don't get into bad habits.'

'I'm a South African,' said Hendriks. 'I'm supposed to know Afrikaans.'

'And I'm not,' snapped Brice. 'So stick to English – always English.'

'English it will be,' agreed Hendriks. 'Even when we're conspiring.'

Brice nodded – a gesture which closed the subject. 'How did you get on in London?'

'All right. That old fool, Farrar, is making the distribution next week.' Hendriks laughed. 'He gave me a cheque for a hundred thousand pounds on account as soon as we got back. Your coffers should be filling up soon.'

'And about time,' said Brice. 'I'm tired of working on a shoestring.' He shook his head. 'The way it was set up in Europe was too complicated. We ought to have had direct control. Farrar asked some sticky questions when he was here.'

'It had to be set up in Jersey,' said Hendriks. 'Do you think we wanted to pay the British Treasury death duties on forty million pounds? This operation wasn't set up to give money to the Brits. As for Farrar, Mandeville kept a tight rein on him. Farrar is a legal snob; he likes working with an eminent British barrister. And Mandeville is a good man. The best.' Hendriks smiled thinly. 'He ought to be, considering what we pay him.'

Brice made a dismissive gesture. 'I never understood the European end of this and I didn't want to. I had my own troubles.'

*You* had troubles! thought Hendriks bitterly, but said nothing. His mind went back to the moment when Alix happily announced that she was pregnant. That had come as a shock because if the child was born before Hendrykxx died it would automatically become one of his heirs and that could not be allowed. The kid would inherit two million of their precious pounds and it would bring Alix right into the middle of the operation.

He had thought of having the will changed and had talked it over with Mandeville but Mandeville had said they would not get it past Farrar. Hendrykxx was then senile and not in his right mind, and Farrar was rectitude itself. So Hendrykxx had to go before the baby was born. It had been risky – murder always was – but it had been done. And all that was on top of the trouble caused by Henry Hendrix who had dropped out of sight in America. Still, that problem had been solved – or had it?

Brice said, 'Your cousin Henry was one of your problems you wished on me. Why the hell was he allowed to come to Africa?'

'We lost him,' said Hendriks. 'And Pretoria was asleep. By the time they woke up back home to the fact that Henry was important because the old man was dead Farrar had employed an American agency and was looking for him himself. The agency man got to Henry about ten minutes before we did.' He snorted. 'Ten minutes and three inches.'

Brice raised his eyebrows. 'Three inches?'

'Our man took a shot at him. Hit him in the shoulder. Three inches to the right and Henry wouldn't have been a problem ever again.'

'Well, he's no problem now,' said Brice. 'I've seen to that. Have you read the papers lately?'

Hendriks nodded. 'It made a couple of paragraphs in the English papers.' He leaned forward. 'You're wrong, Brice. Henry is still a problem. Where's the bloody body? We need the body. His three million quid is tied up until death is proved. We don't want to wait seven years to collect. As it is he's just disappeared.'

Brice sighed. He stood up and went to the window. With his back to Hendriks he said, 'He's not the only one to have disappeared. Two of my men didn't come back.'

'What!' Hendriks also rose to his feet. 'What did you say?'

Brice turned. 'You heard me. I've lost two men.'

'You'd better explain,' Hendriks said tightly.

'It all went exactly the way I planned. You've read the newspaper reports. The stories those tourists told were exactly right except for one thing. They were supposed to see the body and they didn't. It wasn't there – and neither were my men.'

'Could Henry have jumped them and got away? How were they armed?'

'Standard Tanzanian army gear. Kalashnikovs.'

Hendriks shook his head. 'I don't think Henry would have the stuffing in him to tackle those. In any case if he got away he'd be back by now.' He thought for a moment. 'Perhaps the Tanzanians got him. The real ones, I mean.'

'I doubt it,' said Brice. 'The Legislature is in an uproar and the Foreign Minister is putting pressure on the Tanzanians. Some of my boys are on the border with a watching brief. The Tanzanians are scouring the area south of the Masai Mara. Why would they do that if they already had Henry – or his corpse?'

Hendriks said coldly. 'So that leaves one answer. Your men are cheating on you.'

'Not those boys,' said Brice decisively. 'They're two of my best.' He paused, then added, 'Besides, they've got their families back home to think of.'

'So what's the answer?'

'I don't know.' Brice rubbed his eyes and said sourly, 'Who dreamed up this crazy operation, anyway?'

'We did,' said Hendriks flatly. 'You and me.'

Brice said nothing to that but merely shrugged. 'Well, we'll get most of the money in soon.'

'That's true,' said Hendriks as he sat down again. 'But it irks me to have three million tied up. I worked damned hard to get this money in here.' He changed the subject. 'Why did you announce an inheritance of only seven million? Isn't that risky?'

Brice spread his hands. 'Who is going to check back to Jersey? Hell, man; I'll bet not one in a hundred Kenyans even knows where Jersey is. One in a thousand.'

'But what if somebody does?' persisted Hendriks.

'No problem,' said Brice. 'I'll say I was misquoted – misunderstood. I'll say that the seven million is the estimated annual income after the main fund has been invested. We have everything to gain and nothing to lose.'

He checked the time. 'We'll have lunch and then I'll show you around. I didn't show you the real stuff last time you were here. Farrar stuck closer than a leech.'

'I'll stay for lunch,' said Hendriks. 'But the rest can wait. I have got to get back to Nairobi and raise a stink. My long lost cousin has been lost again and what the hell are they doing about it? I must do the grieving relative bit to make it look right. Let's go and eat. I'm hungry.'

# NINETEEN

In Nairobi Gunnarsson was angry. His feet hurt and his back was sore but that was not the reason for his anger. What riled him was that he was being given the runaround in the American Embassy. 'Damn it!' he said. 'I've been kidnapped and my friend is still missing. If I can't see the Ambassador who the hell can I see? And don't fob me off on any third clerk. I want action.'

The clerk behind the counter sighed. 'I'll see what I can do.' He moved away and picked up a telephone. 'Is Mr Pasternak there?'

'Speaking.'

'There's a guy here called Gunnarsson wanting to see the Ambassador. He has some crazy story about being kidnapped by Tanzanians and says his friend is still missing. I think he's a nut, but I can't get rid of him.'

An incredulous silence bored into his ear, then Pasternak said, 'Gleeson; don't you read the papers? Watch TV? Listen to the radio?'

'I've been on safari for two weeks,' said Gleeson. 'Just got back this morning from my vacation. Why? Something happened?'

'Yeah; something happened,' said Pasternak ironically. 'Don't let that guy get away; I'll be right down. And catch up on the goddamn news for God's sake.' He hung up, opened his desk drawer to check that his recorder had a tape ready to go, then went downstairs to meet Gunnarsson.

Gunnarsson was still simmering so Pasternak applied the old oil. 'Sorry you've been kept waiting, Mr Gunnarsson, and sorrier that you've been inconvenienced by idiocy. Won't you come this way?' He slowed his pace to Gunnarsson's hobble as he led the way to the elevator. 'I guess you had a tough time.'

Gunnarsson grunted. 'You guessed right. What's your position here?'

'Nothing much,' admitted Pasternak. 'Third Secretary. You'll realize we're all busy on this thing, especially the Ambassador. He's talking with the Kenyan Foreign Minister right now, trying to get some action. And the rest of our work has to carry on – guys losing their credit cards and traveller's checks and so on.'

'This is more important,' said Gunnarsson acidly. 'You've lost an American citizen.'

Pasternak said, 'We're doing all we can, Mr Gunnarsson; and we're sure you can help.' They left the elevator, walked along a corridor, and he opened the door of his office. 'In here. Would you like coffee?'

'Thanks.' Gunnarsson sat before the desk, thankfully taking the weight off his feet, as Pasternak picked up the telephone and ordered a jug of coffee.

Pasternak sat down, opened his desk drawer and unobtrusively switched on the recorder before taking out a notepad and laying it on the desk. He picked up a pen. 'I've read the newspaper reports,' he said. 'But you know what newspapers are. I'll be glad to hear a first-hand report. If you hadn't come to us, Mr Gunnarsson, we'd have been camping on your doorstep. Now, I'd like you to tell it as it happened. Don't leave anything out even though you might think it irrelevant.'

So Gunnarsson told his story while Pasternak made largely unnecessary notes and dropped in a question from time to time. 'You say these men were in uniform. Can you describe it?' Then again: 'You say the rifles were Kalashnikovs; how do you know?'

'I'm a gun buff back home. I know a Kalashnikov when I see one.'

He got to the end when he said, 'And then we got back to Keekorok and that was that. But Hank Hendrix didn't come back.'

'I see.' Pasternak laid down his pen. 'More coffee?'

'Thanks. All this talk is thirsty work.'

Pasternak poured the coffee. 'What's your relationship with Hendrix?'

'We're business associates,' said Gunnarsson. 'And friends, too.'

Pasternak nodded understandingly. 'Yes, you'd naturally be disturbed about this affair. What business are you in, Mr Gunnarsson?'

'I run Gunnarsson Associates; we're a security outfit based in New York. We run security for corporations and do some investigative work. Not much of that, though.'

'Investigative work,' repeated Pasternak, thoughtfully. 'You're licensed for that in the state of New York?'

'In most states of the Union,' said Gunnarsson. 'We're a pretty big outfit.'

'And what were you doing in Kenya?'

'Well, Hank had some business here. He'd inherited a hunk of dough. I came along for the ride; taking a vacation, you know.' Gunnarsson looked at Pasternak over the rim of his coffee cup. 'The shit's going to hit the fan on this one, Pasternak, because Hank had just inherited six million bucks. The papers will make hay of it back home.'

Pasternak raised his eyebrows. 'The State Department does not run its affairs on the basis of newspaper reports,

Mr Gunnarsson. But you interest me. You say Henry Hendrix had inherited six million dollars from Kenya?'

Gunnarsson shook his head. 'I didn't say that. He inherited from his grandfather, but the will said that a condition of inheritance was that Hank was to spend at least one month a year at some charitable foundation here; helping out, I guess.'

'Which foundation?'

'Ol Njorowa,' said Gunnarsson, stumbling over the unfamiliar words. 'It's near Naivasha.'

'Yes,' said Pasternak meditatively. 'I read they'd come into money but I didn't know about Hendrix.' He thought for a moment, then said, 'How long are you staying in Kenya, Mr Gunnarsson?'

Gunnarsson shrugged. 'For a while, I guess. I'll stick around to see if Hank comes back. And I want to goose the Ambassador. An American citizen has disappeared, Pasternak, and no one seems to be doing much about it. I tell you, I'm going to raise hell.'

Pasternak made no comment. He drew the notepad towards him, and said, 'If you'll give me the name of your hotel here, and your home address, I think that's about all.'

'What do you want my home address for?'

'I doubt if you'll be staying in Kenya indefinitely,' said Pasternak reasonably. 'We might want to talk to you again, even back in the States. And if you intend moving about in Kenya we'd like to know your itinerary in advance.'

'Why?'

'We might want to get hold of you in a hurry. For identification purposes, for instance.' Again it was a reasonable request. Pasternak wrote down the addresses, then pushed a button and stood up. 'That's all, Mr Gunnarsson. Thanks for coming in.' He held out his hand. 'We'll do our best to find what happened to Mr Hendrix.'

'You'd better find him,' said Gunnarsson. 'There's a lot riding on Hank.'

A man entered the room. Pasternak said, 'The messenger will escort you downstairs.' He smiled. 'If you're in the security business you'll realize why we don't like people wandering around the building.'

Gunnarsson grunted and left without saying another word. Pasternak opened the drawer and stopped the recorder, then rewound it. He played it, skipping back and forth, and listened to one part several times. Would a gun nut know a Kalashnikov when he saw one? There were precious few of those floating about loose back home. True, an enthusiast might study illustrations in books. And Gunnarsson was in something known amorphously as 'security' which could be a euphemism for something more dangerous. A couple of loose ends which needed tidying up. He played the tape yet again and frowned when he noted that both he and Gunnarsson had consistently referred to Hendrix in the past tense.

Pasternak turned to the typewriter and wrote a request for any known information on John Gunnarsson, giving the address in New York. He took it to the code room himself.

The telex was addressed to Langley, Virginia.

An hour later Pasternak was interrupted again. The telephone rang and Gleeson said, 'Mr Hardin is asking for you.'

Pasternak frowned, hunting in his mind for a connection, then his brow cleared. 'Not Ben Hardin?'

There was a pause and a few mumbled words, then Gleeson said, 'Yes; Ben Hardin.'

'Have him brought up.' Pasternak depressed the telephone cradle and dialled. 'Send in some more coffee.' When Hardin entered the room he stood up and smiled. 'Well, hello, Ben. It's been a long time. What are you doing in Kenya?'

They shook hands and Hardin sat down. 'A sort of working vacation,' he said. 'I haven't been here in years. Nairobi
has changed some but the country hasn't. I thought I'd drop
in to see if there was anyone I knew from the old days.'

'And you found me.' Pasternak smiled. 'It's certainly
been a long time. What are you doing these days?'

'Working for a British outfit.' Hardin shrugged. 'A guy
has to earn a living.'

'I'd stick in Kenya,' advised Pasternak. 'I wouldn't go
into Tanzania. You'll still be on a list after what you did in
Dar-es-Salaam. I know it was years ago but those guys have
long memories.'

'I'm not going anywhere near Tanzania,' said Hardin.
'Not even to the border. I hear it's not safe even for tourists.'

'You heard about that?'

'It made the London papers, ' said Hardin. 'I read about
it over there.'

'It will have made the New York papers, too,' agreed
Pasternak gloomily. 'If it hasn't yet, it will. One of the guys
who was kidnapped has just been in here bending my ear.
The other American, the one who came back. Gunnarsson
has been threatening to raise Cain.'

'Gunnarsson!' Hardin showed surprise. 'Of Gunnarsson
Associates in New York?' Pasternak nodded. 'Well, I'll be a
son of a bitch!'

'Do you know him?'

'I used to work for him after I left the Company. He's
ex-Company, too.'

'I didn't know that,' said Pasternak. He poured a couple
of cups of coffee while he thought. That would explain the
recognition of the Kalashnikovs, but it did not explain why
Gunnarsson had lied about how he knew unless he did not
want to advertise his one-time connection with the CIA. A
lot of guys were sensitive about it. But Gunnarsson had not
looked the sensitive type. 'What sort of a guy is he?'

'A 22-carat bastard,' said Hardin, and hesitated. 'Look, Mike, I'd just as soon Gunnarsson doesn't know I'm around. We parted on bad terms and now I'm working for the competition. He won't like that.'

Pasternak shrugged. 'No reason for me to tell him, Ben. Who are you working for?'

'Stafford Security Consultants of London. I joined them when Gunnarsson fired me.'

The facts in Pasternak's mind rearranged themselves into a different pattern. Another security crowd! 'You said "a working vacation." How much is work and how much vacation?'

'About fifty-fifty,' said Hardin. 'Max Stafford, my boss, is in Nairobi, too. We're giving Kenya the once-over to see if it's ripe for us to move in.' He thought for a moment. 'Damn it; I'll bet that's why Gunnarsson is here. I'll tell Stafford.' He sipped his coffee. 'Getting any action around here?'

Pasternak smiled genially. 'You know better than to ask that, Ben. You're not in the Company any more and, even if you were, I wouldn't tell you a damned thing and you know it.' He leaned forward. 'I've got the idea you aren't here just to talk about old times, so why don't you spill it?'

'You always were sharp,' said Hardin with a grin. 'It's like this. Stafford has Europe pretty much tied up. Our clients are the multinational corporations and a couple of them aren't happy about their security out here, so they want Stafford to set up shop in Kenya. Well, he's not going to do it blind, and he'll need more than two clients to make it profitable, so he's here to see for himself. Follow me so far?'

'You're doing fine,' said Pasternak dryly. 'Come to the point.'

'We ran across a couple of guys who seem to be the cat's whiskers in our line, very smooth and efficient. Trouble is that Stafford thinks they're connected with the Kenya People's Union and that's bad. If Stafford is thinking of setting up a permanent office here he can't afford to be mixed up with a banned political party.'

'It would be the kiss of death if it came out,' agreed Pasternak soberly. He reached for a pen. 'Who are these guys?'

'A black Kenyan called Pete Chipende and a Sikh, Nair Singh. Know them?'

Pasternak was so taken by surprise that his pen made a scrawled line on the pad. He controlled himself and wrote down the names. 'No, but I guess I can find out, given time.' His mind was busy with the implications of what he had just heard. 'What kind of a guy is Stafford?'

'Not bad – so far,' said Hardin judiciously. 'He hasn't cut any corners yet, not that I know of.'

'Maybe I'll meet him sometime,' said Pasternak. 'What about a drink together?'

'Why not? We're staying at the Norfolk.'

'I'm busy today, but maybe I'll give you a ring tomorrow. Okay?'

'That's fine. Stafford's an interesting guy; he was in British army intelligence – a colonel.'

'Was he? I look forward to meeting him.'

Hardin took his leave and Pasternak seated himself before the typewriter again and composed another request for information. This time the subject was Max Stafford and the telex was to be sent, after coding, to the American Embassy in London. After a moment's thought he wrote another request for information on Hardin and addressed it to Langley.

Kenya was becoming livelier, thought Pasternak.


Gunnarsson was in the Thorn Tree café at the New Stanley Hotel having drinks with Dirk Hendriks. As he had been leaving the American Embassy he had heard a man saying to the marine guard, 'My name is Dirk Hendriks. Where do I go to find out about Henry Hendrix, the man who was kidnapped into Tanzania?'

The marine pointed. 'Ask at the desk, sir.'

Gunnarsson touched Hendriks on the arm. 'Are you Hank Hendrix's cousin?'

Hendriks turned and looked at Gunnarsson in surprise. 'Yes, I am.'

'I'm John Gunnarsson. I was there.'

'You were where?'

'With your cousin when he was kidnapped.' Gunnarsson jerked his thumb towards the inquiry desk. 'You'd better talk with me before you butt your head against that brick wall.'

Dirk looked at him interestedly. 'You mean you were kidnapped, too?'

'Yeah. That's why I'm not too sharp on my feet. They made us walk out and I was stuck full of thorns.'

'I've got my car here,' said Hendriks. 'No need to walk. Where shall we go?'

'I'm staying at the New Stanley,' said Gunnarsson. 'We can have a drink at the Thorn Tree.'

The Thorn Tree was a Nairobi institution, being an open air café serving light refreshments. In the centre grew a large acacia, tall and spreading wide to give pleasant shade and which gave the Thorn Tree its name. The peculiarity which made the Thorn Tree different was the notice board which surrounded the trunk of the tree. Here it was the custom to leave messages for friends and it was a commonplace to say, 'If you want to find out where I am I'll leave a message on the thorn tree.' A local beer company even provided message pads, and it certainly did no harm to the profits of the café.

They sat down at one of the few available tables and Hendriks caught a waiter on the fly and ordered drinks.

He resumed the conversation they had been having in the car. 'And that was the last you saw of my cousin?'

'Yeah. Then we heard shots and the guys around us laughed.'

'But you didn't see his body.'

Gunnarsson shook his head. 'No, but there was something funny about that. They herded us downriver, three of them, leaving one guy to guard the loot. We went maybe half a mile and then they got excited, jabbering away to each other.'

'What were they excited about?'

'I wouldn't know. Maybe because they couldn't find Hendrix. Two of them stayed with us and the third, the guy with the sergeant's stripes, went away. After a while he came back and they had a conference, a lot of talk.' Gunnarsson shrugged. 'They shooed us away then. The sergeant pointed up the hill and the others poked at us with their rifles. We were glad to get away.'

Hendrix frowned. 'The two men who took my cousin away; were they around at that time?'

'I didn't see them.'

The waiter brought their drinks. Hendriks picked up his glass and pondered. 'Could Henry have got away?' he asked. 'But if he did why hasn't he come back?'

'I've thought about that,' said Gunnarsson. 'He might have got away and the shooting might have missed. The two Tanzanians would be chasing him, of course. Still, he might have got away.' Gunnarsson certainly hoped so.

'Then why hasn't he come back?'

'Have you been out there?' asked Gunnarsson rhetorically. 'It's the damnedest country, and every bit looks like every other bit. Hank might have got lost like the guys who followed us in. And remember he was stripped like us. He may still come back, though, if the Tanzanians didn't catch up with him.'

'Who followed you in?' asked Hendriks alertly.

'Another tourist crowd found our abandoned truck and tried to find us. They didn't; they got lost and spent a night in the bush.'

Hendriks was pensive. 'I didn't read about that in the newspapers.'

'I talked to one of them when we got back,' said Gunnarsson. 'A guy called Stafford. He said that . . .'

'Max Stafford!' said Hendriks unbelievingly.

'He didn't tell me his other name.' Gunnarsson stopped, his glass halfway to his lips as he was arrested in thought. The only Max Stafford he had heard of was the boss of Stafford Security Consultants back in London. Now just what the hell was going on?

Hendriks was also thoughtful. Stafford had said he was taking a holiday in Kenya. But was it coincidental that he had been involved in the search for Henry Hendrix? He said, 'Do you know where Stafford is now?'

'No; he left Keekorok and I haven't seen him since. You know the guy?'

Hendriks nodded abstractedly. 'Yes, I think so.'

'Now isn't that a coincidence,' said Gunnarsson.

'Isn't it?' Hendriks badly needed a telephone. He said, 'Glad to have talked with you, Mr Gunnarsson. Are you staying here at the New Stanley?'

'Yeah.'

'Then perhaps you'll have dinner with me before you leave. I'll give you a ring tomorrow morning. I'd like to know more about my cousin's disappearance but right now I have an appointment. Will you excuse me?'

'Sure.' Gunnarsson watched Hendriks get up and walk away. Something goddamn odd was happening but he was not sure what it was. If the Stafford he had talked to at Keekorok was the Max Stafford of Stafford Security then there was definitely no coincidence. He decided he needed a telephone and hoisted himself laboriously to his feet.

Stafford dined with Curtis at the Norfolk that evening and they were halfway through the meal when Hardin joined them. He said, 'I've just seen Chip. He says that Gunnarsson and Dirk Hendriks had a drink and a chat at the Thorn Tree this afternoon.'

Stafford put down his knife and fork. 'Did they, by God?'

Curtis grunted. 'That's not good for the Colonel.'

'No.' Stafford looked at Hardin. 'Ben, do you remember when you followed Gunnarsson and Corliss to Mandeville's chambers in Lincoln's Inn? Did Gunnarsson meet Dirk there?'

Hardin looked up at the ceiling and gazed into the past. He said slowly, 'Gunnarsson and Corliss went in then Gunnarsson came out.' He snapped his fingers. 'Gunnarsson came out just as Dirk and Alix went in – they passed each other in the entrance.'

'Any sign of recognition?'

'Not a thing.'

'Then how did they get together here?' asked Stafford.

'I talked to Chip about that and maybe it can be explained,' said Hardin. 'Gunnarsson went to the police and then on to the American Embassy to raise some hell about them dragging their heels on the Hendrix case. I saw Mike Pasternak and he told me about it.' Hardin retailed his discussion with Pasternak. 'Chip says that Hendriks and Gunnarsson met in the lobby of the Embassy apparently by chance.'

'It's unlucky for us,' said Stafford. 'If Gunnarsson mentioned my name to Dirk in connection with the disppearance of Hendrix then he's going to be suspicious.'

'Suspicious about what?' demanded Hardin. 'I don't know what you have against Dirk Hendriks – he's just a guy who's inherited a fortune. It's Gunnarsson and Corliss who are trying to put one over on the estate.'

Stafford was about to reply when he was interrupted by a waiter who handed him a note. 'From the gentleman at the corner table, sir.'

Stafford saw a man looking towards him. The man nodded curtly and then addressed himself to his plate. Stafford opened the folded paper and read, 'I would appreciate a moment of your time when you finish dinner.' There was an indecipherable scribble of a signature below.

He looked across the room again and nodded, then passed the note to Hardin. 'Do you know him?'

Hardin paused in the middle of ordering from the menu. 'A stranger to me.' He finished ordering, then said, 'Mike Pasternak phoned half an hour ago. He'd like to meet you. Is four o'clock tomorrow okay?'

'I should think so.'

'He'll meet you here by the swimming pool. Maybe he'll be able to tell you who Chip really is.'

'Perhaps.' Stafford was lost in thought trying to fit together a jigsaw, taking a piece at a time and seeing if it made up a pattern. It was true he had nothing against Dirk beyond an instinctive dislike of the man but suppose . . . Suppose that Dirk's meeting with Gunnarsson at the Embassy had not been by chance, that they already knew each other. Gunnarsson had been established as a crook so what did that make Dirk? And then there was Brice at Ol Njorowa who had unaccountably lost tens of millions of pounds. If Dirk talked to Brice and found that Stafford had been at Ol Njorowa *and* Keekorok then he would undoubtedly smell a rat.

Stafford shook his head irritably. All this was moonshine – sheer supposition. He said, 'What else did Dirk do today?'

'He went out to Ol Njorowa, stayed for lunch, then came back to Nairobi where he went to the police and then on to the American Embassy.'

'Where he met Gunnarsson. Did he see anyone at the Embassy?'

'No,' said Hardin. 'He went with Gunnarsson to the Thorn Tree.'

'Could have been pre-arranged,' said Curtis.

'You're a man of few words, Sergeant,' said Stafford, 'but they make sense.'

'But why meet at the Embassy?' persisted Hardin. 'They're both staying at the New Stanley – why not there?'

'I don't know,' said Stafford, tired of beating his brains out. He finished his coffee and nodded towards the corner table. 'I'd better see what that chap wants.'

He walked across the dining room and the man looked up as he approached. 'Abercrombie-Smith,' he said. 'You're Stafford.'

He was a small compact man in his early fifties with a tanned square face and a neatly trimmed moustache. There was a faint and indefinable military air about him which could have been because of the erect way he held himself. He slid a business card from under his napkin and gave it to Stafford. His full name was Anthony Abercrombie-Smith and his card stated that he was from the British High Commission, Bruce House, Standard Street, Nairobi. It did not state what he did there.

'I've been wanting to meet you,' he said. 'We've been expecting you at the office.'

Stafford said, 'It never occurred to me.'

'Humph! All the same you should have come. Never mind; we'll make it the occasion for a lunch. There's no point in having the formality of an office meeting. What about tomorrow?'

Stafford inclined his head. 'That will be all right.'

'Good. We'll lunch at the Muthaiga Club. I'll pick you up here at midday.' He turned back to his plate and Stafford assumed that the audience was over so he left.

# TWENTY

Stafford was ready when Abercrombie-Smith arrived on the dot of midday to pick him up. Hardin and Curtis had taken a Nissan and gone off to the Nairobi Game Park situated so conveniently nearby.

Abercrombie-Smith drove north through a part of Nairobi Stafford had not seen and made bland conversation about the sights to be seen, the Indian temples and the thriving open markets. Presently they came to a suburb which was redolent of wealth. The houses were large – what little could be seen of them because they were set back far from the road and discreetly screened by hedges and trees. Stafford noted that many had guards on the gates which interested him professionally.

'This is Muthaiga,' said Abercrombie-Smith. 'A rather select part of Nairobi. Most of the foreign embassies are here. My master, the High Commissioner, has his home quite close.' They turned a corner, then off the road through a gateway. A Kenyan at the gate gave a semi-salute. 'And this is the Muthaiga Club.'

Inside, the rooms were cool and airy. The walls were decked with animal trophies; kongoni, gazelle, impala, leopard. They went into the lounge and sat in comfortable club chairs. 'And now, dear boy,' said Abercrombie-Smith, 'what will it be?'

Stafford asked for a gin and tonic so he ordered two. 'This is one of the oldest clubs in Kenya,' he said. 'And one of the most exclusive.' He looked at the two Sikhs across the room who were engrossed in a discussion over papers spread on a table. 'Although not as exclusive as it once was,' he observed. 'In my day one never discussed business in one's club.'

Stafford let it ride, content to let Abercrombie-Smith make the running. His small talk was more serious than most. He expatiated on the political situation in Britain, ditto in America, the dangers inherent in the Russian interference in Afghanistan and Poland, and so forth. But it was still small talk. Stafford let him run on, putting in the occasional comment so that the conversation would not run down, and waited for him to come to the nub. In the meantime he assessed the Muthaiga Club.

It was obviously a relic of colonial days; the chosen, self-designed watering hole of the higher civil servants and the wealthier and more influential merchants – all white, of course, in those days. It was probably in here that the real decisions were made, and not in the Legislative Council or the Law Courts. The coming of Uhuru must have been painful for the membership who had to adapt to a determinedly multiracial society. Stafford wondered who had been the brave non-white to have first applied for membership.

They finished their drinks and Abercrombie-Smith proposed a move. 'I suggest we go into the dining room,' he said. He still had not come to any point that was worth making. Stafford nodded, stood up with him, and followed into the dining room which was half full of a mixed crowd of whites, blacks and Asians.

They consulted the menu together and Stafford chose melon to start with. 'I recommend the tilapia,' said Abercrombie-Smith. it's a flavoursome freshwater fish from the lakes. And the curry here is exceptional.' Stafford nodded so he ordered curry for both of them, then said to the waiter, 'A bottle of hock with the fish and lager with the curry.' The waiter went away. Abercrombie-Smith leaned across the table. 'One cannot really drink wine with curry, can one? Besides, nothing goes better with curry than cold lager.'

Stafford agreed politely. Who was he to disagree with his host?

Over the melon they discussed cricket and the current Test Match; over the fish, current affairs in East Africa. Stafford thought Abercrombie-Smith was coming in a circumlocutory manner to some possible point at issue. But he was right; the tilapia was delicious.

As the curry dishes were placed on the table he said, 'Help yourself, dear boy. You know we really expected you to come to us after that unfortunate incident in the Masai Mara.' He cocked an eyebrow at Stafford expectantly.

Stafford said, 'I don't know why. I had no complaints to make.' He spooned rice on to his plate.

'But, still; a kidnapping!'

Stafford passed him the rice dish. 'I wasn't kidnapped,' he said briefly. The curry had a rich, spicy aroma.

'Um,' said Abercrombie-Smith. 'Just so. All the same we thought you might. Would you like to tell me what happened down there?'

'I don't mind,' Stafford said as he helped himself to the curry, and gave a strictly edited version.

'I see,' he said. 'I see. You say you turned back at the border. How did you know it was the border? As I recollect there are no fences or signs in that wilderness. No fences because of the wildebeest migration of course, and the elephants tend to destroy any signposts.'

'Like the telegraph poles,' Stafford said, and he nodded. Stafford sampled the curry and found it good. 'You'll have to ask Pete Chipende about that. He's the local expert.'

'Try the *sambals*,' Abercrombie-Smith urged. 'They do them very well here. The tomatoes and onions are marinated in herbs; not the bananas, of course, and certainly not the coconut. The coconut, I assure you, is perfectly fresh; not the nasty, dried-up stuff you get in England. I recommend the mango chutney, too.' He helped himself to curry. 'Ah, yes; Chipende. An interesting man, don't you think?'

'Certainly an intelligent man,' said Stafford.

'I would tend to agree there; I certainly would. How did it come about that he was with you?'

Abercrombie-Smith was being too damned nosey. Stafford said, 'He offered to act as guide and courier.'

'And Nair Singh? A courier also?' His eyebrows twitched upwards. 'Wasn't that a little overkill, dear boy?'

Stafford shrugged. 'Chip wanted Nair along as driver. He said Nair was the better driver.' That was the exact truth but he did not expect to be believed.

Abercrombie-Smith started to laugh. He laughed so much that he was speechless. He choked on his curry and it was quite a time before he recovered. He dabbed his mouth with his napkin and said, still chuckling, 'Oh, my dear chap; that's rich – rich, indeed.' He put down the napkin. 'Didn't you know that Mr Peter Chipende entered the East African Safari Rally three years in succession? He didn't win but he finished every time and that is an achievement in itself.'

Stafford had heard of the East African Safari Rally; it was supposed to be the most gruelling long-distance motor race in the world and, judging by the condition of the road between Narok and Keekorok, he could very well believe it. He cursed Chip for putting him in such an untenable position and said, 'I wouldn't know about that; I'm a stranger in these parts.'

'So that's what Chipende told you, is it? Well, well.'

Stafford decided to give him back some of the malarkey he had been handing out. 'This curry is really very good;

thanks for recommending it. Do you think I could get the recipe from the chef? I pride myself on being a good cook.'

Abercrombie-Smith's eyes went flinty. He knew when someone was taking the mickey as well as the next man. However, he held himself in. 'I would think it's the chef's family secret, dear boy.' He fiddled with his napkin. 'You haven't been here long, Stafford; but you've mixed with some very interesting people. Interesting to me, that is.'

Stafford thought it would be rather more interesting to MI6 or whatever funny number they gave to foreign espionage these days. He said, 'Who, for instance?'

'Well, Peter Chipende and Nair Singh, to start with. And then there are a couple of ex-CIA agents, Hardin and Gunnarsson. Not to mention Colour Sergeant Curtis, but he's small fry and you did bring him with you.'

'This curry is so good I think I'll have some more.' Stafford helped himself. 'You seem to be taking an inordinate interest in me, too.'

'Colonel Max Stafford,' Abercrombie-Smith said meditatively. 'Late of Military Intelligence.'

'Bloody late,' Stafford observed. 'I left the army ten years ago and, by the way, I don't use my rank.'

'Still, you were a full colonel at the age of thirty-five. You ought to know which end is up.'

'Come to the point. What do you want?'

'I want to know what you're doing here in Kenya.'

'Taking a much needed holiday,' Stafford said. 'I haven't had a holiday for three years.'

'And I know about that one,' said Abercrombie-Smith. 'You take holidays in peculiar places. That was when you went to the Sahara and came back with a bullet in your shoulder.'

Stafford put down his fork. 'Now this be damned for a lark.' He was trying to keep his temper. Besides, he wanted to string this joker along for a while. He was silent for a moment. 'What else would you want to know? There's sure to be more.'

'Of course,' Abercrombie-Smith said easily. 'Principally I'd like to know more about Chipende.' Who wouldn't? Stafford thought. 'And, of course, I'd like to know if Hardin and Gunnarsson really are ex-CIA as they claim. And I'd like to know your interest in the Ol Njorowa Foundation.'

Stafford said deliberately, 'And can you give me any reasons why I should do all this?'

Abercrombie-Smith drummed his fingers on the table. 'What about patriotism?' he suggested.

'Patriotism is not enough, as Edith Cavell said. And as Sam Johnson added, patriotism is the last refuge of a scoundrel.'

'Samuel Johnson was a self-opinionated old fool,' Abercrombie-Smith snapped. 'And I'm not here to bandy literary criticism.'

Stafford grinned at him. 'I didn't think you were.'

Abercrombie-Smith stared at Stafford. 'So patriotism is not enough. I suppose that means you want money.'

'The labourer is always worthy of his hire,' said Stafford. 'But, as it happens, you're wrong. You know what you can do with your bloody money.'

'Damn it, Stafford,' he said. 'Can't you be reasonable?'

'I can; if there's anything to be reasonable about. As it is I resent you probing into my affairs, as you seem to have done quite thoroughly.'

'Well, *I'll* try to be reasonable. Don't you recognize that you are in a most sensitive position? Stafford Security Consultants runs security on a dozen defence contractors back home.' He reeled off the names of half-a-dozen. 'Of course we've had you investigated. We'd have been fools not to. Under those circumstances we couldn't take the risk of you being turned. You do see that, don't you?'

Stafford saw. His own dealings with the intelligence establishment had been with the counter-espionage crowd of MI5 and the police Special Branch. They were thin on the ground and could not possibly undertake the detailed work Stafford guaranteed when he took on a contract. Consequently they were distantly pleased and recognized that Stafford Security was largely on their side. But Stafford could see that they would want to guarantee he was safe. Many a one-time agent has been turned in the past.

Abercrombie-Smith said, 'Well, there you are. I think you'll see the advantage of co-operation now because, if you don't, your firm back in England could get into considerable difficulties.'

He paused as the waiter began to clear dishes from the table. Stafford welcomed the interruption because Abercrombie-Smith's eyes were shifting around as plates were swept away, and he did not see the expression on Stafford's face as he contemplated this naked piece of blackmail.

When the waiter had gone Abercrombie-Smith said, 'I recommend something to take away the taste of curry before we have coffee. What do you say to lychees? They're fresh, dear boy; not like those tinned monstrosities you get in England.'

'Yes,' Stafford said mechanically. 'I'll have lychees.'

So they had lychees and then went into the lounge for coffee. On the way there Stafford excused himself and went into the entrance hall where he found the hall porter and asked him to order a taxi. 'How long will it take?'

'Five minutes, sah; no longer.'

'Let me know as soon as it arrives. I'll be in the lounge.'

'Yes, sah. Immediately.'

When he returned Abercrombie-Smith offered him a cigar which he declined. Abercrombie-Smith produced a silver cutter and nipped the end from his cigar and proceeded to light it with great concentration. When he had got it going to his satisfaction he put the cutter away and said, 'Now, my dear boy; I think we can get down to business.'

'I thought you didn't discuss business in your club.'

'Pah!' he said. 'I was referring to commercial business.'

'You mean the sordid business of making money.'

'Precisely. This is different.'

Stafford put some sugar into his coffee and stirred. 'Sam Johnson, whom you seem to despise, had something to say about that. He said that there are few ways in which a man can be more innocently employed than in getting money. Is the proposition you have just made to me in your club any less sordid than commerce?'

Abercrombie-Smith raised his eyebrows. 'My dear chap; I see you are a moralist. Scruples? I would have thought scruples to be undesirable in your profession; positively a hindrance.' His voice sharpened. 'I suggest you address yourself to self preservation and the protection of your – er – business interests since you seem to have such a high regard for money getting.' He was openly contemptuous.

His contempt Stafford could survive. 'I'm Max. Do you mind if I call you Anthony?' He sipped the coffee.

The switch took Abercrombie-Smith by surprise. 'If you must,' he said stiffly. He came from the formal world of English public schools and London Clubland in which the informality of the use of Christian names is looked down upon.

Stafford said, 'Well, Tony; you're nothing but a cheap blackmailer – a common criminal. If the security of the United Kingdom has to depend on you, or the likes of you, then God help us all. I have nothing against blackmail, of course, but clumsiness is intolerable. Your approach to me had all the subtlety of a Soho whore.'

Abercrombie-Smith was taken aback as though he had been attacked and bitten by a newborn lamb. He reddened and said, 'Don't talk to me in those terms.'

'I'll talk to you in any way I damn well like.'

'So you won't co-operate. That could be dangerous as I have pointed out.'

Stafford put down the coffee cup and leaned back. 'I like your idea of co-operation, but I doubt if it's an acceptable dictionary definition. Do what I say or else – is that it?' He leaned forward. 'I've built up quite an organization in the last ten years. Stafford Security Consultants is primarily a defensive organization but it can be used for attack. If I find any change for the worse in the way I do my business I have the capability of finding the reason. If you are the reason I'll smash you. Not your department or whatever idiot employs you but you, personally. Personal ruin. Do I make myself quite clear?'

Abercrombie-Smith was apoplectic. He gobbled for a moment then said breathily, 'This is outrageous. I've never been spoken to like that before; not by anyone.'

'A pity,' Stafford said, and stood up as the hall porter came into the lounge. 'You might have made a half-way decent man if someone had taken you in hand earlier.' He held up his hand. 'Don't get up. I'll find my own way back.'

By the time the taxi deposited him in front of the Norfolk he had cooled down somewhat. As he paid off the driver he wondered if he had made a rod for his own back. Stafford had always deemed it a virtue not to make unnecessary enemies and he had been hard on Abercrombie-Smith. Still, the man had been nauseating with his casual assumption that he had but to crook a finger and Stafford would come to heel. Stafford reflected that he had better look to his defences.

He picked up his key at the desk and found a message from Hardin saying he was at the hotel pool. He walked through the courtyard, past the aviaries with their twittering and chirping birds, and through the archway to the pool. There he found Hardin who said, 'Where have you been? Pasternak rang again, and said he'd have to make it earlier. He'll be here any minute.'

'I've been having my brains washed,' Stafford said sourly. 'Pasternak wouldn't be boss of the Kenya CIA station by any chance?'

'He might be,' said Hardin with a grin. 'But he's not saying.'

'Tell me more,' Stafford said.

'I didn't know Pasternak when I was here but I knew him from Langley. We weren't really buddy-buddy in those days but we had a drink together from time to time. It's useful that he's here.'

'Where's Curtis?'

'He went downtown.' Hardin looked over Stafford's shoulder. 'Here's Pasternak now.'

Pasternak was a lean, rangy man with a closed look about his face. As they shook hands he said, 'Mike Pasternak. Good of you to see me, Mr Stafford.'

'It's no trouble,' he said. 'But I don't know that I can tell you much. I'm a security man and it's my job to keep secrets. Care for a drink?'

'I'll get them,' said Hardin. 'Beer, Mike?'

Pasternak nodded and Hardin went to the poolside bar. Pasternak said, 'Ben tells me you're interested in Pete Chipende.'

'That's right.' Stafford gestured. 'Let's sit.'

They sat face to face across a table and Pasternak looked at Stafford thoughtfully. 'I'd give a whole lot to know *why* you're running with Pete Chipende.'

'Didn't Ben tell you?'

'Yeah.' Pasternak smiled wryly. 'I didn't believe him. I'm hoping you'll tell me.'

'I'm afraid it's my business, Mr Pasternak,' said Stafford.

'I thought you'd take that attitude. I'm sorry. I hope you know what you're getting into.' Pasternak lit a cigarette.

'Ben tells me you're in the same line as Gunnarsson, but in Europe. He also told me you were in British army intelligence at one time.'

'That's correct. It's a matter of record. And you are CIA but you won't admit it outright.'

Pasternak smiled. 'Would you expect me to?' The smile faded. 'Now, here's a funny thing. Hendrix, a newly hatched millionaire, and Gunnarsson, ex-CIA, are in a party kidnapped into Tanzania. Along comes Stafford, again an ex-intelligence guy, and he chases after the kidnappers together with Chipende and Nair Singh. Then I see Ben, also ex-CIA. Don't you think it's strange, Mr Stafford?'

Stafford said, 'Do you know a man called Abercrombie-Smith from the British High Commission?'

Pasternak straightened. 'Don't tell me he's in on this? Whatever it is.'

'I had lunch with him. And now you are here. Perhaps we'd better hire the Kenyatta Conference Centre for a secret service congress,' Stafford said dryly. 'But what's *your* interest in Chipende?'

Pasternak gave Stafford a strange look. 'Are you kidding?'

'I never kid about serious matters, Mr Pasternak. I really would like to know.'

'It seems as though I'm wasting my time after all,' he said. 'And probably wasting yours. Here's Ben with the beer. Let me put it on my expense account.'

'Don't bother,' Stafford said. 'Just tell me about Chipende. Abercrombie-Smith wants to know, too. He tried to twist my arm this afternoon.'

'Successfully?'

'He got a flea in his ear.'

'I don't want to get the same treatment, Mr Stafford,' said Pasternak. 'So just let's concentrate on the beer.'

Hardin came up with a tray which he placed on the table. They drank beer and chatted about inconsequential subjects such as the necessity for adjusting the carburettor of a car when driving from Mombasa at sea level to Eldoret which is at an altitude of nearly 10,000 feet. Hardin was baffled, as Stafford could see by the odd looks he received.

Pasternak drained his glass. 'I must be going,' he said, and stood up. 'Nice to have met you, Mr Stafford.'

'Come again,' said Stafford ironically.

He walked with Pasternak through the courtyard. Pasternak stopped by one of the aviaries and said, 'Have you noticed that there are no songbirds in Africa? They cheep and chirp but don't sing.' He paused. 'Do you mind if I give you some advice?'

Stafford smiled. 'Not at all. The great thing about advice is that you needn't follow it.'

'Watch Gunnarsson. I got a report on him this morning. That guy is bad news.'

'That's the most superfluous advice I've ever been given,' said Stafford chuckling. 'But thanks, anyway.' They shook hands and Pasternak went on his way.

Stafford turned to go to his room and met Hardin who said, 'Were you two talking in code or something? That meeting was supposed to be about Chip.'

'Ben, I know where I am now.' Stafford clapped him on the back. 'Bismarck was reputed to be silent in seven languages, but I'll bet his silence told more than his speeches. It was what Pasternak didn't say that interested me.'

'Nuts!' said Hardin disgustedly.

# TWENTY-ONE

Next morning after breakfast Stafford said to Hardin, 'Ben, I'm tired of this pussyfooting around; we're going to do some pushing.'

'Who are you going to push?'

'We'll start with Chip. Sergeant?'

Curtis stiffened. 'Yes, sir.'

'You've been liaising with Chip. I want him in my room by ten o'clock.'

'Yes, sir.' Curtis pushed back his chair from the breakfast table and left the room.

Hardin said, 'Why Chip? He's on our side.'

'Is he?' Stafford shook his head. 'Pete Chipende is on no side other than his own. What's more, he has Corliss hidden somewhere and that gives him leverage should he want to use it. You uncovered Corliss but Chip has got him and I don't like that one little bit.'

'You have a point,' acknowledged Hardin. 'But I don't think he'll push easy.'

'We'll see,' said Stafford.

At nine-thirty Curtis reported back. 'Chip will see the Colonel at ten as requested. He asked what the Colonel wanted. I said I wasn't in the Colonel's confidence.'

'You are now,' said Stafford, and told Curtis what he wanted him to do.

Hardin said, 'Max; are you sure about this?'

'Yes, Pasternak told me.'

'I didn't hear him.'

'He didn't say anything,' said Stafford, leaving Hardin baffled.

He spent the next half hour guarding his back.

He wrote a letter to Jack Ellis in London asking that the resources of Stafford Security Consultants be put to investigating thoroughly one Anthony Abercrombie-Smith from the time of his birth to the present day; his schools, clubs, work, friends if any, investments and anything else that might occur to him.

As he put the sheet of notepaper into an envelope Stafford reflected on Cardinal Richelieu who had said, 'If you give me six lines written by the most honest man, I will find something in them to hang him.' That surely would apply to Abercrombie-Smith should he have to be leaned on.

He had just sealed the envelope when Chip arrived. 'You want me?'

Stafford glanced at Hardin and Curtis. 'Yes. Where's Corliss?'

'He's quite safe,' assured Chip.

'No doubt. But where is he?'

Chip sat down. 'Don't worry, Max. If you want Corliss at any time he can be produced within half an hour.'

Stafford smiled gently. 'You keep telling me not to worry and that worries the hell out of me.' He apparently changed the subject. 'By the way, Abercrombie-Smith sends his regards.'

Chip paused in the act of lighting a cigarette, just a minute hesitation. He continued the action and blew out a plume of smoke. 'When did you see him?'

'We had lunch in the Muthaiga Club yesterday.'

'What did he want?'

'Ostensibly he wanted to know why I hadn't reported in to the High Commissioner's office after the kidnapping. He really wanted to know about you.'

Chip's eyebrows lifted. 'Did he? What did you tell him?'

'What could I tell him? I know nothing about you.'

Hardin stirred. 'True enough.'

Chip said, 'Do you know who he is?'

Stafford smiled. 'He'll be listed as a trade advisor or something like that, but really he's the MI6 man in Nairobi, serving the same function that Mike Pasternak does for the CIA.'

Chip sat on the bed. 'You've been getting around. Have you talked to him, too?'

'We had a chat over a beer. Nothing important.'

'For a stranger in the country you get to know the most interesting people.'

'I didn't go out of my way to find them,' said Stafford. 'I attracted them as wasps to a honeypot. We seem to be stirring up some interest, Chip. When can we expect the KGB?'

'It's not a matter for joking,' he said soberly. 'I don't know that I like this.'

'Oh, come *on*,' said Stafford. 'It's not that bad. They approached me openly enough. Hardin knew Pasternak years ago so Pasternak couldn't deny he's a CIA man. As for Abercrombie-Smith, he's a bad joke.'

'Don't be fooled by Abercrombie-Smith,' warned Chip. 'You may think all that "dear boy" stuff is funny but underneath he's as cold as ice. Max, why should you attract the attention of the foreign intelligence services of two countries?'

'I don't know that I have,' said Stafford. 'They didn't seem to be all that interested in me. I think *you* are attracting the attention. They both wanted to know what you are doing.'

Chip smiled sourly. 'And all I'm doing is what you tell me to do. Did you tell them that?'

'I forgot to,' said Stafford apologetically. 'It slipped my mind.'

'Very funny.'

'I'm noted for my sense of humour,' agreed Stafford. 'Here's another sample. Which branch of Kenyan Intelligence are you in, Chip?'

Chip stared at him. 'Are you joking?'

'Not two intelligence services, Chip – three. And maybe another to make four.'

Hardin said, 'You're losing me fast, Max.'

Chip said, 'He's already lost me.' He laughed.

Stafford ticked off points on his fingers. 'One; you could get us rooms at the drop of a hat in any hotel or game lodge I might suggest at the height of the tourist season. That takes pull. Two; you got the information on Brice from Zimbabwe too fast. Three; you could put Adam Muliro into Corliss's party as courier and driver at short notice. Four; in the Masai Mara you could whistle up support to take Corliss into custody at equally short notice. Five; you're too well aware of the identities of foreign agents operating in Kenya to be any ordinary man. Six; when I was talking to Pasternak he rattled off a string of names, all in intelligence, and your name and Nair's were included. I made a crack that we hold a secret service congress and Pasternak didn't disagree. Seven; we were interviewed and photographed by journalists but nothing appeared in the press, and that takes pull too. I'm not surprised you didn't want your picture in the paper – the well-known secret service agent is a contradiction in terms. Eight . . .' Stafford broke off. 'Chip, as you said in the Mara – a man can run out of fingers this way.'

'I didn't say I had no organization,' said Chip. 'The Kenya People's Union . . .' He stopped. 'But I'm not going to talk about that.'

'You'd better not,' said Stafford grimly. 'Because you'd be telling me a pack of lies. I'm saving the best until last. Eight;

when we entered the Masai Mara you didn't pay; a little bit of economy which was a dead giveaway. You showed some kind of identification which you probably have on you now. Sergeant!'

Before Chip knew it Curtis had stepped from behind and pinioned him and, although he struggled, he was no match for Curtis who had mastered many an obstreperous sailor in his day. 'Okay, Ben,' said Stafford. 'Search him.'

Hardin swiftly went through Chip's pockets, tossing the contents on to the bed where Stafford checked them. He searched Chip's wallet and found nothing, nor did he find any form of identification, except for a driving licence, among the scattering of items on the bed. 'Damn!' he said. 'Try again, Ben.'

Hardin found it in a hidden pocket in Chip's trousers – a plastic card which might have been mistaken for any credit card except that it had Chip's photograph on it. 'All right, Sergeant,' he said mildly. 'You can let him go.'

Curtis released Chip who brushed himself down, straightening his safari suit. Stafford clicked his finger nail against the card and said, 'A colonel, no less,' then added dryly, 'I probably have seniority. Military Intelligence?'

'Yes,' said Chip. 'You shouldn't have done that. I could get you tossed out of the country.'

'You could,' agreed Stafford. 'But you won't. You still need us.' He frowned. 'What puzzles me is why you were interested in us in the first place. Why did you latch on to us?'

Chip shrugged. 'There *was* a KPU connection. The address Curtis got in London was a KPU safe house. It wasn't as safe as all that because we'd infiltrated and we intercepted Curtis. Naturally we were most interested in why you, a one-time British intelligence agent, were investigating something with the help of the Kenya People's Union. At least you seemed to think you were working with the KPU. As time went on it became even more interesting. Complicated, too.'

Hardin snorted. 'Complicated, he says! Nothing makes any goddamn sense.'

'Tell me,' said Stafford, 'who were those two men you conjured up in the Masai Mara to take care of Corliss?'

Chip smiled slightly. 'I borrowed a couple of men from the Police Post on the Mara and put them into civilian clothes.'

'And where is Corliss now?'

'About two hundred yards from here,' said Chip calmly. 'In a cell in police headquarters on the corner of Harry Thuku Road. I told you he was quite safe.' He lit another cigarette. 'All right, Max; where do we go from here?'

'Where do you want to go?'

'I'm quite prepared to go on as before.'

'With me picking your chestnuts out of the fire,' said Stafford sarcastically. 'Not as before, Chip. There'll be no secrets and we share information. I'm tired of being blind-folded. You know, there's more to this than Gunnarsson trying to push in with a fake Hendrix. There's a hell of a lot at stake.'

'And what is at stake?' asked Chip.

Stafford stared at him. 'You're not stupid. Suppose you tell me.'

'About twenty-seven million pounds,' he said easily. 'The money Brice didn't declare from the Hendrykxx estate.'

'Balls!' snapped Stafford. 'It's not the money and you know it. But how did you get on to that?'

'Because you were inquisitive about the Ol Njorowa Foundation so was I,' said Chip. 'I rang the Kenya High Commission in London and had someone look at the will. Quite simple, really. But tell me more.'

Stafford said, 'I could kick myself. It's been staring me in the face ever since Ben, here, came back from investigating old Hendrykxx and said there was no Kenya connection. That really stumped me. But then I saw it.'

'Saw what?'

'The bloody South African connection,' said Stafford.

'Bull's eye!' said Chip softly. 'But tell me more.'

'Everywhere I've looked in the case the South African connection has popped up. Old Hendrykxx lived there. Dirk Hendriks is a South African. Mandeville, the English QC, is a right-winger who takes holidays in South Africa. He's there now. I think Farrar, the Jersey lawyer, is a cat's paw and I'll bet it was Mandeville who drew up the will.' Stafford drew a deep breath. 'Brice made a mistake in underestimating the size of the Hendrykxx estate – he was greedy. Are you sure he's in the clear, Chip? Because I'm betting he's another South African.'

For the next hour they hammered at the problem trying to fit the bits and pieces of their knowledge together without a great deal of success. At last Chip said, 'All right; we've got a consensus of opinion; we think that Dirk Hendriks might be a South African intelligence agent, and the same could apply to Brice. What we can't see is where Gunnarsson fits in and who has been trying to kill Corliss.'

'Not Corliss,' said Hardin suddenly. 'Hank Hendrix. Someone took a shot at Hank in Los Angeles and that was before Gunnarsson made the substitution.'

'So you think whoever is trying to kill him is unaware that Gunnarsson made the switch?' queried Stafford. 'It could be.' He looked at Chip. 'That business on the Tanzanian border seemed authentic in the sense that such kidnappings have happened before. What do you think, Chip? How easy is it to lay hands on Tanzanian uniforms and Kalashnikovs?'

Chip smiled thinly. 'Given enough money you can buy *anything* on the Tanzanian border. As for Kalashnikovs,

Kenya is surrounded by the damn things – Tanzania, Somalia, Ethiopia, Uganda. There'd be no problem there. You think the kidnapping was a put-up job to lay the blame on the Tanzanians?' He nodded thoughtfully. 'That could very well be.'

'Then Brice would have organized it,' said Hardin. 'Dirk Hendriks was in England at that time.'

'But all this is supposition,' said Stafford. 'We're not sure of a damned thing. What move will you make now, Chip? It's your country, after all.'

'We can't move openly against the Foundation,' said Chip. 'That would make waves. Newspaper stories and too much publicity. I'll have to take this to my superior officer.' He held up his hand. 'And don't ask who he is.'

Curtis stirred. 'Would the Colonel mind a suggestion?'

'Trot it out, Sergeant,' said Stafford. 'We could do with some good ideas.'

'Give Corliss back to Gunnarsson. Then stand back and see what happens.'

'You've got a nasty mind,' said Hardin. 'That would be like setting him up in a shooting gallery.'

'But we'd stand a chance of seeing who's doing the shooting.' Stafford looked at Chip. 'What do you think? He'd need a good cover story.'

'No cover story would stand up,' said Chip. 'We've had him too long. In any case he's a bad liar; we'd be blowing our own cover.' He thought for a moment. 'No; we've got to get someone inside Ol Njorowa to have a look around.'

'And maybe not find anything,' said Hardin morosely.

'I think there's something to be found.' Chip stubbed out a cigarette. 'Since you drew my attention to Ol Njorowa I've been looking at it carefully. The security precautions are far beyond what's needed for an agricultural college.'

'The Hunts explained that away,' said Stafford. 'Judy said things were being stolen; she said mostly small agricultural tools which didn't matter very much, but when it came to experimental seed it was different. And Alan Hunt came up with a story of a leopard.' He thought about the Hunts. 'Chip, the whole damned staff can't be in South African intelligence. The Hunts are white Kenyans and Dr Odhiambo is an unlikely agent.'

'There's probably just a cell,' agreed Chip. 'Coming back to Hendriks – how long has he lived in England?'

'I don't know,' said Stafford. 'He came into my life two years ago when he married Alix.'

'If he is in South African intelligence he'd be a sleeper planted in England and the Brits wouldn't like that. I think some liaison with London is indicated; and on a high level.' Chip stood up. 'And I'll see if I can get a man into Ol Njorowa.'

'Wait a minute,' said Stafford. 'Dirk knows I'm in Kenya – I told him I'd be taking a holiday here and that I might see him. I think I'll invite myself to Ol Njorowa. Besides, I have an invitation from the Hunts to go ballooning.'

'Going alone?' said Hardin.

'No, I'll take the Sergeant.' Stafford smiled at Curtis. 'How would you like to go ballooning, Sergeant?'

The expression of disgust on Curtis's face was an eloquent answer.

The air of tension in Brice's office was electric as Hendriks said, 'Why the hell didn't you tell me that Stafford was mixed up in this?'

'Because I didn't know,' snapped Brice.

'Christ, he'd been here! You'd met him, damn it!'

'So how would I know who he was?' Brice asked plaintively. 'You'd never mentioned him. All I knew then was that he was a friend of the Hunts; they were dining together at the Lake Naivasha Hotel with an Indian, a Sikh called Nair Singh.'

'Who is he?'

'A friend of Alan Hunt. They were at University together.'

'And then Stafford turned up in the Masai Mara chasing after Hendriks. Couldn't you put two and two together?'

'I didn't hear about it. It wasn't reported in the press. Who is Stafford, anyway?'

'A friend of Alix,' said Dirk broodingly. 'And he's sharp, Brice; damned sharp.' He told Brice exactly who and what Stafford was. 'It's not coincidence that he's popping up here and there at critical times and places. Did he mention me when he was here?'

'No.'

'Why not?' demanded Dirk. 'He knew I was coming.' His mind was busy with possible implications, then he said explosively, 'Good God!'

'What's the matter now?' said Brice tiredly.

'He's seen the bloody will, that's what's the matter,' said Dirk viciously. 'A man called Hardin came to see Alix when I was in South Africa.' He told Brice about it, then said, 'I never met Hardin. Alix said he'd gone back to the States.'

'And you never thought to tell me about this?' said Brice acidly.

'I was too busy thinking about what to do with Hendrix. But that doesn't matter now. What matters is that Stafford knows the Foundation has inherited a hell of a lot more than seven million.'

Brice shrugged. 'We've got a cover for that. I told you about it. I'll just have to report the full extent of our windfall. A pity, but there it is.' He stood up and began to pace. 'This is a damn funny tale you're telling me. Hardin, an American, tells your wife that you had an unknown cousin. Further, Hardin has taken the trouble to get a copy of the will. Why should he do that?'

'He said he was suspicious of the man he was working for, according to Alix. I told you I never met the man.'

'And who was he working for?'

'A private detective agency in New York.'

'The name?'

'I don't know. Alix didn't say.'

'Who employed the detective agency?'

'Farrar, the Jersey lawyer.'

Brice stopped his pacing and faced Hendriks. 'Now tell me something,' he said coldly. 'How did Farrar know there was an American heir?' Dirk was silent. Brice said, 'How many people knew there was an American heir?'

'Pretoria knew,' said Dirk. 'I knew, but I didn't go near Farrar. Mandeville knew, of course.' He stopped.

'Mandeville knew,' repeated Brice. 'The eminent Queen's Counsel knew. Do you know what happened, Hendriks? While Pretoria was chasing Hendrix in Los Angeles he was also being chased by American detectives employed by Farrar at the instigation of Mandeville. Pretoria nearly got Hendrix but he was rescued by Mandeville's crowd. What a balls-up! Hasn't anyone heard of co-ordination and liaison? We've been fighting ourselves, you damned fool.' His tone was cutting. 'What made Mandeville go off half-cocked like that?'

'He always said Pretoria was slow off the mark,' said Dirk. His voice was sullen.

'I think you'd better talk to Mandeville. Find out if our reasoning is correct. If it is, you tell him never to do anything without orders again.' He picked up the telephone. 'Find out the delay on London calls, please.' As he put down the telephone he said, 'And you might ask him for the name of the American detective agency.'

'Why? It doesn't matter any more.'

'How do you know that? Have you got crystal balls?' Brice slammed his hand on the desk with a noise like a pistol shot. 'There's been too much going wrong on this operation. I haven't been sweating blood here to see it torpedoed by inefficiency.' He sat down. 'Now tell me more about Stafford. How did he come to see the will?'

'Hardin had a copy and took it to Alix. I was in South Africa so Alix asked Stafford for his advice. Hardin showed him the will.'

'So he knows the extent of the will, he's been prowling about here, and he was in the Masai Mara when Hendrix was snatched. This man you met . . . er . . . ?' Brice snapped his fingers impatiently.

'Gunnarsson.'

'Gunnarsson told you that Stafford had followed the raiders. Is that it?'

'That's right. Afterwards Stafford told him that his party got lost in the bush.'

'Got lost, did they? I wonder.' Brice cocked a raised eyebrow at Hendriks. 'I lost two men and your cousin is still missing. We discussed it before but we didn't know about Stafford then.' He rubbed his jaw thoughtfully. 'I can see we'll have to find out more about Stafford.' The telephone rang and he picked it up. 'Oh!' He covered the mouthpiece. 'Someone for you. Who knows you're here?'

'No one,' said Hendriks. 'After I talked to Gunnarsson I went to the American Embassy but I told no one where I was going after that.'

'Someone knows.' Brice held out the telephone. 'You'd better find out who it is.'

Hendriks took it. 'Dirk Hendriks speaking.'

'Hello, Dirk; so I've tracked you down at last,' said Stafford, and Hendriks nearly dropped the phone. 'Max here. I thought I'd phone Ol Njorowa on the off chance you'd be there. How are you doing?'

'Fine,' said Dirk. He put his hand over the mouthpiece and said in a low voice, 'It's Stafford.'

'Have you been ballooning yet?' asked Stafford.

'What?' said Dirk stupidly.

'Ballooning with the Hunts. They've extended an invitation for me to go ballooning with them tomorrow. I've just
been talking to Alan. I'll be staying at the Lake Naivasha
Hotel. We must have dinner.'

'Yes, we must,' said Dirk mechanically. 'Hang on a
minute.' Again he covered the mouthpiece. 'He's coming
here. Some crazy talk about ballooning with someone called
Hunt. He'll be at the hotel.'

Brice began to smile. 'Give me the phone.' He took it,
and said, 'Hello, Mr Stafford; Charles Brice here. I hear Alan
Hunt is taking you up tomorrow. Now, there's no question
of your staying at the hotel, we can put you up here. Apart
from anything else it will be more convenient for Alan. Yes,
I insist. What time shall we expect you? All right, we'll see
you then.'

His smile broadened as he cradled the telephone. 'I'd just
as soon have him here where I can keep an eye on him.
"Walk into my parlour," said the spider to the fly.'

# TWENTY-TWO

Gunnarsson lay on the bed in his room at the New Stanley reading a paperback novel in which he had no interest. Several times he had lost the drift of the plot and had to turn back several pages and he was bored and irritable. True, being on his back helped his feet which were still sore, and the doctor had recommended bed rest, but what he was really doing was waiting for a telephone call from London.

The telephone rang and he reached for it. 'Gunnarsson.'

'Mr Gunnarsson, this is George Barbour of Peacemore, Willis and Franks in London. I understand that you want to know the present location of Max Stafford of Stafford Security Consultants.'

'Yeah.'

'To the best of our knowledge Mr Stafford is now in Kenya on holiday. He left London on the eighteenth.'

So the bastard had been waiting in Nairobi, thought Gunnarsson. He said, 'You didn't tip off Stafford Security, I hope.'

Barbour was hurt. 'We know how to make discreet enquiries, Mr Gunnarsson.'

'Okay. Well, thanks.'

He rang off and pulled the telephone directory towards him and began to ring the Nairobi hotels. He struck lucky on his fifth try which was the Norfolk. Yes, Mr Stafford was staying at the Norfolk. No, he was not in the hotel at the moment. It was believed that Mr Stafford was away on safari, although he had retained his room. No, the whereabouts of Mr Stafford were not known. Did the gentleman wish to leave a message?

Gunnarsson did not wish to leave a message so he hung up abruptly and lay back on the bed and tried to sort out his thoughts. He had never met Stafford but had heard much of him from Peacemore, Willis and Franks. There was no Peacemore, nor Willis, nor Franks; the three-barrelled name having been invented by Gunnarsson as having a cosy ring to it suitable for the City of London. The outfit was ramrodded by Terence Ferney who had been vitriolic on the subject of Stafford Security Consultants from time to time. 'Stafford's halo is getting tight the way his head is swelling,' he once said. 'But he's a good operator, there's no doubt about that. He keeps his security tight and he's recruited good men – Jack Ellis for one.'

Gunnarsson had seen Ferney in London and Ferney had been crowing about how they had got past Stafford Security's guard at Electronomics during the Electronomics takeover and Gunnarsson had cut him short curtly. 'You've won one and lost five. Your record's not good, Terry. Get on the ball.'

So it was Stafford who had followed him in the Masai Mara. What sort of coincidence was that? The boss of one of America's biggest private security organizations is kidnapped and the boss of one of Europe's largest security organizations is conveniently at hand. Nuts!

But how had Stafford got on to him? And had he anything to do with the disappearance of Corliss? Did he know about Corliss – that he was a ringer for Hank Hendrix? And why was he horning in anyway? Gunnarsson picked up the telephone again and dialled. 'I'd like to put in a call to New York.'

* * *

Hardin was also lying down, but on a lounger by the swimming pool at the Norfolk Hotel and acquiring a tan. He lay on his stomach, intently watching the bubbles rise in a glass of Premium beer, and reflected that he could not be said to be earning his pay. Stafford and Curtis had gone to Ol Njorowa, Chip and his myrmidons were keeping an eye on Gunnarsson, and there was nothing left for Hardin to do. He felt dissatisfied and vaguely guilty.

He lay there for an hour soaking in the sun, then swam ten lengths of the pool before rubbing himself down and changing into street clothes in the change room. He walked through the bird-noisy courtyard towards the rear entrance of the hotel lobby but, as he entered the lobby, he did a smart about turn and retreated into the courtyard. Gunnarsson was at the reception desk talking to the clerk.

He was about to return to his room when Nair Singh walked into the courtyard from the lobby, his eyes half closed protectively against the sudden blast of sunlight. As he put on sunglasses Hardin tapped him on the shoulder. 'Damn it!' he said. 'I nearly walked straight into Gunnarsson. I should have had warning.'

'I phoned your room on the house phone,' said Nair. 'You weren't there.'

'I was at the pool. What the hell is Gunnarsson doing here?'

'I'd say he's trying to find Stafford,' said Nair. 'He knows who Stafford is. He took the trouble to ring London to establish that the Stafford he met at Keekorok is the same Stafford of Stafford Security Consultants.'

'How do you know that?'

'We put a tap on his phone.' Nair smiled 'Standard procedure. He rang New York an hour ago requesting reinforcements. He's bringing in three men.'

'Who?' demanded Hardin. 'Did he give names?'

Nair nodded. 'Walters, Gottschalk and Rudinsky.'

'Gottschalk I don't know,' said Hardin. 'But Walters is a pretty good man and Rudinsky has worked in Africa before. He's an ex-Company man, too. The pace is hotting up. When are they expected?'

'The day after tomorrow, on the morning flight. Plenty of time to decide what to do. I'll talk it over with Chip; he might have them barred as undesirable aliens.'

Hardin jerked his head towards the lobby. 'You'd better get on with the job. Gunnarsson might give you the slip.'

'He won't. I have three men out there and there's a radio transmitter in the car. He's still at the reception desk.' Nair regarded Hardin blandly. 'I have a radio in my turban; they miniaturize them these days.'

'Neat,' said Hardin admiringly and looked at the turban with interest. The folds of cloth over Nair's ears even concealed the earphone he must be wearing.

Nair held up his hand for silence and cocked his head on one side. 'He's leaving now – getting into a taxi. We'll see him on his way before we check at the reception desk.'

'I wonder how Gunnarsson got on to Stafford,' mused Hardin.

'Could have been through Dirk Hendriks,' said Nair. 'It doesn't really matter. He's out of Harry Thuku Road now. Let's find out what he wanted.'

They went into the lobby to interrogate the man at the desk. Nair said, 'The man who was here just now . . .'

'Mr Andrews? The American?'

'Yeah,' said Hardin. 'Mr Andrews. Was he looking for someone?'

'He wanted to see Mr Stafford. He's a friend of yours, isn't he? I've seen you together.'

Hardin nodded. 'What did you tell Andrews?'

'I told him where to find Mr Stafford.' The clerk looked at the expression on Hardin's face nervously. 'Did I do wrong?'

'I guess not,' said Hardin, thinking otherwise. 'Where did you tell him to go?'

'Ol Njorowa College. Mr Stafford mentioned it before he left. He said he'd be away for a couple of days but wanted to keep his room here.'

Hardin looked at Nair blankly. 'Thanks,' he said. As they moved away he said, 'That was pretty foolish of Max.'

'He wasn't to know Gunnarsson would come looking for him.' Nair stopped with an intent look on his face as he listened to his inner voice. He said, 'Gunnarsson is getting out of his taxi in Muindi Mbingu Street.' He paused. 'He's going into the United Touring Company office. The UTC is a car hire firm among other things.'

There was no discussion. 'I'll pack a bag,' said Hardin. 'Ready in fifteen minutes.' As he walked out of the lobby he saw Nair already reaching for a telephone.

Again Stafford suffered the ritual of inspection before the gates of Ol Njorowa College opened for him. He drove to the Administration Block, parked the Nissan, and went inside where he gave his name to the black Kenyan behind the counter in the hall. He looked around and saw what he had not noticed on his first visit. Chip was right; security was tighter than one would expect in such an innocent organization.

No one could penetrate anywhere into the building without passing the wicket gate, and he was willing to bet that every time it opened it would send out a signal; at least it would if he had been responsible for security. He looked around with a keen professional eye and detected a soft gleam of glass high in a corner of the hall where two walls and a ceiling met, and guessed it was the wide-angle lens of a TV camera. It was unnoticeable and only to be detected by someone actively looking for it. He wondered where they kept the monitor screen.

The man behind the counter put down the telephone. 'Mr Hendriks will be with you in a moment. Please take a seat.'

Stafford sat on a comfortable settee, picked up a magazine from the low table in front of him, and flipped through the pages. It was a scientific journal devoted to tropical crop production and of no particular interest. Presently Hendriks appeared and came through the wicket, his arm outstretched. 'Max! Good to see you.'

Stafford doubted that statement but he got up and they shook hands. 'Nice of Brice to have me here,' he said. 'I could just as easily have stayed at the hotel. It's not far down the road.'

'Charles wouldn't hear of it,' said Hendriks. 'As soon as he knew we were friends. Why didn't you mention it when you were here last?'

'I didn't have all that much time with Brice, and I was with another party – the Hunts, Alan and Judy. Do you know them?'

'No; but I haven't been here all that long. I've just got back from England.'

'And how are Alix and young Max?' asked Stafford politely.

'Motherhood agrees with her,' said Hendriks, and took Stafford's arm. 'Come and see Charles.' He led Stafford through the wicket gate and along a corridor where he opened a door. 'Max is here,' he said.

Brice greeted Stafford genially. 'So you've come to be an intrepid birdman with Alan Hunt. Rather you than me; I don't trust that contraption – it looks much too flimsy.' He waved Stafford to a chair.

As he sat down Hendriks said, 'Bad news about cousin Henry. You've heard, of course?'

Stafford was ready for that one and had already formulated his reply. 'More than heard,' he said. 'I was there. Not with the kidnapped party but with a group who charged off somewhat blunderingly to the rescue. I didn't know that Henry Hendrix was involved, though, and when we got back to Keekorok I got a shock when I heard the name. In fact, at first I thought it might have been you.'

Brice said, 'Odd that your adventure wasn't reported in the press.'

Stafford shrugged. 'Bloody bad journalism. Have there been any developments?'

'Nothing,' said Dirk. 'I've been to the police and the American Embassy but no one seems to know anything or, if they do, they aren't saying.'

'It hasn't done diplomatic relations between Kenya and Tanzania any good,' remarked Brice. 'Not that they were so sparkling in the first place.' He changed the subject. 'I suspect you'll want to clean up. We have some bedrooms upstairs for VIPs – the Trustees visit us from time to time and sometimes the odd government official. You can have one of those while you're here.'

'It's very good of you.'

'No problem at all. You know, we're a rather ingrown community here – something like a monastery but for the few women among us like Judy Hunt. It will do us good to see a new face and have fresh conversation and ideas. Dirk will show you to your room and then . . . er . . . hunt up Hunt, if you'll pardon the phrase.'

'Right,' said Dirk. 'I'll take you up. You have the room next to mine.'

'And you'll join us for dinner,' said Brice.

As they went upstairs Stafford said to Hendriks, 'You're the real VIP here, of course. What do you think of the place?'

'I haven't seen much of it yet. I've been too busy trying to get some action on my cousin. But what I've seen has impressed me. Here's your room.'

The 'monks' in Brice's monastery lived well, thought Stafford as he surveyed the bedroom which would not have disgraced a three-star hotel. Dirk indicated a door. 'That's the bathroom. If you'll give me your car keys I'll have someone bring up your bags.'

'It's not locked.'

'Right. The staff room is at the far end of the corridor. I'll meet you there in fifteen minutes with Hunt. We'll have a drink together.'

'I know where the staff room is.'

'Oh, yes,' said Dirk. 'I'd forgotten you've been here before.'

He departed and Stafford did not doubt that the Nissan would be thoroughly searched, as would his suitcase. He did not mind; there was nothing unusual to be found. He inspected the room with an experienced eye, looking not for comfort but for bugs, the electronic kind. He had no doubt that the room would be bugged; Brice would be interested in the private conversations of the Trustees and government officials.

The table lamp was clean as was the reading lamp over the bed. There were no strange objects attached beneath the coffee table, the dressing table or the bed. He looked at the telephone doubtfully. It would probably be tapped but that did not matter; any conversation he used it for would definitely be innocuous. However, it might have been gimmicked in another way. He unscrewed the mouthpiece and shook out the carbon button to inspect it. It looked all right so he put it back and replaced the mouthpiece. It had taken him fifteen seconds.

As he put down the telephone there was a knock at the door and the Kenyan who had been at the counter in the hall downstairs came in bearing Stafford's suitcase. He put it next to the dressing table, and said, 'Mr Hunt is in the staff room, sah.'

'Thank you. Tell him I'll be along in a few minutes.'
Stafford took his toilet kit and went into the bathroom.
When he came out he looked at the picture on the wall
which appeared conventional enough. It was a reproduction of a painting of an elephant by David Shepherd, typical
of those to be found in the curio shops in Nairobi. He examined it more closely paying attention, not to the picture
itself, but to the frame which was of unpainted white wood
and which seemed unusually thick. Near the bottom of the
frame he found a small knot hole and he smiled.

From his jacket pocket he took a pen torch and examined
the hole more carefully. By angling the light and moving it
rhythmically he caught a repeated metallic wink from the
bottom of the hole – the diaphragm of a miniature button
microphone. As he put away the torch he felt relieved. If he
had not found a bug he would have been worried because
so far all his suspicions about Hendriks and Brice had been
built on a tenuous chain of suppositions. But this was the
clincher; no innocent organization would bug its own
rooms.

Hidden in the thickness of the picture frame would be a
small transmitter and the batteries to power it, and probably somewhere in Ol Njorowa would be a receiver coupled
to a sound-actuated tape recorder. It would be simple to put
the bug out of order by the simple expedient of inserting a
needle into the hole and ruining the microphone but that
would not do because it would be a dead giveaway. Better
to leave it alone and say nothing of consequence in the
room or, indeed, anywhere in Ol Njorowa.

Before leaving the room he took a small pair of field
glasses from his suitcase and went to the window. In the
distance he could see a section of the chain-link fence which
indicated the perimeter of the college. He swept it, the glasses
to his eyes, and estimated it to be ten feet high. At the top
were three strands of barbed wire. Somewhere on the other

side Curtis was making an examination of the fence from the outside, and his briefing had been to make a complete reconnaissance of the perimeter. Stafford put the field glasses away and walked to the staff room with a light heart.

In Brice's office Dirk Hendriks put down the telephone. He had found it difficult to contact Mandeville in London; the lawyer had been engaged in court and Hendriks had requested a return call with some urgency. Now he had just finished talking to Mandeville and the news he got had knocked the wind out of him.

Brice said, 'What's the matter? What did Mandeville say?'

'The New York agency was Gunnarsson Associates,' said Dirk hollowly.

'*What*?' Brice sat open-mouthed. 'You mean the man you talked with in Nairobi was the man who found Henry Hendrix in the States?'

'It would seem so.' Hendriks stood up. 'There can't be many Gunnarssons around and the Gunnarsson in Nairobi is an American.'

'And he was in the tour group with your cousin. They were travelling together, obviously. Now, why should a private detective still stick around after he's delivered the goods? And to the extent of coming to Kenya at that. And why should Henry Hendrix let him?'

'Perhaps he thought he needed a bodyguard after inheriting all that money.'

'Unlikely.' Brice drummed his finger on the desk.

'Oh, I don't know,' Hendriks objected. 'He'd been shot in Los Angeles and there was the business of the car in Cornwall. He might have become suspicious.'

'I suppose so,' Brice said tiredly. 'Another suggestion is that Gunnarsson and Stafford are tied together.' He thought for a moment. 'Whichever way it is Gunnarsson needs watching. We must find out who he sees, and particularly if he gets in touch with Stafford.'

'Do I go back to Nairobi?' asked Dirk.

'No, you stay here and keep an eye on Stafford. I'll send Patterson.' Brice stood up. 'I'll go to the radar office and send him now. You say Gunnarsson is staying at the New Stanley?'

Dirk nodded. Brice was almost out of the room when Dirk said suddenly, 'Wait a minute. I've just remembered something.' Brice turned back and raised an eyebrow, and Dirk said, 'When I was talking to Gunnarsson in the Thorn Tree I had the odd impression I'd seen him before but I couldn't place him. I can now.'

'Where?'

'Remember when I came to Kenya for the first time with Henry and Farrar? We stayed at the Lake Naivasha Hotel. You joined us there and we had dinner together.'

'Well?'

'Gunnarsson was dining at a corner table alone.'

# TWENTY-THREE

Dirk Hendriks walked into the staff room and found Stafford in conversation with Alan Hunt who was saying, 'I'm going up tomorrow anyway. Jim Odhiambo wants some photographs of his experimental plots. The balloon is useful for that kind of thing.'

Stafford beckoned to Dirk and said, 'Alan, I don't think you've met Dirk Hendriks, the grandson of the benefactor of the Ol Njorowa Foundation. Alan Hunt.'

The two men shook hands and Hunt said, 'Your grandfather's largesse has come just at the right time for me. I want a fraction of that seven million quid for a gas chromatograph.'

Dirk laughed. 'I wouldn't know what that is.'

'Seven million!' said Stafford in simulated surprise. 'It's more than that, surely.'

'Per annum,' said Dirk easily. 'That's Charles Brice's estimate of the annual return when the capital is invested. I think he's too optimistic. It's before tax, of course, but he's having talks with the government with a view to getting it tax free. The Foundation is a non-profit organization, after all.'

All very specious. 'I must have misunderstood Brice,' Stafford said.

Hunt whistled. 'I certainly misunderstood him, and so did the pressmen. How much did your grandfather leave us?'

'At the time of his death it would have been about thirty-four million, but probate and proving the will has taken some time during which the original sum has been earning more cash. Say about thirty-seven million.'

Hunt gave a sharp crack of laughter. 'Now I *know* I'll get my gas chromatograph. Let's drink to it.'

He ordered a round of drinks and then Stafford said curiously, 'You said you are taking photographs for Dr Odhiambo. I don't see the point. I mean he can see the crops on the ground, can't he?'

'Ah,' said Hunt. 'But this is quicker. We use infra-red film to shoot his experimental plots. Plants that are ailing or sick show up very well on infra-red if you know what to look for. It saves Jim many a weary mile of walking.'

'The wonders of science,' said Hendriks.

'They use the same system in satellites,' said Hunt. 'But they can cover greater areas than I can.'

Stafford sampled his beer. 'Talking about satellites, who owns the satellite your animal movement people use? They couldn't have put it up themselves.'

Hunt laughed. 'Not likely. It's an American job. The migration study boys asked to put their scientific package into it. It's not very big and it takes very little power so the Yanks didn't mind. But the satellite does a lot more than monitor the movement of wildebeest.' He pointed to the ceiling. 'It sits up there, 22,000 miles high, and watches the clouds over most of Africa and the Indian Ocean; a long term study of the monsoons.'

'A geo-stationary orbit,' said Stafford.

'That's right. It's on the Equator. Here we're about one degree south. It's fairly steady, too; there's a bit of liberation but not enough to worry about.'

'You've lost me,' said Hendriks. 'I understand about one word in three.' He shook his head and said wryly, 'My grandfather wanted me to work here part of the year but

I don't see what I can do. I haven't had the right training.
I was in liberal arts at university.'

'No doubt Brice will have you working with him on the
administrative side,' observed Hunt, and drank some beer.

No doubt he would, thought Stafford, and said aloud,
'Which university, Dirk?'

'Potch. That's Potchefstroom in the Transvaal.'

Stafford filed that information away in his mind; it would
be a useful benchmark if Hendriks had to be investigated in
depth at a later date.

Hunt said, 'Max, if you're coming with us tomorrow it'll
be early – before breakfast. The air is more stable in the
early morning. I'll give you a ring at six-thirty.' Stafford
nodded and Hunt looked at Dirk. 'Would you like to come?
There's room for one more.'

Hendriks shook his head. 'Brice wants to see me early
tomorrow morning. Some other time, perhaps.'

Stafford was relieved; he had his own reasons for wanting to overfly Ol Njorowa and he did not want Hendriks
watching him when it happened. He did not think the
Hunts were mixed up in any undercover activity at the
College. They were Kenya born and it was unlikely they
would have been suborned by South African intelligence.
He thought they were part of the innocent protective camouflage behind which Brice hid, like most of the scientific staff.
He had his own ideas about where the worm in this rosy
apple lay.

Hunt announced he had work to do, finished his beer
and went off. Stafford and Hendriks continued to chat, a
curious conversation in which both probed but neither
wanted to give anything away. A duel with words ending at
honours even.

As Gunnarsson drove to Naivasha he began to put
the pieces together and the conclusion he arrived at was

frightening. He was a tough-minded man and did not scare easily but now he was worried because the package he had put together in New York was coming apart; the string unravelling, the cover torn and, worse, the contents missing.

Corliss was missing, damn him!

He had been so careful in New York. After Hendrix had been delivered by Hardin no one had seen him because Gunnarsson had personally smuggled him out of the building and to a hideaway in Connecticut. The only person to have laid eyes on Hendrix, apart from Hardin, had been his secretary in the outer office and she did not know who he was because the name had not been mentioned. And he had successfully got rid of Hardin; the damn fool needled so easily and had blown his top, which made his dismissal a perfectly natural reaction.

Gunnarsson tapped his fingers on the wheel of the car. Still, it was strange that when he wanted to find Hardin again he had vanished. Probably he had crawled into some hole to lick his wounds. Gunnarsson shrugged and dismissed Hardin from his mind. The guy was a has-been and of no consequence in the immediate problem he faced.

But Hardin's report had been interesting and valuable. Here was Henry Hendrix, a hippy drop-out with no folks, and no one in the world would give a damn whether he lived or died because no one knew the guy existed. No one except that freaky commune in Los Angeles and, at first, he had discounted Biggie and his crowd.

And so, with Hendrix held isolated, he had the material for the perfect scam, and the hit was going to be big – no less than six million bucks. Hendrix had gone along with everything, talking freely under the impression that his interrogation was for the benefit of a British lawyer and quite unaware of the quietly revolving spools of the tape recorder memorizing every word.

And then there was Corliss. Corliss had been easy because he was weak and bent under pressure. He had been uncovered in a routine check by Gunnarsson Associates and when Gunnarsson had faced him and shown him the options he had folded fast. No one in the organization wondered when he quit his job without being prosecuted because everyone knew computer frauds were hushed up. No bank liked to broadcast that it had been ripped off by a computer artist because it was bad for business. And so Corliss had also been isolated but Gunnarsson made sure that Corliss and Hendrix never met.

Then Corliss was groomed to take the part of Hendrix. It was lucky that Corliss was not unlike Hendrix physically – they were both blond and of about the same age – and the passport was easy to fix. After that something had to be done about Hendrix and Gunnarsson saw to it personally. It was a pity but it was necessary and Hendrix now resided encased in a block of concrete at the bottom of Long Island Sound.

Gunnarsson had second thoughts about Biggie and the commune. The sudden emergence of an overnight multi-millionaire called Hendrix could attract the attention of the media. It might make the papers on the West Coast – it could even be on TV with pictures – something which Biggie might see. So something had to be done about *that* and, again, Gunnarsson saw to it personally.

He smiled grimly as he reflected that Hardin had told him how to do it in his report. If a pottery kiln had blown up once it could blow up again, this time with more serious consequences. Exit Biggie and the commune. It was then that he began looking for Hardin seriously and found that he was living in a fleabag in the Bronx, and another rooming house fire in the Bronx passed unnoticed. It did not even rate a paragraph on the bottom of page zilch. That worried Gunnarsson because he was not certain he had taken out Hardin. Discreet enquiries revealed that the bodies in the rooming house were unidentifiable and a further search for Hardin produced nothing so he relaxed.

After that everything had gone perfectly. Corliss had been accepted in London and that old fool, Farrar, had even anted up two hundred thousand bucks as an earnest of what was to come. That was only a sweetener of course; a morsel before the main meal. Then they came to Kenya and the whole goddamn scheme had fallen apart when Corliss was snatched in Tanzania. What griped Gunnarsson was that he did not know whether Corliss was alive or dead.

'Jesus!' he said aloud in the privacy of the car. 'If he's alive I could be cooked.'

He sorted out the possibilities. If Corliss was dead then goodbye to six million dollars; he would cut his losses and return to the States. If Corliss was alive there were two alternatives – either he stayed as Hendrix or he spilled his guts. If he had the nerve to stay as Hendrix then nothing would change and everything was fine. But if he talked and revealed that he was Corliss then that meant instant trouble. Everybody and his uncle would be asking what had happened to the real Hendrix. Maybe he could get out of it by fast talking – he could blame the whole schmeer on the absent Hardin. He could swear he had accepted Corliss as the real McCoy on the word of Hardin. Maybe. That would depend on exactly how wide Corliss opened his fat mouth.

But the stakes were goddamn high – six million dollars or his neck. Gunnarsson thumped the driving wheel in frustration and the car swerved slightly. Corliss! Where was the stupid son of a bitch?

And now someone else was butting in – Max Stafford! It was inconceivable that Stafford could be there by chance; there was no connection at all. So Stafford had caught on to something. But how? He thought back to the time when he and Corliss were in London, reviewing what they had done, and could not find any flaw. So what in hell was Stafford doing and how much did he know? Well, that was the purpose of this trip to Naivasha – to find out. But carefully. And for the moment he was short of troops – he needed legmen to nose around – but a couple of days would cure that problem.

He came off the tortuous road of the escarpment and drove along the straight and pot-holed road that led to Naivasha, and he was unaware of the Kenatco Mercedes taxi which kept a level distance of four hundred yards behind him. There was no reason why he should be aware of it because there were two fuel tankers and a beer truck between them.

As he turned off the main road and bumped across the railway track to join the road which led alongside the lake he thought fleetingly of Hardin's report – the bit where it said Hendrix had been shot in Los Angeles. 'Now, what the hell?' he muttered. Had it started – whatever 'it' was – as early as that? What had Hardin said? A couple of guys with un-American accents – possibly Krauts – looking for Hendrix. And then he had been shot. It would bear thinking about.

He turned into the grounds of the Lake Naivasha Hotel, parked and locked his car, and went to the desk to register. As he signed in he said, 'Which is Mr Stafford's room?'

'Stafford, sir? I don't think . . .' After a moment the manager said, 'We have no Stafford here at the moment, sir. I do recall a Mr Stafford who stayed here some little time ago.'

'I see,' said Gunnarsson thoughtfully. Where was the guy?

'I'll send someone to take your bags to your room, sir.'

'I'll unlock the car.' Gunnarsson turned away, brushing shoulders with an Indian as he walked towards the parking lot, and was again unaware that Nair Singh turned to stare after him. He strode towards his car followed by a hotel servant and unlocked it. As his bags were taken out he looked about him and his attention was caught by the taxi some little distance away. His eyes narrowed and he walked towards it.

He stopped about five yards away and surveyed it. One radio antenna was okay – a guy might need music while he travelled. Two radio antennas? Well, maybe; being a taxi it might be on a radio network. But *three* antennas? He knew enough about his own work to know what that meant. He tried proving it by approaching from the driver's side and peering at the dashboard, and he saw an instrument which was definitely not standard – a signal strength meter.

Slowly he withdrew and returned to his own car where he dropped on his haunches and looked under the rear. He passed his hand under the bumper and found something small which shifted slightly under the pressure of his fingers. He wrenched it loose and withdrew it to find he was holding a small anonymous-looking grey metal box from which two stiff wires protruded. He tested it on the bumper and it adhered with a click as the magnet on the bottom caught hold.

Gunnarsson straightened, his lips compressed, and looked across at the taxi. Someone had been following him; someone who so badly did not want to lose him that a radio beeper had been planted on his car to make the task of trailing easier. He walked briskly back to the hotel and went to the desk. 'That taxi back there,' he said. 'Whose is it?'

'A taxi, sir?'

'Yeah, a Mercedes,' Gunnarsson said irritably. 'Owned by Kenatco – least that's what the sign says.'

'It could have been the Indian gentleman who was just here,' said the manager. 'He went that way.'

Gunnarsson ran back quickly but, by the time he came within sight the taxi was taking off at speed in a cloud of dust. He stood there, tossing the radio bug in his hand, then he dropped it on to the ground and crushed it under his heel. Somebody was playing games and he did not know who. It was something to think about before proceeding too precipitately so he went to his room and lay on the bed before ringing the Kenatco Taxi Company in Nairobi, giving the registration number.

As he suspected, the Kenatco people denied all knowledge of it.

# TWENTY-FOUR

Stafford was wakened at six-thirty next morning by the ringing of the telephone next to his bed. At first he was disorientated but put together the fragments of himself when he heard Hunt say, 'We leave in half an hour, Max. I'll meet you in the hall.'

Half an hour later Hunt said, 'Don't worry; you'll get your breakfast.' They got into a Land-Rover and Hunt drove out of the College grounds and up a winding unsurfaced road which ran next to the chain-link fence. 'The wind is perfect,' he said. 'I think I'll be able to take you through Hell's Gate. Have you ever been up in a balloon before?'

'No, I haven't.' Stafford did not mention that the suggestion that he go through Hell's Gate on a first flight made him feel decidedly queasy.

Hunt swung off the road and the Land-Rover bumped across open bush country. 'Here we are.'

Stafford got out of the Land-Rover stiffly and saw Judy about fifty yards away, standing next to what appeared to be a laundry basket. 'Is she coming, too?'

'Yes; she operates the camera.'

They walked over to her, and she said, 'Hi! Had breakfast?' Stafford shook his head. 'Good! Breakfast is better after a flight.'

He inspected the 'laundry basket' and found it was the thing they stood in while being wafted through the air. Judy was right; it was indubitably better to have breakfast *after* the flight. Stafford was not scared of many things but he did have a fear of heights. He was prepared to climb a cliff but nothing would ever get him close to the edge while walking at the top. Not an unusual phobia. He wondered how he was going to acquit himself during the next couple of hours.

The edge of the basket was padded with suede, and from each corner rose a pillar, the pillars supporting a complicated contraption of stainless steel piping in two coils which was, Stafford supposed, the burner which heated the air. Beyond the basket the multi-coloured balloon envelope was laid out on the ground. It was bigger than he expected and looked flimsy. Four black Kenyans were stretching it out and straightening wire ropes.

He turned to Hunt. 'It's bigger than I expected.' He didn't mention the flimsiness.

'She's a Cameron N-84. That means she's 84,000 cubic feet in volume. When she's inflated the height from the floor of the basket to the crown of the balloon is over 60 feet.'

'What's the fabric?'

'Close weave nylon treated with polyurethane to close the pores. This envelope is nearly new; the old one became too porous and I was losing air and efficiency. It's the ultra-violet that does it, of course. Even though the fabric is specially treated the sun gets it in the end. A balloon doesn't last nearly as long here as it would in England. I'll give the boys a hand.'

Hunt walked forward and began checking rigging. Stafford turned to see Judy working on the basket. She was clamping a big plate camera on to the side. 'Can I help?'

She smiled. 'I've just finished. We'll be leaving in ten minutes.'

'So soon?' He looked at the flaccid nylon envelope and wondered how.

Hunt came back. 'All right; let's get this thing into the air. Lucas, get the fan. Chuma, you're for the crown rope. You others start flapping.' He turned to Stafford. 'Max, you help us get the basket on its side, slow and easy.'

They tipped the basket over so that the burners pointed to the balloon. Two Kenyans were flapping the nylon, driving air into the envelope. It billowed enormously in slow waves and visibly expanded. Lucas came behind with the fan; it was like an over-sized electric fan but driven by a small Honda petrol engine. The engine sputtered and then caught with a roar, driving air into the balloon.

Hunt got into the basket and crouched behind the burners. He lit the pilot flames and then tilted the burners towards the balloon. 'All right, Lucas,' he said, raising his voice above the noise of the fan. 'Join Chuma on the crown rope. Judy and Max to the basket.'

Stafford and Judy stood on each side of the basket. He did not know what to do but was prepared to follow her lead. The balloon was filling rapidly and suddenly there was a growling, deep-throated roar and a blue flame, six feet long and nearly a foot in diameter, shot into the open throat of the balloon. It took Stafford by surprise and he started, then looked towards Judy. She was laughing so he grinned back weakly.

The roar went on and on, and the balloon expanded like a blossoming flower caught in time-lapse photography. Hunt switched off the flame, and one of the Kenyans turned off the fan and there was blessed silence. Hunt looked up as the balloon rose above them. 'All hands to the basket,' he said, and sent another burst of flame into the balloon.

The two Kenyans joined Stafford and Judy as the basket began to stir like a live thing. Slowly it began to tilt upright as the flame poured heat into the envelope. Hunt switched

off again, and shouted, 'Let go the crown rope.'
Immediately the basket became upright as the balloon
surged above them. 'All hands on,' said Hunt, and four pairs
of black hands clamped on the padded edges. 'Max, get in.'

There was a sort of footstep in the wickerwork so
Stafford put his foot in it and swung his other leg inboard.
Hunt caught his arm and helped him regain balance. Judy
climbed in from the other side. She immediately began to
turn a valve on one of the cylinders of which there were
four, one in each corner of the basket. Hunt was giving
short blasts of flame, a few seconds at a time. It seemed to
Stafford as though he was doing some kind of fine tuning.
Once he said, 'Hands off,' and then, almost immediately,
'Hands on.'

Lucas was rolling a cylinder along the ground towards
the basket. Judy unstrapped the cylinder she had been
working on and exchanged it for the one brought by Lucas.
Then she tapped her brother on the shoulder. 'Okay to go.'

He released a sustained flame, then said 'Hands off.' For
a moment nothing apparently happened and then Stafford
became aware that they were airborne. The ground was
dropping away as they rose in complete silence, and the
slight breeze he had felt on the ground had disappeared.

Hunt said, 'The wind is just right. We'll pass over Jim's
vegetable patch, take our pictures, and we're set for Hell's
Gate. But we'll get some height for the photographs.' The
burner roared and Stafford felt heat on his face as he looked
up into the vast, empty interior of the envelope into which
the flame was disappearing. When he looked down again
the ground was receding even faster and the landscape was
opening out.

Hunt pointed. 'The College. We'll pass over it. You ready,
Judy?'

She bent down to look through a viewfinder. 'Everything
okay.'

Stafford produced his own camera. It was a Pentax 110; not a 'spy' camera like the Minox, but still small enough to be carried unobtrusively in a pocket. It also came with a selection of good lenses.

The noise of the burner stopped. 'We'll still rise a bit,' said Hunt conversationally. 'What do you think of it?'

To Stafford's surprise all his qualms had gone. 'I think it's bloody marvellous,' he said. 'So peaceful. Except for the noise of the burner, but that isn't on all the time.'

'There's Dirk Hendriks down there,' said Hunt. 'Talking to Brice outside the Admin Block.' He waved. 'If we were lower we could have a chat.'

'How high are we?'

'Getting on for 2,000 feet from point of departure. That's about 8,000 feet above sea level. The experimental plots are coming up, Judy.'

'I see them.' She took about ten photographs while Stafford took some of his own and then straightened. 'That's it,' she said. 'The work's done. Now for the pleasurable bit.'

'About the noise of the burner,' said Hunt. 'It's difficult to make a quiet burner; I'd say impossible. This one up here is rated at ten million Btu – that's about 4,000 horsepower. You can't keep that lot quiet when it's ripping loose.'

'You're kidding,' Stafford said unbelievingly.

'No, it's quite true. One of the gas cylinders will provide the average household with two months' cooking – we use it up in less than half an hour. But we're not operating at maximum efficiency, so I reckon we're getting about 3,000 horsepower. In England and America they use propane but that's a bit tricky in the African heat so we use butane which has a lesser calorific value. And we have to add pressure with nitrogen; that's what that little cylinder there is for.'

Stafford found the power of the burner hard to believe. Hunt said, 'This dial tells the temperature – not here, but at the crown of the balloon up there.' He jerked his thumb upwards. 'Optimum temperature is 100 degrees Celsius.'

'But that's the boiling point of water.'

'Quite so,' Hunt said equably. 'If it gets above 110 degrees I'm in trouble – the nylon doesn't like it – so I keep a careful eye on the bloody gauge.'

'We're coming up to the entrance of Hell's Gate,' said Judy. 'Alan, come low over Fischer's Column.'

'Okay, but I'll have to go up after that.' He produced a packet of cigarettes and offered one. As Stafford looked doubtfully at the cylinders of butane surrounding them Hunt smiled, and said, 'Quite safe; it'll just add a bit more hot air.'

They drifted into the gorge of Hell's Gate through a gap in sheer cliffs. Hunt occasionally reached up to the burner controls and gave a short blast. Apart from that it was quiet and Stafford could hear cicadas chirping and the twittering of birds. The smoke from his cigarette ascended lazily in a spiral and he realized that was because they were moving at the same speed as the wind. It was weird.

'There's Lucas in the chase car,' said Judy. He looked down and saw the Land-Rover bucketing along a track on the floor of the gorge and towing a trailer. 'That's one of the problems of ballooning; you have to have a way of getting back to where you started.'

Stafford looked up at the immensity of the envelope above, and then down again at the Land-Rover. It seemed strange that a structure the size of a six-storey office block could be folded up to fit in a small trailer. Ahead, rising from the floor of the gorge, was a big rock pillar, tapering to a needle point. 'Fischer's Column,' said Judy. She opened the lid of a box which was lashed to the side of the basket and took out a pair of binoculars. 'We should see rock hyrax. Believe it or not, they're the nearest relation to the elephant. Cuddly creatures.'

'Not too cuddly,' remarked Hunt. 'They carry rabies.'

They were now quite close to the ground, not more than fifty feet high, and Hunt was maintaining this height by short bursts of flame. For a moment Stafford thought they were going to crash into the rock column but they passed about twenty feet to one side. 'There,' said Judy. 'Those are hyrax.'

They were small animals which he would have taken to be rodents. A couple of dozen of them took fright and dashed for crevices in the rocks and disappeared. As they passed Hunt said, 'That's the closest I've been to Old Man Fischer. It's an old volcanic plug, you know.' He operated the burner control and the flame roared in a sustained burst. 'Up we go. There'll be bigger game ahead.'

The balloon rose and the strange landscape of Hell's Gate spread before them. The cliffs to the east were alive with birds which flew faster than any others Stafford had seen. Judy said they were Nyanza swifts. Ahead there was another, but smaller, rock column which he was told was called Embarta. As they rose above the cliffs the crater of the volcano Longonot came into view in the east and Hunt turned off the flame.

Stafford said, 'What kind of bigger game?'

'Oh, eland, zebra, impala – the usual inhabitants. Giraffe, perhaps.'

He saw them all. The zebra herds wheeled as the balloon shadow passed, and the giraffes galloped off in a rocking-horse canter. But none of the animals moved far away; as soon as the balloon drifted by they resumed their grazing and browsing placidly. Stafford said, 'Is this a game reserve?'

'Oh, no,' said Hunt. 'But there is plenty of game outside the reserves.' They were drifting lower and he had the binoculars to his eyes. 'Look there,' he said, handing them to Stafford. 'That tree by the big rock there. There's a leopard on the branch to the right. I wonder if he's the chap who's been visiting the college.' The leopard looked up incuriously, and yawned as the balloon went silently by.

'There's a lammergeier,' said Judy. There was an odd note of warning in her voice. Stafford looked to where she was pointing and saw a big bird circling.

Hunt said, 'That means our flight is nearly over. When the lammergeier goes up the balloon comes down.'

'Why?' asked Stafford. 'Is it likely to attack us?' He could imagine that a sharp beak and talons could make a few nasty rents in the thin fabric of the envelope.

Both Hunt and his sister went into fits of laughter. 'No,' Hunt said. 'A lammergeier wouldn't attack anything. He's a carrion eater. But when he's in the air it means that the ground has heated up enough to start thermals strong enough for him to soar. And balloons don't like thermals; the ride gets too bumpy and it can be positively dangerous. That's why we fly in the early morning.' He looked ahead. 'Still, we'll make it all the way through Hell's Gate.'

They all fell quiet and Stafford found himself in a dream-like state, almost a trance. Ahead, on the crest of the pass, were puffs of white smoke drifting in the breeze and, from the ground, came the clear barking of baboons. They were nearly at the end of Hell's Gate and he saw, at last, why it was so named. What he had taken for smoke was steam escaping from a hundred fissures, and the violent hissing noise competed with the rumble of the balloon's flame.

'This is it,' said Hunt. 'Prepare for landing. Show Max how, Judy.'

She said, 'When Alan says "Now" crouch down in the basket and hang on to these rope handles – like this.' She demonstrated.

They passed over the steam jets and the balloon danced a little. There were flows of jagged lava which Stafford thought would do the balloon envelope a bit of no good should the balloon land among them. They went over those at a height of about fifty feet towards the open grassland beyond. Hunt said 'Now!' and Judy and Stafford crouched, but not before he had seen an eland looking at him with astonishment.

The basket made contact with the ground and he twisted his head to see Hunt yanking on a line. Above him the whole top of the envelope seemed to tear apart and he could see blue sky. Then the basket tipped on to its side and he was thrown on to his back alongside Judy. Everything was still and they had stopped moving.

'End of ride,' she said, and crawled out.

Stafford rolled out and stood up. Behind were the lava flows and steam clouds; ahead was the balloon envelope, looking very much as it had when he had first seen it, inert and dead upon the ground. In the distance the Land-Rover was driving towards them over the grass. Hunt was standing by the basket. He grinned and said, 'What does it feel like to be a hero of the sky?'

Stafford said slowly, 'I think that was the best damned experience I've had in my life.'

'You've not finished yet,' Hunt said. 'There's more to come. But first help me get the gas cylinders out.'

They took out the cylinders and rolled them aside. The Land-Rover drove up and Lucas and the other Kenyans got out. Lucas came over carrying a hamper. 'Breakfast!' said Judy with satisfaction. She opened the hamper and took out plastic boxes. 'Cold chicken; boiled eggs, fruit. I hope I put the salt in – I can't remember.'

'You're forgetting the most important thing,' said Hunt, and stooped to pick up a large flask. 'It's an old ballooning tradition that anyone making a first flight ends up drinking champagne.' He opened the flask and took out a bottle. 'Nicely chilled,' he commented, and smiled. 'That's why we like to take up first-time passengers; that way we get to drink champagne, too.'

They sat on the empty cylinders eating breakfast and drinking champagne while Lucas and his friend packed up the balloon. It folded into a cube with dimensions of under four feet a side. After breakfast they climbed over the lava flows and had a look at the place where the steam was issuing. There was a strong smell of sulphur and the ground was hot underfoot.

Hunt pointed. 'Ol Karia is about two kilometres that way. They're drilling for steam there; gone down over five and a half thousand feet.'

Stafford looked at the steam issuing all around him. 'I don't see the point. Why drill that far down? There's plenty here.'

'Not this flabby stuff; you need high pressure steam to drive a turbine.'

Stafford shook his head. 'I don't think I'd like to live in a volcanic area. I prefer my *terra* to be *firma*.'

'Oh, it's fairly stable around here,' said Hunt. 'There was a quake in the Valley about four years ago but it didn't hurt much apart from taking out a piece of the road coming down the escarpment from Nairobi.'

Stafford turned and look across at Longonot. The crater showed quite clearly. 'Is that an active volcano?'

'Not so as you'd notice. A few fumaroles, that's all. I'd call it quiescent. I've climbed into the crater. There are caves, some quite large, where gases have blown out. There are active volcanoes further south of here in Tanzania, notably Ol Doinyo Lengai.'

They turned to walk back to the Land-Rover and Stafford saw a taxi drawn up next to it and, much to his surprise, Hardin and Nair standing by. Hunt said in surprise, 'Now what are they doing here?'

Nair stepped forward and held the Hunts in conversation leaving Hardin to talk privately with Stafford. 'Things began happening yesterday,' Hardin said. 'We didn't know how to contact you but Nair had the bright idea of following the balloon. You gave us quite a chase.'

He related the facts about Gunnarsson, and Stafford looked at the taxi with its array of antennas. 'You were a damn fool to try a trick like that on an old pro like Gunnarsson. Now he's alerted.'

'It was Nair – not me,' protested Hardin.

'Look, we must have a conference; you, me, Nair, Curtis and Chip, if he's around.' Stafford took the camera from his pocket and extracted the film cassette. 'We'll hold the conference as soon as you get this developed and prints made.'

'How can we let you know?'

'I can see the fence from my bedroom,' said Stafford. 'There's a place on the other side of the fence about a hundred yards long where the grass has been burned over. Curtis will know where it is; he's been scouting the perimeter of Ol Njorowa. In the middle of the burned area there's an acacia. When you're ready have someone take a fairly big sheet of newspaper and stick it on one of the thorns as though it's been blown there. That will be the signal. Where are you staying?'

'I couldn't stay at the Lake Naivasha Hotel,' said Hardin. 'Gunnarsson is there. I booked into a place called Safariland.' He told Stafford where it was,

'Then that's where we'll talk.'

'What about?' said Hardin.

'About using you to spook Gunnarsson and drive him towards the wolves.' Stafford smiled. 'The wolves being at present located at Ol Njorowa.'

# TWENTY-FIVE

Stafford spent the rest of the morning wandering over the grounds of Ol Njorowa, at first with Hunt and then with Dirk Hendriks. He was shown the propagation sheds, the soil testing laboratory, the fertilizer testing laboratory, the this laboratory and the that laboratory, and the scientific terms were pumped remorselessly into one ear only to escape from the other. However, he managed to keep his end up by showing a halfway intelligent interest while keeping his eyes open.

He came to a few conclusions, the first of which was that Hunt was probably not in Brice's pocket. All the time he was in Hunt's company he noted that they were under discreet surveillance by three men, two blacks and a white, who apparently had nothing better to do than potter about in the middle distance. When Hunt excused himself to go about his business they vanished, too, and Hendriks took over the guided tour. The conclusion was that Hunt was not trusted to steer Stafford away from dangerous areas but that Hendriks was.

A second conclusion was that he was being conned and, had it not been for the bugged picture frame in his bedroom, he might have fallen for it. It was being demonstrated to him with some assiduity that Ol Njorowa was an open book in which he might read from any scientific page.

The trouble was that science was a foreign language to him and he could have done with a translator.

At last Dirk looked at his watch. 'Well, that's about it, Max. It's nearly lunchtime. I think you've seen about everything.' He laughed. 'Not that I'm qualified to show you. I don't know all that much about the place myself. Brice was going to give you the tour himself but something came up.'

'Yes,' said Stafford. 'He must be a busy man.' He looked around. 'How big is this place?'

'About six hundred hectares.' Hendriks paused to figure it out. 'A little over two square miles.'

Stafford smiled. 'I couldn't have worked it out so quickly.'

'We have the metric system in South Africa now. It makes you bilingual in mathematics.'

As they strolled in the direction of the Admin Block which was about a quarter of a mile away Stafford thought glumly that one could hide a hell of a lot in two square miles. But could one? Assuming that Ol Njorowa was a going concern as a genuine agricultural college then most of the staff would be genuine agricultural specialists. They would be wandering all over the place and could quite easily stumble across something illicit and wonder what it was. No, thought Stafford; hiding something at Ol Njorowa would not be as easy as all that.

They went into the dining room and threaded their way among the tables to where Brice sat. Judy Hunt was sitting with her brother and waved to him as he passed. He waved back as Dr Odhiambo caught his arm. 'Are you enjoying yourself, Mr Stafford?'

'Very much so,' Stafford assured him.

They sat at Brice's table and Stafford looked around the room which was noisy with animated conversation. Brice said, 'Did you enjoy your flight with Hunt?'

'It was great.' Stafford tasted the soup which was placed before him. 'Alan says hot air ballooning is becoming popular in England. I might take it up when I get back.'

Brice grimaced. 'I don't think I'd like a sport where every landing is a crash landing. And when are you going back to England?'

'Any day now. As it is I've been away too long. I have a business to take care of, you know.'

'Yes.' Brice buttered a slice of bread. 'Dirk has been telling me something of what you do. It must be interesting and adventurous.'

'You mean cloak and dagger?' Stafford laughed. 'Not much adventure behind a City desk, Mr Brice.'

'Oh, please call me Charles.' Brice looked up as a waiter came to the table and gave a card to Hendriks who glanced at it and passed it to Brice. They had a brief conversation in murmurs and Hendriks excused himself and left the table. 'An . . . er . . . acquaintance of yours has just arrived,' said Brice casually. 'Perhaps he'll join us for lunch.'

'Oh?' Stafford raised his eyebrows. 'Who can that be? I know few people in Kenya.'

'I believe you met him in the Masai Mara at Keekorok. An American called Gunnarsson. I wonder what he wants. Never mind; no doubt we'll find out. And what do you think of Ol Njorowa after your morning's exploration?'

Stafford managed to convey a spoonful of soup to his mouth without spilling a drop. 'A truly remarkable place,' he said. 'You're doing good work here.' As he pushed away his soup plate he thought that the next few minutes would probably prove interesting.

'We'll be able to really push it now we have the Hendrykxx inheritance. It's been a hard slog up to now.' Brice looked up as Hendriks and Gunnarsson came into the dining room. 'Would that be Mr Gunnarsson?'

'Yes.' Stafford watched Gunnarsson's face intently and caught the instant change of expression as Gunnarsson saw him sitting next to Brice; from blankness it changed to apprehension and then suspicion.

He and Brice stood up and Hendriks introduced them. 'This is Mr Brice, the Director of the Foundation, and Max Stafford I think you already know.'

'I sure do,' said Gunnarsson as Brice ordered another place set at the table. 'We met at Keekorok.' There was something of a baffled look in his eyes as he stared at Stafford.

'That's right,' said Stafford. 'How are your feet, Mr Gunnarsson?'

Gunnarsson grunted as he sat down. 'Better.' He looked around the table: at Hendriks who was finishing his soup; at Brice who, with bottle poised, was asking blandly if he would like wine; at Stafford who was leaning back to allow a plate to be put before him. Here they all were and what the hell was going on?

Hendriks said, 'I went to the American Embassy and did no better than you, Mr Gunnarsson; a complete blank wall. Have you heard any further news of my cousin?'

'No,' said Gunnarsson briefly. He started on his soup. 'What are you doing in Kenya, Mr Stafford?'

'I'm on holiday,' said Stafford easily.

Gunnarsson grunted, 'If you're like me you don't take vacations.' He looked at Dirk. 'Do you know who he is?'

Hendriks looked surprised. 'Yes; he's Max Stafford.'

'But do you know what he does?'

'We were discussing it before you came in,' said Brice. He sipped his wine. 'Must be very interesting work.'

'Mr Gunnarsson is in the same line of business,' observed Stafford. 'But in the United States. You might say that we're competitors, in a way. Or will be.' He smiled at Gunnarsson. 'I'm thinking of expanding my operations.'

'Thinking of moving into the States?' asked Gunnarsson. His smile had no humour in it. 'It's tough going.'

'It can't be worse than Europe,' said Stafford equably.

'Or Kenya.' Gunnarsson finished his soup. 'Funny things happen here, apart from people going missing. The latest is that my car was bugged. A bumper beeper.'

Stafford raised his eyebrows. 'Now who'd do that?'

Gunnarsson shrugged. 'You have the know-how.'

Stafford put down his knife and fork. 'Now look here. I told you I was in Kenya on holiday. Apart from that I'm a friend of the Hendriks family. You would say that, wouldn't you, Dirk?'

'Of course.' Hendriks smiled. 'Especially since my wife named our son after you.' His tone was a fraction sour.

Brice said coolly, 'We know all about Mr Stafford. What we don't know is why *you* are in Kenya, Mr Gunnarsson. You found Henry Hendrix in Los Angeles and delivered him to London. Why should you then accompany him to Kenya where he mysteriously disappears?' He tented his fingers. 'It would appear that you have to make the explanations rather than Max Stafford.'

Gunnarsson looked at him. 'I don't know that I'm required to give an explanation, Mr Brice, but, since you ask, Hendrix wanted me to come with him.' He smiled. 'He's a nice, young guy and we got on well together when I found him. You might say we became friends and I came with him to Kenya at his request.'

Brice shrugged and turned to Stafford. 'Will you really take up ballooning, Max?' He was obviously changing the subject.

'I might. It seems a great sport.'

The conversation became general with Brice holding forth enthusiastically on the future of the Ol Njorowa Foundation now that it was in funds. Gunnarsson made the odd comment from time to time but his main attention seemed to be on his plate. He was aware of an interplay of tensions about the table but was unable to identify the cause. However, it was enough for him to make up his mind that there was something odd about Ol Njorowa. As he put it to himself, it was 'something phoney'. It was not what was said that drew his attention – it was what was not said. For instance, Brice and Hendriks had not said much about the disappearance of Hank Hendrix.

As Stafford sipped his coffee he had a sudden thought. He could put the picture frame bug to some use – a use that Brice could not have foreseen. He put down his cup, and said, 'Mr Gunnarsson; I'd like to have a few words with you.'

'What about?'

'Well, you know that Stafford Security is broadening its activities. I'd like to discuss a few . . . er . . . ground rules with you.'

Gunnarsson snorted. 'Ground rules!' He smiled grimly. 'I'm willing to talk, sure.'

'After lunch, in my room?' suggested Stafford.

Gunnarsson drained his coffee cup. 'After lunch is now.'

Stafford said to Brice, 'I hope you'll excuse us. It's not my usual policy to talk business in these circumstances, but since Mr Gunnarsson is here and I have the unexpected opportunity . . .' His voice tailed off.

'Of course,' said Brice. 'One must always take opportunity by the forelock.'

Stafford rose and left the table followed by Gunnarsson. There was a moment's silence before Brice said, 'I'd like to hear that conversation. Let's go.' They both stood up.

At the door Stafford cast a glance backwards. He saw Gunnarsson following and, beyond, Hendriks and Brice were just rising from the table. He smiled slightly as he went up the stairs two at a time towards his room. He went in and stood aside to let Gunnarsson enter, then he closed the door. Gunnarsson swung around. 'Stafford; what are you trying to pull?'

'Sit down,' said Stafford. 'Take the weight off your feet.' He looked thoughtfully at the Shepherd print on the wall and thought he had better give Hendriks and Brice time to get settled in their listening post so he took out a packet of cigarettes. 'Smoke?'

Gunnarsson took a cigarette and Stafford snapped on his lighter. He lit the cigarettes, taking his time, blew out a plume of smoke, and said, 'Is it true what Brice said? That you delivered Henry Hendrix from the States to London?'

Gunnarsson glowered. 'What's it to you?'

'Not a damn thing. But if it is true then you have some explaining to do.' He held up his hand. 'Not to me, but questions will certainly be asked. Dirk Hendriks will probably go to the police and they'll be asking the questions. They'll want to know why you came to Kenya after delivering the heir. You'd better have some good answers. I don't believe the yarn you spun to Brice.'

'I'm not here to talk about me,' said Gunnarsson. 'What about you? What are you doing in Kenya? You were in the Masai Mara when Hank was kidnapped, and now you're here. It's too goddamn coincidental.'

'You heard about that downstairs,' said Stafford tiredly. 'I'm a family friend of the Hendriks's.' He paused. 'Well, not really. I'm more of a friend of Alix Hendriks. I might have married her at one time, and Dirk knows it. I don't think he likes me much.'

'Is it true his wife named the baby after you?' When Stafford nodded Gunnarsson said, 'Yeah, I guess he could be sore about that.' He pulled on his cigarette. 'But you were at Keekorok at the right time and pulling heroics. And now someone is trailing me.'

'When did you discover that?'

'Yesterday – about midday at the Lake Naivasha Hotel.'

Stafford spread his hands. 'Then it wasn't me. I was already here talking to Alan Hunt about a balloon trip. You can go down and ask him; he's in the dining room.' He flicked ash into the ashtray. 'I have no interest in you, Gunnarsson. But you must have been doing something for someone to take notice of you, and it's my guess that it's connected with your coming to Kenya with young Hendrix.'

'Aw, hell!' said Gunnarsson. 'It's like this. Here's this young guy still wet behind the ears who's just inherited six million bucks. He talked to me about it. He was worried, see? Hank wasn't exactly stupid; just inexperienced. He talked me into coming along as protection.'

'As a bodyguard?'

'Yeah; something like that.'

Stafford laughed. 'Gunnarsson, this is Max Stafford you're talking to. Better men than you have tried to con me. The boss of Gunnarsson Associates wouldn't take on that job himself; you'd assign it to one of your goons. Now let's have the real story.'

Gunnarsson sighed. 'Okay, why not? The truth is that I was standing right next to six million bucks and I was trying to figure a way to cut me a slice. I talked Hank into letting me come along with him to Kenya.'

'You were going to con him into something,' said Stafford flatly.

'I guess I was. I just didn't know exactly how. I was trying to work out a scam when he was kidnapped and maybe killed. How do you like that?'

Stafford got up and walked to the window. Gunnarsson sounded properly aggrieved and his story was cleverly near the truth. All that Gunnarsson had left out was that he had substituted Corliss for Hendrix in the United States. Stafford hoped that Brice and Hendriks were absorbing all this.

He looked out over the grounds of Ol Njorowa and stiffened when he saw the sheet of newspaper caught against the acacia on the other side of the fence. Nair had wasted no time in getting the prints developed and that meant they were ready to hold the conference.

He turned and said, 'Well, all this has nothing to do with me.' He picked up his suitcase, put it on the bed, and opened it. He took his toilet kit and began to put away his shaving tackle.

Gunnarsson said, 'What are you doing?'

Stafford zipped the leather case closed and dropped it into his suitcase. 'What does it look as though I'm doing? I'm packing. I came here for the sole reason of having a balloon flight with Alan Hunt. I had the balloon flight this morning so that's it. When I've got this suitcase packed I'll be going down to say goodbye to Brice, Dirk and the Hunts. Then I'm going back to Nairobi. If you want a lift you're welcome.'

'I have my own car.'

Stafford became sarcastic. 'And if you want notice of my further movements I'll be leaving for London on the flight tomorrow morning or the day after, depending on whether I can get a seat. Does that satisfy you?'

Gunnarsson watched him folding a shirt. 'Why should you want to satisfy me?'

'I wouldn't know,' said Stafford. 'But this was intended to be a holiday, the first I've had for three years, and it hasn't really turned out that way. I became involved, quite accidentally, in the kidnapping of a group of tourists, and since then everyone has been questioning my motives. Even Charles Brice has been asking pointed questions. Well, I've had enough. I'm going home.' He opened drawers to make sure he had packed everything, then closed his suitcase hoping that Brice was taking it all in.

He said, 'Gunnarsson; what do you think happened to young Henry Hendrix? You were there.'

'I don't know what to think. How about you?'

'I think the group was kidnapped by Tanzanians. It's happened before. I think Hendrix was killed, probably accidentally, and buried. Probably not even buried – the scavengers would take care of him. And I think you're wasting your time, Gunnarsson. You've lost out on your con game. Why don't you go home as I'm doing?'

Gunnarsson regarded Stafford sardonically. 'It'll be a long, long day before I take advice from you. There's something goddamn phoney going on here, and if you can't see it then I can. I'm sticking around to do some probing.'

Stafford shrugged and picked up his case. 'Suit yourself.' He walked to the door. 'I suppose we'll meet again, probably in New York. Brace yourself for a fight.'

'I fight rough,' warned Gunnarsson.

'I don't mind that.' Stafford stood at the door, his hand on the handle. 'Are you coming down or do you think you've inherited this bedroom?'

'Go to hell!' said Gunnarsson, but he stood up and followed Stafford down the stairs. On the ground floor they parted, Gunnarsson going back into the dining room and Stafford to the Nissan to deposit his suitcase. As he walked back to the entrance of the Admin Block he was well satisfied. The conversation he had had with Gunnarsson had been really aimed at Brice and Hendriks and he hoped the picture frame bug had been in working condition.

On his return to the dining room he saw Brice and Hendriks at their table talking to Gunnarsson. As he sat down Brice said, 'Mr Gunnarsson tells us you're leaving.'

'That's right. I'm here to say goodbye and to thank you for your hospitality.' Stafford looked at Hendriks. 'Sorry about your cousin, Dirk. Keep in touch and let me know what happens. I might be moving around when I get home but letters addressed to the office will find me.'

'I'll do that.'

Brice said, 'Did you and Mr Gunnarsson resolve your differences? I hope so.'

Stafford laughed. 'We have no differences – not here.' A waiter put down a cup before him and filled it with coffee. 'Those will begin in New York.' Gunnarsson snorted, and Stafford said evenly, 'That's why I told Dirk I'd be moving around.'

'You think you can muscle in while I'm away?' Gunnarsson chuckled. 'Not a chance, buster.'

Stafford drank his coffee, then turned to Brice and held out his hand. 'Nice to have known you, Mr Brice – Charles. I hope your plans for Ol Njorowa turn out well.' They shook hands and Stafford got up and went around the table. He clapped Hendriks on the shoulder. 'When do you expect to be back in London, Dirk?'

'I don't know. I seem to have my hands full here.'

'You don't mind if I pop in to see Alix and my godson, do you?'

'Of course not. She'll be glad to see you.'

Stafford looked across the room. 'I'd better catch Alan Hunt before he leaves. Goodbye, and thanks for everything.'

With a wave he went striding across the room to intercept Hunt at the doorway of the dining room. 'Alan, I'm going now. Thanks for the balloon flight.'

'I only did it for the champagne,' said Hunt with a grin.

Stafford put a hand on Hunt's elbow and steered him towards the entrance hall. 'I'd like to have a word with you. You were born in Kenya, weren't you?'

'That's right.'

'So it's your native country. What do you think of the way it's run?'

'On the whole not bad. The government makes mistakes, but what government doesn't?' Hunt frowned. 'What are you getting at, Max?'

They walked down the steps into the sunlight and towards Stafford's Nissan. He said, 'Would you consider yourself a patriot?'

'That's a hell of a question,' said Hunt. 'You mean dying for my country and all that?'

'I'd rather you lived for it,' said Stafford. 'Look, Alan; a problem has come up. Do you know where Safariland is?'

'Of course.'

Stafford checked the time. 'Could you meet me there in half an hour? There are a few people I want you to meet.'

'I suppose so,' said Hunt uncertainly. 'What's this all about?'

'You'll be told when you get there.' Stafford opened the door of the Nissan and got in. 'I'd rather you didn't tell anyone where you were going. Maybe you'd better invent a shopping errand in Naivasha.'

Hunt smiled faintly. 'It sounds very mysterious – but all right.'

'I'll see you there.' Stafford reversed out of the parking slot, waved, and drove towards the gates of Ol Njorowa very slowly because of the sleeping policemen. He looked in the mirror and saw Brice walking from the Admin Block to meet Hunt. He hoped Hunt had sense enough to keep his mouth shut as he had been told.

# TWENTY-SIX

Stafford had expected to see Hardin at Safariland but instead he was met by Curtis who walked forward as the Nissan drew to a halt. He got out, and said, 'Good afternoon, Sergeant. Where is everyone? What's the drill?'

Curtis said, 'Colonel Chipende thought it advisable to hold the meeting on Crescent Island. That's an island in the lake, sir. If the Colonel will follow me I have a boat ready.'

Stafford smiled. Now that Chipende was revealed, Curtis was giving him full military honours. He said mildly, 'I think we'll still call him Chip, Sergeant.' He looked at his watch. 'We can't go yet. I'm expecting someone else. Perhaps fifteen minutes.'

So they waited and presently Hunt arrived and, somewhat to Stafford's consternation, he had brought Judy. They got out of the car and Stafford said, 'I told you not to tell anyone else.'

Hunt gave a lop-sided grin. 'I wanted a witness.'

'And I'm a patriot, too,' added Judy. 'What's going on, Max? It's all very mysterious.'

Stafford stood undecided for a moment then he shrugged. 'Very well. You might as well come along.'

'That's not very gracious,' she said.

'It wasn't intended to be,' he snapped, and turned to Curtis. 'Carry on.'

Curtis led the way to the edge of the lake where there was a rough timbered jetty alongside which was moored an open boat with a black Kenyan sitting in the stern. They got in and the Kenyan started the outboard engine and soon they were cruising at a respectable speed towards an island which lay about a mile offshore. 'Why are we going to Crescent Island?' asked Judy.

'I don't know, but we'll soon find out,' said Stafford. He nudged Curtis. 'Who's there?'

'Col . . .' Curtis swallowed and began again. 'Chip and Nair, and Mr Hardin. And there's another man. I don't know who he is.'

Stafford grunted and wondered about that but did not let it worry him. The time to worry was when he thought it might cause trouble. Hunt said, 'Do you mean Nair Singh?'

'Yes,' said Stafford shortly, and watched the island ahead.

At last they drew alongside the rocky foreshore and were able to land. Chip came down to meet them. He looked at the Hunts and frowned, then said to Stafford, 'Could I have a word with you?' Stafford nodded and they walked out of earshot. 'I don't think this is a good thing, Max. Why did you bring them?'

'I didn't bring *them*,' said Stafford irritably. 'I wanted Hunt along; his sister came without invitation.'

'But why even Hunt?'

'We've got to have someone on the inside and I elected Hunt,' said Stafford. 'I have my reasons and I'll justify them. Curtis tells me you've brought along your own surprise.'

Chip nodded. 'You'll forgive me if I don't introduce him. He's here . . . er . . . incognito.'

'One of your bosses?'

Chip smiled. 'Could very well be.'

'So that's why we're here on an island,' said Stafford. 'All right; let's get on with it. We have a lot to discuss.'

Chip hesitated, then nodded. 'All right; let's go.'

Stafford jerked his head at Curtis and the Hunts and they all followed Chip up a slope which led down to the beach, walking among trees. Once Stafford was alarmed as a big animal broke away from quite close and he saw a white-ringed rump as it plunged away from them. 'Water-buck,' said Curtis dispassionately.

'They do very well here,' said Chip. 'They swim across from the mainland. The big cats don't like water very much, at least not to the extent of swimming a mile, so the water-buck are safe from predators.' Stafford thought with some humour that even now Chip could not resist acting the courier, but became alert when Chip said, 'Watch out for snakes.'

They pressed on and eventually came to a piece of level ground on which were the foundations of a building. Whether the building had fallen down or whether the builder had just got as far as putting in the foundations Stafford could not decide. Here, waiting for them, were the others – Nair, Hardin and a stranger. He was an elderly black Kenyan with greying hair and an expressionless face. Chip went over to him and talked in low tones.

Stafford walked over to Hardin. 'Hello, Ben. Who's the old man there?'

'He doesn't say – neither does Chip. I'd say he's top brass. He doesn't talk so you'd notice.'

'He's come to assess the evidence,' said Stafford. 'I have some to give him.'

Chip stepped forward and said to the Hunts, 'I think we ought to introduce ourselves. I'm Pete Chipende, but call me Chip. This is . . .'

'No!' said Stafford sharply. 'Let's not pussyfoot around.' He looked at Alan Hunt. 'This is Colonel Peter Chipende of the Kenyan Army.' There was a flash in Chip's eyes which he ignored. 'You already know Nair but you don't know his rank and neither do I.'

Nair stepped forward. 'Captain Nair Singh, at your service.'

Hunt raised his eyebrows. 'I didn't know you were in the army, Nair.'

'You still don't know,' said Chip flatly. 'This conversation isn't happening. Understand?'

Stafford said, 'Ben Hardin you've already met, and this is Curtis. That gentleman over there I don't know, and I don't think I want to know. Chip is right. What you learn here you keep under your hats.'

Judy laughed nervously. 'All very portentous.'

'Yes,' said Hunt. 'Very cloak and dagger. What's it all about?'

'Tell him, Chip,' said Stafford.

Chip said, 'We have reason to believe that Ol Njorowa is not as it seems, that it is an illicit base in Kenya for a foreign power – a centre for espionage.'

'You're crazy,' said Hunt.

'Alan, you haven't heard the evidence. Wait for it.' Stafford turned to Nair. 'Have you got the photographs?' Nair gave them to him and he said, 'You produced these damned quickly.'

'My brother-in-law is a photographer. He did them.'

Stafford grimaced. 'That joke is becoming pretty thin, Nair.'

'But it's true,' protested Nair. 'My brother-in-law really is a professional photographer in Naivasha. He says because he did them so quickly they won't last; the colours will fade. He's doing a more permanent set now.'

Stafford flipped through them. 'These will do for now.' He sat on the edge of the crumbling concrete foundation and began to lay them out. As he did so he said, 'Has anything happened I ought to know about, Chip?'

'Not much, except that someone was inquiring about Gunnarsson at the New Stanley. He wasn't there, of course; he was already in the hotel here.'

'Who was being inquisitive?'

'We don't know yet. It's being followed up.'

Stafford had got the photographs spread out. 'Right. These are pictures taken of Ol Njorowa during an overflight in Alan's balloon this morning. Anyone got any comments?'

He drew back to let the others inspect them. They crowded around except for the elderly Kenyan who had seated himself on a nearby rock and was placidly smoking a pipe. There was silence for a while then Hardin said, 'Yeah; this tower here. What is it?'

'That's the water tower,' said Hunt. 'The water is pumped up there and then distributed by gravity.'

Curtis coughed. 'Perhaps I could point out to the Colonel that the water tower is in the wrong place.'

'Why, Sergeant?'

'The natural place to build a water tower would be on the highest point of land.' Curtis pointed at another photograph. 'Which would be about there.'

Hunt looked at Stafford curiously. 'Are you a colonel, too?'

'I'm trying to retire but Sergeant Curtis won't let me,' said Stafford dryly. 'All right, a water tower in the wrong place.'

Hardin picked up the photograph. 'It's close to the perimeter fence where it angles. I'd say it's an observation tower. From the top you could cover a hell of a lot of that fence. Good place to put a couple of TV cameras.'

Chip said, 'What about at night? Is the fence illuminated?'

'No; I checked,' said Stafford.

'Could be infra-red,' said Nair. 'You couldn't see that.'

'No infra-red. You're behind the times, Nair. If there is TV coverage of the fence they'd probably use photomultipliers – the things they use as night sights in the army. Even on a moonless, cloudy night you get a pretty good picture.'

'Are you serious about this?' demanded Hunt.

'Very.' Stafford waved his hands over the photographs 'Anything else?'

'Yeah,' said Hardin. 'But it doesn't show in these pictures. He turned to Hunt. 'You said a leopard was getting over the fence and that's why there was an armed guard. Right?'

Hunt nodded. 'Brice had a patrol out. He reckoned the leopard was getting over by climbing a tree which was too near the fence.'

'Yeah, that's what you said.' Hardin jerked his head at Curtis. 'Tell him, Sergeant.'

'Acting on instructions of the Colonel I did a tour of the perimeter from the outside. The vegetation has been cut back on the outside of the fence to a distance of at least thirty feet. There is no tree near the fence. I found evidence of weed killer; there was an empty paper sack. I didn't remove it but I made a note of what it was.' He took a piece of paper and gave it to Stafford.

'Pretty powerful stuff,' said Hardin, looking over Stafford's shoulder. 'It's the defoliant we used in Vietnam, and it's now illegal for commercial use. It looks as though someone wants a clear view along the fence.'

'How long is the fence?' asked Stafford.

'About six and a half miles, sir,' said Curtis.

'A ten foot chain-link fence six and a half miles long,' commented Stafford. 'That's pretty much security overkill for an innocent agricultural college short of funds, wouldn't you say, Alan?'

'I hadn't really thought of it in that light,' said Hunt, 'I was already there when I came to Ol Njorowa.' He shook his head. 'And I hadn't noticed the cleared strip on the outside.'

Chip picked up a photograph. 'This interests me.'

'It interests me, too,' said Stafford. 'In fact, it's the key to the whole bloody situation. What about it, Alan?'

Hunt took the photograph. 'Oh, that's the animal move-ment laboratory. I don't know much about it. I've never been inside.'

'Tell Chip about the pretty wildebeest,' said Stafford ironically.

Hunt retailed all he knew about the work done there on patterns of animal migration. He shrugged. 'I don't know much more; it's, not my field. In any case it's not really a part of the College; we just give them house room.'

'I've been all over Ol Njorowa,' said Stafford. 'I've been given the grand tour; I've been everywhere except inside that so-called laboratory. Alan has been at Ol Njorowa for two years and he hasn't been inside.'

'Well, it's not used all the year round,' said Hunt. 'And the wildebeest migration doesn't begin for another six weeks.'

Judy said, 'We don't see much of those people, anyway. They're not good mixers.'

'So Alan remarked before.' Stafford looked at the sky and said dreamily, 'Up there, a little over 22,000 miles high, is an American satellite for extended weather research, a laudable project and no doubt quite genuine. But it contains equipment used by these people at Ol Njorowa. It occurred to me that a signal sent from that dish antenna to the satel-lite could be relayed and picked up in, say, Pretoria which is about 25 degrees south. Or possibly somewhere in the Northern Transvaal such as Messina or Louis Trichardt which are about 22 to 23 degrees south.' He smiled. 'I've been looking at maps.'

Hunt said, 'This is all sheer supposition. You talk of TV cameras on the water tower, but you don't know they're there. And all this waffle about signalling to Pretoria is just sheer guff in my opinion. If this is what you've brought me to hear you're wasting my time.'

'Alan,' said Stafford gently. 'Does a respectable establishment bug the guest bedrooms?'

'You're sure of that?' said Chip sharply.

'Dead sure. Microphone and radio transmitter disguised as a picture of an elephant.' He described what he had found.

Chip blew out his cheeks in a sigh of relief. 'Thank God!' he said. 'It's the first firm evidence we've had.'

'That's what I thought,' said Stafford. He recounted the events of the day in detail, then said, 'I manoeuvred Gunnarsson into a private conversation in the bedroom because I was pretty sure that Brice would be listening. All the time I talked to Gunnarsson I was really addressing Brice.' He grinned. 'I needled Gunnarsson into saying that he's going to stick around to investigate Ol Njorowa because he thinks it's a phoney set-up.'

'He always was a sharp operator,' said Hardin soberly. 'I'll give him that. He doesn't have cotton wadding between his ears.'

'Yes, but Brice will have heard him saying it.' Stafford laughed, 'It will be interesting to see what happens now.'

Hunt looked at his sister. 'What do you think?'

'Until Max told about the picture in his room I wasn't convinced,' she said. 'But he's really getting to me now.'

'Have you seen the TV camera in the entrance hall of the Admin Block?' asked Stafford helpfully.

Hunt looked startled. 'No, I haven't.'

'That's not surprising; it's hard to spot unless you know what you're looking for. As you face the counter it's behind and to your left in the top corner. Now, don't go staring at it, for God's sake! Just do an unobtrusive check.'

Hunt shook his head in bewilderment. 'You know, last year Brice showed me a couple of papers in a journal about the work done by the animal migration lab. From what I could see it was really good stuff.'

'No doubt it was. The best cover is always genuine.' Stafford turned to Chip. 'When I was talking to Gunnarsson I indicated I was leaving Kenya and going back to London. Brice might believe it or he might not. Can you do anything to support that story?'

Chip thought about it. 'We don't know yet how big an organization Brice has built up, or how far we've been penetrated. I'll have someone book air tickets in the names of you and Curtis. Let me have your passport numbers, and the records will show that you left tomorrow morning. In the meantime you'll have to go to ground.'

'Why not here?' said Nair. 'Here on Crescent Island. It's close to Ol Njorowa and it's quiet. We can bring a tent and sleeping bags and anything else you might need.'

'We'll need a boat,' said Stafford.

Curtis leaned forward and said in a low voice, 'The Colonel might like to know there's someone coming.'

'Where?'

'Up the slope from the water and moving quietly.'

Chip had caught it. He signalled to Nair and they both headed down the slope, angling in different directions. They disappeared and, for a while, nothing happened. Then they came back, strolling casually, and Chip was tearing open an envelope. 'It's all right; just someone bringing me a message.' He took a sheet of paper from the envelope and scanned it. 'The man who was asking for Gunnarsson at the New Stanley. He's been traced back to Ol Njorowa; his name is Patterson.'

Stafford wrinkled his brow. 'That name rings a faint bell.'

Hunt said, 'He's one of the animal migration team. I suppose that does it.'

'Wasn't he the man with Brice when I met him for the first time at the Lake Naivasha Hotel?'

'Yes,' said Judy. 'Alan, I think Max has proved his point.' She looked directly at Stafford. 'What do you want us to do?'

'Chip's the boss,' said Stafford.

'Not really,' said Chip, and nodded his head towards the grey-haired Kenyan who was knocking out his pipe on the rock he sat on. Stafford had glanced at him from time to time during the conference. His face had remained blandly blank but he had obviously listened to every word. Chip said, 'I'll have to have a private talk first.' He walked to one side and the elderly man put away his pipe and followed him.

Curtis said to Nair, 'If we're staying on this island we'll need essential supplies. Beer.'

Stafford smiled, and Hardin said, 'What do I do?'

'That depends upon what Chip wants to do, and that depends upon the decision of Mr Anonymous over there. Or he could be General Anonymous, since this seems to be an army operation. We'll have to wait and see.'

'You know,' said Hunt, 'I can't believe this is happening.'

'You don't know the whole story yet,' said Stafford. 'You'd find that even more incredible.' He turned to Hardin. 'It seems that Gunnarsson is not involved with Brice or Hendriks. He had a ploy of his own which he'd probably call a scam.'

'Ripping off the Hendrykxx estate with Corliss,' agreed Hardin.

Stafford laughed. 'You started all this, Ben. Did you imagine, back in Los Angeles, that you would uncover an international espionage plot in the middle of Africa? It's only because we were suspicious of Gunnarsson that we got wind of it. You know, it puzzled me a long time. I was trying to fit pieces into a jig-saw and only now have I realized there were *two* jig-saw puzzles – one around Gunnarsson and the other around Ol Njorowa.'

Judy said, 'So what happens now?'

'I suspect we fall into the hands of politicians,' said Stafford. He jerked his head. 'That pair over there are

I think, simple-minded military men. If they have their way they'll climb in to Ol Njorowa and disinfect it. The direct way. The politicians might have other ideas.'

Hunt said, 'Curtis refers to you as the Colonel. Are you still active, and in what capacity?'

'God, no! I got out ten years ago.' Stafford sat up. 'I was in Military Intelligence and I became tired of my work being either ignored or being buggered about by politicos who don't know which end is up. So I quit and started my own civilian and commercial organization. I resigned from *Weltpolitik.*' He paused. 'Until now.'

Hardin lifted his head. 'Chip's coming back.'

Stafford heard the crunch of Chip's footsteps. He raised his head and said, 'What's the verdict?' His eyes slid sideways and he watched the grey-haired Mr Anonymous walk down the slope and out of sight among the trees.

Chip said, 'We wait awhile.'

'I might have guessed it,' said Stafford. He shrugged elaborately as though to make his point with Alan Hunt.

Hunt said, 'What about us?' He indicated his sister.

'You just carry on normally,' said Chip, 'If we need you we'll get word to you. But until then you don't, by any action or quiver of a muscle, give any indication that anything is out of the ordinary.'

Hardin said, 'And me? What do I do?'

Chip blew out his cheeks. 'I suppose you come under Mr Stafford. I recommend that you stay here – on Crescent Island.'

Hardin nudged Nair. 'That means more beer.'

Stafford said, a little bitterly, 'Chip, you've talked to that mate of yours. I suppose he was a high-ranking officer. Am I to take it that he's going for instructions?'

Chip shook his head sadly. 'You know how it is, Max. Wheels within wheels. Everyone has someone on his

neck. Any action on this has to be taken on instruction
from the top. We're talking about international stuff
now – a clash of nations.'

Stafford sighed. He leaned back so that he lay flat, and
put his hands over his eyes to shade them from the sun.
'Then get on with your bloody clash of nations.'

# TWENTY-SEVEN

Brice stood looking out of his window over the grounds of Ol Njorowa. His brow was furrowed as he swung to face Hendriks. 'First Stafford, and now Gunnarsson. You heard them. They're on to us.'

'Not Max,' said Hendriks. 'He's going home.'

'All right. But Gunnarsson suspects something. Who is he?'

'You know as much as I do,' said Hendriks. 'He's boss of the American agency which found Henry Hendrix in California. You heard what he said to Stafford. He tried to cut himself a slice but he failed when he lost Hendrix. He's a bloody crook if you ask me.'

'I don't need to ask you,' said Brice acidly. 'It's self-evident.'

Hendriks held up a finger. 'One thing seems clear,' he said. 'Cousin Henry really must be dead. Stafford certainly thinks so.'

'That doesn't do us much good if there's no body.' Brice sat behind his desk. 'And you heard Gunnarsson. He says he's staying around to investigate.'

'So what is there to investigate?' asked Hendriks. 'He's not interested in us. All he wants is to find Henry – which he won't. After a while he'll get tired of it and go home like Max. There's nothing for him to find, not now.'

'Perhaps, but we'll keep an eye on him.'

'Do that,' said Hendriks. He stood up and walked to the door. 'If you want me I'll be in my room.'

He left Brice and went upstairs. In his room he lay on the bed and lit a cigarette, and his thoughts went back over the years to the time it had all started.

He supposed it began when he was recruited to the National Intelligence Service. Of course in those days it was called the Bureau for State Security. Joel Mervis, the then editor of the Johannesburg *Sunday Times*, had consistently replaced 'for' with 'of' which resulted in the acronym BOSS. A cheap trick but it worked and was adopted by newspapers all over the world. Hendriks reflected how oddly insensitive his fellow countrymen were in matters of this nature. It took them a long time to get the point and then the name was changed to the Department of National Security which made the acronym DONS. Even that was received with some hilarity and another change was made to the National Intelligence Service. Nothing much could be made of NIS.

He was thoroughly trained and began his fieldwork, working mostly in Rhodesia at that time. South Africa was desperately trying to buttress the Smith government but, of course, that came to nothing in the end. The death of Salazar in faraway Portugal sent a whole row of dominoes toppling. An anti-colonial regime in Portugal meant the loss of Angola and then Mozambique; the enemy was on the frontier and Rhodesia could not be saved. Now the Cubans were in Angola and South West Africa was threatened. It was a bleak outlook.

But that was now. In the days when it seemed that Rhodesia could be saved for white civilization Hendriks had enjoyed his work until he stopped a bullet fired not by a black guerilla but, ironically, by a trigger-happy white farmer. He was pulled back to South Africa, hospitalized, and then given a month's leave.

Time hung heavily on his hands and he sought for something to do. He was normally a mentally and physically active man and not for him the lounging on the beach at Clifton or Durban broiling his brains under the sun. His thoughts went back to his grandmother whom he dimly remembered – and to his grandfather who was thought to have been killed in the Red Revolt of Johannesburg in 1922. But there had been no body and Hendriks wondered. Using the techniques he had been taught and the authority he had acquired he began an investigation, an intelligence man's way of passing the time and searching the family tree. It paid off. He found from old port records that Jan-Willem Hendrykxx had sailed from Cape Town for San Francisco on March 25, 1922, a week after the revolt had been crushed by General Smuts. And that was as far as he got by the end of his leave.

He did not go back to Rhodesia but, instead, was posted to England. 'Go to the Embassy once,' he was told. 'You'd be expected to do that. But don't go near it again. They'll give you instructions on cut-outs and so on.'

So Hendriks went to London where his main task was to keep track of the movements of those exiled members of the African National Congress then living in England, and to record whom they met and talked with. He also kept a check on certain members of the staffs of other Embassies in London as and when he was told.

Intelligence outfits have their own way of doing things. The governments of two countries may be publicly cold towards each other while their respective intelligence agencies can be quite fraternal. So it was with South Africa and the United States – BOSS and the CIA. One day Hendriks passed a message through his cut-out; Could someone, as a favour, find out what happened to Jan-Willem Hendrykxx who had arrived in San Francisco in 1922? A personal matter, so no hurry.

Two months later he had an answer which surprised him. Apparently his grandfather could out-grandfather the Mafia. He had been deported from the United States in 1940. Hendriks, out of curiosity, took a week's holiday which he spent in Brussels. Discreet enquiries found his grandfather hale and well. Hendriks went nowhere near the old man, but he did go to the South African Embassy in Brussels where he had a chat with a man. Three months later he wrote a very detailed report which he sent to Pretoria and was promptly pulled back to South Africa.

Hendriks's immediate superior was a Colonel Malan, a heavily built Afrikaner with a square face and cold eyes. He opened a file on his desk and took out Hendriks's report. 'This is an odd suggestion you've come up with.' The report plopped on the desk. 'How good is your evidence on this Belgian, Hendrykxx?'

'Solid. He's the head of a heroin-smuggling ring operating from Antwerp, and we have enough on him to send him to jail for the rest of his life. On the other hand, if he comes in with us he lives the rest of his life in luxury.' Hendriks smiled. 'What would you do, sir?'

'I'm not your grandfather,' growled Malan. He leafed through the report. 'You come from an interesting family. Now, you want us to give the old man a hell of a lot of money tied up in a way he can't touch it, and he makes out a will so that the money goes where we want it when he dies. Is that it?'

'Yes, sir.'

'Where would you send the money?'

'Kenya,' said Hendriks unhesitatingly. 'We need strengthening in East Africa.'

'Yes,' said Malan reflectively. 'Kenyatta has been crucifying us in the United Nations lately.' He leaned back in his chair. 'And we have an interesting proposition put to us by

Frans Potgeiter but we're running into trouble on the funding. Do you know Potgeiter?'

'Yes, sir.'

'Could you work with him?'

'Yes, sir.'

Malan leaned forward and tapped the report. 'Your grandfather is old, but not dead old. He could live another twenty years and we can't have that.'

'I doubt if he will.' Hendriks took an envelope from his breast pocket and pushed it across the desk. 'Hendrykxx's medical report. I got hold of it the day before I left London. He has a bad heart.'

'And how did you get hold of it?'

Hendriks smiled, 'It seems that someone burgled the offices of Hendrykxx's doctor. Looking for drugs, the Belgian police say. They did a lot of vandalism; you know how burglars are when they're hopped up, sir.'

Malan grunted, his head down as he scanned the medical documents. He tossed them aside. 'Looks all right, but I'll have a doctor go over them. The Brussels Embassy wasn't involved, I hope.'

'No, sir.'

'This will have to be gone into carefully, Hendriks. The Department of Finance will have to come into it, of course. And the will – that must be carefully drawn. We have a barrister in London who can help us there. I rather think I'd like to move Hendrykxx out of reach of his friends and where we can keep an eye on him. That is, if this goes through. I can't authorize it, so it will have to go upstairs.' He smiled genially. 'You're a *slim kerel*, Hendriks,' he said approvingly.

'Thank you, sir.' Hendriks hesitated. 'If Hendrykxx doesn't die in time he could always ... er ... be helped.'

Malan's eyes went flinty. 'What kind of a man are you?' he whispered. 'What kind of man would suggest the killing

of his own grandfather? We'll have no more of that kind
of talk.'

The operation was approved at top level and that was in the
days when the South African intelligence and propaganda
agencies were riding high. There was money available, and
more if needed. Hendrykxx had his arm duly twisted and
caved in when offered the choice. He was removed from
Belgium and installed in a house in Jersey under the super-
vision of Mr and Mrs Adams, his warders in a most luxurious jail. Jersey had been chosen because of its lack of death
duties and the general low tax rate; not that much tax was
paid – when a government goes into the tax avoidance
business it takes the advice of the real experts. £15M was
injected into the scheme which, at the time of Hendrykxx's
death, had magically turned into £40M. It is surprising what
compound interest can do to a sum which has proper management and is left to increase and multiply.

Frans Potgeiter went under cover and surfaced as Brice,
the liberal Rhodesian, the real Brice having conveniently
been killed in a motor accident while trying to do the
Johannesburg-Durban run in under five hours. He went to
England to establish a reputation, and then moved to Kenya
to manage the Ol Njorowa Foundation. Hendriks returned
to his undercover post in London.

All was going well when came the débâcle of Muldergate
in 1978 and gone were the days of unlimited funds. One by
one the stories leaked out; the setting up of the newspaper,
*The Citizen,* with government funds, the attempted purchase
of an American newspaper, the bribery of American politicians, the activities of the Group of Ten. All the peccadilloes
were revealed.

In 1979 Connie Mulder, the Minister of Information, was
forced to resign from the Cabinet, then from Parliament, then
from the party itself. Dr Eschel Rhoodie, the Information

Secretary, took refuge in Switzerland, and appeared on television threatening to blow the gaff. Mulder did blow the gaff – he named Vorster, once Prime Minister and then President of the Republic of South Africa, as being privy to the illegal shenanigans. Vorster denied it.

The Erasmus Judicial Commission of Enquiry sat, considered the evidence, and issued its report. It condemned Vorster as 'having full knowledge of the irregularities.' John Balthazar Vorster resigned from the State Presidency. It was a mess.

Hendriks, in London, read the daily newspaper reports with horrified eyes, expecting any day that the Hendrykxx affair and the Ol Njorowa Foundation would be blown. But someone in Pretoria must have done some fast and fancy footwork, scurrying to seal the leaks. It was not Colonel Malan because he was swept away in the general torrent of accusations and resigned his commission.

Hendriks had worried about his uncle Adrian whom, of course, he had never met, and his particular worry revolved about the possibility of Adrian fathering legitimate offspring. An inquiry was put in motion and thus he discovered Henry Hendrix, then in his last year in high school. Hendriks wanted, as he put it, 'to do something about it,' a euphemism which Malan burked at. 'No,' Malan had argued. 'I won't have it. We'll do it some other way when the need arises.'

But after Muldergate, when Malan was gone and Hendriks wanted to 'do something', Henry Hendrix had dropped out of sight, an indistinguishable speck of dross in the melting pot of 220 million Americans. From London Hendriks had tried to rouse Pretoria to action but the recent brouhaha of Muldergate had had a chilling effect on the feet and nothing was done.

It was only when Alix became pregnant and it was necessary that Hendrykxx should go that Pretoria took action, half-heartedly and too late. Hendrykxx had left £20,000 in his will to his jailers, Mr and Mrs Adams. Mandeville had insisted upon that, saying that the will had to look good. They responded by killing him, a not too difficult task considering he was senile and expected to die any moment, even though he was inconsiderately hanging on to life tenaciously.

Pretoria bungled in Los Angeles and Hendrix got away. He had survived the car crash in Cornwall, too, by something of a miracle, but now Potgeiter had finally solved the problem in a somewhat clumsy way. Or had he?

Hendriks was roused from his reverie by the ringing of the telephone next to his bed. It was Potgeiter. 'Get down here. Gunnarsson has gone on the run. I've sent Patterson after him.'

# TWENTY-EIGHT

Stafford thought the lake flies constituted the worst hazard of Crescent Island until he nearly broke his neck.

Chip, Nair and the Hunts had departed; the Hunts back to Ol Njorowa, Chip to Nairobi, and Nair to Naivasha to round up supplies. Nair came back in the late afternoon in a boat loaded with provisions and camping gear. They helped him get it ashore, then he said, 'We'll camp on the other side of the island where lights can't be seen from the mainland.'

'Are you staying with us?' asked Stafford in surprise.

Nair nodded without saying anything and Hardin snorted. 'I guess Chip thinks we want our hands held.'

Stafford had a different notion; he thought Nair was there to keep an eye on them. The mystery of Ol Njorowa had almost been solved and all that remained was to bust up the South African operation. But Chip, and possibly others, did not want premature activity and Nair was there to see that Stafford's party stayed put.

They lugged the supplies to the other side of the island, a matter of half a mile, and then made camp. Nair was meticulous about the setting up of the mosquito nets which were hung on wire frames over the sleeping bags, and fiddled for a long time in a finicky manner until he was sure he had got it right. 'Get much malaria around here?' asked Hardin.

'Not here.' Nair looked up. 'Lot of lake flies, though.' He did not elaborate.

Curtis put a burner on to a small cylinder of propane and began to open cans. In a very short while he had prepared a meal, and they began to eat just as the sun was setting over the Mau Escarpment. Over coffee Nair said, 'It's time for bed.'

'So early?' queried Hardin, 'It's just after six.'

'Please yourself,' said Nair. 'But the wind changes at nightfall and brings the lake flies. You'll be glad to be under cover.'

Stafford found what he meant five minutes later when he began to swat at himself viciously. By the time he had got into the sleeping bag and under the safety of the mosquito netting he felt the skin of his arms and ankles coming out in bumps which itched ferociously. Also he found that he had admitted several undesirable residents to share his bed and it was some time before he was sure he had killed the last of them.

Curtis was silent as usual, but from Hardin's direction came a continual muffled cursing. 'Goddammit, Nair!' he yelled. 'You sure these things aren't mosquitoes?'

'Just flies,' said Nair soothingly. 'They won't hurt you; they don't transmit disease.'

'Maybe not; but they're eating me alive. I'll be a picked-over skeleton tomorrow.'

'They're an aviation hazard,' said Nair in a conversational voice. 'Especially over Lake Victoria. They block air filters and Pitot tubes. There have been a few crashes because of them, but they've never been known to eat anybody.'

Stafford lit a cigarette and stared at the sky through the diaphanous and almost invisible netting. There were no clouds and the sky was full of the diamond brilliance of stars, growing brighter as the light ebbed in the west. 'Nair?'

'Yes, Max?'

'Did Chip say anything before he went to Nairobi?'

'About what?'

'You bloody well know about what,' said Stafford without heat.

There was a brief silence. 'I'm not a high ranking officer,' said Nair, almost apologetically. 'I don't get to know everything.'

'They can't stop you thinking. You're no fool, Nair; what do you *think* will happen?'

Again there was silence from Nair. Presently he said, 'This is a big thing, Max. There'll be a lot of talk among the people at the top; they'll argue about the best thing to do. You know how it is in intelligence work.'

Stafford knew. There were a number of options open to the Kenyans which he ticked off in his mind. They could go for a propaganda victory – smash into Ol Njorowa with full publicity, including TV cameras on hand and hard words in the United Nations. Or they could snap up Brice and Hendriks unobtrusively and close down their illicit operation without fanfare. The South Africans would know about it, of course, but there would not be a damned thing they could do. That would give the Kenyans a diplomatic ace up the sleeve, a *quid pro quo* for any concession they might want to wring out of the South Africans – do this for us or we blow the gaff publicly on your illegalities. Stafford doubted if the South Africans would respond to that kind of blackmail.

There was a third option – to do nothing. To put a fine meshed net around Ol Njorowa, to keep Brice, Hendriks and the animal migration team under surveillance and, possibly, feed them false information. That would be the more subtle approach he himself would favour, but he did not give the average politician many marks for subtlety. The average politician's time-horizon was limited and most would go for the short term solution. Had not Harold Wilson said that a week in politics was a long time?

And so there would be a lot of talk in Nairobi that night as factions in the government pushed their points of view. He hoped that Chip and Mr Anonymous had the sense to restrict their new found knowledge of Ol Njorowa to a select few.

He stirred. 'Nair – the men who kidnapped the tour group – do you think they were Tanzanians?'

'In the circumstances I doubt it.'

Stafford leaned up on one elbow. 'Kenyans?'

'Perhaps.'

'But how would Brice recruit them?'

'Some men will do much for money.'

'Even kill, as they were going to kill Corliss?'

'Even that.' Nair paused. 'They could, of course, have been South African blacks.'

Stafford had not thought of that. 'Could a South African black pass himself off as a Kenyan? Could he get away with it?'

Nair said dryly, 'Just as easily as a Russian called Konon Molody could pass himself off as a Canadian called Gordon Lonsdale. All it needs is training.'

Stafford mulled it over in his mind. 'But I can't understand why blacks would work for the white South Africans in the first place. Why should they defend white supremacy?'

'The South African army is full of blacks,' said Nair. 'Didn't you know? A lot are in the army for the pay. Some have other reasons – learning to use modern weaponry, for instance. But in the end it all comes down to the simple fact that if a man has a set of views it's always possible to find another man with the opposite set of views.'

'I suppose so,' said Stafford, but he was not convinced.

'The white man finds it difficult to understand how the mind of the black man works,' said Nair. There was a smile in his voice as he added, 'Not to mention the mind of the Indian. Even the white South Africans, who ought to know better, make mistakes about that.'

'Such as?'

'To begin with, the countries of Africa are artificial creations of the white man. The black does not really understand the nation state; his loyalties are to the tribe.'

'Yes,' said Stafford thoughtfully. 'Chip was saying something about that.'

'All right,' said Nair. 'Take Zimbabwe, which used to be Southern Rhodesia, an artificial entity. They had an election to see who'd come out on top, Nkomo, Mugabe or Bishop Muzorewa who ran the caretaker government. No one gave much chance to Muzorewa. The odds-on favourite was Nkomo and Mugabe was expected to come a bad second. Even the South Africans, who ought to have known better, laid their bets that way.'

'Why ought they to have known better?'

'They've been in Africa long enough. You see, there are two main tribes in Zimbabwe, the Ndebele and the Mashona. Nkomo is an Ndebele and Mugabe a Mashona. The Mashona outnumber the Ndebele four to one and Mugabe won the election by four to one. Simple, really.'

'They voted along tribal lines?'

'Largely.' Nair paused, then said, 'If the South Africans could set up a well-financed secret base here they could stir up a lot of trouble among the tribes.'

Stafford extinguished his cigarette carefully and lay back to think. Because of its position in Africa Kenya was a hodge-podge of ethnic and religious differences, all of which could be exploited by a determined and cynical enemy. Nair was probably right.

He was still thinking of this when he fell asleep.

He awoke in the grey light of dawn and looked uncomprehendingly at something which moved. He lay on his side and watched the buck daintily picking its way across his line of vision. It was incredibly small, about the size of a small dog, say, a fox terrier, and its legs were about as thick as a ball point pen and terminated in miniature hooves. Its rump was rounded and its horns were two small daggers. He had never seen anything so exquisite.

A twig snapped and the buck scampered away into the safety of the trees. Stafford rolled over and saw Nair approaching from the lake. 'That was a dik-dik,' said Nair.

'Have the flies gone?'

'No flies now.'

'Good.' Stafford threw back the netting and emerged from the sleeping bag. He put on his trousers, then his shoes, and took a towel, 'Is it safe to wash in the lake?'

'Safe enough; just keep your eyes open for snakes. Not that you're likely to see any.' As Stafford turned away Nair called, 'There are some fish eagles nesting in the trees over there.'

As Stafford walked to the water's edge he shook his head in amusement. Nair's cover as a courier for tourist groups seemed to have stuck. A herd of Thomson's gazelle drifted out of his way, not hurrying but keeping a safe distance from him. At the shore he sluiced down and was towelling himself dry when Hardin joined him. 'Peaceful place,' Hardin remarked.

'Yes. It's very nice.' Stafford put on his shirt. 'Where's Curtis? His sleeping bag was empty.'

Hardin waved his arm. 'Gone to the top of the ridge there; he wanted to have a look-see at the mainland.'

Stafford smiled. 'Military habits die hard.'

Hardin was staring out into the lake. 'Now, look at that, will you?'

Stafford followed his gaze and saw nothing but ripples. 'What is it?'

'Wait!' Hardin pointed. 'It was about there. Look! It's come up again. A goddamn hippo.'

Stafford saw the head break surface and heard a distant snorting and snuffling, then the hippopotamus submerged again. He said, 'Well, we are in Africa, you know. What would you expect to find in an African lake? Polar bears?'

'Crocodiles, that's what.' Hardin looked around very carefully at the lake shore. 'And I hope Nair was right about lions and leopards not liking to swim too far. We don't have a gun between the lot of us.'

There was an outcrop of rock close by and Stafford thought he would get a better view of the hippo from the top so he walked over to it. As he climbed he found the rock oddly slippery and he had difficulty in keeping his footing despite the fact that his shoes were rubber-soled. At the top he lost his balance entirely – his feet shot from under him and he fell to the ground below, a matter of some ten feet.

He was winded and gasped desperately for breath, and his senses swam. He did not entirely lose consciousness but was hardly aware of Hardin running up to him and turning him on to his back. 'You okay, Max?' said Hardin anxiously.

It was a couple of minutes before Stafford could reply. 'Christ, but that was bad.'

'Anything broken?'

Stafford handled himself gingerly, testing for broken bones. At last he said, 'I think I'm in one piece.'

'It could have been your neck the way you went down,' said Hardin. 'What the hell happened?'

Stafford got to his feet. 'There's something about that rock. It's damned slippery; almost as if it's been greased.'

Hardin took a pace to the outcrop and inspected it visually, then passed his hand over the surface. 'Just plain old rock as far as I can see.'

'Damn it!' said Stafford. 'It was just like walking on loose ball bearings.' He joined Hardin but could detect nothing odd about the nature of the stone surface.

Hardin said, 'If you're okay I'll finish cleaning up.' He returned to the waterside and Stafford waited, watching what he supposed was one of the fish eagles Nair had mentioned as it circled lazily above, and wondering about the curious nature of the rock on Crescent Island.

Hardin finished and they walked back, Stafford limping a little because he had pulled a muscle in his leg. Nair had coffee waiting and gave Stafford a cup as he sat on his sleeping bag. Hardin said, 'Max thinks you have odd rocks here. He took a nasty tumble back there.'

Nair looked up. 'Odd? How?'

'Damn slippery. I could have broken something.' Stafford massaged his thigh.

'Take a look at the soles of your shoes,' Nair advised.

Stafford took off a shoe and turned it over. 'Well, I'll be damned!' The rubber sole was completely hidden by a packed mass of brown seeds.

'You'll be all right walking about in the normal way,' said Nair. 'Just pick your surfaces and don't walk on naked rock or you'll slip.'

All the same Stafford took his pocket knife and de-seeded his shoes after breakfast. The seeds were small and tetrahedron in shape with a small spike at each vertex so that whichever way they fell one spike would be uppermost, rather like miniature versions of the medieval caltrops which were scattered to discourage cavalry charges. Nature got there first, he reflected, and said aloud, 'Now I know why Gunnarsson was hobbling so badly when he got back to Keekorok.' He inspected the sole of the shoe. The remaining small spikes had broken off under his body weight and left a smooth, polished surface as slick as a ballroom floor. He cleaned the seeds out and then looked at the sole of his shoe. It was full of pinholes.

After they had breakfasted and done the camp chores such as flattening and burying the empty cans there was nothing much to do. 'Did Chip say when he'd be coming back?' asked Stafford.

Nair shrugged. 'I doubt if he'd know.'

'So we twiddle our thumbs,' said Stafford disgustedly.

Curtis returned to his position on top of the ridge, taking with him Stafford's binoculars, and Hardin elected to keep him company. Nair and Stafford took a walk; there being nothing else to do. 'We'll be at the north end of the island,' Nair told Hardin before they left.

They strolled along, taking their time because they were not going anywhere in particular. As they went Stafford told Nair of his assessment of the Kenyan options and Nair agreed with him somewhat gloomily. 'The trouble with us,' he said, 'is that we're civilized enough to have intelligence and security departments, but not civilized enough to know how to use them properly. We haven't had the experience of you British. I don't think we're cynical enough.'

It was an odd way of defining civilization, but Stafford thought he could very well be right.

Once Nair stopped and pointed to the ground, ahead of them but to one side. 'Look!'

Stafford saw nothing, but then an ear twitched and he saw a beady eye. 'A rabbit!' he said in astonishment. 'I didn't know you had those in Africa.'

'Not many,' said Nair. 'Too many predators. That's a Bunyoro rabbit.' He moved and the rabbit took fright and bounded away, changing direction with every hop. Nair slanted his eyes at Stafford. 'Too many predators in all of Africa.'

And most of them human, agreed Stafford, but to himself.

It was nearly eleven in the morning when Hardin caught up with them. 'Alan Hunt just landed from a boat,' he reported. 'The Sergeant has gone down to meet him.'

'He might have brought news,' said Stafford. 'Let's go see.'

Hunt, however, had no news. He had been to the service station in Naivasha to replenish the butane bottles for the balloon and to have a pipe welded on the burner and had then decided to see if Stafford knew what was happening. 'We're marking bloody time, that's all,' said Stafford. 'Waiting for the top brass to make up its collective mind – if any.'

'You were right,' said Hunt.

'What about?'

'The TV camera in the entrance hall of the Admin Block. I checked on it.'

Stafford grunted. 'I hope you didn't poke your eye right into it.'

'And your friend, Gunnarsson, stayed over last night. He and Brice seemed quite pally.'

Stafford thought of the directed conversation he had with Gunnarsson in the bedroom. He said, 'Brice is probably measuring him up; assessing the opposition, no doubt.'

Hardin laughed. 'Measuring him up is right. For a coffin, probably.'

Stafford disagreed. 'I doubt it. It's a bad operation that leaves too many corpses around. I don't think Brice is as stupid as that.'

'He wasn't too worried about leaving a corpse on the Tanzanian border,' objected Hardin.

'That was different. There's still no direct connection between Brice and that episode. He's still pretty well covered. I think . . .'

What Stafford thought was lost because a piercing whistle came from the ridge and he looked up to see Curtis waving in a beckoning motion. 'Something's up,' he said, and began to run.

He was out of breath when he cast himself down next to Curtis and thought that this was a job for a younger man. Nair and Hunt were with him, but Hardin was still trailing behind. Curtis pointed to a boat half way across the narrow strait between the island and the mainland, and passed the binoculars to Stafford, 'If the Colonel would care to take a look? It's coming from the Lake Naivasha Hotel.'

Stafford put the glasses to his eyes and focused. In the stern was a young black Kenyan, his hand on the tiller of the outboard motor. And Gunnarsson sat amidships, staring at the island and apparently right into Stafford's eyes.

# TWENTY-NINE

Stafford withdrew from the crest of the ridge as Hardin flopped down beside him. 'What is it?' Hardin asked. He was short of breath.

'Gunnarsson. He's coming straight here as though pulled by a magnet. Now, how the hell does he know where we are?' No one answered him, so Stafford said, 'Ben, you get lost. You, too, Nair; but stay close and available. Curtis and I will form a welcoming committee. Come on, Sergeant.'

'What about me?' said Hunt.

Stafford considered the matter and shrugged. 'That depends on whether you want to get involved. Come if you like.' He peered over the ridge. Gunnarsson's boat was heading straight as an arrow to the roughly-made jetty which formed the landing place.

'I'll come,' said Hunt.

The three of them traversed the ridge heading north and keeping below the crest, then went over at a place where the jetty was screened from view by trees. They moved fast because Stafford wanted to intercept Gunnarsson at the jetty before he set out to explore the island. A water-buck exploded out of a thicket, panicked by their sudden presence, and went galloping across a glade ahead of them. As they went by it stopped and stared and then, reassured, resumed its browsing.

Stafford slowed his pace as he neared the jetty close enough to hear the puttering of an outboard engine. The jetty came into view, half hidden by a leafy screen. He stopped and moved a branch and saw Gunnarsson getting out of the boat. There was a distant mutter of voices and then the raised note of the motor as the boat pulled away. Gunnarsson stood on the jetty and looked at the boats moored there: the one in which Nair had brought the camp supplies and the other in which Hunt had arrived.

Stafford whispered to Hunt, 'Did you come from the Lake Naivasha Hotel?'

'No – from Safariland.'

Stafford frowned. That made it unlikely that Gunnarsson had been following Hunt, so what had brought him? He watched Gunnarsson inspecting the boats. He got into each and appeared to be searching them thoroughly. Not that there was anything to find.

Gunnarsson climbed back on to the jetty, and Stafford said, 'Let's ask him what he wants.' They left cover and walked along the shoreline.

Gunnarsson had his back to them but, as he heard their approach, he turned. A grim smile appeared on his face and he put his hands on his hips and stood with arms akimbo. They got close enough for conversation and Stafford said pleasantly, 'Good morning, Mr Gunnarsson. How are your feet today?'

'By Christ!' said Gunnarsson. 'Stafford, you are one magnificent liar. You had me fooled, you really did. So you were pulling out and going back to London? And I believed you.'

Stafford was comforted by that. If he had fooled Gunnarsson then he might have also fooled Brice and Hendriks. He said, 'What are you doing here?'

'I'm looking for a guy in a turban, but I suppose you wouldn't know anything about him.' He raised his hand before Stafford could speak. 'And don't tell me you don't know anything about him. I wouldn't believe you now if you told me that the thing shining in the sky is the sun.'

Stafford shrugged. 'That sounds like Nair Singh, our guide.'

Gunnarsson looked at Hunt. 'You're from Ol Njorowa. I saw you at breakfast this morning. So you're in this, too.'

'My name is Hunt. What am I supposed to be in, Mr Gunnarsson?'

Gunnarsson looked frustrated. If I knew that I wouldn't be screwing around here in this half-assed manner.' He glanced at Curtis. 'Who are you?'

The reply was characteristically brief and brought Gunnarsson no joy. 'Curtis.'

Gunnarsson's attention returned to Stafford. 'This Hindu guy you say is your guide. Where is he?'

'I wouldn't call him a Hindu; he might take umbrage because he's a Sikh.' Stafford waved his arm. 'He's back there. Do you want to talk to him?'

'Yeah, I want to ask him if he usually drives a phoney taxi equipped to track a beeper bug,' said Gunnarsson with heavy irony. 'It's standing in the hotel parking lot right now. I suppose you don't know anything about that, either.'

'I know now.' Stafford smiled. 'You've just told me.'

Gunnarsson snorted. 'So what is a tourist guide doing with triple antennas and a signal strength meter? Why was he trailing me?'

'Let's ask him,' Stafford proposed. 'I'll lead the way.' He walked away from the jetty and Gunnarsson fell into step beside him. Curtis and Hunt tagged along behind. 'What led you to Crescent Island?'

'That goddamn taxi was in the parking lot when I got back to the hotel this morning,' said Gunnarsson. 'I asked at the desk where the owner was and I was told he'd come here.'

So it had been as easy as that, thought Stafford. Nair had made mistakes; first with the beeper and then not getting rid of the Mercedes. Still, no harm had been done.

They climbed the ridge and went down the other side to the camp site. Stafford shouted, 'Nair!', and Nair got up from where he was unobtrusively lying in the shade of a tree. 'A man here wants to talk to you.'

Nair approached them. 'What about?' he asked innocently.

'Jesus; you know what about!' said Gunnarsson belligerently. 'Why are you so goddamn interested in me?'

'Do you have something to hide?'

Gunnarsson's eyes nickered. 'What's with the double-talk?'

'I think he *has* something to hide,' said Stafford. 'For instance, I'd like to know what happened to Henry Hendrix.'

'We've been through all that before.' Gunnarsson took out a handkerchief and mopped his brow and his neck. 'I'm tired of telling the story.'

'Oh, I don't mean Corliss,' said Stafford casually. 'I know what happened to him. But what happened to Hendrix?'

'Hendrix is . . .' Gunnarsson began, and stopped as the meaning of what Stafford had said sank in. He moistened his lips and swallowed before saying, 'Who is Corliss?'

'Your friend who disappeared in Tanzania.'

'You're crazy! That was Hendrix.'

Stafford shook his head. 'Gunnarsson; you're a bigger liar than I am. The Hendrix you took to London was not the Hendrix found in Los Angeles.'

'Not Hendrix!' said Gunnarsson numbly. 'You must be kidding.' He forced a smile.

'Definitely not Hendrix,' said Stafford. 'And proveable.'

'Look, the guy was brought to me in my office. He had everything right; a pat hand. Everything checked out.' He paused in thought. 'I sent an operative to pick him up in Los Angeles. Could he have pulled a fast one on me?'

'What was his name? This operative?'

'A guy called Hardin. Something of a dead beat. I had to fire him.' Gunnarsson was sweating as he extemporized his story. 'If anyone pulled a fast one it must have been Hardin. He's a . . .'

Stafford cut him short by raising his voice, 'Come out, come out, wherever you are.' As Gunnarsson gazed at him in astonishment Stafford said coolly, 'Why don't you ask him? He's just behind you.'

Gunnarsson whirled and his eyes bulged as he saw Hardin who smiled and said, 'Hello, you lousy cheapskate.'

'You've been under a microscope,' said Stafford. 'Every move you've made has been noted ever since you pitched up in London with Corliss and palmed him off as Hendrix. I won't say we've recorded every time you went to the loo, but damned nearly. And Corliss has been singing as sweetly as any nightingale. The jig's up, Gunnarsson.'

Gunnarsson looked defeated, rather as Stafford had seen him when he hobbled into the game lodge at Keekorok. He mumbled, 'Where is Corliss?'

'Where you'd expect him to be – in a police cell. And that's where you're going.'

To Stafford's surprise Nair stepped forward and produced a pair of handcuffs. 'You're under arrest, Mr Gunnarsson. I'm a police officer.'

Gunnarsson whipped round and began to run. Unfortunately Curtis happened to be in the way and it was like running into a brick wall. Hardin collared him from behind and brought him down. Then Nair manacled him,

right wrist to left ankle. 'Best way of immobilizing a man,'
said Nair. 'He can't run. His only way of getting around is to
roll like a hoop.'

Curtis interrupted the steady flow of obscenities from
Gunnarsson. 'If the Colonel doesn't mind I'll get back up
there.' He indicated the ridge.

'Very well, Sergeant.' Stafford watched Curtis walk away
in his stolid fashion and turned to Nair. 'Are you really a
police officer?'

Nair grinned. 'Police reserve. I always carry a spare warrant card. Do you want to see it?'

Stafford shook his head. 'I'll take it on trust.'

Gunnarsson looked up at Hardin malevolently. 'You
lousy bastard! I'll have your balls.'

'Talk to me like that again and I'll kick your teeth in,' said
Hardin sharply. 'Any injuries can be put down to resisting
arrest.'

'Yes,' said Nair. 'I would advise a still tongue.'

Gunnarsson twisted around to face him. 'What's the
charge? I've committed no crime in Kenya.'

'Oh, we can always think of something,' said Nair cheerfully.

Hunt wore a baffled expression. 'I don't understand all
this. Who is this man, and what has he to do with Ol
Njorowa?'

'His name is Gunnarsson and he has nothing whatever to
do with Ol Njorowa,' said Stafford. 'He tried to get some
easy money but didn't know what he was getting into. Still,
he *did* lead us to the funny business at the College. Hardin
will tell you all about it.'

'Yeah,' said Hardin. 'Over a beer. We've got some six-
packs cooling in the lake; let's go get them.'

As they walked away Stafford called, 'Take a beer to the
Sergeant,' then said to Nair, 'So what do we do about him?'
He indicated Gunnarsson.

'Not much. He'll keep until Chip comes back. Of course, we'll have to feed him.'

'Yeah,' said Gunnarsson. 'If there's any beer going I'd like a can. And what's this about Ol Njorowa? I figured the place wasn't kosher but I couldn't put my finger on what's wrong about it.'

'Hardin always said you were smart,' admitted Stafford. 'But not, I think, smart enough. You got in over your head, Gunnarsson. One of my associates described it elegantly as the clash of nations.'

Gunnarsson looked up at him uncomprehendingly.

One of the nations was preparing for its part in the clash.

Brice looked at Patterson stonily. 'So Gunnarsson went out to Crescent Island. Why?'

'I couldn't ask him; he wasn't within shouting distance,' said Patterson acidly. 'But I think he's chasing after some Indian – a Sikh. He was making enquiries about the driver of a Kenatco taxi in the hotel car park and then hired the hotel boat to take him to the island. The boatman wouldn't wait for him because someone wanted to go fishing. He promised Gunnarsson he'd pick him up in a couple of hours.' He looked at his watch. 'That was nearly an hour ago. I left Joe Baiya on watch and came back here to report. You said not to use the telephone in this business.'

'So I did.' Brice tapped a ballpoint pen on the desk and stared unseeingly at Dirk Hendriks. 'A Sikh in a Kenatco taxi. That's something new.'

'And interesting,' said Hendriks.

'It gets more interesting,' said Patterson. 'I had another look at the taxi – a Mercedes just like Kenatco uses, but I don't think it's theirs. It had three antennas and a signal strength meter on the dashboard. A professional trailing job.'

Brice sat straighter in his chair. 'Gunnarsson told us about that. I didn't know whether or not to believe him.' He stood up and paced the room. 'If it isn't one damn thing it's another. We get rid of Stafford and now we've got this man Gunnarsson pushing in. I'd like to know why.'

'Are we sure Stafford has gone?' asked Patterson.

Hendriks nodded. 'Our man in Nairobi reported in person fifteen minutes ago. Stafford left on the morning flight. He checked out of the Norfolk early and changed his Kenyan money at the airport bank like a good boy. Our man saw the record – he has good contacts at the airport. Both Stafford and his man, Curtis, are on the passenger list.'

'But did anyone *see* them leave?' persisted Patterson.

'Forget Stafford,' snapped Brice. 'Our immediate concern is Gunnarsson and, more important, with whoever is following him. I don't like it.' He stood up. 'Since they're both conveniently to hand on Crescent Island I propose that we find out what they're doing there. Come on.'

The three of them left the office and, on the way through the entrance hall, Brice collected the black who presided behind the reception desk.

Hunt said, 'That's the damnedest story I've ever heard.'

Hardin chuckled. 'Isn't it, though? Not long ago Max asked me if I thought that running down Biggie and Hank would lead to what's happening here in Kenya. Really weird. If Gunnarsson hadn't tried to pull a switch then the Ol Njorowa crowd might have got away with it. Brice and Hendriks are damned unlucky.' He rubbed his chin. 'There's one person I'm really sorry for.'

'Who's that?'

'Mrs Hendriks back in London. I liked her – a real nice lady.'

'Perhaps she's in it up to her neck just as much as her husband.'

Hardin drained his beer can and then crushed it flat. 'Max says not, and he's known her for a long time. He knew her before she married Hendriks. Apparently he got her out of a jam once before; some trouble her brother was in. That's why she went to him when I appeared with my story and Hendriks was away in South Africa. If she was in cahoots with Dirk she'd have kept her mouth shut. No, I think this is going to hurt her bad when the news gets out.'

Hunt looked at his watch. 'I'd better be getting back.'

'Okay.' Hardin picked up a beer can and tossed it to Hunt. 'Give that to Curtis on your way. It must be as hot as Hades up there. Tell him I'll relieve him for the afternoon watch. And check with Max before you go. He might want you to do something at Ol Njorowa.'

'Right.' Hunt looked up at the ridge. 'Funny chap, Curtis. Never says much, does he?'

Hardin grinned. 'The Sergeant is the only guy I know who only talks when he has something to say. Everybody else goes yacketty-yack all the time. But when he does say something, for Christ's sake, take notice.'

Hunt reported to Stafford that he was leaving. Stafford said, 'Alan, is there a way into Ol Njorowa other than the front gate?'

'Not that I know of,' said Hunt. 'You go through the gate or through the fence – or over it.'

'Or under it,' suggested Nair.

Stafford shook his head. 'Brice knew what he was doing when he put up that fence. He's not stupid. My bet is that it's like an Australian rabbit fence and extends four feet underground. Is the animal migration laboratory normally kept locked?'

'I don't know,' said Hunt. 'I've never had occasion to try the door.'

Stafford grimaced. 'Of course not.' He reflected for a moment. 'I don't know if there'll be any rough stuff – nothing like a shoot-out at the OK Corral – normally intelligence outfits don't favour guns. But there may be a bit of trouble when Chip moves in, so my advice is to get Judy out of there. Send her to Nairobi for a week's shopping or something like that.'

'I've already tried that and she's not buying it,' said Hunt.

'Well, tell her to keep her head down.' They shook hands and Hunt departed and Stafford walked over to where Nair was interrogating Gunnarsson. 'Now,' he said. 'You were about to tell us what really happened to Hank Hendrix.'

'Go screw yourself,' said Gunnarsson.

Curtis turned his head as Hunt approached and slid down from the top of the ridge. He accepted the can of beer gratefully. 'Thanks. Just what the doctor ordered.'

'Hardin says he'll relieve you soon,' said Hunt.

'He needn't bother.'

Hunt regarded him curiously. 'Have you been with Max Stafford long?'

Curtis swallowed beer, his Adam's apple working vigorously. He sighed in appreciation. 'A couple of years.'

'Were you in the service together?'

Curtis nodded. 'In a way. A long time ago.'

Hunt decided that making conversation with Curtis was hard work. The Sergeant was polite and informative but brief as though words were rationed and not to be squandered. If brevity was the soul of wit Curtis was the wittiest man alive. But surprisingly Curtis came up with a question. 'Are hippos dangerous?'

'That depends,' said Hunt. 'I wouldn't go too near in a boat and I certainly wouldn't choose them as swimming companions.'

'This one's ashore.' He pointed. 'Landed about an hour ago over there.'

Hunt looked to where Curtis pointed and saw nothing. 'They don't usually venture ashore in daylight. And, yes, they're bloody dangerous. They can move a lot faster than you'd think, certainly faster than a man can run, and those tusks can kill. The thing to remember is never to get between a hippo and the water.'

'I'll tell the Colonel,' said Curtis.

Hunt nodded. 'I'm going back to Ol Njorowa.'

Curtis eased himself to the top of the ridge and picked up the binoculars. Hunt was about to walk past him when Curtis held up his hand. 'Wait!'

Hunt stopped. 'What's the matter?'

'Get down off the ridge – off the skyline.' Curtis was intently watching something below as Hunt dropped beside him. He said, 'A boat coming. Five men; three white, two black.' He paused. 'One is Dirk Hendriks. I don't know the others.' He passed the binoculars to Hunt.

Hunt focused and the approaching boat suddenly jumped towards him. 'Brice and Patterson,' he said. 'And Joe Baiya – he's a sort of handyman around Ol Njorowa – with Luke Maiyani. He's usually behind the desk in the Admin Block.'

Curtis's voice was even. 'You'd better tell the Colonel. I'll stay here.'

Hunt plunged down the hill towards the camp site.

# THIRTY

Stafford's first reaction was to turn to Nair. 'Is this island big enough to play hide-and-seek?'

'Hide from five men?' Nair shook his head decisively. 'And what about him?' He pointed to Gunnarsson who was stubbornly resisting Hardin's questioning.

'Damn!' said Stafford. Gunnarsson was a real stumbling block; if he was left manacled Brice was sure to find him, but if he was freed he might run straight to Brice and blab all he knew, and he knew too much for comfort. Stafford damned the men in Nairobi who were talking instead of acting.

He strode over to Gunnarsson and dropped to his knees. 'Do you want to live?' he asked abruptly.

Gunnarsson's eyes widened. 'That's a hell of a question.'

'Look, I'm not interested in your tricks with Corliss,' said Stafford. 'That's small time stuff compared with what Brice is doing.'

'Yeah', said Hardin. 'You were ripping off a lousy six million bucks. Brice was going for broke – maybe a hundred million.'

'He's coming here now,' said Stafford, and heard Hardin make a muffled exclamation. 'And he's bringing his troops. A few lives are nothing compared to what he has at stake.'

'He wouldn't risk murder,' said Hardin. 'Shots could be heard from the mainland.'

Stafford thought of the man he had killed in Tanzania. 'Who said anything about shooting? There are other ways of killing and the evidence can be buried in the belly of a crocodile,' he said brutally, and Gunnarsson flinched. 'As you are now you wouldn't stand a chance so I'm going to release you, but just remember who is doing you the favour.'

'Sure,' said Gunnarsson eagerly. 'Just let me run.'

Stafford signalled to Nair who shrugged and produced the key of the handcuffs. When Gunnarsson was free he stood up and massaged his wrist. 'This true?' he asked Hardin. He jerked his head at Stafford. 'This guy was talking about something else before.'

'It's true,' said Hardin. 'We've run against South African intelligence and those guys don't play patty-cake. You ought to know that. We've got in the way of one of their big operations.'

'Then I'm fading,' Gunnarsson announced.

'You'll do as you're bloody well told,' snapped Stafford. He was looking at Curtis up on the ridge. 'You said five men. That all?'

'All I saw,' said Hunt. 'There could be another boat coming along behind.'

'Curtis hasn't signalled anything about that,' commented Stafford. 'What do you think, Ben?' The odds are better than even if Gunnarsson comes in. Six to five.'

'You mean a straight fight for it?' Hardin made a wry face. 'We'd lose,' he said flatly. 'Look at us – middle-aged men except for Alan and Nair here, and I wouldn't think Alan has had the training for it. Dirk Hendriks is a husky young guy, and Brice looks as though he eats nails for breakfast. I don't know about the others.' He looked at Hunt.

'Patterson's a toughie and I wouldn't like to tackle Luke Maiyani without a club in my hand,' said Hunt frankly.

'Then if we can't use force we must use guile,' said Stafford.

Gunnarsson said, 'And we can't waste time standing here yapping.'

Nair said suddenly, 'Why is Brice coming here?' It was a rhetorical question because he answered it himself. 'I think Gunnarsson has been followed, probably by Patterson. It was Patterson who went looking for him in Nairobi. And Gunnarsson was following me. I think Brice expects to find only the two of us.'

'Makes sense,' said Hardin. 'And that means . . .'

'Yes,' said Stafford.

Gunnarsson found himself the centre of a circle of eyes. 'Now wait a minute. If you guys expect me to stick my neck out after the way you've treated me you're crazy.'

'Mr Gunnarsson,' said Nair politely. 'You and I are going across the island to meet Brice. On the way we'll think of something to tell him. I'm sure your imagination will be up to it.'

'Keep them occupied while we get rid of this stuff,' said Stafford. He waved his hand at the evidence of the camp site. 'Say ten or fifteen minutes. Then draw them out of sight of the boats at the jetty. We'll be coming in on the flank. And send Curtis down here.'

The engine note altered as the boat neared the jetty. Brice said, 'Two boats here. All right; one brought the Sikh but the boat which brought Gunnarsson went back, you said.' He turned to Patterson. 'So whose is the other?'

Patterson looked at his watch. 'The boatman must have come back for Gunnarsson. Just about time.'

Brice nodded briefly as the boat drifted in and touched the jetty. Baiya and Maiyani held it steady as he went ashore. He turned and said, 'Baiya, you stay here. The rest come with me.'

Baiya lashed the painter around a cleat on Hunt's boat and the others went ashore. Hendriks looked around. 'Where do we start?'

'We'll find them,' said Brice confidently. 'It's not a big island.'

'No need to go far,' said Patterson. 'They've found us. Look!' He pointed up the hill to where two figures stood silhouetted on the ridge.

'Good; that saves time,' said Brice. 'Let's go to meet them. I'd like to know what this is about – but let me do the talking.'

They walked up the hill and met Nair and Gunnarsson on the level base of the foundations of the old building. To Brice's surprise he saw handcuffs on Gunnarsson's wrists.

'What's going on here?' he demanded. 'Why is Mr Gunnarsson handcuffed?'

Nair Singh looked at him sternly. 'Do you know this man?'

'I had breakfast with him this morning.'

'I am a police officer.' Nair took a small leather case from his pocket and flipped it open. 'Nair Singh. This is my warrant card. Mr Gunnarsson is under arrest.'

Brice turned to look at Hendriks who was plainly shocked. He turned back to Nair. 'May I know the charge?'

'He has been arrested but not yet charged,' said Nair. 'You say you had breakfast with Mr Gunnarsson this morning. May I know your name, sir.'

'Brice. Charles Brice.'

Nair's face cleared. 'Of Ol Njorowa College?'

'Yes. Now what's this all about?'

'Ah, then I think you'll be pleased to know that we caught this man before he did too much damage. He's under arrest for fraud.'

'It's a goddamn lie,' said Gunnarsson. 'Look, Mr Brice, do me a favour. Ring the American Embassy in Nairobi as soon as you can. This is a put-up job; I'm being framed for something I didn't do.'

'The American authorities will be informed,' said Nair coldly.

'Now hang on a minute,' said Hendriks. 'What sort of fraud?'

Nair looked at him. 'Who are you, sir?'

'Hendriks. Dirk Hendriks. I'm staying with Mr Brice at Ol Njorowa.'

Nair looked oddly embarrassed. 'Oh! Then you will be an heir to the estate which has benefited Ol Njorowa?'

'That's correct.'

Brice said impatiently, 'Who is Mr Gunnarsson supposed to have defrauded?'

Nair was playing for time. He said to Hendriks, 'Then it was your cousin who disappeared in Tanzania.'

Hendriks and Brice exchanged glances. Hendriks said, 'Yes; and nothing seems to have been done about it. Was Gunnarsson mixed up in that business? Is that it?'

'Not quite,' said Nair. 'How long had you known your cousin, Mr Hendriks?'

The question seemed strange to Dirk. 'What's that got to do with anything? And what's it got to do with Gunnarsson?'

'How long?' persisted Nair.

'Not very long – a matter of weeks. He was an American, you know. I met him for the first time in London.'

'Ah!' said Nair, as though suddenly a light had been shone into darkness. 'That would explain it.'

'Explain what?' said Brice in sudden irritation.

'Henry Hendrix came back across the border two days after he was kidnapped,' said Nair. 'And . . .'

Brice and Hendriks broke in simultaneously and then stopped, each looking at the other in astonishment. Brice said sharply, 'Why was no one told of this? It's monstrous that Mr Hendriks here should have been kept in ignorance. He's been worried about his cousin.'

'As I said, Henry Hendrix came back,' continued Nair calmly. 'But he was delirious; he had a bad case of sunstroke. In his delirium he talked of certain matters which required investigation and, when he recovered, he was questioned and made a full confession. I am sorry to tell you that the man known to you as Henry Hendrix is really called Corliss and he has implicated Gunnarsson in his imposture.'

'It's a lie,' cried Gunnarsson. 'He screwed me the same way as he screwed everyone else.'

'That will be for the court to decide,' said Nair. He studied Brice and Hendriks, both of whom appeared to be shell-shocked, and smiled internally. 'The American Embassy has, of course, been kept acquainted with these developments and agreed that a certain amount of . . . er . . . reticence was in order while the matter was investigated. Mr Gunnarsson will have a number of questions to answer when we get back to Nairobi.' He looked at his watch. 'And now, if you gentlemen will excuse me . . . ?'

There was something wrong here which Brice could not fathom. He watched Nair and Gunnarsson pass by and felt obscurely that somewhere he was being tricked. He said, 'Wait a moment. Have you been following Gunnarsson in that Kenatco taxi?'

Nair paused and looked back. 'In the line of duty.'

'Then why did it happen in reverse? Why did Gunnarsson follow you here to Crescent Island?'

'I tempted him,' said Nair blandly.

'Yeah, he suckered me all right,' said Gunnarsson in corroboration.

Suddenly Brice saw – or, rather, did not see – the missing piece, the missing man. If Gunnarsson had come to the island and the boatman had gone away and had then returned to pick him up, then where the hell was he? Where was the boatman? And if there was no boatman then whose was the other boat? Brice jerked his head at Patterson and stepped forward. 'Look!' he said sharply, pointing at nothing in particular.

Both Nair and Gunnarsson turned to look and Brice hooked his foot around Gunnarsson's leg and pushed. Gunnarsson went flying down the slope and instinctively put out his hands to save himself. In that he succeeded but the handcuffs went flying away in a glittering arc to clink on a rock, and Brice knew he had been right.

Stafford watched Curtis ghost through the trees to his left and then turned his head to watch Hardin on his right. He knew he did not have to worry about a couple of old pros who knew their business, but Hunt was different; he was a civilian amateur who did not know which end was up, which is why he was directly behind Stafford with strict instructions to walk in the Master's steps. 'I don't want a sound out of you,' Stafford had said. Hunt was doing his best but flinched when Stafford turned to glare at him when a twig snapped underfoot.

Curtis held both hands over his head in the military gesture indicating an order to stop. If he had had a rifle he would have held it, but he had no rifle, which was a pity. He beckoned to Stafford who, after stopping Hunt dead in his tracks, made his way to Curtis in a walking crouch.

Curtis pointed and said in an undertone, 'They've left a man at the boats.' He knew enough not to whisper. Nothing carries further than the sibilants of a whisper.

'Where are the others?'

'Somewhere up the hill. I heard voices.'

Stafford turned his head and gestured to Hardin who crept over. 'There's a guard on the boats,' he said. 'And Nair hasn't decoyed Brice away yet. They're still within hearing distance so they can probably see the boats.'

'Tricky,' said Hardin.

'Would the Colonel like the guard removed?' asked Curtis.

'How would you do it?'

Curtis indicated the water glimmering through the trees. 'Swimming.'

'Goddamn!' said Hardin. 'What about crocodiles?'

'I'd poison a crocodile,' said Curtis solemnly and without the trace of a smile.

'I don't know,' said Stafford uncertainly.

'I've been watching the water's edge from the ridge,' said Curtis. 'I haven't seen any crocodiles.' He was already taking off his shoes.

'Well, all right,' said Stafford. 'But you go when I say; and you incapacitate – you don't kill.'

'I doubt if we'd get trouble if he did,' said Hardin. 'We've proved our point and the Kenyans aren't going to be worried about a dead South African agent.'

'Ben, that man there could be an innocent Kenyan brought along just to drive the boat. We can't take that chance.' Stafford went back to Hunt. 'When you answer keep your voice down. Any crocs in the lake?'

Hunt nodded. 'Usually further north around the papyrus swamp.'

'And here?'

'Could be.'

Stafford frowned. 'We might be making a break for the boats in a few minutes. You follow us and your job is to get an engine started. You do that and you don't bother about anything else. We'll know when you've succeeded. And we want to take *all* the boats so we take two in tow.'

'I'll start the engine in my own boat,' said Hunt. 'I know it best. It's the chase boat we use when the balloon blows over the lake.'

Stafford nodded and went back to Curtis who had taken off his trousers and was flexing a leather belt in his hands. 'Where's Ben?' Curtis silently pointed up the hill to the right.

Presently Hardin came back. 'They're still yakking away up there. I couldn't get close enough to hear what they're saying.'

'Can they see the jetty from where they are?'

'I reckon so.'

That was not good, thought Stafford. Only if Nair could decoy Brice away would they stand a chance. Normally he would have sent Curtis off by now to take out the guard at a signal, but the longer he was in the water the greater the risk, and he would not do that. The only thing to do was to wait for an opportunity.

It came sooner than he expected in the form of a distant shout. He said to Curtis, 'Go! Go!' and Curtis slipped quietly into the water to disappear leaving only a lengthening trail of bubbles. There were more shouts and the man in the boat stood up to get a better view.

Stafford, lurking behind a screen of leaves, followed the direction of his gaze but saw nothing until Hardin nudged him. 'Look! Nair and Gunnarsson are on the run over there.'

Gunnarsson and Nair were sprinting desperately, angling down the slope away from the jetty with Gunnarsson in the lead, and Patterson and a black came in sight in full chase. Then Brice and Hendriks appeared. Brice threw up his arm and he and Hendriks changed direction, running down to the shore on the other side of the jetty. They all vanished from sight.

'Now!' said Stafford, and broke cover to run towards the jetty a hundred yards away, and was conscious of Hardin and Hunt behind him. The guard heard the crunch of their feet and turned in some alarm. He froze for a moment when he saw them and was about to turn back to shout for help when something seemed to tangle his feet and he toppled overboard with a splash.

Stafford ran up and jumped into the boat. He leaned over the side. 'Come on, Sergeant,' he said and took Curtis's arm to help him aboard. Hardin had seized an oar and was pushing the boat away from the jetty and from Hunt's boat there came a splutter as the engine balked. Stafford left Curtis gasping on the floor boards and was just in time to grab the painter of the third boat. He fastened it to a cleat and then had time to look around.

Hunt was rewinding the starter cord on his outboard engine and Stafford said harshly, 'Get that bloody thing started.' He was thinking of Nair. Hardin had pushed off vigorously with the oar and the boats were now drifting about ten yards offshore where the guard was standing dripping wet and already raising an outcry. Stafford looked along the shore line and saw Brice and Hendriks turn to look back.

Hunt's engine caught with a stuttering roar, then settled down to an even purr. Stafford shouted, 'Further out and then go south – after Nair.' The note of the engine deepened and the small convoy increased in speed. He bent down to Curtis. 'You all right, Sergeant?'

'Yes, sir. Nothing wrong with me.'

Hardin was staring at the shore. 'Brice looks mad enough to bust a gut.'

Brice and Hendriks had stopped and were motionless, looking at the boats which were now a hundred yards away and moving parallel with the coast. Brice said something to Hendriks and they began to run again. Stafford said, 'Where are Nair and Gunnarsson?'

'Should be on the other side of that point there, if they haven't been caught.'

Stafford raised his voice and shouted to Hunt in the lead boat. 'Open that thing up! Get a bloody move on!'

Curtis had got up and was in the stern, already starting the engine of their own boat. Hardin hauled on the painter of the other boat to bring it alongside, then he jumped in. One by one the other engines started and Stafford cast off the boats so they could operate independently. He said to Curtis, 'Cut in close to the point. I'll watch for rocks.' He signalled to the others that he was taking the lead.

'Hey!' shouted Hardin, and pointed ashore, and Stafford saw that Patterson was in sight but had fallen. He tried to get up but collapsed when he put weight on his leg. Curtis grunted. 'Broke his ankle with a bit of luck, sir.'

Nair thought his lungs would burst. He risked a glance backwards and saw the black about twenty yards behind – and no one else. Ahead Gunnarsson was running steadily but slowing. Nair got enough breath to shout, 'Gunnarsson! Help!' and stopped to face his pursuer.

Luke Maiyani was taken by surprise. The prey was supposed to run, not stand and fight against the odds. By the time he had come to this conclusion he was within five yards of Nair so he also came to a halt and looked back expecting to see Patterson but there was no one in sight. It was this small hesitation that cost him a broken jaw because Nair picked up a rock in his fist and when Maiyani turned to look at him again Nair swung with all the force he could. There was a crunch and Maiyani dropped in his tracks.

Nair turned and found that Gunnarsson was still running along the shore. He stood there with his chest heaving and became aware of shouting from offshore. He looked out at the lake and saw three boats coming in with Stafford in the bows of the leading boat waving vigorously. Behind, Hardin was pointing with urgency and he turned his head and saw Brice and Hendriks just rounding the point.

Without further hesitation he ran for the water and th
approaching boats. He was splashing through the shallow
when Hendriks pulled out a gun with a long barrel and too
careful aim. There was no report but Nair staggered and fell
He rolled over in the water until it was deep enough to sup
port him and started to swim, striking out with his arms an
using one leg.

Gunnarsson's attention, too, had been attracted by th
shouting. He stopped to look out into the lake and Hun
yelled, 'Swim for it!' Gunnarsson hesitated, then made u|
his mind as he became aware of Brice and Hendriks advanc
ing upon him. Hunt steered closer to the shore and wave
encouragingly then stopped in mid-wave.

'Oh, Christ!' he said.

As Gunnarsson ran towards the water there was a move
ment from behind him and a vast grey shape burst out o
the trees. Hunt shouted, 'Sideways! Run to the side
Gunnarsson!' but he was ignored. The bull hippopotamu
behind Gunnarsson was advancing at a steady yard-eating
trot, running much faster than the man. It caught him jus
as he reached the water's edge. Hunt saw the mouth oper
in a cavernous gape edged with white tusks which closed ir
a quick snap. Then the hippo was in the lake and there wa
no sign of Gunnarsson except for a swirl of bloodied water

Hunt wrenched the tiller over and opened the throttle
speeding to get between the hippopotamus and Nair whc
was swimming weakly. He heard no gunfire and did no
know what it was that whined past him like an angry hor
net to hit the outboard motor. The rapid beat of the engine
faltered and then it stopped and the boat lost momentum.

Stafford's boat passed him. Stafford was standing in th
bows holding an oar, and shouted, 'Get down – you're being
shot at!'

'Watch for the hippo!' Hunt replied and twisted around
to look for it but could not see it. But he saw a peculia

wave on the surface of the water and knew the hippopotamus was running on the bottom of the shallow lake. The displacement wave rippled towards Nair but was intercepted by Stafford's boat which lurched violently, almost throwing Stafford off his feet.

Hardin was coming in fast on the other side towards Nair as the hippo surfaced next to Stafford's boat. He raised the oar and struck at its head and as the tough, flexible wood shivered violently in his hands he knew he had got in a good blow. For a moment the hippopotamus looked at him with an unwinking eye then breathed mightily and submerged.

Curtis swung over the tiller and Stafford looked for Nair and was relieved to see Hardin helping him into the boat. A miniature fountain rose quite close to him and Stafford said to Curtis, 'For God's sake, let's get out of here.' He waved to Hardin, pointing out into the lake, as Curtis headed towards the boat in which Hunt drifted.

He slowed as they came alongside and Hunt jumped for it. Even as he jumped Curtis was opening the throttle again and swinging to head out into the lake away from shore. Stafford looked back just in time to see the boat Hunt had abandoned rise bow first and then capsize as the hippopotamus attacked it. There was a splashing and a frothing of water and then the boat had gone leaving only a few shattered timbers floating on the water.

The shore of Crescent Island receded and when they were a good half mile away Stafford said, 'Let's join Hardin and see if Nair is all right.' He looked at Hunt and said quietly, 'That was a bloody bad two minutes.'

Curtis throttled back as he came alongside Hardin and the two boats drifted placidly. Nair had slit his trousers and was examining his leg. Hardin said, 'Nair reckons he was hit in the leg, but I didn't hear any shooting.'

'It was Hendriks,' said Stafford. 'He must have had a silencer. Is it bad, Nair?'

'No, just a hole in the fleshy part of the thigh. The bulle
must still be in there; there's only one hole.' He held up hi
right hand. 'And I broke a finger; maybe two.' He looke
around. 'Where's Gunnarsson?'

'Yeah,' said Hardin. 'Where is the son of a bitch?'

'The hippo got him,' said Hunt.

'I didn't see that,' said Stafford. 'I was too busy trying t
get to Nair. What happened to him?'

'It bit him in half.' Hunt shivered involuntarily.

'Jesus!' said Hardin. 'I didn't like the bastard but
wouldn't wish that on my worst enemy. Are you sure?'

'I'm sure,' said Hunt. 'I saw it. There was a lot of blood ir
the water.' He looked at the sky and added dully, 'They'v
been known to bite crocodiles in half.'

'I'd have reckoned Gunnarsson to be tougher than any
crocodile,' said Hardin in a heavy attempt at jocularity, bu
the humour fell flat.

'We'd better get on,' said Stafford. 'Nair needs a doctor
Any other injuries?'

No one admitted to being hurt, but Curtis said mourn
fully, 'I left my belt back there. It was a good belt, too
Snakeskin.'

'You left more than that,' said Hardin. 'You left you
pants.'

'Yes, but my Amy gave me that belt.'

There was a moment's silence before Stafford said, 'Tha
lot are marooned back there. I think we ought to move int
Ol Njorowa now.'

'Chip won't like it,' warned Nair.

'Chip doesn't know the circumstances. How much staf
does the animal migration lab have, Alan?'

'I don't know,' said Hunt. 'It varies. I didn't think ther
was anyone there now until I saw Patterson.'

'Then there's a good chance that it's empty,' said Staffor
as though arguing with himself. 'I don't think Brice car

have really got going yet. So far he's been working on a shoestring and waiting for the Hendrykxx money. This *must* be the best time to bust him, while he's out of the game. Sergeant; head for the shore.'

'To Safariland,' said Hunt. 'I think I know of a way to get you into Ol Njorowa.'

# THIRTY-ONE

Francis Yongo was boatman at the Lake Naivasha Hotel and Francis was worried. He had promised to pick up M. Gunnarsson from Crescent Island and he had not done so because someone had taken his boat. He talked to the cray fish fishermen by the lake and asked if they had seen it. One said he thought he had seen it going out across the lake with a number of men in it. No, he had not seen where it was going; it had been of no interest.

Dispiritedly Francis walked up to the hotel to report to the manager who spoke acidly about inconsiderate tourists and got on the telephone. An hour later he called Francis into the office. 'I've traced the boat, Francis. It's lying at Safariland – just come in. You'd better take your bike out there and pick up Mr Gunnarsson on the way back. I doubt if he'll be pleased.' He went on to fulminate about thoughtless joyriders while Francis listened patiently. He had heard it all before. Then he went to get his bicycle.

Nair leaned heavily on Stafford as he hobbled up from the dock at Safariland towards the manager's office. Stafford said, 'What went wrong back there? How did Brice catch on?'

'It was Gunnarsson,' said Nair. 'I thought it best to stick close to the truth so I told Brice I'd arrested him

662

That meant Gunnarsson had to be handcuffed but he wouldn't wear them; he said he wanted to be free if anything went wrong so he faked it. Then he stumbled and they fell off.'

'And that was a tip-off to Brice.' Stafford shook his head. 'In a way you could say Gunnarsson killed himself. Will you be all right, Nair?'

'As soon as you've gone I'll phone Chip, then I'll get a doctor.' He sat on one of the chairs on the lawn. 'I don't suppose I can stop you?'

'It's the right time,' said Stafford positively.

'Perhaps, but I have to convince Chip.' Nair took a bunch of keys from his pocket. 'Go to the Lake Naivasha Hotel first. There's a pistol and a spare magazine clipped under the front seat of the Mercedes.' He tossed the keys to Stafford. 'Don't use it unless you have to.'

'Thanks. The others will be waiting. I still have to find out from Hunt how we're to get into Ol Njorowa.'

It was to prove ridiculously easy. He found Hunt, Hardin and Curtis waiting for him in the car park, standing next to Hunt's Land-Rover. Hunt pointed to the trailer attached to the rear. 'You go in there!'

'Is there room?'

'It's empty apart from a few butane bottles and the burner,' said Hunt. 'I left the envelope and the basket at Ol Njorowa when I took the burner in for repair this morning. God, but that seems a long time ago.'

'Aren't you stopped at the gate?' queried Hardin.

'I never have been. Staff members can move freely.'

'Yes, they'd have to,' said Stafford. 'There's a limit to Brice's bloody security. It would look pretty queer if the staff of an agricultural college were searched every time they went in. That reinforces my contention that whatever there is to be found will be in the animal migration laboratory. All right; let's go.'

'I'll put you right outside the door of the lab,' said Hun
'But I can't promise it will be unlocked.'

Hardin said, 'Just deliver us; we'll see to the rest.'

Hunt opened the trailer and Stafford, Curtis and Hardi
climbed in. Hunt hesitated. 'I usually keep it locked,' h
said. 'There's a deal of petty pilfering.'

'Do as you do normally,' said Stafford, so Hunt locke
them in, walked around the Land-Rover and drove o
slowly.

Nair's police warrant card had secured him a telephon
and the privacy of the manager's office. But when he spok
to Chip he had his back to the window and so did not se
Francis Yongo cycle past somewhat unsteadily on his way t
the dock.

Hunt stopped at the gate of Ol Njorowa, gave a blast on th
horn, and waved to the guard. The gate opened and h
drove through, keeping his speed down, past the Admi
Block and onward to the building surmounted by the dis
antenna which lay a little over half a mile further. Ahea
there was a car driving equally slowly and, as he watche
it stopped outside the animal migration laboratory. A ma
got out, unlocked the front door, and went inside. Hur
stopped the Land-Rover and got out.

He looked about him. Everything was calm and peacefu
there were a few distant figures in the experimental plo
but no one nearer. He went back to the trailer and tappe
on the door. 'Stafford! Can you hear me?'

A muffled voice said, 'Yes. What is it?'

'We're near the lab. Someone just went in.'

'Let us out.'

Hunt unlocked the trailer and Stafford crawled out fol
lowed by Hardin and Curtis. They stretched, easing thei
cramped limbs, and Stafford looked over to the buildin
nearby and noted the parked car. 'Who was it?'

'I don't know,' said Hunt. 'I just got a glimpse of him.'

Hardin looked up at the dish antenna. 'Science!' he said, somewhat disparagingly.

'Let's find out.' Stafford waved and the four of them walked to the front of the building. He put his hand on the handle of the door and tested it. To his surprise the door opened. 'We're in luck,' he said quietly.

He opened the door and was confronted by a blank wall three feet in front of him. He raised his eyebrows in surprise and then went inside to the left along a narrow passage and emerged into a room. His hand was in his pocket resting on the butt of the gun.

There was no one in the room but there were two doors, one in the wall opposite and another to the right. There were tables and chairs and, in one corner, a water cooler and a coffee machine together with an assortment of crockery. On the walls were large photographs of animals; wildebeest, hippopotamus, elephant. This he took to be the Common Room where the staff relaxed.

He walked slowly into the room. The polished floor was slick and slippery. He went to the door on the right and motioned to Curtis and Hardin who stationed themselves on either side of it. Gently he opened the door and peered inside. Again, this room was empty so he went in. It was an office complete with all the usual equipment one might expect; a desk and swivel chair, a telephone, a reading lamp, a photocopier on a side desk. Total normality.

There were maps on the wall which were covered with a spiderweb of red lines. He inspected one and could make nothing of the cryptic notations. There were also maps on a large side table which had shallow drawers built into it. Again he could make nothing of those on a cursory inspection.

He left and, on an inquiring look from Hardin, shook his head and pointed to the other door. This, again, was unlocked and again the room was empty. It was a big room with no windows and along one wall, running the whole length, were banks of electronic equipment – control consoles and monitor screens gleaming clinically under the lights of overhead fluorescent tubes. It reminded Stafford of Houston space centre in miniature. He looked about him and saw no other door.

'This is crazy,' said Hardin behind him. 'Where did the guy go?'

Stafford withdrew into the Common Room and said to Hunt, 'Are you sure a man came in here?'

'Of course. You saw the car outside.'

'Three rooms,' said Stafford, 'and one door. There's no back door and no man.' He went to the window and looked out, his shoulder brushing aside curtains. As he turned away his attention was caught by something and he stiffened. 'You know,' he said, 'this place is built like a fortress. A blast wall at the front door, and look here . . .' He pulled aside the curtain. 'Steel shutters to cover the windows.'

'Ready for a siege,' commented Hardin.

'Certainly not innocent.' Stafford looked at Hunt. 'You know more about this scientific stuff than any of us. Take a look round and see if there's anything odd, anything out of place that shouldn't be here. Anything at all.'

Hunt shrugged. 'I don't know much about the electronic stuff but I'll take a look.'

He went into the back room and Stafford returned to the office where he opened drawers and rummaged about, looking for he didn't know what. Hardin checked the Common Room and Curtis stood guard by the front door. Ten minutes later they assembled in the Common Room. 'Nothing in here,' said Hardin.

'All the electronic stuff looks standard to me,' said Hunt. 'But it would take an expert to be sure. I found nothing else out of the ordinary.'

'Same with the office,' said Stafford in a dissatisfied voice. 'But I might have missed something. Take a look at those maps, Alan.'

Hunt went into the office and Hardin said, 'We might have made a big mistake, Max.'

'I'd have sworn on a stack of Bibles six feet high that what we're looking for is in here,' said Stafford savagely.

'So what do we do if it's kosher?' asked Hardin. 'Apologize?'

'It can't be. Not with that damned blast wall and the shutters.'

Hunt came back. 'Standard maps of Kenya,' he reported. 'I'd say the lines are animal movements as recorded by the electronic thingummy on the roof. I told you Brice had shown me papers in a journal. The same stuff.' He saw a strange look on Stafford's face. 'What's the matter?'

Stafford was looking at the door leading into the back room. It was open and a man stood there. Stafford plunged forward and the man slammed the door in his face and it took him a moment to open it as his feet slipped from under him. He yanked it open and then lost his footing completely and fell on his back just as there was the sharp report of a shot.

He rolled over and looked around. The room was empty.

He got up slowly and took Nair's pistol from his pocket. He turned carefully looking at every part of the room and saw nothing. 'It's all right, you can come in.' He picked up one foot and felt the sole of his shoe. 'Damned seeds!' he said and kicked off the shoes.

Hardin appeared at the door. 'Where did the guy go?'

Stafford pointed with the gun. 'He was standing there when I fell.'

'That prat fall maybe saved your life,' observed Hardin. 'That goddamn bullet nearly hit me.' He fingered a tear in the side of his shirt and looked around warily. 'What's the trick?'

'I caught sight of something,' said Stafford. 'Just before I fell. Something big and square.' 'What was it?'

'I don't know. It doesn't seem to be there now.' Stafford studied the floor which was covered with a plastic composition in a checkerboard pattern. Set into it at his feet was a metal plate about three inches square. He bent down and found he could prise it upwards and that it moved on a spring-loaded hinge. Beneath the plate was a three-pin socket for an electric plug.

Hardin said, 'Most of this electronic equipment is mounted on castors. That's why they need floor plugs.'

'Yes,' said Stafford absently. He walked over to where he had last seen the man and found another metal plate. He bent down and lifted it. 'Bingo!' he said softly because it opened to reveal not an electric socket but a metal ring. There's a bloody cellar – this is a trap door.'

He ran his fingers along a hairline crack and found the hinge. The trap door was square and it must have been what he saw when it was standing open. 'Take cover, Ben, and warn the others. He might pop off again.' He pulled open the metal flap, put his finger through the ring, and lifted. The door opened easily and he had lifted it about nine inches when there was another shot and a bullet ricochetted from the wall.

Stafford let the door drop and stood on it. Hardin stepped forward from where he had been pressed against the wall. 'Looks like a Mexican stand-off. We can't get down and he can't get up. But if he has a telephone down there he'll be calling for reinforcements.'

Stafford had not thought of that. 'Sergeant!' he shouted. 'If you find any telephone wires cut them, and keep a watch out there.' Hardin was right, he thought. Unless there was another way out of the cellar which he thought unlikely.

The entrance to the cellar on which he stood was cleverly disguised; another entrance would double the chances of the cellar being discovered.

He snapped his fingers suddenly. 'Got it! I know how we can winkle him out. Go with Hunt and bring his balloon burner and a couple of butane bottles. We've got a flame thrower of sorts.'

'Jesus!' said Hardin. 'That's nasty.'

'We'll tickle him up, just enough to put the fear of God into him. He'll come out.'

'Okay.' Hardin turned to go, but stopped at the door and looked back. 'I wouldn't stand there,' he advised. 'If he shoots through the door you're likely to lose the family jewels.'

Stafford hastily stood aside and, while waiting for Hardin to come back, he wheeled a console across so that two of its castored legs stood on the trap door and held it down. He then walked to the door and said to Curtis, 'Any signs of activity out there?'

'Nothing here, sir; except that Mr Hardin and Mr Hunt are coming back.' Curtis turned away from the window. 'I'll check the other side.' He crossed the room and walked into the office.

Hardin came in carrying the burner and Hunt followed, staggering under the weight of a butane cylinder. They went into the back room and Hunt put down the cylinder. Stafford said, 'Can you rig this thing?'

'Yes.' Hunt hesitated. 'But I don't know that I want to.'

'Look!' said Stafford, on the verge of losing his temper. He stabbed his finger down at the trap door. 'That man has been shooting at us. He shot on sight – didn't even stop to say "Hello!". He could have killed any one of us, and Christ knows what he's doing now. I want him out. Now get that damned contraption rigged.'

'Take it easy, Max,' Hardin said quietly. He looked at Hunt. 'Can I help you?'

'No; I'll do it.' Hunt bent to the burner and Hardin watched him with interest.

'Max was telling me about this,' he said. 'When we were idling on the island. He says it's pretty powerful. Is that so?'

Hunt was connecting tubes. 'It's rated at ten million Btu, but it probably delivers about three-quarters of that.'

'I've never figured out what a British Thermal Unit is,' said Hardin. 'I must have been at a ball game when that came up in class.'

'The amount of heat to raise the temperature of a pound of water by one degree Fahrenheit.'

'And you've got ten million of them in that thing!' Hardin looked across at Stafford. 'Did you say you'd tickle him?'

Stafford smiled slightly. He had cooled down and he knew what Hardin was doing; as an army officer he had done it himself when men were in a jumpy condition. Hardin was soothing Hunt as a man might soothe a fractious horse. Stafford said lightly, 'Quite a cigarette lighter, isn't it?'

The burner consisted of two coils of stainless steel tubing mounted in a rectangular frame so that they could swivel. Hardin said, 'Looks as though you have two burners there. Why?'

'Belt and braces principle,' said Hunt. 'If I'm in the sky and a burner fails I want to have another quickly.' He turned a cock on the butane cylinder then lit a small pilot burner. The pilot flame burned blue. 'I'm ready.'

Stafford said, 'I'll operate it.'

'No,' said Hunt. 'I'll do it. I know exactly how it works.'

'Better think of what's going to happen when you lift that trap,' said Hardin. 'The first thing that'll come through is a bullet.'

'Anyone got a knife?' asked Stafford. Hunt produced a pocket knife and Stafford cut a length of electric wiring from a table lamp. He lifted the small metal flap on the trap door and knotted the end of the wire around the ring beneath. He said, 'I'll pull up the trap from here, standing behind it. The trap door itself will protect my legs from the flame. Let the door be open at least a foot before you let go, Alan; and you'd better lie flat on the floor behind the burner. Bullets travel in straight lines so you should be safe. Ben, move that stuff off the trap and then get clear.'

Two minutes later he looked at Hunt. 'Ready?' Hunt nodded. 'Give it a good long burst,' said Stafford, and hauled the trap door open.

There was a shocking series of chattering explosions as soon as the trap started to move and a stream of bullets came through the opening to strike the ceiling and ricochet around the room. Lights went out as some of the overhead fluorescents were smashed and a monitor screen imploded when hit. Stafford flinched and was about to drop the trap door when Hunt cut loose with the burner. The room was lit by an acid-blue light as a six-foot long flame stabbed down into the basement. The shooting stopped and all that could be heard was the pulsating roar of the burner which seemed to go on interminably.

At last Hunt switched off and the room was quiet. Stafford dropped the trap door back into place and looked around. 'Everyone all right?'

Hardin was clutching his upper right arm. 'I caught one, Max. What the hell was that? A machine-gun?'

'I don't think so,' said Stafford. 'My guess is that it was a Kalashnikov on automatic fire.' He looked at the blood on Hardin's hand. 'A ricochet, Ben. If you'd stopped a direct hit at that range it would have torn your arm off. This is beginning to get bloody dangerous.' He looked down at Hunt. 'Are you all right?'

Hunt was pale but nodded. He said, 'The shooting stopped.'

'But was it because of us?' asked Stafford. 'Or did his magazine run out?' He looked up and saw Curtis standing in the doorway. 'Get back on watch, Sergeant. That doorway is in the line of fire.'

'Yes, sir,' said Curtis smartly, and disappeared from view.

'Are you ready to give it another go?' asked Stafford, and Hunt nodded. 'All right. I'll open the door. If there's no shooting give him a short burst and stop. If he shoots let him have it – a good long blast.' He turned his head. 'Ben, get the hell out of here.'

Hardin jerked his head. 'I'll be behind that bench.'

'Take this then and stay ready.' He gave Hardin the pistol and took up the slack on the wire, nodded to Hunt, and hauled the trap door open. There was silence for a moment and then again the flame stabbed out with a stomach-tightening rumble. Hunt let it play for only a few seconds then turned it off.

Again there was silence.

Stafford shouted, 'Hey! You down there! Come up with your hands empty. You have fifteen seconds or you'll fry.'

There came a distant call. 'I'm coming. Don't burn me.'

Footsteps were heard climbing the stairs and a man appeared. His hair had been burned away and blisters were beginning to show on his face and the backs of his hands. Stafford said curtly, 'Out!' and he climbed up into the room. Hardin moved forward holding the pistol.

'Anyone else down there?' demanded Stafford. The man shook his head dumbly, and Stafford said, 'We'll make sure. Give it another long squirt, Alan.'

'*Nee, man, nee*,' the man shouted. '*Jy kan nie . . .*' His words were lost as Hunt turned on the burner in a long sustained blast. He turned to run but was stopped at the door by Hardin with the pistol. The burner stopped and then things began to happen so fast that Stafford was bemused.

Hardin dropped as though pole-axed as someone hit him from behind. He dropped the pistol which went off as it hit the ground and the bullet screamed past Stafford so close that he ducked involuntarily. When he looked up suddenly Hendriks and Brice were in the room and Hendriks held the pistol with the silencer. 'Everyone freeze,' he said. 'No one move.'

Brice looked at Hunt lying on the floor, his hand still on the blast valve. 'What in hell is happening?' He looked at the scorched man. 'What happened to you, van Heerden?'

'I was down there and they turned that . . . that damned flame thrower on me,' he said. 'Things are burning . . .'

Hendriks gave a choked cry. He thrust his pistol into Brice's hand and ran forward to the trap door, kicking the burner aside as he went. He clattered down the stairs and disappeared from sight. Hardly had he gone when a hand clamped on Brice's wrist from behind and twisted it sharply. Brice screamed as his arm broke and Curtis appeared from behind him to catch the pistol as it dropped.

Stafford expelled a deep breath. 'Get up, Alan,' he said. Hunt got to his feet and turned around. 'See to Ben.' He was about to step forward when there was a muffled thump and the building shook. A dense column of smoke tinged with flame at its centre shot out of the basement through the open trap, and van Heerden screamed, 'It's going to blow up!'

Something fell and hit Stafford on the head and he knew nothing more.

# THIRTY-TWO

'These grapes are not bad,' said Stafford appreciatively. 'Thanks.'

'It is customary to bring grapes to hospital,' said Chip and hitched his chair closer to the bed. 'It is also customary for those who bring them to eat them.' He took a couple of grapes from the bunch and popped them into his mouth. 'When are they letting you out?'

'Another week.' Stafford touched his bandaged head. 'There's nothing broken, but I get double vision when I'm tired. The doctor says it's concussion and all I need is bed rest. How's Nair?'

'He's all right. They took the bullet out of his leg and he's on the mend. He's in a room down the corridor.'

'I'll pop in and see him.'

Chip smiled slightly. 'The population of this hospital has gone up since you began operations. Hardin had concussion like you; Hunt is having a skin graft on his legs – he got scorched.'

'The Sergeant?'

'Nothing wrong with him. He's a real tough one. He'll be coming in to see you soon.'

'All right,' said Stafford. 'What happened?'

'Curtis got Hardin out then went back to help Hunt get you out. Brice got himself out. Hendriks and Miller were both killed.'

'Miller?' said Stafford interrogatively.

'The man in the basement.'

'Oh! Brice called him van Heerden.'

'Did he?' Chip was interested in that and made a note of it. 'His passport was in the name of Miller. A British passport.'

'He spoke a few words of Afrikaans when he was under stress. What did you find in the cellar?'

Chip looked at him oddly. 'Don't you know?'

'I don't know a bloody thing,' said Stafford. 'You're my first visitor.'

'When Nair rang to tell me what you were doing I rounded up some men and commandeered an army helicopter from Eastleigh because I wanted to get to you fast. I thought you were tackling something bigger than you could handle. We were purring the helicopter down next to the building with the dish antenna when it blew up. The helicopter nearly crashed.'

'Blew up!' said Stafford, startled. 'In God's name, what was down there?'

'We've had our forensic people looking at the bits and pieces that are left. Apparently there were a lot of explosives, commercial gelignite for the most part. They say that didn't blow up – it needs a detonator – but it burned hot and that set off the rest of it. They had a small armoury down there, rifles and ammunition, hand grenades and so on.'

'That wouldn't be enough to blow up a building.'

'That's right,' agreed Chip. 'The damage was really done when the fire got to three Russian SAM-7 rockets. We think there were three but it's difficult to tell now.'

'Rockets!' Stafford rubbed his jaw. He was thinking of that hot, blue flame driving heat into the basement. Talk about playing with fire!

'Most of the stuff down there was Russian,' said Chip. 'Probably captured equipment from Angola. The South Africans smuggled it in, probably through Mombasa. We're going into that now.'

'Indirection,' said Stafford. 'What do you think they were going to use it for?'

Chip shrugged. 'There's a lot of talk going on at the top. The general opinion is that the stuff was going to be used to arm various groups in the general interest of stirring up trouble. Those being used would even think they were being paid by the Russians. It could have caused a lot of bad blood.'

'What does Brice say?'

'Brice is saying nothing; he's keeping his mouth shut. Patterson isn't saying much, either. But Luke Maiyani will talk as soon as his jaw is unwired,' said Chip grimly. 'You're going to have visitors, Max. They'll tell you to keep your mouth shut, too. All this never happened. Understand?'

Stafford nodded. 'I think so,' he said wearily. 'How are you going to keep it under cover?'

'I've brought you some newspapers and marked the relevant stories. The matter of Brice hasn't come up yet so it hasn't been reported. I'll tell you what will happen about him. He's under arrest for embezzlement of Ol Njorowa funds; we found enough in his office to nail him on that. He'll go on trial and he'll stand for it because he can't do anything else. We don't know who he is but we do know he isn't Brice.'

'How do you know that?'

'Before Brice left Zimbabwe – Rhodesia – he got into trouble with the Smith government for some reason or other. Anyway, our brothers in Zimbabwe had a look through police records and turned up his fingerprints, and they don't match those of the Brice we've got.'

Stafford began to laugh. 'So Brice goes to jail for embezzlement. He can't do anything else.'

'He'll spend a long time inside, and he'll be deported when he comes out.' Chip smiled. 'We'll probably put him on a plane to Zimbabwe.' He chuckled. 'And the Zimbabweans will arrest him for false pretences and traveling on a false passport.'

'I almost feel sorry for him,' said Stafford.

'Don't,' said Chip in a grim voice. 'We found a safe built into the wall of the cellar. It was strong and fireproof. In it, among other things which I won't go into, we found three passports in the name of Gunnarsson, Hendriks and Rosters. That pins the Tanzanian attack directly on Brice. The Hendrix passport had been tampered with.'

'They'd replace Hendrix's photo with that of Corliss,' said Stafford. 'What happens to Corliss?'

'We'll give him the passport and send him home,' said Chip. 'He knows nothing of what went on. He's a very confused boy and will never tell a straight story.' He stood up. 'When you get out of here you must have dinner with me and my wife.'

Stafford was somewhat surprised. 'I didn't know you were married.'

'Most people are.' Chip flipped his hand in a semi-salute and left.

Stafford picked up the newspapers and read the articles Chip had marked. An American visitor, Mr John Gunnarsson, had been killed by a hippopotamus on Crescent Island, Lake Naivasha. His body was being returned to the United States. A brief editorial in the same issue commented that this should reinforce the warning to all visitors to Kenya that the animals they saw in such profusion *really* were wild and could not be approached with impunity. While regretting the death of Mr Gunnarsson it could not be the function of the Kenyan authorities to wet-nurse headstrong tourists.

In another issue was an account of the disastrous fire at Ol Njorowa College. The animal migration laboratory had been wrecked, mostly by the explosion of butane cylinders stored in the basement. Several people, including the Director, Mr Charles Brice, had been injured, and Mr Dirk Hendriks and Mr Paul Miller had been killed. Mr Brice was not available for comment but the Acting Director, Dr James Odhiambo, said it was a grave blow to the advance of science in Kenya. The police did not suspect arson.

Stafford was about to reach for another newspaper when there was a tap at the door and Hardin and Curtis came in. Curtis said, 'I have taken the liberty of bringing the Colonel some fruit.' He put a brown paper bag on the bedside table. Stafford looked at him with affection. 'Thank you, Sergeant. And I understand I have to thank you for getting me out of the lab before it blew up.'

'That was mostly Mr Hunt, sir,' said Curtis imperturbably. 'I'm sorry I let Brice and Hendriks get past me. I had to watch out on two sides and I was in the office when they came in.'

Stafford thought it was not so much an apology as an explanation. He said, 'No harm done,' then amended the statement. 'Only to Hendriks – and Brice.'

'Is there anything I can get for you, sir?'

'Just a new head,' said Stafford. 'This one feels a bit second hand.'

'I felt like that,' said Hardin. 'But you got a bigger thump than me. We'll come back when you feel better.'

'Hang on a minute, Ben. Do you mind, Sergeant?' Curtis left the room and Stafford said, 'Are you still going to work for me?'

Hardin grinned. 'Not if it's going to be like this month. The pay's not enough.'

'It isn't always as exciting as this. How would you like to go to New York? I want someone across there fast – someone who knows the ropes.'

Hardin looked at Stafford appraisingly. 'Yeah, Gunnarsson Associates will be up for grabs now Gunnarsson has gone. That's what you mean, isn't it?'

'Something like that. I need you there; you know the business. With a bit of luck you could get to be the boss of the American end of Stafford Security.'

'Gunnarsson always kept the reins in his own hands,' said Hardin musingly. 'I guess things could tend to fall apart now. Sure, I'll give it a whirl and see if I can pick up a few of the pieces. To tell the truth I've gotten a bit homesick. All this fresh air seems unnatural; I miss the smell of gasoline fumes. Hell, I'd even take Los Angeles right now.'

'Go by way of London,' said Stafford. 'I'll give you a letter for Jack Ellis. Arrange for whatever expenses you need with him.' He paused. 'Talking of Los Angeles, I wonder what happened to Hank Hendrix – the real one?'

'I'll ask around but I don't think we'll ever know,' said Hardin.

When Hardin had gone Stafford felt tired and was beginning to see double again. He closed his eyes and composed himself for sleep. His last waking thought was of Alix Hendriks who would never know the truth about the death of her husband. It occurred to him that every time he helped Alix she got richer and he achieved a few more scars. This time she would inherit her husband's fortune by courtesy of the South African government, and might even get Henry Hendrix's money with a bit of luck.

He made a mental note that the next time Alix appealed for help or advice was the time to start running.

# THE CIRCUMSTANCES
# SURROUNDING THE
# CRIME

Nineteen-Sixty was not a particularly good year for South Africa. January was not too bad, but on 3 February Harold Macmillan, the British Prime Minister, made his famous 'wind of change' speech to the South African Parliament in which he warned of the storms to come. This did not sit well with South Africans, particularly those of the ruling Nationalist Party, who regarded it as an interference in South African internal affairs.

Then on 21 March an inexperienced police commander made a grave error of judgment when he gave the order to fire with machine guns on a crowd of demonstrating black Africans in the small town of Sharpeville.

Within thirty seconds the death toll was sixty-nine and many of those killed and wounded were women.

On 30 March a State of Emergency was declared in South Africa, and on 1 April the United Nations Security Council adopted a resolution deploring the shootings at Sharpeville which were categorised as a massacre.

On 4 April the Union Expo at Milner Park opened its gates to the public.

By this time Johannesburg had become a magnet attracting the journalistic hot-shots – the international leg-men. World news is where you find *Time* magazine rubbing elbows with *Paris-Match*, both of them trying to get a beat on *Stern*. Noel Barber was there from London, and Robert Ruark represented Scripps-Howard. This was Ruark towards the end of his life – the famous hard-drinking, best-selling novelist and old Africa hand. At this time his idea of breakfast was half a bottle of Scotch and a couple of lightly boiled aspirins. I read one of his two-thousand-word cables and wondered how the desk man back in Chicago was going to make sense of it.

Then there was the brash character who entered the bar of the Federal Hotel, a drinking hole favoured by news-papermen and broadcasters, announcing, 'I've come to interview your Prime Minister – Forwards or Backwards or whatever his name is!'

And, of course, there was the home-grown newspaper talent such as James Ambrose Brown. After Sharpeville all the surviving wounded had been put into Baragwanath Hospital around which the Army had thrown an iron cor-don. Jimmy Brown penetrated the ring by wearing a white coat, an ostentatious stethoscope, and a preoccupied medi-cal expression. He got his exclusive eyewitness interviews and duly made his scoop. Early 1960 was an exciting time for newsmen in Johannesburg.

And where did I come into all this? I, too, was a news-paperman, freelancing for the *Rand Daily Mail* and the Johannesburg *Sunday Times*, and my one aim in life at the beginning of April 1960 was to cover the Union Expo. I was not interested in political matters and scurried about the feet of the journalistic giants doing my own thing. So let us take a look at the scene of the crime, the Union Expo, which was my beat.

Every year at Milner Park in Johannesburg there is an event called the Rand Easter Show. Originally it was an agricultural show – indeed it is still organised by the Witwatersrand Agricultural Society – but it has been overtaken by industry and taken on an international flavour because a dozen nations have built permanent exhibition halls which are brought into use only once each year for about ten days around Easter.

Here the French push their wines, perfumes, military helicopters, and minor guided missiles; the Germans display Bavarian beer and heavy machinery; the British offer Harris tweed, Scotch whisky, and Stilton cheese; the Japanese are there with transistor radios, the Czechs with Bohemian glass, and the Belgians with Browning rifles. The cattle, sheep, pigs, and goats are still there but somehow they seem lost among all the machinery.

Ironically, 1960, the year of disaster, was the Golden Jubilee of the founding of the Union of South Africa in 1910. The Government had decided that this was an occasion for celebration, so a couple of new exhibition halls were built in Milner Park, artists and sculptors were commissioned to decorate them, and the Rand Easter Show was lengthened to three weeks and rechristened the Union Expo, a coinage to chill the blood of anyone who respects the English language. Attendance was expected to top the million mark.

Long before the gates opened on 4 April I had been busy. The *Rand Daily Mail*, Johannesburg's English morning newspaper, was to run a special daily supplement on the Expo and there were many pages to be filled. And I had hopes of pushing material to the *Sunday Times*, the *Mail*'s stable companion. So I was kept busy interviewing exhibitors and anyone else who would provide a good story.

Among these was Kobus Esterhuysen, a relaxed Afrikaner who was an exhibition designer of no mean talent and who was responsible for the Combined Provinces Pavilion. He admitted rather shamefacedly that it was he who had coined the term Expo, and added that he was having trouble with the bats in the Transvaal Pavilion. It seemed he had an animal exhibit and the bats would not hang upside-down properly. It made a paragraph.

By the time the Expo opened I was so busy that I drafted my girlfriend, Joan Brown, into helping me. All that first week we scurried about, me working full time, and Joan in the few hours she could spare from her job in a city book shop.

I had no time to think of the political scene but the politics were there and would not go away. The international pressmen were at the Expo in strength on Saturday, 9 April, because Prime Minister Vervoerd was to be guest of honour and was due to make a speech in the Main Arena, supposedly a 'keynote' speech on the State of Emergency.

Just before three I joined them in the arena, standing before the VIP box where C. J. Laubscher, the general manager of the Expo, was sitting with the Prime Minister, the Mayor of Johannesburg, the President of the Witwatersrand Agricultural Society, and a dozen assorted visiting firemen, including my designer friend Kobus Esterhuysen. Behind us, in the arena, were about 500 prize cattle. There were thirty thousand onlookers in the stands.

I was with Stan Hurst, Features Editor and principle layout man of the *Sunday Times*. Stan was a good friend and was to be best man at the wedding when I married Joan later that year. He looked at Vervoerd, and said, 'He's got to pull a rabbit out of the hat today. He *must* — the country can't go on like this.'

Vervoerd made his speech in both English and Afrikaans, the two official languages of the country. It was of mind-numbing dullness, much to the disgust of the visiting newsmen who were not as hardened as were we locals to the stupifying qualities of South African political discourse. There was not a word spoken that was newsworthy, so when the speech ended they vanished from the arena, some going direct to the airport where they had booked flights for the Congo which was due to erupt at any moment, others back to their hotels, but most drifting into the bar, that haunt of all good newsmen, to swap lies and steal stories from each other.

But for Joan I would have joined them; South African barrooms were for men only.

The next item on the program was for Vervoerd to come down into the arena and inspect the cattle. 'A lousy speech,' Hurst commented. 'Nothing in it for me. I'm going home; maybe I'll take a nap.' He looked at Vervoerd who was chatting with Alec Gorshell, the Mayor of Johannesburg. 'Are you covering the cattle?'

I shook my head. 'I leave that to Terence Clarkson.' Clarkson was an elderly reporter on the *Rand Daily Mail*; he knew less about cattle than I did, but he could disguise his ignorance better. I grinned. 'He'll look up what he wrote last year and rejig it.' I checked the time. 'I promised to meet Joan in the Members' Pavilion after the speech.'

Stan nodded. 'Okay; I'll see you in the office tonight.'

He went away, and 1 walked towards the Members' Pavilion which looked out on to the arena. The only news-paperman left was the photographer from the *Farmer's Weekly* who was stuck with the job of following the Prime Minister as he inspected the bovine regiment in a timeless ritual of South African life.

Joan was lucky enough to have found a table in the crowded Pavilion so I ordered strawberries and cream, dropped a few acid words about Vervoerd's speech, and then we got down to figuring the work plan for the rest of the day.

Less than five minutes later there was a slight disturbance in the arena, merely a couple of shouts and nothing more. None of us heard the gun. A man at the next table stood up and craned his neck, then sat down again. 'Nothing much,' he said. 'I think a bull got loose.'

The thought struck me that a bull loose in the same arena as a Prime Minister might prove interesting and, after

all, I was a reporter. 'I'll be back in a couple of minutes,'
I said to Joan.

I got into the arena by showing my press tag and headed
towards the VIP box fifty yards away. There was a small
crowd of perhaps a dozen men at the bottom of the stairs
and the people who should have been seated around the box
were standing and staring. There was not much noise; just a
hum of conversation and the lowing of cattle from the arena.

As I got closer a struggling man was hauled away by two
policemen. He was not being handled gently. Another man,
a stranger, was lying on the steps, dead or unconscious, with
someone bending over him. I touched the elbow of an
onlooker. 'What's happening?'

'He *shot* him!'

'Who shot who?'

'The bastard shot Vervoerd.' The man's tone was
incredulous.

There wasn't another reporter in sight. '*Who* shot
Vervoerd?'

'Someone called Spratt.'

'Where is Vervoerd now?'

'Lying on the bottom of the box there.'

The photographer from the *Farmer's Weekly* was busy taking pictures. He had problems – three of them. The first was
his camera. It was an elderly Speed Graphic five-by-four,
cut-film camera, a type I thought was obsolete in the 1930s.
Slow to load and heavy to hold. His second problem was
that the VIP box was too high for him to see into. He was
holding his camera above his head with stiffened arms,
leaping into the air, and opening the shutter at the top of
each leap in the dim hope of getting a useable picture.

His last problem was the Mayor of Johannesburg who hit
him on the head with a rolled-up newspaper every time he
leaped up.

I turned and ran back to the Members' Pavilion and
unceremoniously scooped up Joan from her table. I said

in a low voice, 'Vervoerd's been shot; we've got to move fast.'

She got the point. 'Where to?'

'The press room.'

The press room at Milner Park offered jaillike accommodation for frequently protesting reporters. There were a few battered and ink-stained deal tables, a few rickety chairs – and four telephones. In the bar of the Members' Pavilion were half a hundred news-hungry reporters, each of whom would cheerfully give his arm for a telephone in the next fifteen minutes, and I was determined to get mine first.

The press room was empty. I said, 'Ring *Sunday Times* editorial and tell them Vervoerd's been shot by a man probably called Spratt. There'll be more to follow as soon as I can find an eyewitness. And don't let go of that bloody telephone no matter who wants it.'

On the way back to the arena I passed the door to the Members' Bar and hesitated. Maybe I'm not competitive enough and maybe I'm a damned fool but I pushed open the door and went in. There, bellied up against the bar counter, were the Fourth Estate's finest – the international team. Now, because I have a stammer, journalistic legend in Johannesburg has it that I went into the bar and shouted, 'Ver-Ver-Ver-Ver-voerd's b-b-b-been sh-sh-sh-sh-sh-sh-shot!'

My version is that I caught the eye of Bennett, a reporter for the *Rand Daily Mail*, went up to him and said, not too loudly, 'Ver-Vervoerd's been shhhot.'

He grinned at me. 'Pull the other leg – it's got bells on it.' He went on drinking so I shrugged and left them to it.

I needed an eyewitness and then I remembered that Kobus Esterhuysen had been in the VIP box. He and I had got on well together so I elected him as my eyewitness and went in search of him. He was not hard to find because he was standing just by the VIP box.

'Hi, Kobus; hoe gaan dit?'

'Kannie kla nie.'

I switched into English because my Afrikaans, while serviceable enough to establish rapport with an Afrikaans speaker, was certainly not good enough for detailed discussion. 'Got anything to tell me?'

'What do you want to know?'

'Who shot the boss?'

'Pratt,' said Kobus. 'David Pratt.'

'Not Spratt?'

Kobus shook his head. 'I know him. David Pratt of Moloney's Eye.'

That brought me up short. 'Of *what*?'

'Moloney's Eye Trout Farm in the Magaliesburg. Pratt supplies all the Johannesburg restaurants.'

'Spell it,' I said, and Kobus obliged. 'Did you see it happen?'

'Couldn't help it,' said Kobus. 'We were just getting ready to go down into the arena when that *skelm*, Pratt, came into the box, said something to the Prime Minister and then shot him in the head twice.'

'What did he say?'

'I don't know, he didn't speak loudly. Anyway, I grabbed him, and . . .'

'*You* did?' Kobus was not only a model eyewitness but a participant.

'That's right. He was waving the gun about and struggled a bit. Then someone helped me and we got the gun off him – then the cops took him.'

The public address system blatted out, 'Clear the arena of all those cattle. Will everybody leave the stands in an orderly manner and don't panic – don't PANIC – DON'T PANIC.'

Kobus looked across the arena to the stands on the far side. A restlessness was sweeping across the multihued crowd, and he said dispassionately, 'Bloody fool! That's enough to put anyone into a panic.'

I said, 'Where's Vervoerd now?'

Kobus jerked his thumb. 'Still in the box. A doctor's having a look at him.'

'Then he's alive?'

'Only just.'

'Know anything about Pratt?'

'A bit. He . . .'

'Save it,' I said. 'I have to get this back to the office. Where can I find you in the next half hour?'

'I'll be here, or in the Members' Pavilion – upstairs.'

As I went back to the press room the loudspeakers were still blaring, 'DON'T PANIC – DON'T PANIC,' until suddenly the voice was cut off in mid-shout. I later discovered that some resourceful soul had pulled the plug on the idiot at the microphone.

The press room was bedlam, crammed with shouting reporters fighting for telephones. Fortunately, Joan had valiantly defended hers against all comers although she must have had a tough time. I had not known her long and her introduction to the newspaper world had come through me, so she had very little knowledge of how to telephone in a story.

She had rung the *Sunday Times* and, luckily, got hold of Maggie Smith, a reporter whom she knew quite well. She said to Maggie, 'The assassin's name is Spratt.'

'What assassin?' asked Maggie.

'The man who shot Vervoerd.'

'Are you trying to tell me the Prime Minister has been assassinated?' said Maggie incredulously.

It was only then Joan realised that she, Joan Brown – intrepid, amateur girl-reporter – was scooping the world press. She froze solid. It took Maggie some time to unfreeze her, and then she had to cope with the thundering herd of reporters who charged into the press room, but by the time I got back she had regained her efficiency.

I set myself in front of her, fending off the flailing hands trying to grab her telephone, and fed her the facts a line at a time which she passed on to Maggie. Then I said, 'Tell Maggie I'm going to get more from Esterhuysen and some background stuff on Pratt. It'll be about half-an-hour. Then you can give up the phone.'

That telephone was seized very quickly.

When Joan and I left the press room two ambulance men went trotting by carrying a stretcher. On the stretcher lay Hendrik Vervoerd, his hands held to his face. There was a lot of blood. His eyelids flickered and then opened, and I could see that even with two bullets in his head he was quite conscious.

Again, there was not a reporter or cameraman in sight – and I had no camera.

We watched the men carry the stretcher until they turned a corner, then went in search of Kobus Esterhuysen. We drew a blank at the VIP box so we went upstairs in the Members' Pavilion where a reception had been laid on for the Prime Minister after he had made his speech. The black waiters were still ladling out free booze because no one had told them to stop, and every freeloader in Johannesburg seemed to be present. Joan and I took a welcome brandy each, I scooped up a plate of canapés, and we went looking for Kobus.

We found him with a glass in his hand standing by a window. I asked him if he had spoken to other reporters and he smiled and shook his head, so I did my best to drain him of all he knew, glad that the immediate pressure was off and I had reasonable time to spare.

I asked him what it felt like to tackle a man who was waving a gun. He shrugged and said that Pratt did not wave the gun for very long.

'What kind of gun was it?'

Kobus said, 'A .32 automatic pistol.'

'I've just seen Vervoerd,' I said. 'He's still conscious.'

Kobus stared at me. 'He ought to be very dead. One bullet went in at the right cheek; the other went into his ear.'

He did not really know much about Pratt apart from a few general facts. Pratt was reputed to be quite wealthy, was a strong supporter of the United Party, had gone through two wives and had the reputation of being an odd-ball. That bit about the United Party made the questioning a shade delicate because the United Party was largely supported by English-speaking South Africans while the governing Nationalist Party, of which Vervoerd was the leader, was favoured by the Afrikaners. Kobus was an Afrikaner and his leader had just been shot by an English speaker.

But Kobus let me off the hook. 'Hell, man,' he said. 'I have no politics. I'm a painter and a sculptor and have no time for those things.' He paused. 'I'll tell you one thing, though; I'm glad Vervoerd was shot by a white man and not by a black Kaffir. All hell would have really broken loose then. Natives have been beaten up in the show grounds already and the army is moving in.'

That was serious. We already had a state of emergency and we were but one step from martial law and army rule.

There was one point left which puzzled me. I said, 'I saw Pratt being hustled away by the cops, and Vervoerd was in the VIP box. You say Pratt fired only two shots, both at Vervoerd. Right?'

'Right.'

'So who was the man lying on the steps, and how the hell did he get that way?'

Kobus grinned. 'That was Major Richter, Vervoerd's bodyguard. He fainted when he saw the blood.'

I thanked Kobus and we went in search of a telephone and found one in an empty office. I rang Maggie Smith, gave her what I had, and said we were returning to the office but not to expect us immediately. I had a feeling that getting to the centre of Johannesburg was not going to be easy.

There had been 120,000 people at Milner Park that day and they were being shepherded out by the police and the army. The traffic jams were catastrophic. Not that it worried us because we had no car and were resigned to a long walk, but we spotted a *Sunday Times* staff car and hopped aboard.

It was dusk before we got to downtown Johannesburg and it would have been quicker to walk, although not as restful. I used the time to sort out my impressions of the day and to lay out a story in my mind. Driving down Commissioner Street we saw that Broadcast House, the city radio centre, was ringed with armed troops, and so were the offices of the *Sunday Times*. There were also armoured cars parked at strategic intersections.

Because I was a freelance I had no official press card, but we still wore the press tags accrediting us to the Union Expo. Those, some fast talking, and the fact that we were able to give authentic news of what had happened at Milner Park got us into the building.

One of the first persons we saw was Maggie Smith. 'Where is Stan Hurst?' she demanded. 'I thought he was with you.'

'He went home after Vervoerd's speech.'

'Oh, God!' she wailed. 'Half the paper is being remade, everyone is screaming for Hurst, and he has to go home.'

'Ring him.'

'Can't,' said Maggie. 'He's just moved house and his telephone hasn't been installed.' More telephone trouble. Maggie hurried away to give someone the bad news.

Joan said suddenly, 'I know his next door neighbour – she has a telephone.' I stared at her. That was the first coincidence; in a city of over a million people Joan just happened to know Hurst's next-door neighbour.

I took her by the elbow, steered her into Hurst's office and pointed to the telephone, then I appropriated his typewriter and began to put words on paper. Ten minutes later when Stan came on the line he sounded muzzy and was disgruntled at being woken up. 'Stan, you'd better get back to the office. Vervoerd was shot this afternoon and the paper is being remade.'

He didn't believe it.

More urgently. 'Stan, you must get back. You have your own cables to get out to Australia.' Hurst was the Johannesburg stringer for a chain of Australian newspapers.

'Is this straight?'

'I wouldn't joke about a thing like this.'

'When did this happen?'

'Five minutes after you left.'

'Who shot him?'

'A fellow called Pratt – David Pratt.'

Something happened to Hurst; his voice was suddenly alert. 'Not David Pratt of Moloney's Eye?' he said incredulously. There was a lot of incredulity about that day, but Stan had real reason for his.

'That's right.'

'My God!' he shouted. 'Pratt's mistress is my ex-mistress. I'm going to see her.'

That was the second coincidence. Who in hell would ever suppose that the Features Editor of the *Sunday Times* and a political assassin could be linked in such a way? If I put a thing like that into a novel my publisher would scream.

'Aren't you coming into the office?'

'This is more important.' He slammed down his phone.

I looked at Joan and grinned. 'It's a small world.'

To everybody who asked we said that Hurst was on his way back to the office. It was true, even though he was taking a detour and, after all, it was his exclusive story. The groundwork he had laid must have been delightful even though it was damned fortuitous. He strolled into the office three-quarters of an hour later and beamed at me. 'Good lad!'

'That didn't take long.'

'I went up to her flat,' he said. 'I supposed you can call it her flat even though Pratt pays the rent. I hadn't been there more than twenty minutes before two very tall, very broad, Afrikaner Special Branch cops pitched up and tossed me out on my can.' He winked. 'But I got what I wanted.'

'What did she tell you about Pratt?'

'He's bonkers,' said Hurst. 'A nutter who is really round the twist but I knew that already. She told me that he took her to Klosters in Switzerland where they were hob-nobbing with Aly Khan, among others. Then suddenly he announced that he was broke, so they went to London. Pratt booked in at the Savoy and then told her to go out and get a job. What do you think of that?'

'Was he broke?'

'Of course not. Just bloody eccentric.' Stan shook his head. 'Pratt won't hang for this – I don't think he'll even stand trial. And there's a hell of a lot of juicy stuff we won't be allowed to print.'

He sat at his desk and started work.

I was pretty busy myself and Joan was drafted into a strange job for a newspaper office. The news of the shooting had been telephoned to the airport and most of the newsmen who were on their way out cancelled their flights and came streaming back into town. The chattering telex machines also told of others who were flying in.

All these men had to be found hotel rooms; and hotel accommodations in Johannesburg during the Union Expo were as scarce as hen's teeth. So she sat with the telephone book open at the yellow pages and rang every hotel in town and got most of the boys a room. Someone ought to have thanked her for what she did that night but I can't recall that anybody did. She certainly was not paid for it.

In spite of the strange hazards associated with the project the photographer from the *Farmer's Weekly* had got his picture –

just *one* good picture. It showed Hendrik Vervoerd, Prime Minister of South Africa, sitting on the floor of the VIP box and leaning into the corner. Blood streamed down his face.

That night, in a bedroom in the Langham Hotel, the picture was auctioned off by Terence Clarkson, acting as a disinterested neutral. The bidding was brisk but too rich for local blood, and at last there were only two bidders left in the ring – *Time* magazine and *Paris-Match*. The price crept up by jerks to R2,000 (about $2,800), then *Time* shrugged, looked at *Paris-Match* and said, 'What say we split it?' *Paris-Match* agreed and so the *Farmer's Weekly* photographer was a good deal richer than he had been that morning. I hope he bought himself a new camera.

The presses rolled at midnight and five minutes later the first copies were distributed around the *Sunday Times* newsroom. This was a time for relaxation; the first edition was out and away and the pressure was off. Stan brought out a bottle and we drank brandy from paper cups while scanning the front page.

Someone had written an atmosphere piece, the first paragraph of which read:

All is peaceful as the sun sets redly over the Main Arena at the Union Expo. The crowds are gone and all is quiet, and there is nothing to show of the tragedy that happened here this afternoon; nothing, that is, but the Prime Minister's head which still lies on the floor of the VIP box.

I pointed out the error to Joan and she shared my laughter, then I said, 'Hey, Stan; here's something that needs changing. There's a clown on the staff who can't spell hat.'

I turned back to Joan. 'You know; we never did get to eat those strawberries.'

'Which strawberries?'

'Those we ordered in the Members' Pavilion.'

*Epilogue*

Hendrik Vervoerd survived the half-centenary of the founding of the Union of South Africa. And so did the Union – but just barely. The following year, by referendum of the white population, the country voted by a narrow margin to leave the British Commonwealth of Nations and became the Republic of South Africa.

Stan Hurst was right; David Pratt never stood trial. He was found unfit to plead by reason of insanity, and placed in the Old Fort, the high-security section of the Oranje Mental Hospital in Bloemfontein. There, on the evening of 1 October 1961, he took a bed sheet and tied it to the leg of a bed in two places. Inserting his neck in the loop so formed he rotated his body, thus committing suicide by strangulation.

Hendrik Vervoerd, still Prime Minister of what was now the Republic of South Africa, lived until September 1966. In the House of Assembly in Cape Town he was stabbed to the heart four times by a Greek immigrant named Dimitrios Tsafendas, also known as Tsafendakis, Stifianos, and Chipendis. Tsafendas ascribed his action to a huge tapeworm inside him which he variously described as a demon, a dragon, and a serpent.

He did not stand trial, either, being 'detained at the pleasure of the President of the Republic.' He is now in the psychiatric wing of Pretoria Prison, studying computers and computing, and still complaining about his tapeworm.

DESMOND BAGLEY
April 1977